Dear Arabesque Reader,

Thank you for choosing to celebrate 10 years of award-winning romance with Arabesque. In recognition of our literary landmark, BET Books has launched a special collector's series honoring the authors who pioneered African-American romance. With a unique 3-full-books-in-1 format, each anthology features the most beloved works of the Arabesque imprint.

Sensuous, intriguing and intense, this special tenth anniversary series includes four must-read titles. Kicking off the series is *First Touch*, which combines Arabesque's first three novels written by Sandra Kitt, Francis Ray and Eboni Snoe. The series will continue with *Hideaway Saga* by best-selling author Rochelle Alers and *Falcon Saga* by Francis Ray, before concluding with *Madaris Saga* by Brenda Jackson. We invite you to read each of these exceptional works by our renowned authors.

In addition to recognizing the esteemed authors, we would also like to honor the short succession of editors—Monica Harris, Karen Thomas, Chandra Taylor and, currently, Evette Porter—who have guided the artistic direction of Arabesque during our successful history.

Please enjoy these works and give us your feedback by commenting on our website at www.bet.com/books.

Sincerely,

Linda Gill
VP & Publisher
BET Books

Books by Sandra Kitt
Serenade
Sincerely
Suddenly

Books by Francis Ray
Break Every Rule
Forever Yours
Heart of the Falcon
Incognito
Only Hers
Silken Betrayal
Undeniable
Until There Was You

Books by Eboni Snoe
A Diamond's Allure
Beguiled
Emerald's Fire
The Passion Ruby
The Ties That Bind

Published by BET/Arabesque Books.

FIRST TOUCH

SANDRA KITT
FRANCIS RAY
EBONI SNOE

ARABESQUE

BET
BOOKS

BET Publications, LLC
www.bet.com
www.arabesquebooks.com

ARABESQUE BOOKS are published by

BET Publications, LLC
c/o BET BOOKS
One BET Plaza
1900 W Place NE
Washington, DC 20018-1211

All Kensington Tiltes, Imprints, and Distributed Lines are available at special quan-
tity discounts for bulk purchases for sales promotions, premiums, fund-raising, and
educational or institutional use. Special book excerpts or customized printings can
also be created to fit specific needs. For details, write or phone the office of the
Kensington special sales manager: Kensington Publishing Corp., 850 Third Avenue,
New York, NY 10022, attn: Special Sales Department, Phone: 1-800-221-2647.

First Printing: February 2004
10 9 8 7 6 5 4 3 2 1

Printed in the United States of America

CONTENTS

SERENADE

SANDRA KITT

To Alice and Alice,
who made last year possible

CHAPTER 1

One of Grandma Ginny's old wives' tales was that if it rained on the day you got married, the union was doomed to failure. It was a pessimistic, rather sobering notion, but one that kept reverberating with humorous irony in Alexandra's mind as her cab pulled up in front of the modest whitestone church. She struggled with payment, an umbrella, a plastic clothing bag, and the door as the persistent old wives' tale lingered. Alexandra swore to herself she wasn't the least bit superstitious. Still, she hoped it was nothing more than this myth that nagged at her today.

The rain poured down steadily, as if taking revenge on the earth and its occupants for some infraction against Mother Nature. It was not supposed to rain today. It should never rain on anyone's wedding day, Alexandra thought, as she pushed the cab door open and was met by a gentle sweep of cold, damp air—but then, forecasters were notorious for being wrong.

Alexandra swung her legs cautiously out the cab door and promptly stepped into the shallow puddle of water running along the curb. The displacement her step made sent a wave of water into her bone-colored sling-back pumps, making her toes curl with the icy touch. She drew breath sharply between her teeth in exasperation. So far, events did not bode well. If Grandma Ginny's tales had any truth to them, Alexandra was glad she wasn't the one getting married.

With her head lowered and the umbrella braced against the chilling spring winds, Alexandra dashed up the church steps and through the heavy doors, crashing with teeth-rattling suddenness into the tall, gaunt, bespeckled form of Pastor Nichols. The wind was knocked out of them both, and the pastor grunted as he was pushed off balance.

"Good heavens, girl! Where are you off to in such a hurry?" he asked, as he placed a bony restraining hand on Alexandra's shoulder to steady her.

"I'm sorry," Alexandra said, out of breath, trying to shift her clothing bag and attempting to collapse the dripping umbrella.

The pastor chuckled indulgently as he relieved her momentarily of her garment bag while she fought with the temperamental umbrella. "I know they say that girls are all sugar and spice, but believe me, a little rain won't make you melt."

Alexandra smiled as she finally closed the umbrella and retrieved her bag. "I was more concerned about being late, Pastor Nichols. I should have been here thirty minutes ago."

He folded his thin hands over his robes and shook his head gently at Alexandra. "There's really no point in tearing around so. We can't start without the groom, and he's not here yet, either." His eyes twinkled. The pastor now looked at her carefully, making note of the softly upswept hairdo, the sienna-toned oval face with its full, wide, curved mouth. And eyes so dark they were like black buttons in her youthful face.

"Do I know you?" he asked suddenly, wrinkling his brow.

Alexandra's wry smile and raised brows indicated what she thought of the man's memory. "We met at rehearsals last week. I'm to sing in the service this morning, remember?"

Recognition now brightened the pastor's myopic eyes as he gave Alexandra a toothy smile. "Ah, yes. You're the young lady with the incredible voice. I remember now. What a joy it is to listen to you."

Alexandra merely smiled her response, taking a step further toward her destination, concerned about the time even if Pastor Nichols wasn't. But he detained her still.

"You know, I could sure use you in my Sunday morning choir," he hinted broadly.

Alexandra shifted uncomfortably, a guilty conscience reminding her that she had stopped being a regular attendant at church services, here or anywhere else, and that her already busy schedule would not allow for any more commitments. She was spared having to make an admittedly weak excuse when the pastor quickly changed subjects.

"That reminds me, I haven't yet instructed the best man as to his duties. He was the only one not at rehearsals last week. Has anyone else had a chance to speak with him?"

Alexandra shrugged. "I'm sorry. I don't know who the best man is."

"Well, no matter. His job is simple enough, and there's lots of time yet," he said benignly.

Alexandra managed a quick glance at the clock on the wall, and thought not. She took another step away. "Is anyone here yet?"

"Oh, yes, yes. The bride's family has arrived. She's with her mother in that second anteroom off the far corridor." He pointed helpfully.

Alexandra was about to thank him and go on her way when the door opened behind her and a gust of March air blew raindrops on the backs of her legs and swept tendrils of hair against her cheeks. An instant later, someone plowed into her back, pushing her once more into Pastor Nichols. She glanced over her shoulder to find a man breathing down her neck, his hands grabbing her arms to steady her once more. His dark blond hair was damp and windblown, his cheeks a bit ruddy. His strawberry-blond moustache curved at the ends as he grinned wickedly at Alexandra.

"We have to stop meeting like this. What'll I tell my future wife?"

Alexandra rolled her eyes and laughed softly. She watched as Brian Lerner adjusted his black bow tie and smoothed his hair into place with his hand. Then he turned to shake hands with the man who would marry him.

"Hi, Pastor. Hope I'm not late."

The pastor chuckled. "Young man, you can't really be late. You just have to show up." Continuing to hold onto Brian's hand, he steered him into the entrance hall. "I think we should move away from the door. I'm not sure I can survive being tackled a third time."

While the two men laughed in appreciation, Alexandra took the opportunity to move away. "I've got to go get ready. I'll see you in about an hour," she said, and began walking to the room the pastor had pointed out. The long, threadbare red runner down the center of the floor quieted her footsteps as she moved, making Alexandra feel reverent. She might not attend church regularly, but she experienced a quiet, peaceful sense of being whenever she entered one.

Knocking gently, Alexandra opened the anteroom door. Inside, a slender young woman, a few inches taller than Alexandra but about the same age, was having a wedding veil adjusted atop her curly red hair. The short train of the ankle-length Victorian lace dress was being smoothed and arranged by the young woman's mother, at that moment down on her hands and knees. They both turned their attention to Alexandra as she stood smiling in the doorway, and greetings were exchanged.

Alexandra watched the young woman, trying to gauge in her eyes and movement what she was feeling. She found the pretty face flushed and the green eyes bright with excitement. "Well, Debby. This is it," Alexandra said, her voice suggesting that it was getting too late for the young woman to change her mind.

Debby continued to move the veil around on her bright curls. "I can't believe this is finally happening," she whispered, in such wonder that Alexandra knew she had no intention of turning back.

"You'd better believe it," Debby's mother muttered dryly. "After all you've put your father and me through the last six months, if this isn't the real thing, we want to know the reason why."

The two younger women giggled, and Alexandra came closer to examine the beautiful gown. Debby's mother put a hand on a nearby chair and hoisted herself up, shaking out the folds of her own pale blue gown.

"I'm glad I have only one daughter," she sighed. "All of these plans and details have really done me in." But her laugh was nervous, and her voice had a suspicious crack in it.

"Oh, Mom," Debby whispered, putting an arm around her mother's shoulder and kissing her soft, warm cheek. For the moment, the two of them were locked in an intimate moment that no one else could intrude upon.

Alexandra watched the exchange with warmth and a kind of detached envy. She herself had no immediate thoughts of getting married, although a very youthful fantasy still played itself out in her daydreams from time to time—the one in which she'd seen herself in a white dress and veil, about to walk down the aisle to be married to the man she loved. She'd even had a very specific man in mind, bringing the fantasy an inch closer to reality. But a fantasy was all it had ever been. Dreaming was safer and filled a long-ago ache.

That same youthful anticipation had allowed her to realize too late that dreams didn't always come true. That one failed romance was to have other effects on her life. It touched on her relationship to her family and on what Alexandra herself wanted to do with her life. Sure, it had all been disappointing and unbelievably painful at the time, but not the end of the world. She had survived and grown up.

Alexandra watched also the genuine love and tenderness that was exchanged between her friend and her mother and noted another emotion: a sense of emptiness. Her own mother had died when she was fifteen and her younger sister not yet ten. That had been thirteen years ago. She had adjusted to the loss long before she'd reached maturity. Alexandra knew now, as she watched Debby with her mother, that there were certain to be special days when her own mother would be missed a lot.

Alexandra thought how young she'd been when she'd first begun to lose things and people in her life. How young she'd been to take on the responsibility of the family, of others depending on her, inadvertently and helplessly drawing on her strengths and caring until sometimes she felt she'd given it all away and there was little left just for her. In some ways she felt as though she'd grown up too fast. In some ways, she suspected, she had not grown up at all.

Alexandra felt her hands clasp together under the garment bag folded over her arms, suddenly feeling her losses again of having had so much taken away against her will: loved ones, dreams, princes. There were few things she wanted anymore, and these she held onto tenaciously, greedily, to protect them and herself. Alexandra let her tense body relax as Debby's mother spoke.

"Come on, now. Let's not fuss so. After all, you're only getting married, not leaving the country," she said, gently pushing her daughter away. "I'm going to try and find your father, and see if everyone else is here. No doubt he's in Pastor Nichols' office, being fortified with the sacramental wine."

Alexandra and Debby chuckled as the older woman disappeared through the door, leaving the two of them to the last few private moments when they were exactly the same—young women who shared the same interests and were friends. Alexandra had met Debra Geison at the university, where they'd both studied music. It had been Debby who'd willingly tutored her in music theory in exchange for having a steady companion to attend concerts with. Later they'd both begun to teach at the university's conservatory. Alexandra had gone on to give lessons to particularly talented but underprivileged children recommended through a scholarship program by the public school system. The children were all bright, but raw and undisciplined, their attention quickly diverted, and it had taken creative and ingenious steps to make the repetitive lessons fun. Alexandra enjoyed working with children most of all. She and Debby had both been young and idealistic, thinking they could make a difference in children's appreciation of music. Of course, that was before they both realized they were competing with the creative flamboyance of Michael Jackson and Prince. It was before they'd both had their first taste of love, which would change both their dreams and their lives.

For Debby, it had come to a perfect natural conclusion. She was marrying someone who loved music as much as she did, and they both very much loved each other. Another twinge of regret crept in around Alexandra's heart, but quickly dissolved. Alexandra let the true affection she felt for Debby soften her dark eyes with joy for her now.

"Well . . . how do I look?" Debby breathed out, pivoting around much too quickly for Alexandra to see anything.

"Debby, you look beautiful," she responded honestly.

Debby grimaced in mock disgust. "Is that all? Just beautiful? All brides are beautiful. I want to be so stunning I'll knock Brian clear out of his socks. "

Alexandra laughed as she put her things down and shrugged out of her coat. She hugged an arm around her stomach and braced the other elbow on her wrist. Leaning her round chin on her fist, she pretended deep contemplation of Debby's appearance. "Okay. Maybe you're more than just beautiful. I personally think you knocked Brian out of his socks a long time ago. He's going to find you stunning no matter what you wear today."

Debby gnawed her bottom lip. "Do you think so? I'm not sure about my hair . . ." she said, frowning slightly, and turned away to pat and fuss with the glossy curls in an ornate mirror behind her.

Alexandra smiled as she recognized the eleventh-hour nervousness that was attacking Debby with doubts and last-minute questions. Gently placing her hands on Debby's shoulders, Alexandra forced her down onto the vanity chair in front of the mirror. Just as gently, she removed Debby's hands from their blind marauding and once again straightened the filmy veil and train.

"There is nothing wrong with your hair. Everything is just perfect," she voiced softly, and smiled at the suddenly pale reflection of Debby in the mirror. "Are you a little nervous?"

Debby nodded, "Yes, I guess so. This is a pretty bad time to be wondering if this is the right thing to do. Is it what Brian wants to do?" Suddenly, Debby's eyes flew open and she looked positively stricken. "Oh, my God! What . . . what if Brian doesn't want to get married? What if he's only doing this for my sake, and wished he hadn't canceled out on that European tour with his band?"

Now Alexandra did allow herself to laugh. "Oh, Debby, stop it. You're scaring yourself to death for no good reason at all. You know very well Brian adores you. Getting married can't be compared to a European tour. And don't forget, you turned down his proposal twice before accepting."

In an almost comic turn around, Debby blinked at the reminder, considering it. Finally, she began to relax, and squinting, smiled back at Alexandra in the mirror.

"That's right. I did, didn't I?" she remembered gleefully.

Alexandra nodded sagely. "And you also told him you wanted to continue teaching and playing in the orchestra at the Kennedy Center, and he agreed."

"Yes!" Debby brightened even more, her green eyes large and happy again. With her confidence quickly restored, Debby's eyes became coquettish in her pretty face. "As a matter of fact, all things considered, Brian's pretty lucky to be getting such a talented, gorgeous creature!" she continued.

A quick frown passed through Alexandra's dark eyes and then was gone. A thought, a voice, a memory shook her, sending a shiver of feeling all through her body that was unexpected. "Talented, gorgeous . . ." She'd heard that before. Old wives' tales were one thing, but now she was getting waves of premonition that were unsettling; something that would affect *her*, not Debby. Deciding she was being fanciful, she sighed and withdrew her hands from their unnecessary but soothing chore at the elaborate lace headdress and smiled at Debby again. "Oh, I think Brian is well aware of how lucky he is. You both are lucky," Alexandra added, and stepped aside as Debby stood once more to face her.

"Thank you," Debby said in a soft, sincere voice. "Thank you for the pep talk, and for being here, and for taking my classes while I'm on my honeymoon . . ."

Alexandra uncomfortably brushed the words aside. "Don't be silly. That's what friends are for. Besides, I know you'd do as much for me."

"Of course," Debby said at once, checking her makeup yet again. "I don't have the voice that you do, but I'm looking forward to performing at *your* wedding one of these days."

A thought twisted Alexandra's mouth, and she chuckled soundlessly. It was on the tip of her tongue to utter *don't hold your breath* when she realized she'd have to explain her remark, and she didn't want to; but she also didn't want Debby to feel her offer was taken lightly. Yet Alexandra knew with a certainty that she had no intentions of marrying. That idea had been discarded in favor of doing other things with her life. In one way the decision had already been made for her.

Debby turned from the mirror. "Well, that's the best I can do with what I have. Ready or not, Brian, here I come," she laughed lightly. "I decided not to wear my glasses. Pastor Nichols could marry me to the best man and I'd never know it."

At that moment, Mrs. Geison opened the door and stuck her head in.

"For heaven's sake, you two. Everyone's almost ready. Come along, Debby. The pastor is ready for you to take your place."

Debby quickly gave Alexandra a hug. "I'd better let you change." She stood back and stared at Alexandra. "Do you realize that in twenty minutes, I will be Debra Geison-Lerner?" Before Alexandra could respond, Debby giggled joyously and went through the door, her train like gossamer behind her.

The amused smile on Alexandra's face lasted another few seconds before it slowly faded, and she stood alone and somber in the suddenly quiet room. Automatically she took out her gown from the garment bag, and went about quickly changing from her street clothes. She applied a teak blusher to her cheeks and chin, mascara to her dark, thick lashes, and gloss to her lips. She recaptured a few wayward strands of hair on her nape, and tucked them back into the bunched curls pinned high on her head in an arrangement with seven pale pink rosebuds. There was a quiet thoughtfulness to Alexandra's features, as if she always had a thought in mind. Her eyes were large and dark and sometimes sad, people had told her. Alexandra mentally compared her face to that of her younger sister, Christine. Sighing, she knew there was no comparison. Christine was without a doubt the real beauty in the family.

Alexandra could never see her true image in the mirror and didn't recognize the attractive, poised woman of twenty-nine she'd grown into from the thin, gawky, all-knees-and-elbows, large, chocolate-eyed girl she'd been. She had also convinced herself that beauty gave a person many more advantages than being talented did. Having watched most of her life as a younger, capricious Christine got her own way just about every time had led Alexandra to believe that she herself was in on a pass.

A young man named Parker Harrison had once promised Alexandra that she was like a swan that wouldn't reach its full glory until after it was fully grown; like a wine that ripens slowly, a flower that blooms late but then is the most magnificent of all. Romantic claptrap, Alexandra thought airily . . . it wasn't true then, and it wasn't true now. But at nineteen she'd been romantic, and young enough to believe the silken magic words of a man she'd thought herself in love with. Parker had seemed so sincere and had been so convincing that now, without him in her life to provide the image, to believe in it and enrich her, it all seemed to have been nothing more than mere fantasy, only pretty words.

Alexandra never believed she could possibly be pretty enough to hold a man's attention. But she had something else: a beautiful voice. And with her voice, the one thing that was purely her own, Alexandra was ready to set the world ablaze with her music. With it she had a career and life already mapped out. She was reaching for much more than singing at weddings.

As for the romance in her life, she had been only nineteen, but Parker had given her her first real and strong taste of love. It had helped her cross that mysterious invisible boundary between innocent teen and young woman. It had given her a soft feminism from the angular youth of inexperience, and had nearly broken her heart and left her cold.

He had given Alexandra just enough that it could not be mistaken for promises and commitments, and he had taken enough to make her wary and selective. She knew there was never any love like the first one; the next can only be second best. So Alexandra had turned completely to music and teaching it to children who hadn't yet realized their own potential. Teaching might be a poor substitute for love, but at least it was something she was sure of.

In the mirror, her large, dark eyes lacked a glow of total happiness. Her well-shaped, full mouth smiled frequently with warmth, but her smile lacked a certain depth. And her pretty brown countenance often spoke of a certain wishfulness. She was like a sleeping beauty, waiting.

Hearing the bracing cords of the church organ finally changed Alexandra's pensive expression to one of quick surprise. She was going to be late.

Hastily putting her street clothing away in the garment bag and getting things in order, Alexandra grabbed her music, pulled open the

door, and rushed out. She ran lightly down the corridor toward the choir room, where she'd join the church members asked to sing during the short wedding service. The thought that she might cause the delay of her friend's wedding caused her to gnaw on her lips as she tried to remember which of the four doors on the adjoining hallway was the one she needed.

Suddenly, as she reached the junction, someone rounded the corner and Alexandra slammed right into a moving blur of black and white. The air was knocked out of her, forcing out a surprised gasp. She was bounced back several steps with the force of the impact. Her music sheets, shaken loose from her hand, drifted to the floor around her. A pair of strong hands immediately reached out to grab her arms and steady her.

"Hey! I'm sorry. Are you all right?" a concerned, masculine voice sounded in Alexandra's rattled brains.

She blinked rapidly to clear her vision and raised both hands to hold on to her sudden source of balance.

"I . . . I think so," Alexandra murmured, and then shook her head ruefully. "I've been bumping into people all morning. I'm not usually so clumsy . . ."

The man, somewhat taller than her five feet six inches, released her and bent to retrieve the scattered pages. But as he stood to face her once more, the rest of Alexandra's words were left unspoken as she stood gaping openmouthed at him. Blindly she accepted the sheets from him even as she continued to stare in disbelief.

"I just hope I didn't hurt you. We collided pretty hard, and I . . ."

"Parker!" Alexandra breathed, her heart feeling like it was flipping over and over in her chest. "What . . . what are you doing here?" she asked.

The man frowned at her, stared, and slowly began to shake his head. His brown eyes were intent and careful as his gaze searched her face. there was no sign of recognition. A curious smile lifted a corner of square mouth as he continued to frown.

"I'm sorry. You have the advantage," he said apologetically.

Alexandra blinked at him and the sudden involuntary light that lighted her eyes faded, along with her initial shock. He didn't reme her. He had no idea who she was, or what connection they migh Her voice completely failed her now.

A door opened and a buxom, middle-aged woman dressed i robes stood in the doorway looking up and down the hall, until s —— ted the two people staring rather fascinated at one another.

"Are you the soloist?" she asked urgently.

Alexandra pulled herself back from the past and looked at th "Yes, I . . ."

Sandra Kitt

"Well, come on, come on!" she gestured impatiently. "We're waiting for you!"

"Oh . . . yes," Alexandra said vaguely, feeling herself caught in an odd sensation of time-warp. Her eyes, still round and bright, looked back to the man, who apparently still hadn't gleaned any insight into her identity, although his interest was obviously caught now. "I'm sorry. I've got to go . . ."

"But wait . . ." he began calling after her.

But feeling foolish and beginning to experience a crushing, heavy sadness, Alexandra hurried into the room away from him.

Alexandra knew a kind of piercing breathlessness. The man who'd changed her life nearly ten years ago had no memory of her at all. It made her feel insignificant, unimportant. It made everything that had been between them seem a mere chance passing, and the crushing tension now in the pit of her stomach told her that perhaps for Parker, that was all it had been. But her own memories recalled that time as more special than mere chance.

She had no time in which to recover her shattered senses. The processional began and the choir, with Alexandra in the lead, headed out a side door that placed them eventually to the left and rear of the altar, facing the wedding party and the congregation of guests. Her stomach muscles began knotting alarmingly, and a sickening swirl of emotion rose to her throat. She felt hot and cold at the same time. Numb . . . and also alert.

Alexandra felt her eyes searching the seated guests, quickly scanning for the familiar head and face. She found Parker in place as best man next to Brian. Alexandra irrelevantly remembered Debby's recent words about being married to the best man without benefit of her glasses to tell the difference and a short, hysterical giggle escaped her. Debby would have to be stone blind not to know the chiseled brown features of Parker, a night-and-day contrast to the fair and blond Brian.

Parker was pursing his lips and staring thoughtfully into space when the eight-person choir reached their elevated spot in a balconied tier behind the pastor. His eyes caught the movement, he found Alexandra in front, and their eyes locked and held.

Alexandra swallowed hard and felt a breath catch in her throat as she returned his look with frank, unavoidable curiosity of her own. Her lips parted somewhat in awe at the handsome picture he made, dressed for this auspicious occasion. The stark white of his formal dress shirt contrasted richly against the tobacco brown of his skin. The black of the tuxedo made his slender six-foot frame sleek. His hands were crossed over one another in front of him, his legs braced a little apart, and he gave a virile image of a man totally in control. Alexandra raised her attention to him again, wondering if he really was. Certainly, he didn't ap-

pear to be as shaken as she had been by the brief encounter in the corridor.

Alexandra had a momentary sense of surprise that she had been anything at all to this man in the past. The fact that their lives had touched in every imaginable way for a period of three months now seemed some odd dream that she'd made up. She clearly remembered every second of their romance.

Parker had moved on to fame and fortune. There was no need for Parker Harrison, successful composer and songwriter, to look behind him to the young girl whose life he had stepped in and out of so quickly.

Alexandra gathered her wit, made a determined effort not to look at Parker again, and gave her attention to the service. She led the choir through the ceremony, her rich alto soprano voice clear and melodious, drawing an emotional response from the listening guests. She knew she'd been blessed with a strong singing voice, but she was generally unaware of its effect on people. She didn't take her abilities for granted, but she was more aware of concentrating on simply singing well. She listened to her own sounds, always wanting them to be the best she could produce.

Hearing Debby and Brian exchanging their vows, however, brought unexpected tears to her eyes. As of that moment, a new life started for both of them. Alexandra hoped their lives together would be everything they wanted. She hoped their love would last.

Then the organ began its final introduction and Alexandra softly launched into "The Lord's Prayer." She closed her eyes to feel it as she sang. The classic version of this hymn had always been a vocal challenge because of its sweeping climbs and drops in octaves. It never failed to move Alexandra, never failed to make her believe in the existence of something greater than herself which filled her with joy and gave her peace and hope. It was to this that she raised her splendid voice in song gratefully, as much as it was to celebrate the joining of Debby and Brian.

There was an eerie silence when she finished, and the chords of the organ finally faded away. Pastor Nichols's voice finally broke into the near-reverent silence to finish the service. Alexandra missed the final words, the final benedictions, as she was acutely aware of Parker's gaze on her. She suddenly found it difficult to breathe evenly, and she resented that she felt so uncomfortable and unsettled.

The guests and wedding party filed out of the room and crowded into the church vestibule. Because of the rain, pictures of the happy couple could not be taken on the steps of the church. Instead, the service was reenacted to allow the photographer to record it. Alexandra hung back, watching the photography session, since she only knew the bride and was only recently acquainted with the groom's immediate family. The other members of the choir had departed for the reception, leaving her now alone.

From a distance, she indulged her desire to observe Parker Harrison covertly as he was photographed with the rest of the wedding party. Alexandra sat in a pew quietly, still dazed by his presence.

Belatedly, Debby realized that she'd not been included in the photo session, and spotting her, exclaimed, "Oh, there you are! I wondered where you'd disappeared to. Come here, I want you in the pictures, too."

Debby grabbed her hand and unceremoniously dragged her down the aisle to the waiting group. Alexandra had no time to protest or demure as she was suddenly conscious of Parker silently watching her approach, his gaze more intent on her now than before. As a matter of fact, he was openly staring. She ignored him, however, and walked over to Brian. Placing her hands on his shoulders, she tiptoed to kiss his cheek.

"Congratulations," Alexandra said stiffly, trying to smile. Brian rested a hand on her waist.

"Thanks. Come over here. I want you to meet someone. You've probably heard of him," he teased coyly.

Alexandra felt her stomach knot as Brian gently swung her around to face Parker, who was standing to the side. The warmth drained completely from her body, and her apprehension raised gooseflesh on her bare arms. Right now, she'd be just as happy if he never remembered who she was. But she raised her chin proudly and looked squarely at Parker.

His gaze upon her this time was different. The curiosity was still there, but it was mixed with a kind of soft probing that thoroughly examined her. Whatever he saw he found pleasing as one dark, straight brow quirked and a lazy, appealing grin shaped his mouth.

For a quick instant, Alexandra lowered her gaze, then raised it again. She'd never before gotten that kind of look from Parker. In a way, it was flattering, because his eyes and mouth were flirting with her, liking what he saw in her. Alexandra hid a smile, perversely enjoying the knowledge that they knew each other far better than he realized.

Parker's jacket was unbuttoned for the moment and forced back as he stood with his hands in the pants pockets, watching her approach.

"Hey, man . . ." Brian began, slapping Parker on the shoulder. They were about the same height, but Parker was decidedly more slender. "I want you to meet the pretty lady behind the pretty voice. This is Alexandra Morrow. And this . . ." he smiled cheerfully at his friend, "is the famous Parker Harrison."

"Or infamous, as the case may be," Parker said in a quiet, deep tone as he continued to look at Alexandra. "Hello," he said, putting out a long, slender hand.

Hesitating, Alexandra put her hand into his and felt his fingers close warm and firm around her cold limb. She could tell he was aware of it as he tilted his head and gently squeezed her fingers.

"I'm aware of Mr. Harrison's reputation in music. Hello," Alexandra said softly. She was proud of the poise she could command, even as her insides knotted with tension. She frowned askance, however, as Parker just held onto her hand, not allowing her to pull away. She looked at him only to find that he was once more scanning her face thoughtfully.

"Parker and I played in a tour together across the country for a couple of years," Brian explained, with obvious pride at their friendship. He slapped Parker's shoulder again. "While Parker here went on to become a household word, I went on to get married."

"You didn't do so badly," Alexandra scolded him softly.

"I agree," Parker voiced caustically, finally releasing Alexandra's hand and turning his head to Brian. "As a matter of fact," he said in amusement, "anyone who can put up with a temperamental musician deserves sainthood."

"I'll drink to that."

They all turned to see Debby moving between them. She slipped her arm through that of her new husband and hugged it. "Not even married a full hour and already I'm deserted."

"All for a good reason, Honey. I wanted Parker to meet Alexandra."

"Yes, and that reminds me," Debby said sheepishly, turning her appealing green eyes to Parker, "Would you mind very much bringing Alexandra to the . . ."

Realizing what her friend had in mind, Alexandra stopped her.

"Oh, come on. I can go alone. After all, Mr. Harrison might have other plans later this evening," Alexandra tried to excuse Parker. She wasn't sure how much longer she could claim anonymity.

He turned his dark, piercing gaze on Alexandra, and his eyes sparked. "Parker," he insisted. "I'll be happy to bring her," he interrupted Alexandra, directing his comment to Debby. He looked at Alexandra, once again amused, "Unless Ms. Morrow really objects to being in my company."

They all waited for Alexandra's answer, Debby's expression making it clear she would be out of her mind to refuse. Alexandra knew there was only one response left to her.

"N-no, of course not," she said lamely.

"Good! Now that that's settled, Brian, the photographer wants a family shot." Keeping her hold on his arm, Debby led him away. "Don't go anywhere," she whispered over her shoulder to Alexandra before she was out of earshot. "I still want you in some of these pictures."

Alexandra followed more slowly behind them for a short distance and stood by a pew, feigning an interest in what the photographer was doing. But her heart was racing in her chest, and her body was trembling with the anxiety of the last few minutes. She was still stunned that Parker was right here in the same space, together with her after all these years, and didn't remember who she was. And as much as Alexandra tried to deny it, it hurt that he didn't. Alexandra tried to let her spine stiffen with resolve. She had obviously left no lasting impression on Parker Harrison; she'd been completely forgettable.

She hadn't counted on Parker moving closer to her just then, so close that she could smell the faint, pleasant chemicals of mothballs from the recent storage of his tuxedo, and the clean, starched scent of the professionally laundered shirt.

Alexandra's body stiffened and she held her breath. Her back was to him, but she almost felt that at any moment he would reach out a hand and touch her. Was she waiting for it? What finally touched her, rasping on her nerve ends and sending a chill quivering through her, was his deep, low voice.

"Hello, Alex," he murmured.

CHAPTER 2

Parker's memory of Alexandra was almost ten years old. She had been barely a young woman then, truly still a girl. She had been incredibly young and endearingly naive. With him, she had had her first encounter with a man who wasn't her father, a teacher, or a friend. In many ways he had been all three.

Parker allowed his eyes to travel from the appealing angle and slenderness of Alexandra's neck to her shoulders, which were straight and erect, unlike the uncertainty she'd shown physically at nineteen. There was a discreet dip to the back of her formal gown, showing smooth skin and subtle curves, down to a small waist and narrow hips. He smiled appreciably to himself. There was at least one way that Alexandra Morrow had grown up. Parker felt painful regret and sadness and impatience overwhelm him. Damn it! She *had* been too young then. He felt a terrible crush to his gut that he had not recognized her right away, although he could not be blamed completely. Alexandra Morrow had finally come into her own.

It wasn't until she'd stood behind the Reverend Nichols. It was in the church light's diffused glow spotlighting her; then it came to him. And then Parker had been spellbound. Against all reason. Beyond mere surprise. Deeper than shock. For seeing Alexandra Morrow so suddenly had swept him back to a time in his life when he, too, had been too young.

It was a long, poignant moment before Alexandra could bring herself to turn around and face him. In a matter of seconds, she had to recover from the shock and disappointment of his not knowing right away who she was. And she had to show, just as she had moments ago, seeming indifference to him and to the past.

When she turned, Parker's gaze roamed over her face with memories as well as recognition reflected. There was wonder and surprise, curiosity and thoughtfulness, and as the seconds swept silently by, the slight smile on his mouth was mixed with sadness, shaping his mouth with irony as well as warmth.

Alexandra could see now, however, that their meeting again had been just as much a shock for him.

"I didn't think you remembered," Alexandra said honestly, meeting the steady gaze, alert to his every movement and reaction to her.

"No . . ." Parker said vaguely, his eyes not finished with their inventory of her yet. "That wasn't it. I didn't recognize you," he admitted.

"Oh," she murmured, feeling let down somehow. But it should not have surprised her that a man of Parker's experience should have forgotten a wide-eyed teenager with big dreams and innocence, an inexperienced teen who'd hung on his every word, every musical chord, as though he were a prophet. She didn't remember Parker ever having been impressed by adoration, but not to recognize her . . .

"That is, not until Brian said your name and I saw the freckles."

She glanced up, a hand self-consciously reaching to touch her face where a handful of brown dots dusted the bridge of her nose. Parker quickly cut short the movement by touching her hand and pulling it down. He looked down at her hand caught in his, running his thumb over the smooth, soft back. Her hand was still delicate and slender, although for the moment, she left it limp in his.

"Your hand is still cold. Were you wondering when I'd figure it out?" he asked in wry amusement.

"I think I was hoping you wouldn't," Alexandra stated evenly, extracting her hand, too aware of the warm strength of his fingers. But Parker raised a brow at her withdrawal. "It . . . it would have been too difficult trying to explain how we knew one another," she said.

"Oh, I can recall that," Parker said easily, with a slow smile, and it brought the heat of embarrassment to Alexandra's cheeks as she also wondered if he recalled how well and deep the knowledge went. Suddenly, she felt both the pain and exhilaration of having been so young.

Parker read both her expressions, and it surprised him. It had been a very long time, but was it possible Alexandra had not forgotten? Certainly part of the proof was in her easy and quick recognition of him. But it was too hard to think of more than that.

Parker half squinted an eye closed and tilted his head. "Let's see. It was seven years ago . . ."

"Almost nine," she corrected without thinking.

He nodded, conceding the point. "You had an apartment down the hall, and liked my piano." His eyes took in the rest of her now, in her peach formal dress that flattered her slender form. The appreciation and surprise were back again in his gaze. It was new to Alexandra.

"I remember that you were studying music. You were going to become rich and famous," he said, lifting a brow, his mouth in a smile.

Alexandra couldn't tell if he was teasing her or not, but even the thought that he might be added to the mixed emotions tumbling through her system. She had overcome too many past adolescent heartbreaks to stand and have Parker make light of her youthfulness of years ago. She didn't want him to turn his scant recollections now into an easy laughable account that might hold no meaning for him beyond this chance encounter. Because that was all it was. It had taken Alexandra a long time to come to the conclusion that what they had been to each other had been important only to her. For Parker, it apparently had held no significance beyond that point and space in time. But since he was here before her now, she wasn't going to let it change anything.

"I still plan to," Alexandra bantered lightly, and a frown settled on Parker's brow.

"Yes, I can see that," he said absently, knowing she wasn't just making conversation. She was still serious about that.

Parker turned his head to see how the photo session was going, and seeing that the photographer was going for every angle and shot possible, he sighed and faced her again.

"Look . . . I could use a cigarette. Do you think I'll be excommunicated if I smoke in the foyer?"

"I think your soul is safe for now," Alexandra chuckled softly.

"Good," he tilted his head to the left. "Come keep me company." Parker began walking toward the end of the aisle leading to the foyer, and a little reluctantly, Alexandra fell into step beside him. The light touch of his fingertips on the back of her waist guided her to the one lone wooden bench along the wall, and they sat down together, Alexandra making sure that there was some room between them. Only the filmy fabric of her dress floated and rested against his thigh.

"I'm convinced there's a church ordinance which dictates that there be only hard wooden benches to sit on," Parker said dryly, and Alexandra laughed softly, letting him charm her all over again with his easy ways.

"It's just to make sure your mind stays where it should," Alexandra said, rolling her eyes heavenward.

"No doubt," Parker murmured.

He was staring at her again, but this time Alexandra found it more disconcerting. She couldn't imagine what held him fascinated, what he looked for in her oval face. Parker reached for his cigarettes, never tak-

ing his eyes off her while he slowly lit one. A crooked smile formed
around the burning cigarette held in his firm lips. A deep slash was revealed in one cheek, a masculine groove that was attractive and added a
rakish air to his handsome face.

What he saw was a face that had filled in with feminine maturity and
softness. Gone was the stubborn little ball of a chin Alexandra used to
possess. Gone were the too-thin hollow cheeks, and the eyes that seemed
too large for her face. But one thing remained; it was true then and it was
true now—Alexandra possessed a calm, comfortable prettiness that
made him want to smile.

Unaware and unashamed of her own staring, Alexandra reacquainted
herself with Parker's face. His hair was curled into a short, even cut that
defined the shape of his head. He didn't seem to have changed physically. Perhaps the face was more filled out and mature, the eyes a bit
more worldly and thoughtful in their gaze; there were two parallel furrows across his forehead. He had always been capable of deep intensity.
The wide, square mouth was more experienced. Alexandra lowered her
gaze, and her wayward thoughts. He seemed the same, but she knew he
couldn't be.

"Almost nine years. That *is* a long time," he said, removing the cigarette and expelling smoke. His voice was a disturbing, distinctive drawl. It
was too caressing—a unique way, Alexandra remembered, he had of
using his voice. It could make him nonthreatening, pleasantly friendly,
unintentionally seductive, intentionally soothing.

"So . . . how have you been?" she asked rather stiffly, still feeling as
much on guard with him as she was with herself. There was a part of her
that wanted Parker to see how much she'd matured, how self-possessed
and grownup she was. She wanted *him* to be impressed and overwhelmed
this time. But again, in view of his life now, she wondered if he'd care.

Parker chuckled silently, noticing an aloofness in her again. He could
well imagine what was the basis for it. The past, and him. He slowly shook
his head. "I'd rather talk about you. How have *you* been?"

Alexandra shrugged indifferently, lacing her fingers together. "Okay, I
suppose. I teach now, I study music, I sing . . ."

"Anywhere besides church?" he teased.

"I sing at The Outer Edge," she stated confidently.

Parker's brows raised, and he nodded, taking another pull on the cigarette. "I've heard of it, but I've never been there." He tilted his head in
question. "But I remember that you wanted to sing light opera . . ."

"That's true," Alexandra said, looking away from him and down the
corridor. She knew they were both thinking that her opera career should
have happened by now.

Alexandra's opportunity to do so at nineteen had been lost when

Parker had suddenly and mysteriously departed from her life, leaving her emotionally devastated. At the same time, her father had been diagnosed as having a weak heart, an additional emotional burden for her. Christine, who'd felt restrictions upon her time and activities as a result of their father's condition, was frequently uncooperative. Alexandra had lost precious weight and sleep; she hadn't been able to concentrate on anything for months, least of all the demanding practice and preparation necessary for the prestigious audition.

Alexandra had been determined to go to the audition anyway, but after the second required movement she had disqualified herself, claiming illness. But the truth of the matter was that in that moment, standing on a brightly lit stage in the presence of peers, of stiff competition and strict censoring judges, she had been on the verge of embarrassing herself by collapsing into tears. In that instant, she didn't care about the competition, only what was happening to her father, and what had happened to cause Parker to leave.

It was only much later, as she began to pick up the trail of Parker Harrison's rising career, that it had come to her. Like the song, they had been strangers in the night. Meeting, touching, passing briefly, until his dreams and ambitions took him elsewhere.

A sudden bewilderment made Alexandra's hands clench together, and a sense of injustice turned her eyes bright and sparkling. He had no right to do that, she thought, as her throat threatened to close tight around the emotion of indignation. He had no right to make her care, and then to just walk away.

Alexandra stood up abruptly, and she knew that Parker's frown deepened at her sudden motion. His questioning eyes followed her as she walked to a small leaded-glass window. She looked out absently at the rain still falling on the streets of Washington, D.C., the slick surface distorting images, colors, and shapes. She was shocked to find that a mere half hour in his presence could revive so many feelings she'd thought were done and gone. Alexandra took a deep breath, and turning slowly, once more composed, she walked back to where Parker sat forward, resting his elbows on his knees, watching her.

Parker could tell that for whatever reason, Alexandra was angry with him. He could feel it. He wondered if it had anything to do with what they both had in common—music. It was true that he had gone on to incredible recognition, more money than he either wanted or needed, and the supreme satisfaction of knowing that his music was heard everywhere. Obviously, Alex had not achieved such lofty levels yet. But who was to say which of them was to be envied? Whose life was more normal? It seemed to be a question of a private life versus a public one. It didn't seem all that clear to Parker.

There was a sadness in his eyes, which he quickly shielded when she turned to face him. Parker took a final drag on his cigarette and flicked the butt into a nearby trash bin.

"You have a beautiful voice," Parker began, to break the silence. "It's grown strong."

"I think it's good enough. I still hope to be accepted by the Light Opera Company here in D.C."

"You probably will be. You seem . . . determined." Parker said.

"Oh, I am," Alexandra said, raising her chin in a stubborn, defiant manner.

In the past nine years, she'd fought down her pain and hurt to go on to other things in her life. She'd once given her all to Parker, but there was no more she intended to give of herself to him or the past. She had her music. Slowly but surely she had her future; she had her own dreams.

"I remember you could accompany on piano . . ."

Alexandra shifted her face from his scrutiny. "I don't play piano very well," she demurred. "It's not one of my strong points."

Parker stood up now, tall and straight, to look down at her. "That's all right," he said softly. "I seem to recall you had many others." He rebuttoned his jacket and checked to make sure his satin bow tie was straight. Then he smiled at her, charming again, and so appealing. "I promised my first dance to the bride. Will you save the next one for me?"

She was surprised. She'd expected him to probe deeper into the past nine years, to ask more questions. She'd expected that somewhere along the way would come unnecessary excuses and apologies and explanations. And Alexandra wasn't sure if she was relieved or frustrated that he wasn't going to offer either. Perhaps it was best not to. What they were to each other only had to do with now—today.

Her sense of humor slowly began to return, and she could feel herself gaining both confidence and control. Parker Harrison was attractive and accomplished, and he was her escort for the day. She would enjoy it for what it was—no more, no less. She smiled now, her eyes softening, brightening her face. "Thank you."

Parker bent an elbow and held it out for her. Alexandra curved her hand around his arm. "You realize that this whole thing was a set-up, don't you?" he said in mock seriousness.

She looked at him. "You mean Brian and Debby wanting the two of us to meet?"

"Umm-hmm."

"It *is* a bit embarrassing," she said ruefully. "I was hoping you wouldn't notice."

Parker laughed low, showing his strong teeth in a flashing grin. "So were they," he commented dryly, as he escorted her back to the group.

"Maybe I should make it easy on them and explain that we've . . ."

"No, don't," Parker objected firmly. He stopped for a moment to look at her upturned face with its questioning eyes. "Let's continue to pretend this is the first time we're meeting and we're getting to know one another."

The request was made so quickly that it surprised even Parker; it had come out of nowhere. Well, maybe his subconscious. Some of the past memories were distinctly uncomfortable, but he didn't want them to spoil today. Alexandra Morrow had popped back into his life, and he found her so attractive, so intriguing now as a woman, that he wanted a chance to know her again. It was also an opportunity to settle a few things.

"All right," she agreed reluctantly, feeling caution come into play again as Parker gave her another warm smile and they walked on.

"So far, I like what I see," he drawled.

But if he was pretending that they could start over completely, Alexandra thought tightly, then he was in for a big disappointment.

The ride to the reception hall began in uncomfortable silence, at least for Alexandra. Parker seemed to be concentrating on the wet, slippery roads and the traffic through Washington D.C. But Alexandra was concentrating on him.

She'd half expected that Parker would have some kind of entourage at his disposal—waiting in the wings for a word or signal to do his bidding. But there was none. When they'd left the church, everyone heading for a car for the drive to the reception, Alexandra had found herself alone with him. She assumed that his car would somehow reflect his enormous financial success, something totally obvious and flashy. But it was a white Volkswagen, a well-preserved convertible Karmen Ghia Champagne Edition, that he led her to. Although in very good condition, it was not a flashy car. It did not lend itself to chauffeurs or entourages. It was strictly a two-person vehicle, closed and private.

He deposited her things in the back seat and carefully helped her into the front. In the tight confines of the small car, Alexandra was suddenly aware of his manliness. Alexandra had allowed herself only a passing interest in the opposite sex over the last few years, and disappointingly, their interest in her hadn't extended much beyond sex itself. She had convinced herself that involvement of any kind could not possibly work to her advantage. She had only once allowed herself a brief flight of fancy, and it had very nearly destroyed her. What she had in mind for her life now did not require a man or love. She would fulfill her life on her own, alone. Yet it was a surprise to find that she could still remember, still be moved by the maleness, the warmth that Parker emitted sitting in the driver's seat next to her. Unbidden images of delightful intimacy filling her mind and imagination as she wondered if he, too, remembered.

Parker was exuding a sensual quality that was almost tangible. Alexandra found herself squeezing uncomfortably against the door of the car as if to avoid it, as if it reached out to her.

Parker didn't seem inclined to talk, only asking a question or two for directions or making an innocuous comment about their surroundings. He was also busy remembering the places he'd been, the things he'd done so long ago in D.C. with Alex. Parker's mouth curved into a slight smile at the mental image of their youth. He remembered how confused and unhappy he'd been with his life at the time, even with his music. But Alexandra's presence had been a surprise which, for a while, had made it all bearable.

Alexandra found that she, too, was capable of only meaningless conversation during the ride to the reception hall. For a frightening heart-stopping moment, she wondered just how indifferent she really was toward Parker Harrison. She wondered if she could actually be afraid of his persuasive powers, coupled with the knowledge of what they'd been to each other in the past. Was there any possibility she'd forgive him?

From the moment they came through the door of the restaurant, with a fresh cigarette pressed into the corner of his wide mouth, Parker captured everyone's attention. All afternoon he was politely but persistently besieged with questions, requests for autographs, and adoration.

At one point, while she was sitting alone, Alexandra absently twirled the stem of her champagne glass. She was half listening to the laughing conversation taking place at her table among people she didn't really know. At the tables to her left and right were the immediate families of the bride and groom. Behind her, at the fourth and last table, were musician friends of Brian's, and Parker.

Alexandra had found herself seated next to him at the reception table. But beyond the dance he'd claimed with her after proposing a toast to the bride and groom, they'd been separated all afternoon, and he'd wandered from table to table, speaking with everyone.

She'd been asked to dance by Debby's father, and then by Brian, and then by a few of the musicians. Each time she'd returned to the table, Parker was somewhere else, surrounded by female admirers.

Alexandra grimaced in resignation. She supposed that when you were as well known as Parker, anonymity was impossible. But it was hard to ignore the constant outbreak of cheerful voices and laughter around him, hard to enjoy herself when she found herself surreptitiously following his movements and feeling so left out. Parker sat like a king holding court, smiling amiably and giving each member of his audience a slice of his time and attention. Alexandra had to admit he handled himself well. He'd become quite polished and sophisticated in comparison to the Parker she remembered, with his many doubts and insecurities. Of course, those had to do exclusively with his music, his public life, and his questions about his career, now that he was beyond the stage of child prodigy. It was those concerns which had made it possible for them to meet so fortuitously when Alexandra was nineteen. Often over the years Alexandra had tried to convince herself that Parker had found resolutions to his questions and that those answers had taken him away from her. It wasn't really satisfying as an explanation, but it was all she had. There was always the possibility, however, that Parker hadn't cared enough about her.

An attractive blonde flirted outrageously with him now, but she was no more successful than the other women trying to be special in his eyes. It was easy for Parker to be gracious and charming. Much of it came naturally because, although not very gregarious, he was approachable and friendly. Some of it had to do with his being a performer. He was probably used to having an audience even when he wasn't on stage.

As friendly as he was in this moment, no one could detect Parker's desire to slip away and go back to his table, back to Alexandra. She astounded him. She was so much more than he remembered. The raw, youthful vulnerability was gone and had been replaced by . . . he wasn't sure what. Certainly she had matured. And she had grown more lovely than ever.

What also caught Parker's attention almost at once was Alexandra's apparent lack of attention to him. Actually, it bordered on indifference. It was a refreshing turn-about from what he'd come to expect from people, both male and female. The Alexandra he'd known before, in her youth and honesty, had kept him grounded, had reminded him that he had a natural ability in music, that he had a responsibility to it and to himself. He realized now, as he listened to the overly bright laughter of those around him and catered to their expectations of him, that he'd missed Alex's honesty and insights.

A vision in intricate white lace suddenly blocked Alexandra's frowning contemplation of Parker, and she looked up to find Debby in his vacated chair. Alexandra at once gave her a warm, bright smile while disguising her own emotional confusion.

"So, do you feel any different now that you're married?" Alexandra asked.

Debby lifted a brow saucily at her friend. "I'll let you know after tonight."

Alexandra laughed. "That's not exactly what I mean."

Debby shrugged. "Mom used to always say, the first time you have a fight is when you know you're really married. You can't very well tell him to go away."

"I think she was only teasing you," Alexandra offered.

Debby tilted her head thoughtfully. "On the other hand, fighting can have its advantages. Think of all the fun we'll have making up."

Alexandra shook her head at her friend's outrageous line of thought. "I think Brian is marrying you just in time."

Debby sobered a little and shrugged a shoulder. "I think it was time. Being separated while he was on the road was hard on both of us. We spent a fortune on long-distance calls. Believe me, it's probably cheaper to be married."

Alexandra took a small sip of her pink champagne. She stole a thoughtful look at Debby over the rim of the fluted glass. "Well, now you're married, but Brian will still go on the road, won't he?"

"This is his last tour. He's applying for a seat in the Washington Symphony. I think he wants to follow Parker's example."

Alexandra felt a lurching of her heart in her chest. She stared at Debby. "What do you mean, follow Parker's example?"

"Just that Parker told Brian he was tired of life on the road himself. He doesn't have to prove himself anymore, heaven knows. I think he'd like to settle down in one place to pick and choose what projects he wants to do." Debby looked anxiously at Alexandra. "That's . . . sort of why Brian wanted him here today. What do you think of him? Isn't he something?"

Alexandra ignored the question and narrowed her eyes suspiciously. "And I suppose that Brian thought Parker could follow his lead and find someone, er . . . interesting?"

"Well . . ." Debby hesitated, seeing the stubborn, defensive set to her friend's face. "Brian just thought it would be nice if you two . . ."

"I knew it," Alexandra moaned. "Brian's playing matchmaker."

"Well, not exactly," Debby hedged.

"Did he mention me to Parker before today?" Alexandra probed on.

"No, I don't think so. He thought you two should just meet and let things kind of take their own course."

Alexandra's eyes grew stormy. It was on the tip of her tongue to tell Debby that Brian's efforts had been wasted and that he was about nine years too late. Things *had* taken their own course.

"Look . . ." Debby said soothingly, not getting the response she'd expected and seeing the storm rising in her friend. "I'm sorry if it seems like we interfered. But Brian thinks the world of Parker, and I'm so fond of you that . . "

"That naturally you figured that Parker and I would sort of hit it off and have a happy ending—just like you and Brian."

Debby looked shamefaced. "I guess it sounds awfully silly."

Alexandra knew at another time, under other circumstances, it wouldn't have been. And there was no way on Earth for either Debby or Brian to know that. She smiled with a reassuring effort and patted Debby's hand. "It's not silly at all. And I'm touched at your concern for me, but . . ." She struggled to find the right words to express her sentiments now. "I'm busy with my own music right now. And I'm sure Parker would like to arrange his own life. I doubt if it's going to include me," Alexandra said with a false lightness.

Debby sighed. "That's too bad. I was sure you two were right for one another. Parker is successful and popular and talented. But I don't think he's all that happy. There's something in his past he doesn't talk about, something that hurts him." Again she turned her eyes hopefully to Alexandra, but already her friend was shaking her head adamantly.

"We all have hurts in our pasts, Debby. I'm sure Parker will survive his," she said rather coldly, even as she swept aside her own curiosity at Debby's observations of Parker's present life.

Debby shook her head sadly. "I was so sure you'd like him."

Alexandra felt the warmth drain from her face, neck, and bare shoulders. "I didn't say I didn't *like* him. I just don't think you should marry us off so quickly."

"You haven't exactly been setting dating records, you know. I've never met anyone as picky as you are. Some really great men have asked you out."

She stared blankly at Debby for a long, silent moment knowing that the word "like" was not nearly adequate enough to describe her feelings. There was no way, not enough time to do so, and in any case, it didn't matter. She wasn't going to let it matter.

A large hand settled on her shoulder, and Alexandra jumped. She looked up into the quizzical gaze of Parker standing at her side. Alexandra merely stared at him, lost for the merest second in the past, and recalling with crystal clarity how she'd once felt about him.

"Oh, you've come to ask Alexandra to dance?" Debby instigated, getting to her feet.

"As a matter of fact, yes," Parker said. He gave Debby his champagne glass and reached for Alexandra's hand, and pulled her slowly to her feet. He'd already learned very quickly that it was best not to give Alexandra too much time to reply because the answer would likely be "No." He wanted to change that. Parker never questioned why it was important that he make a positive impression on Alexandra Morrow. She was intriguing, even in her coolness toward him. Still, wanting to charm her smacked of wanting to redeem himself in her eyes. Parker knew that there was something he'd done in the past which continued to bother her deeply.

The warmth and strength from his fingers sent a quiver of emotion through Alexandra again and, with a feeling of panic and defeat, Alexandra realized that she'd always responded to being near Parker. *That* apparently had not changed in all those years.

Parker led her to the dance floor, where a light Latin number played. The beat of the music didn't really allow for body contact, but every now and then Parker would take her hand to swing her through a series of intricate turns, drawing unexpected cheers and applause from a small group of guests who followed his every move. Alexandra kept up with his lead, excited by their matched timing, synchronized as if it were natural. She kept her eyes focused on his loosened bow tie, just a zig-zag of black fabric draped carelessly around his neck, the top two buttons of his formal shirt opened as well.

When the number ended, Alexandra was breathless, her face warm from the exertion and her eyes bright. Unexpectedly she had enjoyed the dance. When she raised her gaze to Parker, she could tell he'd enjoyed it, too. And she saw that it wasn't over yet. He held out his hands, wanting the next dance as well, which was slow and romantic.

One hand slid slowly, sensuously, around her waist, drawing Alexandra in until thighs rested against thighs. The other hand threaded with her fingers intimately. They moved in time to the music. Parker was deliberately careful in holding Alexandra to him. There was a delicacy about her, a lightness that required subtlety and slowness. Sudden moves and actions could easily spook her. Parker thought with some irony that he'd apparently done just that to her a long time ago, and never realized it.

It had been a while since Alexandra had been so close to a man; an age since she'd been so close to Parker. She had a sudden mental image of a dark, secret moment with them together, and convulsively she squeezed his shoulder. Parker pressed her waist, and Alexandra blinked and looked up at him to find his scrutiny dark and serious.

"Your hands are still cold. What are you thinking now?" he asked in a low voice.

Alexandra studied him for a moment, seeing all the things that had ever made him attractive to her. "That you never answered my question before. How have things gone for you?" she evaded.

Parker lifted a corner of his mouth as if he found the question amusing. "Things have gone okay. I have few complaints." He turned her to the music.

Alexandra raised her brows. "You have some? I'm surprised."

"Why?" he asked puzzled.

"Oh . . . I don't know. You've done well for yourself. Some would even say you lead a charmed existence. What could there be to complain about?"

His eyes grew very dark and scanned her upturned face thoughtfully. "Maybe 'complaints' is the wrong word. I should have said I want for very little."

"There's something missing?" Alexandra persisted.

Parker didn't answer her, but continued to watch her, and move her to the music. He asked a question rather than answering hers. "Tell me, what do you want out of life, Alex?" he asked softly, trying to understand the slight edge to her voice.

Alexandra stiffened slightly, and she silently chuckled. "What you have," she answered firmly.

"Perhaps you know something I don't," Parker said cryptically. "Why don't you tell me what it is I'm supposed to have?"

Although Alexandra thought he was teasing, his eyes were still targeted on her, and his stare showed he expected a serious answer. It made her nervous suddenly. "Well, for one thing, your music is heard everywhere. You are paid well to perform, and you get to work with exciting people." She stopped and looked up at him. Parker seemed totally unmoved.

"Go on," he said flatly.

Alexandra frowned. He sounded disappointed. What more could there be? "You have the attention of hundreds of thousands of fans, record sales in the millions," she continued. "You have everything."

Again Parker lifted a corner of his mouth, but this time without any show of humor. He'd heard all that before. The image of him was not new, but it was tired. It was almost as if people couldn't really see *him*, only what he did and what he had. It was all so superficial. And it was sad, because Alexandra used to know him better than anyone and now she apparently believed the misconceptions about his life. My, how the mighty have fallen, Parker thought wryly.

"No . . . not everything, Alex," he said evenly, and a muscle began working in his jaw. His voice became wishful and soft. "My apartment accommodates one person. Me. I come back to it after a road trip, alone. There are lots of people in my life, but not many friends, and no one person who's special." His hand moved slowly along her spine. "If I go out for a walk, to just enjoy a day like someone who leads a normal life, I can count on being recognized and surrounded by scores of people. Strangers. They'll all know my music, but not one of them will really know me. I found out how lonely it can be in a crowd," Parker finished with a lift of his brows and a soundless chuckle.

The music had stopped again, and the band was taking a break. But neither Parker nor Alexandra noticed. The lights dimmed on the dance floor leaving the two of them locked in semi-privacy. Behind them the wedding guests were moving among themselves and shifting chairs. Alexandra and Parker remained in the middle of the dance floor.

Alexandra stared at him. The Parker she remembered had been a solitary man, often plagued with self-doubts and insecurities. He'd been well known and respected even then, but for different reasons. Then, Parker had said he'd performed to please and to cater to everyone but himself. He'd suffered a period of not wanting to play at all. It was during that time, Alexandra knew, that Parker discovered he wanted to compose his *own* projects; play his *own* music.

When he'd suddenly left Washington, D.C., all those years ago, she discovered later, it was to pursue that music and develop his own unique style, which would take him to the forefront of the musical world for the second time in his life. The first time he'd followed the dictates of his parents and his instructors. The second time Parker had taken control of his career and his life. But Alexandra had to admit, Parker didn't seem all that pleased or happy about his fame, just as Debby had hinted at earlier. She didn't understand what more he could possibly want.

Suddenly standing in his arms, her hands pressed lightly against his chest, Alexandra surprisingly saw in his face and eyes all the things that had brought her so close to him once before. Did he still have the need for approval and support and faith? Was he still uncertain whether he was any good? Against her will, she felt empathy for that part of his life that might remain empty and unfulfilled, but she fought against it. He had made a choice. He had a life-style to die for. If he didn't "have it all," he certainly, at least, had the next best thing.

"Are you saying that fame isn't all it's cracked up to be?" Alexandra asked softly.

Parker frowned and shook his head. "Fame was never what I was aiming for. I thought you knew that," he finished, just as softly.

There was an implied criticism, an implied disappointment that made Alexandra suddenly angry. Who was he anyway, to assume so much of her after so many years? "Maybe I did at one time," she said sharply. "But I was very young and believed a lot of things that weren't true. I don't believe everything I hear anymore." She dropped her hands to her side.

Slowly, Parker released Alexandra and stood back a step. He surveyed her lovely, lithe body in the peach silk gown, and looked deeply into her eyes.

"What do you believe in?" he asked. "What's important to you?"

"Myself," Alexandra answered without hesitation. "My ability to sing."

"Is that all?"

No, she thought, *I always believed in you.* But her large, dark eyes never wavered from his. "Yes, that's all."

Parker slowly took a deep breath and slowly let it out again. He slipped his hands into his pants pocket. "You've changed, Alex," he commented. A strange pain settled in Parker's chest. It was disconcerting, but familiar.

His regret immediately caused Alexandra's heart to turn over, her resolve to slip, her teeth to clamp tightly together to keep her eyes from misting with tears. He was wrong in ways she'd never let him know, so wrong that for an instant she forgot the pain of the past and was tempted to blurt out what was really in her mind and heart at that moment. There was a time when she would have settled for just having his love. She would have given up her own dreams of a musical career for that.

"No, Parker. I haven't changed at all. I've only grown up. And I've learned that we all have to be responsible for what our lives become; some people are lucky and get everything they want. Others have to work very hard."

"Are you suggesting that I didn't really earn my good fortune?" Parker asked, his eyes staring bright, angry sparks at Alexandra.

She shook her head. "No, of course not. No one knows better than I the cost of your success. But I also learned an important lesson from you: never let anything stop you from getting what you want in life."

Alexandra turned and walked slowly back to the cheerful gathering, swallowing the tension inside herself. She was chilled and shaking with emotions, sorry that she'd let her feelings get away from her, but perversely glad that she could get them out.

By the time she'd pulled herself together, the wedding party and the guests were grouped for the next ritual in the afternoon's celebration. A chair was placed in the center of the floor and with great ceremony and applause Debby was led to it and seated by Brian. Brian bent to one knee and lifted the hem of his wife's wedding dress, exposing a comely turn of silken leg. There were whistles and cat calls as Brian slowly slipped Debra's "something blue," a lace garter, down and off her leg. Then he stood on a chair with his back to the group as the men gathered closer. Twirling the garter risquely around a finger, Brian let it go, flinging it into the crowd.

It was caught by Debby's school administrator, a timid, scholarly man in his sixties who gingerly examined the lace confection as though it was a curious insect. He turned beet red at the laughter around him and, with a sheepish grin, hastily stuffed it into a pocket.

Next, Debby was helped onto the chair as she, too, presented her back to the group while holding onto her floral bouquet. Alexandra continued to hang back on the edge of the group, her mind still on the conversation with Parker, and only half attentive to the rollicking. She wasn't in the mood right now to participate, but she made the effort to be part of the group.

At the boisterous count of three, the bouquet was flung up and over Debby's shoulder. Hands flew up and there were squeals and laughter. But Debby's arm strength was a lot better than her aim, and the flowers flew over everyone's head.

It was a fast second before Alexandra realized the flowers were headed straight for her, and all she could think to do was close her eyes and duck her head out of the way.

There was a surprised gasp and then a roar of more laughter. When

Alexandra opened her eyes, it was to turn and find Parker holding the bouquet with an embarrassed grin on his handsome face. Everyone applauded. For a moment Parker turned his attention to Alexandra. Something fleeting and electric passed between them, causing Alexandra to quickly avert her eyes. Forgetting her anger at Parker, Alexandra remembered another of Grandma Ginny's tales: that the one to catch a bouquet at a wedding would be the next bride. There was an immediate appeal to the idea that was just as quickly dismissed in her mind.

He was tempted to give the bouquet to Alex, and he could see that she dreaded that he would. She had done a very good job of putting him on the spot all day whenever they were alone. Maybe it was even deserved, but Parker couldn't help wishing Alexandra had been a little more forgiving. Parker also knew she hadn't intended to be spiteful, but it did speak volumes for the way she felt toward him. He wasn't going to go tit for tat. Revenge could be wreaked in much more pleasant ways.

Parker walked past Alexandra and over to the six-year-old flower girl, who was also Brian's niece. The little girl's face lit up when she was given the flowers, and she rewarded Parker with a childish wet kiss to his cheek. There was additional applause.

Alexandra was pleased and soothed that Parker had handled the situation in the best way possible. It was further proof of the tenderness she recalled, and it made Alexandra feel all the worse for her petulance of a moment ago. But she had no intention of apologizing to him.

The reception soon broke up and the bride and groom made another receiving line to make farewells to their guests.

Alexandra thought to escape alone and quickly. Saying goodbye to Parker was going to be as awkward as saying hello had been, and she suddenly had a panicky feeling that she couldn't handle it. While everyone else was kissing each other goodbye and making hasty plans for future gatherings, she slipped away to the coat room unnoticed. She had her coat on and was actually at the restaurant door, ready to leave, when she realized that everything, her garment bag, her umbrella, was in the back of Parker's car. Of course the car was locked, so she couldn't quietly get her things. As she stood wondering the best way to solve this latest complication, Alexandra became aware of someone behind her. The hair bristled on the back of her neck. With a fatalistic sigh, she realized that the rest of this evening had to be played out with Parker to the bitter end.

Slowly, Alexandra turned her head to look over her shoulder. Her large, wary eyes encountered Parker standing a few feet behind her. His eyes were dark and cold. His mouth was no longer sensuous and mobile, but hard and tightly closed. There was a purposefulness in his stance, in his stiffly held body, that made it clear to Alexandra a reckoning was coming. She thought to avoid it. But as she opened her mouth to speak, she was abruptly cut off.

"I'm taking you home," he stated firmly, eliminating any possibility of argument. And then, not bothering to put on his top coat against the cold, he headed out the door.

CHAPTER 3

"I can sense this day taking a turn for the worse," Parker said stiffly. "It doesn't have to," Alexandra said. "You can still let me go home alone."

Parker shook his head. "It's not over yet." He didn't want the day to end with him feeling remorseful and guilty, with the resurgence of so much regret. He knew the decisions he'd made years ago were the only ones open to him at the time. Any alternative would have doomed him to failure. He'd hoped that Alexandra would have understood. But how could he expect her to? She didn't have all the facts he possessed about what had really happened.

They stood like combatants outside the restaurant's reception area, squaring off stubbornly, each wanting to have his way. Grimly, Parker realized he couldn't force the issue. Alexandra was going to win.

"Wait . . . wait!"

They both turned at the sound of Debby's breathless voice behind them.

"I thought you and Brian began your honeymoon ten minutes ago, when you said goodbye to your guests," Parker said in amusement.

Debby grinned sheepishly. "It begins when the plane takes off from Dulles. I just wanted to make sure Alexandra would get home all right. I didn't want to leave her stranded in Maryland . . ." Debby's voice faded as she saw the mutinous transformation on her friend's face.

Alexandra did an admirable job of containing her annoyance and ill humor. She tried to remember that this was Debby's special day; she had no right to be difficult. She remembered that Debby only thought to see after her welfare. And finally, she remembered that Debby had no knowledge—how could she?—of Parker's past relationship to her. Alex took a deep breath.

"You know, it wasn't very fair to make me Parker's responsibility all day. He shouldn't have to be a chauffeur as well. What would his manager think?"

"I didn't mind," Parker said tightly.

Debby looked silently and wide-eyed from one to the other, hoping for redemption from either one.

"I wouldn't have missed this afternoon for the world," Parker said wryly, but took little satisfaction in watching Alexandra's discomfort. He reached for her hand, raising his brows at her still chilled fingers. Parker gallantly bent over the hand and kissed it lightly. "I'm looking forward to taking Alexandra home."

Alexandra averted her gaze and stood stiffly. She let him hold her hand. She could hear Debby's relief.

"Oh, thanks, Parker. You're a prince and a gentleman."

Parker chuckled, still holding Alexandra's hand. "It's a matter of opinion."

Alexandra forced a smile and looked at Debby. It became warmer when she saw Debby's obvious confusion. "I'll be fine." She gave Debby a quick hug and pushed her away. "Go on. Brian is waiting."

"Impatiently, I hope," Debby giggled, then turned and ran.

The sudden quiet turned chilly again, and Parker released Alexandra's hand. With a further flourish, he stood aside for her to precede him. Alexandra pulled her collar up around her neck, wishing that at least Brian and Debby had decided to marry in June, like other normal people.

As though informing a cab driver of her destination, Alexandra, as impersonally as she could, gave Parker her address, and then sat back to gaze stonily out her window. She was so deep into her own reflections, wondering how she was going to handle Parker once they reached her apartment, that when he spoke his voice made her jump.

"You know, I get the feeling you don't like me very much," Parker said, in a tired, reflective tone.

Alexandra's eyes widened, and she cast a quick, surprised glance his way before once again staring into the dark, wet night. "I'm sorry," she said softly. "I didn't mean to give that impression."

"Oh? Just what feeling were you trying to give me?" he asked, puzzled.

Alexandra bit her lip. "None at all, Parker. I mean . . . what is it you want me to say? We haven't seen each other in a very long time, and we only knew one another for a few months." She shrugged nervously. "There just doesn't seem to be very much to say."

There was a small silence, and then, in the quiet tenseness of the car,

Alexandra heard him sigh. In it she heard exasperation, impatience, even defeat, as if he'd hoped and tried to elicit another reaction from her. She had been surprised and unprepared for seeing him again like this, but she hadn't forgotten that he'd been the one to walk away.

"I remember those few months as being pretty terrific in lots of ways. I thought we got to know each other real well. I have good memories of that time, Alex." His eyes searched her profile briefly before returning to the road ahead. "We shared a lot. We were good together."

"But you left," Alexandra whispered in a small voice, hoping none of the bewilderment showed. Again she bit her lip and clenched her hands. She hadn't meant to say that. It was too much like an accusation. She sounded too hurt.

"You always knew I would."

She swung her head sharply around to him. "I *never* knew that. I always thought if you left, I would . . ." Alexandra closed her mouth to stop the confession.

"In the end, I had to leave, Alex. But I didn't . . ."

She didn't allow him to finish. "Yes, and now it's all history," she said, taking a deep breath, closing her eyes momentarily and opening them to stare out the window again. "Why don't we just leave it at that? Tell me, how long will you be in D.C. this time?" she asked quickly, to change the subject. "You must have lots of commitments. Are you staying for long?" she asked, unsure of which she hoped it would be.

"I haven't decided yet," Parker answered. "I may drive up to Philadelphia to see my folks. Or I might hang around Washington for a while. I forgot how much I like it here," he answered, glancing at her briefly. Did she remember the fun they used to have? The good times that had been of her making, though he'd been too serious to relax and enjoy them?

"Are you staying with friends?" Alexandra asked carefully, again trying not to be too curious. She wondered if there was a current lady in his life. She was annoyed with herself for even thinking it, and dismayed to feel a brief twist of jealousy grabbing at her.

In the darkness of the car Parker lifted a brow and pursed his lips as he considered her innocent question. It told him instantly so much. It was a facet of Alexandra's personality which remained that he'd always liked. A certain natural naïveté that peeked through the young woman then, the adult woman now. It was a kind of youthful hopefulness and eagerness maintained for all things, despite the need to be seen and treated as mature and worldly. Alexandra *had* changed in nine years. But not as much as she thought.

"I'm staying at the apartment of my manager. He and his wife are in Europe, making a tour arrangement for another one of their interests.

It's for my use for as long as I want. Or until the middle of April, whichever comes first."

Alexandra looked at him. The car turned slowly onto a residential street of row houses in northwest D.C. "What happens then?" she asked.

Parker squinted through the streaked window, trying to find her house number as he drove slowly. "Then I go to New York. I'm doing a benefit concert for the United Negro College Fund." He pulled the car into a spot in front of the line of nearly identical buildings, and turned off the windshield wipers.

"You did a benefit concert several months ago for UNICEF," Alexandra stated.

"That's true," Parker said, now turning off the engine and swiveling a little in his seat to face her.

"How nice of you," she said stiffly, just a touch of sarcasm in her tone. She looked at Parker's face without being able to see the details. The shadows showed the twitching of a jaw muscle, the high, prominent line of his cheek, and the corner of his mouth. Only bits of nighttime light reflected in his eyes, and they shot off sharp sparks in her direction. He was annoyed.

She was being difficult and she knew it. But Alexandra couldn't seem to help herself. It was as if some angry, enraged super-ego had taken possession of her and was determined to be unpleasant, uncommunicative, unforgiving. She baited, pushed, and dared, thinking that her cold, ungracious demeanor was justified and would hurt him deeply before she left him for the night . . . or for eternity.

Gone were all elements of the warm, even-tempered young woman she was normally. Invisible was the ready smile that brightened her eyes and face and made her a pleasure to be with. Hidden was the empathy she was capable of that often allowed her to consider someone else's feelings and needs above her own. Alexandra didn't know herself, and she didn't like at all what she was as she sat opposite Parker. The humidity began to fog the car windows, closing them in an eerie pocket of silence as they sat like adversaries. The entire day, indeed their pasts, hung between them. It didn't seem possible to get past it.

The one-word question "Why?" had sat on her tongue all day long, needing to be asked of Parker, but her pride prevented her from asking it. What had gone wrong? What had *she* done? It had always infuriated her that she thought herself to have been at fault; after all, Parker had been the one to walk away. The question and the need for an answer had remained. Yet she wouldn't ask him; she couldn't. Alexandra felt so righteous in her anger, and she knew instinctively it would be a poor, unworthy victory.

"Doing free concerts has nothing to do with 'nice,' Alex," Parker finally said, interrupting her thoughts. "It's my way of saying 'thank you' to all the people I'll never meet who believed in me, and who put me where I am today."

His voice was low and caressing, as if he was explaining something she should have understood. She was sure there was a sad note of regret in his tone, as if he shouldn't have to explain to her, of all people. He had always been sensitive to the wishes and needs of others, and she well remembered how torn other people's wishes had left him years ago. Which made his abrupt desertion of her, for that was the word, so unreal and so painful to bear. He had not shown much care for how *she'd* take his departure. Didn't her feelings count, too?

She lowered her head and fought to control the trembling of her lips. *What is the matter with me?* Alexandra wailed silently to herself. She felt like she was coming apart, wanting to forgive him, whatever his reasons, and wanting to strike back in retaliation.

"I'm sorry," she said, in a broken voice. "That was unnecessary of me. I . . . I don't know why I said that," she finished helplessly.

Her head was still bent, and she saw one of Parker's hands reach over to cover both of hers clenched in her lap. But she couldn't bring herself to look at him, although she suddenly wanted to grab and hold onto his offering.

"Alex," he said to her, "*I* know why you said it."

Now she did look at him, but she could read nothing in his expression. It was controlled, and *in* control, and Alexandra recognized what she hadn't allowed herself to see. Parker had changed, too. The earlier flicker of doubt was gone from his eyes. He was much more self-possessed and confident. He seemed to have made peace with himself, while her own peace of mind was shattering virtually before her eyes.

He closed his fingers around her hands and squeezed. "Your hands never did get warm," he said. "I'm hoping that means you still have a warm heart."

Before she could respond Parker released her and turned to open his door to climb out. He quickly came around to her side and helped her out as well before retrieving her things from the back seat. Placing his hand beneath her elbow, he led her firmly toward the brightly lit entrance of her building.

Alexandra had the entire second floor of a three-story limestone townhouse. When they reached the top of the stairs, she had regained some command of herself. She dug her keys out of her bag and silently took her other things from Parker.

He knew that if he asked to come in, she would refuse immediately. It would be just another way for her to deny him as she'd done all day. But Parker also knew with a certainty that unless she could get beyond the anger of their past before they said goodnight, he might never see her again. He didn't want that to happen.

"It was nice seeing you again, Parker," she said formally. "You look well, and I'm glad you're so successful." She held out her hand awkwardly for him to take. She felt so foolish. This was the man who had taught her about love, and she was now about to shake hands with him as if they'd never met before. "Thank you for driving me home."

Parker suddenly leaned against her door frame, ignoring the hand, watching the play of emotions on her smooth countenance after a long afternoon of trying to control them. "Did you ever get your piano?" he asked quietly with a smile, out of left field, but it succeeded in diverting her for the moment.

Alexandra blinked at him. When they'd first met, she'd been very envious of the grand upright he owned. "Yes, I did," she finally answered.

Then Parker held out his hand. After a moment's confusion, Alexandra placed her apartment keys into his palm. Silently, he opened the door and turned the knob, letting the door swing open into the interior. He waited, and finally Alexandra preceded him into her apartment. She flipped on a wall light as he closed the door, and continued through the small foyer to a darkened room to her left. Another light switch was turned on and she stood at the entrance waiting for Parker to catch up to her. He stopped next to her looking at the baby grand piano which dominated her living room.

A low, appreciative whistle came between Parker's pursed lips. "For someone who says she doesn't play so hot, you sure went all out."

Alexandra couldn't help but be pleased that Parker thought she'd chosen well. She'd saved for two whole years to be able to afford this one. Parker walked over to the piano and automatically turned on the small reading lamp positioned over the sheet music stand. Idly he fingered the keys. Alexandra felt herself go still inside, and she just stood and watched. She felt time slip slowly away.

Parker, his attention totally on the beautiful instrument, slipped off his coat and dropped it over the back of a nearby chair. He sat down at the keyboard and was contemplative before he lifted his hands, and the long, masculine, well-trained fingers touched the keys.

Parker surprised her by starting with a classical fugue as he became familiar with her piano. He then played several short classical pieces with such concentration that he might have been totally alone. His eyes closed as he tilted his head to catch his own sounds. His mouth moved and pursed with inner reactions and emotions, his jaw tensing, brows furrowed.

Alexandra knew that Parker did not often delve into his classical background anymore—at least, not in public. He did not often search among the keys for the music that had begun his auspicious career when he was just a child. But it was obvious he still loved it. Alexandra knew that this, too, satisfied his joy of music.

Parker himself had said he never fully understood where the love had come from. At what point did he begin to *feel* music in his bones, to absorb it into his soul so that he felt nourished and fulfilled? When did he know that this would be his life, playing and creating music?

Alexandra had met Parker in a period of transition, and had learned quickly that he wanted more from his talents than performing just the classics. She'd always assumed it had been in pursuit of recognition, but words he'd spoken to her earlier in the day echoed softly through her head, and she realized with a small shock that there were many things she didn't know or understand about him.

Then Parker switched to something by Aaron Copeland, and moved briefly into a jazz piece she didn't recognize. Without consciously being aware of it, Alexandra put down her things and shrugged out of her coat, and, as if mesmerized, her eyes followed Parker's sure hand movements and her ears filled with the sounds of his music. Her heart remembered well the wonderful presence of him, the admiration, joy, shyness of being near this extraordinarily gifted and handsome man.

She stood just behind him and nearly held her breath as the music floated like magic on the air, and all her first young emotions were reborn.

"Do you remember this one, Alex?" Parker reminisced with a smile. He launched into *All Because of Love,* and then *Memories.*

Her throat started to close, and she swallowed hard. Oh, yes . . . she remembered.

Parker's glance bounced off her quickly. "Sit down," he said as he switched melodies and, with a knowing look at her, started with something fast and intricate and breathtaking, the movements across the keys requiring skill as well as a sense of feeling for the piece. Alexandra smiled.

Instinctively she lifted her slender hands and, at the right moment, came into the piece with Parker, their duet in syncopation. A smile curved her lips as the near-forgotten became instantly familiar again as she and Parker played a piece they'd improvised together during that time he was helping her to improve her skills. It had been so much fun.

Now Parker added some chords, instantly new, and Alexandra kept up the harmony, sensing rather than actually knowing the way of his mind with the music. But she'd always understood his music.

He nodded. "Hey! Well all right, now!" his brows raised in surprised pleasure. "You've been doing a bit of practicing, Miss Alexandra Morrow," he crooned over the piano music.

Alexandra felt at once elated and then, just as quickly, wanted to pummel the keys in frustration. It shouldn't matter what he thought. His praise should mean nothing . . . *nothing*. But her music was better because of all the time Parker had spent with her at the piano, *his* piano, teaching her about rhythm and pacing and how to touch the keys. Her musical ear and the touch of her fingers had become more sensitive because he'd told her not to think so much, but to feel how her fingers moved when she played. *She* had become more sensitive, because of Parker.

With eyes bright and large, Alexandra looked at him and caught his scrutiny. Her hands faltered once, and then again. Suddenly she stopped. Parker's fingers continued for several more chords, and then he stopped as well.

They looked at one another and Alexandra knew that the pretense had come to an end. The natural joy of just a moment ago became a sadness that began to weigh heavily within her. Alexandra felt confused again, betwixt and between, no longer sure what she was feeling or what was real. But she knew that the longer she remained in Parker's company, the less sure she became.

"Stop. That's enough. I . . . I think you'd better leave," she said, in a shaky whisper.

"Alexandra . . ." Parker said hoarsely, using her full name for the first time. Hearing him say her name with his own unique enunciation always made her feel she belonged with him. He used her full name to get her attention, make her listen and to make her believe what he said.

Alexandra stood up abruptly. "Please! I want you to go."

"I never meant to hurt you." He let out a harsh chuckle. "I swear, there were times years ago when I didn't know if I was coming or going. Don't you remember how confused I was?"

"Well, I guess you decided you were going. So fast, as a matter of fact, you never bothered saying goodbye." Alexandra marched over to the chair and yanked up Parker's coat. "Here," she said holding it out to him. Her hands were shaking.

Parker stood up and slowly advanced toward her. He ignored the coat. "It was best that I did that, Alex. I was no good for you then. Hell, I could barely keep myself together. I had a lot of things to work out," he explained angrily, his jaw and mouth taking a proud and stubborn line. He saw her struggling with tears, saw her soft hair loosening under its pinned restraints, and the tendrils adding a lost, vulnerable, wary look to her face. "Alex, I needed you. But if I'd stayed I might have taken everything from you and left nothing in return. I wanted you to have your music, your chance, your own life."

"How noble of you. You should have told me that before I cared so much," she whispered brokenly.

"I cared," he said clearly. "But until I got my head together, it wouldn't have worked," he said softly. "It was harder for me to leave than you think. Believe me, I was only thinking of you."

She shook her head. More curls came loose and lay against her neck. Her vision was blurred with tears. "You were thinking of yourself," she said angrily. "You probably had a good laugh because this silly teenager was so infatuated with you."

"Alex . . ." he began coaxingly.

"Take your coat." She thrust it into his chest, but Parker grabbed her wrist, holding her still for a moment.

He plied his cashmere coat from her rigid fingers and carelessly tossed it back on the chair. Then his hands wrapped around her arms and slowly began to pull Alexandra toward him. She braced her hands against his chest as fear clutched at her heart.

"I never laughed at you, Alex." He slid a hand around her back and down her spine, drawing Alexandra in closer until his thighs and hips were tight against her own. There was a gentle trembling in her entire body, like that of a small, frightened animal that has been trapped and cornered. Parker knew he'd have to be careful and prove to Alexandra that he wasn't going to hurt her. Not again. He wasn't even responding to the past, but to the now.

Alexandra felt wholly feminine and fragile in his arms. It seemed so sudden, so inappropriate. But it was instantly exciting to feel that physically she affected him the same as when he'd last seen her; that emotionally no one else seemed to have gotten next to her the way he had.

Alexandra leaned back, vowing not to give in to Parker. Her chest rose and fell with the extent of her emotions and she no longer had the ability to hide them. A tear slipped down her cheek to the corner of her mouth. She felt the start of a sudden quivering heat from inside. She was frightened. She was angry. And she was responding to the mere closeness of Parker.

"*Li-liked you? Cared* about you?" she mouthed blankly. Her elbows bent, and her hands were flattened on his chest as Parker finally closed the distance. "Oh, Parker . . ." she moaned brokenly, her emotions winning out. "I was foolishly, hopelessly in love with you," she confessed plaintively, and let the distance close between them.

Parker kept one hand around her waist, and with the other he automatically tried to brush the tears from her cheek. "I know," he whispered gently, and bent to ply a feather-light kiss from her lips.

It was over before Alexandra realized it had happened. Belatedly she registered the firm, sensual width of his mouth on hers, the fleeting warmth of his breath, and the intoxicating power of being held by him again. But it was just enough to involuntarily trigger all her senses to another response, one that made her breath catch with surprise. A sensation of melting assailed her system. She was suddenly terrified of what was happening between them.

"It was the most wonderful gift anyone had ever given me, Alex. Absolute faith and all your love." His head was still bent over her, and his words melted all resistance in her. He had always known that Alex loved him; it was hard to miss. He'd left not because he'd been afraid of her love, not because he didn't return her feelings, but because the timing was all wrong. Had he stayed with Alexandra, he truly believed neither of them would have grown. Each had to become his own person so that they'd know for certain what they shared between them. Had he stayed, he would not have realized his music and she would have been disappointed in him. He would have disappointed himself.

Was it unfair, then, to hold her now after all these years, to use the moment to say how sorry he was?

Alexandra rested her forehead against his chest. She'd just admitted she'd loved him. She hadn't known how to handle it at nineteen but had hoped that eventually Parker would tell her first that he loved her, too. Then she would have been free to express her feelings. But he'd known all along how she felt and had never said a word.

"You were the best thing that ever happened to me," he said with such force and seriousness that Alexandra held her breath and stared at him as though she were nineteen again.

In slow motion Parker bent his head to kiss her; Alexandra watched his features until they blurred and her eyelids naturally drifted closed. When she again felt Parker's lips, they were slightly parted and settled purposefully on her own. He pursed his mouth and gently pulled at hers until her lips parted, too. Then she felt his tongue gently explore. Without another hesitation, she gave him entry and became pliant against his firm length. Another tear trailed down her face as her body surrendered to the gentle passion. Parker's hand squeezed her tightly around the waist, the other hand lay along her jaw, the thumb touching her bottom lip and urging her to answer his kiss.

Alexandra felt her senses spin. She had no strength to fight him or to deny the near-dizzying effect being touched by him had on her. She didn't care. She only knew the need to press her slender, trembling body closer to him . . . to let his kiss reclaim her as his mouth manipulated and moved eloquently until a moan deep in her throat escaped. She lost herself in the feeling. But slowly his mouth lightened the pressure, his lips teasing and nibbling until they separated from Alexandra.

Her fingers clenched in his shirt front. She could barely breathe; she felt weak. Parker's mouth trailed teasingly along her jaw, her cheek, until he reached her ear and gently bit the lobe, making her stomach muscles curl with the tingling sensation. Parker's hands stroked her back and shoulders as he whispered something into her skin. The words were hot and absorbed into her neck. She only wanted him to kiss her, hoping the intimate dance of their lips and tongues would ease some of the hurt, wash away the past, and finish what had been begun before.

"It was so damned hard to leave," Alexandra heard him say finally, before she tilted her head back and turned it to meet his mouth halfway. A long, quivering sigh eased out as she allowed Parker's large hands to hold her head, while his mouth gently but thoroughly ravaged her own.

A shudder coursed through Parker, and Alexandra felt it in his tightened embrace, in the forward thrust of his thigh and hips against her, blatantly outlining his aroused state against her trembling body. She heard it in his deep moan, and gave no thought to what she was doing, only what she was feeling and needing.

Suddenly Parker literally tore his lips from hers and, on a deep breath, rested his forehead against Alexandra's. "Do you realize what we're doing?" he asked harshly through clenched teeth. "Do you know what you're doing to me?"

Alexandra opened her eyes. She wondered if there was a struggle going on in him, too, a need for her. Their emotions had escalated beyond belief. She knew that her whole being, body and soul, yearned unashamedly for Parker's complete caress. But she didn't know if she would be opening a Pandora's box of more problems, when the last ones had yet to be resolved.

"Parker . . ." she began in confusion, wanting him to make the decision.

"Look," he began, bringing his mouth to within inches of hers again, so close that she could feel his warm breath. "Maybe this shouldn't be happening. This afternoon, I got the impression from you that if looks could kill, I'd be dead," he growled. His mouth touched her cheek and rubbed along the silky surface, erotically coming back to within a hairsbreadth of her parted lips. "But right now," his voice grew low and hoarse, and he again pressed his lips to hers, "you feel so good to me."

Again his mouth took hers, the pressure of his lips taking the kiss deeper, forcing her to give him full access. Parker put his arms tightly around her, one hand smoothing over a hip, his fingers digging gently into her.

Alexandra was beyond a single clear thought. She was experiencing a pure joy, outside of reason, which made her feel she was right where she belonged.

Parker again released her mouth and Alexandra knew that the moment of truth had arrived. Parker frowned deeply, his eyes searching over her soft features, her dreamy eyes and moistened lips. He shook his head ruefully. "I don't know if I should make love to you or get the hell out of here," he said.

Alexandra looked clearly at him. "You didn't give me a choice last time," she responded quietly.

A slow, uncertain smile shaped Parker's mouth. "No, I don't suppose I did. There were reasons."

"*Your* reasons, not mine. I didn't want you to leave."

His thumb brushed over her lower lip as he continued to try and gauge her feelings. He moved his finger and began to kiss her slowly again. "Where's your bedroom?" he asked against her lips, making the decision.

It was then that a warning bell went off in Alexandra's head. There would be no turning back. Was she doing the right thing? She couldn't answer Parker's question and stood stiffly until he gently took her by the shoulders and turned her until her back was to him. There was a momentary rustling of fabric until Parker's arm swung past Alexandra to drop his tuxedo jacket and shirt on the cocktail table before the sofa. Then his fingers found the zipper of her dress and slowly opened it. Alexandra closed her eyes as the material drifted. His arms reached around her. Her breasts were firm but small and fit perfectly in the palms of his hands. While there were no callouses on Parker's fingers the tips were hardened, and their slow sweeping movement on Alexandra's heaving chest made her nipples instantly erect and sensitive. The motion raised gooseflesh of anticipation along her arms, but Parker's body emitted a stirring heat. Alexandra's senses became heated by the erotic stimulation of Parker's hand.

Parker's mouth descended to find the hollow in her neck and nuzzled at the skin to trail random kisses along the slim column until he reached her ear. Then slowly he released Alex, and walked over to turn off the wall light. They were left in only the tiny reading light on the piano.

It made crazy dark shadows in the room, and Parker seemed an almost ominous figure as he approached her.

To Parker she looked waiflike, her eyes large and uncertain. Her dress was slipping off her shoulders, but her gaze was riveted to his face as if trying to understand him, and the moment. He wasn't at all sure what there was to really understand. They wanted each other, and that was perfectly clear. He'd always been able to exercise good sense in matters concerning the opposite sex. But Alexandra was different. She'd always been different because she'd come of age with him. He had been her first lover. That also made her special.

Alexandra held her breath, and her gaze held his as he removed the rest of his clothing. Then he slowly began to remove the last of hers. The warmth of his arms closing around her and drawing her to his hard, lean body was electrifying. She wordlessly raised her mouth so that he could kiss her and love her again.

Parker lowered her to the sofa and neither mentioned the bedroom again. Parker stretched out his own body atop hers. He removed several of the pale rosebuds still pinned in Alexandra's hair, crushed earlier by his fingers. He placed them on the table with his shirt and jacket, and settled against her.

Parker looked into her eyes, searched over her creamy brown face for several long moments. Alexandra shifted her legs so that he was nestled comfortably between them.

"I used to dream about this," he said thickly, gently moving against her.

"What?" Alexandra asked, resolutely burying a rising anger beneath the onslaught of her desire. "What it would be like to see me again? To make love to me again? To have me so foolishly willing?"

Parker shook his head and smiled sadly. "No. What it would be like never to have left. I feel like tonight is *our* honeymoon."

The words were a complete surprise. But his kiss once again distracted her. His lips held her captive, but it was just a prelude to stimulating the rest of her senses into molten desire. They would have been so much more comfortable in Alexandra's bed, but Alexandra wasn't ready for that step. No, not yet.

Parker rubbed his body against hers and Alexandra felt a twisting, grabbing need spiraling throughout her body. Her loins seemed to melt and soften beneath him, and his quick, sure possession of her eliminated the need for talk as they clung together to bridge the past.

Alexandra's mind was a blank. She wasn't at all sure what she'd done or what she'd hoped to prove in the last three hours with her and Parker entangled in each other's arms. She only knew she couldn't have pulled herself away. Whatever anger she'd held, whatever remorse Parker had been trying to overcome, had been forgotten in three hours of primal passion. Her body felt warm, relaxed, sated. Achy. His touch had been expert and sure, his caresses and kisses leaving her limp with a need for fulfillment. She loved and delighted in every moment. It was obvious that they were still perfect together as lovers. But it had not settled the past; it had not changed anything.

Parker was propped up against the sofa cushions, Alexandra lay against his chest. There was a long silence between them that was both strained and embarrassed. Parker was not the least bit sorry he'd made love to Alexandra. To him it had been more than just lovemaking; they had begun to reconnect, to find the spiritual and emotional kinship they'd once known. But now Parker suspected they were back to where they'd first been when they'd arrived at Alex's apartment.

Parker had located his cigarettes and was smoking, the smoke a pale gray veil over them. Alexandra, her cheek to his chest, listened to the small puckering sound his lips made around the cigarette as he inhaled. Her head moved with his chest as he exhaled. She was deceptively fascinated with his coordination of smoking and breathing. Anything to take her mind off the last three hours, and the emptiness she felt inside.

She'd wanted to make love with Parker but she didn't know why.

Parker had maintained complete control over their passion, tempering the pace when it seemed to spiral ahead too fast; picking it up when the ache in them both stretched out too long. He'd known—remembered how to touch her and make her respond at will; but then he had been the first to teach her how. They'd brought each other to a precipice and the fall over the edge into fulfillment had been sweetly torturous. After long moments of silent recovery, they'd begun it all again.

To Alexandra, the loving, instead of having brought them closer, seemed to have driven her farther away from Parker.

He finished his cigarette and put it out in an ashtray on the low table. He made a movement to get up, and Alexandra shifted to allow him to. She immediately felt bereft of his support and warmth. She watched as he retrieved his clothes and silently began to dress.

"Why did you let me make love to you, Alex?" he asked suddenly, the words not loving and seductive, but harsh and cold. He didn't even look at her, but sat on the edge of the sofa to put on his socks and shoes.

Alexandra's nakedness made her feel too exposed, too vulnerable, and she quickly got up. She retreated to the bathroom for a floor-length robe, slowly returning to find Parker buttoning his shirt.

He stopped for a moment to stare at her. "Why?" he asked again.

Alexandra balled her hands and stuffed them into the pockets of her robe. "Because we both wanted it," she said softly. "It's been a very long time."

Parker began shaking his head as he resumed buttoning his formal shirt. "No, Alex. *I* wanted to make love to you. *You* were just looking to punish me."

Alexandra hugged herself, a flush of warmth flowing over her. "I don't see why you should feel that way," she began evenly.

"Don't you?" he said. "What were you trying to do, Alex, remind me of what I'd given up by leaving you years ago? You don't credit me at all for having made a real hard decision."

"That's not what I was thinking. I wasn't thinking much of *anything* a moment ago. But you're one to talk. It couldn't have been so hard for you to leave," Alexandra said stiffly. "I'll remind you again, you never said goodbye."

"All right, damn it. Never saying goodbye was a mistake. But if I'd tried, I might never have left. I *had* to go, Alex. For more reasons than you know."

"Reasons," Alexandra answered back. "Obviously, you didn't care at all how I'd feel," Alexandra angrily whispered.

He looked at her strangely then, his eyes at first puzzled, and then only thoughtful. "I figured you'd get over it. You were very young."

Alexandra swung away from him, the quick motion dislodging the rest of her hair and causing it to fall in a haphazard way around her face.

Parker walked over to her and grabbing her arm, swung her back to face him. His expression seemed incredulous. "And this is how you deal with men who've hurt you? You tease them into your bed then let them go, with only memories?"

Alexandra pulled her arm free, and with the other brought her hand stingingly against Parker's cheek. He barely flinched, but his jaw muscle worked quickly, tightly, as he regained control of his emotions.

"I didn't want you to bring me home at all, remember?" she reminded him in a tight voice.

"I guess I deserved that. Except for one thing. I could have had sex with anyone, Alex. I didn't come here tonight for that."

"What did you expect? That everything was the same, and I'd just be here waiting for you?" she asked raggedly, ashamed, angry, hurt all over again.

"The past is over." He got his jacket and slipped it on. "I think tonight has taken care of that." He reached out his hand. But he thought better of touching her. "I wish to God things had worked out differently. But we can't change the past."

"The past is all we'll ever have between us, Parker. I *hated* you for what you did to me then. I hate you for making a fool of me now."

Parker calmly reached for his coat and threw it over his other forearm. "I don't know if you love me anymore, and I'm not sure if you really hate me, either. You can't have it both ways, Alex." He turned and walked into her hallway and stopped to regard her again. "It's either one or the other. And I mean to find out which it really is and what it is you really want."

Alexandra stood as if in a trance as she heard Parker let himself out, and the door clicked closed behind him. For another few seconds she stood like that until she gave way to the overwhelming sea of emotions that washed in waves over her. She collapsed on the piano bench and cried. She cried because it was already clear to her what she really felt for Parker, as she had known all those years ago.

Talk was cheap. Some things never change. She hadn't stopped loving Parker at all. And her vindication was a poor substitute for it.

CHAPTER 4

It was nearly dawn and the only sound from the bedroom, dimly lit by one bedside lamp, was the crackling of stiff acetate pages being turned in a photo album. Alexandra turned the pages slowly, her reddened eyes sweeping with familiarity over the layout of photographs and clippings, reviews and music sheets. It was fat and heavy and warm on her lap as she lay propped by pillows against the headboard. As she slowly turned the pages, surprised by some of the contents as if reading them for the first time, or smiling thinly at more familiar, dear pieces, she was amazed at the wealth of documentation that marked the public and very prolific career of Parker Harrison.

Attempts to sleep had been futile. After Parker had left, she'd cried herself into hiccoughs and exhaustion for a full hour. Later, Alexandra's immediate reaction was that she felt surprisingly better. The horrible tensions of the day and evening, the surprise elements that had forced her to maintain a control she was far from feeling, had been purged from her system. She felt calmer. And she was hungry. She realized, after Parker had left, that with the trauma of seeing and dealing with him all afternoon, she'd been unable to eat a thing. After taking a long, hot bath during which she reflected even further on their evening, Alexandra saw it as a healthy sign that she wanted to consume anything she could get her hands on in the kitchen.

As she sat eating French toast at midnight, Alexandra recalled Parker's prophetic departing remark, that he had every intention of finding out how she really felt about him. She recognized it as a challenge, and she grew excited by the prospect. Yet there was not even the smallest hint from Parker as to how he might now feel about her—except regretful. Nor had there been any suggestion as to how he would carry out his challenge. Alexandra did wonder, for a moment of make-believe, if Parker intended to kiss her into submission, force *her* to declare herself, or sweep her away by the sheer force of his desire.

She was old enough to know that men found her appealing. But it did occur to her that the very volatile consummation with Parker in her living room was new. It was intense and very physical. It was adult. Years ago, Alexandra would not have been able to handle the passion which had been generated so quickly and so thoroughly between them. The earlier innocence and naïveté of their relationship was gone. What happened definitely indicated unresolved feelings. But Parker had said he'd wanted more from her than mere sex.

After making herself French toast, Alexandra went to the bookcase in the living room and searched out three thick binders. One was a photo album, and the other two were scrapbooks. She'd taken the albums with her to bed and sat up the rest of the night reviewing the contents. When she opened the first one, several unsecured articles on Parker Harrison slipped out onto her lap. Alexandra read every word of every article, feeling both comforted and regretful.

Sadly, she had to admit that Parker had been right about one thing: she had hoped to punish him. She had hoped for instant retribution, vindication, but she also wanted a sign, not so much an indication of guilt, but of love. That he had loved her. The fact that they had been so easily, so quickly drawn to one another again, spoke of an affinity between them that had always been there. It had not happened all at once, such as the physical eruption of the early evening, but had taken time and youthful uncertainty and trust. Alexandra still resented that Parker Harrison had taken her trust lightly, that it might not have meant more to him.

She'd always thought that Parker truly understood her driving need for her own life, for her own music. Even her own father, with his music background, limited as it had been from lack of nourishment, had not understood what music gave her. Parker always had. Sometimes she wished she could have been more like her younger sister, Christine, who wasn't the least bit interested in music beyond whether or not she could dance to it. Besides, she and Christine were not remotely alike; Christine didn't have to want to *do* or *be* anything to get what she wanted. Opportunities fell into her lap.

Alexandra read the pages in the album, savoring each event of Parker's career which she'd preserved forever on the black pages. She felt pride in Parker's accomplishments because she had encouraged him and believed in him.

Alexandra lay back against the warm comfort of her pillows, feeling a perverse delight in having followed Parker's career and in realizing that her collection of memorabilia may have actually bridged the gap between the past and present, keeping her connected to him vicariously while she continued slowly to grow up and become a woman. With a deep sigh, Alexandra recognized another truth: the past was indeed finished. Making love with Parker tonight had not been so much for whatever might be between them now, as for what was. It closed a chapter; it said goodbye.

Again Alexandra's mind came back to Parker's words, "I mean to find out." Did that mean he would stay? If so, for how long? This time she would know for sure and not indulge in fantasies that were impossible. This time, if they were to start over, Alexandra promised, beginning to recall the first time she and Parker Harrison met, she would be careful how she loved . . .

Alexandra had been four months shy of her twentieth birthday when she'd moved into her first apartment in Washington. For the very first time she was on her own, not responsible for a semi-invalid father, or a younger sister who was annoyingly self-centered and capricious. Sheer determination and single-mindedness to get out from under the demanding home life had made her work hard enough to win a scholarship to study music and voice at the music conservatory of George Washington University. Then she'd had to arrange for a local health care provider to check in on her father two days a week, although by then, her younger sister, Christine, was old enough to bear some responsibility. Her father had been proud of her and had wished her well.

Alexandra didn't have the sultriness or funkiness, as her sister liked to remind her, to be a popular singer, but it didn't matter, since she was aiming to sing light opera.

Her apartment outside of Georgetown was just a sublet for eighteen months, long enough to eventually find something else. Alexandra had been settled for only a few weeks when one evening, after she'd returned from a voice class, the muffled strains of a concerto came through her walls from another apartment. She'd opened her door and stood trying to figure out which apartment had someone who played so beautifully. Then the music had abruptly stopped. Alexandra waited, hoping it would continue, but finally gave up with a sigh and turned back to her apartment. Suddenly the music started again.

Quickly she turned around, back into the hall, putting out a hand behind her to catch the door. But she misjudged the distance and made a frantic grab for the knob as the door swung heavily closed, automatically locking her out of her apartment.

"Oh . . . no," she groaned, grimacing in frustration. Futilely, she twisted the knob back and forth. Annoyed, she kicked at the metal door, and it sounded like a shot echoing around the narrow hallway. She quickly recoiled as a pain shot through her bare foot.

Alexandra didn't notice the music had stopped again as she considered her dilemma. She couldn't believe she'd been so completely careless. She stood there, her mind totally blank, as she wondered what she was going to do. How embarrassing to have to ring the bell of a neighbor who was a stranger, in her bare feet, and admit she'd locked herself out! Shortly, a door opened down the hall and a tall, very slender man stepped partway out, looking up and down the corridor. Alexandra protectively pressed back against her door. But the man, a lit cigarette hanging from his lips, couldn't help but see her.

A straight black brow arched up after he'd leisurely surveyed the stiff length of her. She stood dressed in ancient jeans and T-shirt and balanced on one foot as she favored the injured one. His dark eyes sparkled from his square face. He took the cigarette from his lips and exhaled as he lounged in his doorway. A smile slowly began to spread over his sharp brown face, and even in her embarrassment, Alexandra saw he was very good-looking.

"If you're trying to break into that apartment, kicking the door won't do it."

She stared silently at him.

"And you'll give burglary a bad name dressed like that." He was laughing at her.

"I live here," Alexandra said, examining him.

"Do you?" He crossed his arms completely over his lean torso. He was dressed in a pale blue shirt, at that moment hanging open outside his close-fitting faded jeans and exposing a slight, smoothly muscled chest. Alexandra was suddenly acutely aware she was braless under the T-shirt, as she watched the way his gaze traveled over her body.

"The best way of getting into your apartment is with a key," he teased. "Don't you have one, or did you lose it?"

Alexandra's mouth suddenly curved into a small smile at the absurd conversation he was having with her.

"That's better. Now, what happened?" he asked.

She lifted her shoulders in resignation. "I locked myself out."

"Not too cool," he said shaking his head. "How did you manage to do that?"

Alexandra liked the low timbre of his deep male voice. She self-consciously fingered her loose hair, wishing suddenly that she was dressed more attractively, wishing she didn't look like an adolescent. "It's actually your fault," she accused.

He raised his brows incredulously. "Me?"

"I wanted to find out where the piano music was coming from. I stepped into the hall for a second . . ."

"And the door closed shut behind you," he finished.

"That's it."

He let out a sigh and stood straight, being careful not to close his own door completely. He walked to the incinerator and flicked the cold butt of his cigarette down the chute. "You have a real slim case, but I guess I'm partly to blame. Why don't you come in and we'll call the super to bring up a passkey?" He held his door open, expecting Alexandra to enter. But she didn't move, and he looked quizzically at her. "Hey, we can't do anything if you just stand there," he reasoned in amusement.

"I don't know who you are," Alexandra explained suspiciously, with a quick shrug of a shoulder.

He stared at her for a moment and laughed in disbelief. He scanned her vulnerable position and questionable dress and grinned ruefully. "Right. I'm Parker Harrison, your piano-playing neighbor. Now, come on in . . ."

"I'll wait here, thanks," she said stubbornly, feeling both absurdly young and foolish.

Some exasperation began to show on his face. "Look, I can't leave you in the hallway. And I promise, your body is safe with me."

His eyes were filled with amusement again as she continued to hesitate. Chewing on the inside of her bottom lip, Alexandra knew a moment of feminine ire as she realized he was sincere. She would be perfectly safe with him.

"Besides, if I bite, you can always bite back," he said wryly.

She grinned nervously then, but still felt butterflies in her stomach. She walked toward him, keeping her eyes down, and slowly entered his apartment. She had never been in a single man's home before, and she slid past him, avoiding any chance of their touching by accident. But a new warm sensation snaked through her body at her physical awareness of the handsome stranger. And she remembered once more that she had no bra on.

"The piano's in there." Parker pointed to a room at the length of the apartment. He walked past her into another room and she heard him pick up a phone and began dialing.

Shyly, Alexandra continued on into the front room, absently noting the framed posters and artwork on the walls. She spotted the piano at once. It was dark and shiny, an expensive Steinway baby grand. What also caught her attention, however, was the haphazard scattering of paper all over the room. On the piano bench, the floor, the piano top, the coffee table, lay sheets upon sheets of music. Fascinated, Alexandra moved to the piano stand to see what he played. She walked slowly about the room, tilting her head this way and that as she craned to read titles. She stepped over piles on the floor. The answer was, he apparently played everything. There was Chopin, Beethoven, Ellington, Bach, Satie, Rachmaninoff, Hancock. There were notebooks with notes and partially finished music. Alexandra was lifting a page, trying to decipher it, when Parker entered the room. He stopped for a moment in the doorway, then casually walked over to her.

"The super is on a call somewhere in the building." He gently took the notebook from her and closed the cover over the written page. "He should be up in half an hour or so." He looked down thoughtfully at the notebook in his hand.

Alexandra knew at once that she had not only breached good manners, but had invaded a part of this man which was private and sensitive. "I'm sorry. I didn't mean to touch your things," Alexandra began, noticing a tightness around his previously smiling mouth.

Parker shrugged indifferently, but Alexandra could sense the tension in his body. "No problem," he said.

But Alexandra knew he did mind. He threw the notebook carelessly on a pile and sat on the piano bench, facing her as she stood awkwardly in the middle of his papers. Alexandra watched him furtively, the silence between them stretching out as he slowly let his eyes appraise her. His mouth had lifted in amusement when he'd spotted her narrow bare feet, the toes curled under on the wood parquet floor. When his eyes again assessed the curving of her breasts under the T-shirt, Alexandra quickly and modestly crossed her arms over her chest. He made her feel so young.

Alexandra stood looking covertly around the minimally furnished room, dominated by the beautiful piano. On the walls were framed programs and photographs of Parker, but much younger and formally dressed. In one he was seated at a piano. There was another of him accepting an award of some kind. In none of the photos did he smile or give any indication of being pleased at the recognition accorded him. In none did he seem relaxed, or proud, or exhilarated. Alexandra became fascinated by the sense of dissatisfaction that was apparent on the many different faces of this man. She somehow knew that it wasn't the recognition that irritated him, but his playing. He hadn't been satisfied. He hadn't felt he'd done his best. Alexandra felt a sudden kinship. She *understood* that look.

"So, what do you think of the piano?" he asked, his eyes scanning over her slender body thoughtfully once again.

"I didn't touch it," Alexandra disclaimed quickly, turning around to face him, her attention diverted from the gallery of pictures.

"You can," he shrugged indifferently, and moved to make room for her on the bench. "Come on. Try it. Do you play?" Parker swiveled on the bench to face the keyboard.

Alexandra smiled slowly at the invitation and she approached the bench somewhat in awe. "Not very well. Not enough practice. I'll probably sound terrible." She sat down and aimlessly played a few bars and exercise chords. Then, because he seemed to be expecting it, she tried something a bit more advanced, concentrating on her movements. She looked expectantly at Parker when she was finished, her sable brown eyes unknowingly seeking approval, her pretty brown face open and instantly trusting.

"Not bad. Where did you study?" Parker asked, drawing on his cigarette.

"I've only had two years of formal study," she said carefully, not adding that two years was all that could be afforded from the household budget. She had fought to get that much for herself. "My father taught me to play."

"Oh? And where did your father study?" Parker persisted.

"He didn't. He's self-taught," she said, shaking her head and continuing to move her fingers along the keys until the sight of his almost bare chest so near made her stop abruptly.

Parker nodded briefly. "If you learned that from your father, I'm impressed." Then he suddenly moved closer to her on the bench, squinting at her face.

Alexandra once again tensed at his closeness, as he seemed to be examining every square inch of her face. She could smell the tobacco smoke on him, but also the hint of soap on his skin from a recent shower or bath. There was still another essence, something that awakened Alexandra's senses to him as a man. She felt an unexpected tension and tingling in her stomach. There were stirrings, and the start of new physical sensations that felt good, but which were frightening. It was much too intimate a circumstance suddenly, and she felt threatened because she didn't know how to handle either her awareness of or her fascination for this good-looking, confident man.

"Well, I'll be damned! Should I call you 'Freckles'?" he teased in surprised wonder. He obviously wasn't reacting to her in quite the same way.

Alexandra was indignant and moved to stand up. "Don't call me that. I don't like it," she ordered softly, in a firm, noncompromising fashion.

Parker grabbed her arm and forced her to stay seated, then quickly released her again. "Then what should I call you?" he asked, ignoring her anger.

"My name is Alexandra Morrow," she responded primly.

Parker raised his brow and hid a smile. She was suddenly so correct and polite. "Alexandra," he enunciated each syllable carefully, making the name sound like a disease or a proclamation. He paused before slowly saying it again, this time lyrically, in such a way Alexandra loved the sound of it on his lips. "That's quite a mouthful for such a little girl."

"I'm not a little girl," she corrected. Again he'd seemed to ignore her indignation, and it seemed to Alexandra that he wasn't treating her seriously at all, that he was amused by everything about her.

"What do people call you?" he asked curiously.

"Alexandra," she said clearly, but it didn't have the least quelling effect on him.

"No, no, no," Parker said, shaking his head sadly. "It takes too long to say all that. Just Alex is enough," he decided. He put out his hand for her to shake.

"That's a man's name. And I don't like nicknames, either," she frowned. "Alexandra" had always made her feel older and more mature.

Parker shrugged. "I think Alex suits you. It's clear, precise, and strong. Some nicknames aren't very nice, it's true. But some are used out of friendship or love. Haven't you ever had friends or love, Alex?"

Again there had been that teasing glint in his eyes. Alexandra was about to answer honestly, "No." Instead, she merely looked away indifferently and shrugged a thin shoulder. Let him think what he wanted.

"Anyway," Parker continued, swinging back to the piano and letting his right hand absently perform magic upon the keyboard. "I'll call you Alex. I'm sure no one else ever thought of it." He turned to regard her thoughtfully, his gaze warm and suddenly playful. "You don't have to tell anyone. It will be just between the two of us."

She knew that he was teasing her again, but she didn't know how to tease back. There had never been much time in her life for boyfriends and flirtations. Except maybe for Nathan, when she was in high school. She'd really liked him because he'd seemed as shy and serious as she had been. He'd gone away one summer after school was out, and had come back the next fall, older and more demanding. Alexandra hadn't been in love with Nathan. What he'd wanted from her in their junior year she hadn't been prepared to give him. Alexandra certainly didn't kid herself that someone as smooth and handsome as Parker Harrison was attracted to her. He might tease, and show indulgence, and some curiosity. He might recognize that she had a lithe, innocent beauty and a nice way about her, as her father used to say, but he wasn't going to be seriously interested in her. Yet Alexandra also felt that something had just been created between them which was going to be unique and different. It was going to be something for herself that she didn't have to share with her sister. She liked that.

"I wasn't making fun of you," Parker said earnestly.

Alexandra relaxed. "I'm sorry I got angry. I guess I'm too sensitive about them." She put a hand up briefly to her cheeks as if hoping to brush the scattering of freckles away.

Parker smiled kindly, drawing on his cigarette and finishing it, adding the butt to an already overflowing ashtray. "You shouldn't be. They are very attractive."

Alexandra felt uncomfortable with the gentle words and compliments, not used to them at all. Nervously, she got up and moved around the room.

"Where did you study?" she asked, using Parker's earlier question to bring the conversation back to safer ground.

Parker groaned and grimaced. "Everywhere," he said dryly, "since I was six years old." He didn't seem thrilled by the memory. "Private lessons, Juilliard, more private lessons, the Sorbonne in Paris."

"Paris," Alexandra sighed enviously, her eyes popping open.

"And more private lessons. I was what they call a 'wonder,'" Parker said, somewhat indifferently.

"Are you someone famous?" Alexandra breathed, again looking quickly to the framed photos on the wall.

He laughed out loud at her question. Alexandra smiled to herself dreamily, liking the rich, resonant sounds.

"Not at all. I could have been another Andre Watts, but . . ." he trailed off end shook his head.

"But what?" Alexandra persisted, leaning carelessly on the piano top and regarding him in near awe, forgetting that her breasts bobbed against the T-shirt.

For a moment, Parker's smile was warm and indulgent, his eyes scanning her face and seeming to enjoy the novelty of being unique in her eyes. Then, Parker got up restlessly, and frowned at the stack of music on the floor. He stuffed his hands into his jean pockets. "I wasn't interested. I got tired of concerts and recitals, limited engagements, and special appearances. I'd had enough," he ended impatiently.

"Your parents must have been very disappointed."

"You're right, they were. I felt very guilty telling them I wanted out. After all, they'd done everything to see that I got the best training and the best instructors. They told me that they understood how I felt, but . . . they were hurt. They had my future all planned out." There was a trace of irony in his words. "They'll get over it."

"Yeah. But will you?" Alexandra asked astutely. "If you were that good . . ."

"Why throw it all away?" Parker blinked thoughtfully, and his eyes became distant. His face, that of a man probably in his late twenties, was now curiously young and fleetingly uncertain.

"Because I'm sorry I missed going to regular school like all the other kids on the block. I missed Saturday morning football because of

Saturday piano lessons. I hated traveling to different cities to give a concert, because I never knew anyone there. There were times when I just wanted to hide in a penny arcade and play pinball all day."

His eyes slowly focused and settled on her face. Alexandra had a fleeting glimpse of longing in his eyes, some distant vision or hope that perhaps he'd never really known. But it quickly cleared, and that derisive spark came back. He got up abruptly from the piano bench.

He moved to the coffee table and carelessly leafed through the music sheets. "Besides, I have my *own* music," he tapped his temple, "up here. I didn't want to interpret and play the world masters; I want to *be* one.

"There's a lot of music inside of me, Alex," he continued, his words spilling out. "I have to try and work it out. Even if everyone, including my parents, think I'm crazy, I need time to work it out. All artists have their own style. Well, so do I."

Parker had looked over several of the composition sheets, his eyes quickly scanning the notes, and for a moment Alexandra knew he had music running through his head. For just that instant he was far away, in another world. She felt a jolt of understanding go through her. It was exactly how she felt when she was singing.

Alexandra was mesmerized by his energy and convictions. She found that she liked the shortened form of her name when Parker said it. It seemed so friendly and personal. It *did* make her feel very special.

"I'm going to be famous someday," she whispered confidently into the suddenly quiet room, unconsciously raising her chin at some unnamed objection or obstacle.

Parker raised his brows and looked at her, gently studying her for a long moment. "Is that what you want? To be famous?"

She nodded. "I want everyone to love my voice and singing. I want to sing at Carnegie Hall and at the Metropolitan Opera. I want to travel, *be* somebody."

Parker's eyes softened and he shook his head slightly. "Hey, you *are* somebody." Then his empathy changed and his expression became serious and fixed. "Be careful what you wish for, or you're likely to get it, Alex."

His tone brought her sharply back to the present, and the dreams that were going to come true suddenly became clouded by this new prophecy.

She shook her head. "No. I want to be famous."

The doorbell rang shrilly then as the super arrived with his passkey. Regretfully, Alexandra had to say goodbye.

"Not goodbye, just goodnight," Parker had said, walking her to the door. "Come and visit my piano anytime," he teased lightly. "And me, of course. I'll even give you some pointers on the keyboard, if you like."

"Am I that bad?" Alexandra asked.

Parker grinned. "Not at all. But everyone can be better. We'll work on it together."

She shyly thanked him for his kindness, but Parker grinned wickedly at her. "Don't thank me yet, Alex. I'll probably expect retribution . . ."

That had been the start. And retribution, when it came, had been the end of it. Quickly, mysteriously. Silently, without goodbyes or goodnights.

Alexandra slowly closed the album, running her hand over the smooth leather which protected the treasured contents. She put the albums away with a sleepy sigh, but the reminiscence stayed tenaciously with her, keeping her nervously awake. She turned off the bedside light and stared into the dark, her memories vividly alive. Parker, then and now, was different. Then, he was too thin and too intense, and had too much energy. Parker was still slender, but matured and confident. With a frown of concentration, Alexandra realized that he was a man fully grown, and rather different from the young man who had so captured her heart and attention. For all her memories, she had to admit this new Parker was more of a stranger. He had outgrown his uncertainties. He had outgrown his youth. He had outgrown much of the past, and perhaps her, too.

Reluctantly, Alexandra also admitted to finding him appealing in a way that stirred the woman in her and made her restless. It was confusing, because it was not as she'd remembered it from years ago. At that time, the feeling had been fantasy and dreaming—not based on much more than her awakening to her own feminine capabilities, and the flexing of her charms and innocence. Her reactions now were primitive and basic. She had some experience and memories behind her, which allowed the ready response to Parker Harrison's kisses and embrace, which had allowed the precipitous lovemaking the night before.

Parker was calm and self-possessed. He had cooled out a lot with accomplishing what he'd set out to do. But what did he really mean, fame wasn't all it was cracked up to be?

Parker, years ago, had been indulgent toward her, teasing her playfully, much as one would tease a favorite younger sister. Except that Alexandra had quickly developed much deeper feelings than that. She was infuriated with him for not recognizing them, but never having been in love before, she hadn't a clue as to how one proceeded, or even how to deal with him and the knowledge of her growing feelings for him. How do you tell someone you love them when they treat you like a favorite relative?

Alexandra also remembered that Parker smoked too much, and often forgot to eat, causing her to assume the role of protector. He sometimes had dark, brooding periods. He frequently locked himself inside his apartment, burying his telephone under sofa cushions, disconnecting the answering machine, not answering messages slipped under the door while he worked with a vengeance on his music. Just as unpredictably, he'd call her to come and hear some work in progress, as if he was uncertain and needed her to act as a sounding board. He asked for input and suggestions, teaching her, inadvertently, what he needed from her. Once, Parker got her out of bed at three-thirty in the morning, excited and tired and fulfilled with a composition that had worked just perfectly. Alexandra smiled as she remembered him pounding on her door, telling her to hurry and get up because he had something new she had to hear. She became like a shadow in the hallway between the two apartments, floating back and forth between his life and her own.

Afterward, Alexandra would curl up on his sofa, offering sleepy praise and encouragement. She'd then fix breakfast and they'd talk about the music some more until Parker's energy was replaced by sheer exhaustion. He would kiss her cheek affectionately and go off to sleep for hours, leaving her to let herself out of the apartment where beautiful music was made. One of her greatest joys with Parker had been that he'd honestly sought her opinion and listened to her suggestions.

He was like a man possessed at times, switching back and forth between classics and jazz, as if not sure what he really wanted to play, or as if choosing one could mean giving up the other, or as if torn between the need to take a risk with his life or seek the comfort and safety of an assured concert route. Many times Alexandra had come across telegrams crumpled among the debris of his studio. Telegrams from an agent, a concert hall manager, a professor begging him to return to the fold. But when even she, who saw how obsessed he was at times, suggested that perhaps he was being foolish to give it all up, Parker had only said flatly, "I can't go back." He had been dead serious about finding his true place in music.

When Parker had taken to disappearing for a day or two, Alexandra unexpectedly realized the depth of her feelings for him, and the fear that he'd never know. He'd told her from the start his stay was short. She always knew he planned on going elsewhere, wherever he needed to go to speak and play with new musicians, hear new music, get his perspective straight. He had only recently said he'd already stayed in the apartment down the hall months longer than he'd intended to.

"You're the only person who understands the music and what I'm doing," he'd often teased. "Sometimes, even I'm not sure it's worth anything."

"I believe in you." Alexandra had told him. Did he ever understand the depth of that belief?

Alexandra turned on her side and hugged her pillow. She closed her eyes against the subtle blue glow of dawn through the window blinds. She sighed sleepily. They *had* been so good together. And then it had gotten even better, as she recalled the first time he'd kissed her.

It had started out playfully enough, just after she'd run to him with the news that she'd been chosen to sing in a chorale at the Kennedy Center during a Christmas performance. The congratulatory kiss that had been a mere pressing of his lips to hers had changed things subtly between them. The woman in her was gently touched. She became aware of his masculinity, of the sleek hardness of his lean body, his wonderful deep voice, his beautiful hands. The safe, friendly distance that had existed between them was suddenly gone, and their awareness of each other grew into a sensual tension that was quite mysterious to her at the time. From then on, Parker would touch her affectionately, hugging her, holding her by the waist, holding her hand. It made her giddy with anticipation, made her yearn for much more from him, though she could not put the feelings into words. And she was afraid to actually admit to herself what that yearning might be. That early exploration had been in the first month. By the second month, curiosity between them had reached a vibrant, tantalizing peak.

Everything between them seemed to culminate right after Parker had written a beautiful new piece of music. It was a sweeping melody with romantic tension. In it, Alexandra could hear lovers' heartbeats, breathy excitement, and the anxious anticipation of being in love. She saw herself in it.

Several days later, Alexandra had surprised Parker with words to go with the music. After playing it through several times and changing a note here, a word there, it was finished—and absolutely perfect.

"That's it!" Parker said in wonder. "That is just what I wanted. Awright . . ."

He'd grabbed her and started kissing Alexandra all over her face, making her laugh happily. Then the kisses reached and stayed on her lips, becoming slow, sensual, and serious. For a breathless moment they stared at each other with the sudden excitement of their discovery changing their breathing, the heat of their bodies, the tension. Suddenly they sought the deeper embrace of each other's arms. They kissed and then kissed again, suddenly aware of the texture of each other's lips. Alexandra noticing that Parker's mouth was mobile, firm, teaching her how to kiss him. The kiss deepened, Parker expertly parting her hesitant lips to explore beyond the small white teeth and stroke against her tongue with his own.

Parker found the feminine curve of her lips and waist, felt the soft, delicate roundness of her breasts. When he'd hesitated and stared into her face with a thoughtful frown, Alexandra had hoped he wouldn't see her inexperience, but only her trust in him. She'd wanted him to take her beyond friendship.

Parker had cupped her face and smiled tenderly. The moment had become special forever.

"This is a love song, for you," he'd whispered.

Parker had taken her into his arms carefully, but she knew he must be feeling her insecurity. He'd kissed her sweetly to ease her nerves; had reassured her silently as his mouth started the sensual dance. Parker's hands roamed her body, eliciting soft gasps of surprise as he introduced her to physical love. In his darkened room he undressed her, uncrossing arms modestly protecting herself, allaying her fears with murmured words and tender touches. But the kisses were potent and searing, demanding a response that was impossible for her not to return. She kept her eyes averted from the undressing of Parker's own body. She was familiar with the expanse of his torso but had never touched him or seen it so close to her before so that she could feel the warmth of his skin. He had long, muscular, athletic legs, his hips narrow, the swollen male part of him sending eddies of apprehension and anticipation through her body, but in a dizzying, pleasurable way. She felt herself a mass of quivering raw nerve ends waiting to explode or burn out. Parker had led her slowly to his bed, and she had never considered not following or letting him pull her down to the quilted top, drawing her slowly into his arms as his mouth sought hers again. Alexandra had been surprised and awed by the incredible feel of his warm, naked body pressed to her with such intimacy, startled by the way they seemed to naturally fit together. She had been mesmerized by Parker's lack of inhibition in exploring and touching her skin, feeling safe in his knowledge and know-how.

Parker led her though an intricate maze of new sensations, one escalating on top of another, so exquisite as to leave her weak and breathless. His hands were a caressing joy upon her body, sensitizing her quivering skin, tickling the smooth surface into responding to him, and recognizing and satisfying her own raw needs. Alexandra felt herself waiting for the next wonderful sensation. But the apprehension returned when Parker lay his full weight on her body and maneuvered her legs apart. He poised over her before lowering his hips and thighs, and thrusting gently forward between her legs.

When it came, she was shocked into stillness by the unavoidable pain from him. But Parker had soothed her, whispering low and kissing her hot skin. He was slow and easy, until she became used to the total fullness of him deep within her body. She was lost for a moment in a combination of tingling pain and pleasure.

Parker had demonstrated such care for her, holding her against his long body, his movements oddly possessive and comforting. The stroking of his hands was sure and knowledgeable. She clung to him with total love. She trusted him completely. Alexandra marveled at the rhythm their bodies swayed into, rocking in union, the personal and intimate movements she'd never known, until Parker reached some pinnacle still beyond her reach, releasing himself into her, relaxing on her.

Then, with all the time in the world, with a giddy sense of discovery and magic, they'd started all over again. Parker had shown her slowly, completely, what loving was like between a man and a woman, until finally she, too, had known the heart-stopping moment of fulfillment.

She'd stayed with him that night, the first of many in which they played and explored and loved each other with an affinity that neither questioned, but which Alexandra thought would last forever.

And then Parker had left.

Two weeks before she had an important audition.

Two weeks after they'd started a new song which went unfinished.

A month before her twentieth birthday.

Alexandra turned over restlessly in her bed. She threw the covers off, and then, two minutes later, reached to pull them up again. She felt again the familiar, horrible pain of betrayal and humiliation, thinking of the way Parker had just walked out of her life. She had gone over every detail of their last phone call together, and after all these years, had never been able to find any one moment that might have alerted her to what was about to happen.

They were going to spend the evening working on their song, although Parker had admitted he'd thought of nothing new for the melody. But Alexandra had called to say she had to spend the day with her father, who needed to be escorted to a medical appointment.

"Don't worry about the song," Parker had soothed her. "We'll get back to it later."

"But I might have to stay the night. And I have classes and a rehearsal tomorrow."

"Alex . . ." Parker had interrupted. "There'll be time for everything. Your father is more important now."

"You won't try and finish it without me?"

"It's our song. We'll finish it together," he'd promised. "Sooner or later."

Was that it? Had he hoped that she would know he'd made a decision, accepted a band position, was going to leave immediately? Was she supposed to assume that of course he'd be in touch? And when he wasn't, how long was she supposed to wait before realizing the painful truth— that he had no intention of contacting her again?

The break had been quick and clean, surgical. She had always known Parker would move on. She would hope and pray for a romantic miracle, but she had yet to finish school, and he was trying to find himself.

She'd always known . . .

Alexandra had barely gotten through the rest of the semester. She had moved back home to her father's house to mope, cry, and function in a daze all summer as she sought to understand why. Thankfully, her father had asked no questions, but had made it clear that he was glad she'd come home. She, in turn, did not want to burden him with her heartbreak. Mostly, Alexandra wanted her father to hold her and comfort her.

Christine, on the other hand, had shown mostly disappointment at having her home again. Perhaps she had believed that with Alexandra on her own, she'd outgrown the need for a surrogate mother in the form of an older sister. But Christine was also curious about her life away from home. Christine had no sympathetic offerings to make, although, Alexandra was to admit later, her sister's voiced opinions held their own wisdom, borne of both innocent observation and awakening teenage conjecture.

Alexandra had been listlessly unpacking her things when her fourteen-year-old sister had come into her room, not heeding Alexandra's silence as a sign that she'd rather just be left alone.

Christine, who had long ago shown signs of being a beauty, was a full three inches taller than her older sister, and more self-possessed. Her near-black hair was thick with fat locks loosely curled and layered from her face to her shoulders. The budding feminine softness was completely misleading, hiding within it the hard determination of Christine that was often demanding and often got her her own way.

Christine had perched on the edge of the bed, idly watching as her sister removed things from her suitcase. She began to swing her leg back and forth against the mattress.

"So what happened?" she'd asked boldly.

Alexandra hesitated only a second in her chore, her stomach lurching with the sure knowledge that Christine was going to ask questions she didn't want to answer. She refused to meet her sister's gaze, pretending an indifference to the question.

"What do you mean, what happened?" Alexandra asked, carefully turning her back to open a dresser drawer.

"I mean," Christine sighed, "why did you come back home?"

"Aren't I allowed? After all, I do live here, too."

"Well, you were the one who wanted to leave, to become famous, remember?" Christine taunted.

Her recent disappointments flooded Alexandra, sending chills through her system and making her shiver. She had been so boastful, so sure of herself. She didn't respond.

"You sure didn't become famous since you left," Christine chided with a light laugh. "You don't look famous. I bet you never even tried to sing anywhere."

"Will you please stop?" Alexandra begged, in a thin voice. She didn't even have the strength to be angry, just hurt all over again.

Christine had suddenly stopped as if she could see the genuine look of pain on Alexandra's face. It had always been easy for her to tease and goad her older sister, but Alexandra recognized that she'd never done so to deliberately hurt her. Shrugging at her sister's plea, Christine had gotten up from the bed and wandered over to Alexandra's bureau, poking idly among the few pieces of jewelry laying on top.

"Did you meet anyone interesting?" she had asked, lifting a bracelet to examine the design.

Alexandra looked furtively at Christine, hoping that her own face and expression gave nothing away.

"Of course, I did. There were plenty of people in my classes whom I got to know."

"No, I mean someone *special*. You know—as in falling in love," Christine patiently explained.

Alexandra's hands tightened around the garment she held, and she knew she couldn't lie, but she didn't know how to answer. It somehow seemed strange to be talking about a feeling like love or an emotion like hurt with a fourteen-year-old, when she was struggling so hard herself to understand what she'd been through. And as she'd never been in the habit of confiding in Christine the things that were closest to her, she found herself being cautious now, even though there was a desperate need to unburden herself. She decided, instead, to play it safe and tell a half-truth.

"People don't fall in love in just three months," Alexandra had responded, but the lie caught in her throat, and she'd wondered if her voice, or her overly warm face or clenched hands, would give her away. Apparently, that answer had satisfied Christine, who now dropped the bracelet noisily, and turned to regard her beautiful unusual features in the bureau mirror.

"Anyway, you can't fall in love and be famous at the same time," Christine murmured, practicing the enticing arching of a brow, and pursing her full mouth this way and that.

Alexandra frowned at her sister, caught by the curious nature of her words. "What makes you say so?"

Christine wrinkled her nose quaintly and grinned at her image. Then she looked over her shoulder at her sister. "Well, you know, if you really want to be famous, you have to work real hard at it. You don't let anything or anyone stop you. *I* wouldn't."

Alexandra had believed this was true of her sister. It had been true of her until she'd met Parker, who'd left her not sure of what she wanted anymore.

"Christine, what do you want most? What do you want to do with your life?" Alexandra asked her sister, eager to know if she had any dreams, any ambition beyond being pretty and popular. Did she have any fears at all that life would just pass by without her having done anything with it?

Christine shrugged and giggled. "I just want to have fun. I want to have lots of friends and lots of money. Maybe I'll be a dancer or an actress."

"But what if *you* fall in love?"

Christine had raised her chin, showing surprising confidence. "I'm not going to fall in love until after I do what I want."

Alexandra chuckled grimly at the memory of Christine's words, which were a mixture of naïveté and inexperienced bravado. But she'd known Christine meant it. Christine was not the kind of person to let herself be overcome with grief. She would have shrugged her shoulders and quickly dismissed it as unimportant. Christine would have turned to the next adventure, the next admirer waiting in the wings. Life was too short for constant reflection.

Alexandra considered the coldness and odd truth of Christine's observation. But, she reasoned, if Parker had loved her, they could have worked it out, even though she couldn't see how. Would he have left her if he loved her? And how would it have affected his music? How would it have affected her own? But why did it have to be either love or success? Why couldn't there be both?

Alexandra sat on the bed. Maybe Christine was right, maybe she had to be single-minded with her music. There should be no distractions.

She had privately hoped all spring and summer that Parker would call, filled with remorse and with a desire for her forgiveness. Each time she'd return home after her job or a class, Alexandra would ask if anyone had called for her. After a while, it seemed that her father came to dread the question, and to dread having to tell her "no."

It had all been so confusing. She had been too upset to go through with her audition, but she had also been too scared; terrified that she was no good at all. Her confidence left the same day Parker had. She had been left to wonder why she'd backed down when the moment of truth was at hand. Had Parker's leaving been just an excuse?

"We make beautiful music together, Alexandra Morrow," Parker had once said to her.

They had.

* * *

The memories stopped abruptly, and Alexandra rolled onto her back feeling totally wrung out and incapable of shedding another tear for the past, yet recalling with a clarity that was frightening how much pleasure she'd known with Parker Harrison. It was very obvious that that, at least, had not changed. They'd made love together just hours ago and the magic was still there. But her pleasure tonight had been a mixture of seduction and revenge, although it was hard to decide whether it was worth it.

Alexandra no longer felt depressed. The day-long stress of being with Parker seemed like a catharsis. Right now, it no longer surprised her that after so many years she could still be moved by the emotions that had so affected her life at the time.

Alexandra had thought that with her maturity, her love and anger for Parker, the two extremes, would cancel each other out. But that had not been the case. She was finding now that the anger had become a need to question why. And the love had become a persistent, gnawing ache needing to be fulfilled.

Parker left Alexandra's apartment feeling angry and shaken. He had tried to deal with the unexpected encounter with her in a mature fashion. But the Alexandra Morrow he remembered from years ago had grown up with a vengeance.

He had carried with him a sweet memory of a pretty, talented young girl who'd clearly idolized him. It had been charming and amusing, but he'd never tried to play into that. It was only after they'd started a serious affair that Parker had realized Alexandra could easily fall in love with him and he could hurt her just as easily. One more reason for the decision he'd made.

Parker was shaken because the changes in Alexandra destroyed some of the memory he had of her which had been safe and romanticized. He was angry because he'd allowed his ego to be manipulated by Alexandra's cool aloofness toward him. He'd wanted to see that she was still the sweet, innocent wide-eyed girl he'd introduced to love, and who'd believed in him with her heart. Parker was angry because despite everything, he'd hoped not to hurt Alexandra, and it was abundantly clear that he had nonetheless. At the time, he had been deathly afraid of making a wrong decision for both of them.

The events for his leaving came back with force: the invitation to attend a creative artists' community for the following summer, the former mentor wanting to see and hear what he'd been working on incognito, Alexandra's father. Parker had thought the time perfect.

That day . . . that last day, with everything packed and him ready to leave, Parker had written a letter, but then had stood outside Alexandra's apartment, debating whether or not to slip it under the door. He'd desperately wondered if there was another way to do this. Why not be open and just tell her? Because it would have been too easy to have been persuaded by Alexandra . . . by *himself* . . . to change his mind. He was a coward, he had chided himself. But he truly believed it was best. Her face appeared in his mind. He was going to miss her intuitiveness and her faith in him; miss the sweet, open response of her body during their lovemaking.

Even now, Parker knew he couldn't tell Alex that he'd tried to reach her after he'd left, because to do so would mean having to fully explain what had happened. He wasn't at liberty to do so, and it might do more harm than good. It was much too late to wish that he'd left the handwritten letter after all.

Parker got back into his car and sat there a long time before he started the engine. When he'd left Washington years ago, he'd found what he'd been looking for: freedom, energy, new music—and himself. He'd made musician friends in smoky little dives in towns no one had ever heard of, where local talent was raw and natural. He'd learned from a bunch of much older men and women whose music had survived by word of mouth, not because they were famous or ever likely to be. He'd met alluring, sexy women who'd satisfied his physical needs, but who could not connect with him in any other way. Parker had found his own unique voice in music, but had lost a human consideration that was pure and open and honest, like that he'd had with Alexandra. He'd sometimes felt the loss, but he'd always gone on without it.

Parker had no idea that Alexandra was to be the soloist at the wedding. Perhaps the surprise element had worked in their favor: they could only be absolutely natural with each other. He'd been forced to deal with the fact that at that first instant of seeing Alexandra, he didn't recognize her. So firmly had his earlier memory of her planted itself that Parker had been surprised, shocked, maybe even disappointed, to find not a wide-eyed, animated, lovely young teenager, but a woman who was cool and self-possessed, and who held herself very much in control.

The second thing he'd had to deal with was the unavoidable sense that Alexandra harbored a great deal of resentment toward him.

It began to feel cold and damp in the car, and Parker started the engine. He didn't want to continue to sit in front of her building, but he wasn't ready to head home, either. He'd had quite enough to drink at the reception, between the cocktails and champagne, so going to a bar would do him no good, either. Parker decided instead to just drive into D.C. and meander around the streets of the capital.

He'd always been sure he'd made the right decision when he'd left

D.C. years ago. But that had not stopped him from waffling over the wisdom of leaving Alexandra. Parker could now admit to himself he'd found no one quite like her since.

Parker tensed his jaw and sighed into the chilly silence of the car, although parts of his body were suddenly, unexpectedly, recalling the incredible warmth of having held her and kissed her, of having made love to her. She'd felt more than good beneath him. He'd felt more than satisfied loving her. And Parker knew that this time, he couldn't just walk away. The past had caught up with him.

CHAPTER 5

The final lyrical strains of the song ended, the last note held for a prolonged beat as the clear voice faded. The drummer rat-a-tatted dramatically, then hit his cymbals to clearly end the performance. The audience came to life then, spurred on by the momentary silence. The applause and whistles were scattered and almost halfhearted, while the spotlight on Alexandra's face grew into a small circle until she was no longer clearly visible. Finally, the dim house lights came up.

Alexandra smiled and nodded demurely. She gracefully brought her left leg back and dipped into a stage curtsy, her aqua blue strapless dress shimmering under the stage lights. She made one more bow, sweeping her arms to include the three-man combo accompanying her. Quickly, feeling chilly in her stage outfit, Alexandra headed for her cubicle-like dressing room. She struggled not to cough, her lungs affected by the air which was heavily polluted with cigarette smoke. Alexandra thought it was probably not a good idea to let her voice teacher know the conditions under which she sang, even though Signora Tonelli was delighted that she'd found a part-time singing position.

"Hey, Morrow . . ." the bartender yelled after Alexandra's retreating form. "There's some guy here to see you."

Alexandra never stopped walking, but raised her chin and waved briefly as she opened the door leading from the narrow, dark hallway to the absurdly small dressing room. Ruefully, she thought there was always "some guy" waiting to see her. She never knew any of them, of course, but they were usually more than willing to introduce themselves and change all that. Anyone else would have been flattered. Anyone else might have held out the slim hope that one of those guys might be a producer or director, or another nightclub owner or a musician, ready to offer a bigger opportunity. But Alexandra had learned quickly, after first attempting to be polite and gracious to those men, that they'd obviously had other thoughts in mind than her career. And she was not about to be part of the school of thought that said you had to sleep your way to the top of the music field. She was determined to become a good singer on merit alone—or not at all.

Alexandra sang at the club for only two reasons. Foremost, for now, was the extra money, which allowed her to afford private voice lessons in preparation for the upcoming light-opera tryout. She had finally decided to audition for it this year. The second reason was that it gave her performance experience, teaching her to cope with the jittery nerves and unexpected stagefright that happened no matter how often she sang. She was also getting a first-hand, up-close lesson in how to deal with the occasional malcontent or patron who'd had too much to drink and who often found it necessary to voice his opinions on almost any topic, but usually while she sang.

Alexandra had also found the musical range that was best for her. She could manage love ballads and light popular music. She could not manage the gospel-laced inflections and impromptu arrangements of an Aretha Franklin. And she was good at weddings. Nevertheless, she'd not been happy with her performance tonight. It went beyond the fact that the combo, permanently fixed musicians of the club, played without passion and care. Alexandra knew her concentration was off as her mind had wandered during the course of the evening to Parker Harrison. She had been thinking a lot about him, remembering their emotionally charged lovemaking, which had held little tenderness, but which had sparked within Alexandra the fires of desire and passion she'd only had for one man. She thought that that occasion had meant the permanent closing of a chapter of her life. She'd heard nothing from Parker the whole week, and Alexandra was wondering why.

With a sigh, Alexandra entered the small room and closed the door. She began stripping out of the sequined dress. The garment, which left her shoulders and neck bare, was heavy and stiff. When she wore it, or something similar, Alexandra would give her performance feeling cold and exposed. She hated having to wear the dress, but the club manager insisted that she needed something flashy to make her more noticeable on stage. It was annoying to think that, as the manager seemed to be suggesting, without the "flash," she wouldn't be noticed. She'd given in to him, now thankful that she did only one show on Friday and Saturday night, which was finished by eleven-thirty.

She hated the stale air of the club, the noise, and the often unsavory people, who seemed none too interested in her voice. She also didn't care for the feeling that her part in what the club offered its customers was really insignificant. The manager had always been clear that he made money from people who drank, not the few who might quietly sit and listen to an unknown performer. In other words, she was not much more than window dressing.

With another weary, resigned sigh, Alexandra reminded herself she was just paying her dues. Everyone had to start somewhere. But it was with a noticeable lack of enthusiasm that she came to the club each weekend evening, and the feeling only got worse. She convinced herself to keep returning by remembering the ultimate dream that kept her going, that hopefully she would soon be performing in a better place, with a more attentive audience.

Alexandra was just stepping out of the dress when her door suddenly opened. She gasped and quickly pulled the dress back into place to cover herself. She was apprehensive but not surprised to find the club manager, Joe Jefferies, standing in her doorway. Alexandra forced herself to remain calm and hoped that she appeared indifferent and in control.

"Do you mind? I'm changing," she said, trying to speak firmly. "I'll be out in a moment."

Ignoring her protest, a short, squat man closed the door and leaned back leisurely against it. "Good show," the rough male voice said.

A smiling leer spread over Joe Jefferies's blunt features, his thick moustache making him look sinister. His eyes roamed appreciatively over Alexandra's creamy brown shoulders and throat, the upper curves of her breasts visible over the top of the loosened dress. Alexandra clutched it tighter.

"We'll have to see about getting you another dress, Sugar. Something a little more . . . revealing. An audience likes to see as well as hear what they're getting for their money."

Alexandra's eyes narrowed at him. "I don't think you get the kind of audience that really cares. For the money, they don't get my body—only my voice."

Joe chuckled at her, shaking his head at her naïveté. "Well now, Sugar, it ain't enough. A pretty face helps. There's a nice crowd tonight. We always do a good first show when you're on," he crooned.

Alexandra raised a shoulder indifferently. "It's crowded because it's Friday night and everyone got paid today."

"Maybe . . ." Joe said absently, his eyes locked on the rising and falling of her chest as Alexandra clutched the dress to her. "But you sure don't hurt, either."

Three months of working with Joe Jefferies at The Outer Edge had been more than enough time to show Alexandra that she was a ready target for his male interest. It hadn't occurred to her when she'd first taken the job that he could pose a problem. She never imagined she'd spend so much time fending off his unwanted advances.

"Look, can't we talk about this later?" she said quietly. "I'd really like to . . ."

"So would I," Joe filled in, his voice low and suggestive. He came away from the door moving slowly toward her.

Alexandra caught her breath and tried not to panic. She could scream, but how embarrassing if everyone came running in while her dress hung loose around her. She could try reasoning with him as she'd done in the past, but her mind was suddenly blank as he continued to come closer. She could fight him . . .

"Ummm. You sure are fine." A wide, thick hand reached out to rub a palm over the soft round point of Alexandra's shoulder.

Goosebumps rose quickly on her skin, and she shrugged her shoulder out of his reach with distaste, taking a quick step backward.

Joe was just Alexandra's height. He was stocky, with a thick neck and hands that were callused. She could look right into his face and hear his raspy breathing.

"Joe . . . don't," Alexandra whispered firmly.

He grabbed her arm to hold her. "When are we gonna get together, Sugar? I've been waiting weeks for you to say the word."

"We're together two nights a week," Alexandra said nervously, being deliberately obtuse. "I see you more than I see my own father."

A grin cracked his face, showing slightly crooked, slightly yellowed teeth. "I ain't your daddy, Sweetheart. I have something else in mind."

"Will you get out of here? Can't you understand I'm not interested?" Alexandra said, trying to push against his chest with one hand.

Joe now took hold of both her arms against her protests. "Yeah . . . but you know you don't really mean it. All you women love to play hard to get. But I know what you want." He pulled her toward him abruptly, making Alexandra unsteady on her feet.

Alexandra began to struggle in earnest, feeling scared now. "Let me go, Joe," she said, anger also lending strength to her words.

"I could do a lot for you, Sugar. I know a lot of people," he panted, as he tried to kiss her.

Alexandra quickly turned her head and felt his mouth on her neck. She closed her eyes in revulsion and pushed against his chest with her fist. She lost her grip on the fancy dress and it sagged heavily to the floor around her feet.

"Oh, Sugar . . ." Joe groaned, gathering Alexandra tightly in his arms.

Tears of anger and frustration welled in her eyes as she squirmed and wiggled to pull herself free from him. She couldn't move except for her legs, and she instinctively brought her knee up sharply to try and use it as leverage against the man. Her knee jutted into Joe's middle and he immediately released her, cursing as he doubled over in pain, grabbing himself. Alexandra stumbled backward.

Suddenly, there was a knock on the door and Alexandra hastily reached for her dress again. Joe was still cursing as the door opened.

Parker stood there in the doorway.

Alexandra felt rooted, her breath catching in her throat as embarrassment sent a rush of heat over her body. But just as quickly, a chill followed in its wake, leaving her shoulders and arms raised with goosebumps. She blinked at Parker, so surprised at seeing him that for a second Alexandra forgot she was standing there with almost nothing on.

A cigarette burned in Parker's mouth, and Alexandra watched while he slowly removed it. A frown gathered over his dark brows as he surveyed the scene before him, looking pointedly at Joe Jefferies before his narrowed gaze shifted slowly back to Alexandra. Alexandra's own eyes were enormous with relief as she saw instant understanding for the situation darken Parker's eyes to cool black and his jaw muscles knotted. He stepped into the already tight space and closed the door.

"Parker . . ." Alexandra managed in a combination of relief and surprise.

Joe at last tried to stand straight and he turned an angry, still contorted face to the taller man behind him. "Who the hell are you? You're not supposed to be back here."

Parker's expression remained the same, but his study of the shorter man was hard and steady. Parker slowly drew on his cigarette, then exhaled. He swung his gaze back to Alexandra. "Do you want me to leave?" he asked her smoothly.

Joe's head swung from Parker to Alexandra, finally jerking a thumb at Parker. "Do you know this guy?" he asked rudely.

Alexandra suddenly realized the absurdity of the situation and just wanted them both to go away and leave her alone. "Yes," she answered in a tight voice. "This is Parker Harrison. Parker, this is the club manager, Joe Jeff . . ."

"Parker Harrison," Joe interrupted, impressed despite himself. He forgot his injury, forgot Alexandra standing in a stiff huddle as he turned to Parker. "Hey, man, I follow your style," he said, straightening his jacket and tie, and trying to look as cool and pulled together as Parker appeared.

Parker raised a brow at the stocky manager. "I hope not. It's not my style to come on to women who have to fight me off."

Alexandra caught her breath and looked fearfully at Joe. She was well aware of Joe's short fuse. He could be mean and cruel and unfair, and there weren't many men who would tangle with him. Alexandra could clearly see now that he was stunned for an instant, but then anger made him take a threatening move toward Parker. Alexandra quickly intervened.

"Joe was just discussing my . . . my singing," she interrupted quickly. With a dawning sense of horror, Alexandra realized that it wouldn't take much for the two men to start swinging at each other. She hoped that Parker, at least, would not let it go so far.

"Do you always discuss business in your underwear?" Parker asked sarcastically.

His tone was cutting, and Alexandra stared at him. And then her look became defiant at his unwarranted attack. Parker's jaw muscles continued to twitch angrily in the otherwise smoothly controlled features of his handsome face.

"I don't think that's any of your business, man," Joe said, but there was no threat in his tone as he took a step toward Parker and then stopped.

"Maybe you're right," Parker acknowledged, still looking at Alexandra.

Joe glanced back and forth between Parker and Alexandra. "I've got a club to run," Joe said impatiently now, but looked once more at Alexandra. "We'll finish our talk later."

There was no apology, and no show of blame or guilt for the way he'd compromised her. He brushed past Parker and out the door, leaving the small room charged with tension.

The silence was awful as Alexandra tried to read Parker's suddenly closed expression. She wondered if he thought that what he'd walked in on was her fault or had been at her bidding. His look made her feel even more angry, as if he was judging her.

Parker, however, in that first instant as they stood silently appraising each other after Joe's departure, was suddenly seeing Alex as he'd first seen her, standing barefoot in the hallway outside her apartment. Then, as now, her pretty, youthful face had seemed impossibly guileless and open, her eyes enormous and direct with interest. And then Parker saw her sense of humiliation, a perplexed look that asked, *What should I have done?* It made him angry, too, but not at Alex. Parker was angry because her life, unlike the smooth passage of his own, had led her to this unpleasant circumstance, a circumstance she didn't deserve. He knew that Alex, here at this club, was out of her league.

Alexandra gave in first, her chin beginning to quiver as she fought tears. She turned her slender back to Parker, biting into her bottom lip.

"Alexandra," Parker said, his tone still angry.

She didn't answer. She stood silently and heard him put out his cigarette in an ashtray on the vanity. Then she could feel him moving closer to stand right behind her.

"Alex," Parker tried again, the voice now hoarse and gentle.

Alexandra felt the light, cool touch of Parker's fingers at the back of her neck. It was tentative, and so light that she felt a warmth begin to cover her. Parker's fingers splayed over her neck and shoulders and forcibly turned her around into his arms. "Come here," he whispered.

Once again, Alexandra released the dress and let her hands be sandwiched in between the two of them. She crossed her arms to cover herself modestly, garnishing more warmth from Parker's arms. Alexandra rested her forehead on Parker's shoulder and closed her eyes. She felt comforted and safe against the black woolliness of his turtleneck sweater. She could smell the leather of his brown trench coat, and hear the unique stretching and caressing of it as he moved his hand up and down her back.

She was grateful he was there, for if he hadn't come, she didn't want to think about what might have happened with Joe. She was grateful that for the time being he said nothing and asked no questions.

Parker, for the moment, didn't need to. It was very obvious what had been going on the instant he'd walked into the dressing room. He'd been out on the professional circuit long enough to know and to have witnessed the sacrifices and compromises people made to get what they wanted.

Parker let his hands move along the slender, very fragile curvature of Alexandra's back. Right now, holding Alex helped him as much as it comforted her. Nothing probably would have happened, Parker knew, because Alexandra would not have let it. That realization pleased him and confirmed every impression he'd ever had of her.

She snuggled unconsciously closer as his lips pressed lightly into her hair.

"Are you all right?" he asked in a low voice.

She merely nodded into his shoulder. His arms tightened just a little, and Alexandra forgot she'd had angry, hateful words with him just a week ago. She forgot that they'd made tense, passionate love, fraught with raw, angry need, the emotions torn from both of them as if they were combatants. She suddenly felt totally safe and protected. She knew Parker wouldn't let anything happen to her. There was complete silence in the dressing room, but unlike last week, it was not awkward, but had a kind of familiar comfort to it. Parker must have felt it, too, for he chuckled silently.

"It's been a long time since I just held you like this," he growled in a low, throaty tone. "You feel different."

Alexandra sighed. "I'm not as skinny," she said playfully.

"Yes, I noticed last week," Parker said, a note of seduction in his voice. "But this is different. Not at all like last week," he added, and then abruptly stopped.

Alexandra could feel the stiffening in his arms, and knew he regretted his easy words. Last week, there had been more anger than anything between them.

Parker slowly but firmly pushed Alexandra away from him, lifting her chin so he could see her face. "Jesus. Your lip is bleeding," he whispered tightly.

Alexandra drew the bottom lip inward and tasted her own warm blood. She'd fought so hard against crying that she'd bitten into her lower lip. Parker bent to examine it, using his thumb to gently pull her lip out again. Alexandra was held captive by the look of pure concern and anger in his dark eyes, his face close, and the familiar odors and scents of him assailing her.

"Did he do this?" Parker said shortly, his jaw muscles tightening again.

"No. I guess I did," she responded.

Parker raised his eyes to hers, and she had not recovered sufficiently to remember that he was still somewhat out of favor with her, or that he had recently stepped back into her life to play havoc with her uncertain emotions. She just let his thumb press to the broken skin of her mouth before he replaced his finger with his lips gently, as though to heal.

Alexandra held perfectly still because she liked his gesture, and didn't protest when he tilted his head to press closer, seeking a deeper kiss by encouraging her to answer him. It was quick and thorough, his firm male lips pulling at her until Alexandra let her mouth open slightly and Parker's mouth branded himself on her, seeking to mate his tongue with her own. He was reclaiming her, staking out a territory he wanted from her. She complied reluctantly but naturally, until she remembered her undressed state. She turned her head away, breaking the unexpected kiss, keeping her gaze lowered. Parker didn't push her, but finally pulled back to try and see into her face.

"Has this happened before?" he asked roughly.

Seconds passed before Alexandra realized he was referring to the encounter with Joe. "Not exactly," she answered softly, embarrassed, not willing to add that there had been hints of Joe's intentions in the past, but nothing overt, like tonight. Actually, Alexandra had done a very good job of innocently avoiding Joe, needing only to tolerate his leering looks and suggestive smiles.

Alex knew what Parker was leading to; that it could happen again. The very possibility made her stomach tense. She didn't want to get into a wrestling match with Joe Jefferies just to keep her job.

Parker looked deep into her eyes, his own dark and stony, although his voice was even. "Will you know what to do next time?" he asked. Alexandra's eyes widened, and she knew she wouldn't.

She hadn't considered a "next time." She knew a lot about music, a lot about what she wanted, but she clearly had no idea the price that her career goals might exact.

Parker said nothing because he also understood the drive, the need. He slowly shook his head and grinned at her ruefully. "You obviously haven't thought about that part."

She frowned. "I don't understand."

"The ways you'll be asked to pay in order to achieve what you want. Joe Jefferies is a piece of work, but he's not uncommon in this business, Alex. All along the way there are going to be people, *men,* asking for your body and your soul to help you become a performer."

"I can always say no," she countered.

"If they're not animals," Parker said darkly. "There's also coercion and compromise."

"You're not painting a very pleasant future," Alexandra said with some annoyance.

Parker's grin became an indulgent, warm smile. He ran a knuckle down the side of her face. "It may not be. It's not easy; this can be a dirty business."

"But you do it. You're successful."

"At a price. Everything comes at a price," Parker murmured sagely.

Parker knew, however, that his own successful career had meant life constantly on the go, and a loneliness he hadn't expected and never wanted. It meant leaving Alex behind so that she could grow up and he could find out what he wanted to do with his life.

"You're not sorry about how your life has gone, are you?" Alexandra asked.

Parker rubbed her arms. "For the most part, no. Even the tough times had something to teach me. I certainly don't regret the year I dropped out of sight; that's when I met you." He watched her avert her gaze with its hint of regret. "Just be careful. Nothing is worth giving up your soul for."

"Have you lost your soul?"

Parker let his thumb touch the small abrasion on her lip again. He gazed into her eyes. He shook his head. "Sometimes I think it's the one thing I haven't lost." Alexandra opened her mouth to respond, but he gave her a quick silencing kiss. "I'll wait outside for you to change," Parker said quietly, and left her alone in the tiny room.

Alexandra hung up the aqua dress and began to change into a rose-colored sweater with dolman sleeves, and a pair of black corduroy jeans. She combed her hair out from its severe pulled-back styling with the huge fake gardenia attached and twisted the medium-length strands into a soft, easy bun at the back of her head.

All the while, Alexandra knew Parker waited for her outside the door. She had a few questions about his fortuitous appearance. How had he known where to find her? What did he want? Alexandra also knew an unexpected excitement at Parker's sudden presence. She had not forgotten his parting words of the week before, and couldn't help but wonder now if he'd indeed been serious. Even she was not sure if the final realization would be love or hate. Her eyes seemed overly bright in the mirror, and her lips were moist and parted. Her freckles stood out pertly as ever, but all in all, she didn't seem any the worse from her tussle with Joe. Her annoyance with him had been replaced with the new expectation of what would now happen with Parker. Once changed, Alexandra stepped in the corridor and found Parker slowly pacing the small hallway, smoking. When she closed the door and turned to face him, he drew on his cigarette and slowly exhaled.

He eyed her carefully, noticing the feminine hairstyle which emphasized her heart-shaped face and large, dark eyes. He felt a sudden regret that his Alex of jeans and T-shirts was gone, perhaps forever.

Alexandra suddenly felt uncertain with him as she met his steady, considering gaze. She spoke first to break the sudden awkwardness.

"What are you doing here?" she asked.

Parker concentrated on the growing ash at the end of his cigarette. With his thumb he flicked the cigarette to loosen the embers and send ash drifting to the floor. "I owe you an apology for last week," he began. He stared at her, his eyes narrowed. "I should have realized you'd be angry at me. What happened at your place was my fault. I should have had more control."

Alexandra felt a rush of heat to her face at his confession, but she looked him in the eye. "It wasn't like it used to be between us," she whispered with poignant honesty. "We couldn't just pick up where we left off. We've changed."

Parker nodded in agreement. "I know."

Alexandra waited, hoping he would voice his feelings more about the intimacy that had swept through them both last week. How was he going to explain that? Did it need to be explained? It had come quickly, but Alexandra now recognized that more than anything, their impromptu lovemaking had been an uneasy, but less destructive conclusion to the things left between them. They'd hidden behind hot embraces and erotic kisses, behind the physical euphoric release of energy and feelings that were almost a decade old.

"I caught your show," Parker said abruptly, changing subjects. "I saw an ad in this afternoon's paper that a 'bright, new singer, Miss Alexandra Morrow, is performing the seven-thirty show at The Outer Edge every Friday and Saturday night,' " Parker quoted verbatim. He lifted a brow. "Didn't the bartender tell you I was waiting?"

Alexandra shrugged. "He said there was some guy waiting, and I thought . . ."

"You thought it was some jerk with a fast come-on," Parker guessed. Alexandra only nodded. "Obviously a lot of guys try it. Even the manager," Parker observed dryly.

He was absolutely right. She took a silent moment to smooth back an errant strand of hair. When she looked at Parker once more, an appreciative smile played at the corners of his full mouth.

"You were good out there tonight."

Alexandra only lifted her shoulders diffidently. "I was okay. I could have been better." She did an admirable job of hiding the bubble of joy and appreciation his words brought.

Parker nodded once, conceding the point. "That's true, but all in all, I don't think it mattered."

Alexandra frowned at him. "What do you mean?"

"I mean, your talents were wasted. Your efforts to entertain the audience were noticed by me, but not by them. I mean that your renditions on a couple of songs were original and clever, but no one seemed to care or could tell the difference. The backup combo was barely adequate and didn't know how to pace with you. I mean, Alex, what are you doing in a place like this? You don't belong here."

"I'm getting practice, experience, and exposure," she said, somewhat flippantly.

"You belong in a better club than this," Parker said firmly.

Alexandra smiled ruefully. "I'd *love* a better club than this, but no one wants to hear from someone like me with no experience."

"Someone like you has to be more aggressive. You want to sing and you know you're good, right?" She nodded. "Then you have to tell the other club managers flatly they'd be making a mistake by not at least hearing you sing. You have to make them give you a chance."

Alexandra grimaced. "I hate that part."

"What? Auditioning?"

"Selling myself."

"I thought you wanted a career. The first thing you have to be besides ambitious is assertive. You want people to pay attention to you. Can you do that?" Parker asked bluntly.

A blade of doubt sliced through her. "I don't know."

"Ten years is a long time not to know. What does it mean when people listen and then applaud you afterward? What does it give you to know that all those years of work and study meant something?" Parker said, almost urgently.

Again she shrugged. "I . . . I don't know. I want to be sure. I want to be really good before I move on. It's like, I'm not really paying attention to the audience, but to how I sound. I need to know."

"You can look into a mirror, sing to yourself, and get the same results.

You have to start paying attention. If you lose your audience, you have no career. That audience will grant you a career."

Alexandra couldn't help but realize that on one level, Parker was talking about himself, and the double roads of his own career.

"What if no one takes me seriously?"

"That's part of the risk of putting yourself out there on the line. Believe it or not, I've been turned down. If you believe in yourself, it won't matter. Only a handful of people make it on luck alone. If you want it, you have to show you deserve it." He was firm and hard with the truth.

Parker looked with distaste around the dim and dingy cracked walls backstage at the club, annoyed that Alex would settle for such a second-rate place.

"The Outer Edge can't do a thing for you. Come on," he said, and taking her by the arm, led her back out through the smoky and crowded main room.

"Where are we going?" Alexandra asked, bewildered, nonetheless allowing him to lead her.

"I'm taking you to Blues Alley."

"Blues Alley," she gasped. "Parker, that's one of the best clubs in D.C.! Getting auditions with them is next to impossible."

Parker stopped to look into her face. "Don't you think you're good enough? Fish or cut bait. It's that simple," he said bluntly.

It was a question that she'd honestly never been able to answer.

"Tonight we're just going to go and listen to the competition. And then you tell me."

He started heading toward the door, and Alexandra knew with a kind of panicked excitement that Parker was right. She could be months or years working up to Blues Alley just by playing it too safe.

As she followed Parker through the smoky lounge, Alexandra spotted Joe at the bar, brooding into a Scotch glass. She knew he had not forgotten her or what had happened in the dressing room. She knew Joe was thinking up new ways to compromise her. Alexandra needed this job at The Outer Edge for the time being, but she wasn't going to let someone like Joe Jefferies intimidate her.

She turned to Parker and touched him lightly on the arm. "Can you give me a minute? I have to take care of something."

Parker looked at Alexandra with a frown, and then automatically to the club manager sulking at the bar. "Are you sure you want to?" he asked.

Alexandra pursed her lips and nodded. "It's important."

Parker reluctantly gave in. "I'll wait by the door."

Alexandra paused momentarily before taking a slow breath and approaching Joe. She glanced once over her shoulder to see that Parker was carefully watching her, and it felt good that he stood ready to come to her aid again, if necessary. Alexandra knew, however, that it wouldn't be.

She touched Joe on the arm and he gave her an unfriendly, baleful look before turning back to his drink.

"I want a lock on the dressing room door," Alexandra said in a quiet, calm voice. "And I want to choose some of my own dresses for the show."

"Where do you get off being so uppity?" Joe questioned in annoyance, scowling at her.

"Yes or no?" Alexandra persisted.

"You sure give me a hard way to go, woman," Joe mumbled.

"Does that mean I'm fired?" Alexandra asked evenly.

"Hell, no," Joe said gruffly. "I'm no fool. You're a good singer. You're good for the club."

"Thank you," she said automatically, not particularly flattered. "Then I'll see you tomorrow."

He grunted into his glass as she turned to leave. "Oh, and another thing . . ." he looked warily at Parker. "That other business tonight. It never happened, okay?"

Alexandra lifted a corner of her mouth into a triumphant smile. "And it will *never* happen again."

"Yeah, yeah," Joe said, dismissing her.

Alexandra met Parker at the door, and he could tell from the bright gleam in her eyes that whatever was said between her and the manager had accomplished what she wanted. But Parker knew men like Joe Jefferies, and he was not inclined to be as trusting or forgiving. People like the burly manager were persistent, insensitive, and had short memories. Sooner or later, his interest would turn to Alexandra again.

The thought enraged Parker, because it was so obvious. He knew he'd only alienate Alexandra if he tried too hard and too often to tell her what to do. He realized that there were other ways around it.

Alexandra, who didn't own a car, followed Parker to his, and recalling their ride together a week earlier, again sat uncomfortably next to him. But whereas before she had tried valiantly to deny the effect his male presence had on her senses, even after so much time gone between them, there was now the tangible evidence in her cold hands and nervous stomach and rampant imagination that something more *would* happen.

Their lovemaking a week ago had effectively crumpled old barriers and bridged a yawning gap in their sensual awareness of each other. It had also proved that the strong attraction they had for each other was still there, even though in other ways they might be worlds apart.

"How long have you been singing in that place?" Parker suddenly interrupted her thoughts.

"About two months."

Parker made an impatient sound. "I hope you're not planning on going back there."

"Why shouldn't I? Besides, I need the money," Alexandra said stubbornly, her previously languid thoughts giving way to defensiveness.

"What for? Are you buying your own opera company?" he teased, and she had to smile.

"No. But I need the money for private voice lessons. I don't have much time left to prepare for the auditions for the Light Opera Company."

"When is that?"

"About a month, the week before Easter."

Parker was quiet for a time. "You shouldn't go back there, Alex." And He sounded so serious.

Alexandra was a bit annoyed that he would presume to tell her that. Her earlier romantic musings shriveled.

"Look, I realize I've taken my time to achieve my goals, but that doesn't mean they're not important to me. This may well be my last chance to try out for the opera. Don't be so cavalier with my future." She refrained, however, from reminding Parker that she didn't have the resources or opportunities he'd had.

"I don't want you to go back because Joe Jefferies thinks from below his waist and he's not going to leave you alone, no matter what he promised," Parker emphasized sharply.

"You can't expect me not to, Parker," Alexandra said stiffly, her voice laced with hurt and anger. "I missed my last audition for this company because of you. I won't do that again."

Parker considered that and let out a deep sigh. "At least consider singing somewhere else. Somewhere that's not a dive, somewhere the manager has respect for you as a person and will keep his hands off you."

His voice was slowly rising, and Alexandra was surprised at the vehemence. When she didn't say anything, Parker chuckled dryly.

"I know I have a lot of nerve, and I know you think I'm meddling and I don't understand, but . . ."

"Yes?" she coaxed, turning to look at him.

He hesitated. "I care about you, Alex. I care what happens to you. I know you don't believe that, but it was always true."

"Even when you left?" she questioned softly, her heart pounding, waiting for his answer.

"More so, then," he answered in a low, hoarse voice, recalling the events at the time which had left him so little choice. Should he tell her about the phone calls he'd made to her home? It seemed pretty obvious to Parker that Alexandra knew nothing about them. He glanced briefly at her and back to the traffic.

"Where else have you been singing?"

She tilted her head thoughtfully. "Oh . . . I'm part of the chorus at the Kennedy Center. Last year I did a Christmas special with a local TV station. You didn't see me, but you heard my voice. I sang at Howard University's commencement ceremony several years ago. And I tried auditioning for a musical that was opening here before it went up to New York."

"What happened?"

Alexandra shifted restlessly in her seat. "Well, I made the third round of callbacks, but I discovered I couldn't act."

"They couldn't use you in some other way?"

"Not really. It was pretty laughable. Even my own sister thought I was pretty bad and should just stick to singing."

Parker thought quickly for a moment. "Your sister . . . I almost forgot you had one. How is she doing?" When Alexandra didn't answer, he continued. "And your father?" Parker asked quietly. "Is he still dependent on you?"

"He's doing well. He's stable as long as he follows his diet and tries to get some exercise. Unfortunately, that only entails walking from one end of the house to the other."

Parker chuckled silently. "And is Christine all grown up now?"

Alexandra silently thought what an understatement that was. "I would say so," she replied quietly.

Their car finally pulled into the side lot for Blues Alley, and after parking, they proceeded into the club. As soon as they stepped inside, Alexandra sensed that there was a world of difference between this more popular and well-received club and the questionable one they'd just left. But she was already feeling intimidated by its long history of featuring distinguished performers.

Parker gave her a look that asked if she wanted to forget going in. He could see the uncertainty that made her silent, and he drew her close to his side. Alexandra lifted her chin and rose to the silent challenge.

The interior was visible under dim atmospheric lighting that made the room warm and welcoming. There were only a few vacant tables, yet the room was not overpowered by cigarette smoke or noise. The maître d' recognized Parker, but didn't carry on about it or draw unnecessary attention to his presence.

Parker led her to a table and ordered them both drinks. They sat talking about the surroundings, and except for one casual mention that he'd studied music with one of the owners of the nightclub, they studiously avoided any other mention of the past. The show started with a solo saxophone player, followed by a female singer.

The saxophonist was a virtuoso, clever and lively with his music, playing pieces that had the attentive audience tapping their feet and moving shoulders and heads to the beat. Alexandra got as much pleasure listening to the audience's response as she did listening to the extraordinary playing. Parker would occasionally whisper little comments or observations about the saxophonist's technique, or a tricky musical departure. At one point they joined the audience in spontaneous response to a particular rendition, and they caught each other's gaze for a moment.

Reflected in each one's eyes was a mutual love of hearing wonderful music. For this moment, gone were Parker's stardom and her performance at The Outer Edge, the unsettled emotions of last week, and earlier tonight, and ten years ago. For the moment, it was all about them.

The saxophonist got the warm round of applause he deserved, then the singer came onto the stage. The first thing Alexandra noticed was that the woman was not wearing a suggestive gown. In fact, her plump body was well covered. Her ensemble was loose and without sparkles or shiny beads, and she was given a comfortable stool to sit on.

Alexandra listened and watched in total absorption, observing the woman's act, and noticing her ability. Alexandra liked her very much, and her admiration made her doubt her own ability to perform. Not to sing . . . but to *perform*. The woman's voice was good, but certainly nothing special, yet she had a presence and style that captured the audience's attention and made everyone follow her every move and note.

Between songs she had an easy repartee with the crowd, and a sense of humor that emanated naturally from her. She seemed totally at ease on the stage, and in total command. She wasn't thrown or confused when specific requests came from the patrons. Alexandra knew that her heart would have been in her throat if there had been a deviation from her own chosen set of songs.

Alexandra suddenly realized that she didn't know how to be spontaneous and to just go with the flow. With a light dawning in her mind, Alexandra recognized that there were only two ways in which she'd ever performed and been totally comfortable with herself. One was in teaching and demonstrating to her children. The second had been with Parker.

Alexandra frowned as these new thoughts took hold in her mind, as a new perspective allowed her to see and examine her heart, her dreams, her past. She cast a furtive look at Parker only to find him watching the female singer. Alexandra could see that he was entertained by her. Alexandra suddenly questioned whether she had the ability to hold Parker's attention. But not just Parker's . . . *anyone's*.

Parker hoped Alex was paying attention. He didn't want her just to hear how the singer sang, he wanted Alex to see how she performed. It took more than just having a great voice and a long repertoire of songs. There was also presence, style, ease, and even acting. The audience had to believe that she was up there performing only for them. Parker's attention roamed over her quiet profile. *Is this what you want?* he asked silently.

The songstress took several bows after her performance and promised to return for the midnight show.

"Well, what do you think?" Parker asked, as he signaled for the waiter and ordered two fresh drinks.

Alexandra gnawed on her lip, forgetting that she'd already done injury to it once tonight. "She was excellent. So lively. I enjoyed it," she said, not sounding very happy about it.

Parker took a thoughtful sip of his drink, still watching her, his eyes watching for a particular reaction. "What about you, Alex? Can you hold an audience? Make them glad they came to hear you?"

His voice was low, but the questions were pointed, going deep into her and the heart of the matter, which she'd not considered before. After a long moment, Alexandra raised her dark eyes to Parker. "I think so."

He raised his brows. "You only *think so?*"

"I'm sure I can," she said softly.

"Then what are you going to do about it?" he asked now. "And I'm not counting your engagement at The Outer Edge."

Alexandra felt as though he was putting her on the spot. "I'm doing everything I know how."

Parker twisted his glass around on the coaster. "Blues Alley holds open auditions every Saturday. Are you going to be here tomorrow?"

Again Alexandra detected a gentle challenge in his question. "I teach tomorrow. And I'm taking my class to the Kennedy Center to hear the children's program."

"Fine." Parker nodded. "I'll pick you up there." He lifted his drink. "We'll come together for the tryouts."

Alexandra stiffened her back and her eyes went quickly from confused to stormy. She heard the challenge again, and resented that he thought so little of her commitment. She, after all, had never had a moment's doubt about his, and look how far it had taken him.

"What's the matter. Afraid I won't show up? You don't have a lot of faith in me, do you?"

Parker hesitated in mid-air with his glass, and then put it back on the table. "If I didn't have faith in you, Alex, I wouldn't have dragged you away from The Outer Edge and brought you here. Do you have the desire and the guts to show up tomorrow?" Parker asked bluntly, no longer mincing words.

"Yes," Alexandra said through clamped teeth, angry that he was pushing, and angry that already the tension of anticipation had grabbed at her stomach.

"Then you're not afraid?" he pushed.

"Of course I am. I don't want to make a fool of myself," Alexandra said.

Parker slowly grinned at her. "Good," he nodded. "A little fear will keep you hungry and honest. That helps your music."

"Are you speaking from experience?" she asked flippantly.

"Absolutely," Parker readily admitted. Then slowly he leaned across the table, closer to her. "As you recall, you used to prod me quite a bit. You wouldn't give an inch. You'd never let me get away with saying that there was something I couldn't do. Don't you remember what you'd tell me, Alex?"

She was fascinated by the calm in Parker, by the dark, caressing regard in his eyes, by his sultry voice, which whispered their history without rancor, but with seeming regret and fondness. "An audition will only cost you carfare there and back," she said by rote. "You'll never know if you never try."

Parker arched his brow. "Are you going to eat those words?"

Alexandra sighed. Her anger began to dissipate. "No. I know I'm good, but nothing like you."

He shook his head. "Don't use me as an excuse. We don't do the same kind of music. And you're wrong. You're *going* to be great."

Parker pulled some bills from his pocket to pay for the drinks, and they stood up to leave. He helped her put her coat on and then reached out to take her hand. Without thinking, Alexandra put hers into his firm grasp. She looked at the joined hands, loving the instant familiar feel of his long, narrow fingers. She looked up at Parker and into his handsome face, with its gentle, ironic smile. He had extended the olive branch.

"And besides," Parker murmured, as they headed for the exit, "how many people go to auditions with their own fan club?"

She smiled at him. Parker winked at her and squeezed her fingers, and Alexandra relaxed. It was amazing how much Parker's firm belief in her mattered.

The drive to her apartment was very different than the drive the night of Debby and Brian's wedding.

"What music will you sing?" he asked, as they discussed the open audition.

"I guess soul ballads, torchy love songs. I have a couple of jazz compositions I do well with."

"Just don't try to practice tonight. It's too late to do you any good. Be prepared to give it your best shot tomorrow. Another thing—get some rest. Sleep as late as you can in the morning. And don't yell at the kids, no matter what they do to drive you crazy . . ."

She began to laugh. "You sound like a coach getting his athletes ready for a major tournament."

"I am. I know you can nail this, Alex."

Parker's faith in her made Alexandra feel so terrific. "Thanks, coach," she murmured in amusement.

Alexandra realized that this evening had changed the relationship. Last week had caught them both off guard, and swept them back into an unresolved chapter in their lives. Somehow, tonight they'd gotten forever past it. Whatever the past had been, it was now over and done. It served no useful purpose to continue the resurrection of it. The hurt still lingered, but only because she had loved him so much. And even recognizing that that love might still be the same only made for a bitter sweetness of how glorious the future might have been for both of them together.

At her door, she turned to face Parker. He made the moment easier for both of them by stating it was too late for him to come in. Alexandra nodded gratefully in agreement.

"Were you ever nervous at your auditions?" she asked him, as they stood outside her apartment door.

Parker shrugged. "I was probably too busy being annoyed," he grinned sheepishly, slowly starting to light a cigarette.

"Why annoyed?" she asked. Parker grimaced, but his brows were ominous across his forehead.

"I was never all that interested in performing, Alex. I just wanted to create my music. I could have been just as happy letting someone else play it."

She'd never known that. She shook her head. "No one could have done it as well."

Parker began to smile at the compliment. "Thank you," he said quietly.

"Thank you, too," she chuckled nervously.

"Don't thank me yet," Parker said.

As they stared at one another in the silence of the hall it seemed a small moment of déjà vu to Alexandra. She suddenly recalled the first night she'd ever met Parker. She remembered his teasing, his kindness and care. She remembered thanking him, just to have him say, "Don't thank me yet." *It's happening all over again,* Alexandra thought.

His eyes searched her face, settling on the pretty curves of her wide mouth. He was charmed by the freckles on her cheeks, which only served to make her seem young and unworldly. Parker knew in a way she was. And he was grateful for it. His hand stroked her cheek tentatively, to test how much she'd actually forgiven him.

"Alex?" he questioned quietly, and when she said nothing, he slowly bent his head until their lips met.

Alexandra's lips parted of their own will, and she knew again the heady feel and taste of his lips. There was faint alcohol and tobacco, and for some reason, her senses responded to the residual stimulus. She enjoyed the gentle play of his tongue against hers. His movement was so erotic and tantalizing that Alexandra swayed toward him, wanting him to put his arms around her.

Parker made no move to hold her, only taking control of the kiss, probing deep within her warm mouth with his tongue, boldly imposing himself before slowly pulling away to separate them with a moist little sound. He could smell the sweetness of her skin, the perfume on her clothing.

When Alexandra opened her eyes, she found Parker regarding her with tenderness.

"Goodnight," he whispered against her mouth. His hand slipped from her cheek, and he backed toward the stairs. "I'll see you at ringside tomorrow."

Alexandra smiled and waved goodbye.

CHAPTER 6

Alexandra felt like her coat was totally useless against the cold March wind. The sunshine was deceptive, promising more warmth for the day than was truly possible, and she clamped her teeth together to stop the chattering and hunched her shoulders deeper into her wool coat. The ten children in her charge seemed totally unaffected by the weather as they laughed and squealed playfully in youthful abandon.

"Michael, please, come away from there," Alexandra shouted at one boy, who'd decided that throwing bits and pieces of his lunch into the Potomac was more fun than eating it. But he scampered away at the strident sound of her voice, and joined several other youngsters in a game of tag.

Twice a year, Alexandra brought her young music students to the Kennedy Center to hear concerts or watch films. Last September they'd seen *Fantasia* and seemed to enjoy hearing classical music used as a background to the famous Disney animation.

Today, it had been the Young People's Orchestra, playing *Peter and the Wolf*. The audience had been filled with children, some there with parents just to hear the music and the narration that went with the story. But many more in the audience were future musicians themselves.

As a child, Alexandra had never had the opportunity to hear a live performance, and so the outings were just as much a treat for her as for the children.

Alexandra had always hoped that seeing and hearing other children perform would inspire her own kids to greater efforts. At least she tried to convince herself of that as she sat almost frozen, watching their energetic play, music far from their thoughts as they waited to be picked up by parents.

She was also very much aware that for some of these children, the study of an instrument was done more to please their parents; many of them were in her class reluctantly. Still, all the children enjoyed the biannual outings because each one meant a Saturday afternoon away from practice.

Two thin bodies streaked past Alexandra, one little girl in hot pursuit of a boy who'd been teasing her. The little girl's braids and ribbons were being pulled about by the wind. Alexandra gasped at the sight of the child hatless and gloveless, with her coat hanging open.

"Marsha, button your coat, before you catch a cold."

Marsha hastened to obey, but Alexandra suspected that she herself was the only one who was cold and uncomfortable. She could feel the chill seep into her very bones, stiffening the joints. She kept recalling how cold she'd been the night before in the strapless blue dress while performing. She remembered, also, the draft which had blown from the narrow hallway leading to the dressing room, to the small stage where she sang. The fact that Alexandra had awakened this morning with a headache and slightly stuffy nose did not bode well for the state of her health. She couldn't afford to be sick right now. There was still work to be done for her audition. There were all her classes, and those of Debby's until Debby returned from her honeymoon. And now she was also wishing she hadn't agreed so readily to the tryout session this afternoon at Blues Alley.

Alexandra could still envision the ease of the female singer the night before, the woman's calm assurance and professional performance, and she began to experience quelling self-doubts. Her years of amateur singing hadn't made her *that* confident and at ease. She began to blame Parker for urging her on. Maybe she wasn't ready yet. After all, Joe Jefferies notwithstanding, what was so bad about The Outer Edge?

"Well, for one thing, it certainly isn't Blues Alley," she muttered wryly to herself, knowing full well the great reputation of the famed Washington club. But the question was, was *she* ready for the big time?

Alexandra sighed, blew her nose miserably into a tissue, and stood to call her brood together. A number of parents were already waiting in the red carpeted lobby when she hustled the children inside. There were brief conferences with some parents who wanted to know their children's progress, and gentle words to the children themselves, reminding them to practice. After thank-yous, most of the children and their parents left.

Alexandra, scanning the group hastily, caught sight of one woman just as she was leaving with her son.

"Mrs. Evans, can I speak to you for just a moment?" Alexandra called out, hurrying through the dispersing group to the woman's side.

The woman, a little shorter and plumper than Alexandra, looked over her shoulder and smiled.

"Of course. David, don't wander too far. I'll only be a minute," she said to her son, who was already wandering off with mischievous ideas of playing on a nearby escalator. Then she turned back to Alexandra. "Yes?" she asked.

"I feel that David isn't practicing as much as he should between classes."

Mrs. Evans relaxed, the frown clearing from her round brown face. "Quite honestly, Miss Morrow, I'm not surprised. He likes music but hates the practice. I try to keep after him, but David has baseball on the brain and not much else."

"Perhaps you could talk to him. I mean, he's so talented. He's months ahead of the other children. He seems to understand the concepts so easily. I know David enjoys playing, but his attention wanders."

Mrs. Evans had already begun rolling her eyes heavenward during Alexandra's entreaty. "I know, I know," she said. "Right now, he can't decide if he wants to be on stage or on Astroturf. I have to tell you, baseball's got an edge. It's not your fault his mind is elsewhere. He likes you very much and tells his father and me about the great games you invent to make practice more fun. But with David, you almost have to sit on him to make him work hard."

Alexandra wanted to scream in her frustration; David was one of her most talented students. "Then maybe he can come to me three afternoons a week and I'll work with him."

Mrs. Evans sighed and shook her head. "We can't afford more lessons, Miss Morrow. We put off getting a new car this year so we could get David a decent piano . . ."

"I wouldn't charge you anything more. It's just that David is so promising."

Mrs. Evans sighed again, looking toward her son with both pride and exasperation. "So everyone seems to think. My husband and I were truly happy when David's teachers said he had a good ear for music, and recommended you for lessons. But what good are all the lessons if he simply doesn't care, or if he's not sure? Sometimes he'll sit at that piano and play for hours without me saying a word. Other times . . ." she merely shrugged.

Alexandra couldn't respond, and she felt defeated because Mrs. Evans was right: all the talent in the world meant nothing if one wasn't willing to put in the time or work or if there was no encouragement. Against her will, Alexandra thought fleetingly of her father's own wasted talents and lack of opportunity. She thought of Parker and his easy success. But she frowned now as she suddenly remembered his own evaluation of his career and his training. Parker was lucky and he didn't know it, she thought. She knew that if someone had offered her music lessons at ten, she'd have been in heaven.

Mrs. Evans shrugged and shook her head helplessly at the other woman. "Maybe the lessons are a waste of time and money. I've been thinking of not making him come for a while. I could just put the money aside. Maybe he'll miss the classes."

Alexandra shook her head vigorously. "Don't worry about the money. It's not important," she said generously. "I just don't want David to lose this time."

"I appreciate that."

"I was hoping he'd try out for the Young People's Orchestra in September. He's that good. He still has a few weeks left to apply and fill out the application forms."

David's mother laughed softly. "I know he enjoyed today's outing. He just said to me, 'Ma, I can do that. I can play as good as those kids.' "

"He can," Alexandra agreed, her eyes bright with hope.

"You're very patient," Mrs. Evans sighed.

"It's easy with David. He's a very talented little boy. Look, why don't you just let him come to classes as usual? He can come to me during the week. If he needs motivation to practice, I'll work with him and we'll practice together. It doesn't have to be every week, just whenever he wants. 'Half a loaf is better than none,' " Alexandra grimaced with a smile.

The other woman chuckled, already summoning her son. "That's real nice of you, and I'll keep your offer in mind. His father doesn't want me to push him. After all, he's only ten, and naturally he's more interested in sports. He's got all of those heroes in sports. It's a little tough to beat."

"But there are many heroes in music, too. Luther Vandross hasn't done so badly."

Mrs. Evans laughed softly at the truth of Alexandra's words. "You're right, of course. All those professional musicians lead such hard lives."

"Please don't discourage him. He may only want to play for fun. But he should learn as much as he can *now*. He can always decide what he wants to do later."

Mrs. Evans smiled. "I'll try, Miss Morrow. But it's really all up to David."

The boy came back and pulled on the sleeve of his mother's coat. "Mom, could we stop for pizza before going home?"

"Didn't you eat your lunch?" his mother asked.

David shrugged. "I'm still hungry."

Mrs. Evans looked at Alexandra. "That's where the rest of our money goes—into his stomach."

Alexandra smiled and winked playfully at the young boy. "What's your favorite food, David?" she asked.

David thought for a moment. "I like hamburgers, brownies, and grilled cheese sandwiches."

"I tell you what. If you come to an extra practice next week, I'll make brownies for you, and we'll go have hamburgers afterward."

"Ms. Morrow, that's not really . . ." Mrs. Evans started.

Alexandra gave her a silent pleading look and the woman hesitated.

"Can I, Mom?" David piped up, surprising his mother.

She raised her brows. "Well . . . that's up to you. You could practice at home, you know."

"I'd rather do it with Ms. Morrow."

Alexandra laughed. "Is it the practice, or the promise of a hamburger?" she asked. "I'll give you a call on Monday and we'll pick a time, okay?"

"Okay," David said, already moving toward the exit, and the hope of pizza on the way home.

"Thank you," Mrs. Evans said sincerely.

Alexandra watched as a moment later David left with his mother.

Music had always been important to Alexandra. When she was a youngster, it offered an escape. Like reading a book, it was something she could do alone for entertainment that took her out of her ordinary world and transported her to someplace wonderful and new. It made her feel good. And all she wanted was to let children like David learn, as she had, that good music was like magic.

Alexandra sensed she was not alone and turned to look into the face of Parker Harrison. She was startled at suddenly seeing him, and had a surprising mixed reaction. She was glad to see him, and then again, she was not. Her stomach knotted apprehensively as she recalled the upcoming afternoon audition, and the thought of Parker listening to her perform.

"Hello," he said quietly, and there was gentle amusement in his watchful dark eyes. "Why do I get the feeling that you were about to bolt like a scared rabbit?"

"Because I probably was," she admitted dryly. Her voice cracked and she softly cleared her throat.

Parker raised a brow and frowned slightly.

"I think I'm coming down with a cold," Alexandra told him.

Parker studied her face alertly for a second, listened to her excuse, and shook his head. The collar of his leather coat was pulled up, framing his neck and jaw. He drew on a lit cigarette held in his hand.

"Are you saying you would rather not try out this afternoon?" he asked casually, exhaling and watching her through the gray haze.

Alexandra thought about it. She had always been waiting for another time, the right time. There was never going to be a right time unless she made it for herself. "I want to sound my best," she equivocated, but she wasn't being totally honest with herself or with Parker.

Parker's brows furrowed in further thought for a moment, and he glanced briefly at his watch. "Tell you what—let's get warmed up. Then we'll see about the tryout."

Alexandra let out a sigh of relief and lifted dark, warm eyes to his handsome face. She wondered if he guessed her inner thoughts. She sensed he was perfectly capable of it. "That would be nice," she responded.

He winked and gave her a reassuring smile. "Good. I'll leave the car parked here. Let's walk to the Georgetown Inn. It's not too far away."

Automatically Parker held out a hand to her, and Alexandra let his hand close around hers as he led her out into the cold but bright day.

Her fluffy blue turtleneck sweater was swathed protectively around her throat and chin, and a matching beret was pulled over her hair and ears. Her wool coat was buttoned up to her throat. Nonetheless Alexandra was cold. With a great deal of effort, she held back the shivers. Parker seemed right in his element. His leather coat flapped open in the wind. Alexandra was glad when they finally reached the restaurant.

Alexandra removed her coat and hat. As Parker also removed his coat and muffler, it struck her, certainly not for the first time, how good-looking he was. Even more so than she'd remembered. Parker seemed to have come to full adulthood so much in command, so unlike the younger man she'd known. There was a strength about him now that had obviously been gained over the last several years. She had been so stunned into letting down her anger at him a week ago that she'd missed the subtle differences. He might almost be an entirely different person. Now that she'd been able to spend some time with him, no matter how awkward or emotionally confusing, she could see him through different eyes, more adult and realistic ones. Alexandra liked this Parker better. And while she didn't want to change the earlier memory she had of him, of that time when they'd first met, she was at last putting the relationship in proper perspective. She had been awfully young when Parker had come into her life.

Parker was also enjoying his assessment of Alexandra, but it only confirmed what he'd seen and recognized the week before at Brian and Debby's wedding. Alex was very much a woman now, no longer the young girl he'd last seen.

The thought came to Parker that he'd never told his parents about the student he'd met who'd had more of an influence on him than he would have admitted at the time. They'd never been overly impressed with the women he'd dated or known primarily from being on the road and being so visible. But Parker wondered what they'd think of Alex and her stubborn pride, her determination, and her youthful prettiness. She ordered a pot of hot chocolate, too nervous to think of eating, but Parker ordered coffee and a club sandwich. They sat comfortably opposite each other, waiting for the order.

Unaware of Alexandra's thoughts or her melting change of heart, Parker leaned toward her, resting his elbows on the table. "So, how did the kids enjoy the outing? Are you hoping a serious interest will seep in through the pores?"

Alexandra grinned ruefully. "I think they enjoyed being away from piano lessons and my prodding. But they're a good group. Some were impressed by the show and a few felt intimidated, but I think it's important for them to see what's possible for themselves."

Parker grinned. "Remind you of anything?"

"You mean last night at Blues Alley? The thought crossed my mind. I guess the difference is I've already made up my mind what I want to be when I grow up." Parker laughed lightly with her. "The kids still need all the training they can get *before* they make their decision."

Alexandra suddenly became excited about her really exceptional students, like David Evans, and told Parker how she hoped he'd change his mind about practicing seriously and come to appreciate his unique gift.

In her glowing report, Alexandra missed Parker's quiet enjoyment of her animated features. "You obviously like teaching," he observed.

"Oh, I do. You have no idea how wonderful it is to get a talented child and watch his progress, to feel that I might have contributed to it. I want them *all* to go on to great things."

Parker watched Alexandra closely, somewhat surprised at her excitement and wholehearted enthusiasm for her work. Did she realize that she seemed to have much more faith in her children than she had in herself?

"But you know most of them will only be just competent. You realize, of course, that most of them will give up in a few years, or be discouraged in high school. A precious few will go the distance, Alex. In any case, you can follow their progress long distance—after you become rich and famous yourself, that is," Parker said casually.

Alexandra's focus became sharp, and the glow of her eyes began to burn out, to be replaced by confusion and deep thought. It was as if she'd never considered that if her own career took off the way she'd dreamt, her teaching would end. There'd be no time for it.

"Yes, of course," Alexandra mumbled, distracted.

Parker chuckled soundlessly, but shook his head as he reached for his cigarettes to light one. "Nobody gets to have it all."

"You did."

He shrugged. "You can't judge by my career. I wouldn't want anyone else to think I've had it so easy. It's relative.

"Just don't forget that they're still kids, Alex. Sometimes a movie or a house party, a softball game, or a date is more important."

Alexandra shrugged and smiled. "You're right. I think sometimes I do forget. The ones who are serious are serious about music no matter what. Some of the others take lessons because of parents or friends."

". . . And hope to just coast along and not be noticed," Parker added. "As I recall, the students are late a lot, or call in sick, or just don't show. The excuse is that there's too much homework, or relatives are visiting, or the dog has to go to the vet again."

A smile of surprise and recognition played on Alexandra's features as Parker recounted some of the ingenious excuses of students.

"Once or twice a grandparent has passed on, usually of some awful, unknown disease. Do you have any idea how many grandparents have gone to heaven to spare a kid music classes?"

Alexandra nodded, laughing softly as their order was served. The waitress seemed to linger over the simple chore, her gray eyes, under a droopy mop of skewered blond curls, taking furtive looks at Parker.

Alexandra, still amused by Parker's revelations, felt a momentary twinge of annoyance and pride at the waitress's attention to Parker. He was totally oblivious to the young woman's interest.

"Can I get you anything else?" the young waitress asked, hoping to draw Parker's attention. But he merely shook his head and gave her a vacant smile.

"This is fine, thanks," he said, returning his attention to Alexandra.

It was in that moment that it occurred to Alexandra that there were probably women who came on to him constantly, who tried to capture his interest, to be drawn into his charmed circle. But here he sat with her, telling amusing anecdotes, and willingly giving time to encourage her goals, but also to instill reality. Parker could have walked away last week, and seen their brief and volatile encounter as just "for old times' sake." But he hadn't. He'd returned not once, but twice, and it was to her that his time was given. Parker was not playing at being a celebrity. He was being a friend, and one who certainly knew her better than anyone else, except her father.

As Parker poured himself coffee, his eyes narrowed with further memory and the storytelling continued. "Another good excuse I've heard is the one where the dog ate the music sheets, or they got thrown out in the trash by mistake. But my all-time favorite is the one where the music sheets were *accidentally* used to line the cat's litter box."

Tears of laughter filled Alexandra's eyes as Parker sipped from his cup, grinning broadly at her amusement.

"So how did you know all that?" she asked, wiping away the tears.

"I made up most of them," Parker admitted wickedly. "And there are some others that come to mind now."

"Maybe you should tell me so I'll be warned," Alexandra urged.

He squinted at her. "I don't think so. I wouldn't want to spoil the efforts of some creative kid."

Her amusement slowly faded. "You surprise me," she whispered, watching him as he chewed his sandwich. "You're so good, I assumed you always were, that you *always* worked hard and practiced."

Parker nodded. "I did. But sometimes it wasn't by choice. Believe me, I know how your students feel sometimes," he observed.

"You sound like you approve of what they do."

Parker put his sandwich down and he began to play idly with his napkin. "You're wrong, Alex. I don't approve at all. But I do understand. When you're eight, nine, ten years old, piano lessons are not the beginning and end of the world. Only parents and teachers think so."

Alexandra shifted uncomfortably, acutely aware of the conversation just that afternoon with David Evans and his mother. "You resented it, didn't you?" Alexandra observed.

Parker didn't comment at first. His eyes were following her movements, the small, narrow hand that smoothed her hair, the bright glow of her face with the dusting of freckles which made Alexandra look so appealing. For the moment, he seemed more fascinated with her as he raised a hand to smooth her dark hair. The gesture was caring and personal, something he used to do often, affectionately, long ago. It was as if the talk of music and classes was merely a smokescreen to disguise the fact that they were each in turn still filled with questions about what they were to each other. The talk of music was an easy, common link, but it hardly dealt with their real feelings, whatever they were.

Parker let his hand drop just short of stroking her cheek, and turned his attention to Alexandra's last comment.

"I suppose I resented the constant reminders to practice," Parker said around a mouthful of sandwich, his brows furrowed. "Music was always easy for me. I didn't understand why I had to practice all the time if I was supposed to be so good."

Alexandra suddenly recalled Parker's ambivalence about all his earlier years of training. But until this very moment, she'd never considered the powerless frustration he must have felt as a child urged onward by doting parents and encouraging teachers. David Evans again came to mind, and Alexandra could see the beginning of similarities between the child and Parker. She understood now that David had to make the choices himself, something Parker had not been allowed to do. A whole new vista of enlightenment brightened her eyes as she regarded Parker over the rim of her steaming mug.

"Are you still sorry?" she asked.

"No, of course not," he shook his head. "My parents did what they thought best, and believe me, Alex, I'm grateful. Look how far it's taken me. I just would have liked other things in my life besides the obsession with music. I've missed a lot." As he spoke, he reached out and suddenly lifted her hand and turned it palm up. "I hope you don't make the same mistake. Don't make music the center of your life," he added softly, almost to himself, and rubbed his thumb over her soft palm. "What were you like as a little girl?" he asked with a small smile.

Alexandra pursed her lips. "I don't remember being a little girl," she replied thoughtfully. "I think I was always serious and always had responsibilities."

"And who took care of you?" Parker crooned.

His thumb made circles lightly on her skin, leaving a path of tingling sensations that radiated outward through her. Alexandra briefly closed her eyes, fighting the lovely languid feeling that was spreading through her limbs. She didn't feel so cold now. "I didn't need to be taken care of." When he didn't respond, she raised questioning eyes to his brown features. Parker was watching her intently.

"I'm not so sure about that," he murmured. Then, with an effort, his mood lightened and he looked at her mischievously. "Shall I tell the lady's fortune?"

Alexandra nodded with a smile. Parker pretended deep concentration over the delicate lines etched in her hand.

"Swami says the lady will have a bright future . . ."

"As in, under spotlights?" she grinned.

"Very possible," he hedged. He frowned over the slender limb. "I see that she is very talented. There is a great opportunity coming her way that will bring her many followers."

"That sounds intriguing," Alexandra chuckled.

"Ahhh, I also see someone with her."

"You do?" Alexandra asked, forgetting this was make-believe, and bending forward earnestly.

Parker nodded sagely, tracing the lines along her fingers. "Yes . . . yes, his image is coming in clearly now."

"*His* image?" Alexandra questioned.

"Yes. He's tall . . . dark . . ."

"And handsome," she finished the predictable description with a grin. "No doubt we're talking about you." She was going to pull her hand free, but Parker held fast.

"I didn't know you thought me tall, dark, and handsome," Parker said, with provocative intent. His brow arched.

Alexandra grimaced at him, but was embarrassed that she was so readily caught in her admission. "It could be you," she murmured.

"Could be. Is there anything wrong with that?" he questioned smoothly. "What if someone came into your life and you fell in love, Alex? Would there be room for him, too? Or are you only dedicated to your career?"

Alexandra became alert now, as Parker examined too closely the questions she hadn't asked in a long time. He had already been the someone she was in love with. And she might very well have given up her singing, her golden chance, for him. But he had made one decision, ending that possibility, and she had made another. She would not give up her goals so easily a second time.

Parker leaned across the table, his hand squeezing her fingers almost painfully as he questioned and searched, pinning Alexandra in place with his intensity. Her heart began to race, and she sat staring at him.

"I want a chance, Parker," she began softly. "You had yours. My father even had his. My sister seems to get more chances than seems fair because everyone finds it hard to tell her no. I just want to try for myself. I *need* to."

There was a long silence as Parker's brows drew together. He did see how much it meant to her. He tried to hold his feelings in check, but there was a tight, forceful plea to his whispered words to her.

"I know you do." He stared at her as though determined to make that clear. "But it's hard and lonely out there, Alex. I know, I've been there, and I just don't want to see you hurt. I don't want to . . ." He stopped suddenly, clamping down on the rest of the sentence.

Alexandra felt the chill of strong emotion crawl over her, bringing moisture to her eyes. "I've been hurt before," she whispered.

Parker's jaw tensed and twitched and he clasped her hands warmly and protectively in his own. "Will you ever forgive me, Alex?"

She blinked to clear her vision. Suddenly, the anger was all gone. There was only regret, because she could still love him, and there seemed to be no chance for them now. She swallowed hard, and was actually able to smile. "I already have," Alexandra said. So now he knew she didn't really hate him. But she would not let him know she loved him more than ever. There would be no point in that kind of confession.

They were interrupted when the waitress brought their check and began clearing the table. Then, coyly smiling with youthful feminine charm at a good-looking man, she asked if he was Parker Harrison.

"I'm afraid so," Parker said dryly.

The young woman found that amusing and laughed. Then she wanted an autograph. Then three other people made uncertain approaches to their table with the same request.

The electric intimacy they shared had been intruded upon thoughtlessly, Alexandra noted. Watching Parker sign autographs politely, she also had a glimpse into what his life must be like day after day, being well known and so visible, the demands made, the concessions granted, the compromises.

The waitress departed, as did the patrons who'd recognized him.

Parker had given them his attention, as he had the guests the week before at the wedding, but the moment was gone and he quickly was, once again, the Parker she knew.

Parker stood and looked at his watch, and back to her. "Ready?" he asked, making no further reference to their unfinished exchange.

Alexandra swallowed and nodded and pulled her hat on once more against the cold. She knew grimly now that Parker meant was she ready for much more than just the audition at Blues Alley.

It occurred to Alexandra that everyone gathered around the small stage and lit piano would probably know who Parker Harrison was. But he didn't enter the club at all beyond escorting Alexandra into the dim entrance. Once there, he'd turned to her, his face shadowed and solemn.

"Remember what you used to say when I was working on a new piece of music? Even before you'd heard it?" he asked throatily.

Alexandra hesitated, then she remembered. "Yes. I'd say, 'I'm going to love it, Parker. So will everyone else.' "

He nodded. Then he stepped forward, gathering Alexandra into his arms. He was holding her close, with his cheek bent to touch her own, and their skin began to warm up as he surprised her with the sudden embrace.

"They're going to love you, Alex, but so will I," he whispered.

And before she could say anything, before she could question what he'd said or if she'd heard correctly Parker moved his head to settle his frosty lips over hers. Her response was immediate; she was melting against him and answering the serious urging of his mouth and tongue.

His kiss confused her, fogged her thinking, made her forget what she was going to ask, even made her forget her fear. His hands rode up her back to hold her head as he purposefully gentled his kiss and let his lips caress and tease at her until Alexandra wanted to press closer to him and have him send her senses reeling delightfully again.

He wanted her. She knew he did, and admitted to herself that this time it would mean something different, something more to her as a woman and not as a teenager, to have him love her. Alexandra wanted to feel, too, how they'd changed and grown.

Parker abruptly released her, and pulled open the club doors to step back into the cold before she could recover herself, or change her mind about the audition. Alexandra stood still for a shaky moment, her breath caught in her throat while she still savored the feel of his mouth. The door swished closed behind him. She pulled herself together with a sigh, and went through an inner door.

There were several men and women gathered near the piano and stage, a number of others still wearing outer coats, like herself, who were hopeful auditioners. They sat quietly, scattered in chairs through the room, which looked different and imposing with its house lights up, the magic of late night lighting and decorations gone.

Alexandra slowly approached the small group of people. Spotting her through a curling haze of smoke and stale air, the pianist snapped his fingers at her and held out his hand.

"Let's see your stuff, baby," he mouthed abruptly around a smelly cigar. There was no greeting and there were no accommodations.

For a moment, Alexandra had no idea what he meant, until she remembered the music sheets in her shoulder bag. She hastily pulled them out and gave them to the burly man. He glanced indifferently at them, and added the sheets to a small pile on the piano top.

A man and woman seated at a small, cluttered table beckoned her forward. They barely looked at Alexandra as they asked her name and where she'd last performed. She felt mildly annoyed at their offhanded attitude, and when she was asked what she was going to do, Alexandra foolishly answered, "To sing."

The man and woman looked at each other and laughed. "We kind of figured that out. We want to know *what*. What's your style, your program? Know what I'm saying?" the woman said patronizingly.

Taking a deep breath, Alexandra answered, "I guess I do ballads and some love songs. One or two slow numbers."

"Show tunes don't go over so big here. Can you give us some deep soul?"

Alexandra mutely shook her head.

"Okay, Baby. Take a seat." The woman gestured toward the open room.

Looking around at the others, Alexandra noticed two women, a musician testing out his trumpet, and a pianist reading the *Washington Post*. One of the women was doing her nails, and the other hummed quietly to herself.

What struck Alexandra as odd was the way everyone ignored everyone else, seemingly unconcerned about the competition, or as if being here for the same reason precluded being friendly and open. Alexandra found it cold, but couldn't bring herself to break through the imposed silence to ask where they'd performed before or what their career goals were. She wanted to ask if they were nervous too, and to ask the two attractive women how they would dress for their shows if chosen. Just simple questions that would have established a common ground of support and understanding for all of them, something Alexandra needed. But no one else there seemed to need that connection. So Alexandra sat alone, waiting her turn, feeling isolated and insignificant, and wishing Parker

SERENADE

was holding and kissing her again. She began to daydream and lose track of her surroundings, her imagination entertaining her.

Two hours later, the trumpet player was hired, as were one of the two women and Alexandra. The managers told her she had a nice, easy presence, almost romantic. They hired her for two weekends, and she would begin in a month. She'd be paid a salary plus tips, and she had to provide her own outfits.

It was quick and professional; and once the shock wore off, Alexandra felt more bewildered than elated. The excitement that she'd expected would accompany her selection never materialized. She felt relief that the audition was over and had been a success, as Parker had said it would, but already she could sense her worry, and the anticipation of performing in front of an audience that was going to be much more discerning than the patrons at The Outer Edge. She was given a contract to look over, sign, and return sometime before the start of her show.

There were no signs of pleasure or encouragement from the management. With a curious sense of disappointment, Alexandra went to find Parker, who was waiting outside the club.

He was standing under the now-lit canopy, smoking a cigarette, deep in thought. He turned at the sound of the door opening and watched Alex exit. He scanned her smooth, calm face for a long moment. She only frowned at him.

"Were you standing out here all this time?"

"No. Too cold for that. I went to a record store a few blocks from here and got some tapes." He patted one of his pockets. "And I stopped to shop for a gift." He patted the other pocket, but didn't elaborate. "When do you start?" Parker asked confidently, tossing away the cigarette, and pulling up the collar of his coat.

"Next month," Alexandra answered breathlessly.

She expected Parker to kiss her or hug her, or in some way, bring back the magic he'd created before she'd gone in to audition. She suddenly felt as if she desperately needed it, as if it was the only thing she was sure of in the last few hours. But Parker made no move toward her. He only curved a corner of his mouth and stuffed his hands into his pockets.

"Congratulations," he murmured.

Alexandra was disappointed, not hearing the pleasure she'd expected from him.

"This calls for a celebration. How about dinner and champagne?" he asked.

Alexandra shook her head. "I can't. I have a show tonight at The Outer Edge, and I always cook for my father on Sundays." She saw his even acceptance of this and thought quickly. "Would you like to come home to dinner with me tomorrow?"

Briefly, a hesitation and wariness passed over Parker's strong features, and his jaw tensed nervously. Then his face relaxed, and finally he smiled warmly. "I can't tell you the last time I had a home-cooked meal. I'd like very much to meet your father. It's time," he ended mysteriously, and Alexandra nodded in agreement.

CHAPTER 7

The house where Alexandra and her sister were raised was a small, simple, two-story wood frame house in a neighborhood where all the houses looked pretty much the same. The middle-class black community was a quiet suburb in Virginia, just an hour outside of D.C., and accessible by Metro and bus. The colors and wood trim of the neighborhood houses changed here and there, and some residents had done more elaborate landscaping than others. Some homes were in disrepair and needed work, some looked freshly sided or painted. Alexandra's childhood home fell somewhere in the middle.

As Parker got out of his car, he slowly looked over the neighborhood. Even though it was night, he had a clear sense of order, quiet, and community. He smiled to himself wistfully. He, who had grown up in a large, attached townhouse, locked in between a long row of like structures, had always wanted to live like this, with trees and lawns and spaces between the houses, with driveways and backyards and neighbors who invited you over. The apartment he'd had in Washington the year he'd first met Alex had certainly not come close to fulfilling his fantasy of home, but then, being in D.C. served another purpose: it placed distance between him and his family and was temporary enough not to matter.

He and Alexandra had never spoken of their childhood or of where they'd grown up. In a way, when they'd first met, perhaps they were both trying to get away from it, to live it down; both were anxious to begin a life that was different from the past. But Parker had traveled enough, had gone and come back enough to realize he'd always wanted to return home to something like this.

Alexandra had always been less sure. As she stepped out of the car, she unconsciously scanned her old neighborhood, as if deciding whether it was good enough, wondering what Parker thought of it. Even now, as they slowly approached the porch of her family home, Alexandra wondered nervously why Parker was smiling. Was he amused or surprised?

Alexandra herself was more than a little surprised at the meeting between her father and Parker. There was an almost imperceptible moment when the two men shook hands and silently measured one another before Mr. Morrow stated with an odd pensiveness, "Well, well. It's a real pleasure to finally meet you."

Parker was impressed with the firm grip of George Morrow, whose hands were thin, long-fingered, and sinewy, the hands of a piano player. He also had the dark, intense eyes of his daughter, observant and filled with feeling. He was hardly taller than Alex.

"Same here," Parker responded to Mr. Morrow's quietly cordial welcome. "I told Alex it was time."

Alexandra smiled at the way they greeted each other, as if they'd always known one another and hadn't been in touch for years. Of course, her father knew who Parker Harrison was. It was just interesting to have him treat Parker comfortably and easily as he would any longtime friend visiting the family. Mr. Morrow showed no surprise or curiosity about how his eldest daughter had come to know someone of Parker's standing and reputation. Alexandra wondered why he didn't.

Alexandra was further surprised to see the two men hit it off right away, as if they already knew and understood a lot about each other, but they were an incongruous pair. Parker, neatly and expensively attired, towered over her shorter, slightly built father in his loose, limp trousers, a favorite worn plaid shirt with too-short sleeves, and bedroom slippers. Neither of the two men was the least interested in putting on airs or in impressing the other. Once introduced, it was as though they'd always known each other. Parker barely had a chance to remove his leather topcoat before her father was engaging him in a comfortable conversation about how he enjoyed having company. This led, in some mysterious way Alexandra couldn't follow, into sports and spring training for baseball.

Her presence was suddenly ignored, and with a rueful chuckle, she slipped away to the kitchen at the back of the split-level house, where she made a weekly inventory of what was needed from the market. As she wrote out her shopping list, she listened to the low murmuring and occasional laughter from the living room and smiled at the sense of warmth and family she felt with the two men together.

It was surprising that her father was being more than just polite with

Parker. Her father had never spoken kindly of professional performers. He was honest in admitting that most of them were very talented and real nice, too, but he didn't feel any of them lived in the real world. Alexandra knew that this attitude accounted for her father's less than enthusiastic acknowledgment of her own desire for a music career.

Alexandra peeked into the living room at one point and found her father and Parker deep in what seemed to be a serious conversation. She retreated back to the kitchen, but hoped her father wasn't doing something totally embarrassing, like asking Parker what his intentions were.

Alexandra began preparing Sunday dinner, which consisted of mashed potatoes, sauteed chicken in a lemon sauce, kernel corn, and a salad. She then set the dining table in the small alcove off the kitchen. These simple chores of making dinner for her father always managed to bring her back to earth, the "real world," as her father reminded her. And there was certainly a sense that her father's welfare and needs had more importance than music. In this, Alexandra also believed she could do both. After all, other people managed.

As she laid out place mats, her movements were stilled when she heard the strains of the old family piano. It was Parker playing, and although his touch and selection of keys were idle, it was easily recognizable, even on the ill-tuned and ancient keyboard. He finally settled into a melody he'd composed several years ago that had firmly established his own special style in the music world. As she continued her preparations, Alexandra experienced almost personal pride because perhaps she, better than anyone else, knew how far Parker had come.

In the living room, Parker was impressed by the pride Alexandra's father showed in his piano. It was a good, serviceable instrument, and when Parker ran his fingers absently over the keys, the sound was still clear. He smiled to himself. This was where Alex had learned to play! She had watched her father and followed his example.

Now that he'd finally met George Morrow, Parker realized he liked him. George seemed to be a simple man who was happy with his life, one who didn't moan or regret that it could have been something more. His credo was simply to live honestly and try not to hurt anyone. As a father raising children alone, he was as protective of his daughters as Parker imagined. It was good that they had this chance to meet and to dispel any possible misconceptions.

"Never could afford a better piano," George Morrow said with a wry shake of his head. "But this old baby, it's held up pretty good. I used to sit in the middle with a daughter on each end, and Lord, the sounds that would fill this house." He rasped out a chuckle at his own memory, as he watched the wistful playing of the younger man. "I wish I could have given my girls the training you had."

Parker raised his brows, his wide mouth slanted into a slight smile. "I'd say your daughters had the best kind of training—it came straight from your heart. I envy them that."

From the kitchen, Alex heard the music stop for a while, and then begin again, but now with her father seated at the bench. His style was untrained and chaotic but lively and definitely musical. He was bold and inventive at the keyboard, unmindful of techniques which he didn't know while bringing into play his own. Parker's playing was smooth and neat. But only now that she was able to hear a comparison did Alexandra gain an awareness of her father's individual and unique style. Absently considering the differences in ability, Alexandra went to inform the two men that dinner was ready.

Her father watched her approach from over his left shoulder, beaming from a thin, excited face. Her father brought his music to a flourished, noisy end.

"Did you hear that?" Mr. Morrow laughed. "There's life in the old joints yet." He wiggled his thin, knobby fingers in the air.

"Yeah, you sound real good. Carnegie Hall next?" Alexandra teased.

Her father merely grunted out a derisive laugh of doubt as he rubbed his aching fingers. "Maybe not Carnegie Hall, but I can certainly start some feet tapping in church."

She turned smiling eyes to Parker, grateful because her father was having such a good time. "I'm glad that there's no rivalry between you."

The two men exchanged quick glances and her father's expression was guileless.

"Why should there be?"

Parker pursed his lips and said quietly, "We've just had a chance to talk and get to know one another." He smiled at George Morrow. "Your father is a wise man."

Alexandra was slightly astounded by Parker's confession. Her father waved the comment away, and Parker began to read the music sheet on the piano stand.

"Your father told me he wrote that piece," Parker began, but was interrupted.

"Oh, that was years ago. It wasn't anything," George Morrow said, embarrassed, as he half turned toward his daughter.

Alexandra's gaze swung back sharply to her father. "I didn't know you wrote that." Not only was Alexandra surprised, she was fleetingly disappointed that she never knew of her father's input into the work.

Mr. Morrow was looking very uncomfortable now, not used to being the topic of conversation. He shrugged and plunged his hands into his trouser pockets. "What's to know? I was just fooling around a bit. I didn't think it would come to much, and it didn't."

"Perhaps the timing was all wrong," Parker said introspectively. "Sometimes those who care least about the recognition will find themselves pushed into the limelight. And those who want it most never find it."

Mr. Morrow was shaking his head vigorously. "I never wanted all that. I just enjoyed the music. I played just for myself."

"All the same, your music is good. I'd like to hear more," Parker said to the older man.

"We'll see, we'll see," Mr. Morrow responded demurely, but he was still pleased.

As her father slowly got up from the piano and Parker moved out of his way, Alexandra caught sight of two glasses on the piano top. She glanced quickly at her father. She indicated the glasses with a tilt of her head.

"You know this isn't a good idea, Daddy."

"Aw, come on, girl. That's the only drink I've had in days."

Alexandra ignored her father's mild protest, not wanting to debate the point right then. She headed back to the kitchen, taking the glasses with her and leaving the two men to follow.

Alexandra poured the contents of the glasses into the sink and began digging for serving utensils from a drawer. When she turned, Parker was standing in the doorway, watching her. Alexandra leaned a hip against a counter, and stared down at the utensils in her hand.

"My father has a heart condition and high blood pressure. He's not supposed to drink."

"I'm sorry. I'd forgotten, and he never said anything," Parker replied apologetically.

Alexandra sighed heavily. "I'm not surprised. I can't begin to tell you the time I've spent trying to convince that man to take better care of himself. If I'm not around, he doesn't."

Parker chuckled at the picture she drew of her father. "He sounds stubborn; just like someone else I know."

Alexandra shrugged at the comparison and chose to ignore it. "Anyway, there are so few things he enjoys anymore—like fooling around on the piano, or a drink now and then. And he's often alone, now that Christine and I are on our own."

"Do you see your sister often?"

Only when she wants something, Alexandra thought to herself ruefully. "No, not often." Alexandra answered vaguely. She turned around to the cabinets again and reached for glasses on an overhead shelf.

"You never talk about her. Is she musical, like you and your father?" Parker asked, moving closer to stand behind her.

"No," Alexandra chuckled dryly. "Christine has other talents."

"Like what?"

Alexandra hesitated in her motions, acutely aware of Parker's near-ness. She was aware that suddenly it seemed only to set her on edge, as if she expected it to lead to something more complex between them.

"If you ever meet her, you'll know," she responded absently, nearly los-ing track of the conversation. He was standing so close now that she could feel his subtle body heat.

"And does she have freckles like you?" His voice had gotten curiously low and seductive, and frantically Alexandra wondered why he was doing this to her now. He was deliberately attacking her senses. Slowly she turned to face him, giving him a chance to see the dots sprinkled across her face.

"No. No, I'm the only one."

"You see?" Parker murmured, his eyes ignoring the freckles, and seem-ing to search everywhere else, particularly her mouth. "I always said you were different and special."

Parker only smiled at the expression in Alexandra's eyes. He didn't know how to say she was also different to be around in the home where she grew up, with her father, who was a lively, funny, very talented man of extraordinary good sense. He particularly didn't know how to tell Alexandra how much softer and more feminine and more comfortable she seemed here.

Here, in her childhood home, Parker could forget about their mutual involvement in music, which seemed all-consuming. Here, the music was for pure pleasure, adding to the quality of their lives, which was normal, real, grounded. Parker saw clearly in Alexandra, as she stood here in her family kitchen looking both pretty and unusually domestic, what he wished he could come home to, what he knew he could never leave.

There was a quickening of Alexandra's heartbeat as she felt the virile magnetism of Parker standing so near. His presence made her feel softly vulnerable, and she, too, was seeing him differently. She wondered what he was thinking. What was it that was causing Parker to seem so intimate?

"Alex . . ." he began, and then stopped as she watched curiously the play of emotions over his strong, dark features. He raised a hand and with a bent index finger ran his knuckle down the side of her neck just below her ear. He could see Alexandra let out a shaky breath, her skin re-acting, quivering. "I'll bet no one knows how sensitive you are right there," he teased in a low, hoarse voice.

"I haven't just been sitting around for ten years, Parker," Alexandra said, with a touch of coyness.

"Has there been someone else?" he asked, suddenly curious.

Alexandra's chin lifted, the stubborn pride clear in her eyes and mouth. "I hope you don't expect me to answer that."

Parker tilted his head for a moment to study her further, his eyes once again more interested in her pouting mouth. "You just did," he replied, his mouth twisting in sad irony. He slowly took the silverware and glasses from her hands and put them on the counter behind her. Then he placed his hands on her narrow waist and in the same movement pulled her closer to him until he could rub his hard chin against her temple.

The action was slow, but still happened too fast for Alexandra to do anything beyond bracing her hands on his upper arms and letting her thighs rest intimately against his.

He sighed. "I'm not surprised there may have been other men in your life. But I don't want to know about it. Pretty arrogant of me, isn't it?" he said tightly. "I remember everything about you."

His voice grew husky, the utterance of words warm on her skin, creating a tingling that began to drift down and throughout her. Parker closed his arms gently around her until her breasts were pressed into his chest. Alexandra clutched his upper arms, her heart beginning to race.

"I can remember holding you just like this against me, knowing you trusted me."

"Parker . . ." she began, only to have him squeeze her silent. She sensed that he needed to talk and say these things. She needed to hear them. But not now.

"But the best part was making love to you. I remember making love to you most of all. I have all the memories of those moments."

It was an incredible admission to make just then, and Alexandra could only stand stunned, quiet, and enormously excited as she listened. The intimacy of their bodies together sent a curl of warm passion coursing through her. She could sense that Parker was trying to say something important and personal to her, without actually saying it. Alexandra's stomach twisted into little knots of desire and tension. Her fingers dug gently into his arms.

Parker pulled back so he could see her face again. "No one else has what you gave to me. I know that now," he said, in a voice that was somewhat poignant and wistful. "And no one else will."

The silence that followed was suddenly like a deep, empty pit that Alexandra felt herself falling into. She blinked away a sort of slumberous desire. She opened her mouth, and not a single word came out.

She never thought of a relationship anymore, because Parker had been the only man she'd ever wanted, and that hadn't worked out. He'd left her. He'd never said he loved her. But did he want her back now?

Alexandra pushed slowly but firmly out of his arms and took a step back. It was by pure chance that Parker Harrison had walked back into her life. His leaving had allowed her to see that she didn't have to rely anymore on someone else to make her happy. And his sudden arrival into her life meant she could stand the risk of letting him go this time in order to fulfill herself.

Alexandra suddenly realized that Parker had probably made the best decision years ago. She could do him a favor and not let him continue to feel guilty for it. She would not let him pretend to love her, either.

Alexandra smiled sadly at him, shaking her head. "I've learned to be careful who I give my affections to."

"You should be," Parker remarked smoothly. "I want you to be very selective."

For a moment longer, they stared in silence. And just as Parker bent his head to kiss her, the kitchen door swung open and George Morrow's head popped through.

"Are we eating tonight, or what?" he asked, apparently not fazed at finding his daughter in Parker's arms.

"My fault," Parker apologized, his eyes still thoughtfully on Alexandra. "I had to find out something important."

"I'm serving now," Alexandra said, squeezing past Parker, and reaching for pot holders and the oven door.

"Good," Mr. Morrow boomed. "You two can . . . er . . . finish your private affairs later." And with that, he left.

Parker and Alexandra managed to grin sheepishly at each other before Parker picked up the glasses and followed behind her father.

Dinner started out a little awkwardly, but with Mr. Morrow's unconcerned air of what he might have heard or witnessed in the kitchen, there was soon lots of laughter and funny little stories. Mr. Morrow told Parker all about what his eldest daughter was like as a child. Parker, in turn, told of his upbringing as an only child. Alexandra assiduously avoided mentioning how they'd met, but then Parker, in recounting another anecdote, made it obvious that he and Alex had known each other before. George Morrow silently nodded, but clearly did not seem surprised.

There was, of course, talk of music. Parker was particularly interested in George Morrow's compositions and his lack of attempts to do anything with his work. He asked a lot of questions, and Alexandra was stunned to learn that her father apparently had dozens of pieces he'd "tooled" with. George Morrow said he wrote them for the simple love of doing it, and that had always been enough. As far as he was concerned, he *had* done more. He'd passed his talent on to Alexandra, and there was pride and quiet joy in his words.

His admission surprised his daughter, who suddenly realized her father thought far more of her abilities than he'd ever let her know. With a slight tinge of anger, she wondered why he hadn't thought to encourage her more.

"That was good," Mr. Morrow declared with a satisfied sigh and a pat to his flat stomach.

"It sure was. Thanks for sharing it with me," Parker added sincerely, watching Alexandra.

"Oh, anytime," her father offered magnanimously.

Alexandra grimaced at her father's generous sharing of her time.

"Unfortunately, I only get such good cooking on the weekends, myself. For years, she's had some grand ideas about becoming a singer, and most of the time she's busy living, breathing, and thinking music."

Quickly Alexandra looked at Parker, who pursed his lips and raised a brow as if in complete understanding.

"My singing is important to me," Alexandra defended stiffly, as she began clearing the table.

"It should be," Mr. Morrow nodded. "But I think you go overboard, Baby. Just because you want it bad doesn't mean it's going to happen. It hasn't happened yet. I don't want to see you count on it so much and be disappointed."

"I won't be," Alexandra argued, but there was a lack of conviction and strength behind the words, as well as an apprehensive tightening of her insides—almost like a warning, or a prediction.

"Besides, I thought you really loved teaching. I would think that would keep you busy enough," Mr. Morrow said.

Parker merely sat there as an interested observer, listening and watching how Alexandra responded to her father. Parker wasn't surprised that she was just as stubborn with him.

"I don't want to just be busy. I want to find out if I'm any good as a singer," Alexandra said, her rising annoyance manifesting itself in the way she rattled the silverware and noisily stacked the dinner plates.

"You are," the two male voices said at once, and Parker and her father looked quickly at each other. Mr. Morrow nodded sharply, glad to have someone in his corner.

"That's fine for you both to say," Alexandra argued heatedly, putting the stacked plates down so hard they clattered dangerously together. She rested a small fist on one saucily elevated hip and looked at her father. "You decided you didn't want a career. Maybe you were worried you weren't good enough, or that others wouldn't think so. Maybe you thought there were too many sacrifices to make." She swung bright, sharp eyes to Parker. "And you're past the years of practice and struggling and can enjoy your talent and success. You *both* decided what you wanted to do and you went for it. That's all I want to do. Why won't you let me try it my way in peace?"

The two men exchanged looks again and Alexandra was suddenly suspicious of some kind of conspiracy against her. She sighed in exasperation. "All I need is a chance. My voice will do the rest."

Mr. Morrow sighed in equal exasperation and threw up his hands in surrender.

"Look at what almost happened last night," Parker reminded her softly.

Mr. Morrow frowned. "At the club? What happened last night?"

"Nothing," Alexandra ground out shortly, coldly eyeing Parker and angry that he had to remind her of that embarrassing moment as well. Parker met her stare with one of his own. "I know what I want," she added firmly.

"Alex, what you want is freedom," Parker said softly.

His words hit so clearly on the truth that Alexandra felt as though the wind had been knocked out of her.

"And something else," he whispered mysteriously. "But what you'll get are managers, agents, hotel rooms, and propositions. You'll spend more of your time on the business of singing than on singing. You'll eat lots of horrible food, not get enough sleep or exercise, not do anything. Everyone you meet will want something from you. And let's say you finally make it. There's your name on the billboard, or the marquee, you've gotten your first record contract, and now come the tours. Forty concerts in three and a half months, until you forget what city you're in, or don't care. When do you see family? Will you have any friends? Not other musicians, but friends who tell you about their perfectly ordinary, unfamous lives, but who make you feel real and at home and don't treat you differently than they ever did. When do you meet a man, fall in love? You believe in love, don't you? How do you squeeze in having a marriage, a family?"

Alexandra was breathless with Parker's observations. "Are we talking about my life, or yours?" she asked astutely.

Parker acknowledged her counterattack with a rueful tilt of his head and a sad smile.

"You're not being fair. I'm capable of compromise," Alexandra added. "You've been able to manage, and you look none the worse for a life of being in the spotlight. Would you have me believe that you wouldn't love to go all the way and someday receive a Grammy?"

Parker shook his head and stared at her. "My happiness doesn't depend on a Grammy. I won't let it."

"But I'll also get recognition, appreciation, and a sense of accomplishment," Alexandra reasoned.

"You already have it," Parker declared, "if only you'd let yourself see that."

"What are you two talking about?" Mr. Morrow asked, dazed. He sensed that the conversation had changed to something far more personal between the two young people. His head swiveled back and forth between them.

"Well, from the sound of it, they're *not* talking about music."

All heads at the table turned simultaneously to the entrance, where a young woman stood.

"Hello, Baby," Mr. Morrow beamed.

While Parker sat staring, Alexandra glanced at him quickly to test his immediate reaction to her younger sister, feeling a sinking in her stomach as Parker seemed riveted in place. All conversation about music careers came to an abrupt halt, and for the moment Alexandra was no longer the central topic.

Christine Morrow moved slowly into the room. She acknowledged her father with a brief touch of her red glossed lips to his sunken cheek. She gave her sister a quick smile and passing glance, and then turned the full force of her considerable female charms on Parker.

Alexandra watched the male response to her sister with her usual sense of the inevitable. As she watched the intent brightening of Parker's gaze, she felt a quickening of annoyance. She listlessly brushed table crumbs onto a napkin, and shook it out over a plate. She didn't have to actually watch the unfolding scenario to know what was happening. Her sister was laying claim to the kingdom.

Alexandra had always been assured that she was a very attractive young woman, with appealing youthful features that made her likable. She was not always aware of her own assets, but she'd guessed correctly when she'd decided long ago that she and Christine could not be compared.

At five feet nine inches, Christine Morrow was beautifully proportioned. Her body was slim and curved in total femininity in all the right places. Her skin was more amber than Alexandra's, flawlessly smooth and clear. Christine's hair was cut very short, no more than two inches in length all over, but curly and glossy over her well-shaped head, making her look almost ethereal. She had thick, dark, lovely long lashes that she'd learned to use well since adolescence, keeping her lids demurely lowered until just the moment she wanted to achieve a complete coup and reveal stunning, pale gray-green eyes. The results were always predictable, and Parker was no less a victim now than anyone else who'd never met Christine.

Alexandra was also willing to admit that at twenty-one, Christine knew some things about the world in general, and men in particular, and how to make the best use of both, which made her seem years older than Alexandra. Christine was supremely aware of herself and her effect on others. There was no question that she basked in the attention and admiration, earned or not. Commanding so much attention had also given her undue power over most circumstances in which more than two people were present. She had an instant audience on whom to practice her charms.

"I didn't know you were coming tonight. We would have waited on dinner," Mr. Morrow said.

Christine charmingly wrinkled her pert nose, briefly lifting her sultry gaze from Parker to look with disinterest over the dinner plates.

"Probably something fattening. Besides, I can't stay." Her eyes returned openly to Parker, who was still watching her with a curious intensity that made Alexandra's spirits plummet. "I'm Christine. Should we know each other?"

Despite her turmoil, Alexandra had to raise her brows at her sister's imperial attitude. Not *"Do* we know each other", but *"Should* we." Already she was making her interest known. Alexandra watched as Parker merely smiled, tilted his head in consideration, and showed silent amusement at her question.

"This is Parker Harrison," Mr. Morrow made the introductions.

"Hello," Christine said with delight, smiling at him. She put out a slender, beautifully manicured hand, forcing Parker to stand formally and take it. "I didn't realize you were a friend of the family."

"Well, this is his first visit," Mr. Morrow confessed carefully.

"I'm a friend of Alex's," Parker said smoothly.

"Alex?" Christine questioned, looking to her sister in blank surprise. "He calls you Alex. You never even mentioned you knew Parker Harrison. I *love* his music."

Alexandra pursed her mouth against a retort, and merely smiled. "How thoughtless of me."

"Well, that's okay," Christine cooed. "Now that we've met, we can get to know one another."

She gave Parker a smile that had been known to make more than one man foolish. Alexandra stood up and began to carry the dirty dishes from the table. "I'm sure Parker will like that," she said evenly to Christine. Then Parker stood up as well.

"I would, but in a moment." He lifted a stack of plates. "I'll help with this," he said agreeably to Alex.

She was surprised by the offer. She glanced at her sister and found Christine somewhat nonplussed, as though the dishes could wait, but she shouldn't have to. Alexandra smiled at Parker, but shook her head.

"Thanks, but I can do this. Let Christine entertain you," she said, with a hint of dry humor in her tone. She headed for the kitchen alone. In her wake she could hear Christine's exuberance over meeting Parker, her father's laughter, and Parker's deep-voiced response to Christine's questions.

As she rinsed the utensils and scraped the plates, Alexandra recalled how, when she and Christine were small children, strangers or even friends would fawn over the gorgeous child Christine had been, forgetting the other, older girl standing quietly on the sidelines. In a funny way, she felt a certain pride that Christine was her sister, and she could even admit to a vicarious pleasure at seeing her predictable effect on people, men in particular. But Alexandra also wondered if her sister would ever outgrow her ego-centered need to conquer the entire male population of the civilized world.

She was almost finished with her cleanup when Christine came into the kitchen. Alexandra had half hoped it was Parker, coming to keep her company after all and maybe to secretly hold, caress, and kiss her as he had before. Christine was dressed in a white angora sweater that complimented her brown complexion, a slim black mid-calf skirt, and high-heeled patent leather boots. It was a simple, understated outfit, but Christine had always shown a talent for making simple clothing look very expensive and haute couture. Christine had always wanted to work with fashion, either as a stylist or as a designer. Since finishing school eight months ago, she was still looking for an opportunity to move to New York. Alexandra had no doubt her sister would succeed. She could get anything she wanted.

Christine stood and watched as Alexandra put away dishes. "How did you ever meet someone like Parker Harrison?" she asked innocently.

"Parker and I met when I was in school. I haven't seen him in ten years. He was best man at Brian and Debby's wedding," Alexandra admitted, as she turned to put leftovers in containers or wrap them in foil.

Christine leaned a hip against the edge of the sink and smiled. "I suppose that was better than finding out he was the groom," she commented dryly. "So . . . Parker's the one, huh?"

Alexandra dropped a spoon and quickly stooped to pick it up. "What do you mean by that?" she asked softly, not meeting Christine's sure gaze.

"I mean, dear sister, that he's probably the one who sent you home from school that year looking like you'd lost your best friend. You moped and dragged yourself around all that spring before finally going back the next fall. Was it all because of Parker?"

"No," Alexandra admitted honestly. "I was just scared and confused and inexperienced. Parker had his own set of troubles that had nothing to do with me."

"What about now? Is he strictly hands-off?" Christine asked, with smooth casualness.

Alexandra was thrown by the question. She already wondered if Parker's presence in her life now could lead to anything, but she couldn't assume it would.

"Parker doesn't *belong* to me, Christine. He's a grown man. He can make his own decisions."

Christine pursed her lips and flexed a foot, absently examining the shiny surface of her boot. "Does that mean you're not going to fight for him?"

Alexandra's brows shot up and she laughed at her sister's unexpected question. "How? In a vat of mud, or should we just pull hair? Don't be foolish."

Christine shrugged a shoulder. "I bet he's rich and knows just about everyone. And he's very good-looking," she added with a sly smile.

Alexandra thought with irony at the order of her sister's priorities. "He's quite a bit older than you, too."

Christine made an impatient sound. "That doesn't matter. I like a man who's mature. And the way he looked at me says he doesn't think I'm too young," she said with assurance.

Alexandra saw no reason to point out other differences, such as her sister's short attention span and her lack of interest in music. She smiled benignly at her. "If Parker's interested, then you have nothing to worry about," she said with false levity, and then forced her mind away from the thought of Parker and her sister together. "We didn't expect you tonight. I thought you and your roommate were going to Baltimore."

"No wheels. I came to see if Daddy would lend me the car for a few days." She dangled the car keys from thumb and index finger and smiled triumphantly.

"If you take the car, I won't be able to food shop for Dad for next week," Alexandra reminded her.

"Have the market deliver," Christine shrugged.

"And what about his doctor's appointment on Wednesday?"

"I'll have it back by then."

"Then you'll drive him."

"I can't," Christine moaned contritely. "I have an interview at I. Magnin that I can't miss."

"What's the interview for?"

"Well, not much. One of the perfume houses wants a half-dozen models to walk around squirting customers with their product . . ."

Alexandra chuckled.

"And we get to wear some great clothes from one of the boutiques. Maybe we'll even get to keep them."

"Will this lead to anything?"

"I hope. The marketing rep is dating my roommate."

Alexandra sighed and gave up. "Please return the car with gas this time," she said smoothly to Christine, who only waved airily and left the kitchen.

Alexandra stood silently and alone for several moments, listening absently to the laughter coming from the next room. She felt her slow burn begin to roil dangerously inside her. It annoyed her no end that Christine operated on the premise that what she wanted, she got. While Alexandra didn't deny that her sister was genuinely talented, it still frustrated her that so many opportunities came Christine's way simply by virtue of her beautiful face.

For a moment Alexandra, reviewed the recent communication and levels of intimacy that she and Parker had been able to establish after such a long time. She was not indifferent to him, and she wondered now if she really stood in jeopardy of losing what they'd gained together to her sister's interest in Parker.

Alexandra finished the last of the cleaning up in the kitchen. She was reluctant to go back to the living room and sit as an observer while Christine, with her bright personality, controlled the rest of the evening. And Alexandra did not want to see if Parker was going to succumb before her very eyes.

When Alexandra ventured forth at last, Parker was shrugging into his heavy leather coat. He swung around at her approach. She tried not to show her disappointment that he was already leaving.

"Your father told me you'd be staying over tonight."

"Yes, I try to at least one night a week to give him a hand with some household chores."

Parker picked up a couple of composition-type notebooks and tucked them under his arm.

"What's that?" Alexandra questioned, nodding at the books.

Parker looked sheepish. "Your father has agreed to let me see some of his original work. I promised to guard them with my life."

Alexandra had to smile. "That's quite an honor." She looked around. "Where is he?"

Parker gestured toward the door. "He stepped outside to say goodbye to your sister."

"Without a coat on, no doubt," Alexandra commented dryly.

Parker laughed at her worry. "You're a good daughter."

"I hope that's not something to make fun of," she mumbled with a pout.

"No, Alex," Parker said gently, putting a hand on her shoulder and massaging the joint with his fingertips. "It's something to admire." Then he sighed deeply, looking briefly over his shoulder toward the front door, which stood ajar. "So . . . that was Christine." It was a kind of statement that had finality to it, as a fact of irrefutable certainty.

Alexandra crossed her arms over her chest to stop the start of nervous tremors. "What do you think of her?" she asked lightly, her eyes searching Parker's expression.

He chuckled with a short shake of his head, and arched a brow. "She's one of the most beautiful women I've ever seen. I bet she was deadly at sixteen."

"Long before that," Alexandra admitted without rancor.

"And I bet she always gets her own way."

Alexandra smiled again. "Some find it hard to say no to her."

"What she needs is a very firm hand from someone who can see beyond that gorgeous exterior."

"You seem to read her pretty well," Alexandra commented tightly. Could Parker possibly be interested?

"Believe me, I know the type," Parker said.

He stared at Alexandra, seeing the vulnerable lift to her brows and the soft drooping of her mouth. He would guess that Alex had made more than her share of concessions to someone people found easy to adore. And where had that left Alex? Wanting something that was purely her own that people could admire or find enviable. Her music. Her magnificent voice. For a moment Parker had a realization of what it must have been like, growing up with a sister like Christine. Alexandra had always spoken of her goals and dreams with such iron-clad conviction. Now he understood why.

Parker slowly pulled her closer, releasing her shoulder to slide his fingers around the slender column of her neck, to gently tug until Alexandra's face tilted up to his. Quickly and gently, Parker nibbled and pulled a kiss from her mouth. He kissed her again.

Alexandra felt like he was releasing a tightness that had gripped at her insides ever since Christine's arrival. It frightened and surprised her how much she needed Parker to touch her. Parker's kiss was as personal and private and every bit as intense as it had been before Christine's arrival. She sighed with relief.

"Thanks for dinner. And the chance to meet your family," Parker whispered softly to her.

"You're welcome," Alexandra croaked out, more formal than she wanted to sound. Parker suddenly bent his head toward her until his forehead touched hers. She could feel the warmth of his breath.

"Do you still hate me, Alexandra Morrow?" he asked in his deep voice.

"I've never really hated you," Alexandra answered honestly. He relaxed his fingers as he let go of her neck and let out his breath. He kissed her briefly again, his lips firm, but so warm and mobile.

"Then that only leaves one other question to be answered, doesn't it? Think carefully what it will be, Alex," Parker suggested quietly.

They stared at one another and then there was a short, impatient tooting of a car horn. Alexandra blinked in a startled expression as she realized he intended to follow Christine, in his own car, back to town.

Parker didn't say any more. Instead, with a pat to her cheek, he turned and went out the door, and shortly the cars motored off into the night.

Alexandra beckoned her father back inside and closed the door. For a moment she felt a shot of jealousy grip her as her sister and Parker drove away. She knew perfectly well what Christine was capable of, and Alexandra's own past inexperience made her feel insecure. Yet she had only to recall that Parker had come to hear her sing on Friday, had encouraged the audition the afternoon before, had kissed her goodnight just moments ago. She smiled thoughtfully as she followed her father back into the living room. She was by no means ready or willing, yet, to concede the evening to Christine.

* * *

George Morrow was again seated at the piano where, as Alexandra finished reading the Sunday papers, he'd provided a kind of melancholy background of slow, moody music. It was random and the melodies couldn't be placed to any one composer or musician. Alexandra had wondered idly, though, how much of it was his own. She put the papers aside, approached the piano bench, and sat down unobtrusively next to her father so as not to disturb this rare recital. The musical play continued for another ten minutes before Mr. Morrow let his arms drop away from the keys and he turned his thin, tired face to his elder daughter.

"It's been a long time since I've felt so much like playing. A long time since music brought back so many memories," he smiled wistfully.

"Oh, Daddy, I didn't realize. I'm sorry if bringing Parker home made you uncomfortable or . . ."

Mr. Morrow chuckled softly, shaking his head and raising a hand to hush her. "No, no, Baby. You don't understand. I wasn't uncomfortable at all. It was a *good* time. *Real* good. I like Parker. He reminds me of my younger days . . . my passion."

Alexandra had to smile silently to herself. It was hard to imagine her father having a passion of any kind. Her father again played chords upon the keys with just one hand. The music sounded vaguely familiar to Alexandra, and as he played she could almost anticipate the unfolding notes as the soft, sweet melody touched the quiet air of the room.

"I wrote that for you the day you were born," he said, and smiled fondly at her.

She was surprised, and her widened eyes expressed it. "I didn't know that. I've always loved that piece."

"Yep. Wrote one for Chrissy, too, when she came along. Only she'd never sit still long enough to hear it through. But when you were just a little thing, you'd make me play your piece over and over again. You were four years old when I first realized you were interested in music. Your mother and I heard you banging away on the piano one day. You'd pulled yourself up on the stool, and knelt there with your tiny fingers poking at the keys—and singing! You *know* what it must have sounded like." They both laughed over the image.

"Your mother used to say you came by your talent honestly." He sighed again and stopped his playing. "She was always sorry we couldn't afford to give you real music lessons."

Alexandra leaned forward and touched her father's cheek with her lips. "I *did* have real music lessons, Daddy. I had *you* to teach me."

"I did my best. But you know what I mean. My postal salary wasn't bad, but it didn't allow for a lot of luxuries. Then your mother got sick, and I got sick, and . . ."

"You don't have to apologize. I have no complaints," Alexandra said emphatically, but feeling an uneasiness in her heart of hearts, wishing now that she'd been more sensitive, more understanding of how her parents had both worked so hard to give her and Christine the best they could.

Her father nodded in contradiction. "I do have to apologize. You were too young when you suddenly had to take over for your mother when she passed. Too young to have to be a second mother to your sister and a helpmate to me. I knew that your music meant escape in a way and having something of your own. But lots of things happen that you never count on, and I really believe that things usually turn out for the best." He sighed and, shaking his head in some private reminiscence, stood up and stretched his body. Alexandra stood up, too.

"You're tired. Let's just forget this for a while and get you to bed. Tomorrow I'll do some marketing and maybe we'll have lunch somewhere."

As she spoke, Alexandra looped her arm through her father's and walked him to the den behind the stairwell, which had been converted into a small bedroom so he would not constantly have to climb the stairs. Her head was filled with the music played by Parker and her father that evening; but also, she couldn't help but notice the different paths each man's life had taken.

"Daddy?"

"Yeah, Baby?"

"Why didn't you follow through with your music?"

Mr. Morrow looked at his daughter and smiled sadly. "I did. I just didn't have any plans to build a career with it. I just wanted to play a piano. Well, I did, and I was pretty damned good even without training, like Count Basie. I had some good times jammin' with my friends, but that's all it was.

"Then I met your mother, and what with getting married and starting a family, why, music wasn't all that important. I still have it, you understand. The music is still in me, and that's enough for me. I guess the bottom line was, I loved you girls and your mother more than a life on the road all the time."

Mr. Morrow stopped one more time and he looked at his daughter. "Your friend Parker is a sight more talented than I ever was. His music has taken him straight to the top. Now, that's a dream come true. But he's not happy, and I don't envy him."

Mr. Morrow yawned expansively as Alexandra stared blankly at him. "Do you know why? What did he say to you?"

Her father moved into the room and turned to face her with his hands on the doorknob. "He didn't have to say anything, but I could see what it was. The minute I met him, I knew." He made to close the door. "I see that same thing in you, sometimes. I also see that you're in love with that young man," he chuckled, shaking his head. "Lord, don't I remember what it's like."

"Daddy," she began, with as much calm as she could manage. "It's only been a week or so since Parker and I met again."

He cackled mischievously. "I know, I know. But you've loved him long before now. I *know*."

Alexandra only stared at her father, absolutely speechless at his observation, and helpless to deny it.

"Don't look so surprised," Mr. Morrow said.

"But what has any of this to do with Parker not being happy? Why shouldn't he be?"

Her father sighed and rubbed his chin with its stubbs of black and grey hair. "You're a smart girl, Alexandra. You'll figure it out," he said, as he gently closed the door.

CHAPTER 8

Parker had trouble following the aged Toyota. Christine Morrow drove by her own reckless rules. At first, Parker thought she was just an erratic driver, until it occurred to him that Christine was deliberately leading him a merry, unsafe chase.

The lady liked to be in control.

Once Parker realized what Christine was up to, he had no trouble following her unpredictability. It was her idea that he follow her back into the city, and Parker had agreed. He was familiar enough with D.C. that he didn't believe he could get lost if Christine outmaneuvered him, but he wasn't going to let her do it. Parker had a very clear impression that Christine Morrow liked to test people and push the envelope.

Parker admitted to himself, however, an ulterior motive for agreeing to Christine's idea: he was intrigued by her because she was, as he'd been able to realize in an hour, a total contrast to her sister.

Alexandra had never talked about her younger sister in any detail. Christine had always been mentioned in an off-handed way without being assigned characteristics, personality, looks, or opinions. Now Parker knew why: Christine was a phenomenon that had to be experienced. Although he was not drawn to her as he imagined most males over twelve would be, there was no denying that Christine didn't need to throw out any lures.

Her car turned into a street of restaurants and cafes and she pulled up in front of Emerson's. Parker pulled in behind her, lifting a corner of his mouth in a knowing smile and put his car into neutral. Then he waited.

After thirty seconds, Christine got out of her father's car and walked back to Parker. He rolled down his window.

"Is there a problem?" he asked.

Christine smiled demurely and tilted her head. "I don't know. Is there?"

Parker looked through the windshield. "This isn't the block you told me you lived on."

"That's right. This is a block that happens to have a really nice cafe. I thought maybe we could have a nightcap before . . ." Her lashes lowered. "Before going on home."

"It's not a good idea to drink and drive, especially given your driving skills," Parker said wryly.

Christine shrugged. "Coffee, then."

Parker considered that it might be interesting to watch Christine in action. It might even be entertaining. He inclined his head. "After you . . ."

Christine gave him a triumphant smile and got back into her car to pull it into the lot. Parker followed right behind her.

It was a little after ten, and the dinner crowd had thinned out considerably. Christine's height and regal carriage, her outfit, so understated and so obviously more fashionable than anything else in sight, announced her arrival. She didn't wait to be seated, but found the table she wanted and proceeded in graceful feminine strides. Parker held her chair as she sat, and a waiter left them with menus. Christine draped her coat back over her shoulders and smoothly slid her arms free of the sleeves.

Parker reached for his cigarettes. "Mind if I smoke?"

"Please," she gave permission with a negligent wave of her slender hand.

Parker took his time, openly watching her as she wiggled in her chair to get comfortable. She propped her chin on her hand and quickly looked over the menu. Parker only had to glance briefly about him to see that interested eyes struggled not to stare at the beautiful woman seated across from him.

"So, what is this all about?"

Christine raised a beguilingly innocent face to Parker. "What's *what* all about?"

Parker slowly smiled and exhaled his smoke. "What is it you want to know?"

"I thought it would be nice to get better acquainted, but not in Daddy's living room while he listened. It's obvious you and Alexandra know each other—well, I take it?"

Parker gave nothing away in his expression and didn't respond. How well he and Alexandra knew each other was not Christine's business, and he hoped his silence conveyed that to her. He saw a fleeting doubt in Christine's exotic eyes. "We're good friends."

"I felt left out when I got to the house," she complained.

Parker tapped his cigarette into the ashtray. "We could have gotten better acquainted back there. You didn't stay to visit, and you left rather quickly."

She shrugged. "Don't you think it's nicer this way? One to one?"

Parker chuckled silently. "Christine, with you I honestly don't think it matters."

Christine stared, not understanding his point. She closed her menu. "What were you fighting about when I came in?"

Parker arched a brow and needlessly shifted the ashtray. "It wasn't a fight. We were having a discussion."

"About what?" she asked persistently.

"Music," he said vaguely.

"You're very good at it," she complimented.

"So is Alex."

Christine shrugged lightly. "Did . . . *Alex* talk about me?"

"Actually, no."

"I'm not surprised."

"Why?"

She wiggled in her chair again, her expression charming and thoughtful. "Alexandra and I are different. She's too dreamy."

"And you're full of life, a go-getter, and if you're not famous someday, you're certainly going to be rich."

Christine smiled. "How did you guess?"

"You and your sister *are* different, but you're more alike than you realize."

Christine looked disappointed at the comparison. "Let's not talk about Alexandra."

"What would you like to talk about?"

"You and me," she said softly.

Parker narrowed his eyes against the cigarette smoke and inhaled. He suddenly thought of the concert halls and arenas, the stages and clubs where he'd performed worldwide. He thought of the hundreds of women he'd met, some beautiful, some exotic, some incredibly sexy, and all with an interest in him that always had a hidden agenda. He thought of the gushing compliments, the sometimes painfully obvious ploys of trying to gain his attention and affections. He thought of all the lonely times when he wished he could just relax and not be *on*, when he wished not everyone was expecting him to be, when everyone didn't want *something* from him.

Parker thought of all the people, but especially the women, who tried to link themselves to him. Not for him, but *because* of him. He could only think of one person who'd always treated him like a normal person: Alexandra.

"We've only just met, Christine. There is no 'you and me.' "

"But that's why I thought it was a good idea to stop. We can get a chance to know each other."

"What do you think of your sister's talent, her ambitions?" Parker asked quietly.

Christine became impatient. "Why are you so interested in Alexandra?"

Parker waited.

She shrugged. "Her voice is nice. It's pretty, but nothing special. All this fuss and bother over her. She's been singing for years. She doesn't even know how to go about getting well known."

"How would you do it?" Parker asked.

"I'd meet people. I'd always be where things were happening, and believe me, I wouldn't let anything stop me."

Parker nodded, putting out his cigarette. "That's how you have to do it sometimes," he agreed.

Christine beamed. "See? We're two of a kind."

"What would you do if you didn't become famous?"

She leaned across the table. "Marry someone who was. Alexandra would never do that. She's the kind who would marry for love. She believes in it." Christine tilted her head. "I don't know what went on with her when she was in school that first semester, but she suddenly gave up and came home. She moped and cried and was depressed. I think she was in love. Who needs that?" She tilted her head. "Was it with you? You didn't let love get in your way."

Parker frowned and burned under the painful truth of Christine's cold observation. It struck him as doubly ironic and sad that Christine, whom he wouldn't have credited an hour ago with having much depth, was showing a remarkable degree of intuitiveness. Parker was less reluctant to admit how her insights were causing him to freshly evaluate the year he and Alex had first been lovers. For one thing, it wasn't that he hadn't let love get in the way. It was only that he hadn't realized that what he was feeling was love. He had never known it before. Not like what Alex had given him: faith, hope, and herself.

"What if I told you I believe in love, too?" Parker asked.

"Then maybe you can change *my* mind," Christine laughed lightly.

"That's an interesting challenge," Parker murmured with a smile. "How would you like to come with me to hear Alex perform next weekend?"

"What has that got to do with you and me?"

"I'm trying to change your mind about love, remember? You might learn something," Parker said with a wink.

* * *

"Welcome back, Mrs. Geison-Lerner," Alexandra exclaimed over the phone, and was answered with a laugh.

"Thank you, thank you. I'm still not used to being called 'Mrs.,' but it sounds just lovely."

"How was the honeymoon? Did you guys ever leave your hotel room for air or to eat?"

Debby giggled. "Eventually. When we started getting weak and noticed dark circles under our eyes. Then we made up for the lost time by sitting in the sun for days. When my sunburn fades, I think I'm going to have a great tan."

"I'm happy to say I don't have such problems," Alexandra teased.

"Lucky you."

"In any case, welcome home."

"I'm not so sure," Debby murmured dryly. "It's rather disappointing to leave Barbados in sandals and arrive in Washington to four inches of snow."

"Well, spring is coming. April showers should be next, followed closely by the cherry blossoms."

Debby groaned. "Can't wait that long. I want to go back to Barbados." Alexandra's laugh was muffled in a tissue as she blew her nose. "Oh, I'm sorry, Alexandra. Here I am complaining and moaning, and you're fighting a nasty cold."

"The battle is over; I lost," Alexandra corrected on a sniffle.

"Has the weather been so bad?"

"No more than can be expected for this time of year. My resistance was low. I think I've been overdoing it," Alexandra confessed, tucking her feet further under her robe. She pulled it closed around her throat and reached for more tissues from the box next to her.

"Did any of my classes give you a hard time?" Debby asked contritely.

"Oh, no. They were fine, no trouble at all."

"I had my first class yesterday since getting back, and all I heard was how much fun Ms. Morrow's classes are, and how come *we* don't play games."

"I'm glad they enjoyed the sessions."

"I think you've spoiled them forever," Debby lamented.

"But I also made them work very hard."

"How's prep coming for your audition? It's just a few more weeks, isn't it?"

Alexandra snuggled more into the corner of her sofa, and took a tiny sip of the orange juice she'd poured over ice. In all honesty, the audition had not been paramount in her thoughts, and because it wasn't, she didn't know if she should be concerned or relieved.

"Well, I haven't had one voice lesson in the whole time you were gone.

There were the classes to teach. I'm doing extra tutoring to prepare some of my kids for the Kennedy Center auditions in August, and my father has his ups and downs, and then I switched clubs after Parker took me to Blues Alley . . ."

"Parker," Debby interrupted sharply. "Wait a minute. Did you say Parker?"

Too late, Alexandra realized that Parker's name had slipped out, and of course Debby had noticed. There was no way to retract her innocent comment, but Alexandra also knew that having said this much, she'd have to explain more. She didn't want to explain a relationship which she still didn't understand.

Alexandra hesitated. "He came to hear me at The Outer Edge and persuaded me to try out for Blues Alley. I was accepted, and I start in another week. If I ever get rid of my cold . . ."

"Boy, you *have* been busy the last two weeks," Debby remarked. "And I thought you weren't interested in Parker. At the wedding, you gave the impression you found him annoying."

"I know, I know," Alexandra said hastily. "But the fact is, Parker and I had met before, when you and I were in school."

Debby was very silent for a moment, and then she sighed deeply. "Oh, I get it. A love affair gone sour?"

"Not sour, just gone. It's a long story," Alexandra said lamely. She really wasn't inclined to go into details over the phone.

Debby groaned. "Oh, Lord. When I think about how Brian and I plotted to get you two together! You must have wanted to kill us."

Alexandra shrugged. "It was awkward. But Parker and I thought it best just to play along. I didn't want to spoil your day." Alexandra chuckled soundlessly. "He didn't even remember me right away."

Debby sighed again. "Well, it sounds like he got over *that* quickly enough. Can I ask what you two have been doing the last two weeks? On second thought, maybe I'd better not."

Alexandra thought instantly of Debby's wedding night and the sparking of passion between herself and Parker. She certainly couldn't tell Debby about their having made love when it had been born of both anger and regret. She couldn't even tell Debby of her ambivalent feelings because so much was predicated on a past that now seemed so unreal, and so long ago. Whatever she and Parker were to each other now probably had little to do with the past.

"Mostly we've been getting to know each other all over again," Alexandra said. "I took him to meet my father, and he had dinner with us." She paused significantly. "He met Christine."

Debby chuckled softly. "That must have been worth the price of admission. Did he lose his cool altogether and go ga-ga? Or is he still interested in you?"

"All it is *is* interest. Maybe no more than morbid curiosity because we knew each other before," Alexandra sighed. And no, Parker had not lost his cool over her sister. At least, not so she could tell.

That night, after Parker had left with Christine, Alexandra was angry with her sister for smartly manipulating the rest of the evening, and at Parker and herself for allowing it to happen. If she'd wanted to, Alexandra knew she could have made it impossible for Christine to have her father's car. She could have changed her mind about staying the night with her father and had Parker drive her home. But Alexandra had *never* allowed herself to be drawn into her sister's plotting, and she wasn't about to start now.

In any case, it had become a mute issue. Parker had called her later that night to thank her again for dinner and for the chance to meet her father. And Christine had not talked about what had happened after she'd left the house with Parker, a very clear indication that absolutely nothing had happened.

"Well, how about you? How deep is your interest in Parker these days?" Debby hazarded cautiously, sensing the conflict in her friend.

For a quick second, Alexandra thought of denying her feelings, but she couldn't see the point, and knew that perhaps saying it out loud would ease the tightness in her chest, the holding in of real feelings. She took a deep breath and plunged into the truth.

"I've always been in love with Parker Harrison, Debby. That's never changed. But I don't know how he feels about me. I've never really known. I never expected to see Parker again, and I'm confused. And if you repeat any of this to *anyone,* Brian is going to be a widower," she added tightly.

"I don't understand. You love him, but . . . you're resisting?"

"Yes," Alexandra said vehemently. "Parker once made a choice between me and his music, and I lost. Yes, I'll resist, if this is just another phase in his life, like last time. Yes, if he doesn't understand how important a music career is to me, just as his music is to him."

Debby laughed at that. "Given my choice, I'd rather have Parker."

"Why can't I have both?" Alexandra asked quickly.

"Oh," Debby said softly. "So you *do* want him."

Alexandra bit her lip and wiped the raw skin under her nose with the tissue. "It sometimes doesn't matter very much what we want, Debby. Things have a way of not always working out."

Debby sighed. "Maybe it's because we sometimes want the wrong things. Things we only think we want. Sometimes we go after things that aren't good for us."

Alexandra shifted restlessly. "I wish someone would write a user's manual so a person would know," she said with a sarcastic chuckle.

Debby laughed. "You wouldn't believe it anyway. So, tell me about Blues Alley."

Even the mention of it caused Alexandra's stomach to churn. She knew that in all honesty, she was nervous. But somewhere, there was another fear. Alexandra pretended that the nebulous feeling churning within her had no significance and wasn't real at all.

"There's nothing to tell, except that I have a show Friday and Saturday for two weeks. If they like me, perhaps I'll get invited back."

"I don't hear a lot of enthusiasm," Debby chided lightly. "You're about to make your debut."

The uncomfortable gnawing kept at Alexandra's insides. "I . . . I think it's my cold. It's made me a little tired, and I'm trying to get over it before my first weekend at the club," Alexandra improvised. "Besides, I don't want to get too excited. I can still flop, you know."

"I don't believe that, but I understand how you feel. Brian's going to be thrilled when he hears. Would it bother you if we came and acted as your official fan club? We'll bring lots of applause."

"Only if I deserve it," Alexandra advised, with a small shrug of her shoulder.

"How about your Dad, and Christine? Will they be there?"

"My father said he'd come on Saturday. He says he's giving me one night's grace to get over the jitters. I have no idea about Christine. She's not impressed with my singing anyway."

"And Parker? Since it was his idea, I suppose he'll be there, too?"

Alexandra shredded the tissue in her slender hand. She tried to infuse offhanded indifference into her tone. "I don't know. He didn't say he would."

"You could have asked him," Debby said in a soft voice.

Yes, she could have. But Alexandra was silent because it had never occurred to her to do something that straightforward. And she wasn't giving herself or Parker enough credit that it was important that he be there. She was not at all sure of what Parker expected of her. In any case Alexandra believed Parker had to make the next move.

"I never got a chance to." Alexandra stretched the facts a bit. "As I said, Christine made a timely grand entrance and everyone's attention was diverted."

Debby groaned. "Yes, that would do it. I can guess what happened next. Parker was dazzled right before your very eyes."

"Something like that," Alexandra admitted with wry humor in her voice.

"Well, I wouldn't worry about it. Parker has been around the track once or twice. He'll know that batting-eyelash routine when he sees it."

Alexandra laughed in sad amusement. "You underestimate Christine when she decides she wants something."

"No," Debby corrected smoothly. "You're probably underestimating Parker."

Alexandra hugged herself to stop the shivers, but it didn't help much. It seemed that every part of her body was being attacked by nerves. Suddenly she was overly warm and perspiration pricked at her scalp until she was afraid the moisture would cause her careful sidesweep of curls to go limp. Her stomach was a mass of knotted tension that seemed to have movement of its own as she pressed her fingertips against the churning and wondered in a panic if she was going to be sick.

She'd heard of this kind of reaction in famous people just before they were to perform, but she'd never before understood it. She'd always felt that if you were good and knew what you were doing, the positive energy would naturally transmit itself to the audience. She couldn't believe that Parker ever went through such trauma. She never thought that *she* would. But as Alexandra stood in the wings, she knew that she was about to eat her words.

A peek through the silver lamé curtains showed a full house. The three-piece band that she'd rehearsed with only twice during the week were taking their places and idly warming up on their instruments. The people nearest the platform were shifting their chairs around for the best vantage point. And everyone was waiting for her.

As quickly as the panic seized her, it melted away. It was replaced with the dawning realization that she was about to give her first professional performance. In her mind, she didn't count the few awful weeks spent at the Outer Edge because she was sure that no one there even remembered her. Certainly the clientele there was not as appreciative of her talents. This was different; this was a true testing ground.

Alexandra rubbed her palms together. They were no longer damp and clammy.

She could do this.

She was ready.

It was what she'd always wanted, she reminded herself as she straightened her shoulders and took a deep breath.

"Are you ready, Baby?" a technical assistant asked Alexandra in passing, but he didn't wait for an answer. He was checking the position of the overhead lights, the microphone, and the amplifiers.

A piano chord cracked the air and Alexandra came alert with a start. She thought instantly of Parker. She'd missed not hearing from him all week, but she herself had been working on reserve energy while battling a cold, teaching, and seeing after her father. She didn't want to consider if he was now preoccupied with Christine. She did believe, however, that Parker would be there to hear her sing.

As Alexandra waited to be introduced to the world, she couldn't help but realize the irony of her circumstances. It was *she* who had declared over and over how much she wanted to be a professional singer. Yet after all those long years of her steady pace, it was Parker who'd made tonight possible. It was Parker who'd eased her out of the past. She also had to recognize that she was not just willing to step aside so that Christine could have a clear shot at Parker. If she wasn't willing to put herself on the line for her music and for Parker, then she was going to lose them both.

The lights suddenly dimmed in the club room, drawing Alexandra's anxious thoughts back to the situation at hand. The introduction for her happened so quickly that any lingering thoughts about Parker were suddenly pushed to the back of her mind. She was on.

"Ladies and gentlemen, Blues Alley is proud and pleased to present a hot new singer from right here in D.C. How about a warm welcome for *Miss Alexandra Morrow.*"

To the sound of encouraging applause and the curtains magically parting before her, Alexandra placed a confident smile on her glistening rouged lips and stepped through the curtains and stood before the microphone. She moved carefully, her walk unwittingly seductive. She heard a half dozen or so wolf whistles from the invisible depths of the room. Her cobalt blue chiffon dress, shirred and gathered over one shoulder, exposed the other and fell in soft folds to her ankle. It flattered her slender form and lent an air of regality to her. Her controlled movements successfully disguised the quaking inside her, the suddenly hammering heart, and the irrational fear that she'd forgotten how to sing. A slender hand reached for the microphone to pull it a fraction of an inch closer as she felt the need to hold on to something solid.

The musicians continued the notes of the introduction to the first number until the applause had died down, and then the guitarist signaled for her entry. Alexandra took a deep breath, opened her mouth, and sang.

The first number was fast and snappy, grabbing the audience's attention at once and holding it as they waited to hear in those first bars and lyrics whether or not she'd been worth the cover charge. For the first half of the song, Alexandra was gripped with a fear that she was performing badly, and it took the rest of the song for her to calm down and realize she was in command of her song and the audience. Alexandra did not go in for theatrics on stage. Her performance was her voice, although unbeknownst to her, her slight feminine gestures added to the image, and set that image with the audience. They knew after the first few numbers that she definitely came across as a lady with her own soft, romantic style.

Alexandra sang numbers best suited to her abilities. She concentrated on the emotion in each piece, drawing all she could from it, and gave it back to the audience. She reached out to touch their hearts with her voice. And the audience, in turn, showed its appreciation for her efforts with genuine applause.

At the end of her fifth number, Alexandra began to feel a shift from her audience. It was almost tangible, as if she knew they were trying to be polite, trying to give her their full attention. Then someone shouted a request. Alexandra's stomach muscles twisted into knots again. She hadn't thought of that happening, and she wasn't sure how to respond. In the mere second or so she took to consider, two more requests came. Her hands grew damp again and her throat dry. She stole a quick glance at her band and found them waiting, watching for her decision. This was, after all, her show.

For a moment, Alexandra felt as though everyone was sitting in judgment; when they issued an opinion she'd be found wanting. They were not going to be happy with what she gave of herself, and they weren't going to let her get away with just being good.

She swallowed hard and held the mike tighter. "I have a song I think you'll like better," she said smoothly into the audience, and tempered it with a slow smile that earned her some applause and a few shouts of approval.

The number was "Delta Dawn," a popular ballad about a woman wearing a faded yellow rose as she waited day after day at a train station for her lover to return. The song started out slow, a story being told. Then the sadness and hopelessness of the forsaken woman became a refrain repeated over and over and increasing in tempo and pitch until the music and words were almost like a cry of pain from her heart.

Alexandra had not been sure she should include this song, knowing that it called for a kind of bluesiness of tone and voice that was not her style. But she worked hard with it, maybe because the audience expected so much. Maybe because she related in some way to the anguish in the song.

She ended the song on an unexpected drawn out "Oh, noooo . . . ," the woman realizing the futility of waiting for the man who was never to return.

The response this time was enthusiastic and vocal. Alexandra nodded her thanks. But she knew in her heart that she had just squeaked by, and she doubted if she could do it again. Rather than exhilaration, she felt relief.

She sang two more songs, but at the end of her performance the response was polite again. It said she had done a very nice job—no more and no less.

"A rising young star, ladies and gentlemen. Let's hear it for Alexandra."

Alexandra took one more demure bow and gratefully left the stage. Almost in a daze, and feeling as though the last hour had never happened, she made her way to the dressing room, and nearly collided with the young woman who was to perform next. The young woman was stunningly dressed in an outfit that was revealing and suggestive.

"You did real nice, honey. You have a pretty voice," the woman said, with a sympathetic smile.

"Thank you," Alexandra murmured, a little surprised.

"But you gotta give them more on stage than a pretty voice," the performer said with a small movement of her shoulders.

"What do you mean?" Alexandra asked, but she knew.

"The audience wants an 'act.' You know; they want you to move around and speak to them. They want to see you work. And you need a little more . . . 'hot sauce' in your numbers. More 'Delta Dawn,' " the woman explained like an expert. She put her hands on her hips and took a posture.

Alexandra took a deep breath and plucked absently at the fabric draped over one shoulder.

"I don't think 'hot sauce' is really my style," Alexandra confessed simply.

The woman shrugged and touched her hair to make sure it was in place. "Honey, you give them what they pay for. That's what this business is all about. Don't worry, you'll get the hang of it." She smiled again and walked past Alexandra.

Alexandra felt an immediate stiffening in her spine, felt indignation rise. Not at the woman's words, for she sensed the truth in them, but in the implication that just because she performed for people, she somehow belonged to them. The idea was unsettling, and she wondered at what Parker had repeatedly said to her about being a performer. Understanding was just dawning on her.

Parker had always said that what he loved most was *creating* music. Anyone could *play* it. It had just worked out that he played it better than most. Parker had told her from the very start, all those years ago when he'd given up concert hall recitals to do what he truly wanted to do, that he would have loved to have been more normal, *not* so well known, *not* so public. It seemed incredible to Alexandra that when you were willing to give so much of yourself for someone's enjoyment, they could possibly think of asking for more. Could she tolerate giving up so much?

Something clicked inside.

A puzzle piece, long missing, fell into place while scenarios and conversations Alexandra had had with her father, with Parker, even with Christine, came flashing like neon in her head. Blindly she began to walk toward the dressing room, feeling as though a key had been used inside her to open a door. Alexandra knew that she had a gifted voice. She knew how to sing. But only this moment did she suddenly truly wonder why she wanted to sing, and for whom.

The door was partially open when Alexandra entered the bright room the female performers used. It was empty, except for Parker, whom she saw half-sitting on the edge of the Formica vanity. He was dressed in black slacks and a black turtleneck sweater worn with a stylish wool sports jacket of a subtle black-and-white tweed. Alexandra had only a second to register his appearance before she unthinkingly rushed forward into Parker's arms. Her realization had twisted the very center of the dream she'd maintained her whole life, now asking her point blank, *are you sure this is what you want?*

Parker stood to take the gentle impact of her body, his arms closing tightly around her. Alexandra tunneled into his coat and wound her arms around his waist. She was so glad to see him, even as she was surprised at her need to have him there now. Parker was a haven from the unpredictability of the evening and the audience. But she also knew he would recognize some of her feeling.

"Alex?" Parker whispered, caught off guard by her sudden action. "Are you okay?"

Alexandra raised her eyes to look into his curious gaze, his mobile mouth lifting at a corner, his brows furrowed in question. What they both needed and wanted in that instant came together and communicated between them.

A look of sudden understanding softened Parker's eyes. He immediately saw the dawning in her bright eyes that recognized what being a performer was all about. One needed a spark, a drive, determination to play for the audience, to make them love you. And the strength to continue against all odds.

He kissed Alex, claiming her and calming her with his control and care. He gave her back a sense of reality after the taut strangeness of performing.

Alexandra melted willingly into him, feeling him stiffen the hard muscles of his thighs to take her weight against him. She welcomed the warm, rough texture of his tongue, and Parker held her captive until the emotions within her changed slowly from confusion to calm, from chilled tension to warmed flesh.

Parker sensuously rode her lips with his until their shortened breaths demanded air and he released her. Alexandra let out a deep sigh and allowed her eyes to drift closed. She leaned against him, her cheek on Parker's chest. She wanted to stay there forever. She didn't have one thought at the moment for the performance she'd just given, or the one that remained. She was just feeling overwhelmingly lonely. She felt

Parker's lips in her hair, felt a large hand stroke her back and shoulders, sliding over the soft fabric of her gown.

"Now, that's a welcome to warm a man's soul. What did I do to deserve it?" Parker teased in a low drawl. "And how can I get it more often?"

I needed you. Alexandra heard the anguished reply in her head but bit her lip from actually saying it. She pulled back a little out of his embrace so she could see up into his face. "I'm sorry. I shouldn't have come running at you like that."

"Don't be sorry," he said, tilting her chin up so he could see her features, running his gaze over her face, making note of a warm sort of glow in her creamy skin. "I'd much rather have you rush into my arms than anyone else."

"Even Christine?" Alexandra heard herself ask pertly, unable to stop herself.

Parker tilted his head down and narrowed his eyes. "Even Christine," he answered softly.

Alexandra averted her eyes against a sudden light of determination in Parker's. That's when she noticed the clear glass vase filled with fresh water and a dozen deep red roses. She smiled gently and reached out to touch a velvet petal with her finger tip.

"They're beautiful," she said softly, in surprised awe.

"They're for you," Parker said, setting his arms comfortably on her lower back and smiling at the joy on her face. He was not unaware that the flowers had brightened her eyes far more than her first show. "They're to mark the debut of your singing career, and to wish you luck." He lifted a hand to cup it against the side of her face. "I'm happy for you, Alex. I know this is what you've always wanted."

"Parker," she interrupted, in a soft, anxious voice, but he went on.

"Let me finish. Many years ago you gave me something that even I didn't know I needed: belief in what I wanted to do, and belief that I could do it. You gave me understanding and love," Parker said sincerely.

Alexandra felt a rush of blood warm her face, and her hands inadvertently tightened on his forearms.

His thumb rubbed gently over her rounded chin, and his voice dropped. "I took all you had to give me, Alex, and gave almost nothing in return," Parker said reflectively, almost to himself. He carefully examined her features to gauge her response to his words. He wondered, was it now too late to admit how much he still needed her? If he told her he loved her, what would happen to her dreams, all of which were about to come true?

"That's not so," Alexandra demurred, surprised by Parker's unexpected confession and filled with an unexpected, swirling feeling of dread.

"I want you to know it never meant I didn't want to give as much to you. I always wanted you. Always," Parker said firmly, his eyes serious and searching, his words tender and sincere. He clenched his jaw muscles, but his hand was still gentle against her face. "I'm proud of you, even if I give you a hard time about it. I realize now how much singing really means to you." Parker dropped his hands to his side and released her. He could see the slight frown in her eyes as his arms slipped away, but he didn't want to hold onto her as he said his next words. He knew if he wanted another chance with Alexandra, he'd have to let her go . . . the same way she'd let him go so long ago, when she'd had no say in his leaving. The decision he'd made was suddenly haunting him. He hadn't given Alex a choice then. Was it fair that he ask for one now?

In all the years since he'd known Alex, Parker had frequently found himself making a comparison between her and the packaged and polished facade of other women. Now he realized that the comparison was too simple, because the image he'd carried of Alexandra had been of her at nineteen, sweet and unpretentious. It had been a jolt to meet her again and find that not only had she grown up and matured and blossomed into beautiful womanhood, but that she had rekindled all the feelings for her he'd set aside. Now, Parker wasn't even sure he could admit them to her. He didn't want to win her over from her dreams; he wanted to join her in them.

He let out a small sigh. "I have another surprise for you. I persuaded my manager to consider letting you open my concert in New York next month. I talked to him long distance a few days ago."

Alexandra's mouth opened in surprise as she just stared at him. Parker was being too helpful, too accommodating.

"That's kind of you," she said, disappointed in a way she couldn't explain. "But I'm not ready for that."

"Why not? You have as much talent and experience as anyone I'd find to open my show. Remember that the whole idea is to give you exposure. Let people see and hear you and remember who you are," Parker reasoned.

Alexandra swung away from him, clasping her hands together. "Why are you pushing me?" she asked angrily. "First it was Blues Alley; now it's your concert in New York." She swung back to him. "I don't know if I can do that. I'm not even sure it's what I want."

The words were suddenly out. The silence that followed seemed to stretch on forever.

Parker was watching her, a look of surprising calm on his face, even after her outburst. "Then what *do* you want?" he asked softly.

Alexandra slowly unclenched her hands and let them fall to her side. She was wondering nonsensically why he couldn't read her mind. She wanted *him*. It was the only thought that was absolutely clear to her. But she couldn't say so. The reasons she couldn't had nothing to do with a fear that Parker wouldn't understand. She *knew* he wanted her. But that wasn't the same as love. That wasn't the same as commitment. It wasn't the same as a future that they could build together.

Alexandra knew she need not fear Christine staking a claim to Parker and then pursuing him relentlessly, or even of Parker being enthralled with Christine's beauty; Parker had never been that shallow. No . . . Alexandra knew all the answers and decisions lay within herself, and as she stood facing Parker, she was afraid of making the wrong one.

"Parker . . ." she began softly, taking a hesitant step closer to him.

Suddenly the door burst open and Debby and Brian came tumbling in, their words running together and not making much sense, beyond the pair's obvious excitement and congratulations. Parker's question went unanswered.

"Hey, you were terrific," Brian said, gathering Alexandra into a crushing bear hug and swinging her in a half-circle off her feet.

Alexandra came out of her trance. "Brian, be careful. I have another show to give in this dress," she said, laughing softly.

Brian obligingly set her down, and Debby hugged her next. "Oh, Alexandra, I can't believe you actually did it. I'd be scared to death in front of all those people."

Alexandra stood back, straightening her gown, and forced herself to smile at the exuberance of her friends. "What makes you think I wasn't scared to death? I kept expecting someone in the audience to boo me off the stage."

"You were very good," Parker said smoothly.

Alexandra gave him a wan smile as a slight frown gathered between her brows. "I'm not sure 'very good' was good enough. I'm not sure I had the audience with me all the way."

There was silence as Parker studied her intently, his eyes half closed. "Sometimes you don't. Sometimes you're not with them all the way, either. Audiences can be very fickle—loving you one performance, hating you the next."

Brian and Debby shook their heads. "They *loved* you out there. 'Delta Dawn' stood the place on its ear. Even Christine 'yeahed' you through the number." Debby looked behind her. "Where is she? I thought she was right behind us."

"Is Christine here?" Alexandra asked, looking at Parker.

"She came with me." He looked right into her eyes. "I thought she should hear her sister perform. I wanted her to appreciate how talented and special you are."

Alexandra clenched her hands together, trying to decide if the warmth she and Parker had just shared was real or not. Suddenly, she had a vivid image of Christine being held by Parker. "I'm surprised. She's always told me I'm wasting my time."

"Well, *she* was surprised. She heard the audience's reaction as well as we did. She even liked your dress," Debby said in dry humor.

"Although she admitted she likes other singers more," Brian added.

Alexandra chuckled. "All of whom have more 'hot sauce' in their act," she said, a private joke, but Parker understood.

The door opened yet again, and all heads turned as Christine entered, looking bright-eyed and excited. She was wearing a magenta knit dress, the electric color of the outfit bringing Christine's beautiful brown coloring into exquisite clarity. The dress, with its fashionable dolman sleeves and cowl neckline, was a perfect foil to anyone around her who was more likely to be dressed in simpler fare. Even Alexandra had to admit that her sister had a wonderful dramatic flair with clothes and colors. But now, Christine's eyes danced quickly over the four people gathered until she spotted Parker, and she reached for him beseechingly.

"What are you doing here?" she asked, and grabbed Parker's arm, trying to guide him toward the door. "The manager is going to announce you to the audience, Parker. They want you to play something."

Parker easily lifted his arm free, not moving. "Whoa . . . wait a minute. I came to hear Alex sing tonight. I have no intention of getting up in front of an audience."

Christine smiled charmingly. "But you can't let everyone down. They're your fans, and they want to hear you."

"No," Parker said unequivocally. Brian and Debby exchanged anxious glances. "You should have asked first."

"I didn't think you'd mind," Christine reassured innocently, with a shrug of her shoulder.

"I don't mean me. You should have asked Alex."

"She won't mind," Christine said. "She was very good tonight, but *you're* famous. Everyone knows who you are."

"Alexandra is going to be famous," Debby suddenly said in defense.

While Alexandra realized that Christine meant no deliberate malice, her maneuvering stung.

"I don't mind," Alexandra intervened, struggling to keep her feelings hidden. "If I was any good out there tonight, they'll remember. Maybe you should go out. Everyone is expecting you now," she said to Parker.

Parker seemed about to protest further. For a long moment he seemed to weigh the decision in his mind. Then his brow cleared.

"All right," Parker said finally. To Christine, he said dryly, "You're not going to understand why, but I thank you."

"Brian and I are going back to our table," Debby said, giving Alexandra a quick peck on the cheek before she left.

Christine, with Parker's arm in her grasp, headed for the door. "Hurry. Everyone's waiting."

Parker gave Alexandra a private look. "The evening isn't over yet," he said, and winked at her before disappearing with Christine.

Alexandra let out a sigh in the silence that followed, feeling as though she'd just witnessed a badly written comedy routine where the joke was on her. She felt tired and just wanted to go home. She had no idea where she was going to get the energy or enthusiasm for her second show. She would have been just as happy not to have to.

Through the still open doorway, Alexandra could hear the manager giving a glowing and flowery introduction to Parker, and listened to the applause and enthusiasm building even before he'd finished. She wasn't angry or jealous that Parker could command such instant consideration at an impromptu set at a club where he hadn't been scheduled to play. She stood alone in the doorway of the dressing room, distinctly aware of the difference in the reception Parker was receiving and that which had welcomed her. Alexandra slowly began to smile. She had opened for Parker, anyway.

Alexandra tilted her head, listening to the excitement building in the audience and quickly became infected by it. Three years ago she'd attended one of Parker's concerts in Baltimore. As much as she loved Parker's music and understood his creative motivation, as much as she loved Parker, it was the only time she had ever seen him perform. On stage he had been cool, gracious, phenomenally talented and versatile. He had an aloof style with the audience. And the audience loved him.

Alexandra walked back to the stage, under the double spotlight from the side of the performing platform, in time to see Parker take a seat at the piano. He shook hands with the musician who'd stepped aside for him. He'd removed his sports jacket and looked like magic, dressed in black, as he nodded politely to the audience, which had come to its feet, the room filled with the sound of applause.

Alexandra joined in the adoration, a smile of pure pride curving her mouth as she watched him. He had a presence that was very unique. She felt so much love for him in that moment that her heart began to race.

"Thank you. Thank you very much," Parker said, as he repositioned the microphone near the piano. "Hey, I'm supposed to be on vacation and incognito," he said easily to the audience, and received warm laughter. "I came this evening for the same reason you did. To hear a beautiful lady sing some beautiful songs . . ." There was more generous applause. "I'm honored that you want to hear me. But I'm going to need some help.

"As you know, I do a fair job of writing music." There were whistles and shouts of agreement. "And I can hold my own on the keys. But I guarantee that you *don't* want to hear me sing. So, I'd like to call upon a very special friend of mine to give me a hand. This is someone I admire and respect tremendously, who many years ago was there to listen to some of my music being composed. Sometimes even wrote a lyric or two."

Parker turned his head, finding Alexandra, knowing she was there waiting. "Alex . . ." he whispered to her. Surprise swept through the audience, and the applause began anew.

"Go on, Baby. Don't just stand there," the manager hissed behind her.

Alexandra was taken unawares, and her eyes widened as she saw Parker look pointedly at her. His eyes held a mixture of emotion. There was tenderness and a sort of all-knowing look because he had managed to surprise her yet again.

Once more Alexandra found herself before a microphone. But this time there was a confidence and giddiness to being there that was attributed to Parker and to having him seated at the piano. She felt safe with him and not at all nervous. He immediately took his seat again and started to play. Alexandra needed no coaxing, no cues or intros to his music or style. She knew it by heart. She knew what to expect and how to work with it. When she sang the words to his music, some of which she had indeed written, the love of the music and the man lent power and emotion that was second nature. Their performance together was spellbinding.

Alexandra was not singing to the audience, nor was Parker playing for them. This was private. It was a long overdue duet that was just between them. It brought them together on every level that was important to either of them in their music.

Parker cross-faded one song into the start of another, and Alex followed his every beat perfectly. She felt the charisma that had been between them years ago born anew. A special aura was warming her, lighting her eyes, enveloping them both. Everything around her faded away except for Parker. It was just the two of them, surrounded by her voice and his playing. They were each other's private audience. When the music finally ended, Alexandra caught her breath in the momentary silence. She felt like it would never be so perfect again as it was right then. She let her breath out slowly, and blinked back to the reality of where she was.

At the end of the second number, Parker stopped and stood up. The audience exploded in an electrifying response.

Parker took Alexandra's hand and gave it a hard squeeze, communicating volumes through the touch. Together they faced the audience and bowed. They faced each other. Alexandra, who was preparing to curtsy to

Parker, was pulled into his arms instead and given a brief, sweet, gentle kiss. Parker chuckled softly at her embarrassment as Alex released his hand and left him alone with the final tribute. She hurried back to the dressing room feeling breathless and exhilarated.

There was a second convergence upon the dressing room, but there was no more opportunity for Alex to be alone with Parker. She could tell that Christine was a little put out by all the attention everyone was giving to Parker and Alexandra, yet she had only herself to blame.

"How much time before your second show?" Brian asked.

"Only forty minutes," Alexandra responded. "Are you planning on staying for that one as well? You don't have to. The songs will be different, but . . ." she spread her hands almost shyly, "you've seen my act. I can't be any different."

"Oh, I'd like to stay," Debby argued.

Parker said nothing, knowing that at that moment Alex probably would have liked nothing more than some time to herself.

"I don't. Besides, I'm hungry," Christine said bluntly. "Can't we go have dinner somewhere?"

"That's a good idea," Brian seconded, taking hold of his wife's hand and kissing Alexandra on the cheek. "I think Alexandra has had enough of us standing on top of her all evening."

She laughed. "I'm so glad you all could make it," Alexandra said.

"You were *so* good," Debby breathed, kissing her friend. "I'll call you tomorrow."

Somehow, Parker managed to be the last one to leave, and Alexandra felt her heart begin to flutter in her chest. There was still a kind of heated, sensual warmth between them that would not be explored tonight, and Alexandra wondered anxiously when it ever would. She wanted him to say something to her, something that would keep the hope alive within her and tell her how he felt. Her communication to him was silent, and private, and she hoped Parker understood. But beyond smiling warmly at her, he conveyed no other message to her.

"Are you happy, Alex?" Parker asked her softly, watching for her reaction.

At the moment, standing there with him so close, she'd hoped he'd know. "I think so," she hesitated with a whisper, and was surprised when his eyes clouded over.

"Then that's all that matters." Parker kissed her tenderly, chastely, and left without another word, giving no hint if or when they'd see each other again.

Disappointed, Alexandra slowly made her way to the makeup counter, and again spotted the bouquet of roses. She cupped her hand around one, and saw the edge of a small white card stuck between two stems. She hastily pulled it out, thankful that there was this last contact from Parker, hoping it would say something more to her.

"Congratulations on a dream come true," the card said simply.

Alexandra sighed in disappointment. She thought with some irony that poor "Delta Dawn" had nothing on her in that moment.

CHAPTER 9

Alexandra closed her apartment door and carefully leaned against it for support. She tilted her head back and a deep sigh escaped through the slight parting of her dry lips.

Water dripped from her raincoat and umbrella to the bare floor, its light "pat-pat" sound in harmony with the throbbing in her head. With an effort she forced herself from the door, and after placing the umbrella in a stand, proceeded to the kitchen, where she carelessly dropped the wet coat over a chair. The apartment was well heated, but nonetheless Alexandra felt chilled clear through to the bone. She felt she'd never be warm again.

She put on a kettle of water to boil and stood staring blankly into space, her mind drained of thoughts, her body drained of energy. Her insides, however, the core of her being, was a whirlwind of confused emotions. She felt as though she no longer had control, or any idea of what she was doing with her life.

After making herself a cup of hot tea, Alexandra made her way slowly to the living room to curl up in a corner of the sofa. Every joint in her body was sore and she was afraid to move too fast. She tried to ignore the persistent and steady pounding in her head, but there had been no sign all afternoon that it would let up, and miserably she endured it.

She could still feel the damp chill of the strong spring winds, from having been out and around D.C. that morning, and that, too, seemed to have settled into her bones. A quiver of discomfort rippled through her huddled body and she closed her eyes on a shudder.

Alexandra reflected, through the foggy cluster of thoughts already in her mind, that if she could just get through tonight, everything would get back to normal. Her life seemed to have gotten so complicated, and unreasonably, she blamed it all on Parker. Everything had been fine until he'd come back into her life. Since that first few weeks after they'd met again, when they'd both reacted with foolish intensity, followed by slow caution, he'd assiduously become part of her life again.

He'd gone rather quietly from unannounced appearances to being a fixture in her life in one way or another from day to day. It had gotten so that she expected to see him, and that both angered and frightened her. Alexandra knew her anger was rooted in the belief that Parker could walk out of her life again as unexpectedly as he'd walked in. It had happened before, and seemed to be something he was capable of doing easily. But Alexandra knew also the wreckage that would be left behind of her emotions and love. She didn't want to give in to it, afraid she wouldn't survive a second time. Yet she felt compelled to follow the inclinations of her heart to love Parker and to trust him as he'd asked, while he developed a friendship with her sister.

There seemed to be a certain familiarity between them, and Christine could, more often than not, be found at their father's home. In a way, Alexandra didn't mind that; she actually preferred it, because it suggested that Parker was not spending time at Christine's place. Alexandra had no intention of getting into a cat fight with her sister over Parker Harrison, or *any* man. He'd have to decide whom he wanted without an ounce of coaxing from her. Yet to be fair, there was no indication that Parker found Christine more than fascinating and amusing. It infuriated Alexandra that she felt like she was waiting with baited breath.

Parker hadn't ignored her, either. He had been to every one of her performances at Blues Alley, falling into the easy habit of taking her there, sitting through the shows, and bringing her home. He'd make casual suggestions about how to do a song, or perhaps replace one tune with another. He gave her hints on how to work an audience, and while Alexandra was getting better at it, it never became easy or comfortable. She just wanted to sing, but she was fast realizing that performing involved much more than just ability. Sometimes she and Parker would have a late supper together, talking music, of course. Or, after he drove her home, they'd sit on the sofa with coffee and talk about her audition, or of his upcoming concert in New York.

Parker was still insistent on her being the opening act for the concert, and toward that end he had his management office mail a contract for her to read and sign. She still had not done so. And the longer she delayed, the more difficult her decision became. It wasn't so much that she didn't want to do it. It was just that she was unsure.

Alexandra knew it was a terrible admission to make, given her ranting and raving about wanting a professional career. The dream was much more appealing than the reality. Was Parker trying to prove that point, or did he sincerely want her to start his show, to give her the golden opportunity she'd always wanted? Alexandra had to admit that when she and Parker performed together, whether professionally, or just when they were fooling around, she was never nervous. It was always natural, always perfect.

Parker had further surprised Alexandra by showing up during one of the piano lessons for three of her advanced students on Wednesday of the previous week. He'd quietly sat and watched her for an hour as she'd taken her three charges through a series of advanced exercises. Although it had thrown her off guard to see him there unexpectedly, she was soon able to put him out of her thoughts as she gave her full attention to her kids.

She imagined Parker had come out of curiosity. Her teaching was just another facet of her life he really didn't know much about. He had only known the driven person she was, with a dream and ambition she fervently believed in. The Alex who had talked so passionately as well about her music students was a direct contradiction.

Sometimes Alexandra thought she was at her best when she was encouraging small children. She was sincere and attentive and showed enormous patience while being firm, creative, and tireless. This was her real forte, her real challenge—teaching the *love* of music.

She joked with the children and knew how to tease them, make them laugh, and keep them interested. She never connected so well with her adult audiences.

On that Wednesday, Parker had chatted easily with the kids for a while. Afterward, when one of the girls, giggling, asked if he was Miss Morrow's boyfriend, he'd laughed lightly and responded, "I think you'll have to ask Miss Morrow," and he'd given Alexandra a sly, playful hug.

Alexandra quickly reminded the kids that their parents were probably all waiting outside in the cold for them to appear. The children had made a noisy exit, waving to Alexandra, still smirking and laughing over the presence of Parker. To Alexandra's dismay, he didn't let the matter rest.

"So, what's the answer?" Parker had asked seriously, when they were alone. "Am I your boyfriend?"

Alexandra instantly became busy gathering sheet music, closing exercise books, and shifting piano benches in the conservatory studio. She was thinking that Christine would call Parker a boyfriend, implying he was hers. But Alexandra had never seen Parker as someone who was hers, but someone with whom she belonged. At least, she'd thought so years ago.

"Am I your girlfriend?" Alexandra flippantly answered his question with a question. But when she'd turned her clear, challenging gaze to his, she was stunned to find Parker's eyes gentle, his mouth in a sensual smile. He was shaking his head very slowly.

"You are much, much more than that to me."

Alexandra stopped her nervous movements around the music room to stare at Parker. There was so much confidence in what he'd said and in the way he'd said it. What was he saying? What was he *admitting*?

Alexandra lowered her puzzled gaze to the music in her hands. "What about Christine?" she asked smoothly.

Parker pursed his lips and put his hands into his pockets. "I like your sister very much," he began, and watched Alex's head snap up, her eyes wide and their expression briefly surprised and troubled. "I think she's beautiful. I also think she's stubborn, headstrong, immature, and manipulative. All of which will hopefully change when she finishes growing up. The way I see it, Christine uses it all as a defense because she's jealous of you."

It was a moment before his last remark registered, and for a while Alexandra just stared blankly at him. Then she arched a brow, rolled her eyes, and struck an attitude. "Give me a break. Are we talking about the same Christine?"

Parker nodded. Then he walked slowly toward Alexandra and took the music sheets from her hand. He glanced through the titles one by one. When Alexandra made to quickly take them back, Parker smoothly turned away. Two of the sheets were music he'd composed when he was not even twenty. They were harmless little pop rock numbers.

Parker looked at Alexandra, his expression unreadable; but his dark eyes were intense and probing. He smiled slowly.

"Think about it, Alex. You share your father's talent with music and the sheer joy of playing it. There was something you both could discover together. I'm not saying he ignored Christine. It's pretty obvious he loves her dearly. But in Christine's eyes, you were probably always just a bit more special."

Alexandra shook her head, surprised at the observation. It had never occurred to her that she had any attributes Christine would envy. Alexandra was still very uncertain that what Parker was saying held any validity.

"It's not true."

"Sure it is. You took music lessons. And then, not only do you get to study at one of the top conservatories in the country, you get to perform at the Kennedy Center, you perform in a chorale at Rockefeller Center, you perform on public television.

"You teach children. Imagine, people come to you, Alex, to teach their children, because you have something special to offer. Christine can knock 'em dead on first sight, but you have staying power. You have a talent."

"Christine has lots of talent," Alexandra defended, with such sudden temper that Parker held up his hands in surrender.

He did not want to seem like he was attacking Alex's younger sister. "I know. She's very persuasive. She's very good at talking people *into* things. She's going to do very well for herself, with the right guidance and advice."

"From you, I suppose," Alexandra said archly, crossing her arms over her chest.

Parker was highly amused, but he dared not laugh again. It was clear to him that Alexandra, while loyal and loving of her sister, was still stubbornly taking a "wait and see" attitude with him.

"Alexandra . . ." he began gently.

She could instantly detect his seriousness in how he said her name.

He slowly shook his head. "I'm not in love with Christine. And I'm not going to be."

Alexandra stood still, appropriately tongue-tied. Parker had effectively answered one of her most persistent questions, but he had not addressed all her concerns.

He allowed no time to let the comment sink in, or for her to respond. He declared a moratorium on work and decided it was time to play. He immediately swept her away for the rest of the afternoon. They rambled in and out of music stores, then went to a movie that was so bad they sat and laughed all through it.

They were having a date.

It struck Alexandra that she and Parker had never really dated, or had a true opportunity to know one another. They'd really just come together out of circumstances. Alexandra had to admit that starting over definitely had its advantages. On one level they knew each other very well, and there was a comfortable melding of minds and attitudes. On another level, it was a discovery. They were finding out about each other as adults.

Later, at her apartment, Alexandra had made them both a light dinner of a pasta and chicken salad. And after talking in a desultory manner, easy and languid and familiar, for several more hours, Parker had left for his own temporary lodgings. Alexandra didn't want him to go, but she also didn't ask him to stay. Everything had been perfect so far, and she didn't want to risk it changing. Her day with Parker was exactly as she'd always imagined it. Comfortable, invigorating, and fun.

She'd walked Parker to the door and allowed him to put his hands on her narrow waist. He drew her closer so that he could kiss her. Even the kiss was comfortable. It was filled with easy warmth and affection. It had liking and simple pleasure that wasn't in any way demanding or too casual.

Alexandra had had a wonderful time with Parker, knowing a companionship and comfort that was far more natural than their first relationship. He'd shown caring, support, understanding in the last few weeks. She could talk freely with him now about her music. He listened to her sing, let her air her doubts over the choice of arias that were good or not good for her voice during an audition. He calmed her unspoken fears about the competition for the Light Opera, the judging, the outcome. It was all she'd wanted and needed from a friend, boyfriend or not, but not *all* she needed or wanted from Parker . . .

The rain continued to fall outside, and Alexandra continued to feel chilly. A frown furrowed the otherwise smooth skin of her forehead as her musings played further havoc in her mind. She was on her way to getting somewhere with her music. It was what she'd worked toward single-mindedly for six or more years, wasn't it? She had resolutely intended for nothing and no one to interfere. But there was a persistent nagging sense that everything was not going according to plan.

Alexandra put her teacup on the table at the end of the sofa, and slid her body down further into the plush cushions. Her body ached with each movement. She thought she'd just rest for a little while before getting ready for the evening's performance at Blues Alley. *One more,* Alexandra thought, with an unconscious rush of relief. But then, there'd be no reason for Parker to be there at the beginning and end of her evenings. In any case, he'd have to leave soon for New York and preparations for his own concert. She would go on to her audition, on with her music, on with her life. And she'd be alone.

The frown deepened and Alexandra twisted her aching body into a more settled position. With a small mew of protest wrung reluctantly from her by her weakened condition, by her sudden vulnerability, Alexandra let her truth out.

She wanted Parker.

She was in love with him.

At nineteen, perhaps she had known him prematurely as a lover, but nonetheless, brief lovers they had been. Now, after an explosive reunion which had turned into gentle, affectionate caring, Alexandra found herself wanting him more than ever. This time she would know fully what she was giving, and what she wanted in return. She was prepared to reconsider her priorities without giving anything up. Somehow, before Parker left for New York, she had to know where their relationship was headed.

With a wrenching of her heart, Alexandra further recalled the evening she'd gone for a voice lesson with Signora Tonelli. The former Italian diva had been relentless in her pushing, forceful in her prodding, and stingy with her praise. The signora, not mincing words, had told Alexandra that the key to doing well in the competitions was to remember that she was very good in what she sang and performed, and to simply concentrate on singing well what she knew.

"However . . ." the diva had said airily, as she'd ended one two-hour session with Alexandra, "tonight you had the concentration of a turnip. I suggest you forget everything else in your life, at least for the next month. Forget your love life, paying bills, and the laundry. Nothing else must exist but your singing. I've never known a turnip to win the competition yet."

Alexandra had left the cramped little apartment of her instructor feeling a wave of panic, a crush of self-doubt so strong that she couldn't swallow around the lump in her throat. She needed reassurance and encouragement.

Parker had been waiting to take her to dinner as he'd been doing for weeks, and this time when she saw him, Alexandra let the tears of frustration slip down her cheeks. Parker approached her with strong concern reflected in his eyes. He'd instantly discarded the lit cigarette to comfort her. He put an arm around her shoulder and squeezed gently.

"I was godawful." She'd tried laughing only to have it come out as a wretched little sob.

"What happened?" Parker had asked, folding her into his arms, while standing outside in the cold.

Alexandra shook her head forlornly and turned watery, dark eyes upward to gaze at him. "She says I'm not concentrating enough."

Parker had watched her curiously for a long moment, his hands rubbing up and down her arms.

"Why aren't you concentrating?" he'd asked softly, carefully. It was the first sign that Alexandra's whole mind and heart were not into what she was doing.

Alexandra pressed her hand against her temple as if trying to evoke an answer. "I don't know. I . . ."

And then, unexpectedly, Parker had closed his mouth over her falterings, forcing the words and thoughts back down her throat. His arms had held her closer to him, until it seemed his heat seeped right into her chilled body. The persuasive pressure of his firm masculine lips and the sensual possessive stroking of his warm, rough tongue were like a balm to her senses and rippled along her spine, causing Alexandra to press closer to him, to open her mouth willingly to further exploration. Certainly right then she wasn't thinking about the competition, or Signora Tonelli, or her music.

The kiss was meant to calm and comfort her, but Parker didn't intend for Alexandra to forget that she had a serious concern that needed immediate attention.

Just when Alexandra was about to sink into Parker's comforting caress, he slowly released her. His eyes were blazing and dark with intense emotion, and his hands had tightened on her arms.

"Why aren't you concentrating?" he asked again.

Alexandra blinked at his tone of voice, the fire in her blood, quickly aroused, now quickly fading.

"Well, I certainly can't think when you kiss me like that," she said, feeling lightheaded. Her heart was racing, and she missed the warm security of his arms.

"Then I won't kiss you like that," Parker said evenly. "I won't even touch you like that, but I want to hear what's on your mind."

In that instant, Alexandra was on the verge of confessing everything. But it dawned on her that just because she loved Parker and wanted a life with him didn't mean she couldn't have a career as well; it was just that she was ambivalent about how badly she wanted that career.

If she changed her mind again about the audition or about doing another club engagement, it had to be her decision and her responsibility. Parker had not suggested it, but if she'd really wanted that audition ten years ago, she'd have done it, no matter what. She'd have taken her chances, risen or fallen on her own efforts, and not because he'd suddenly left.

Alexandra stopped crying. She stopped waffling because her life and future had never depended on fate, timing, connections, or love, but in knowing what was best for her. So as Parker stood waiting for her answer, she gave the only one possible.

"Nothing that I can't work out."

"Good. Remember, this is your show, Alex. It's all up to you," Parker said firmly.

The truth of his words had not sat well with her. But it had served as an appropriate reminder of her priorities. The signora had no complaints about her lessons the rest of the week. Alex performed as if her very life depended on them.

But if Parker's treatment of Alexandra had seemed more tutorial than romantic, Alexandra was even more hard pressed to explain the affinity that had developed so strongly between him and her father.

Very soon after the two men first met, Alexandra returned from her weekly shopping expedition one Saturday afternoon to find the two men comfortably seated at the dining table in the alcove, laughing, talking, and finishing off a lunch that consisted of tuna salad sandwiches, leftover spice cake, and apple juice.

Alexandra had stopped in the doorway between the kitchen and the alcove to view this unexpected sight, her arms burdened with bags and packages.

SERENADE   153

"Hi, Baby." Mr. Morrow greeted his daughter with cheerful complacency.

Alexandra looked curiously at Parker. He wore a pair of well-worn denims and a blue sweatshirt with the word "Mellow" written jazzily across the chest in red. He looked appealingly handsome and casual, and very much at home.

"What are you doing here?" Alexandra asked, as Parker quickly got up to help her with the groceries and headed for the kitchen counter.

"I came to visit," he said easily. He began unpacking as she stood staring at him. There was something rather warm and familiar about Parker pressing himself into her life this way, into her entire family.

"How did you know I'd be here?"

Parker put down a package of frozen vegetables and grinned at Alexandra. "I remembered that you did his marketing every week about this time. But I didn't come to see you, Alex. I came to visit with your dad," he said.

The surprise effectively silenced Alexandra and she stared blankly at him. "Oh . . ." she responded softly, then turned slowly and thoughtfully away to finish the unpacking. "You seem to have developed a fascination with my family. First Christine, now my father."

That was because her family was so much more normal, more ordinary than his had been, Parker considered silently. Even in the few hours he'd shared with Alex and her father earlier, Parker could see that.

His own parents were not any less loving or caring than the Morrow family. But he'd been born to a lawyer and a private school administrator, parents who could afford to indulge him in not only their whims, but his own. Except where the whims diverged from music.

Parker's parents had been attentive to all his needs, except the one to just cut loose and be like everyone else. They had always made him feel more than special, way above average, destined for greatness. He hadn't disappointed them, and he was happy that he hadn't. But he had missed something basic and simple and easy.

He found it here, with Alex and her family.

"It began first with you," Parker interrupted quietly. "I'm sort of making up for lost time." He came to stand behind her, close enough to make her nervous, and close enough for her to be aware of his warm aura, something she found herself susceptible to. "I'm finding out there are lots of things I didn't know about you, Alex. I want to," he said, in a strangely hoarse voice, "because so far, I like everything I've seen."

Parker raised his hands to rest on her shoulder, reaching further around her for the opening of her coat. For a moment, Alexandra was cocooned loosely in the shelter of his arms. The tips of his fingers brushed innocently over the roundness of her breasts.

"Why don't you take off your coat and stay awhile," he teased into her ear. Absently, Alexandra obeyed, letting him help her with the leather jacket.

"So . . . what have you two been talking about?" Alexandra asked lightly, continuing to put away the food, feigning casual indifference. She turned her head to gaze at Parker as he laughed softly.

He took the cans and jars out of her hand and put them back on the table. Then he half sat on the edge of the table, sweeping an arm around Alexandra's waist and drawing her to him.

"Well, we talked about his music. Did you know your father once played backup for one of Pearl Bailey's nightclub acts?"

Alexandra felt Parker's hands as he pulled her to rest her hips against his. The intimacy of it left her speechless. She merely shook her head.

"Well, he did. I've persuaded him to finish some of the music he began writing years ago. There's a lot of good stuff there. I'd like to see some of it performed one day."

Alexandra let her hands rest on his chest, slowly relaxing her body against his. "You two do have that in common."

Parker wiggled a brow at her, pulling her even closer. "We have more in common than you realize," he drawled softly.

Alexandra looked into his eyes. "Maybe I should let you go back in to him. He might begin to wonder . . ."

"He might," Parker whispered. "Don't you want to know what else we talked about?"

Alexandra lowered her gaze to his chest. She used a finger to lightly trace out the word "Mellow." "Let me guess. Christine." She gave him a coy glance.

Parker sighed. He lifted Alexandra's chin and gently forced her to look at him, his expression serious. "I knew everything I needed to know about Christine the moment I met her. But you are a different story. I didn't know nearly enough about you." He paused for a moment to scan her face. "I didn't know that strawberry is your favorite flavor ice cream or that you love old Gary Cooper movies. I never knew you always wanted to fly a plane or learn to speak French. All those things make you *you.*"

He released her chin and let out an impatient sigh, but still he kept his possessive hold on her. "Do you realize how little we knew of each other back when we first met? We never talked about each other, only about music," he said, with both amazement and exasperation.

She nodded.

"You were finally getting started with your life. Your voice was going to be the magic carpet to the rest of the world. But I had already been on the magic carpet, and I wanted to get off. You couldn't keep me from that, any more than I can keep you from your dreams now."

"So you left," Alexandra said with finality, though without anger.

"You're right. We knew little about each other. Maybe you did the right thing by leaving. A clean break, so we could each go on with our lives, and grow up."

"I still should have said something to you. I was a young boy myself." Parker's hand stroked her face, following the contour from cheek to jaw. His thumb rubbed along her bottom lip. "You were completely unexpected, Alex. You weren't part of the program I had planned for that year." He bent forward, his lips a hairsbreadth away from her own. "I knew I was your first love. I thought it was a little crush you'd get over. I never counted on becoming involved myself and needing you so much."

His lips opened to gently stroke a soft kiss across her mouth, and then again. Her eyes stayed open to see his face. She wanted desperately to understand what she never had before. Parker pulled back a little and let out a small sigh. "I thought it would hurt less and you'd forget if I disappeared. I can see now you didn't. Neither have I. But at the time, I didn't have a choice. If I'd stayed, or brought you with me, neither of us would have done what we needed to do."

Alexandra looped her arms gently around Parker's neck, his hands gliding up her back. She felt no anger anymore, only regret that time and circumstances had played against them, had not given them both a fair chance to see where the feelings might have taken them.

"I admit I was pretty hurt and angry with you for a long time. You have a choice now, Parker. Why are you staying?"

He shook his head silently, slowly standing up so that Alexandra was pressed against the entire length of him. "In a way, it's to say I'm sorry. And I want to be here to cheer you through your audition. I want to give to you what you gave to me when I needed it. I want to *be* there."

Alexandra searched his face, looking for the one thing she wanted from him and had yet to really receive.

"Will you leave again?" she asked quietly.

Parker's jaw tensed suddenly and his eyes were pensive. "That's up to you this time around, Alex. When I go, *if* I go, you'll be the very first person to know." Once again, he reached out to grab her chin and turned her face up to his. "But let me be very clear about this, I won't just disappear this time. Do you understand?"

Alexandra was about to kiss him when the kitchen door opened and her father came in carrying the luncheon dishes.

"Can't you two find anyplace else to make out besides my kitchen?" he lamented, shaking his head, walking past them.

Unlike last time, neither Parker nor Alexandra was embarrassed to be caught. Perhaps, Alexandra thought, it was more a statement than they realized of how far they'd come in their feelings for one another.

"We were just taking care of some old business," Parker said smoothly, finally releasing Alexandra.

Mr. Morrow chuckled wickedly. "Things sure have changed. Now, when I was a young blood, we had very different ways of taking care of business."

Alexandra was incredulous. "That's not what Parker meant, Daddy."

Parker laughed at her. "Oh, yes, it was. But we'll finish later. Right now, your father and I have other things to finish talking about, and you are definitely in the way."

The rain hadn't stopped.

And she felt worse.

Alexandra slowly got up from her prone position on the sofa. If she stayed there any longer, lulled into a stupor by her aching body, she'd never get up at all. Her head felt like it could roll off her shoulders, but with an effort she stood up to walk with heavy weariness to her bedroom. She had a show to do tonight, and the show must always go on. The audience was not going to understand that she'd stood in the rain for twenty minutes this afternoon, for the distinct privilege of meeting Christine to lend her a hundred dollars. They were not going to be impressed that one of her students was going to give his first recital, or that another had mastered a difficult piece during class. The audience would simply want to be entertained.

Alexandra laid out the gown for the evening and twisted her hair into some semblance of order and headed for the bathroom. She stripped off slacks and sweater and stared at her naked body in the mirror. Slender and lithe, she had nothing to be dissatisfied with. Except it ached. But the ache that Alexandra was feeling in that moment was not the physical exhaustion her mind refused to recognize, but the ache from wanting to be held and loved.

It had begun the night she and Parker had so precipitously made love. And although they had not done so since, the ache—the need and gnawing—had gotten worse. The touching and teasing, the gentle caresses and strokes that began as a sensory stimulus, had been growing in intensity until she didn't know what to do. But Parker had kept her at arm's length, in total control, despite the fact that Alexandra sensed he wanted her, too.

She turned on the shower water, until the hot steam began to cloud and fog the small room, engulfing her. But it couldn't keep from her the truth that what she wanted most in the world was to love Parker and have him love her. To have a life with him that was of their own music and making. To share love songs sung only for each other. But Parker had also been right when he'd said it was up to her now. The trick was that Alexandra truly enjoyed singing. She also loved teaching. And she loved Parker. She wanted to be greedy and have it all. She knew she couldn't.

She stepped into the shower, thinking that she'd spent what seemed the whole day getting wet. But the shower was soothing, the water massaging away her tension, sloughing off the concern and questions. For one more night she belonged to Blues Alley. For one more night she'd give herself up to the audience and their pleasure, before she stepped back and considered how to go about winning her own.

With a determination that was admirable, even if totally foolish, Alexandra dressed and prepared for Blues Alley. Her actions were automatic, no thought really necessary to slip on high-heeled sandals, or to adjust the wide gold belt at the waist of the black crepe dress. But if her head had been clearer she might have considered the absurdity of it all and gone to bed instead.

She listlessly applied eye shadow, mascara, and blusher, looking suddenly, in her own eyes, like a garishly painted wind-up doll who moved and performed on command. The thought was distasteful, but not so wrong.

When the doorbell rang, Alexandra knew it was Parker. Lamenting the need, somewhat giddily, for further unnecessary movement, she walked lethargically to the door, every joint in her body, every muscle and nerve, screaming in protest.

When she opened the door, she couldn't even focus on him properly. The swaying, blurred image of a neatly dressed Parker made her stomach churn, and a sudden heated wave of nausea and light-headedness made her knees weak. It wasn't like the weakness she got when he kissed her with passion, and the thought made Alexandra suddenly grin drunkenly at Parker.

Parker's lazy, seductive smile slowly changed as he viewed Alex in considerably more detail. He was all set to say hello, but couldn't help but notice that she looked ill. He stepped past her into the apartment, and a frown deepened the grooves of his face. His expression turned into quick concern and question.

"Are you all right?" he asked sharply.

Alexandra shrugged and immediately regretted the careless move. Her grin faded. "Of course, I'm all right. I'm almost ready." She turned to walk away, but had to stop to think where she was headed. Thinking seemed to accentuate her headache, which was already accelerating with alarming intensity. Alexandra gingerly touched a finger to her forehead.

"I'll just get my coat and things and . . ."

"Wait a minute. *Wait* a minute," Parker commanded, quickly catching up to her. He was totally alarmed by the blank look in her eyes. She was not at all steady on her feet. He took hold of Alexandra's slender forearm and, halting her unsteady steps, faced her anxiously. "You look terrible," he muttered.

Alexandra made a sound of annoyance between her teeth. "Parker, there's no need to scream at me. I can hear you."

Parker's eyes quickly looked over Alexandra's face, making note of the too-bright eyes and the slow, careful way she spoke. He looked down at her arm, which his hand held lightly, and rubbed his thumb over the unusually cool surface.

"Parker," Alexandra began, trying to pull free. "We have to go. I'm late."

As Alexandra made to continue in search of her coat, Parker, now with a firmer grip on her arm, purposefully steered her to the sofa. "We're going nowhere. You're sick."

Alexandra pulled her arm free and swayed in front of him. Again her hand pressed to her temple. "Don't tell me I'm sick. I'm *not* sick. Please, can't you stand still and stop moving back and forth?"

Parker's eyes narrowed as he looked at her, and he began to remove his overcoat. "I think we'd better sit this one out. You're not going anywhere tonight but into bed."

"I can't do that. I have a show to do," Alexandra tried to reason, managing to look both helpless and confused. But she no longer resisted Parker's hold on her.

He got her seated and her head dropped heavily back against the sofa.

Her eyes closed, Alexandra felt like she was falling slowly into a spinning black abyss. It was like being on a merry-go-round with nothing moving past you but more blackness. She sighed.

It was so peaceful . . .

Parker, reaching for the telephone, looked hard at her. "Forget the show. If you go tonight, you'll probably pass out on stage. That's all the audience will remember, Alex. Not that you're having an off night because you're sick. They'll only remember the show was bad." He began dialing a number, and turned his back to her.

Inside, Alexandra knew instant and pure relief. The very fact that someone else had said she was truly sick somehow made it okay to feel perfectly terrible. Slowly, she felt her body begin to give in to the weakness, and she felt entirely too heavy even to stand.

To the drone of Parker's deep voice making explanations and apologies to the club manager, Alexandra got up from the sofa with painful, excruciating slowness and walked with increasing unsteadiness to her bedroom. She sat down heavily on the bed, her body moving in a different direction than her insides. She could hear Parker's smooth conversation as he carefully manipulated a possible new engagement at Blues Alley for her in a few months.

Alexandra lowered her body to the cotton coverlet, thinking that she didn't want ever to sing at the club again. She'd have to buy another skimpy dress. She'd have to take requests. She'd have to sing songs that pleased *them,* and not her. She'd have to pretend it was just what she'd always wanted.

It was not. She must remember to tell Parker later.

She had no idea how long she lay there, but she was more than half asleep when her arm was touched and her name softly echoed in her head. She felt her body being gently pulled into a sitting position, and forward until her head rested on Parker's chest.

"Were they angry?" she mumbled in a hoarse croak.

"Only disappointed," Parker answered, his fingers feeling for the zipper to the long gown. "People had heard about you and were coming to hear you sing. Did you hear me, Alex? The word is out about you and people are coming to hear you. They'll come next time."

The zipper was opened and the dress slipped from her shoulders. Alexandra's arms were pulled free and the room air was a momentary shock to her sensitized skin, and she shivered.

Parker murmured something soothing, and Alexandra gave herself up to his care. The belt was removed and the black dress tugged over her hips and legs. Her slip followed, and shoes thudded to the floor.

Alexandra continued to lie against him, left in only bra and panties, loving the feel and gentleness of his hands. She wanted to become a part of him, let him take care of her. She wanted to let go of herself, let go of the past, change the present, and rethink the future. She didn't want to be strong. She didn't want to be lonely. She just wanted to be happy and to be with Parker forever.

Parker was a little alarmed at how hot her skin was. She was running a fever. It felt strange, having Alex so pliant against him and unaware of what was happening to her. He had never known her to be anything but alert, quick, bright, and animated.

Alex was not a forceful person, but she had always been in control. Except for the moments when he'd inadvertently stripped her of that power, like years ago. Except when nature stepped in to pull back the reins, like now.

But Parker felt a certain odd excitement, surely not because Alex was sick, but because he'd have an opportunity to take care of her, give back a little of the enormous care she'd given him; just love her.

Parker's hands were sure and direct. He released the clasp on her bra and removed the wispy fabric. Alexandra lifted feverish eyes to his face. Her skin was all at once hot with an odd mix of exhaustion and anticipation.

"Parker?" she whispered, watching as his eyes thoroughly examined her breasts and their erect, agitated peaks, moving with her deep, erratic breathing. She saw the interest, the hard desire in his eyes.

"Lie down, Alex," Parker said, pulling back the covers and sliding her between the sheets. The cover was pulled to her chest.

"Parker?" Alexandra tried again, not sure what it was she was trying to say, but hoping Parker would understand. Her eyes drifted closed.

He brushed a soothing hand over her cheek, letting the fingers trail down until they rested on her throat and upper breast.

"When you're feeling better," was all he said, because he *did* understand.

For Alexandra, it was enough. It answered at least one question.

With a sigh of relief, she closed her eyes, drawing comfort in knowing that Parker was there with her. All sense of time was lost, and eventually, even whether it was night or day. Alexandra had only the sensation of falling down a deep black well, spinning round and round into an abyss. Someone held her hand tightly, and whispered loving words, and the fall became a floating sensation. She didn't care where she was, or what she was supposed to be doing, as long as Parker was there to catch her free-fall into space and keep her safe. There were moments in which she could hear the continuing fall of early spring rain outside her window, and she'd imagine herself still wet and miserable. She shivered and sought comfort and warmth deep in the coverings on her bed.

Parker appeared in and out of her dark world with shirt sleeves rolled up. He sat next to her, his image warm and welcome, but unsteady. He carefully spooned some tasteless liquid into her, and an equally tasteless and dry substance that crumbled in her mouth and felt like bits of broken sponge and rubber. But Alexandra ate it all and went wearily back to sleep. Later still, he was back again with pills and juice, and a warm washcloth to wipe her face. But the world, her room, Parker, still seemed very dim and unreal.

Throughout it all, something rang incessantly in the background. It clanged in her head, forcing her under the covers for quiet. But in Alexandra's confused dreams, the sound was an alarm clock, making her twist and fret anxiously that she was going to be late for lessons. It was a kitchen timer; had she burned her father's dinner? Or was it a bicycle bell? There was a brief image of one of her less-than-enthusiastic students riding a bike and chasing her, shouting, "I don't want piano lessons. I want to play."

It was an elevator alarm. She was stuck between floors at the audition hall and was going to miss her tryout for the Light Opera Company . . . again.

There was, for a while, a need to cry and scream helplessly. But no sound came from Alexandra's dry parched throat, only moans.

She thought she heard Christine, argumentative and fussing, but there was an equally strong and determined male voice. When the apparition of her sister seemed to appear towering over her, Alexandra just wanted to shout, "Go away." Alexandra had no idea what Christine wanted of her now, but she couldn't help her. She couldn't help herself.

Yet there was also an uncharacteristic look of worry and regret on Christine's pretty face, her image moving too quickly. Alexandra felt Christine straighten the tumbled bed linens over her feverish body.

"Everything's under control. We're taking care of it all," Christine seemed to be saying.

Alexandra believed her. Her fretting quieted down. Rolling onto her stomach, she at last fell into a deep sleep, content to let others take charge.

Parker let Alexandra's hot, damp cheek rest in his hand. He watched her face closely, concerned that she might suddenly clamp down with her teeth on the thermometer he'd placed in her mouth. He took a quick glance at his watch and, finding that adequate time had passed, removed the instrument to read Alex's temperature.

One hundred and two.

Parker frowned, absently shaking out the thermometer and putting it into a glass of water on Alex's nightstand. Her pulse had been a bit fast for more than an hour, but he still didn't think there was cause for alarm.

He wiped Alex's face with a slightly cool, wet cloth, watching her as she moaned softly, turning her head restlessly on the pillow. She looked so young and vulnerable under her coverlets, with just her head sticking out, and Parker was suddenly reminded again of how young she'd been when they'd first met. He stood watching her for a while longer and then quietly got up.

Of course, she couldn't be left alone, and he never even gave it a thought. But he'd have to call her family and let them know what was going on. Parker took off his suit jacket and pulled his tie loose, reaching for the phone. It was after nine because, of course, club acts always started late in the evening. But Parker knew that George Morrow was no longer up to long days and late nights. If he was awakened, he'd know at once something was wrong. Even as he dialed the number, Parker was already wondering how to tell a father that his daughter was sick, but that he shouldn't worry.

The phone was picked up and there was a moment of coughing before Alexandra's father rasped out in a sleepy and slightly peeved voice, "I was asleep . . . If this is Christine, the answer is no."

"George, this is Parker Harrison."

The surprise was evident in the long seconds of delay. Parker could imagine from the sounds on the other end that he now had Mr.

Morrow's attention, and if he was only half awake a moment ago, he was most definitely alert now. The older man cleared his throat.

"What is it, Parker?" he asked, his tone serious but firm.

"I'm with Alexandra at her apartment. She couldn't make it to the club tonight."

"Why? What's wrong?"

"I think she's caught some sort of chill, maybe a flu virus."

"Is she okay?"

"I don't think it's serious. Her temperature is over 100, and she's a little out of it. She's not going anywhere for a few days."

"Well, I'll come over and . . ."

"I'll stay with her. That's why I'm calling. I knew you'd be concerned about her being here alone."

"You'll stay?" George asked quietly.

"I'll bunk on her sofa, but someone should be giving her liquids, and using cool cloths to bring her fever down. Where's Christine?"

"Christine? Lord knows. She was going to come over 'cause she wanted to borrow some money, but I didn't have it for her. She was going to call Alexandra."

"Then if you haven't heard from her, she must have seen Alex sometime this afternoon."

"Ummm . . ." Mr. Morrow uttered. "In all that rain. What do you want with Christine?"

"I want her to bring some aspirin. I want her to bring some juices, and I want her to help with Alex."

Mr. Morrow sighed. "Well, then . . . I'll certainly call her first thing in the morning."

Parker waited. "But?"

Mr. Morrow sighed again. "You know, Christine is a good girl . . ."

"I know that, George," Parker agreed. "I also know she's not as indifferent to things and people as she lets on. All that attitude," Parker chuckled softly, "a lot of it is insecurity."

After a moment, George Morrow gave an answering throaty laugh. "You know my girls pretty well."

Parker shrugged. "I have a vested interest," he said.

"Well, assuming I reach Christine, I'll give her your message."

"She'll come," Parker said confidently.

"What's the payoff for her?" George asked, certainly understanding his own daughter. "She's going to want one, you know."

"She's not going to miss a chance to be able to tell her older sister what to do."

Parker didn't get much sleep that night. Despite his soothing words to George Morrow, he was concerned about Alex. Not because he believed her to be in any danger, but because he cared and didn't want anything to happen to her. He missed her feistiness and quick spirit. He missed the companionship that let them laugh together, be angry together, be honest together.

It is called love.

Parker checked on Alexandra several times in the next few hours. There was little change in her temperature. Although her sleep was fitful, she didn't seem to be too uncomfortable. He finally set up a makeshift bed on the sofa, but wasn't inclined to get any sleep himself. Instead, Parker lay in the dark of the living room, wondering how he was going to convince Alex that what they both wanted and needed was each other.

The doorbell woke Parker on Sunday morning. He quickly pulled on his trousers and shirt from the night before and went to answer the persistent buzzing. Christine was at the door.

It was obvious that it was still raining outside from Christine's dripping umbrella and the beaded wet surface of her black patent leather raincoat. It was also obvious that no matter what the circumstances, weather or conditions, Christine managed to look bright, fresh, and unscathed.

"Good morning, Christine," Parker said, and stepped aside so she could enter.

"What's wrong with Alexandra?" she asked coolly, removing her outerwear to reveal black leather slacks and a bright red angora sweater. She also wore a red beret pulled down at a saucy angle over her dark short curls.

"Alexandra's sick. She's caught some kind of bug," Parker said, yawning, buttoning his slacks and rolling up the sleeves of his wrinkled shirt.

Christine pulled off the hat and expertly used one hand to fluff up her springy curls. "Alexandra is never sick."

Parker shook his head and went into the small kitchen to put on coffee. "Did you bring the medicine?"

"Yes, I did," Christine sighed.

"Good. You can take it in to her. Here's a glass of juice. And she'll probably want help to the bathroom."

"Me?" Christine complained.

"Yes, you," Parker said firmly.

Christine took the proffered glass, and with a long-suffering sigh, turned away.

Frowning, Parker watched her go.

Christine entered her sister's room without knocking. She was impatient, and she was disagreeable. It was not so much that she didn't want to help her sister, it was just that she'd only ever seen or known Alexandra as someone who could always manage on her own. It was Alexandra who'd taken care of both her and her father after their mother had died. It was Alexandra who'd set the rules, kept things going, gotten things done. And it had always seemed that she didn't need anyone's help herself. Except for that time she'd come home from school in the middle of the semester. In all the years since then, even though she'd dated, Alexandra had never shown much interest in other men. Now Christine understood why.

It was a blow to her ego that Parker hadn't come running after her like most men did. She hadn't ever imagined that Alexandra could be in love, or that anyone would get close enough to love her. But life was full of surprises.

To Christine, Alexandra hadn't been so much an older sister as she'd been a very young surrogate mother. But as Christine stood over her sister, she had a strange reaction. Alexandra looked so small in her bed. In fact, she looked like a little girl curled on her side with her hand sandwiched in between the pillow and her cheek. She looked sort of helpless and sad and lost in the bed, and not so strong and self-sufficient at all.

Christine had always resented her sister, telling her what to do, and even how and when. On the other hand, Alexandra had always been there for her. Christine knew she'd always taken that for granted. It felt very odd suddenly to feel that Alexandra needed her, and she might never had known if Parker hadn't sent for her.

Alexandra dragged her eyes open and they closed again against her will. She frowned and moaned, "No." Christine sat on the edge of the bed and began opening the newly bought package of flu medication.

"Don't you worry," she said in a low voice that hid sudden realization and concern. "I'll take care of everything."

Which is exactly what Christine tried to do, resulting in an argument between her and Parker over who was going to take care of Alexandra. It was after Christine had returned to the living room to find Parker on the phone with her father. She'd declared in a suddenly commanding tone that her sister needed her, to which Parker had told her not to get carried away. Alexandra needed *both* of them.

"Well, I'm her sister," Christine countered.

"And I'm in love with her," Parker was prompted into responding impatiently.

Christine struck a pose and crossed her arms over her chest. "I figured that out," she said sarcastically. "When are you going to tell Alexandra?"

It was a good question, but now was not the time to consider the answer.

Parker won the argument. He told Christine that her instant sisterly devotion was admirable, but that more than anything, Alexandra needed rest, peace and quiet. So he dispatched Christine instead to his manager's house to get a change of clothing.

By six that evening, much of Christine's enthusiasm as a savior had cooled, but the image of a wan and weak Alexandra, who hadn't been able to do much without her help, had left her thoughtful. Christine had always been able to do what she wanted because Alexandra had always been right there when things went wrong. And Christine had always been able to criticize and find fault, because she'd never had to be responsible for anything or anyone. Where did that leave her sister? Who was there for her when Alexandra needed it?

Debby came late in the afternoon, bringing with her some chicken soup and one of her grandmother's cold remedies. Brian sent flowers. Mr. Morrow called. And Alexandra had no idea of what went on in her behalf.

On Monday, the fever stabilized, and Alexandra slept soundly. And Parker found the albums she'd kept of him.

At first, he thought they held photographs, perhaps of her family, of her and Christine growing up. But to Parker's amazement, they were meticulously kept, chronologized memorabilia of his career.

He was surprised, then amused. And then he realized what he was looking at: the collection of someone who cared. It was the treasure of someone who had a hero who was respected, admired, and loved. Parker looked through the albums once, and then he started all over again, slowly seeing how his career had grown and developed, made possible in no small way by the belief and encouragement of Alexandra.

When he returned the albums to the bookshelf, he was humming. His mind had suddenly turned to melodies and new music. He sat down with pen and paper and composed a love song.

He was interrupted at three-thirty by a knock on the door. He opened it to find a young boy of about ten or eleven with a Batman knapsack over one shoulder, tossing a baseball back and forth. The ball dropped to the floor and the boy stared bug-eyed at Parker.

Parker grinned, caught the ball on the bounce, and gave it back to the youngster, who was still confused and speechless.

"Don't worry. You have the right apartment," Parker grinned.

"Where's Miss Morrow?" the boy asked.

"Miss Morrow is here, but she's not feeling very well. Did you come for a lesson?"

"Yeah, but that's okay," the boy said, snatching the ball and trying to make a quick retreat. "I can come next week."

Parker smoothly reached for the dangling strap on the sack and easily pulled the youngster up short. "You must be David."

David went bug-eyed again and looked suspiciously at the tall man. "How'd you know?"

"Alex . . . Miss Morrow told me all about you. She said you could someday play like me, but you probably want to be another Claudell Washington."

"That's right. He's bad. He's a real good fielder." He frowned. "Who are you?"

"Parker. I'm a friend of Miss Morrow's."

David began tossing the ball again. "You play the piano?"

Parker grinned. "A little. Why don't you come in. I'd like to hear about Claudell Washington. And your music."

"Well . . ." David hesitated.

Parker pushed the door open. "Just a few minutes. You won't even have to practice on the piano today because we have to be very quiet."

David thought a moment and then shrugged. "Okay."

He was there the rest of the afternoon.

Parker was charmed by the ten-year-old. They talked about music and a lot about sports, and Parker was relieved that, unlike him, David was given rein to just be a kid.

David wanted to know where Parker played. Parker told him about the tour he'd just finished, and the concert coming up in New York. The boy's eyes grew round at the mention of Stevie Wonder, Elton John, and Anita Baker on the program.

"I guess you're real good," David said in wonder, making Parker laugh.

"It all came with practice," he hinted.

"Yeah, I know," David sighed, and then looked shyly at Parker. "Can you show me something? Maybe you can play real soft so Miss Morrow won't hear."

Parker grabbed at the youngster's sudden interest, and bought into carefully selecting some pieces to play that could hold David's attention. At the end of the day they were practically best friends.

When David's mother called to check up on her son, Parker introduced himself and explained, listening patiently to her gasp of surprise. She came to get David half an hour later, with Parker extracting a promise from David to keep in touch.

He was exhausted.

He recalled all the phone calls that had come in for Alex, about commitments and classes and another wedding and rehearsals. He had a whole support team, courtesy of his manager, to take care of details. In some ways, Alex's life seemed so much more complicated . . . and so much more fulfilling. Parker crawled onto the sofa for another night of thinking it was too bad Alex wanted the life he had; he would much rather have hers.

* * *

She'd slept around all the funny noises and people in the other room, around Parker and Christine's arguments and their careful entry into her dream world to whisper to her or touch her. There had been other voices, and the phone had rung incessantly. Only when it became perfectly quiet did Alexandra come fully, alertly awake.

She sat up slowly in bed, listening to the silence, convinced that she had dreamt everything else. She got cautiously out of bed, a little lightheaded and unsteady, and walked out into the living room, not bothering even to don a robe.

There was a lamp near a window, but otherwise the room was dark; it was late evening. It was dry and very clear out, and she wondered when the rain had finally stopped. As a matter of fact, she wondered what day and what time it was. She frowned, and peered around the room, nearly jumping out of her skin when she saw the body stretched out on her sofa. It was Parker, asleep.

He was bare chested, and his feet were raised on the sofa arm, sans socks and shoes. He'd located an extra blanket, and although it was spread over his thighs and stomach, mostly it trailed on the floor. The rest of his clothes, the black trousers and white shirt, and other articles of clothing obviously belonging to him, were folded on the coffee table.

Moving quietly, Alexandra stood looking down at him. He had stayed. How long had it been? One day? Two? It had been longer. He had never left.

Sacrifices are made because of love, compromises arranged and carried out for it, hurts and misunderstandings endured, dreams given up . . . or started anew.

Having Parker here, when she most needed someone . . . when she most needed *him* . . . made her see that he did care. She *was* important to him, and he had not been mouthing empty words.

Carefully, Alexandra replaced the blanket over Parker's prone form, and stepped back quietly when he half turned in his sleep. Feeling the room air on her naked limbs, Alexandra wrapped her arms around herself, a very satisfied sigh of peace escaping from her. She glanced with amusement at the disarray of her living room, evidence that Parker had kept the world at bay so that she could rest and overcome exhaustion. Sheets of music lay on the floor, accumulated mail and messages on tables and chairs. A child's worn wool glove and a baseball. Overflowing ashtrays, a half-filled cup of coffee, cold for God only knew how long. She smiled at how comfortable he'd made himself.

Parker had once said, "Be careful what you wish for, because you're likely to get it." Well, Alexandra had just learned that it was true only when it was something she really hadn't wanted in the first place. But now she knew what she truly wanted, and she also knew why.

Parker had also said he meant to stay until he found out whether she hated him or loved him. Alexandra's smile broadened as she left him to go and draw a hot bath for herself, needing to wash off days of being in bed. When she was done, she had every intention of giving Parker the answer he'd been waiting for.

CHAPTER 10

The hot water felt wonderful steaming around her, scenting the air with the floral essence of bath oil. The room was warm and the bath was soothing and rejuvenating, giving Alexandra a lazy, peaceful sense of well-being. It was in direct contrast to the way she'd been feeling recently, pulled and torn in so many directions, confused and indecisive, longing for some order to her harried, not completely satisfying life.

Alexandra smiled dreamily as she thought of Parker taking care of her while she'd been sick. She wondered how his manager and agent and lawyer would respond to the information that the world-renowned musician had fed her aspirin, spooned soup and juice into her parched mouth, gotten her into the bathroom and back, all with the most endearing tenderness and love a man could show.

She finally heaved herself from the tub, finding that languishing in the bath had left her a little weak, hungry, and sleepy.

She wrapped a large yellow towel around her body, absently patting herself dry as she recalled the gentleness of Parker wiping her damp brow, moistening her dry lips with a cool cloth, smoothing back her tangled hair, all the while whispering endearments which had made her feel so safe and cared for.

Clutching the towel around her slender body, Alexandra opened the bathroom door and stopped abruptly.

"What the hell are you doing out of bed?" Parker's voice boomed, causing her to start violently and gasp at his sudden appearance.

He was standing with nothing on but an intriguing pair of briefs, white and distinct against his dark skin. His lean, muscular legs were spread and his hands were planted on his narrow hips. The thunderous expression on his weary, handsome face slowly transformed into one of concern and relief. Parker surveyed Alexandra carefully as she stood before him.

Her hair was twisted into a knot at the top of her head, and her face looked delicate and drawn. Her skin was still moist and shiny from the bath oil, making the smooth skin of her bare shoulders and arms look silky and soft. All in all, Parker had to admit she looked rather enticing, and much more rested than the forlorn person she had been several days earlier.

"Are you all right?" he asked, his tone soft with concern.

"I'm fine," Alexandra smiled, twisting the bright towel higher over her breast while exposing more of her long legs. "I just had to get up. I felt like I was becoming fused to the bed."

Parker arched a brow, letting his gaze roam up and down the length of her, unaware of the sexy figure he himself made to her eyes. He smiled slowly. "The rest didn't hurt you any. You should go back to bed."

"Not yet," Alexandra protested. "I want to know what's been going on. How long was I asleep? I don't even know what day it is. Did I see Christine here, too? The phone rang a lot." She pressed a hand to her stomach. "And I'm hungry."

Parker listened to this recital before suddenly starting to laugh. He moved slowly toward her. "Well, I guess there's no doubt that you're feeling better." He came closer and began to briskly run his hands up her toweled back and sides to dry her thoroughly.

Alexandra felt a tightening in her chest. She was acutely aware and highly sensitized to the fact that very little separated their flesh. Parker had his arms around her. Her own were half imprisoned in the folds of the terrycloth. The brisk rubbing grew slower, but not before the movements of Parker's hands had succeeded in making Alexandra feel warm. She'd fought long and hard to deny what was so obvious in this moment—that she longed to have Parker touch her, longed to be in his arms. She just wanted to surrender to the overwhelming knowledge that she loved and wanted this man.

Alexandra stood relaxed and limp under Parker's massaging hands, mesmerized by the sensual, repetitive stroking until she felt a flow of desire quivering throughout her body. It was all the need she had held inside and kept secret from Parker, and she wasn't going to ignore it any longer.

The growing heat, the building wave of sensuality, made Alexandra's heart race. She felt a sudden urge to lean forward and kiss Parker's smooth, firm chest. She realized that Parker's stroking had become less functional and more caressing. He seemed to be slowly pulling her forward until their bodies were a mere inch apart. His breath was warm on her cheek, and every movement from him only melted and softened her more.

Parker, too, seemed entranced by the slender feel of Alex under his hand. He was glad to see her up, relieved to hear strength in her voice. But his body was struggling not to react to the alluring and erotic picture she made standing before him nearly naked.

They stared at one another for an intense silent moment. Alexandra made the first move, because she didn't want to happen now what had happened too fast so many weeks ago. It was truly up to her now; she was center stage, with the spotlight marking her every motion and gesture.

"Is there anything to eat?" she asked in a wispy voice.

Parker slanted a wry smile at her. "I think we can put together something. I'm a little hungry myself," he said, but something in the gravelly texture of his voice made her doubt he was speaking of food.

It really didn't matter to her what they ate. It was the time together that was important, the wonderful sense of well-being that she'd never known before. After a dinner of spaghetti with a light butter sauce, they sat on the sofa, catching up to three days of activity that had gone on while she had been ill. She listened to the details: the great Parker Harrison had acted as wet nurse and baby sitter for her. It was so domestic, so personal, that Alexandra found herself studying Parker for any sign that he'd felt inconvenienced. There was none.

Alexandra sipped her tea, shaking her head in bewilderment. "I can't believe it's Tuesday. I can't believe I've lost four whole days."

Her feet were curled under her and Parker had wrapped her in the blanket he'd been using at night. He'd pulled on a pair of jeans, but remained without shirt or socks as he sat next to her.

He tilted his head back to expel his cigarette smoke toward the ceiling. His legs were stretched out on top of the coffee table and his other arm stretched along the back of the sofa, absently fingering the blanket which had loosened around Alex's shoulder.

"You didn't lose four days. You just used them differently than you otherwise might have." Parker looked at her as he tapped his ashes onto a paper napkin. "You were completely out of it. You needed the rest, Alex."

Alexandra looked at him thoughtfully over the rim of her cup. "Was I that bad?" she asked softly.

"Worse," Parker said with a soundless chuckle. "You'd gotten yourself on a treadmill and something was bound to give, with the kind of crazy pace you set for yourself. What gave out finally was you."

Alexandra silently nodded, willing to admit to herself that she'd been using music to fill a void in her life that she didn't know how else to fill. Alex gulped the last of her tea and put down her cup. The most important revelation was still to be made.

"Have you been here all the time I was sick?" she asked quietly.

Parker turned his head to study her. "Yes."

"You must have been very uncomfortable, sleeping on the sofa." She looked into his eyes.

"I was. A chiropractor could make a lot of money off me right now," he said with a straight face, but his eyes were sparkling and he made Alexandra smile.

"I'm sorry. You should have just left me to sleep," she suggested.

Parker's expression changed, becoming tight and serious. "I only made that mistake once, Alex." The past no longer concerned him; it was the future that needed clarification. As he watched the light in Alexandra's eyes, the way her body was poised stiffly in her corner of the sofa, he knew that something had to be settled with Alex here and now, or it wouldn't happen at all.

"Besides," he began, "I had a lot of help. Christine, for one."

"So, I *didn't* imagine her."

"No. I had her bring me a change of clothes, and some juice and stuff for you. She made some meals, and then I sent her off to see about your father. I didn't want him to start worrying about you."

Alexandra grimaced. "That's why I heard the fussing. She couldn't have been very happy about being a nursemaid."

Parker frowned. "You're wrong. She wanted to stay. She wanted to take care of you."

Alexandra's eyes widened in disbelief. "Really?"

Parker smiled. "Yes, really. We fought over it, because I was afraid in her enthusiasm she'd do you more harm than good. But she was right there. Christine is not as good at taking care of people as you are, but she's capable enough."

Alexandra looked skeptical, but Parker nodded to contradict her. "You may not have given your sister enough credit for being able to think about more than herself. Yeah, she's beautiful and she knows it, but she's never sure if people see anything else. She's not sure there is anything else. So what does she do? She plays the vamp to get attention." Parker's fingers rubbed her shoulder through the material of the blanket, forcing it to fall away and expose her soft joint. "She wanted to take complete charge here, but I vetoed that."

"Did you? Why?" Alexandra asked quizzically.

"She hides her concern by being overcritical, overfussy. Something like the way you hide behind your music because you think that's all *you* have."

Alexandra began to fidget at Parker's words, realizing he was right.

"Christine is jealous of you and has been all her life. Pretty girls are a dime a dozen, but she can't do what you do."

Alexandra stared at him and shook her head. "She's always teased me about my music. She's always said I'd never be a world-class singer because I let my feelings distract me and get in my way."

Parker hesitated as he considered Christine's observation and his response. "To some degree, she's right. You know, it takes a lot of determination and work. It's difficult to concentrate on this kind of career and anything else. You give up a lot because, more often than not, it's one or the other," he said with some knowledge.

"Is that how you did it? Not caring about anything else?"

Parker sighed impatiently. "It's not that I didn't care. But what I did was not for fame, fortune, or friendships. My music was for *me*. Recognition is fine and I appreciate it, but my music would still have been for my own satisfaction, with or without all the other stuff."

"That's easy for you to say now, but what if no one ever said you were good?" Alexandra queried bluntly.

Parker shrugged. "I can't answer that, Alex. You seem to feel the trappings will make you somebody. Don't you know you *are* somebody? And you *are* important: to your father, your students, and your friends; even Christine admires you more than you know, and more than she'll admit.

"Now other people *are* telling you that you're very good." He gave her a wry, ironic look. "Whether you realize it or not, Alex, with Blues Alley, you have arrived."

Alexandra stared at him and gnawed on her lower lip. She wanted to tell Parker that she was now sure of what she really wanted. But inside, she felt the fear of letting go of so many dreams, and all the plans which had sustained her for so long. The other truth was that even if her feelings for Parker were not returned and she hit a dead end, the other considerations would still not be any different.

Alexandra took a deep breath and felt her insides somersault as she looked at Parker. Now, finally, she had nothing to lose.

"I don't want to sing at Blues Alley anymore. Even if they ask, I don't want to go back."

Parker looked intently at her. He sat very still. He'd tried very hard to be honest and fair with Alex this time, but he wasn't going to deny that her answer was very important to him. She was very important to him. His fingers stopped their caressing movement on her shoulder. "Why?" he asked softly.

Alexandra laced her fingers together and the truth lay like a hard lump in her throat. "Because it doesn't make me happy," she answered simply.

She didn't meet Parker's intent gaze and she missed the imperceptible pursing of his wide mouth and the gentle lift of a brow.

"When I'm on stage at the club I only think about doing the numbers to finish my act, and then getting off. I don't always feel what I'm singing.

I sometimes feel . . . empty," Alexandra finished, somewhat surprised by her own revelation.

Parker drew his legs down from the coffee table and turned to face her more fully. "I know," he said, apparently not surprised by her confession.

Alexandra looked curiously at him. "How do you know?"

"Because that's how I'd gotten to feel about my music when I met you years ago. You described what I went though every time I gave a concert. My music *is* important to me, just like your singing is important to you. But I had to do it *my* way."

She shook her head. "The question is, what is *my* way?"

"Only you can answer that, Alex. But it may not be performing at all. Maybe that's not where you should be heading."

Alexandra frowned at him. "But then, why did you insist that I try out for Blues Alley?"

"So that you could find out for yourself by simply trying," Parker said, and rubbed his hand along a bristled jaw that needed shaving. "When I first turned up again, you were piddling by, here and there, never putting the energy into performing. I made the mistake of trying to convince you of how difficult a stage life is. Experience is still the best teacher. That's why I backed off. It was how *I* found out. I had to *do* it first." He paused for a moment. "So you know. Now what?"

Alexandra glanced quickly at him. Her heart was beginning to beat faster as she realized that a reckoning was about to take place between her and Parker. "I don't know. I'm not sure. There's still my audition next week." Her voice dropped to a mere whisper; it was now or never. "And there's still you."

Parker lifted his hand slowly to stroke her hair. "Is there?" he asked, in a thick, low voice.

The very sound sent a spiraling of feelings cascading through Alexandra. It was very personal and touched the sensitive core of her. It made her feel that in this moment they were closer than they'd ever been before.

"Parker, why did you stay?" Alexandra asked earnestly of him. "You didn't even remember me when we met at Debby and Brian's wedding."

"It wasn't that I didn't remember you, but you'd changed. I left a young girl, Alex, just on the verge of womanhood. I stumbled back into your life to find you'd grown up beautiful and strong, but," he paused and smiled, "confused. I stayed because I couldn't just leave. Not again; not like last time. I never had a chance before to know the things I've learned about you now. I wanted to know *all* about you, all about your family."

"Is that why you spent so much time with my father, and with Christine?"

He nodded, reaching to grasp both her hands. "I like your father. He's much more down to earth than mine, and a lot easier to talk to. As for Christine, I also learned that for someone so beautiful, she's also insecure. You're right—she's very talented in her own way. I've told her she should be in New York studying design, and I know that's what she wants to do. So I've arranged for her to stay in Philadelphia with my folks until she gets started and knows what she wants to do. With your father's permission, of course. My folks can keep an eye on her."

Alexandra looked at him in awe. "Why are you doing all of this? First me and Blues Alley, then my father with his music, and now Christine."

Parker smiled at the naive bewilderment in her voice.

"Haven't you figured it out yet?" His voice was soft, his eyes gentle and understanding.

Alexandra stood up very suddenly, dropping the blanket but holding tightly to the yellow towel. She walked over to lean against the piano.

"No. Tell me," she said in a strangled voice. A sudden apprehension was building inside. She heard Parker get up behind her, knew he was approaching. She gripped the edge of the piano as an astounding truth quickly came to her. Parker had said everything, and really nothing at all, to make her see the truth. Her mind rifled through years of memory rapidly to try and figure out why she'd missed the obvious key to what had happened when Parker had gone away.

"Alex, your father . . ." he began, and then gently put his hand around the column of her neck, his fingers soothing over the skin. She finally understood, and Parker knew that the information, the instant realization, hurt.

Alexandra turned around quickly to face him, and Parker was stunned to find tears in her eyes. She didn't give him a chance to say anything further. She was swallowing to keep control, but a tear slid down her cheek.

"My father? What did he have to do with it?" Her voice filled with shock and surprise. Alexandra stared at him. His expression was one of concern and deep regret.

"I wanted your father to know. I spoke to him a day after I left and told him my reasons. He reluctantly agreed with me that it was the best decision at the time. He asked me not to contact you for a while. A while turned into years, unfortunately.

"I called you once, several months after I'd left. Your dad said he didn't think you were ready to leave home yet. He asked me to give you more time; you needed to give yourself more time."

Alexandra was openly crying now. "Oh, Parker." She moaned and covered her face.

Parker gathered her into his arms and held and stroked her, while the shock of truth shook her from head to toe.

"Alex, you can't blame him. He was doing what a father is supposed to do. Don't even be angry with him. Not saying goodbye was still my fault."

"He never said . . . he never even hinted," she sobbed.

There was a part of her that wanted to be furious at her father and at Parker for deciding the direction of her life. She wanted to rage that they'd had no right to exclude her. But after nearly ten years, what was the point? She'd been angry nonetheless, and Parker had taken the full brunt of it.

Her father had been so understanding when she'd been forced to return home from school, so comforting when she'd missed her auditions. It was her father who'd reminded Alexandra that the world had not come to an end and she would survive, finish school, and go on with her life. But it had been odd that he'd also never asked any questions, never probed into those magic months which had soured for her. He'd known all about them.

Alexandra had believed all those years that Parker had really just walked away without caring. And now, of course, so many things said and done recently and in the past made it all clear to her that it hadn't been so cut and dried.

All Parker could do for the moment was hold her and let her cry. It was a release of tension. It was the realization of the truth. It was the relief of doubts proved wrong and the surprise of knowing that ultimately all that had gone before and recently had been to love and protect her.

"I'm sorry, Alex. I thought that after a while your father would tell you. I thought all these years you knew. When I ran into you at Brian and Debby's wedding, I couldn't figure out why you were still so angry with me. That night when I brought you home, I knew you believed I'd just walked away." Parker squeezed her to him, murmuring, and she held on tightly, her tears making wet splotches on his brown skin. "I knew that I had a chance to stay and *show* you the truth. But I couldn't betray your father. He loves you very much, and he did what he thought was best for you at the time. He said things would happen when they were supposed to happen, and he was right.

"Well, things have changed. Your father knows he can trust me. He can trust that my folks will keep an eye on your sister. And he can trust that I'll love you."

Alexandra's crying turned to hiccoughs as she purged herself. Parker felt the calming in her and leaned back to cup her tearstained face and tilted it up to his. "I couldn't even tell you how much I loved you, Alex," his voice was husky with emotions, "because I knew if I did, it wouldn't have mattered what your father wanted for you. When I suddenly found you again, I knew I was going to do everything in my power to make it up to you. To us. I cared, and I always have. My reason for being here, right now, is because I love you." He kissed her forehead and tried to wipe the tears from her face.

Alexandra shook her head slowly in continuing amazement. "I can't believe what he did," she sniffled.

Parker smiled kindly. "You were nineteen years old. How could he not? Think of how hard it must have been for him, trying to do the right thing."

"But to let me think it was all your fault. I thought I hated you."

Parker pulled her close again, soothing her and inadvertently loosening the terrycloth towel wrapped around her slender body. "I've already gotten a confession that you don't hate me, Alex. But you haven't mentioned love."

Alexandra's crying had stopped, and she gazed at Parker through wet, spiky lashes, and from eyes that were shimmering and bright.

"Of course I love you. That was the one thing I never doubted." Alexandra's chin quivered as she tried a weak smile and lifted her shoulders in a shrug. "There goes my pride."

He hadn't realized how anxiously he'd awaited that response until Alex had actually said the words. Parker just stared at her. "I'd rather have your love," he said, letting his fingers trace along her jaw and touch her still trembling lips. "Pride never kept anyone warm at night, and I think we're much better together than we are apart."

Very slowly Parker lowered his head, his mouth lightly touching Alexandra's. It was a tender new discovery of love. It was much more than the past or the present because their feelings, now spoken and shared, laid the groundwork for a future.

Alexandra let out a deep sigh of relief, love, joy, and wonder as she leaned into Parker, feeling safe and secure in his solid presence.

"Alex, I love you," he said earnestly against her mouth. "I've always loved you."

He pressed his lips against hers. She reacted by lifting her face, bringing her waiting mouth closer to accommodate him.

This time Parker took gentle possession, carefully brushing against her mouth, settling into a position that allowed his warm tongue to test and tease and seek entry. His hand released her face and glided down her arms. Parker's arms, closing around her back, tangled in the towel, pulling it loose. His right hand continued a journey to her hip, his fingers massaging her flesh through the towel, pressing her to the bold, hard outlines of his growing desire. He was slow, taking his time to earn Alexandra's trust again, taking his time to prove his love.

His mouth slowly became heated, more insistent and hungry, his tongue and lips making passionate demands that Alexandra was more than willing to meet. He finally released her mouth, taking in a deep breath of air. He moved his mouth along her skin, leaving kisses from the corner of her mouth to her ear and neck.

The towel was slipping away, leaving Alexandra's breasts exposed. Parker groaned deep in his chest, and he looked down. He could see the hard, brown nipples, the softness surrounding the centers as her breasts pressed against him.

Parker rested his forehead against hers, closing his eyes, controlling the potent surge of feelings that made his breathing ragged. His middle was hard and undulating against Alexandra's hips, his hands seeking her warm skin under the towel, until he grabbed it and simply pulled it away.

Alex gasped softly at the sudden exposure of her skin to the cool air and Parker's exploring hands. The touch of his hands was an erotic warmth on her skin, heating her all over. Her own desire lent boldness to her actions, and Alexandra began to press a series of kisses across Parker's chest. She kissed his nipple and turned her head to rest a cheek against his chest.

"I love you," Alexandra whispered. The absolute truth of it was heartfelt. Alexandra's admission was more for herself than it was a confession for Parker. It didn't matter if he heard her or not.

Parker stroked her shoulders. "When I finally met your father face to face, the night you took me home to dinner, he and I both knew."

"Knew what?" Alexandra asked dreamily, following the sensual wanderings of Parker's hands, the alternate hesitancy and daring of his touch.

"That my feelings hadn't changed in all those years. I haven't lived the life of a monk, Alex, but I've never been in love with anyone else. Not even close. You are still the only woman I can just be myself with."

Parker slowly began kissing Alexandra's face, his breath whispering over her skin, his lips teasing at her mouth again, moistening the surface with his tongue. He was feeling a certain level of wonder and reverence toward her. He was feeling lucky that after so many years, he'd found his true love. That conviction lent power to Parker's next words.

"I don't know what I did to deserve seeing you again, but I'm not going anywhere unless you're with me. I don't care if you want to be another Leontyne Price or Shirley Bassey, as long as we can love each other." His hands smoothed down over the contours of her back and gently gripped her buttocks, Parker pulled her to the heated need of his body and moaned deep in his throat. "I don't want to talk anymore about your father, your sister, the past, or music. I want to love you, *make* love to you."

Parker released her and Alexandra retrieved the yellow towel to hold in front of her as she watched Parker unsnap his jeans and push them and his shorts down over his narrow hips.

Seeing the blatant display of his masculinity sent a wave of pure longing rippling through her. All Alexandra wanted, too, in that moment was to have Parker make love to her. She wanted to *feel* his love within her.

Her eyes were bright with need and love when she met his intense gaze. He stood naked and magnificent before her. Mesmerized by the message he sent her with his slumberous gaze, she dropped the towel and stepped toward him.

He reached for her hand and led her back to the bedroom. He pulled her into his arms and began to kiss her with deep erotic urgency, as if he was using this instant to ask for forgiveness, declare his love, give to her and take from her all the moments they'd both needed all the time they were apart.

His mouth manipulated and demanded, and Alexandra was too overwhelmed and helpless to do anything but comply. The muscles in her stomach twisted and tensed with a need that seemed out of control. She didn't have to ask him, for Parker, too, needed a gratification that would bind them together.

Parker lowered Alexandra to the cool linens, their mouths and tongues still fused. He levered his long, trim body over hers, and settled easily and comfortably to fit her soft contours.

Alexandra felt protected and safe under the weight of Parker's body. It was very like the trusting feelings she'd granted Parker the very first time they'd ever made love. And now, having reestablished that connection and trust, Alexandra experienced the heightening of her senses, her desire growing and leaving her limp in Parker's embrace. He began to move against her, to rub his thighs and stomach against her so that his intentions were so clear that Alexandra drew in her breath sharply as she felt herself melting and wanting him almost with desperation.

"Oh, Parker . . ." Alexandra sighed, as his mouth once again robbed her of words. There was an eloquent demonstration of his love as he stroked her sides and thighs lightly with his hands, and his hips pressed against her.

Alexandra's legs separated, and she and Parker both moaned deeply at their joining together, which was quick and electrifying. For long moments they lay entangled, until Parker began a rhythm, a cadence that created more sounds, deeply felt utterings of satisfaction and delight. There was music that played perfectly between them, through movements fast and slow, until the ending was a crescendo, expertly pitched and timed. But there was no way such heights could be sustained. The ebb and flow of their playing peaked. Alexandra's back arched from the bed, allowing Parker easy access to her pert, uplifted breasts with his warm, rough tongue. Her climax was enough to trigger his own, and Parker buried his mouth in her neck and groaned deeply at his release and pleasure.

Their movements were a gentle swaying together until their bodies finally came to rest. Heavy breathing and little mews of expression were the only sounds thereafter for a long time.

Alexandra kissed Parker's neck, her nose buried in the strong male essence of him. Parker began slowly with her shoulder, kissing his way along a collarbone to her throat, her chin, her slightly parted lips. His voice was raspy and thick when he finally spoke, coming up on his elbows and letting his gaze search over the shadowy glow of Alexandra's face.

"That was to settle any doubt in your mind that I've always loved you and wanted you. God, it's been such a long time," Parker said with feeling.

Alexandra sighed, tilting her head to let Parker's lips continue their journey. "I never knew," she whispered in a trembling voice, tears of happiness gathering in her eyes again.

Parker chuckled lightly. "That's my fault," he said, moving his body, rubbing against her sensuously. "But I plan on taking the rest of the night to apologize."

"And after tonight?" Alexandra asked softly. She could see Parker beginning to smile rather lovingly at her.

"Then we talk about being a two-career family," he responded, kissing her and putting an end to further talk for the time being. "You sing, and I'll play."

EPILOGUE

When Alexandra stepped off the elevator, four pairs of alert eyes greeted her with varying degrees of expectation. The sight both surprised and amused her and, walking toward the support group of family and friends, she began to laugh merrily.

Debby looked maternally anxious as she gnawed on her bottom lip, her eyes rounded behind her glasses. Her expression seemed to convey sympathy without yet knowing if it was needed. Mr. Morrow, looking decidedly uncomfortable in a dark blue suit that hung on his spare frame, had his hands stuffed in his pockets and looked like an expectant father-to-be. Christine's tapping foot and impatient air hid her need to ask "Well, how did it go?"

And then there was Parker, lounging casually against a pillar in the main lobby of the empty recital hall.

Alexandra wore a white angora knit dress, its hem hiding the top of her brown high-heeled boots. Her hair, full and loosened in waves around her face, was topped by a black beret pulled saucily on an angle. Her outfit, at once bright and warm like her dark eyes and sunny smile, was like a harbinger of spring which had finally arrived. The four silent adults before her were as much stilled by her appearance as they were with their own anticipation of the outcome of Alexandra's audition.

"You all look like I've just been given a reprieve by the governor." Alexandra laughed. She squeezed her father's arm reassuringly as she passed him, but continued past her sister and Debby, right up to Parker.

"Well, are you going to end the suspense and put us out of our misery, or what?" Debby begged plaintively.

Alexandra gave her friend a brief smile over her shoulder but still said nothing. Christine made an impatient sound and flounced over to her father.

"Boy, she is going to play this for all it's worth. We already know she won," Christine said with conviction, but still she cast a speculative glance at her sister, who, for all intents and purposes, only had eyes for Parker.

For Alexandra, it was impossible to describe to the other three witnesses what passed between her and Parker. It was a secret communication between kindred spirits.

Parker's brows raised and he lifted a comer of his mouth in a half-smile. He was thoroughly enjoying the animation on Alexandra's teak-brown features, the dark, sparkling eyes that showed a joy that truly only the two of them could know. It was a sense of "being there," of having reached the very top of her form, of having executed something very well, and knowing that others realized it, too. But beyond the *others,* the judges and pianist and nervous competitors, Alexandra knew that this day she had at last truly achieved her dream. And wherever else today led her, *today,* this moment, was the epitome and culmination of all she'd worked for. If it all ended in the next hour, or the next year, she still would have accomplished what she'd set out to do so many years ago.

Cupping a hand at the back of Alex's head, Parker gently pulled her forward to kiss her. The kiss said everything—I love you, congratulations, you look gorgeous. "You look like the cat that was given a bowl of rich cream," he drawled in amusement.

"And lapped up every ounce of it," Alexandra said softly. She sighed. "I was good, Parker, *very* good. I did everything right, and I'm happy with how I performed."

"But?" he asked easily.

Alexandra turned to encompass the rest of her entourage. "But I didn't place first," she said comfortably, with neither rancor nor disappointment.

"What? Are they *crazy?*" Christine burst out in surprising defense.

Alexandra gave her sister a wry affectionate grin.

"Oh, Alexandra," Debby moaned her disappointment, clicking her tongue against her teeth in a soothing manner, as though Alexandra was a child.

"Well, I know you did your best, Baby. That's all that's important," George Morrow said awkwardly, not sure how to ease his daughter's defeat.

Alexandra raised her brows and her eyes quickly glanced at each person around her. "Come on, guys. This isn't the end of the world. I was first choice for the chorus, and I'll understudy the female lead in next fall's production."

There was a long moment of stunned silence while this information sank in before Debby let out an uncontrolled squeal of delight, and everyone converged at once on Alexandra, surrounding her with love and hugs. Everyone started talking at once, and Alexandra laughed and shook her head at all the confusion, appealing to Parker over the top of everyone's head to be rescued.

Parker came to stand next to Alexandra, draping an arm around her shoulder and pulling her against his side. "Look, let's give her a chance to catch her breath, and she'll tell us everything."

However, the talking began at once as Parker led them all to a bank of leather banquettes. They all sat, with Alexandra in the middle, and Parker next to her, holding her hand.

"So, talk," Debby urged excitedly.

Alexandra took a deep breath and gave them the details they wanted to hear. Only Parker knew that beneath the routine of waiting in a dim hall, and on an even dimmer backstage with a dozen or so other hopefuls, was the essence of the experience.

He acknowledged, as Alexandra had, that her talent, her God-given gift from which she might personally derive so much pleasure, was to be judged and censored by a group of strangers who knew nothing at all about why she did what she did. Still, within that spectrum was the need for their approval. He knew that there was validation Alex received for all the years of belief in her own talents and worth. There was the knowledge now that all the years of work and worry had paid off.

As she talked, Alexandra repeatedly sought Parker's attention, as if to say to him, *Now I know what it's like.*

When she was finished, she shrugged. "Well, that's all of it," she said, and looked around at the pleased faces. "I just want you all to know I couldn't have done it, couldn't be here today, without your love and support. You deserve congratulations, too."

Christine gave an exasperated sigh, her beautiful face grimacing with charm nonetheless. "I still think you should have won."

Alexandra smiled. "It's not a matter of winning, but of earning a place. I earned not one but *two* spots, Christine."

"That's even better," Debby exclaimed.

"Does this mean you're going to be famous, after all?" Christine suddenly asked.

Alexandra laughed at her sister, easily seeing the drift of her thoughts.

"I hope not," Alexandra said, and looked at Parker. "One famous musician in the family is quite enough," she conceded. It meant much more to her to be loved than to be well known.

Parker basked in Alexandra's glow. Yes, he knew what it was like, how it felt to have the recognition and accolades. But he also knew what it was like to come home to an empty place after the fans and your manager have told you how hot you are. It doesn't last forever. Realistically, it shouldn't. What he always wanted to have instead was something that required more of a commitment, real compromises and work. A family. *That* he could have forever.

"So, what happens now?" Parker asked her, squeezing her hand.

"Well, I told them I was opening a concert in New York, and I told them I am getting married in June."

"See? I told you you'd let your private life get in the way of your music and career," Christine said.

"No, you don't understand, Christine. I won't let *music* get in the way of my private life." She looked with glowing eyes to Parker again. "After all, there *are* priorities. I love to sing. But it's *not* the most important thing in my life."

"But what if you have to go on tour?" Debby asked.

Alexandra was shaking her head. "One of the reasons the Light Opera Company of Washington is so perfect for me is because the repertory never does tours." She looked at Parker. "I never really expected to do concerts and nightclub acts."

"If either of us goes on tour, the other will go along, if it's possible," Parker added. "But I'm going to begin to limit my tours to a few a year."

"What about your teaching?" George Morrow asked.

"Oh, I'll continue with that, too, but I'll probably limit it to advance preparation for recitals and tryouts. Like David Evans. Thanks to his impromptu meeting with Parker while I was sick, he's discovered a new interest in music and he's back to his piano lessons."

"And I suppose you'll start having babies?" Christine said, with a bored but still curious tone.

At that, however, Alexandra became tongue-tied. She glanced at Parker. They had not, as yet, talked about having children, although there was no question that they both wanted them.

Parker arched a disapproving brow at Christine's question. It was still too personal to be bandied about like cocktail conversation.

"Alex is going to take her shot at performing first. Our babies will come after a year or two. There's no rush."

"How many?" Christine asked impertinently.

"Okay, that's it. Enough questions," Parker said, standing up abruptly. "I've made reservations for dinner at a great restaurant in Georgetown. There's a whole lot of celebrating that has to be done."

"How nice," Debby chirped. "I sure wish Brian could have been here, instead of at a recording studio."

"I could use something to eat," George Morrow said, patting his flat stomach. "I'm getting too old for all this excitement."

"Are you trying to get rid of us?" Christine asked suspiciously.

"Yes," Parker didn't deny. "The reservation is for the three of you. I have something else in mind for Alex and myself." He stood and helped Alexandra into her coat, and turned to usher Debby, Christine, and George Morrow to the exit.

"But . . ." Christine started to protest.

"Good. It's settled," Parker overrode her, and everyone laughed. Parker knew exactly how to keep Christine in line.

Alexandra was very curious about what Parker had in mind, but made no objection as they waved to the departing cab headed for Georgetown. She turned to him, trusting whatever decision he'd made. She was happy that it meant they could be alone and away from the curiosity of everyone. Alexandra didn't mind sharing her victory and her excitement, but she'd rather have Parker to herself. They still had a lot to catch up on.

"Now . . ." Parker said with a deep sigh, as he faced Alexandra and put his arms around her. "I had plans for a candlelight dinner, and soft, romantic music. *Not* mine." She giggled. "Champagne, and maybe even dancing."

Alexandra smiled up at him, and circled her arms around his waist. "Ummm. That sounds lovely. I hope I have enough time to change before we have to be there."

"No problem. The reservation will hold."

Alexandra was curious. "Really? You must know a maître d' in high places."

"Ummm," Parker said noncommittally. "And there's no need to change. As a matter of fact, this is an occasion to dress down, not up."

Alexandra's frown deepened. *"Really?"* she said again, more intrigued than ever. Parker began kissing her cheek, trying to distract her as he signaled for another cab. "Just where are we going?"

Parker kissed her nose. "My place," he said hoarsely, hugging her close. "I figure it's going to take at least five or six hours for me to congratulate you," he said wickedly.

Alexandra looked coyly at him. "Oh? And what happens after dinner?"

Parker's grin grew broader and broader. "Dessert, of course," he said softly, and bent to kiss her soundly as the cab pulled up before them.

FOREVER YOURS

FRANCIS RAY

For daddy, Mc Radford Sr, for all the usual reasons and so much more.
I couldn't have made it without you.
—K.

Special thanks to Laree Bryant and June Harvey for their invaluable assistance,
to Cleo L. Hearn who introduced me to the extraordinary African-American men
and women who follow the rodeo circuit, and to my mother, Verona Radford, who
instilled in me a love of reading.

CHAPTER 1

"Have you chosen which one of your young gentlemen you're going to marry, Victoria?"

Stunned, Victoria Chandler stared over the silver tea service at her grandmother. Heart pounding in her chest, Victoria carefully set the clinking cup and saucer on the antique clawfoot cocktail table in front of her. From out of nowhere came the childhood chant "liar, liar, pants on fire". "I . . . er . . . no. I'm still trying to decide."

Clair Chandler Benson's nut-brown face creased into an indulgent smile. "You told me you were having trouble choosing from your four young men. It's a dilemma not many women are faced with. But you've been blessed with the same striking looks as your great-grandmother. Like you, she had long black hair, hazel eyes, and honey-colored skin, a vision. However, I have complete faith your heart will guide you in the twenty-one days you have left."

Feeling as if the floor shifted beneath her feet, Victoria fought the panic that threatened to overwhelm her. "Grandmother, why don't I wait and decide at the end of summer, when things aren't so hectic at the stores?"

Clair shook her blue-gray head of hair. "That won't do at all. It will be beyond the cutoff date and you'll lose Lavender and Lace."

Victoria's tenuous hold on her emotions slipped. Fear widened her eyes and left her momentarily speechless. "You-you're serious, aren't you?"

"I've never been more serious about anything in my entire life," Clair answered. "I know we haven't discussed it in some time, but I thought I had made myself quite clear. I remember our agreement well. We were sitting in this very room and I gave you six months to get married or I would call in the loans for your three stores. Victoria, you did mark your calendar didn't you?"

Slowly Victoria rose to her feet. Her eccentric grandmother wasn't playing. She meant every word. Fool that Victoria was, she thought she could evade the issue by telling her grandmother that she couldn't choose between four men. The trouble was, there were *no* men in her life—and that was the way Victoria wanted to keep it.

"Grandmother, marriage is a serious matter."

"Of course it is. You're talking to someone who celebrated her thirty-fifth wedding anniversary last month." Clair smiled, showing natural white teeth. "I completely understand your apprehension. After my first husband died I never dreamed I'd find anyone like him. Then I met Henry at a charity dinner. I'm sure you'll be as fortunate as I was in finding a wonderful second husband."

"Men have changed since then. They aren't all honest and forthright like grandfather," Victoria said with a tinge of anger.

"I know that, dear, but you've picked the best Fort Worth has to offer; a doctor, a lawyer, a cattleman, and a banker." Clair looked at her only grandchild with unabashed pride. "Although, I must admit I rather favor the cattleman, since you mentioned his ranch is in the area. It would be nice to have a horseman in the family again. Your great-great-grandfather, Hosea Chandler, was a buffalo soldier with the Ninth Cavalry unit."

Victoria groaned inwardly. Those nursery rhymes again. Doctor, lawyer, Indian chief. At the time, she knew even her unconventional grandmother wouldn't have believed Victoria was dating an Indian chief. Out of nowhere a "butcher" and a "baker" had popped into her head. Before she knew it they became a cattleman and a banker.

"What if I can't make up my mind?"

"Oh, dear." Distressed, Clair paused in adding a dollop of cream to her specially blended tea. "Then you might have a problem."

"What do you mean?" Victoria's stomach muscles clenched.

"You know how much your grandfather and I love you, and I was afraid I'd lose my nerve and call off the whole thing. On the other hand, you know how much pride I take in a person keeping their word. So, I turned everything over to my lawyer."

Victoria slumped into the nearest chair. "Grandmother, how could you have done this to me?"

"Because I love you. You're thirty years old and still dragging your feet about remarrying and carrying on the Chandler name. I simply decided to help you."

Sheer panic propelled Victoria once again to her feet. She felt trapped as she glanced around the sitting room full of overstuffed furniture, antiques, and heirlooms that had been handed down through five generations of Chandlers. The Chandlers had been a prominent and well-respected family in Texas since reconstruction and each generation coined the name with pride.

She wondered if the hardships her ancestors endured were any greater than hers had been when she was married to a selfish, greedy man who demeaned her and took from her until nothing was left . . . not even her self-respect. The thought of marriage tied her stomach in knots.

Unconsciously, Victoria shook her head. "I need more time."

"You have twenty-one days." Clair picked up her tea and took a sip, then assessed her granddaughter critically. "Perhaps if you bring your young men over, on separate visits of course, your grandfather and I can help you choose one. You're so compassionate, you're probably worried about the three losers, but it can't be helped."

Victoria looked at the seventy-two-year-old woman who sat before her, lovable and cuddly in chiffon and pearls, and wanted to shake her. But experience had taught Victoria that when her grandmother was in one of her stubborn moods, she developed tunnel vision. It was easier trying to reason with a two-year-old child. Still, for Victoria's own sanity, she had to try. "I'm not marrying anyone in twenty-one days."

"You will if you want to keep Lavender and Lace, " Clair reminded her, then leaned back on the blue silk couch. "I told you, it's in my lawyer's hands now. I can't change it. And it isn't as if you don't have any prospects. At least you can choose your own man. In the past, women seldom had that luxury."

True fear began to creep up Victoria's spine. "Grandmother, don't do this. You know how much my shops mean to me. If you love me, you'll stop this now."

"It's because I love you that I won't stop. Besides, I have complete confidence that you'll decide within the time left." Clair looked at her granddaughter with steadfast brown eyes. "When your precious father and mother were killed in that tragic boating accident eighteen years ago, you became the daughter I never had. Each night I say a prayer for that man who pulled you to shore safely. Victoria, your father would have wanted me to guide you in this matter. I've only got a few good years left and I want to see you happily settled before I go."

"I *am* happy," Victoria cried.

"You can lie to yourself, but not to me. I see the wistful look in your face when you see a baby or a small child." Clair set the delicate china on the table. "You are a sensitive, caring woman. You want and deserve children of your own."

Her grandmother's perceptiveness caught Victoria off guard. She had tried to forget her dream of children just as she had tried to forget her failure as a wife. Apparently, she was successful at neither. Her shoulders straightened, causing her emerald green wrap dress to tighten across her hips and rise above her knees.

"Many women want children. My wanting them doesn't prove anything," Victoria said, taking a seat beside her grandmother.

A gentle hand caressed Victoria's shoulder-length hair. "It might not, if you didn't also crave what's required in order to *have* children."

Blushing, Victoria stood and walked to the open French doors on the other side of the room. "I don't know what you're talking about."

"Yes, you do." Shrewd eyes swept Victoria's rigid posture. "You stayed with Stephen out of a sense of duty, not love. You've yet to find the man who can kiss you senseless."

"Grandmother!" Victoria whirled, her mouth open in shock.

"Oh, my darling Victoria," her grandmother said, her eyes twinkling mischievously. "Sometimes you're such an innocent. It's going to be a pleasure to watch you fall in love and blossom."

"Where is grandfather?" Victoria asked as she stepped onto the terrace and looked out over the immaculate lawn to the flower gardens beyond. "Perhaps he can talk some sense into you."

"Henry is in the rose garden and he and I are in perfect agreement." Clair folded her hands in her lap. "We both decided the best way to get you to the altar was through Lavender and Lace. You wouldn't raise an eyebrow if we threatened to cut you out of our will."

Anger replaced irritation and fear. Victoria stalked back to her grandmother. "I earn my own way, just like I earned Lavender and Lace. I slept in the back office to cut expenses, did without, and worked fourteen hours a day to make the first store successful."

Clair was undisturbed. "Against my advice and wishes, but you proved me wrong. I've never been prouder of you."

"Then give me the time to pick my husband," Victoria said, unable to keep the pleading note out of her voice. She'd spent the last eight years regaining her self-respect and her independence; she wasn't about to let a man destroy her again. "Let me choose in my own time."

Her grandmother shook her coiffured head. "You have twenty-one days or the lawyer will call in the loan. I'm thinking about letting DeShannon manage the stores for me. They'll give Henry's niece a reason to get up before noon." Clair took a sip of tea. "Although I don't know what she'll do once she gets to your office. She's as flighty as a hummingbird," she said almost to herself.

Clair picked up a wafer-thin cookie and critically eyed the cherry center. "Hard to believe your grandfather is related to that family," she continued. "Oh well, that's their side of the family. What I intend to do is preserve mine. The Chandler bloodline will continue in you."

Discarding the cookie, Clair picked up her cup of tea and drew in a long, deep breath. "Smell those roses. Your grandfather is working hard to keep them pretty in hopes you'll change your mind about a civil ceremony and get married in the garden. I hate that you won't be a June bride, but you can't have everything. April is a beautiful month to get married."

Clair glanced sideways at the silent Victoria. "Do you think you could manage to get pregnant right away?" The older woman looked wistful. "I don't want to rush you, but we're all getting older. A boy would be nice, but we could name a girl Chandler to carry on the name, or you could hyphenate Chandler with your married name. Which idea do you like best?"

"Why ask me when you obviously have everything planned?" Victoria said tightly. "You probably have my obstetrician all picked out."

Clair looked thoughtful. "I haven't. Perhaps I should begin looking into the matter. The best ones are difficult to get."

Her head pounding, Victoria plopped into an ornate straight-back chair near the terrace window. How could you love someone and want to throttle them at the same time?

Two days later, the anger and frustration Victoria felt about her grandmother's unimaginable proposition hadn't diminished. She sat in one of downtown Fort Worth's most elegant restaurants and couldn't have cared less. Her salad fork pinged against her plate as she speared an olive. "Grandmother, how could you do this to me?" she said absently.

Seated across the restaurant table from Victoria, Bonnie Taylor lifted a perfectly arched brow and slowly smiled. "So that's why you've been so preoccupied during lunch. I thought there was a problem with one of your stores."

"If grandmother has her way, they won't be my stores in nineteen days."

"So, she was serious about her ultimatum?"

"Yes," Victoria said. "My sweet, loving grandmother deliberately badgered me into borrowing money from her to open another store, planning all along to use the loan as leverage to force me to remarry. I could kick myself for thinking she was just being fanciful and that she'd forget all about her plan in a couple of months."

"I take it the old girl proved you wrong."

"In spades. Unwittingly, I helped her scheme by insisting I put up the other two stores as collateral in case something happened to me. If I default on the loan, I'll lose everything."

Bonnie's light brown eyes sparkled as she looked around the posh dining room, with its high crystal chandeliers, breathtaking murals of angelic cherubs in a blue sky, and hovering waiters in white dinner jackets.

"Well, you picked the right-place to find a husband." She waved a slender hand toward the floor-to-ceiling draped window twenty feet away from them. "The hotel across the street spans three city blocks. There has to be at least two hundred eligible men registered there and probably half that many are prowling the halls in the attached convention center. Minutes from here is the historic stockyards district, where I bet you'll find another hundred men."

Bonnie ignored Victoria's warning look and continued. "If you don't feel like going to all that trouble, there's a man sitting about four tables behind you near the balcony who hasn't taken his eyes off you since you came in. I'll bet—"

"I'll bet he either has one of those smoldering looks guaranteed to make a woman's knees weak or he's showing a toothy smile that helped an orthodontist put a hefty down payment on a Porsche," Victoria said without looking behind her.

Bonnie smothered a laugh. "I think he was trying to pull off a combination of the two."

"Men! Most of them think all they have to do is show some muscle, be reasonably good looking and a woman will swoon at their feet."

The teasing look vanished from Bonnie's face. "I haven't seen you this steamed in a long time."

"Can you blame me?" Victoria asked, leaning back in her seat. "I've boxed myself in. If I don't find someone to marry, I'll lose Lavender and Lace."

Bonnie frowned. "I know you're scared and angry, and you have a right to be, but marriage isn't that bad. I love being married."

"Of course you do. You're married to a man who worships the ground you walk on. My ex-husband only worshiped my bank account," Victoria said bitterly.

"I know Stephen betrayed you, but not all husbands are monsters. Dan is the best thing that ever happened to me." Bonnie's voice softened. "I can't imagine my life without him."

Victoria nodded. "Maybe because he's an architect, he wants to create, not destroy. The best decision you ever made was getting bids on renovating that old building for your art gallery. I vividly remember your jaw coming unhinged when Dan came by to give an estimate. He was just as taken with you. I think he loves you now more than he did when you were married five years ago. Stephen's so-called love for me didn't last past the honeymoon cruise." She crunched on a piece of lettuce. "I've been attracting the rejects ever since."

"Part of that is your fault, Victoria," Bonnie replied gently as she picked up her wine glass.

Jerking upright in her tapestry upholstered chair, Victoria stared at Bonnie. Despite being complete opposites in background and temperament, they had been best friends since they were in the sixth grade. They met when Victoria, painfully shy and lonely, had enrolled in Eastwood Academy after the death of her parents. The outspoken Bonnie had looked at the scrawny kid clutching her books, her eyes wide and frightened, and taken her under her wing. "My fault?"

Setting the long-stemmed glass aside, Bonnie explained. "You're beautiful, independent, and successful. That's intimidating enough to a lot of men. And since your divorce from Stephen, a trifle hard on a man's ego. Only a fool, a schemer, or a man in love is going to let you tramp all over him."

Victoria's delicate features hardened. "After the fiasco with my ex-husband, can you blame me?"

"No, I can't, but Stephen has been history for a long time. That is," she paused. "Until last week."

"I can't believe he had the nerve to call me," Victoria snorted. "I hope the sound of the receiver crashing down gave him an earache for a week." She played with her salad. "Yesterday I learned the reason for his sudden interest. He lost another job."

"He certainly made a mess of his life. On the other hand, you've got to get on with yours. I think your grandmother realized your hesitancy and decided to give you a little push."

Victoria's fingertips drummed out an angry beat on the white tablecloth. "But why did it have to be over a cliff?"

Bonnie laughed. "I'm glad to see you haven't lost your sense of humor. Does it also mean you've decided to quit fighting and get married?"

For once Victoria didn't have a quick answer. No matter how she tried to find a way out of the trap her grandmother had set for her, she came up empty. Clair Benson had Victoria's signature on a legal document. The only way she could find a way out was to sign another legal document. A marriage license. Her stomach clenched. Never again had she wanted to give a man any control of her body or of her life.

"Well?" Bonnie prompted.

Victoria looked at her friend waiting for an answer and knew she had only one choice if she wanted to keep her boutiques. Her face settled into determination. "I'll do whatever it takes to save Lavender and Lace. Only this time the marriage will be on my terms. Not my grandmother's. Not the man I choose. This time I'll make the rules."

"I don't suppose you're going to make this easy and fall in love in the next nineteen days?"

Victoria's eyes narrowed. "Love has nothing to do with this. It'll be a business arrangement. A simple transaction for which I'm willing to pay."

Bonnie looked as if she wanted to argue, but all she said was, "How long do you plan to stay married?"

"A year, tops. Anything shorter and grandmother can demand payment in full on my loan." Victoria twirled her fork.

Bonnie pushed aside her salad plate. "I hate to bring this up, but how do you plan to keep your grandparents and everyone else from finding out the marriage is a sham?"

"My husband will travel a great deal. His being gone so much will lend credibility to the eventual divorce." Glancing at the lobster chowder the waiter placed in front of her, Victoria picked up her soup spoon. Her appetite had returned.

Deep in thought, Bonnie didn't pay any attention to the lasagna of shrimp, scallop and spinach set before her. Instead she said, "What you need is a man who has enough integrity not to want your money after the divorce, or one who has enough money not to want yours."

"I know," Victoria said. "I want him to quietly disappear when the time is up. Call it pride or whatever, but I don't want it known that the only way I can get a man is to pay for one. Once was enough."

"Then we need to add 'discreet' to his qualifications," Bonnie said.

Victoria put her spoon down. "You might as well add 'kind,' 'sensitive,' and 'caring' while you're at it."

With a secret smile, Bonnie looked at Victoria. "I have your man."

"What!" A wave of silence followed as stylish heads turned toward their table. Victoria ignored them. "Tell me you're not kidding."

Grinning, Bonnie shook her head, her dark, layered hair brushing against her cheeks. "My cousin, Kane Taggart, is thirty-six, single, and has all the qualities you're looking for."

"Kane?" Victoria's dark brows furrowed. "That name sounds familiar."

Bonnie sucked her teeth. "Why, Victoria Chandler. I never thought you'd forget the name of the man you first slept with."

Outrage and indignation swept across Victoria's face. "Stephen is the on—"

Laughter erupted from Bonnie. "I meant 'slept' literally. How could you forget the night you spent at my house, when that violent storm roared across the city around midnight? We had just graduated from high school, and my parents and your grandparents were out of town. We were shaking as much as the trees." Bonnie fingered the stem of her wine glass. "Tornadoes had been sighted in the area and hail was so loud on the roof we had to shout to hear each other. The phone was out and there was a loud pounding at the door just as the lights went out."

Victoria completed the story. "It was Kane. He had driven through high winds and rain to check on us. Your parents called him when they couldn't reach us."

"It's a wonder we didn't knock him down the way we launched ourselves at him," Bonnie laughed. "I don't see how he managed to get out of his raincoat, because neither one of us would let go of him."

Victoria giggled, Bonnie's laughter infectious. "Yet somehow he got us settled in the hall, with pillows, blankets, a flashlight and a small portable radio he had brought. You went to sleep a couple of hours later, but I don't think I dropped off until around dawn. Sometimes we talked, sometimes we just listened to the rain."

A vague memory about that night tugged at Victoria. A deep, soothing voice and the gentleness with which she was held returned to her. Her parents' hugs had been frequent, but quick. Her grandparents patted her on the hand or on the head. Victoria hadn't realized how wonderful and reassuring it would feel to be held until Kane's arms tightened each time her voice quivered or she shivered. Somehow she had never experienced the same sense of well-being in a man's arms. She quickly attributed the reason to youthful embellishment.

"That morning he was gone. I don't think I ever saw him again," Victoria said quietly.

"You must have. He was in and out of my house the entire summer and so were you. But you started dating Johnny Evans around that time and he was all you talked about until you went to college." Bonnie picked up her fork. "Anyway, Kane's in town for a few days and he came by the house last night to say hello. He wasn't there ten minutes before he asked about you."

"Me?"

"You may not remember him, but he definitely remembers you," Bonnie explained. "I detected a lustful gleam in his black eyes when he said your name."

"I don't want lust. I want a business arrangement," Victoria said, her voice tight and final. She owed Kane her gratitude, not her body.

"That's up to you and Kane." Bonnie took a bite of pasta. "Come over to the house tonight around seven and meet him. Dan should be home from work by then."

"I don't know, Bonnie. Do you think he'll agree to my terms?"

"Kane has a big heart for anyone in trouble. Besides, what have you got to lose?"

Knowing what she had to lose right down to the last square footage, Victoria sighed and said, "I'll be there."

At exactly five minutes to seven, Victoria walked up the curved stone steps to Bonnie's home. A wide expanse of glass showcased the rosewood staircase and elegance of the house in the development Dan had helped design. Working together, Bonnie and Dan had built their dream house. Immediately, Victoria thought of Stephen. He had destroyed her dreams by working for nothing and grabbing with both hands for any and everything, she thought bitterly.

With grim determination, Victoria brought her mind back to the present. Shifting uneasily in her three-inch heels, she took a deep breath, then brushed an unsteady hand over her magenta-colored raw silk jacket and skirt. She had come this far, she couldn't back down now. No matter how repugnant marriage was to her, she couldn't add another failure to her already seemingly long list.

She was the only child of brilliant parents, yet she was an average student. Not once did she get the lead in a play, make the honor roll or the cut for the drill team. She hadn't dared try out for cheerleaders. Her success on the girls' softball team in her senior year hadn't made up for the failures that continued to dog her after graduation from high school. Because she had dropped out of college at the end of her junior year to get married, she had failed to get her business degree from Texas Southern University.

Lavender and Lace was the one and only success in life that she could look upon as totally hers. She would keep it at all cost. Squaring her shoulders as she always did when faced with a problem, she ran a distracted hand through her wind-tossed hair, then rang the doorbell.

Her hand lifted again just as the heavily carved door opened. Her jaw slackened. Standing in front of her was the brawniest man she had ever seen. He had a rugged, dark brown face. Winged brows arched over piercing black eyes edged with thick lashes. A neatly-trimmed mustache defined an uncompromising mouth.

Separately, his features weren't noteworthy, but combined, they created an unusual picture of sharp angles and hard planes, as if someone had done the impossible and sculptured his face from a mountain of granite.

His tall, powerful body reinforced her impression of a mountain. At least six feet five, his white-shirted torso lent new meaning to the term "yard-wide chest." Broad shoulders tapered to a surprisingly flat stomach and narrow waist. A hand-tooled belt, with the initials K.T. on the silver buckle, looped through faded jeans that displayed his muscular build with shameless disregard for propriety.

Her drying throat caused her to snap her mouth shut. *Oh, God! How could I have forgotten a man this overwhelmingly masculine and intimidating?*

CHAPTER 2

"Hello, Tory. It's nice seeing you again."

Victoria blinked. The soft, modulated voice contrasted dramatically with the towering giant standing in front of her. It was as if Mother Nature had tried to make up for the excess in his size by subduing his voice, then making the tone irresistibly hypnotic.

"Please, come on in."

When she didn't move, gentle, almost caressing fingers closed around her silk-covered elbow and drew her inside. Absently, she wondered why she allowed him to continue holding her once she was over the threshold.

"I take a bit of getting use to," he said easily as he guided her past the formal living area toward the den in the back of the house.

"Er . . . I . . . no. You just startled . . . I mean . . ." She stammered, then flushed.

A deep melodious sound floated over her head. She glanced up to see the walking mountain laughing. The sound was as soothing and as alluring as his voice.

He peered down at Victoria with what she thought were the most compelling eyes she had ever seen . . . soul-stirring and midnight black. She shifted under his penetrating stare, annoyed with the tingling sensation in the pit of her stomach.

"Beautiful women can be forgiven almost anything, Tory. Hope you don't mind me calling you Tory. Victoria sounds too formal," he explained easily. "Let's go find Bonnie. Dan's still at the office and she's using us as guinea pigs to test her cooking skills." He waved Victoria toward a teal leather couch.

Automatically, Victoria perched on the edge of the cushion, her gaze on Kane. She was still trying to get her bearings, though he lounged easily against a winged leather chair with one booted foot crossed over the other. There had been no hesitation when he met her, no awkwardness. She had the feeling that there weren't many situations where he felt as overwhelmed as she did at the moment. A man his size probably hadn't faced too many things that intimidated him.

A thunderstorm with wind gusts of sixty miles an hour hadn't stopped him. She wasn't foolish enough to think he'd let her wishes sway him. Stephen had never listened to her opinion and he had been nowhere near Kane's formidable size.

It would take a special kind of man not to use such obvious strength indiscriminately. The man who calmed her fears while the wind howled and the rain slammed against Bonnie's house had been that type of man. Victoria had learned the hard way that people often let you see what they wanted you to see.

"Can you cook?" Kane asked abruptly.

"I . . . why . . . er . . . yes."

A slow, teasing grin lifted his mustache. "Good."

Victoria blinked. His smile revealed the sensual curve of his lower lip. Warmth curled through her. Unconsciously, she leaned forward to study him closer. How could she have thought his mouth was uncompromising? The sudden knowledge of what she felt, what she was doing, raced through her like wildfire, fierce and frightening. She jerked upright in her seat. The last thing she needed was a man who made her remember she was a woman.

Bonnie entered the room, carrying a clear oblong tray. "Hi, Victoria. Let's try these cheese appetizers while you and Kane get reacquainted."

Kane groaned. "You promised to feed me, not tease me with something the size of my thumb."

"Man does not live by bread alone," Bonnie said meaningfully, then winked at Victoria.

Victoria surged to her feet. "Bonnie, we need to talk."

"In a minute," Bonnie said, setting the tray on a glass coffee table. "Let's eat these while they're hot."

"Now," Victoria said, unable to keep the panic out of her voice.

Hands braced on her slim hips, Bonnie straightened. "What's so important it can't wait?"

Victoria was unable to keep from glancing at Kane. What she saw didn't reassure her. She had never seen a person so still and watchful. She swallowed. "I'm sure Kane won't mind excusing us."

"No, I wouldn't. But you don't have to take Bonnie into another room to tell her I'm not what you had in mind as marriage material," he said bluntly.

Victoria whirled to face Kane. She realized she hadn't been able to hide the wild desperation in her voice. He returned her look with an unblinking stare.

"But you're exactly what she had in mind!" Bonnie argued, clearly puzzled as she looked from Victoria to Kane.

"Why don't we let her tell us that," Kane said.

The words wouldn't come. Kane might look as if he was carved out of granite, but nearly twelve years ago he had comforted her and asked for nothing in return. Just as he asked nothing of her now except the truth.

It had been a long time since she had met a man who valued honesty so highly. If nothing else, he earned her grudging respect for that. *If* she was crazy enough to be looking for a real husband, the man watching her with the predatory inertness of a cat might have deserved a closer look.

"Are you always so outspoken?" Victoria asked.

Crossing his arms over his chest, his black eyes narrowed as he peered down at her. "I find it saves time and bother."

"Next time, take the time. I wanted to ask Bonnie how much you knew," she improvised, then lifted her chin at his arched brow. "Obviously, that's no longer necessary."

"You need a husband who doesn't want your money, who won't interfere in your business, and one who, when a year is up, will get lost. Did I leave out anything?" Kane asked.

Voiced by him, her words sounded crude and demeaning, but Victoria had been through too much to back down from the unflattering truth.

"As a matter of fact, you did. This marriage will be a business, not a personal, transaction. We'll see each other exactly twice; once at the wedding ceremony and twelve months later when we sign the divorce papers. My husband will conveniently travel a great deal. I don't want flowers, candy, or whispers of sweet nothings, or anything from the man I marry except his signature on the license."

Kane's posture relaxed but his eyes were no less penetrating. "Was your first marriage that bad, or that good?"

Victoria's nails dug into the soft leather of her clutch handbag. "My previous marriage will not be open for discussion."

"Under ordinary circumstances I might agree, but if I decide to go along with this, you'll be carrying my name for a year and I think that entitles me to know." He glanced at the silent Bonnie. "Why don't you check on something in the kitchen?"

"We haven't decided—" Victoria began, but her friend had already turned to go. Bonnie hesitated, then walked soundlessly from the room.

"Changed your mind again?" Kane asked, his voice flat and emotionless.

Victoria glanced up at him, watching her with his unnerving black eyes, and realized that if she said yes she would be revealing more than she wanted to reveal. "No."

"Then I suggest we get started. Would you like to sit back down?"

"No." Sitting would only make the next few minutes more difficult. Kane had effectively backed her into a corner. Either she proceeded or she walked. Walking was infinitely preferable to telling him the humiliating and embarrassing truth about the events surrounding her marriage.

"Tory, I hope you realize that Bonnie would never have asked me to help if she thought I couldn't be trusted," Kane said, his voice soothing.

Restlessly, she turned toward the double doors in the back of the room, which allowed a view of the rock garden and the swimming pool. "Is this necessary?"

"If you were in my position, wouldn't you want to know?"

Again the voice was soft and gentle, but no less insistent. Years ago the same voice had been the center of her world for a few hours. She might have become callous, but she hadn't stooped to repaying kindness with cruelty. She'd complete the interview with Kane, tell him she'd get back to him, and start looking for someone else.

"My first marriage was also a business transaction, although at the time I didn't know it. Eleven months and a hundred thousand dollars from my trust fund later, I filed for divorce. Stephen got half of the remaining twenty thousand dollars, and I got my freedom."

"Did you love him?"

Something about Kane's voice had her turning toward him. He was within ten feet of her and again his eyes searched her face with an intensity that unnerved her. Stephen had swept her off her feet with his handsome face, easy charm, and polished manners. They had met at a Christmas party and spent every day together until she went back to college after the winter break. She had been flattered when he came to Houston to see her, and proud of the way the other women in her dorm practically drooled over him.

With stars in her eyes, she had accepted his proposal on Valentine's Day. She had thought it so romantic. It was only after she said "I do" that she realized he intended them to live off her money. He quit his job with an advertising firm and started running up her charge accounts. The considerate, loving man she thought was Stephen didn't exist.

In his place stood a cruel, heartless stranger who made no secret that he loved himself and her money more than he could possibly love her. Nothing she did pleased him, and he was quick to point out her imperfections. Unwilling to admit she had failed again, she stayed in a prison of her own making until his betrayal slapped her in the face. Seeing Stephen and another woman in her bed filled her with an almost uncontrollable rage. The graphic scene she had witnessed also gave her the courage to walk away, taking nothing except her tattered pride.

Victoria finally answered the only way she could. "At one time I thought I did."

Kane took a step closer, bringing with him a disturbing heat that increased her uneasiness. "And now?"

"I think of my stupidity in trusting a man who took with no thought of giving in return," she said, unable to keep the bitterness out of her voice. How could she have been so weak and spineless? "No man will ever make a fool of me again."

"Tory, don't judge all men by Stephen." Kane lifted his callused hand toward her cheek. She reflexively drew back and nearly tripped over a chair.

Quickly, she glanced away from Kane's narrowed eyes. "I don't. In fact, I think as little as possible about men."

"What do I get for my signature?"

Victoria's head jerked up, her brows furrowed as she tried to determine if the suggestive note in his husky voice was real or imagined. "Ten thousand dollars."

"You pay off one husband and plan to buy another one with the same amount of money. Is that your going price for a man?"

"It worked in the past. Besides, I don't expect a man to marry me for nothing." An arched brow on his hard-looking face told her quicker than her brain that she had said too much. "I . . . I mean that—"

"I get the gist of your meaning." He studied her for a long time. "Do you know that every time I come near you, you flinch or turn away?"

She flushed. Her grip on her purse tightened.

"Well, I guess some things aren't meant to be. Good luck and goodbye, Victoria." Whirling on booted heels, Kane strode toward the kitchen. Despite his size, he moved with the strength and grace of a large cat. "Bonnie, get yourself out here."

A grinning Bonnie came rushing from the kitchen, a portable phone in her hand. "I'm talking to Dan. When's the wedding?"

Kane's face might have been carved out of stone for all the emotion he showed. "I decided that I'm not ready to get married." He hugged a frowning Bonnie. "Tell that husband of yours I'll stop by before I leave for home." He headed for the door.

"I'll call you back, Dan." Throwing the phone on a chair, Bonnie advanced on Victoria. "What did you say to him?"

"Nothing." Victoria watched Kane cross the room and retrieve his black Stetson from the hall tree. There was no doubt in her mind that this time she would never forget him, nor the look of censure on his face before he turned to leave.

"Then why is he leaving after telling me he was going to help you? He's the nicest man I know." Bonnie glared at Victoria. "Some people act stupid when they meet Kane, because of his imposing presence and strong will, but I thought you had more sense."

Victoria almost blurted out that she bet those acting stupid were women. Annoyed with her wayward thoughts, she tunneled her hand through her hair. "You heard him. He's the one saying no, and I have to agree with him. If I get married, it will be on my terms. Kane is probably like a runaway bulldozer when he wants something. Nothing is going to stand in his way."

"You're afraid of him," Bonnie cried incredulously.

"I'm not afraid of any man," Victoria shot back.

Bonnie rolled her eyes heavenward. "Oh, come on, Victoria. This is a girlfriend you're talking to. I've seen that wide-eyed look too many times not to know what it means."

"Kane is not the man for me," Victoria cried stubbornly.

"Oh, I suppose you think you'd be better off with a man who acts like a doormat? If so, you better think again," Bonnie advised. "Because any man you can control with money or intimidation can just as easily be controlled by someone else. Have you considered what will happen if your grandmother starts rambling and your *Mr. Malleable* is stupid enough to think he can outsmart or outthink her? He won't know what hit him."

Victoria thought of her grandmother, whose diminutive size, soft voice, and impeccable manners often deceived people into thinking she was a pushover. She wasn't. Victoria had named her boutiques Lavender and Lace because it reminded her of the strength and durability of her grandmother, who always carried a lace handkerchief and wore a lavender scent. Whomever Victoria introduced as her husband had to be able to hold his own with Clair.

Bonnie crossed her arms in a good imitation of her cousin. "You're right about Kane. He can be controlled about as well as a thunderstorm. But if he likes you, he'll use that same iron will to stand by you no matter what. I'd say he's exactly what you need. Now, are you going to go after him and change his mind or are you going to stand there shaking in your shoes?"

"You know I hate it when you're right."

Bonnie was undisturbed. "Instead of glaring at me, don't you think you better go after Kane?"

Victoria ran for the front door. If anyone had told her an hour ago she would be chasing after a man to get him to marry her, she would have called that person insane. Somehow, once she caught up with Kane, she had to get him to change his mind and help her. If she accomplished that task, she still had a greater challenge of keeping her body from reacting so strongly to his.

He thought she was bothered by his rugged, almost overpowering masculinity. She was, but not in the way he imagined. He was the most riveting man she had ever had the misfortune to meet. He disturbed her in ways she didn't understand and didn't want.

Outside, she saw a mud-splattered truck parked on the other side of the tree-lined street. A man sat inside. His black Stetson-covered head stared straight ahead. One arm was draped across the steering wheel.

Kane. Without hesitation Victoria went to the vehicle and got in on the passenger side.

His head swung around. "What are you doing here, Victoria?"

Neither his eyes nor his voice invited conversation. The tip of her tongue moistened her dry lips. His gaze followed. She felt again the unwanted tightening sensation in the pit of her stomach. "Why . . . why did you stop calling me Tory?"

One large hand clenched and then slowly unclenched on the steering wheel. "I don't think you'd like my answer."

She shifted against the black leather seat. "Kane, I know things didn't work out the way either of us planned, but I had things all worked out in my head and then I met you."

"You're not what I expected either," he drawled, disappointment heavy in his voice.

Victoria decided to ignore his baiting words. "This whole situation is awkward for both of us. Maybe if we got to know each other better."

"I don't think that would help." A flick of his wrist ignited the engine. "If you don't mind, I'd like to be on my way."

She did mind. "I know you want to wring my neck, but—"

"Is that what I want to do to you?" he interrupted, his voice stroking her.

There was no mistaking the husky inflection in his voice this time. Her heart thudded in her chest. This wasn't supposed to be happening to her.

"Kane, all I want is a business transaction. That way, both parties know where they stand and no one will get . . . the wrong idea."

"We've been through what you want. Now please get out of my truck." *The woman he remembered was gone, and there was no sense staying.*

"I need your help."

"I'm not interested."

"Eleven thousand dollars."

A finger and thumb kicked back his hat. "Not everyone has a price tag. Or is your ego so big you can't stand the idea of a man rejecting you?"

She leaned toward him. "That's the stupidest thing I have ever heard."

"Then get out of my truck."

"No."

"You've got three seconds," Kane warned.

"Twelve thou—"

"Time's up." Strong hands grasped her forearms, twisting and turning her in one deft motion. His mouth captured hers.

Victoria gasped in shock, inadvertently allowing Kane's tongue inside the warm interior of her mouth. Her body stiffened at the unwanted intimacy. But as the velvet roughness of his tongue touched hers, unexpected desire swept through her. She fought the need to join in the kiss until his teeth nipped her lower lip, then suckled the sweet pain away. By the time his mouth covered hers again, she had ceased to think.

Her tongue sought and found his. He tasted hot and sensuous. She had never known a kiss could be so potent. There was nothing she could do to control the fire racing through her body except hold on and try not to be consumed by it. But as their kiss deepened, her own hunger grew, and she made her own demands.

Slim arms circled his neck, knocking his hat off as her fingers plowed through his thick, black hair. From somewhere she heard a moan, then realized it was hers just as a callused palm covered the hard peak of her breast.

Suddenly, her mouth was free.

Her eyes blinked, focused. She lay across Kane's lap, her arms circling his neck. Kane stared down at her, looking as dazed as she felt. The sound of their labored breathing filled the truck's cab.

His hands tightened and his head dipped. Her lips parted.

Kane thrust her away. "God, woman! Don't you have any sense?"

Victoria's trembling hand touched her tingling lips. *No,* she thought, *because a man has finally kissed me senseless.*

Briefly, her eyes closed against the unwanted but undeniable truth. Kane had touched her in a way that no man ever had. She didn't like her response, but there was nothing she could do about it.

At least she knew that Kane wouldn't take advantage of her body even if her mind didn't have the sense to say no. She couldn't say the same thing about Stephen or any other man she knew.

She sat up. "I . . . I guess that shows you I'm not scared of you."

"It just shows that neither one of us is thinking clearly," Kane said, the ache in his lower body making him grind his teeth.

Victoria Chandler made a man forget everything except her honeyed skin, sweet lips and tempting body. A man would be a fool to willingly spend time with a woman who could tie his guts in knots. He had lived with that undeniable knowledge for nearly twelve years.

That night, so long ago, during a thunderstorm, he had tried to downplay his reaction to her. He was a man and she was a beautiful young woman. Why wouldn't he feel a healthy dose of sexual attraction? There had been only one problem. Early the next morning after the storm had passed, he had carried the sleeping Victoria to Bonnie's bed and hadn't wanted to let her go.

Disturbed by his desire for a woman he had been sent to protect, Kane made sure he left while she still slept. He stayed away from his aunt and uncle's house for a week. When he returned, Victoria had a new boyfriend.

Kane had gotten on with his life and wished her happiness in hers. Only it hadn't worked out that way. She had married a man who abused her emotionally. Kane now had a second chance to see what might have happened between them.

No other woman haunted his thoughts the way Victoria had. At the oddest times he'd catch himself trying to recall her softness, the scent of her perfume, the sound of her voice. The other women he had dated hadn't helped. He enjoyed them and promptly forgot them. He might feel lust and protectiveness toward them, but he never felt a need to shake the world and make it right for them.

When Bonnie had explained Victoria's problem, he had jumped to help. He hadn't been able to step five feet away from his cousin's front window since six-thirty that night. The first glimpse of Victoria had jolted him. She looked beautiful and frightened and determined. The night of the storm, she had looked the same way. Once again he wanted to slay dragons for her, but she had shrunk from his touch. Each time she pulled away it had been like someone flaying his back with a bullwhip. Yet, he had stood there. Now he needed closure.

He needed to know that the compassionate, sensitive young woman who had been more concerned about her grandparents and Bonnie's welfare than her own safety no longer existed. In her place was a woman who looked no deeper than the surface for a man's worth. He hadn't wasted his time with anyone so shallow since high school.

"Kane, reconsider." Tentative fingers touched his arm. His muscles bunched. This time she didn't pull back. "I need your help."

Kane looked into her rare-colored yellow-green eyes. Cat eyes, soft and pleading and full of passion and need. Just as her body had been against his earlier. Outwardly, she might pretend to be self-assured, but underneath dwelt the same insecure teenager he had held so long ago. And her kiss touched him as nothing ever had.

"I don't know, Tory." She smiled shyly when he said her name and Kane felt the kick in his stomach again.

"I'm glad you're not angry with me any longer. Why don't you come by my place tomorrow and we can have din—" She tucked her bottom lip between her teeth, then glanced away. "Perhaps we should go *out* to dinner." Finding a pencil and paper on the dashboard, she wrote her address and phone number.

"You're going to pretend that kiss never happened?"

"It won't happen again," she said, careful to keep her gaze averted from his face.

"Want to test your theory?"

His voice stroked her. Victoria breathed in sharply. It was a mistake. The scent of his cologne, spicy clean and compellingly sensual, invaded her nostrils. The imprint of his hand lingered on her waist, on her breast. Helplessly, she turned toward him.

"Do you?" he asked.

She was caught between his voice and his eyes, one minute soothing, the next crackling like leashed lightning. "I-I don't want this."

"Your mind may not know what you want, but your body does," he tossed out. Picking up his hat, he rammed it back on his head.

The truth of his words jolted her. "Now who has an ego problem? I know perfectly well what I want—a man who keeps his hands to himself and who does what he's told." Getting out of the truck, she took particular pleasure in slamming the door.

Victoria stalked back into the house and slammed the front door as well. "Who the hell does he think he is?"

"Your future husband," Bonnie said, her laughter echoing around the high ceiling of the foyer as she unrepentingly turned from spying through the window.

Victoria's glare only made her best friend laugh harder. "Your cousin is the most antagonistic man I have ever met. If there was the slightest hope of finding someone else, I'd tell him to go . . . go jump off a mountain."

"You're just upset because Kane is the only man who hasn't backed down from you."

"Whose side are you on, anyway?"

Bonnie held up her hands as she walked back into the den. "From now on, I'm staying impartial. This is one time I think Cupid could end up getting an arrow in the back."

CHAPTER 3

Clothes, from beaded and sequined evening dresses to functional day wear in silk and linen and cotton, in various lengths and colors, littered Victoria's king-sized bed. Standing before her mirror, she eyed her red jacket with its matching slim skirt and white shawl blouse, then nodded her head in approval.

The well-cut suit clearly stated the evening was to be a business meeting, not a social one. No more senseless kissing. The word "senseless" caused her to gnash her teeth.

She had been emotionally upset the previous evening. Kane had caught her off guard. This time, however, she planned on keeping the upper hand. Swallowing her pride and asking for his phone number from Bonnie had been bad enough. Then she had had to call twice before Kane had time to talk with her. All he said then was "I'll be there" and hung up.

"If I didn't need you, Kane Taggart, I'd boil you in oil," she said as she applied her lipstick.

Hearing the doorbell, she picked up her red handbag, draped the gold chain strap over her shoulder, and headed for the door. There was no reason to sit and chat. The sooner they left, the sooner she'd know Kane's price. She had found that most men had one.

Taking a deep breath, she opened the door. Her mouth dropped open. Kane, arms folded, leaned casually against the doorjamb as if he had expected her to keep him waiting. He wore a smile on his face as easily as he wore a western-cut gray suit. His gray-and-wine colored tie was silk.

His black eyes captured the reflection of the hall lights and twinkled. "Are you always going to do that when we meet?"

Heat flooding her cheeks, Victoria snapped her mouth shut. A man with eyes that compelling should have to wear dark sunglasses. "You look different."

"You don't," he said, his gaze leisurely running from her black hair in a loose coronet atop her head to her red pumps. "Ready?"

"Yes." Resisting the urge to slam the door again, Victoria stepped into the hallway. She wasn't vain, but he could have said something about the way she looked after all the time she spent selecting the right outfit. No sooner had the thought materialized than she quickly chastised herself. She didn't care one way or the other what Kane thought about her.

Kane leaned over to test the lock, and for a charged moment Victoria was trapped between him and the door. Her heart rate surged. He smelled of spice and man and danger.

Righting himself, he placed a hand beneath her elbow and started toward the elevator. "Are you always ready for your dates?"

"This isn't a date. It's a business meeting."

"Is that the reason for the suit?" He punched the elevator button, then gave her another leisurely inspection. "That red outfit is sending out mixed messages, or is that what you intended?"

"Mr. Taggart—"

"I thought we dispensed with the formalities yesterday."

"What we shared yesterday was a way of releasing tension. Nothing more," Victoria said tightly.

His index finger slid up and down the shoulder strap of her purse. "I didn't mean the kiss. I meant the reason for our meeting."

"Oh."

Kane smiled and Victoria thought again of boiling oil. The elevator doors slid open. Bristling, she stepped inside. The man infuriated her. Mixed messages indeed. She didn't want anything beyond a signature from him. Strumming her finger and thumb up and down her purse strap, it took her a few moments to realize she was stroking the exact place he had touched. She jerked her hand away.

Kane leaned against the paneled elevator wall and tried hard to keep the grin off his face. Never in a million years would he have thought he could make Victoria's body sing for him. Sure, he had dreamed; hell, he had even fantasized, but he never really thought it was possible until he had become angry enough to kiss her. He still couldn't believe she had turned to fire and need in his arms.

The night of the storm he had sat in a hallway with Bonnie on one side and Victoria on the other as torrential rain, golfball-size hail, and sixty-mile-an-hour winds beat against his uncle's house. Each time thunder shook the house, Tory burrowed closer to him. Yet despite her own fear, she kept trying to reassure Bonnie. She'd touched him with her compassion.

Bonnie had gone to sleep, but Victoria stayed awake most of the night and they had talked. He learned she was unpretentious and oddly unsure of herself. The lack of confidence in someone so beautiful and wealthy was surprising. He found himself trying to reassure her and holding her just a little bit closer. He had never felt so strong or so helpless as he did that night.

Out of the corner of his eyes, he saw two young women on the elevator whispering and pointing at him. Experience had taught him they were either discussing the best way to come on to him or marveling over his size. He had been born big and grew to a formidable height. Trying out for sports in junior high proved disastrous. He kept tripping over his size-thirteen feet.

It had taken him and his body a long time to come to an understanding. By the time he reached the tenth grade he accepted he wasn't going to wake up one morning and be a cover model unless it was for cigarettes. For whatever reason, all the classic good looks had gone to his younger brother, Matt.

Matt was the pretty boy. Yet they were as close as two brothers could be. That was one reason Kane hated to see Matt so cynical about women in particular and life in general, hated to hear people call him Hard Case.

His brother had two categories for women, the ones you slept with and the ones you called friend. So far, no woman had been able to be both. That didn't stop them from trying. Victoria probably would have gone weak-kneed over Matt, like every other woman. But Kane wasn't giving her the chance to meet Matt until after the wedding.

Kane looked at Victoria again. She was glaring at the two women. He grinned. Imagine, Victoria being protective of him. Apparently she hadn't seen the wink the younger woman had sent him. No matter how Victoria acted, she was a caring woman. And she was going to be *his* woman. If she agreed to his one condition.

"What brought you to Fort Worth, Kane?" Victoria asked mildly.

A black brow arched, then he said, "My horse."

"You rode a horse here?"

He laughed at the incredulous expression on her beautiful light brown face. "I drove a truck. Devil Dancer came in the trailer. He's entered in the calf-roping competition at the National Black Rodeo at the Fort Worth Coliseum."

Astonishment touched her face. "You're a rodeo performer?"

His smile vanished. "You have something against rodeo performers?"

"N-no, of course not. I just assumed . . ."

Kane straightened, giving her his full attention. "Assumed what?"

Victoria glanced around the elevator before she answered. "I just assumed the cowboy regalia wasn't real."

"Does it bother you knowing it is?"

She beamed. "Oh, no. I'm quite pleased, in fact. Don't some rodeo people follow the circuit year round?"

"Yes, they do," Kane replied in a clipped tone and watched as Victoria's smile broadened.

The elevator door opened, and people shifted to make room for an oncoming passenger. Something poked Victoria in the side. Frowning, she turned around and looked straight into Mildred Booth's face. Seventy, the old woman swore she was fifty, and was the worst gossip in town. Three years earlier, when the older woman had moved into the apartments, Victoria had seriously considered moving out. Now she wished she had. Unconsciously, she glanced at Kane.

Leaning over, Mildred whispered, "Big and mean looking isn't he? I don't blame you for staring."

Afraid that he might have heard Mildred, Victoria's mouth tightened. "That remark was uncalled for, and I wasn't staring."

Mildred waved Victoria's words aside with a wrinkled hand weighted down with rings on every finger. "High-strung, just like your grandmother. I do hope you're both coming to my party this weekend at the country club." Her voice dropped to a hushed whisper. "Everyone on the 'A' list will be there, including Harold."

"I have plans," Victoria said, staring straight ahead. Harold was Mildred's spoiled nephew, who thought he could buy anything, including a woman.

"My dear, surely you must be jesting," Mildred said, genuine astonishment on her sagging face, layered with powder and rouge. "Harold is one of the most sought-after men in the state."

"Then he shouldn't miss my not being there."

The elevator door glided open on the lobby floor. Passing by Victoria, Kane leaned over and whispered in her ear, "I'll meet you outside." Then he merged with the other passengers.

"Victoria, are you listening to me?"

Irritation flashed through Victoria; to think that she had to ignore Kane because of a gossipy woman like Mildred! "Sorry, I can't come to the party. I do my laundry on Saturdays." She brushed past the open-mouthed matron. Victoria's steps quickened as she saw Kane go outside through the revolving glass doors.

Standing on the sidewalk, she quickly scanned the cars lined up in the circular driveway of her high-rise apartment. No truck and no Kane. Feeling foolish and a little put out, she started toward the park across the street. Occasionally, she parked there if all the spaces in front of the building were taken and she didn't have time to park underground.

One of the reasons she moved to the apartment was beautiful Turtle Park. People from all over came to see the five-foot-tall red and white azaleas in bloom, picnic on the lush green grass, or simply watch the ducks meander in and out of the winding stream. At night the park was almost deserted, although lights dotted the walkway and shone down from the towering oak trees.

Two trucks were parallel parked in front of the park. One was dented and mud-splattered. The other one was clean. They were both black. Each had a trailer hitch. She bit her lower lip. Yesterday, she really hadn't paid much attention to Kane's truck. All she remembered was that it had been big and black and muddy. Unfortunately, vehicles of the same body style all looked alike to her.

Straightening her shoulders, she started toward the mud-splattered truck. She wasn't afraid of a little dirt or of Kane Taggart, for that matter.

Crossing the street, her heels clicking on the pavement, she went around to the passenger side of the truck and grabbed the handle. The loud, vibrating sound of an alarm blared from the truck's interior. Snatching her hand away, she staggered back.

"Hey, you! Get away from my truck!"

Victoria spun toward the rough voice. Two burly, unshaven men ran out of the park's darkness and into the revealing light. A frisson of fear shot through her. One of them pulled something out of his front pocket and pointed toward the truck. The grating noise stopped. The men, in dirt-smeared jeans, tattered shirts and steel-toed boots, closed in hemming her in between them and the truck.

"Hey, looks like we got lucky," said the one who had shut off the alarm. Rubbing his protruding stomach, he took a swig of beer from a can in his beefy hand. The two men traded laughs and elbow jabs.

Although both men towered over her, Victoria forced herself to relax. "I made a mistake. I thought this was my date's truck."

They jeered and hooted louder. "I heard you uptown babes like to go slumming. Don't chicken out. Me and Sam deserve something soft and nice after working on the high-rise all day."

She averted her head from grimy, questing fingers. "That may be; however, it won't be me. Now please step aside and let me pass."

The man who had spoken moved closer. Stale beer and body sweat assaulted her nostrils. "What if we don't wanna?"

"Then I'd say you're making a big mistake."

The coldness of the voice caused Victoria and the two men to whirl in unison toward the sound. Kane stood by the back of the truck. "Come here, Tory. They'll let you pass."

Although his stance was casual, there was something menacing and lethal in Kane's glittering black eyes. The men slowly and carefully backed away as if they were afraid any sudden move might make Kane's implied threat a reality.

Trying to mask her relief, Victoria went to Kane. His eyes never left the two men as he placed a possessive arm around her slim waist. Unable to help herself, she leaned into his comforting warmth.

"Apologize to the lady, then be on your way," Kane ordered with icy anger.

"You can't—" started the one who had done all the talking. Kane took his arm from Victoria's waist.

The man held up his hands and stepped back. "Hey, man. I didn't mean no harm to your woman. Sorry, lady."

"I could almost believe you meant it. If I see you bothering another woman, I won't ask for an apology, because when I'm through with you you won't be able to give one," Kane promised with controlled rage. The man's eyes widened in fear.

Kane inclined his head toward the truck. "Get out of here and re-member what I said."

The man scrambled around the front end of the truck and jumped inside. His buddy followed. Tires shrieked as the truck left the curb.

Kane didn't speak until the taillights disappeared around the corner. "Are you all right?"

She nodded. "Thank you."

"Do you mind telling me what you were doing bothering that man's truck?" he asked, leading her back across the street.

"I wasn't bothering his truck. Well, I was, but I thought it was your truck," she told him.

"That banged-up thing looks nothing like my truck," he said, stopping beside a gray Mercedes sedan.

"It did to me." At his disbelieving look she continued, "Automobiles of the same style look alike to me. The only way I can tell my car is by the license plate or the stuff inside. You'd be surprised how many red cars there are. I always have to write down where I park." She wrinkled her nose. "The security guards at the area malls know me by name. A couple of them let me park in restricted areas. They say it's easier that way."

Kane looked at her for a long moment, then burst out laughing. Victoria punched him on the shoulder. He laughed harder. His laugh was worth the last few anxious minutes, she thought. She liked the deep, rumbling sound of it.

Finally, he straightened, forcing himself to stop chuckling. "Does this car look familiar?"

She glanced at the gray car. "It's the same color as Bonnie's, only it's cleaner inside. Is this her car?"

"Not many rodeo performers could earn enough money to own a car like this," Kane said and opened the door.

She started to remind him that if he agreed to marry her, the money she'd pay him would be a nice down payment on a luxury car, then decided to wait until after dinner. "Why didn't you tell me earlier we were going in Bonnie's car?" she asked, getting inside and fastening her seat belt.

Kane waited until he pulled away from the curb before answering. "From what you said, you could have just as easily mistaken another car for it."

"I wouldn't have made that mistake if you would have waited for me," she said accusingly.

Accelerating, he took the entrance to the expressway. "I thought you might not want your friend to know that we were together."

"Mildred Booth is no friend of mine."

"Does the same go for Harold?"

With a feeling of dread, she asked, "Did you hear what Mildred said?"

"With these ears, there isn't much that I miss," Kane said, his voice flat.

Replaying the conversation in her mind, Victoria felt a strange need to touch Kane and reassure him. Knowing he might get the wrong idea, she tried to explain. "Mildred is tolerated only because her late husband was a noted civil rights activist before his death three years ago. She is an unkind woman who still wants to be the center of attention, and she doesn't care who she hurts in the process."

"You haven't answered my question about Harold."

"Harold is her nephew and almost as bad."

Kane sent her a quick glance as he exited the freeway. "Don't you know any good men?"

"No," came her quick reply. She refused to think that that might be her own fault, as Bonnie had pointed out.

"I guess that means I won't have to worry about some man trying to stop our wedding," he said easily.

Her heart thudded. Ignoring the tug of the seat belt, she turned until she faced Kane. "Then you've decided to say yes."

Kane looked at her with unreadable black eyes. "I've decided to get to

know you," he corrected. "Beyond that, I'm not making any promises except one."

"What's that?"

"I always kiss my date good night and, regardless of what you say,
tonight you're my date."

CHAPTER 4

Victoria recoiled. Her heart rate soared. "There'll be no more sen—*unnecessary* kissing."

"It might have been unnecessary, but we both enjoyed it," Kane said bluntly.

"*Tolerated* might be a better word," Victoria said, sitting against the door and staring at the downtown skyline.

"Are you always this dishonest about your emotions or is it just for me?"

Her head whipped around. "You have no right to say anything like that about me."

Kane cut her a quick glance. "Maybe not, but I told you I believe in honesty, and if you want my help, you better remember that."

"Just because I won't stroke your ego, you call me dishonest."

"If I wasn't driving this car, we'd both be stroking something else," Kane said, pulling into the Wellington Restaurant's crowded parking lot.

Victoria's throat dried. "Why do you keep saying things like that?"

Shutting off the motor, Kane unbuckled his seat belt and twisted toward her. "Because I remember a young woman who refused to give in to her fears, yet twelve years later, this same woman has locked herself behind a wall she dares anyone, especially a man, to try and climb over."

The truth of his statement annoyed Victoria She had cut herself off, but she had never regretted it until now. Kane might have been her friend under different circumstances. "You make me sound like some princess in a tower."

Kane shook his dark head. "A princess wants to be rescued. You're happy locked away from the world. The only thing I can't figure out is why you have to get married."

She watched him wearily. "I thought Bonnie explained everything to you."

"Only what I told you," he admitted and sent her a raking glance. "With a life like yours, you have about as much use for a man as I have for another head."

She opened her mouth to berate him for his cavalier judgment of her, but nothing came out. Instead, she studied the tight set of Kane's shoulders, the tighter set of his mouth. Thus far, he had asked nothing from her except honesty and she had given him anything but.

He awakened too many old fears. He was closer than he thought in scaling her wall of defense. "You wouldn't understand."

His eyes narrowed. "I might if you told me. I want to be your friend, Tory."

Seeing no way out of her problem, she drew in a deep breath and told him about her grandmother's ultimatum, including her own fabrication of having four men to choose from. She concluded by saying, "I'm as much to blame for this as my grandmother, but I've worked too hard to lose Lavender and Lace."

"I'm your last hope, huh?"

She gripped her purse. Letting Kane know how desperate she was wasn't a good idea, yet her being with him told its own story. "Let's just say I don't see anyone else trying to scale the tower wall."

"Some men are afraid of a few thorns. Come on, let's eat dinner and, if you're nice, I'll pretend not to hear you moan when I kiss you good night."

She had never been so embarrassed in her entire life. After Kane's outlandish remark, the night had gone downhill. They hadn't been seated five minutes before she knocked over her water glass. Each time she looked at Kane his gaze strayed to her lips and her stomach muscles clenched. His velvet laugh made the knot tighten and her annoyance rise. She had barely made it through dinner. She didn't want to feel anything for the man now patiently holding out her door key for her.

"Tory, don't be so hard on yourself. How could you have known that by trying to snatch the check from our waiter you would hit another waiter in the stomach, causing him to drop all those dishes?" The teasing smile on Kane's dark face was in direct opposition to his soothing words. "Don't worry, I left a big tip and paid for all the spilled food."

Victoria gritted her teeth against recalling the shock and humiliation of hearing the waiter's surprised grunt, the ominous sound of clinking china as the plates slid off the tray. Even worse was the memory of Kane literally snatching her out of the way of raining salad, oysters and soup.

"Tomorrow night we'll go someplace where it won't matter if you break every glass in the place," Kane placated.

First thing tomorrow, she thought menacingly, she was going to check on buying a pot of oil. In the meantime, she'd give him his kiss. But she'd give absolutely nothing of herself. "Just get it over with." Shutting her eyes, she tilted her head back.

Something soft and warm brushed against her forehead. Then nothing.

Opening her eyes, she searched for Kane. He was headed for the elevator. Without thought she ran after him. "You come back here, Kane Taggart. For the past hour and a half you had me worried about you kissing me and then you barely touch me?"

He turned. Black eyes twinkled. "Complaining?"

Her head snapped back. "Certainly not."

"I think you are. Tomorrow night we'll do it longer and slower."

"We will not."

"We will if you want my help."

"You're not touching me again."

His gaze darkened with promise. "Wanna bet?"

Gasping, she stepped back. "You are no gentleman."

"I don't remember that as being one of your requirements." Spinning on his heels, he started down the hallway.

"We don't have to go out again. You can tell me your decision now." She'd had all of the man she could stand.

"I never make any important decisions without sleeping on it first. Be ready at nine P.M." He never slowed his pace.

Fury swept through her. She was fighting for her life and he was being stubborn. "You make me so mad I could scream."

Stepping into the empty elevator, he faced her. "Someday I'm gong to make you scream for an entirely different reason."

Her insides clenched. She closed her eyes against the sensual promise in his eyes from thirty feet away. When she had the courage to open them again, he was gone. She groaned. Things weren't working out at all the way she had planned. She had wanted her future husband to be malleable and easily disposed of. Kane was neither. Worse, he was intent on making her sexually aware of him, and so far he was doing a darned good job.

Returning to her apartment, she saw a door a few feet ahead of her close. A tenant had moved in a few weeks ago and Victoria still had not met the new occupant. Mortification caused her to quicken her steps. This was all Kane's fault. Well, tomorrow night she'd show him she was in charge, then she'd get on with her life without a man cluttering it up.

Feeling more herself, Victoria gave serious thought to locating a pot for the boiling oil.

Victoria was restocking sachets in an eighteenth century armoire when she saw them through the plate glass window of Lavender and Lace. Something was wrong. Her grandmother's usually perfect gray hair looked windblown and two of the buttons down the front of her chiffon dress were unfastened. The pearls she always wore were missing—Henry Benson had given them to Clair on their wedding day and Victoria couldn't remember a single time seeing her grandmother without them.

Her grandfather, who prided himself on wearing dapper-looking ascots, was without one. The wind lifted his blue sports jacket, revealing the absence of his trademark red suspenders. Her always impeccably groomed grandparents looked as if they had dressed in a great hurry. Something disastrous must have happened for them to appear in public so disheveled.

They hung onto each other as if they were past their endurance. Worse, her strait-laced grandfather wasn't stopping at the door, as he usually did. On an ordinary day, he was embarrassed just looking at the lingerie-clad mannequins in the window.

Fear propelled Victoria across the room. "What is it? What's wrong?"

"My poor darling Victoria," cried her grandmother as she sniffed into a linen handkerchief with a two-inch border of lace.

"I'll beat the scoundrel like the dog he is," Henry Benson flared, his five-feet-five frame quivering with indignation.

Frowning, Victoria looked from one to the other. "What are you talking about?"

"The second cousin to God of course," Clair said, as if her statement made perfect sense.

"Perhaps we should continue this in my office." Victoria turned to the young sales clerk. "Lacy, I don't want to be disturbed."

Leading her grandparents into her office, she sat them on the couch and drew up a chair in front of them. "Now, start from the beginning."

"It's . . . it's all my fault. I never dreamed something like this would happen." Clair leaned her head against Henry's shoulder.

"Grandmother, what are you talking about?"

"The scoundrel you had the argument with last night at your apartment," Henry explained. "We know all about you having to submit to his baseness. Margaret Tillman heard you arguing with him."

"It's my fault." Clair dabbed her teary eyes, but it was clearly a losing battle. "As soon as I hung up the phone from talking with Margaret, we got dressed and rushed over here. Victoria, you must believe me when I say that I never thought things would turn out this way. I can't stop the loan being called in, but there has to be something we can do so you don't have to . . . have to . . ." She looked at her husband for support.

The hand Henry had around his wife's shoulder tightened. He looked at his granddaughter with blazing anger in his brown eyes. "You will maintain your honor."

The pieces clicked into place for Victoria. Apparently Margaret Tillman was the new tenant who had been listening to Victoria's and Kane's conversation. Margaret must not have heard the word "kiss," only words like "touching" and "it." Victoria looked at the two people she loved most in the world and hugged them both. "We were talking about a kiss."

"Margaret said he towered over you and the floor shook when he walked and his voice boomed like thunder," Clair persisted, apparently thinking the description aptly described a celestial being.

"Kane is big, but even he can't shake a sixteen-story building when he walks. His voice is melodious, not boisterous," Victoria said, not realizing her voice had softened. "I wouldn't go out with the kind of man you just described."

Clair and Henry traded glances. Relief visibly washed over them. Victoria found herself being hugged once again amid murmurs of apology.

"No apology needed. I'm glad you care." Victoria straightened. "Although, I think I'm going to have a talk with my new neighbor. She sounds like a busy-body."

"As a matter of fact, she is," Henry admitted. "I guess she wasn't wearing her hearing aid last night. I can't imagine a woman in her sixties being that vain. Mildred Booth recommended the apartment to her."

Victoria threw up her hands. "I knew I should have moved."

"Your marriage should take care of that nicely." Once more in control, Clair placed her handkerchief into her black patent handbag, then set about restoring some semblance of order to her clothes and her hair. Henry did the same.

"Grandmother—"

Clair smiled. "You don't know how you relieved our minds. For a while I thought I might have made a mistake. Might we assume since you're discussing a goodnight kiss that you have narrowed the field without our help?"

Only someone of her grandmother's generation would consider a kiss significant. "You might."

"Is he the cattleman?"

Victoria twisted in her seat. "Yes, Grandfather. He is."

Henry helped Clair to her feet. "Come, Mother, we mustn't overstay. First, I think you forgot something." He pulled a strand of lustrous pearls out of his coat pocket and fastened them around his wife's neck.

Clair took a snowy white neck scarf from her purse and tied it around Henry's neck. For a long moment they shared a special smile.

He turned to Victoria. "We're sorry we doubted you. It will be our pleasure to tell Margaret to mind her own business the next time you and your young man are having a discussion."

Considering she and Kane had a tendency to strike sparks off each other, Victoria thought that might be a wise thing to do.

Gravel crunched beneath the tires of the Mercedes as Kane pulled into a vacant parking space between two trucks. "We're here."

"Here" was the Cuttin' Inn, a country-western dance club. Somehow Victoria wasn't surprised. She glanced around the crowded parking lot. "It's a good thing I didn't try to find your truck here."

"That's a fact," Kane said, loosening his tie.

"What . . . what are you doing?" she asked unsteadily, glancing around the dimly lit parking lot.

"I'm taking enough of a chance going in there wearing dress pants. A coat and tie would send the boys into a fit of laughter so hard they'd probably fall down." He looped the tie over the mirror. "Only thing is that when they got up, they'd tease me into next year."

"These boys are your rodeo friends?"

His fingers hesitated over the top button of his white shirt. "Some of them are. Now, what are we going to do about you?"

"Me?"

"Suits and dance halls don't mix, and if someone got out of hand, I might hit and think later. The double-breasted jacket goes and the hair comes down."

"No. They'll accept me as I am or not at all."

Kane leaned back in his seat. "They'll accept you. I just want them to like the woman I might marry."

Victoria played with the clasp of her handbag. "I was planning on telling as few people as possible."

"Well, that's out. If there is a marriage, my family and friends will be there. Understand that now. That's one thing that's not negotiable," Kane said through stiff lips, his mustache a slash of black.

"You can't have everything your way."

"If I had things my way, you'd be too busy kissing me to do any arguing."

Victoria went hot, then cold. "This is a business—"

"Arrangement. Yeah, I know. So this business partner says we're going inside and dance. Tonight, when you met me at the door with a smile, I thought we might be able to get through one evening without arguing. I guess I was wrong." Opening the car door, he got out and slammed it shut. Victoria winced. Her door opened. "Come on," he said.

Slowly she got out of the car. Kane was right. She had started the evening determined to stop reacting to him emotionally and physically and show him her best side. That was easier said than done. "You, you didn't take off your coat," she stammered.

"It doesn't matter."

Victoria knew why his jacket didn't matter. One look at Kane's face and only someone with a death wish would laugh at him. Besides, he was right about the marriage. If there was one, her grandmother would shout it from the rooftop.

"Don't I have any say in whether we go inside or not?"

"Over my shoulder or walking?"

Kane didn't mince words. Whether she liked it or not, his meaning was out there for her to examine. Where else was she going to find an honest man on such short notice? She needed Kane. She mustn't forget that.

One hairpin, then another came out of her hair until all six were in her hand. Her hair fell into a luxurious black disarray around her shoulders. Putting the hairpins into her purse, she combed her fingers through the dark tumbling mass of curls, then removed her raspberry colored jacket and tossed it onto the front seat.

"Do you always pout when you don't get your way?"

"Men don't pout." His blue coat landed on top of hers. His fingers laced her own. "You'll enjoy the place."

"That remains to be seen. Let's see what the boys have to say about us."

Not a word.

Seven mouths were open, but nothing came out. Their owners were too busy looking. The five men and two women sitting in a curved booth at the back of the huge room hadn't said one word since Kane introduced Victoria as his friend. The only thing that moved were their heads as they looked from Kane to Victoria then back again.

"Are they always like this?" Victoria asked, her voice raised to be heard over the live band and the male singer's mournful voice lamenting his lost love.

Kane smiled tightly. "I think your beauty has made them speechless. But enough is enough," he said to his friends. "Or you'll make Tory nervous."

The man sitting closest to her jerked his straw hat off his balding pate and scrambled to his feet. The rest, including the two women, followed. "Beg your pardon, Miss Chandler, it's just that Kane never brought a lady—ouch!" He turned to the person who had elbowed him. The man nodded toward Kane.

Victoria's gaze followed. Kane's face was stern and forbidding, his body rigid.

"Pay no attention to Kane," Victoria said. "He's probably unhappy because he wants to dance."

The eyes went back to Kane, their mouths opened. "Is there anything wrong with that?" Kane asked.

Seven heads whipped back and forth.

"No."

"Not a thing."

Victoria took Kane's large hand in hers. "Come on and let's dance, before you turn into a bigger grouch."

Once on the wooden floor, couples swaying around her, her bravado faded. No matter how she tried to pretend otherwise, Kane did strange things to her equilibrium. She didn't understand it, she certainly didn't like it, but it was there nonetheless. "If you'd rather not dance, I'll understand," she said.

"Not a chance." Both hands settled gently on her waist. Victoria tensed in spite of herself. Kane's expression didn't alter. "Look around you, Tory."

She did. Every woman on the dance floor was being held the same way. She looked back at Kane. He waited with the patience of a mountain, apparently undisturbed that people were looking at them oddly because they were just standing there. It was her call. If she stepped into his arms it would imply more trust in him than she had given any man since her divorce. No matter what, she knew she could trust him. She lifted both hands and laced them around his neck. With incredible slowness, he drew her to him.

Awareness ripped through her. The heat of his body seemed to envelope her. Strangely, this time it comforted her rather than made her nervous. She didn't try to analyze why. She simply knew she was tired of being on guard around Kane, and he had proven he'd protect her, even from her own foolish emotions if necessary.

She relaxed and her eyelids drifted shut as his arms tightened around her waist. He moved with surprising ease, his steps sure and graceful. Her cheek rested on his chest. A smile curved her lips at the fast tempo of his heartbeat. Her smile faltered as she realized that he probably felt her erratic heartbeat as well. The music ended and she quickly stepped back and glanced up at Kane.

"Don't look so scared. You're safe . . . for now," Kane said, then winked. A devilish smile on his face, he led her back to the booth.

Several new faces waited for them. Someone pulled up a cane-back chair for her. She sat down and Kane stepped behind her, his fingers curled around the top slat of the chair back, his possessiveness obvious.

This time, no one had any difficulty talking. With a firm handshake and a smile, people introduced themselves. The names of their home-towns were as varied as the hues of their skin.

Surprise widened Victoria's eyes on learning that the short barrel of a man who had the courage to speak first was a "bullfighter." Ben said he preferred that name over "rodeo clown." Victoria understood once Kane explained Ben's job was to protect bull riders by playing dodge with two-thousand-pound angry animals.

Not to be outdone, the men who were bareback riders, steer wrestlers, and calf ropers were just as vocal. Jason, Oklahoma Slim, and Manuel got into an argument over who had won more belt buckles in previous competitions. Victoria glanced at Kane's waist and he shook his head.

"This time I bet you'll win one," she whispered, then turned her attention to Stony, a muscular young man with a wad of chewing tobacco stored in his cheek.

"I'm going to be the best pickup man in the business." Stony shifted the tobacco to the other cheek, then continued, "When the eight-second buzzer goes off and a man's lucky or skilled enough to still be ridin' a buckin' bronc and he's lookin' for a way off, I'll be there to lift him off as gently as if he were a baby."

Victoria saw the determination in the man's eyes and wished him luck. She soon learned some of the people were in town for the rodeo, others lived nearby. Everyone seemed to respect and defer to Kane. Victoria sensed it had nothing to do with his size. He was genuinely well liked and respected. Somehow she wasn't surprised.

Someone pushed a beer into her hand. Not wanting to remark that she didn't like beer, she accepted the foaming mug with a smile. After several minutes had passed and she hadn't taken a drink, Kane took the glass. She glanced over her shoulder and smiled her thanks, then turned to see everyone staring at her again.

"I'm afraid it didn't work, Kane."

His large hand tensed on her shoulder. "What didn't work?"

"Leaving our jackets in the car. We're still somewhat of an oddity, the way we're dressed," she said with wry amusement.

"No," a pretty brunette rushed to say. "I've been admiring your outfit." She looked at Kane. "Since I know you won't punch a woman, I might as well tell Victoria, before she thinks we all have fallen off our horses one time too many."

"Penny, some things are more dangerous than barrel racing," Kane answered.

Uncertainty crossed the young woman's face. Victoria hadn't seen Penny, an insurance adjuster from Oklahoma, so quiet since they were introduced. The other woman by her side appeared just as unsure of herself. Victoria stood. "Penny, could you and Kisha show me to the ladies room?"

Smiling sweetly into Kane's scowling face, Victoria linked arms with the two women. Five minutes later she had discovered that Kane hadn't brought another woman to the Cuttin' Inn in over two years, and when he had, they hadn't danced. The knowledge saddened her. Hadn't any other woman had the sense to recognize what a good man Kane was?

Penny must have read the expression on Victoria's face, because she said, "Don't think it's because he hasn't had the opportunity. He has. He's just particular. Kane's not the type of man to date just to have a woman on his arm. Unlike his brother, Matt, who changes women faster than he can rope a calf. He was the '91 champion."

Victoria frowned. "Kane didn't mention he had a brother."

"Kane nor any other man with good sense," Kisha said, repairing her lipstick. "Matt's as handsome as sin and he has a smile that could make an angel weep." She sighed. "His black eyes will make your heart go into overtime, *if* you're lucky enough to catch his eye."

"Catching his eye is not the problem. Keeping it on you is," Penny said. She and Kisha shared a look.

It was evident that both of the women had tried to interest Matt. Obviously they hadn't been successful.

Penny glanced at Victoria. "You're lucky to have a stable man like Kane."

"You make him sound as dull as week-old dishwater," Victoria said, aware that she sounded defensive.

The two women laughed. Kisha shook her head. "Kane? Dull? Cross him or do something to one of his friends and see how dull he is. Most men would rather tangle blindfolded with a bear than get on Kane's bad side. Like Penny said, you're lucky."

Victoria followed them out of the ladies' room, her mind on Kane. What had possessed her to take up for him? He could take care of himself. As for her being lucky . . . her luck had run out six months ago.

"You all right?"

Victoria looked up to see Kane standing near the end of the fifty-foot bar. She saw something she never expected to see in his eyes . . . uncertainty. It touched her as nothing had in years. "You have some very loyal friends. You're a fortunate man."

The tension seemed to ease out of his broad shoulders. He took her hand. "Come on. Since you said you never learned the "Cotton-Eyed Joe," the boys decided to have the band do it in your honor."

She grinned and held up her full skirt. "Lead on."

When the line went forward, Victoria went backward. Dancers kicked forward, she kicked backward. Kane never stopped laughing. His warm laughter flowed over her, through her, making it harder to concentrate. Finally, his powerful arm circled her waist and held her against the hard line of his body with an easy strength that fascinated and amazed her.

"Put your arm around my neck, honey," he grinned.

She did, despite the tingling in her body, despite the people in the line behind her and on her line shouting that she and Kane were cheating. Once or twice she asked Kane to put her down. He did, until she made a misstep and back up she went. When the dance ended, she still had one arm looped around his neck.

People circled around them, applauding. She hadn't had so much fun in years. With a start, she realized she had also forgotten the reason she was out with Kane. On some deeper level, she didn't fear or distrust Kane as she did other men. She didn't know whether to be pleased or not.

Reluctantly, Kane put her on her feet. One possessive arm remained around her waist. "I'm going to get Tory something to drink. She's probably thirsty from all that dancing," Kane said, a wide grin on his dark, craggy face.

Catcalls and good-natured jeers followed them to the bar. Victoria slid onto a wooden stool. Kane hooked one booted heel over the chrome footrest circling the bar and stood beside her.

"What will you and the lady have, Kane?" the bartender asked, wiping the scarred oak surface of the bar with a dry cloth.

"A diet cola," Victoria replied.

"A diet cola and a long neck, Jake."

Nodding, the bearded man turned away. Kane gently brushed the wisps of black hair off her forehead. "You really are having a good time."

Before she could answer, a tall glass clinking with ice cubes and a bottle of beer were plunked on top of cardboard coasters. She took a sip of cola. "You doubted?"

He rolled the bottle between finger and thumb. "I wasn't sure. I just wanted to bring you here."

"Why?"

"These are my friends. I wanted to see if you could be comfortable with them and they with you."

She tilted her head to one side and stared up at him. "I might have believed that two hours ago, but not now. You respect and like your friends, but you wouldn't care two hoots and a holler, as Penny would put it, what they thought about the woman in your life."

"You think so?" He took a swig of beer.

"I know so. Now, care to tell me the real reason we're here?"

For a long moment he stared at the foam disappearing in the brown bottle, then his gaze captured hers. "I wanted to hold you, and the only way I could think of was to take you dancing."

She felt humbled, special, and in trouble. She searched her mind for something to say and could think of nothing that wouldn't lead him on or hurt him. Her grateful gaze touched the beer bottle. "Thanks for taking my beer earlier. I can't stand the taste."

Kane spluttered, almost choking as he jerked the long-neck bottle out of his mouth. Alarmed, Victoria jumped off the stool to pat him on the back. "Are you all right?"

"Yeah." The bottle thumped on the bar. "Must have gone down the wrong way." Pulling out some bills, he laid them beside the discarded beer. "Ready to go back to your place?"

"Yes," she said, realizing instantly why Kane had stopped drinking his beer. The good-night kiss. Did he plan to kiss her on the mouth tonight? She had certainly acted like they were on a date. Her body tensed. Whether it was in fear or anticipation, she didn't know, and she wasn't going to look too deeply for the answer.

They walked back to their table and said their goodbyes. To requests that she come to the rodeo starting in two days, she gave a noncommittal "I'll see."

Becoming better acquainted with Kane's friends wasn't a good idea. If Kane agreed to help her, the least she could do was save him the awkward embarrassment of trying to explain what had happened to her after the divorce . . . as she had had to explain about Stephen.

Neither spoke on the way to her apartment. The only sound was the country and western music on the radio. Every song described a broken-hearted woman or man that was cheated on or left behind.

"Aren't any country and western songs happy?" Victoria asked, the lyrics increasing her nervousness.

"Some are, but I guess most of the time you have to hurt before you know what it is to love."

She glanced at him as he pulled under the covered driveway. "Have you ever been hurt?"

"Once."

"What happened?"

"She married someone else," he said softly.

The sadness in his voice tore at her heart. "I'm sorry."

"No sorrier than I am." He switched off the engine. "Come on. I guess it's time we talked."

Kane opened his door, feeling the tension back in his body again. In a matter of minutes he'd either lose or win the only woman he wanted for his wife. Victoria had her jacket back on, but her hair was still down. His hands itched to run his fingers through that hair, shimmering in the light, but he knew he couldn't. Not yet.

His hand gently rode the curve of her waist as they entered the elevator. Feeling her stiffen, he withdrew his hand and stepped back. Maybe he was crazy thinking his plan could work. But what did he have to lose? On the sixteenth floor, the doors slid open and they stepped off.

Inside the living room, Victoria asked, "Can I get you anything?"

"No." Kane looked around the room. Chic and stylish and feminine. It reflected the woman, with soft colors of peach and ivory and blue. There was nothing soft about him or the life he led, yet he wanted her to share that life.

Victoria sat on the sofa and took a deep breath. "What is your decision?"

Kane rammed his hands in his pockets, then just as quickly ripped them out again. "The decision will be yours, once I tell you what I want."

Something inside her heart twisted. "You mean you want more money. Is fifteen thousand dollars enough?"

"It isn't money I want."

She swallowed. "Then what is it, Kane? What do you want?"

"You, Tory. I want you to be my wife for real."

CHAPTER 5

Shock ripped through Victoria, widening her eyes, sending her heartbeat soaring. He reached for her. She shrank back in the chair.

"No. I-I told you I wanted a busi—"

"Forget the business agreement," Kane said fiercely. "I'm asking you to be my wife."

Panic-stricken, she rose. Her legs trembled. Blindly, she groped for the back of the couch to steady herself. "Kane, I don't want this."

"You think I don't know that? It's all I've thought about all night. Do you think I'd choose for a wife someone who can't decide if she wants to run *to* me or *away* from me?"

Victoria was too stunned by his counteroffer to try and explain the reasons behind her erratic behavior. "I'll double the money."

"I don't want your money. I want a wife."

She shook her head in bewilderment.

Kane clenched his fists to keep from dragging her into his arms. "Listen, Tory. I'm not some crazed fool who is going to abuse you or take advantage of you. You're Bonnie's friend, for goodness's sake. The first time I saw you at your and Bonnie's commencement, the other girls wore dresses, you wore a collarless white suit with a single strand of pearls and pearl earrings. Your hair was up. The whole family had come up for Bonnie's graduation."

"I don't remember seeing you."

"Would it have made any difference if you had?"

Victoria wanted to tell him that she would have smiled, but she knew at eighteen, she had been eager to test her womanhood. Kane had held her and soothed her fears, and she had never thought to seek him out and say thank you. At the time, she had been too busy with a new boyfriend. Stephen had taught her that cruelty worked both ways.

"You trusted me the night of the storm twelve years ago," Kane said softly. "Trust me again. Marry me, Tory. I'll make you a good husband."

She shook her head, her hand clutching her churning stomach. "I told you what I expected from you. I don't need a good husband. I only need a signature."

"What about someone to care for you, laugh with, share your dreams with?"

His voice, soft and coaxing, reached out to her. Her spine stiffened. "I don't need caring. I have my boutiques."

"Then what about what you feel when I hold you?" he asked gently. If he could get her to stop running from her feelings long enough to face them, they might have a chance.

Her churning stomach worsened. "I admit there's an unexplained 'something' between us, but I don't plan to give in to it or act on it."

He studied her for a long moment, his fist tightening. He had lost. He didn't want a woman whose barriers he had to knock down every moment they were together. Without trust, they had nothing to build on. "I don't guess you could have made it any plainer."

"Kane, I need you."

"What about *my* needs, Tory? Have you for one moment considered my feelings?"

"I offered you money," she wailed. Didn't he understand? Money was the only thing she could give him that wouldn't put her emotionally at risk.

Black eyes blazed. "I'm not Stephen. I want to give, not take."

The throbbing sincerity in his voice made her throat sting. "Don't you understand? I can't give in return. I don't know how and, even if I did, I won't be that vulnerable again."

Kane's face softened. "You're wrong, Tory. You give just by being you. I saw the way you looked at those two women on the elevator, the way you made my friends feel at ease around you. You have so much to give if you'd just let yourself."

"I'm not so giving that I'm going to jump into bed with you to save my business!"

"Your body is as hungry as mine, Tory. We both know it!" Kane's voice curled through her.

"Will you stop saying things like that? A few kisses doesn't prove anything."

Kane took a step closer, his eyes dark and compellingly sensual. "How many men have you kissed like you kissed me?"

Victoria ran a distracted hand through her hair and looked away from the temptation of Kane's mouth. "That's not the point. Anyway, what would you do with a wife while you're following the circuit?"

"I'm not with the rodeo," he said softly.

"What?" As if her legs were unable to hold her any longer, she sank into a chair. Her head bowed, her trembling fingers massaged her pounding temples. Kane kept throwing her one curve after the other.

Black cowboy boots came into her line of vision. Her head jerked up. "What is it you do?"

"I have a small place about a forty-five-minute drive from Fort Worth."

She looked at him with accusing eyes. "You could have told me that instead of letting me think you were a rodeo performer."

"You seemed to like the idea of my not being around. Besides, it doesn't matter what I do unless we can come to a compromise."

She sat up straighter. "What kind of compromise?"

"I still want a wife." He held up his hand when she opened her mouth to speak. "However, I'm willing to admit that asking you to be my wife for real might have been taking advantage of your situation. But, remembering how you kissed me, I didn't think you'd fight so hard." Victoria's back became straighter. "Therefore, I'm willing to give you your own bedroom. In return, you'll live with me for the length of our marriage. To the outside world, you'll be my wife."

"Live with you! I can't do that. I have a business to run."

"If you don't get married in sixteen days, there won't be a business," Kane reminded her.

For a moment, Victoria was speechless. How dare he use her deadline on her! The pounding in her temples began anew.

"Look at it from my viewpoint, Tory. People are going to talk anyway when they learn we married so quickly. If you stay in Fort Worth while I stay in Hallsville, people will have a field day. With all that talk, your grandmother is bound to become suspicious."

"What do you get out of it?"

He smiled wistfully. "A wife. Someone to worry about me if I'm late, have coffee with in the morning, share the day with."

"I'd be a substitute for the woman you lost?" she asked.

Once again his face became shadowed. "What does it matter as long as you get my signature on a marriage license?" When no answer came, his face strengthened into resolve. "I'll stick around until noon tomorrow. After that I'm gone and I won't be back."

She stood. Her hand clenched the back of her chair. "Twenty thousand dollars."

He countered. "Six months in my house in your own bedroom."

Again she ran a distracted hand through her hair. "Why can't you be sensible and understand that what you're asking for is impossible?"

"I understand more than you think I do. You're still locked behind the tower and letting Stephen run your life."

"That's crazy. I hadn't spoken to him in over two years until he called last week. His life is going down the drain and he obviously thought I was foolish enough to care. He was wrong. I can barely stand to be in the same room with him."

Kane's eyes darkened. "Or any other man. You've let your hatred for him dictate your reactions to everything. Instead of being thankful you wasted only eleven months of your life, you keep it before you like a mirror."

Her temper flared. "You can't stand there and judge me. You don't know what it was like. He made my life hell, then left me with nothing."

"Tory, stop feeling sorry for yourself. Your marriage to Stephen made you stronger, not weaker." His gaze bore into her. "Do you think you would have had the courage to go against your grandparents' wishes and start your stores if living with him hadn't made you stronger?"

"How do you know—" she started to ask him, then knew the answer. "How much has Bonnie told you about me?"

"It was less than I wanted. She's your friend first, my cousin second. Cheer up, Tory. Maybe the next man will free you for good." The door closed softly behind him.

Hands clenched by her side, Victoria headed to her bedroom. The phone rang as she passed the end table.

"Yes," she snapped, then grimaced at her caustic tone.

There was a long pause before the caller said, "I guess I don't have to ask if tonight went any better than last night."

Victoria plopped in a chair. "No, Bonnie, you don't. Kane wants me to live with him. In separate bedrooms."

"Seems reasonable to me. After all, you're asking him to give up other women. The least you can do is keep him company," Bonnie pointed out.

"I might have known whose side you'd be on."

Bonnie laughed softly. "I told you, I'm staying out of this. I love you both."

"Bonnie, why didn't you ever mention Kane was asking questions about me?" Victoria fretfully twirled the telephone cord around her finger.

"Didn't seem important, I guess. Kane is easy to talk to, and I admit I worried about you when you and Stephen were married. But you know I'd never betray a confidence," Bonnie hastened to add.

Victoria did know. She had told Bonnie more about herself than anyone else in the world, but there was one shameful secret Victoria would never tell anyone. "Kane does have a way of slipping past your defenses."

"But he'd never use it against you."

"Tell that to someone he isn't trying to blackmail."

Laughter floated through the receiver again. "Good night. I want a full report tomorrow."

"Good night." Victoria hung up the phone and stared at the front door. He'd be back. No man would give up twenty thousand dollars to live with her for six months.

"Victoria, you're going to rip the lace décolleté if you aren't careful. Why don't you just take off the arm, as you usually do?"

Slender fingers clutched the silk chartreuse camisole briefly, then continued to ease the spaghetti strap up the arm of the mannequin. "Did you need something, Grandmother?" Victoria asked.

Clair's sigh was loud and eloquent. "I thought you might be a little put out with me. My lawyer called this morning."

Victoria picked up the matching floral kimono and began slipping it on over the chemise. "Why should I be a 'little put out' as you call it just because I received a certified letter this morning giving me fifteen days to repay a loan of two hundred and fifty thousand dollars or turn over the keys to my stores?"

"Dear, you know that won't happen, because you're going to be married by then." Clair thoughtfully fingered the pearls at her throat. "You did take into consideration the length of time it's going to take to get the marriage license and blood tests, didn't you?"

Victoria turned, her yellow flared shirt swirling around her legs. Her headache was back with a vengeance. "Grandmother, was there something you needed?"

"No, not really. I called last night and didn't get an answer. I guess you were out with your cattleman again. All those late hours are putting circles under your eyes."

The tenuous hold on her patience snapped. "He's not my cattlema—"

She pivoted as the little gold bell over the stained glass front door jangled. Two young women came in and Victoria's assistant, Lacy, moved to help them. Victoria's hands clenched. Her gaze strayed to the wall clock. 10:45.

"What do you mean he's not your cattleman? Did you have another fight? Is that why you keep looking at the front door every time the bell rings? Is he coming here?" Clair asked in an excited rush.

"No, Grandmother, that's not what it means."

"What is it, dear? I haven't seen you this upset since you discovered Stephen was being unfaithful." Clair gasped. "He isn't married, is he?"

"No."

Clair relaxed. "For a moment you had me worried. Don't think this entire matter hasn't disturbed me." Frail fingers touched Victoria's cheek.

"You're all I have left of your dear father, all the hopes and dreams of the Chandlers rests with you. For all of us, you have to remarry."

Feelings of dread climbed up Victoria's spine. There was no way out of the web of lies she had helped spin. "If I don't?"

Fear darkened Clair's eyes and pinched her lips. "Then you will lose Lavender and Lace and I will lose you." Tears sparkled in the older woman's brown eyes. "I don't see how I could stand that."

Fighting her own tears, Victoria hugged her grandmother's small frame to hers, smelled her familiar lavender scent, felt her grandmother's arthritic hands try to squeeze her granddaughter into acceptance. If Victoria lost the shops, there would be no winners.

Choices were gone.

Kane's counteroffer flashed through her mind. She shied away from the thought of living with him. Not because the thought repulsed her, but because it didn't. She didn't want anything in her life she couldn't control. But she no longer had the luxury of having things her way.

Gently pulling away, Victoria opened her grandmother's black patent purse, found the lace handkerchief she knew would be there and dried her grandmother's eyes. "Everything will be all right."

Clair looked doubtful. "Are you sure?"

"Yes." Victoria answered with more assurance than she felt. Sealing her fate, she said, "I'm seeing him today."

"When can we meet him? Does he come from a big family?"

Victoria answered the only question she knew the answer to. "I'll see if he can come to the dinner party you're having tonight."

"Please assure him he'll be welcomed." Clair shook her graying head. "I'll need a distraction with your grandfather's side of the family there."

"He may have other plans," Victoria pointed out quickly.

Clair gave Victoria one of her stubborn looks. "Then it's up to you to change them." She tugged on her white lace gloves. "One question?"

"No, you don't know him."

"That wasn't the question."

"All right."

"Has he kissed you senseless yet?"

Victoria's cheeks flushed. Her hands flew up to palm her face, but it was too late. Her grandmother smiled and began humming the wedding march from *A Midsummer Night's Dream*. The boutique's front door closed softly behind her.

One hour, three phone calls, and two wrong turns later, Victoria pulled her red Jaguar into the back parking lot of the Fort Worth Cowtown Coliseum holding the National Black Rodeo. Trucks and trailers, in every description and size, from chrome-plated and air-conditioned to faded and dented, littered the area.

Stepping out of her car, her nostrils were assaulted with the earthy scent of cattle and horses. Recalling the statue of Bill Pickett, the first black rodeo performer, at the entrance to the coliseum, her uneasiness returned. The inventor of bulldogging was portrayed biting the lips of a steer as he brought it down. Apparently rodeo performers were unique individuals, and so were the men who worked with them. Brushing an unsteady hand over her white suit, she started toward the bold red entrance sign to find Kane.

The white leather heels of her pumps clicked on the hot pavement. Dressing in white to remind Kane of their meeting years ago had been her last-ditch effort to sway him, although Kane didn't strike her as a man easily influenced.

"It's about time you came to rescue us."

Victoria glanced around to see Penny. With her was a man wearing jeans and a blue chambray shirt. The brim of a black Stetson shaded the upper part of his brown-skinned face.

"Hello, Penny," Victoria greeted. "What are you talking about?"

"Kane. He's been as grouchy as a bear." She glanced at the tall man beside her. "Victoria Chandler meet Matt Taggart, Kane's brother."

Victoria's gaze swung back to the silent man. His nutbrown face was unbelievably handsome, yet no warmth shone from his piercing black eyes. He was as still as a shadow and appeared to be as unfeeling. She found nothing but his black eyes and powerful build to indicate any relation to Kane. She couldn't see what fascinated Penny about him.

"Hello, Matt."

"So, you're the one," Matt said, his voice low and deep, his eyes studying hers intently.

"The one what?" Victoria asked. When Matt didn't answer, just continued to study her with unblinking black eyes, she dismissed him and asked Penny, "Can you tell me where I can find Kane?"

"I'll take you to him," Matt said.

His offer surprised Victoria, since he had yet to show any friendliness toward her. "Penny can show me."

"She needs to practice and Kane is in a restricted area. If you want to see him, you'll have to go with me." Without looking at the other woman, Matt asked, "Penny, don't you think you should get going?"

After one longing look at Matt, Penny left. Victoria felt sorry for the other woman because Matt seemed to have already dismissed her from his mind.

"To have attracted Kane's attention, there must be more to you than a beautiful face," he said bluntly.

"From what I've heard about you, I can't say the same," Victoria tossed back.

He laughed, a gravely noise that sounded as if he hadn't laughed in a long time. Victoria's eyes widened at the change it made in his face. It was wickedly sensual. At last she saw the fire behind the shadow. Women would line up in droves to draw the real man from behind his facade. Yet she wouldn't try for all the gold in Fort Knox. That kind of man would leave you crying and never even notice there were tears on your cheeks.

"Come on. Penny's right about Kane. Let's go put him out of his misery."

They followed the white fence until they came to the gate of a small arena. As soon as Matt opened the gate, Victoria saw Kane. Her heart rate kicked into overtime. Arms folded, he leaned back against the fence. He didn't look any happier than she felt.

Matt let out an ear-piercing whistle. "Kane, a lady is here to see you."

Kane glanced up. He and Victoria's gaze met, held. His expression softened. Pushing away from the fence, he took several running steps then stopped abruptly. His face became hard and shuttered as he looked from her to Matt, who was holding her arm.

"I think I'd better leave. So long, Victoria." Tipping his Stetson, Matt walked away.

Uncertainty kept her from moving. Thirty feet separated her from Kane, yet neither moved. Then he started toward her again. Too nervous to smile, she clutched the strands of perfectly matched pearls around her neck.

"What's your answer?"

"You're asking too much."

"Of which one of us? Is it asking too much for a wife to spend six months out of a year with her husband or too much for a husband to give up the pleasure of his wife's bed?" He glanced at his watch. "Make your decision, Tory. It's twelve, straight up."

CHAPTER 6

"Why do you want a woman interfering in your life, asking you to take out the garbage, pick up your clothes, wash the car?"

"You're evading the issue and you know it," Kane responded smoothly.

Knowing that Kane easily saw through her diversion didn't help. Victoria swallowed. "How about a week?"

"Goodbye, Tory." Gently he pushed her out of the way and closed the gate. He turned away with her looking through the slats.

Just keep walking, Kane told himself. Put one foot in front of the other.

His body obeyed, but that didn't help the pain twisting his gut. He hadn't realized how much he wanted her to say yes until she turned him down. He had gambled and lost the only woman he had ever loved. Before the kiss in his truck he only wanted a woman who had haunted his thoughts. Somewhere between then and now, desire had strengthened into love. When it happened didn't matter. He loved a woman who was afraid to love.

He knew himself well enough to realize that having Victoria for a wife and not being able to touch her would have slowly killed him inside. But it would have been worth the gamble to get her to love him and share his life.

Maybe it wouldn't hurt so bad if he didn't know she was fighting her attraction to him. No matter what she said, she still judged every man by Stephen. And until she took the first step to put her ex-husband behind her, she'd never be free to love Kane or any other man.

It was time he left Fort Worth and went back to his ranch. Victoria wasn't going to change her mind and he wasn't going to change his. But the plunging neckline of her suit jacket had almost done him in.

From his height he could detect a bit of white lace against the rounded curve of her honey-colored breasts. If that wasn't enough of a temptation to Kane, her skirt reached six inches above her beautiful knees. Lord, but he had almost been enticed into swallowing his pride and taking her on any terms.

The chute across the arena opened, and out burst a three-hundred-pound calf. Matt, riding Devil Dancer, was right behind the animal. With a practiced twist of his wrist, Matt widened the rope's noose as it twirled over his head. At the exact moment he released the twenty-five-foot lariat, the black Angus spun in the opposite direction.

He missed by three feet. Knowing a second loop took precious seconds and usually kept the roper from receiving prize money, Matt didn't attempt another throw. To the sound of good-natured jibes and instructions, Matt took the slack from his rope, the animal forgotten. All the on lookers knew the calf would run for the gate expecting to get out as was the customary practice during a real rodeo event.

All except Victoria.

Please, don't have followed me this time. Even as Kane thought the words, he turned. What he saw made his heart stop. Victoria, standing in the gate, looking at him.

"Get out of the way!" he yelled, and started running, calling out for Matt.

Finally, Victoria saw the black streak running straight toward her. Instead of moving, she screamed one word, "Kane!"

Booted feet pounded the dirt-filled arena. Animals were unpredictable. The calf might veer around Victoria but it could just as likely run over her. Knowing he had one slim chance to keep Victoria from possible injury, Kane kept his eyes on the Angus, praying he'd intercept the animal before it reached Victoria.

His heart hammering, his lungs bursting from want of air, Kane ran. Just a few more feet.

Determined hands grabbed around the animal's neck. The calf immediately protested by bucking and twisting sideways toward the unwanted obstruction. Kane hung on, digging his heels into the ground and twisting the calf's head back, its nose up.

Both elbows ripped through Kane's white shirt sleeves. The animal went down and didn't move.

Matt jumped off his horse while the chestnut was going full speed. Using "piggin string," Matt tied three legs of the downed calf in two seconds.

Kane's midnight eyes blazed as he stood and faced his brother. "What the hell do you mean letting the damn calf get away?"

"He ran for the gate. I didn't know she was there."

"You shouldn't have brought her here!"

"Kane, do you really want to tear a strip off me or see to your woman?" Matt asked calmly.

"She's not my woman!"

"And it's eating you up inside."

Kane raised his fist. The younger man didn't flinch. "I'd let you beat hell out of me, big brother, if I thought it would make you feel better. It won't. Take Victoria to my trailer."

Kane looked at Victoria. What he saw made his gut twist violently again. Her face was pinched in fear. Her arms were folded protectively around his damn hat, her purse lay a few feet away.

He grabbed her purse in one hand and her elbow in the other.

His hands were trembling, but his voice was as sharp and as biting as a bullwhip. "I told you to go home. Don't you ever think before you do something?"

He stalked through the open gate without a backward glance. "Everyone knows how unpredictable animals are, and nobody but a fool would stand in front of the gate unless they know how to scale a fence."

Going up the steps of a trailer home, he opened the door and pushed her inside. "Can you scale a fence, Tory?"

She mutely looked at him.

Without benefit of undoing the buttons, he tore the ruined shirt from his body leaving only his white T-shirt. He twisted the faucet on the kitchen sink and water gushed forth. He washed his hands. Finished, he jerked a paper towel. The entire roll hit the floor.

He cursed.

She whimpered.

His hands fisted.

His angry gaze settled on his hat. "Stop clutching that damned hat," he ordered. Snatching the Stetson from her fingers, he flung it to the floor. "It doesn't mean a thing to me. It can't feel pain . . . it can't . . ."

His eyes closed, his hands shook. He drew in a ragged breath.

"Kane, if you're going to fuss, do you possibly think you could do it while you're holding me?" Her voice was a wobbly thread of sound.

"Oh, God, Tory. If I touch you . . ."

She bit her lip. If Kane didn't put his arms around her, she was going to lose what little control she had managed to hang onto. She needed to feel his strength. "P-please," she whispered. "I—" Her voice broke.

He swept her into his arms, felt her body tremble. His arms tightened. "You're safe, honey. Don't cry." He sat on the couch because he wasn't sure how much longer he could stand. He settled her in his lap. "I'm sorry for yelling. Don't cry, honey. The calf probably would have run on past you. I'll bet being bulldogged scared him as much as he scared us." Knowing he shouldn't, yet unable to help himself, Kane kissed her eyelids, the curve of her lips.

"I-I don't think that's possible. I was so frightened."

"I should have made sure you were safe." Self-condemnation laced his voice.

She pushed away from his chest and studied his dark brown face. "It wasn't your fault." Trembling fingers tenderly stroked his cheek again and again as if in reassurance. "It was mine. I shouldn't have followed you." Her body shuddered. "If anything had happened to you, I never would have forgiven myself."

Ebony eyes held hers. "You were scared for me?"

"When you grabbed that animal, all I could think of was that if you were hurt it was because you were trying to protect me. You told me you weren't a rodeo performer." She swallowed. "Kane, I know you're probably tired of hearing it, but I am sorry."

"Now that you're safe and my heart is out of my throat, I'm not. I got you into my arms again." His hands stroked the curve of her back. "If you don't want to be thoroughly kissed, speak now or be prepared not to speak for a long time."

Victoria glanced up through tear-spiked lashes. "I don't think we should."

"Probably not, but we are if you aren't off my lap in three seconds and counting."

Knowing how much she wanted to stay gave her the will power to move from the security of his arms onto the couch.

Kane immediately pushed to his feet. "If you're feeling better, I'll help you find your car."

She didn't move. Instead she watched Kane pick up the roll of paper towels and slip them back into the holder. Despite her refusal of his counteroffer, he had not hesitated to protect her from danger, then from himself. He always put her first.

How many men wouldn't have taken advantage of her vulnerability or would have remembered she needed help in locating her car? How many men would be that generous or caring? Kane deserved better from her than she had given him.

The words began softly, cautiously, then gathered strength and momentum. "Lavender and Lace is the only thing I've ever been successful at. Mother finished summa cum laude at Spelman: Daddy finished magna cum laude at Morehouse. They were number five and six in their med-school graduating class at the University of Texas.

"My parents balanced their social and professional lives as skillfully as they wielded a scalpel. They lectured all over the country. The best I ever did was the seventieth percentile. They never said anything, but I always felt somehow I had let them down." She closed her eyes for a moment, then focused on her clasped hands in her lap.

"They died in a boating accident when I was twelve. I went to live with my flamboyant grandmother and indulgent step-grandfather who loved me, but again I was overshadowed. I couldn't get over the feeling that I should be smarter, wittier, prettier." She looked up and met Kane's intense gaze without faltering.

"I met Stephen when I was a junior in college. He was handsome, a smooth talker, and a hustler. He made me feel important. I got a marriage license instead of the degree in business I always wanted." Her lashes lowered, concealing the pain in her eyes. "Lavender and Lace is the only thing I'm good at."

Kane was stunned by Victoria's confession. He remembered sensing her insecurities the night of the storm, and couldn't believe she hadn't outgrown them. Despite her devastating divorce, despite her grandparents' wishes to the contrary, she had taken charge of her life, stood on her own feet and succeeded.

"My life revolves around my stores. I'd do anything to save them except put myself at risk emotionally. You want something from me I can't give," she finished softly.

Kane heard the fear and vulnerability behind Victoria's words and wanted nothing more than to lift her chin, pull her into his arms, and kiss her until she was breathless and aching with desire. But that was what she was afraid of . . . the mindlessness that overtakes a woman when passion rages through her body. She didn't want anything in her life she couldn't control or couldn't walk away from. She didn't want another failure. Not even in a sham marriage.

But what made his heart swell with pride and love was knowing she was trying to protect him from being hurt as well.

It had taken a great deal of courage to bare her soul to him, to confess her so-called failures. Obviously, she thought it would lessen her in his eyes. But it had only strengthened his feelings for her. *This* was the caring, compassionate, courageous woman that he had carried in his heart for so long. If it was within his power, he was going to take that haunted look from her eyes and show her the good things about herself she didn't see.

To accomplish that, he needed her to say yes to his proposal. He now realized he had gone about trying to convince her the wrong way. She was too stubborn and too wary of men to be pushed into a marriage that wasn't on her terms, but she could be *lured*. Thank goodness, he finally knew how to entice her. He was going to appeal to her greatest strength, her compassion for others. He only hoped he was a good enough actor to pull it off.

"I guess I came on pretty strong at times," Kane said mildly.

Her head lifted. "A little."

"Sorry, Tory. I guess after we kissed in the truck my brain went south." As Kane expected, Victoria ducked her head and began fiddling with the clasp of her purse again. "I can't believe I found someone to solve all my problems and I blew it."

Her head snapped up. "Problems?"

This time it was Kane who ducked his head. "I'm usually pretty self-sufficient, but lately I've gotten tired of going home to an empty house and eating meals alone." He sent Victoria a slanting glance. "If I go out with my married friends and their wives, I feel like a fifth wheel. Or I'm given the unwanted name of some woman their wives think would be perfect for me. If just the married guys and I go out, I have to listen to them talk about their wives. If I go out with my single friends, by the end of the evening they're ready to pick up anything breathing. I'm left alone again. That ever happen to you?"

Slowly she nodded. "I learned to take my car whenever I'm meeting single friends for dinner or drinks."

Kane's broad shoulders slumped as he crossed his arms and leaned against the counter top in the kitchen. "Then, there are the times when I stay home. I'm hungry, but nothing in the refrigerator appeals to me and even if I felt like driving, I don't know what it is I want to eat. Nothing on the TV is worth watching, and the book I wanted to read can't hold my interest past a couple of pages."

Kane sighed loud and eloquently. "I don't realize I'm lonely until the phone rings and I break my neck getting to it. Nine out of ten times it's a solicitor and it takes all my willpower not to hang up on them."

This time Victoria spoke without being prompted. "I guess most single people feel lonely once in a while."

"You been to your high school reunion yet?"

Victoria blinked at the seemingly arbitrary change of subject. "No."

Kane suspected Victoria probably thought bulldogging the calf had rattled his brain. "Last year at my high school reunion, I was the only one out of my class of two hundred and seventy eight that hadn't married. Some were working on marriage number two or three." He shook his dark head. "I'm going to pass on going to my college reunion in July."

"Why?" Victoria asked, unwittingly walking right into Kane's trap.

"Everyone will be asking if I got married and I'll have to say no. I've already heard from a few of the guys. As soon as I tell them I'm single they start trying to match me up with someone." His gaze sought hers. He couldn't tell if she was swallowing his line or not. For good measure, he tried to make his voice sound as sad as he hoped his face looked. "You would have been perfect and saved me a lot of trouble. No one would have suspected that you were pretending to like this face of mine."

"There is nothing wrong with your face," Victoria snapped defensively.

He didn't smile, but his heart did. "After Bonnie explained your problem, I really started looking forward to going back to Prairie View. You would have been by my side, my arm around your waist, maybe a kiss or two."

Victoria bit her lip.

Kane wondered if he should have left the kissing out. No. She needed to know up front they were going to act like a happily married couple in public. He only hoped one day it wouldn't be acting.

"If we had gotten married it sure would have helped me out. You don't know how tired I get of the measuring looks from my friends when they talk about their wives and families. Even my mother has started giving me a hard time. I stopped telling her when I was coming home because I don't want to be cornered by some woman my mother thought would make me a good wife."

At least that was the truth. The last time he had gone to Tyler to visit his parents, not less than three women just happened to drop by. Any fool could have seen it was a setup. After the last one had gone, he warned his mother if she ever did that again, he would get in his truck and leave.

"She sounds like Grandmother," Victoria said.

Kane sighed. "She keeps telling me she wouldn't worry about me so much if I had a wife to take care of me. I can take care of myself, but it would be kind of nice having someone who worried about me if I was late coming home. Being married would have given me some breathing space with my mother and friends, a wife for the reunion, and someone to come home to."

Unfolding his arms, Kane pushed away from the counter. He wished he could tell if she was weakening. "We could have really helped each other out. I guess I better see you to your car."

He walked over to her, grasped her gently beneath the elbow and helped her to her feet. As soon as she was upright, he stepped back. "I'm sorry I blew things with you by coming on too strong. I'd ask for another chance, but I know how difficult it is for you to trust men."

"I trust you, Kane," she defended.

"Enough to give me a second chance?" he asked. The ringing silence and her downcast head was his answer. "I bet Matt wouldn't have any trouble finding a wife."

Her head snapped up. "He'd have even more trouble. Pretty men usually have pretty big egos. You're kind and dependable."

"You just described a dog I once had."

She hit his chest with a closed fist. "Don't say that!"

His dark brows drew together. "Tory, you sure you feel all right? You want to lie down?"

"No, I don't." She took a deep breath, looked into Kane's eyes, which held so much concern for her, and knew what she had to do. "I hope you continue to be this solicitous about me after we're married."

He went still.

"We both have reasons for getting married. I don't see why we can't help each other." She wasn't going to find a better man than Kane to marry. She doubted if one existed. "Three months living together should be enough time to get your mother off your back and get you through your college reunion."

"Done," Kane blurted and extended his hand.

She lifted hers. "My grandmother and your mother will just have to be happy with a year of marriage."

He expected a lifetime with her. His hand closed over hers, his thumb stroked her skin. "You'll make a beautiful bride."

The velvet softness of his voice caressed her as much as his thumb did. Liking both too much, she quickly withdrew her hand. "My grandmother wants to meet you. The entire family will be there, but I don't want to mention our engagement. I couldn't stand all the questions."

His dark brow arched. "Are you sure that's the only reason?"

She frowned. "What other reason could there be?"

"I'll give you one guess," he answered with a wicked smile.

Her eyes blazed. "Will you give it a rest! If we're going to be married I can't be bothered watching every thing I say for fear you're going to take it the wrong way." Victoria gave him her grandmother's address. "Dinner is at seven. It's up to you if you want to come." The door shut with a decided snap behind her.

"Well, I'll be." Kane threw back his head and laughed. Victoria really knew how to dig her spurs into a man's hide. He rubbed his hand across his face. He had pushed too hard, but more than his next breath he wanted to see pride and love in her eyes when she looked at him. He should have known he'd be greedy where she was concerned.

After putting on one of Matt's shirts, Kane snatched up his misshapen hat, rammed it on his head and followed Victoria. He had a feeling this time she would wander the parking lots located around the stockyards all afternoon without coming back to ask him for help.

Kane caught up with her less than thirty feet away. "Promise me you'll put me in my place if I get out of line again."

The rigidness left her shoulders. She stopped and looked up at him. A shy smile curved her lips. "I will . . . if you promise to help me find my car."

"It's a deal, but there's one thing we forgot about our engagement."

"What?" she asked wearily.

"This." His head dipped, his lips took gentle possession of hers.

"Would you care for more apple pie, Kane?" asked Clair.

Swallowing the last bite of his second large slice, Kane shook his head. "No, thank you, ma'am."

Clair beamed at him, then at Victoria, as if they had given her something precious and rare.

Kane studied the petite yet regal older woman in ecru lace and pearls. Clair Benson wasn't what he had expected. She was charming and genuinely warm. She treated him like the proverbial prodigal son. Within two minutes of his and Victoria's arrival it was also obvious that his new fiancée was Clair's favorite among the fourteen other assorted relatives.

Despite their being late, Clair had insisted two chairs be brought into the living room so they could sit next to her. When they went in to dinner, Clair's husband escorted Victoria, and Kane took Clair's surprisingly firm arm.

"Do you come from a large family, Kane?"

"Grandmother, please. You've been quizzing him all evening," Victoria said.

"Kane doesn't mind. Do you, dear?"

Kane smiled. "I've got a feeling that whether I minded or not, you'd still want an answer."

"Age does have its privileges."

Victoria groaned.

"I'm the oldest of three children. The baby's a girl." Kane grinned. "But since she is about to get her chemical engineering degree from A&M, she doesn't want us calling her 'baby' any longer."

"I thought it was just you and Matt," Victoria said, before she thought.

"It never came up."

Victoria sat back in her chair. It had never come up because she hadn't asked him anything, except how much money he wanted for his signature. "You must be proud of her."

"We all are."

"You should be." Clair nodded to Henry and rose. Everyone followed suit. "Victoria, take everyone into the living room. I'd like to show Kane something that I'm proud of."

"Grandmother, I—"

"I know you'd be happy to do it for me." Clair laid a hand on Kane's arm, then placed one on her husband's, who had come to her side. "We'll be in shortly."

Victoria heard the buzz of her relatives around her and knew they were speculating about her grandmother's attachment to Kane. If she wasn't so grateful that her grandparents had appeared to like Kane on sight, she might have balked. "Shall we go into the living room?"

"Wasn't she a beautiful baby? She's so special."

Kane looked at the black and white picture of the thin child who had her thumb in her mouth while holding the hem of her mother's flared skirt in the same hand. "I don't think we came in here to talk about Tory's childhood."

"Perceptive of you, young man," Henry said, looking over the wire rim of his glasses.

"Do you think a lesser man would have our Victoria in a dither?" Clair asked her husband.

"What did you say?" Kane asked.

"Don't go dumb on us now." Clair closed the oversized photo album. "What we'd like to know is why, since you and Victoria obviously care about each other, you had her so upset earlier today. If it's because you need money—"

Kane came to his feet. "I think I'd better go."

"Do sit down, Kane, and stop glowering at me, or Henry will have to take you to task," Clair said.

Kane glanced at Henry, who remained unmoved in his leather easy chair, his legs stretched out in front of him on a hassock, his hands folded across his lap.

"Please do as she asks or I'll have to defend her, and I don't relish any of my bones being broken, especially at my age," Henry said mildly.

"If we thought all you wanted was money, we'd never let you through the door. We learned our mistake with Stephen," Clair said with heat.

"You should have protected her from that pile of—" Kane flushed and took his seat. "Sorry."

Clair patted Kane's hand. "I don't like to speak ill of others, but in Stephen's case, it's justified. It occurred to Henry and me that cattle ranching is a very unsteady business and you might be a little hesitant in asking for a woman's hand."

Kane almost relaxed at the antiquated term of asking a woman to marry you. "The ranch is solvent."

"Then there is no reason why you can't ask Victoria to marry you."

"That, Mrs. Benson, is between me and Tory."

"Did you know you're the only person she allows to call her anything besides Victoria?" Clair persisted. "There has to be a special reason."

"No, I didn't. As for a reason, I stopped trying to figure out why women did things before I got out of high school." He rose. "If you don't mind, I'd like to join the others."

Clair smiled indulgently. "I do believe you're as stubborn as I am."

"No," Kane said. "That dubious honor goes to Tory."

CHAPTER 7

The alarm clock's strident buzz woke Victoria. A groping hand shut off the intrusive noise. For the first time in days, worry hadn't prodded her from sleep and driven her from her bed long before the alarm sounded. It was all because of her engagement to Kane. He had given her back Lavender and Lace. But in his giving, he had taken as well.

He had taken away her ability to group him with other men. He was Kane. Rugged, aggressive, yet so tender with her that she felt better just being around him. Rolling from her side, she lay back in bed staring at the gathered peach moire half-canopy overhead. What was there about Kane that slipped past her defenses, making her want to take the frown from his face? Whatever it was, she was going to remember they had a business arrangement and nothing else.

Throwing back the comforter, she got out of bed. Kane was picking her up around twelve to go get their marriage license, then they were going for lunch. Today he'd see a poised Victoria, not someone who shivered at his slightest touch. Today she would not spend her time wondering about a man who could be as rugged as a mountain or as gentle as the stream that wound through it.

However, once at Lavender and Lace, she continued to think about Kane. He clearly puzzled her. No one in the past had put her needs above theirs. Her parents had loved her, but she had understood from an early age that they had social and professional obligations to meet.

By forcing her into marriage in hopes of continuing the Chandler line, her grandmother put her own wishes above Victoria's.

Only Kane had put her first. He hadn't taken advantage of her moments of weakness in his arms or of her need for a husband. She paused in hanging up a slinky black chemise.

A man as giving as Kane deserved a woman who would cherish him as much as he would cherish the woman he loved. She would have to do a delicate balancing act of giving him a make-believe wife while not becoming too emotionally involved. Perhaps she should have said no kisses.

"I hope I'm not the cause of that frown?"

She pivoted. "Kane! What are you doing here so early?"

He stepped closer. Her body heated. "I needed something."

"W-what?"

A long, tapered finger traced her quivering lower lip. "Guess?"

Her throat dried. What must she have been thinking to agree to a public display of affection? Kane was too good at making a woman feel special and needed. "I can't leave the store now."

His black Stetson jerked in a clerk's direction. "Can't she take care of things?"

"Melody is very competent, but I usually help and it's almost time for her lunch break." Victoria stepped around him and away from temptation. This time when they talked, she was going to be sensible. No more kissing. "Melody," she said, going behind the solid oak counter. "You can go to lunch now."

Melody, petite, pretty, and a redhead for the past three days, glanced at Kane who leaned against the eighteenth century armoire, his arms folded as if he lounged daily in the midst of a lingerie shop. He tipped his hat, his dark gaze returning to a fidgeting Victoria.

"Is he yours?" Melody inquired.

Used to the young co-ed's direct way of speaking, Victoria simply gave her the answer she sought. "Yes."

"Does he have a brother?" Melody persisted, her voice carrying as she gave Kane a thorough once over.

Kane grinned. "One, and he's a lot harder to catch."

"Melody, you're wasting your lunch time." Victoria reminded her, then grimaced as she heard the irritation in her voice.

"Sorry, but it isn't often you see a man so well built. He's got some killer eyes, too. I'll just get my purse and leave." Retrieving her purse from the back, she did just that.

Kane pushed away from the armoire, his steps slow and predatory as he came to Victoria. Reaching over the counter top, he lifted her chin with finger and thumb. "Thank you."

"For what?"

"For pretending to be a little jealous."

"I don't know what you're talking about," she informed him, turning away.

"Oh, no you don't," Kane said, his incredibly gentle hands palmed her face. "I've seen compassion and desire in your eyes. Jealously, even pretending, is something I never hoped for, and you're not going to deny it."

"We *are* engaged," Victoria said, thankful he didn't realize she hadn't been acting. What had happened to her earlier plans to keep things on a business level?

"That we are." A rough-tipped thumb stroked the smooth line of her jaw. Her stomach somersaulted.

Her hands closed over his. "Kane, you can stop now. No one is in the shop."

"Yes there is." He inclined his head toward the front door.

Victoria snatched her hand away and quickly skirted the counter. She hadn't heard the bell. Thankfully, the young woman was a repeat customer and knew what she wanted. As soon as Victoria finished the sale, she returned to Kane.

"I think we sh—"

"How do you buy those things?" he interrupted.

Following his pointing finger, Victoria saw a reclining mannequin wearing a black lace merrywidow with plunging underwire cups. Garter straps hung down over a black G-string bikini and attached to lace-trimmed black stockings. "By sizes."

Kane looked at her, his eyes hovered briefly on the rise and fall of her breasts beneath her yellow silk blouse, and he asked, "Sizes of what?"

Heat climbed from her breasts to her face. The twinkle in his eyes gave him away. "You should be ashamed of yourself."

"Didn't you know that when a man takes a wife he has no shame?" he asked softly.

"I-I'm beginning to."

"Finally, I'm getting somewhere. Now, wrap everything up," he ordered.

"You're serious?"

"I am." He leaned closer. "Maybe if I get lucky, I'll get to see my wife wearing them."

Excitement and uncertainty vied for her attention. Uncertainty won. "Kane, you shouldn't have to get lucky to see your wife wearing lingerie."

"Considering we're only pretending, I do," he teased. "But I am looking forward to sharing other things with you, like watching the sunset, having breakfast, going on a picnic."

"I haven't gone on a picnic since I was a little girl," Victoria said wistfully. "I bought a basket a while ago but I never got around to using it."

"You will now. I know the perfect spot." His fingertips gently touched her cheek. "You're going to knock the guys' socks off when we go to Prairie View for my college reunion. Now, let's see what else there is."

Taking her hand, he stopped in front of a red satin teddy. Fingering the lace at the bodice, he looked back at Victoria. His eyes narrowed. For a second his hand tightened on her arm, then loosened. He stepped away.

The front door bell sounded again. The customer and the one after her needed Victoria's assistance. Pointing to the front door, Kane mouthed "twelve" and left. Her gaze followed until the matronly lady asked Victoria about bath crystals in a tone that clearly stated she had asked the question before.

Showing the customer the different fragrances, Victoria glanced back at the closed door. Kane was apparently enjoying their engagement, but she was in deep trouble and sinking further each time he came near her.

Precisely at twelve, Kane returned. Victoria tilted her head toward the back office. Nodding, Kane walked in that direction. After she finished ringing up a sale, she followed.

"Business seems good," Kane said, looking around the room cluttered with several opened boxes.

Obtaining her purse, Victoria nodded. "This time of year is always busy with vacations and weddings." Her eyes slid away from Kane's.

His large hands spanned her waist, drawing her and her gaze to him. "You won't be sorry, and you'll never have to be afraid of saying no." His head bent, his warm breath flowed over her lips.

Victoria inhaled sharply and tasted something mint flavored. Instead of stepping back as she had intended, she licked her lips. Kane did the rest. Warm lips brushed against hers so fleetingly that Victoria's lashes barely settled against her cheek before they lifted again.

"If I kissed you the way I wanted, we'd miss lunch and I'd get into trouble for overstepping our bargain." Her hand in his, he started from the room. "Now, let's get going. We have a lot to do."

The phone rang just as they reached the door. Quirking a dark brow, Kane released her hand. "Make it quick or I might have to start nibbling on you."

Flushing, Victoria picked up the phone. She wondered if there would ever come a time when her body would be immune to Kane's teasing. She sincerely hoped so.

Her voice was breathless when she spoke, "Lavender and Lace." Pause. "Hi, Bonnie. Yes, he's here." She handed Kane the phone. "She wants to talk with you."

"Hey, Bonnie, don't you get tired of bothering us?" Kane spoke jokingly into the receiver. His smile abruptly faded. "Mama?"

His uncertain gaze flicked to Victoria. "Yes, ma'am, it's true."

A hard knot settled in Victoria's stomach. Instinctively, she stepped closer to Kane.

"Don't cry, Mama. I was going to call you." He paused. "Yes, I'm with her now. Addie? Sis, don't tell me you're on the line too. No, you can't have a discount, and get off the other phone. Now!" He rubbed his hand across his face. "Sure, Mama, you can talk . . ." He glanced heavenward. "She won't think you're strange for crying." There was another pause. "That sounds fine, Bonnie." His expression looked anything but fine. "All right, Mama. Goodbye."

Hanging up the phone, he leaned against the desk. "Since it's Friday, my sister came home from college for the weekend. She called Bonnie to thank her for her graduation gift, and Bonnie told Addie one of her brothers was getting married. She yelled out to Mama, who thought it was Matt. Bonnie finally explained that it was me. Then Bonnie hooked us up to a three-way call. I guess you heard the rest."

He rubbed the back of his neck. "I wanted my parents to hear about the wedding from me. Mama was crying and talking about losing her firstborn."

"How did you plan to explain to them that a woman is using you to regain control of her business?"

"I'm a grown man, not some idealistic kid. I don't have to explain anything to my parents or anyone else," he said fiercely. "I run my own life and make my own decisions. I meant they deserved to hear about our engagement from me first. I'm getting as much out of this marriage as you are."

"I shouldn't have told Bonnie last night when she called," Victoria admitted ruefully.

"It's all right, but there's something else."

"Why do I have the feeling that I'm not going to be pleased?"

"The whole family is coming up tomorrow evening at six to meet you. Before they do, I think it's about time I showed you where I live."

Kane was in trouble.

He knew it the moment he drove across the cattle guard to his ranch. Victoria's entire body tensed on seeing the initials K and T on each of the ten-foot black iron gates. Gripping the truck's steering wheel, Kane continued the mile-long drive on the paved road to his house.

A winding stream meandered on his left. On his right, red Herefords lolled beneath cedar and oak trees or at the salt block. The white-faced cows' mooing broke the silence of the countryside. Kane wished something would break the strained tension inside the truck.

He pulled up in front of his two-story frame house bordered by a bed of dark gold zinnias. Kane grimaced on seeing his quarterhorse, Shadow Walker, run to the corral fence and nicker in greeting.

Getting out of the truck, he walked around and opened Victoria's door. "Come on, I'll show you around."

Without a word, she complied. Deciding to save the house for last, Kane started toward the outer buildings. Victoria became stiffer as he pointed out the barn, the stable for his registered quarterhorses, the tractor and hay combine under the galvanized shed, the bunk house for the three full-time hired hands.

Finally they started back. The house, painted white and trimmed in blue with blue shutters, had a wraparound porch. Three large baskets of ferns and a porch swing shifted in the gentle spring breeze. Kane opened the front door and stepped aside for her to enter.

Gleaming oak hardwood floors stretched from the front room to the staircase and beyond to the glass-enclosed porch. Hundred-year-old oaks shaded the enormous back yard. His worried glance flickered around the large open room filled with overstuffed chairs and antique furniture he had rescued and lovingly restored. It wasn't classy like her home, but it had a casual comfort that he liked.

"Grandmother would love this room."

Kane let out a sigh of relief. At least she was talking to him. "I'm more concerned with what you think."

She swung around. "The two-car garage I saw in back. Would it happen to have a gray Mercedes in it?"

Kane's expression turned grim. "Yes."

"Is this the reason you didn't want the girls at The Cuttin' Inn talking to me alone?" Victoria asked.

"Partly," Kane answered truthfully. "You seemed to think money was the determining factor for us getting married. It never was for me. I thought it more important for us to like and trust each other than for you to know I didn't need your money."

"How many acres does this 'little place,' as you put it, have?"

"Tory—"

"How many?"

"Just under a thousand."

Her hazel eyes glittered. "You're rich!"

"Depends on your definition of rich," Kane said, trying to lighten the mood. At Victoria's continued glare, he explained further. "I grew up on a small farm on the outside of Tyler in East Texas. The football coach in high school thought I'd be perfect for the defensive line, but I kept tripping over my feet or someone else's."

"Kane, there is nothing remotely clumsy about you," Victoria said without thought. "You move with the self-assurance of a man who knows who he is and where he's going. You must have been going through an adolescent phase of awkwardness."

Kane smiled. Even being upset with him, Victoria rushed to his defense. But the resurgence of the glitter in her hazel eyes told him he wasn't off the hook. "Coach Phillips also happened to be my algebra teacher. He discovered that what I lacked on the football field, I made up for academically. He liked to dabble in the stock market and got me interested. By the time I went to Prairie View on a math scholarship, I was pretty good at it."

"What happened to get you from there to here?" Victoria asked, her body no longer rigid.

"Nothing, for a while. I got my MBA in banking and finance, went to work as a financial consultant for an investment firm, and kept in touch with Coach Phillips." Kane shrugged his broad shoulders. "While I made some good investments, I quickly learned the only way I was going to stop being nine-to-five was to get in on the ground floor of a company before it went public. I started saving so I'd be ready."

Admiration shone on Victoria's face as she leaned against an overstuffed chair and waited for Kane to finish.

"The chance came with a phone call from Coach Phillips four years after graduation. A small cosmetics company in Dallas specializing in moderately priced skin care and makeup products for African-American women was going under and looking for backers. I checked it out and quickly discovered the company also needed a strong marketing plan and sound financial management to survive. After getting good feedback from mother and some of her friends who tested the products, I knew my chance had finally come."

"I only knew I wanted to be my own boss. Luckily, I was friends with a savvy businesswoman who owned a specialty dress store. She gave me a lot of good advice," Victoria said.

"Why did you choose lingerie?"

"Women deserve to feel pampered and beautiful." Victoria folded her arms. "Nothing can do that more than having something soft and luxurious next to her skin."

Kane started to argue that the right man could make a woman feel the same way, but decided he'd do better to keep the conversation in relatively safe waters. "I told the owner I could save his company, but in return I wanted a twenty percent share and a voice in the operations."

Victoria rolled her eyes. "Why doesn't that surprise me?"

"If you don't believe in yourself, who will?" he asked pointedly. Victoria remained silent. "Anyway, my investment paid off. Cinnamon is among the top cosmetics firms in the country. About two years ago, I decided it was time to cut back on the time spent with the company and enjoy life more. My partner and the original owner, William Conrad, thrives on the hassle of running a corporation almost as much as he enjoys being solely in charge. I enjoy the ranch. This way we both get what we want and I don't have to worry about the fluctuating price of beef."

"I've heard of your company. You should be very proud of yourself." She straightened and looked him squarely in the eye. "I only have one question left. Why did you want to marry *me?*"

Kane was in trouble again. He had to be very careful how he answered. "I told you why I wanted a wife."

She glanced around the antique-filled room and shook her head. "Not all of it. I might have believed I was your last hope yesterday, but not after what you just told me and seeing this place. You wouldn't have had any problems getting a wife. Some women can be as heartless as men when it comes to being greedy. Why me?"

It was on the tip of Kane's tongue to blurt out everything until he realized Victoria wasn't ready for the truth. She might be attracted to him, but she was fighting it every step of the way. Nothing would make her run from him faster than telling her he loved her.

"Well?" she prompted uneasily. "And remember, you believe in honesty."

"Some of the women I've dated saw my money and not me. Others only wanted a good time. A few just wanted to get married to the first man they could drag to the altar," Kane said without bitterness. "I needed a woman I could trust. A woman who had as much at stake as I did."

Victoria nodded in understanding. "With me, you knew I stood to lose Lavender and Lace if anything went wrong."

He may not have been able to tell her he loved her, but he could tell her how special he thought she was. "With you I get a woman who is compassionate, kind, loyal and beautiful. If I prayed to God on bended knees for a thousand years, I couldn't have gotten better. And . . ." His eyes twinkled. "You're really getting good at this pretend kissing stuff."

Her face softened moments before she tucked her head. "You shouldn't say things like that."

"I know, but it's such a pleasure to tease you and watch you blush. I never thought I'd find a woman like you. Maybe this will help you forgive me." Reaching into his shirt pocket, he withdrew a ring. At her continued silence, unease twisted through him. "Don't you like it?"

Victoria looked at the square-cut diamond surrounded by emeralds. The brilliant stones glowed with an inner fire reflecting the sunlight filtering through the large double windows behind her. "You're doing it again," she said, her voice barely audible.

"Doing what?" Kane frowned, clearly puzzled.

"Overdoing it. Giving and expecting me to take. Ours isn't a real engagement. I don't need a ring."

"I thought we settled this last night. To all outside appearances our marriage will be the real thing. Everyone who knows me would be suspicious if you didn't have a ring on." One long finger stroked her cheek. "Wear my ring, Tory."

"I can't," she said quietly. "You should save it for your real wife."

"Then I guess you better put this on, because for the next year you're going to be my real wife," he said, picking up her left hand and sliding the ring on the third finger. He never planned for her to take it off.

"Will you listen to me," Victoria said, trying to free her hand. "I'm not wearing your ring."

"Wanna bet?"

"You're weak, Victoria. Weak. Weak," Victoria mumbled to herself as she walked out the leaded glass front door of her grandparents' house at ten minutes to six. Ruefully, she looked at the beautiful ring glittering on her left hand. She should have been stronger. But Kane had looked at her with those "killer eyes," as Melody had called them, stroked her with his velvet voice, and she'd forgotten about resisting.

For so long now she had prided herself on being her own woman, making her own decisions. Since Kane had entered her life, she didn't appear to be able to do either. Now, she faced the added responsibility of meeting his family.

Kane and his parents would be coming down the boxwood-edged driveway and pulling up within minutes. Brushing a hand over her beige linen suit, she shifted from one foot to the other. Her stomach had been in knots since leaving Kane's ranch the previous day.

On the return trip to town they decided the best thing to do was to stick as close to the truth as possible. A call to Bonnie confirmed that she hadn't told his mother where or how Victoria and Kane had met. Although Bonnie had an early-morning flight out of DFW Airport to New York for an art show, she promised to come and give moral support that evening.

A gray car appeared, followed by two trucks, one of them black. Kane opened his door first and started toward the car. A few feet behind him walked a stunning young woman with stylishly cut short black hair. She wore a cropped herringbone jacket, a white blouse, and wide-legged black trousers.

Bonnie and her mother, Doris Fisher, emerged from the front seat of the car. Out of the back stepped a slender, gray-haired woman whose smile was slightly hesitant. Kane put his arm around her waist, then took the arm of the raw-boned man who had climbed down from the truck Matt drove. Releasing the older couple, Kane came to stand by Victoria.

"Mama, Daddy, Addie, I'd like you to meet Victoria Chandler, my fiancée."

Victoria extended her hand. "I'm pleased to meet you."

Mrs. Taggart's black eyes misted. "Kane, she's beautiful. I always knew you'd choose someone extraordinary."

"Why should a son be any different from his father?" Mr. Taggart said, his gaze warm and loving on his wife.

"Hello, Victoria," Addie said. "He's the best there is, so treat him nice."

"Hey," Matt called as he walked up to the small group. "What about me?"

Addie snorted. "Why would any sensible woman marry you when she could have Kane?"

Matt smiled, and this time it almost reached his eyes. "I once knew a sensible woman who stood in front of a calf running for the exit gate in order to get a man's attention."

Victoria flushed.

"Don't mind Matt, Victoria," his mother said, giving her middle child a stern look. "We have so much to talk about. I want to know everything. Where and when you met? Why I'm the last to know?"

Victoria's smile slipped only for a second. "Please come inside. We'll talk there. My grandparents will want to meet you."

"They've already met Kane?" asked Mrs. Taggart crisply.

Victoria glanced at Kane. "He came to dinner the other night."

"They know about the engagement?" Censure laced Mrs. Taggart's voice.

Victoria and Kane exchanged another look. "We called them after Kane talked to you," Victoria said, glad to be able to tell the truth about something.

Mrs. Taggart's expression softened. "Then I wasn't the last to know."

"No, Mama, you weren't," Kane said. "But from what I know about Victoria's grandmother, she probably already has the wedding planned."

"I hope not," his mother said. "There are a few things I'd like to have a say about."

Kane and Victoria exchanged another look and groaned.

"The rose garden will be perfect for the wedding."

"All the Taggarts have been married in church."

"The colors will be pale pink and white."

"Peach would be prettier."

"She'll carry roses."

"Gardenias."

They agreed on nothing. Although Clair Benson and Grace Taggart sat close to each other, their ideas were light years apart. They had started planning "the children's wedding" five minutes after the introductions. Dinner and protests from Victoria and Kane were seen as minor obstacles. To Victoria it was no wonder the men left as soon as they finished dessert.

Their excuse was to watch Matt in the calf-roping finals at the rodeo. The look of relief as they almost ran for the door told its own story. The Taggarts might be a rodeo family, but hers wasn't. Yet her own grandfather had supervised the fast exit. Bonnie, Doris, and Addie gave Victoria sympathetic glances and tried to remain out of the war zone.

Victoria kept her eyes on the sitting room door. One hour ticked into the next. How long did it take to rope a calf anyway? "Matt's best time is 5.3 seconds. The record is somewhere around 4.8 seconds."

Victoria's startled gaze swung to Addie, who had an impish smile on her beautiful almond-colored face. Realizing she had spoken aloud, Victoria glanced around.

"Pay attention, Victoria," admonished Clair. "It's nice to know you miss Kane, but we have work to do. You can't even decide on a simple thing like the flowers for your bouquet, let alone big decisions like china or crystal patterns."

Panic swept through Victoria. There was no way she was going through that again. "Grandmother, Mrs. Taggart, perhaps we can just spend the time getting to know each other and finalize the plans for a small wedding later."

"That's just it, Victoria," Mrs. Taggart chimed in. "We don't have the luxury of putting anything off. I can't believe Kane only gave you two weeks. You both deserve a proper wedding."

"As long as the minister pronounces us man and wife, it will be," Kane announced from the doorway.

"Kane!" Without thought, Victoria was on her feet and running to him. His arms closed around her waist and pulled her close. The comforting warmth of his body reassured her. She pressed even closer.

"That bad huh?" he asked gently, and smiled down into her upturned face.

The rumble of his deep voice vibrating through Victoria made her want to curl up in his lap. Her eyes widened with the realization of where her thoughts had strayed and what she was instinctively doing.

She tried to pull away. His arm became a steel trap. The smile on his face remained, but the eyes were unrelenting. She wasn't going anyplace.

"If anyone is interested, I came in second," Matt stated laconically.

"What stopped you from being first?" Addie asked.

"That's right, Kitten. Keep him humble," Mr. Taggart said as he and Henry brought up the rear.

Matt grunted and leaned against the door frame.

The Taggart family laughed. Victoria glanced around and again saw the family closeness. No one noticed that she had panicked. They were too involved in sharing Kane's illusion of happiness.

"Matt, you know I care, but at the moment we're trying to plan a wedding on an impossible schedule." Mrs. Taggart picked up a color chart. "Victoria has yet to pick out her colors."

"I don't know about hers, but mine is any color she's wearing," Kane said, a lazy smile on his dark face.

Warmth Victoria didn't want to feel, shouldn't feel, spread through her. Kane always said the right words. Why couldn't she do the same without getting restless? She pulled away and this time he let her go.

"I think we should have the reception with a sit-down dinner at the Four Seasons," Mrs. Taggart suggested.

Clair straightened in her seat. "Well, I don't. If the wedding can't be here, I insist the reception be held in the garden."

Mrs. Taggart shook her head. "You have a beautiful home and I'm sure the grounds are just as lovely, but ours is a big family, plus all of Kane's friends. If they can make it, I'd say we're looking at two hundred people easily."

Victoria's eyes widened. "You're planning on feeding over two hundred people at a sit-down dinner?"

"It will be our wedding gift to both of you. Thanks to Kane's financial advice, his father and I can afford to be generous," Grace said proudly.

"No." Victoria said. "It's too much. We're having a simple wedding. Isn't that right, Kane?"

"Whatever you say, Tory. Thank you, Mama, Mrs. Benson, but it's up to Tory. Go get your things, honey, and I'll follow you home."

"Kane, you can't take her home. We have too much to decide," Clair said, looking at Grace Taggart for support.

"Kane?" Grace said hesitantly.

"We're leaving," Kane said, a note of finality in his voice.

Grace leaned back in her seat. "I'm sorry, Clair. When he gets stubborn, there is nothing anyone can do to change his mind. Since his decisions are usually sound ones, the family learned to give in a long time ago." She sent her eldest a penetrating glare. "Now I'm beginning to wonder if that was such a good idea."

Kane grinned. "I love you too, Mama."

"I'm ready." Victoria reentered the room, her car keys in one hand and her purse in the other.

"Good night, everyone, and thank you for sharing tonight with us.

Thank you for having us, Mr. and Mrs. Benson. Mama and Daddy, I'll call tomorrow." Kane brushed a kiss across his mother's cheek, then led Victoria to her car.

"Thanks for the rescue. I wasn't sure how much more I could take."

"It will be over soon."

"I may not last that long."

"Kane, Victoria. Wait a minute," Addie called as she ran down the walk to them. "Please don't kill the messenger, but both of you are expected back here after church tomorrow to continue discussing wedding plans."

Victoria looked at Kane. "We should have escaped while we had the chance."

Things are getting out of hand, Victoria thought as she drove to her apartment. Tomorrow, her grandmother and Kane's mother would politely ask Victoria and Kane their opinion, then do exactly as they wanted. Unfortunately, what they wanted was to turn a quiet ceremony into a social event.

A large wedding would only make things worse for her and Kane. Instead of acting like an ecstatic bride-to-be, she knew she would act the way she felt, scared and unsure of herself. Deceiving hundreds of guests would be next to impossible. She'd embarrass and humiliate Kane. She couldn't do that to him.

Another increasing concern was her growing attraction and dependence on Kane. His size and strength might once have intimidated her, but she was beginning to rely on that same size and strength. And reliance on a man, even one as nice as Kane, was sheer stupidity.

Neither of them spoke as they took the elevator to her floor. Inside her apartment, Kane said, "Sorry, Mama means well."

"Kane, I'm the one who should be apologizing." Victoria tossed her purse onto an easy chair. "Your mother is doing what any woman in her place would do. It's not her fault I'm a fraud."

"Tory, don't." He reached for her, but she moved away to pace the length of the fireplace.

"You should have heard her after you left. She was so pleased that some unscrupulous woman wasn't marrying you for your money." Shaking her head, she glanced away. "I can't go through the next thirteen days planning a big wedding I know is going to end in divorce."

"I'll have a talk with my mother."

"That still leaves my grandmother, and no one is going to keep her from doing what she wants."

He nodded. "What do you suggest?"

There was only one way out of this. "Do you have any objections to signing a premarital agreement tonight?"

His face remained impassive. "No. After what happened with Stephen and your grandmother, I didn't think my word would be enough."

Victoria winced on hearing the bleakness in his voice, but she couldn't turn back now. "I'll call my lawyers."

"Why won't it wait until tomorrow?"

"Because if you can possibly change your mind about a church wedding, I'd like to get married tonight."

CHAPTER 8

"We're home."

Shutting off the truck's ignition, Kane glanced at his bride. Nothing moved except her head as she looked at the dark house. She hadn't said a word since they walked out of the justice of the peace's home an hour ago. It was as if only then did the full magnitude of what they had done finally hit her. She was scared.

So was he.

Getting married had been the easy part. Signing the premarital agreement at her lawyer's house had taken less than thirty minutes. Tracking down a district judge who could waive the seventy-two-hour waiting period took a little longer, but less time than it would have taken for them to drive across the state line to Oklahoma.

Luckily, the judge's neighbor was a justice of the peace. Neither the JP nor his wife seemed the least bit bothered that he was being asked to marry someone at one o'clock in the morning. Nor was the JP concerned that he had to repeat the vows several times to the bride.

When he pronounced them man and wife, Kane had turned to kiss Victoria. He was unsurprised to see the fear in her drawn face, taste it in the coolness of her lips. He had a bride, but it remained to be seen if he had a wife.

Teaching her to love him was going to be the hardest and most important job he had ever undertaken. Yet, what if he couldn't get her to overcome her fears and learn to care for him? What if at the end of the three months she walked out of his life? Callused hands clamped on the steering wheel. That wouldn't . . . couldn't happen. Until tonight, each time she was with him she became less wary, more accepting of him, of his touch.

Until now. Now she was as wary of him as a chicken at a fox convention. He knew it would get a lot worse before it got better.

"I'll get your suitcase out of the back." He got out of the truck, relieved to hear the passenger door open and the glide of material across the leather seat.

Unlocking the front door of his house, he flicked on the light. Her back ramrod straight, Victoria's heels clicked loudly on the hardwood floor as she walked into the living room. Woodenly, she faced him. Seeing the continued cautiousness in her large hazel eyes, he fought the growing urge to draw her into his arms and tell her he loved her.

Since nothing would send her running from the house faster, he pushed the words down inside his heart and hoped one day he'd be able to set them free. "Do you want me to put those papers in the safe?"

Her grip on the large manila envelope tightened. Her gaze lifted to his, then skittered away. "I . . . er . . . no."

"Tory, listen to me. I outweigh you by at least a hundred and twenty pounds and you're clutching a piece of paper that says we're man and wife." She flinched and he cursed under his breath. "I know you don't have a very good opinion of men, but you don't have to act as if we're on a deserted road and I've dragged you into the back seat of a car and you can't decide how far you want to go or if you should grab for the door handle and get the hell out of there. With me you'll always have a choice."

Her head snapped up. Kane met her gaze squarely. He saw her too clearly.

Women always talked about wanting an intuitive, sensitive man. Victoria doubted seriously if they knew what they were getting themselves into. What woman in her right mind wanted a man who could easily determine her mood, her thoughts?

A man who knew what you wanted before you did was bad enough, a man who looked into your heart and read your soul was lethal. Her ex-husband hadn't been nearly so perceptive and he had made her life a living hell. She turned away.

"Tory?"

Impatience. It vibrated through that one crisp word. Sometimes Kane wasn't a patient man. In her mind's eye she could see him standing behind her, hands on hips, his black eyes narrowed. If she didn't answer in his time frame, he'd touch her. Heaven help her, she liked being touched by him.

"If you can't find it in you to try and make this work, we're going to have the worst three months of our lives," Kane continued. "Despite your grandmother meaning well, she made you trust a little bit less. I'm willing to let you take your time, but you have to be willing to try."

Finally, she faced him. "What if I can't?"

Sadness swept across his rugged brown face. "I'm betting you can. I'm betting you're stronger than you know. I'm betting you'll remember you can trust me. A judge didn't have to tell me to honor and cherish you. Trust me, Tory. Trust yourself, because I don't think I can take you scurrying away from me or looking at me with fear in your eyes for the next three months."

Neither could she take the disheartened look in his face. Kane deserved better from life, from her. She just wasn't the woman to love him the way he deserved. Memories of her first marriage were too painful for her to want to remain in another one.

Tonight, standing before the justice of the peace, repeating her vows, had brought back all the foolish hopes she had during her first marriage ceremony. She hadn't known until her wedding night just how cruel and cunning Stephen was. Then it was too late. She was trapped by pride, by embarrassment, by her own foolish dreams.

Just like she was trapped in a marriage now to save her stores. She could only hope that she was a better judge of character than she had been ten years ago, and that Kane didn't change after he said "I do." In any case, she had to be as strong as he thought she was. "You better put these in the safe."

His face creased into a smile. "Come on, I'll show you the combination. Then we'll have a glass of champagne to celebrate the beginning of trust."

Kane's office was an interesting mixture of new and old. Worn blue leather armchairs, books, small western statues, and scattered rugs on the hardwood floor decorated the room. Bordered by two large windows was a massive desk with a computer and a printer on one end. In the far corner of the room sat an antique Wells, Fargo & Company safe that could have been used for an old western movie.

"You have got to be kidding."

"What other kind of safe would a real cowboy have?" He grinned boyishly. "It would take three strong men to lift it onto a dolly and ten sticks of dynamite to open this baby. Come on, I'll show you the combination so you can open it if you need the papers."

With only a moment's hesitation, Victoria knelt in front of the safe. Kane came down behind her. The heat of his powerful body wrapped around her as he reached past her to show her the combination. She had to concentrate to keep her hands from shaking as she repeated the maneuver. Three twists, a pull on the handle, and the heavy black door swung open.

Without a word, Kane handed her the manila envelope. She quickly placed it on top of a stack of papers, then swung the door shut. Warm fingers grasped her elbow and helped her to her feet.

"Let's go get the champagne out of the refrigerator."

"Do you always keep champagne chilled?" Victoria asked as she followed him into the blue and white kitchen. Obviously, Kane liked blue. She did too.

"A husband can't tell his wife all his secrets." Releasing her hand, Kane went to the refrigerator. "Grab a couple of glasses out of the cabinet."

Doing as he requested, she walked back to the round oak dining table for four. She glanced back to see Kane bent over, the snugness of his jeans over his hips. She jerked her gaze away from the oddly disturbing sight and looked around.

The kitchen was as spotless as the other rooms she had seen. She appreciated neatness, since she knew how much effort it took to achieve it. She disliked housework intensely. One of the first things she had done once her store began showing a decent profit was hire a housekeeper. What if he expected her to keep house?

"Here you go." Bubbling gold liquid filled her long-stemmed glass. Finished, he sat across from her as if realizing they both needed space.

"Your house is very neat," she ventured.

He cocked a dark brow. "Men aren't the slobs we're made out to be."

"I know that," she hastily said. "It's just that you didn't expect me, and yet the house is immaculate. That's more than I can say for my place."

"There wasn't a thing out of place when we went by your house tonight."

"Because I have a full-time housekeeper." Again she glanced around the kitchen with its glass-front white cabinets trimmed in blue.

"Tory, I didn't marry you to cook or clean house. I have a woman in twice a week to give the place a good cleaning." He studied the disappearing bubbles in the wine for a moment before meeting her eyes. "My father warned me it was easier to live with a happy woman than an unhappy one. Since most women like neatness, I never forgot it once I got a place of my own."

"Just your luck to get a woman who isn't neat," she bantered.

"There are other compensations," Kane said, his black eyes studying her closely.

The subtle shift in the conversation disturbed Victoria. "I think I'll go to bed."

He picked up his glass. "We haven't toasted yet."

Helplessly her gaze went to his strong hand gently holding the fragile stemware. After a moment, she raised her glass. "What do we toast to?"

"To lasting happiness and love," Kane said.

Victoria's delicate eyebrows lifted. After the horrors Stephen had put her through, she no longer believed in love and happiness.

"Tory," Kane prompted.

"To love and happiness." Victoria drank and allowed Kane to keep his illusions.

Draining his glass, Kane took both pieces of crystal and rinsed them in the sink. In the living room, he picked up her suitcase and started toward the stairs. "Willie keeps the room ready in case my family decides to spend the night."

"Is Willie the housekeeper?"

"Yes. Willimina Russell. She's been with me since I bought the place. She's always complaining about climbing the stairs. Now she won't have to."

Victoria pulled up short. "Why?"

Kane gave her an indulgent look. "Willie is almost as pushy as my mother. I'll see to our rooms. If she had any idea we weren't sleeping in the same bed, she'd ask questions."

"I can take care of my room," Victoria mumbled. The idea of Kane in her room, touching her things, was too intimate.

"She's also nosy." Kane's booted feet were muffled by the hooked rug running the length of the hallway. "I'll hang a few of your things in my closet and tell her you're using the connecting bedroom for your dressing room."

Something moved inside Victoria at the thought of her clothes hanging beside Kane's. Before she could analyze what, her mind scurried away. "You seem to have thought of everything."

"Not quite, but I'm working on it." Opening a door, he switched on a light.

Stepping inside the room, Victoria was instantly delighted with the white iron bedstead, washstand, and trifold mirror atop a double dresser. A nightstand by the bed held collections of miniature blue bottles and old Western photos of black cowboys.

"Is it all right?"

"It's wonderful," she said. "I've always liked antiques. It's as if you have a link with the past."

"I know." Brushing by her, he placed her luggage atop the bedspread. "There are a lot of antiques in the house. Are you a collector?"

He shook his dark head. "No. I just like the idea of restoring old furniture no one wants and turning it into something beautiful and useful." He ran his hand lovingly across the washstand.

Victoria watched Kane's large hand stroke the oak wood and wondered if he thought of himself as something no one wanted. Sometimes she'd catch a glimpse of a vulnerable man; other times she didn't think a jackhammer would dent his hide.

"I have a friend in the antique business who keeps an eye out for pieces I might like. Some I can repair, but others . . ." He shrugged his broad shoulders.

Drawn by the soft lull of his voice, Victoria walked closer to him. "When do you find the time?"

"Nights mostly. Well, I guess I better let you get some rest. The bathroom is through that door. The door next to it connects to my room. It doesn't have a lock unless you want one."

"No." She answered without hesitation.

The tightness in his brown face eased. "Good night, Mrs. Taggart." Warm lips brushed across hers. The door closed.

Fingertips pressed against her lips, Victoria stared at the door. She hadn't expected the kiss, but it hadn't annoyed her. Fact was, it had calmed her. No one had ever kissed her or treated her as tenderly as Kane. Best of all, he hadn't changed. Things were a little awkward between them, but nothing they couldn't work out.

Opening her suitcase, she picked up her nightgown. Light filtered through the wispy white cotton material. Fingering the spaghetti straps, she frowned. She didn't remember the gown being so revealing.

A noise lifted her head. She turned toward the floral covered wall she shared with Kane. It sounded like booted feet against a wooden floor. He must be getting ready for bed. She wondered if he slept in pajamas or nothing at all. Warmth spread through her. Her hand fisted. That kind of thinking would lead to trouble. In three months she planned to be back in her own apartment, in her own bed.

Going into the bathroom, she took a bath, then slipped on her gown. Yawning, she turned back the covers and crawled beneath the cool sheets. Her hand was on the lamp's switch when she noticed the bouquet of red roses painted on the porcelain base.

Roses like the twelve individually wrapped ones Kane had insisted on buying from an all-night grocery store. He had arranged them into a bouquet and given them to her. "No bride should marry without flowers," he had said.

Instead of clinging to the roses, she had clung to the marriage license and the premarital agreement. Instead of berating her about being callous, he had asked her if she wanted the papers put in his safe. Instead of thinking about Kane's goodness, she had remembered Stephen's cruelty. Getting out of bed, she went downstairs.

He had fulfilled his end of the business arrangement; it was time she kept up her end. He wanted a woman who cared if he was late getting home. Such a woman wouldn't leave her bridal bouquet to wither. At the front door, she flipped on the porch light, then went outside to the truck. Opening the door, she leaned inside.

"What are you doing out here?"

In one motion she straightened and whirled. In her hand she clutched a long-stemmed red rose. A barechested Kane stood a few feet from her, his unsnapped jeans held up only by the flare of his hips. With difficulty, she pulled her gaze upward. "My flowers. I forgot."

Slowly his eyes moved to the rose, then to Victoria in her nightgown. He took in a deep breath, then let it out. A shudder of relief racked his body. She wasn't running away from him.

Listening to her leave her room and hearing the retreating footsteps panicked him as nothing else had. Finding her in his truck was almost unbearable. Seeing her sheer nightgown molded against her uptilted breasts and sleek curves wasn't any better. "Where are your shoes?"

She glanced at her feet, then at his. "Same place yours are, I'd imagine."

"My feet are a lot tougher than yours. Pick up your flowers and let's go."

"I hope you aren't going to be the dictatorial type of husband. You can't boss me around the way you did the owner of Cinnamon." Gathering the flowers, she closed the door. "Thank you for the roses. They're beau—"

Powerful arms picked up Victoria and held her against a muscular chest. Kane stared down at Victoria's lips, slightly parted and tempting.

"K-Kane, put me down!"

Since there was nervousness instead of panic in Victoria's voice, Kane ignored her command. Slowly his gaze moved to her watchful eyes. He gathered her closer. He remembered the same cautious look when he had first held her twelve years ago. Then it had been the threat of a thunderstorm; now it was the threat of a husband.

"Kane, put me down," she repeated, her voice suddenly husky.

"Once we're inside." Kane started for the house. He tried to ignore the fullness of her breasts, the heat of her body through the sheer gown. "Besides, it gives me another chance to carry my bride over the threshold. Earlier you might have given me a black eye."

She heard the teasing note in Kane's voice and reacted to it, not the pounding of her heart. "Not if I didn't want a broken hand. I'll have to think of something more subtle if I'm displeased with you."

He laughed, a deep, booming sound, and gathered her closer. Victoria felt the heat and hardness of his body, tried to remain impassive in his arms, and lost the battle before he had taken another step. One arm inched around his neck.

Inside, he continued across the room and up the stairs. In front of her door, he released her so slowly that she slid against his body. A firm hand kept her there, his other hand brushed back her hair. For a long moment, he stared at her lips. "You better start thinking of my punishment."

His lips touched her, gently, then with growing hunger and need. His hands searched her body in a restless assurance, then settled on her hips to fit her lower body against his growing desire. With a small moan her fingers opened. Her hands slid around his neck.

Abruptly he tore his lips away. He pulled her arms from around his neck and stepped back. "Sorry. You make a man forget."

Dazed hazel eyes blinked open.

"I hope you won't hold this against me," Kane rasped.

"I—I No." Fumbling for the doorknob behind her, she finally grasped it, opened the door, and went inside.

Closing his eyes, Kane leaned his head back and drew in a deep shuddering breath. What had started out as a good-night kiss had exploded into something wild and untamed. He hadn't expected her eager response in his arms, and he sure hadn't expected his mind to whisper they were married and she was willing. He had almost lost it.

He knew he had made the right decision to make light of the kiss, but his body was paying the price. He wanted Victoria so much he ached. But he wanted a lifetime, not a night, and that was all he'd get if he made love to her now.

Knowing sleep was impossible and that nothing short of a tornado was going to get Victoria out of her room before morning, he went to his room to get dressed. He was going to his workshop.

He enjoyed working with his hands. The first piece he restored had been a chifforobe given to him by his maternal grandmother. It had taken him two weeks to get the old coats of paint off. He quickly discovered he liked seeing the worn, rough surface change before his eyes into a hidden treasure.

Victoria was another hidden treasure. To the casual observer, she was beautiful and untouchable. But if a man took the time to get past her defenses, he'd discover a vulnerable and sensitive woman who wanted to love and be loved. He was determined to be that man. If his plans went well, he'd finally put to use the small piece of furniture his mother had insisted on giving him after he bought the ranch.

He rubbed his broad jaw. Too bad he couldn't use sandpaper and varnish on himself. Passing Victoria's door, he stepped on something.

Roses were scattered around his feet. Bending, he picked them up. Hope stirred.

He realized something he had initially been too scared, then too aroused to fully understand. Victoria cared enough about him to go outside and get her flowers. She hadn't even taken the time to put her shoes or robe on.

Whether she knew it or not, she was weakening. A smile lifted the corner of his mustache. He didn't need varnish or sandpaper. Just a sassy, sexy lady named Victoria Taggart. Pushing to his feet, he went to get a vase.

* * *

I can't hide in this room all morning. It's after nine. So I was in my nightgown clinging to Kane like lint to a sweater. He is my husband. So I'm attracted to him. Anyone can have a weak moment. At least the morning after my second marriage I'm not crying my eyes out the way I did after my first marriage.

Victoria had been arguing with herself all morning and had yet to come up with the courage to face Kane. She brushed aside the ruffled curtain to stare out the window. Brownish-green pastures and rolling hills spread out before her. In the foreground were the buildings Kane had pointed out two days before. An hour ago she watched a thin, wiry man tramp back and forth between the stable and the bunk house, but nothing since then.

She still didn't understand why when Kane touched her, her brain shut down and her body went into overdrive. Before now, memories of how Stephen had deceived, then almost destroyed her, had enabled her to remain emotionally detached from men.

Until Kane.

Well, that was about to end. Her chin lifted. She would not allow him to mess up her life. And she wasn't going to stay in her room all day. Walking to the door, she yanked it open.

Kane, his rugged face impersonal, filled the doorway. He lowered his balled fist. "How long had you planned on staying up here?"

"I was on my way down," she answered.

"Good, I need some company." Taking her by the arm, he took her to the kitchen. "Have a seat and help yourself."

The first thing she saw was the roses. Their long stems had been cut and they were in a short, wide-mouthed vase. Her fingers touched a dark red petal. A sensitive man like Kane could get a woman into a lot of trouble.

A large platter plopped on the table in front of her. Her mouth gaped. The blue stoneware overflowed with bacon, sausage patties, ham, French toast, scrambled eggs, biscuits, hash browns. "Who is going to eat all this?" She sank into her chair.

"I plan to give it a good try." Kane helped himself to a bit of everything.

"Do you always cook this much?"

"This morning I got carried away," he admitted. "I didn't know what you liked. Do you want coffee?"

"No. Juice is fine." She picked up her glass.

"After breakfast I'll introduce you to the hands."

"They're going to be surprised you have a wife." She sipped her juice.

"So are your friends." He looked at her empty plate. "Why aren't you eating?"

"I usually don't eat breakfast."

"You do now." He put two sausage patties, hash browns, and eggs on her plate.

Victoria folded her arms. "Didn't I warn you about being dictatorial?"

"Yes, but I'm willing to take a chance. Eat up. We have to go into town and tell our families."

"They aren't going to be happy," Victoria said, and picked up a fork.

"That's their problem." Kane's gaze fixed on Victoria's face. "But I'm going to enjoy every second of the time we have together. How about you?"

CHAPTER 9

The alternate knocking on the door and the ringing of the doorbell came as a welcome diversion for Victoria. "I think someone is anxious to see you."

Getting up from the dining table, Kane brushed aside the ruffled white curtain. "They're anxious all right. For both of us. It's my folks and yours."

"What?" Victoria rushed to the window. Two cars were parked behind Kane's truck. She didn't know about the blue car, but the burgundy one belonged to her grandparents. She might not be able to find her own car, but the fins and oversized headlights on her grandparents' '52 Cadillac were unmistakable. "How did they know?"

"Only one way to find out." Letting the curtain fall, he started for the den. With each step the noise at the front door become more pronounced. A few feet away, Kane glanced over his shoulder at Victoria. The corner of his mustache tilted upward. "Well, partner, do we slip out the back or face the angry mob?"

Despite her uneasiness, Victoria smiled. "Why bother? The back door is probably guarded."

"Victoria, I know you're in there."

"Kane, open this door."

Ignoring the demands of Clair Benson and his mother, Kane came back to Victoria. His hands settled on her shoulders. "I don't know about Mrs. Benson, but Mama blows out of steam quickly once she's spoken her mind. Everything will be all right." After a light squeeze of reassurance,

Kane went to unlock the front door. The Taggart and Benson family were crowded on the porch. Only Addie and Matt were smiling.

Grace glared at her eldest. "Kane, I can't believe you were so irresponsible. I'd already called Pastor Hill."

Clair, her face pinched in disapproval, went straight to her granddaughter. "How could you do this to me?"

Before Victoria could answer, Kane placed himself between Clair and his wife. "There's no need to bully Tory."

Clair's brown eyes widened. "Get out of my way. Victoria is my grandchild."

"She's my wife."

One bony finger jabbed Kane's chest. "Sneaking around and getting married is nothing to be proud of. How do you think I felt learning my only grandchild eloped? And in the middle of early morning church service of all places! The judge's wife just leaned over and told me. I thought she was playing until she mentioned your name. I can only be thankful she didn't blurt it out."

"It seems to me that you should be congratulating us instead of being angry," Kane pointed out.

"No one has *ever* eloped in *our* family." Clair glanced around for her husband. "Henry, kindly move Kane out of my way."

From behind her came a groan and a chuckle. Kane knew Henry must be thinking of broken bones and Matt was enjoying the whole thing.

"Now, everyone. Calm down," Mr. Taggart said. "Kane is right."

"I think so, too." Addie smiled devilishly. "By the way, Victoria, I don't want to appear greedy, but how much of a discount do you give family members?"

"Addie, that's enough," Mrs. Taggart warned. "Your brother has acted totally irresponsible."

"It's not Kane's fault. I'm the one who asked him to get married last night," Victoria said and moved in front of her husband. Every pair of eyes in the room converged on her. Silence reigned. Her chin lifted. "If you want to blame someone, blame me."

"You only had to ask once." Kane's strong arm circled her waist. "Mama, Mrs. Benson, we're sorry if you're upset, but Tory and I are responsible adults. The choice was *ours*. If anything, our marriage does credit to the way you raised us. We needed to be together and we wanted it to be right. I'm sure both of you can remember when you couldn't spend another minute apart."

For a charged moment both women stared at the newlyweds. Then with cries of happiness, the elderly women threw their arms around Victoria and Kane.

"Kane, I'm sorry."

"Victoria, forgive me."

"Come on, Grace and Mrs. Benson," Kane's father said. "Let's have a little feeling for the newlyweds and get out of here."

Grace and Clair sent Bill Taggart a hard glare, which he ignored. "Congratulations, son. Welcome to the family, Victoria." Mr. Taggart exchanged a masculine hug with Kane and kissed his new daughter-in-law on the cheek. "Henry, if you'll grab your wife, I'll get mine."

Henry did as requested, but not before he shook Kane's hand and kissed his granddaughter. Smiling broadly, Addie hugged and kissed both the newlyweds. Matt winked at Kane and tipped his hat to Victoria. The door closed behind them.

"You were very convincing," Victoria said. If she hadn't known better, she would have believed his touching speech just as their relatives had. It annoyed her that she could still be so easily duped by a man.

"Was I? Come on and let's finish breakfast, then we can go pick up the rest of your things."

"There's no hurry. I thought I'd pick them up as I needed them."

"Well, think again," Kane told her. "Only a fool would believe our marriage is on the level if you go by your old place every day to pick up clothes. You'll have to find another excuse for staying away from me."

"That was not my intention," she flared. "You have no right to say such a thing."

"Saying what I want is about the only right I have with you and I'm going to do it whenever I please." He took her by the arm and started for the kitchen. "Our breakfast is getting cold."

Resisting the childish impulse to dig in her heels, Victoria decided to show her displeasure in another way. "I'm not hungry."

"Suit yourself. You can watch me eat."

Kane is a mean, spiteful man.

Snatching a sleeveless blouse from her closet, Victoria tossed it in the direction of the overflowing suitcase on the bed. He had to know she was hungry. It was after three in the afternoon. They had already made one trip back to his ranch with her car and a load of clothes, then returned for the second haul.

But had he asked if she was tired or hungry? No. And she wasn't going to give him the satisfaction of asking him to stop and eat. Of course he wasn't hungry after the huge breakfast he had put away. He lounged against her dresser, watching her pack as if he hadn't a care in the world.

Her stomach growled again. Her teeth gritted.

"You have any clothes sturdier than these?"

Victoria glanced over her shoulder to see that Kane had finally moved.

Hands on his hips, he stood by her bed, frowning down at the array of cotton, rayon, and silk blends scattered across the bed. All of them light and airy for the hot Texas summers. "They suit me," she said coolly.

Midnight black eyes swept upward. "Not on a ranch they won't. I don't want to hear you complaining if something gets caught on a nail or you get a splinter in your rear because you leaned against a piece of rough wood."

She clenched her teeth so hard her head hurt. "I promise I won't complain, but since you're so concerned, I'll confine myself to the house."

"No you won't. I want you with me."

"I've had enough of you. You've been bullying me ever since breakfast. It's about time you learned I push back. I'll wear what I want, when I want, and it's none of your business. If you want a constant companion, that's your problem."

"Are you finished?"

He looked mean and hard, but at the moment she didn't care. "For now."

He hugged her. "I knew you could fight back if I pushed hard enough."

She blinked, bemused by the hug and his statement. "You wanted me to get angry?"

"Not exactly. I just don't want you to be afraid to tell me off." He smiled. "I'm not always sure I'll listen, but you can try. How about on the way back we stop and eat?"

"You knew I was hungry?"

"Your stomach was growling so loud it shook the truck."

She punched him on the shoulder. "I'll get you for this."

"You can try."

They stood smiling at each other until slowly their smiles faded. Her heart rate sped up. He looked at her lips. She looked at his.

He stepped back. For a moment she thought she saw regret in his eyes, then it was gone. His fingers uncurled from her waist. "We better get a move on."

"I suppose so," Victoria mumbled, feeling bereft and not understanding why.

"You want to wait or find someplace else to eat?"

Victoria glanced around the packed parking lot. There wasn't a space left. When Kane had driven by the front entrance of the popular seafood restaurant, she had seen people crowded against the stained glass door.

"Since it's Sunday afternoon, it's probably going to be the same everywhere," she told him. "Besides, I love the food here."

"That settles it then. You go inside and get our names on the waiting list. I'll stay here until I can park the truck." Kane pulled over to let a car pass. "Don't worry about your suitcases, I'll put them in front."

"Kane, that's a lot of trouble. We could eat someplace else."

"We could, but we aren't going to."

Victoria smiled. "Since my mouth is practically watering for some fried shrimp, I'll let you get away with being dictatorial this time." Getting out of the truck, she began to weave her way through the cars. She and Kane were really going to have to talk about his attitude.

"Victoria."

Shock ripped through her. Every nerve in her body went on alert on hearing the unmistakable sound of her ex-husband's voice. For a confused moment, she didn't know whether to continue to the restaurant or find Kane and leave. Remembering Stephen Malone's cruel streak, she decided against both. She turned.

Smiling as if he owned the world and everything in it, Stephen approached her. Rage built inside her against the man whose greed had nearly destroyed her.

No matter how she tried to feel relief that he was out of her life, anger always twisted and shimmered through her.

It always would.

Seeing her former husband was a harsh reminder of how pathetic and malleable and stupid she had been. In him, all her failures were magnified a thousandfold.

Stopping in front of her, his smile broadened. Dimples winked in his nut-brown face. "You're looking beautiful, Victoria, but then you always do."

"What do you want?" Victoria asked, her voice as chilling as the look she turned on him.

His smile faded. Nervously, he fingered the tan silk square in the breast pocket of his wheat-colored sport coat. "There is no reason why we can't be friends."

She laughed in his face. "I could give you a long list, starting with a hundred and ten thousand dollars. Do you want more?"

"Can't a man be forgiven for his mistakes?" he asked, a pleading note in his voice as he reached out to touch her arm.

A hard glare from Victoria stopped him inches from his goal. "Why this sudden interest in me?"

"Frankly, I've never gotten over you. Only I didn't realize it until recently. Richard saw you with a giant of a man at Wellington's last week and when he told me, it made me jealous. Today I was coming to see you and saw the same guy Richard must have been talking about help you into a truck at your apartment. On a hunch you were going out to eat, I followed," he explained, obviously proud he had been correct. "I've asked around and know you haven't dated much since our divorce. You must still care for me. Baby, I've never gotten over you either."

For a moment she was speechless. Of all the egotistical jerks! "You think I haven't dated because I wasn't able to get over you?"

Stephen's smile showed perfect white teeth and supreme confidence. "There's no reason for you to settle for such a mean-looking man. I know how insecure you are. I'm willing to take you back and we can start over."

"*I* wouldn't take *you* back if you were gold plated and had an apple stuck between those caps I paid for," she said furiously. "I didn't *settle* for less, I was lucky enough to get more. You are the one who is mean and cruel. My husband is more of a man than you could ever be."

Shock widened his eyes. "You married him!"

"Don't ever try to contact me again," she said tightly. "I know you lost your job and you need another meal ticket. This time, it won't be me."

Something cold flashed in his eyes. "Still trying to act more than you are just because you come from a wealthy family. You're no better than anyone else. How much are you paying him to tolerate a cold, shrewish woman like you?"

She flinched; he smiled.

"How does it feel knowing you're nothing but a beautiful shell?" he continued with malice. "A man might look at you, but your money is the only reason he'll stick around."

"You bastard!" Untamed fury swept through Kane. Before Stephen could move, Kane grabbed the smaller man by his throat and shook. Stephen's eyes bulged as he gasped for air.

"Tory is my wife and what's mine I protect. I never want to hear of you or see you within a hundred yards of her. Do I make myself clear?"

Gasping for air, Stephen clawed at Kane's unrelenting fingers. Kane's hand tightened. Stephen nodded. Kane unclamped his fingers. Stephen crumpled to the pavement.

Kane waited until Stephen looked up. Kane's smile was feral. "Stay out my wife's way. You'll be healthier. Now be smarter than you look and get out of here. Don't let me see you again."

Nodding, Stephen dragged himself to his feet with the help of a car bumper and staggered away.

Kane whirled to see several people watching him. Victoria wasn't among them. Brushing past the bystanders, he caught up with her and led her to his truck. He had rushed to her side as soon as he recognized the man Victoria had stopped to talk with. Kane closed her door. Victoria jumped. He hadn't been in time. Quickly, he got in on the other side.

"Tory."

"I was such a fool." Her voice trembled.

Kane's hand, reaching toward her, halted in midair. His eyes shut. A hellish agony twisted through him. "Don't listen to him. He's a sorry bastard who wants to hurt you any way he can."

She looked at him with dark, pain-filled eyes. "I'm not hungry. Can we please leave?"

Kane's hand fisted. She was in pain and shutting him out again. He started the engine. He'd wait until they were home to finish talking to her.

But talk she would. That was her problem now—she kept too many things inside. He only hoped when she started talking, she wouldn't say something neither one of them could forget or forgive.

"Tory, I'm back with dinner." Kane sighed and knocked on the bedroom door again. He knew she was in there. Once they returned home, she had gone straight to her room. When he followed with her luggage, she hadn't acknowledged him in any way. Not even when he told her he was going to pick up something to eat.

Stopping at another restaurant was out of the question. From the shattered look on her face, he would have had to forcibly take her inside. She was hurt and angry. Unfortunately her anger was directed at herself and the closest man in her life. Kane.

He opened the door. She turned sharply away from the window. Despite the anger emanating from her, he walked further into the room. "Dinner is ready."

She looked back out the window. "Close the door on your way out."

"I will, but you're coming with me. Walking or over my shoulder. Your choice."

Her shoulders jerked. For a charged moment he wondered if he had pushed her too far. Giving him a look that would have made a lesser man run, she stalked from the room. Kane followed.

Two feet inside the kitchen, she halted. Knowing the reason, Kane stepped around her and began opening the seven Styrofoam servers stretched across the blue counter top. "I didn't know what you liked, so I got a little bit of everything. Catfish, shrimp, crab cakes, flounder, french fries, hush puppies, and several different kinds of salad."

As he opened the last container, he glanced up. She had moved closer to the food. Her gaze was fixed on the batter-dipped butterfly shrimp. He snagged two plates from the table, handed her one and began to fill his own. The last thing she needed was him watching her. Finished, he sat his plate on the table and got a pitcher of tea and a diet cola from the refrigerator.

He joined her at the table, glad to see she had put a decent amount of food on her plate. Without asking her anything, he opened the soft drink and poured it over a glass of ice. Head bowed, he said grace and heard her faint "Amen."

Kane ate with an eye on Victoria's plate. He made sure he kept it full. When he tried to give her the last fried shrimp, she shook her head. "Please, I'm stuffed."

"What about some pecan pie for dessert?"

"I'm too full to lift a fork, let alone have the energy to chew."

"Good. You sit there and I'll clean this up." Going to the refrigerator, Kane crouched down and began rearranging the food on the shelves. As he moved to get up, he saw Victoria standing with the containers in her hands.

"Working together, we can finish sooner," she said simply. She had wanted to hold on to her anger, to nourish it, stoke it against becoming vulnerable again. Kane's thoughtfulness had snuffed it out. Kane wasn't Stephen. He wouldn't hurt or use her.

"Thanks." He put the food away and stood up. "How about a walk to make room for the pecan pie?"

She lifted a brow. "I must be hearing things. You're actually asking?"

His mouth quirked. "I admit I'm a bit bossy. If you go with me, I'll try to mend my ways."

"Somehow I doubt you will."

"This is my favorite place," Kane said, spreading a blanket beneath a gnarled oak tree on a high hill overlooking his house. The ranch sat in a valley below, shedding its winter brown for spring green. Two horses played in the corral. Cows grazed a hundred yards away. "When the former owner brought me up here and I looked around and couldn't see another building, I knew I'd found my home."

Victoria carefully sat on the far corner of the blue blanket. "How long ago was that?"

He looked down at her before answering. "Eight years ago last month." Her body tensed again. He had bought the place two weeks after her divorce was final.

"You never looked back?"

"I made mistakes, if that's what you mean."

"None like mine." Self-reproach rang in her voice.

"It's time you stopped blaming yourself." He dropped down to his knees. "You're afraid you'll make the same mistake in judgment. Afraid you'll trust the wrong man again."

The truth of his words took her by surprise. Intuitive and dangerous.

"Do you think I'd use you?" he asked softly.

She had no defense against the need in his beautiful black eyes. "No.

You're not like Stephen. I looked at him, really looked at him today, and couldn't believe I was ever fooled for a moment by his so-called charm and good looks. He used me, and I was stupid enough to let him."

With all his heart Kane wanted to take her into his arms, but if he did, she might stop talking. She needed to be able to put Stephen behind her, to know trusting him hadn't made her a lesser person. "You were young and impressionable. Blame Stephen, not yourself."

Her arms wrapped around her updrawn knees, she rocked back and forth and remembered. Stephen's attitude changed toward her the moment they boarded the cruise ship for their honeymoon. The gentle, considerate man she had fallen in love with was replaced by an argumentative, abusive stranger. The steward had barely closed the door to their cabin before Stephen pulled her down on the bed. He said he couldn't wait to make love.

She quickly learned the rough sexual act that followed had nothing to do with love. Stephen didn't care that it was her first time or that she was scared and unsure of herself. He wanted her and he had taken what he wanted. Afterward she lay crying as he hurled insults. He said it was her fault he had finished so quickly. He thought he had married a woman, not a cry baby. Without asking, he had taken some money from her purse and slammed out of the door saying, "At least I can have a good time in the casino."

Victoria shook her head, sending her black hair dancing around her tense shoulders, trying to stop the memories, but it was useless. Stephen had returned to their cabin hours later and apologized. The captain of the vessel had asked about her and wanted them to sit at his table. Excited about the honor, Stephen had promised not to resume their "lovemaking" until they were home. Once again, he became the old Stephen. At the time, she was naive enough to think he was concerned for her instead of concerned about presenting a picture of a devoted husband and happy wife.

His changed behavior made her think he might be right about things being her fault. After all, she had failed so many times in the past. Perhaps she just wasn't a sexual person. Once home, she had tried to make up for her deficiency by giving in to his demands of moving to a high-rise condominium, and letting a design studio do all the decorating.

A month after they were married, he wanted her to co-sign a loan for a new sports car. Neither one of them had a job and they both already had good cars. She refused. That night she had to endure his sexual demands for the first time since their honeymoon. The next day, she signed the papers. She learned to loathe Stephen, sex, and herself. But she learned the power of money over a greedy man.

"The things I let him say to me, all the humiliation I suffered at home and in public. The countless times I gladly came home knowing he was being unfaithful and not caring. I only cared that I wouldn't have to be bothered by a man whose touch sickened me. When there were no other women, I used his greed to keep him away from me."

Something clicked in Kane's mind. "You paid him to keep out of your bed, didn't you?"

CHAPTER 10

Her eyes widened on realizing what she had unintentionally admitted. No one knew that awful secret, not even Bonnie. With a strangled cry, she tried to get up.

Kane caught her. Ignoring her fists, he pulled her into his arms and down onto his lap. "It's all right, Tory. It's all right. You did the only thing you could think of."

Shame swept through her. "Let me go."

"No. Maybe this will convince you he was wrong." His lips sought hers.

Victoria turned her head and clamped her mouth shut. Kane veered to her throat and kissed the cord of her neck. He nuzzled the curve of her jaw, then ran the tip of his tongue across the seam of her closed mouth. With a delicate shudder, she opened for him.

Kane rewarded her by cherishing what she offered. He kissed her with all the tenderness and need he had held within him for so long. His tongue dipped and swirled, stroking the smooth inside of her mouth, the delicious heat of her tongue.

A long time later he lifted his head. He stared down at her tangled hair he had lovingly mussed, her dazed eyes, her lips moist and swollen from his kisses. With knives cutting through him, he waited until her gaze cleared and she focused on him.

"I'm not Stephen. Don't ever confuse us." His breathing ragged, Kane rolled away and stood. They both needed the space. "It's not your fault Stephen's a bastard." For a long moment he let the words lay between them.

"Don't you understand? There's not a cold bone in your body. He didn't know how to appreciate what he had. It wasn't your fault." At her continued silence, he reached for his waning control and sat down on the blanket again.

"You're a beautiful, sensual woman. He tried to make you less because that was the only way he could control you. Don't let him win. Put the blame where it belongs and get on with your life. Stop looking for him in other men. In me."

Mutely she stared at him, then looked away. "I'd like to go back, please."

Her voice was polite and correct and distant. Kane wanted to smash something. Instead he grabbed a fistful of blanket as soon as she stood.

Victoria looked at Kane's rigid profile. Misery twisted inside her. She didn't want to have her emotions probed. She wanted to be left alone. Even as the thought ran through her mind, she knew she lied. That was the reason Kane frightened her as much as his kisses thrilled her—she wanted to open up to him.

Yet she knew if she forgot the painful lesson Stephen taught her, and yielded to Kane, he would touch her in ways Stephen never had, leaving her exposed and defenseless. This time, if something were to go wrong, she wasn't sure if she would heal again.

He grabbed her arm and started down the hill. "Let's go. But we're not finished with this."

"Why do you keep pushing me to talk about him?"

Kane stopped and faced her. "Because you're my wife, and even pretending, I don't like the idea of your ex-husband having any influence over you."

Mixed feelings surged through her. "I don't want to be vulnerable again."

"No one does." His voice softened. "Just take the first step. I'll be with you all the way."

She bit her lower lip. "I may try your patience."

"You already have," he stated bluntly. "But we're a team now. We have to work together." He started walking again. "Can you play dominoes?"

Victoria thankfully grasped for the change of subject. "Grandfather says I can."

"After we get your things unpacked, we'll find out."

Her arms crossed, Victoria watched Kane put the dominoes back into the box. "You cheated," she said with a pout.

Kane never looked up. "You're such a lousy player, I didn't have to."

Victoria leaned over the table and punched Kane on the arm. "I am not. Grandfather and I played all the time and I seldom lost."

"Knowing what a poor loser you are, he probably let you win to keep the peace," Kane said. He rose and put the dominoes back on the bookshelf.

Victoria pursed her lips. "Maybe. I hate to lose."

"That's what your grandmother was counting on."

Her playful mood evaporated. "I guess so."

"You're going to have to stop doing that."

"Doing what?"

"Withdrawing each time the reason we got married comes up."

She sighed. "I'm working on it."

"Good." Walking over, he pulled her to her feet. "You better go to bed if you expect to go to work tomorrow."

At her door, he gave her a brief, nonthreatening hug. "Good night, Tory."

"Good night." Victoria entered her room, then leaned against the closed door. Today her emotions had ranged from self-pity to rage to passion. Through it all, Kane had been there. He had seen her at her worst, and continued to believe the best. The knowledge warmed her. Perhaps caring for someone wasn't so bad after all.

Sunlight filtering through gauzy white curtains woke Victoria. She glanced at her watch. 8:18. If she didn't hurry she'd be late getting to the shop for the first time in years. Throwing back the covers, she got out of bed and got dressed. The aroma of coffee greeted her the moment she reached the bottom of the stairs.

Kane glanced up when she entered the kitchen. "Good morning. Your timing is perfect. Grab a seat," he said, sliding a fluffy omelet onto her plate.

Victoria looked at the large amount of food on the table. "Do you cook for the hands as well?"

Kane sat down. "Are you saying I overdid it again?"

"I'm not saying anything." She bowed her head for Kane to say the blessing. "Amen." Picking up her fork, she cut into her cheese and ham omelet and took a small bite. Her lips closed around the food and she groaned in delight. "I might start eating breakfast every day. You're a good cook."

"I've been a bachelor for so long, I had to be." He selected a biscuit from a two-inch stack. "I gassed up your car and washed it. I hope you don't mind?"

"When did you have time?"

"This morning. I told you I'm an early riser."

Victoria was touched. "I don't mind at all. Thank you."

He nodded. "We got calls from both your grandmother and my

mother this morning. They wanted to speak to you, but I told them you were asleep."

Her face heated. Slowly she put down the glass of juice she had picked up. "What did they want?"

"To get the inside track on having us to dinner first, and to see if we liked our wedding announcement in the newspapers."

"What!"

Calmly, Kane handed her two newspapers. "At least *you* look good. I can't believe Mama put my old picture in the hometown paper."

Victoria stared at their pictures. Kane looked hard. She looked sullen. "It's a tossup which one of us looks the worst," she said, then glanced up quickly at Kane to see if she had made him angry.

Kane grinned. "I think I take the honors."

"I could wring Grandmother's neck. This is all I need."

He studied her closely. "Are you worried some of your friends might have seen you yesterday at the restaurant?"

"No," she denied quickly.

Kane didn't look convinced. "Maybe I should go to the store with you."

She shook her head and stood. "No need. I'll be fine. What are your plans today?"

His narrowed gaze told her he was aware she had deliberately changed the subject. "I have a meeting at Cinnamon around ten, then I plan to do some work around the ranch."

"Then I'll see you this evening." With a forced smile, Victoria left the room.

"Kane, have you heard a word I've said?"

Slowly Kane turned from staring out the office window on the twelfth floor of the Cinnamon Corporation. A frown marched across his brow as he stared at the rotund man sitting behind a massive teak desk. "I'm sorry, William, did you say something?"

William Conrad, founder, president and CEO of Cinnamon, clamped his teeth tighter on his imported cigar and studied Kane over the rim of his bifocals. With a controlled motion, he sat upright in his chair. "I said, what do you think of the plans we've come up with to expand into men's skin care?"

The furrows on Kane's brow deepened.

"It's in the report I gave you." A manicured finger pointed to Kane's right hand.

Kane glanced down at the blue portfolio as if he hadn't seen it. In truth, he didn't remember taking it. Just as he didn't recall the view from the window. The landscaped grounds and surrounding office buildings hadn't existed for him. His mind was filled with visions of Victoria's determined but frightened face. She was intent on facing her problems alone.

Kane's gaze went back to William. At sixty-six, his once coal-black hair was generously sprinkled with gray and his athletic body of college days had rounded. One thing remained the same: his passion for Cinnamon. Kane didn't even think Helen, his wife of thirty odd years, came before the company. While Kane admired William's keen intelligence, he didn't agree with his priorities.

"It makes my ulcer act up just thinking of things that could go wrong with this new venture." William knocked the ash off his cigar. "Of course, I'd feel a lot better with you back here every day."

"One of us with an ulcer is enough," Kane said flatly. "I'll always appreciate being a part of the company's growth, but being a consultant on occasion is enough time spent away from my ranch."

William looked from beneath bushy brows. "You make it sound as if I welcomed you with open arms."

"You did eventually," Kane said mildly. He had expected William's resistance in taking on a partner instead of acquiring investors as he had originally planned. Kane just hadn't accepted William's decision.

"It was you or bankruptcy court, just as it was let you go gracefully two years ago or face the prospect of losing the driving force behind this company's growth," William said with a touch of irritation he didn't try to hide. "Now that you're married, you'll never come back full time. I didn't even know you were serious about anyone."

"Sometimes these things happen quickly," Kane explained. It was just his and Victoria's luck for her picture to be in the same section of the newspaper where they were running the second excerpt from a tell-all book about the rich and famous in Dallas/Fort Worth.

"As I told you earlier, she's beautiful. I probably wouldn't want to leave a woman like that either," William confessed.

"I'm not sure Helen would take that as a compliment," Kane said.

"I'm not either, so let's not tell her."

"I wouldn't think of it," Kane said, and placed the folder back on the desk, then headed for the door.

William rose out of his seat. "Where are you going? We've got to—"

"I'm well aware we have to finalize a decision in a couple of weeks if we're to hit the stores in December." Kane never slowed down. "I have something to do that can't wait."

The door closed and William slumped in his chair. "One day I'm going to have the last word with Kane."

Lavender and Lace was a madhouse. People were waiting for her when she arrived, and more came as the day wore on. Customers came into the store she hadn't seen in years. They wanted to hear all about the courtship. They ogled her ring and cast veiled glances at her stomach. The hot-pink jersey minidress she wore afforded them a good look. If it wasn't for her real friends who came by as well, she would have closed the store.

She wasn't naive enough to believe everyone had dropped by to wish her luck because she had gotten married. From the way Stephen's name kept popping into their conversation, she wondered if a few of them had heard about her altercation with him. Yet none of them were bold enough to ask outright. She had never seen so many watchful eyes and twitching ears on the alert for any hint of juicy gossip.

By 11:15 A.M. she had a raging headache. When her grandmother's lawyer stopped by, she was glad to escape. Immediately, she ushered him into her office. He stared at the marriage license she handed him so long she began to think he believed it was a forgery.

Finally, he lifted his gray head and acknowledged she'd beaten the deadline, but her grandmother could still call in the total amount of the loan if the marriage ended in less than a year. Feeling the pounding in her head increase, she walked to the front with him and said her good-byes.

The door had barely closed behind the lawyer before it opened again. Kane's powerful body filled the doorway. Dressed in form-fitting jeans and a crisp white shirt, his appearance reminded her of their first meeting. His sweeping gaze locked on Victoria. He started toward her with a slow and purposeful gait.

A hush fell over the store. Customers parted. Kane didn't seem to notice or care. His intense gaze never left Victoria. He stopped in front of her. For a timeless moment midnight black eyes probed hers as if searching for something.

"Hi. Didn't you have a meeting?" she asked.

"Seeing you was more important."

Warmth curled though her. She realized he had been worried about her. Without thought, she placed her hand on his chest, and from somewhere, found a smile. "I'm fine."

"In that case, I'll get to the second reason I'm here." His head lowered until he heard the collective indrawn breath of several women. Grabbing Victoria's hand, he took her into her office and closed the door. Without a word, he drew her into his arms.

Her heart pounding, her eyes wide, she pressed both hands against his chest. "Th-there's no need to go any further."

"Yes, there is." His thumb grazed her lower lip. She shivered. "A woman who's been thoroughly kissed has a certain look about her. You don't have that look, but you will before you leave this room. When you go back outside there'll be no doubt why we married or why I'd fight through hell to taste your lips."

His last words ringing in her ear, his mouth closed over hers. This time she didn't think of resisting. She simply enjoyed being held and cherished. He always knew exactly what she needed.

Too soon Kane's lips and body were gone. Slowly she opened her eyes. He looked no happier than she felt. "Come on."

He didn't stop until he reached the front door. "I'll expect you at six." He opened the door and left.

Victoria touched her lips as she watched Kane get into his truck and drive away. Absently she heard the excited chatter of the women around her and knew Kane had accomplished what he had set out to do. Her reputation and her honor were intact. His timing had been perfect. Once again her knight had rescued her, but in doing so he also presented her with an even greater danger. Himself.

Returning to her office, she dialed Bonnie's art gallery. Victoria desperately needed a calming presence. She was worried about her boutiques. She was worried about being vulnerable to a man who made her blood sing. She was also sinking in quicksand and had no idea how to pull herself out. There was something to be said about living behind the safety of a castle wall.

A short time later, Victoria hung up the phone. Bonnie hadn't returned from her buying trip to New York. Victoria didn't doubt for a moment that someone in the Taggart family had called Bonnie. What concerned Victoria was that the one person she expected to receive a call from, hadn't phoned. Maybe Bonnie hadn't gotten over her fear of cupid getting an arrow in the back. All Victoria had to say was that it would be better than one in the heart.

Victoria pulled up in front of Kane's ranch house at six-thirty. She meant to be home at six, but she had gotten tied up in traffic. It wouldn't hurt this one time to give in to Kane. Especially after his help that morning. But he really was going to have to learn to ask and not tell her what to do. Her pace quickened as she crossed the porch and opened the front door.

"It's about time you got home. I'm starved."

"Bonnie," Victoria shouted and ran to embrace her best friend. "I tried to call you all afternoon."

Grinning broadly, Bonnie pulled away and glanced at her husband sitting across from Kane. "Blame Dan. Kane wanted to surprise you."

"Guilty." Dan's deep mahogany face creased into a smile. Chocolate eyes sparkled devilishly. Broad shoulders and six feet of conditioned muscles, Dan was easy to talk to and fun to be with. He was the perfect husband for the light-hearted Bonnie. "I warned Kane that when you two get together, no secret is safe. I must say I never thought she'd stand not calling you all day."

"I told you, Kane asked me not to," Bonnie defended.

"I don't suppose it occurred to you to call me anyway?" Victoria asked mildly.

"It occurred to me, but I think you once compared my cousin to a bulldozer. Try bulldozer with an attitude if he doesn't get his way," Bonnie said.

"Tell me about it." Victoria smiled and looked at Kane. "It's a nice surprise. Sorry I'm late."

"Late? You're exactly on time," Bonnie said.

Victoria glanced from Bonnie to Kane. "Traffic held me up. You almost slipped up this time."

Standing, he walked to her. "A man needs a woman who'll keep him on his toes. If you want to change out of those heels, you better hurry. We don't want to make a bad impression on our guests."

"I won't be a minute." She started for the stairs, then stopped. "Where are we going?"

"Some place to have fun," Kane promised.

He was right. From the moment they entered the sports restaurant, and threw darts to select their table, to playing bingo until their orders arrived, to bowling afterwards, the evening was fun. Until Kane decided to challenge Dan to a game of pool.

"The loser has to pay the bill," Kane announced, his arm curved around Victoria's waist.

Dan rubbed his hands together. "Rack em up, then get out your wallet."

"You and Bonnie don't have a chance against a team like us."

"Us?" Victoria echoed. "I don't know how to play pool."

Kane shrugged broad shoulders. "It's easy. I'll teach you, Honey."

Learning the "Cotton-Eyed Joe" had been child's play when compared to the coordination and eye control needed to shoot the cue ball from where it lay and strike the object ball into one of the six pockets. Victoria never accomplished one shot correctly. She couldn't concentrate. Kane had *insisted* on "helping her" when it was her turn.

Every time she bent over the table with her cue stick, her hips brushed intimately against Kane, who stood behind coaching her. Her insides tingled. She had the strangest urge to rub her hips against the bluntness she felt. Half ashamed and half aroused, she missed shot after shot. The game ended in total defeat for the Taggarts.

She handed Kane her cue. "Sorry. At least Bonnie managed to pocket one ball."

"Winning isn't always important. It's how you play the game," he told her, his voice deep and husky.

Victoria didn't say anything, she couldn't. Her body's sudden need overrode everything else. The same need was mirrored in Kane's beautiful eyes. She felt hot, restless and up to her waist in quicksand. She wanted him. Badly. She didn't know what frightened her more, her emotional vulnerability or her fear that if she gave in to her desire, Kane would find her lacking as a woman.

Arriving home, she started for the safety of her room. Kane's deep voice called after her. "How about a game of dominoes?"

She spoke without turning. "I've lost enough for one night." Spending more time with Kane was asking for trouble.

Kane's velvet laughter followed her up the stairs. "Good night, Honey."

After breakfast the next morning, Kane waved goodbye without asking what time she planned to be home. Victoria made it a point to be home by six. For once she was going to win the mind game.

Seeing no food on the stove, she smiled. Until she opened the refrigerator and saw two large T-bone steaks marinating and a mixed salad. She was leaving the kitchen to change clothes when the back door opened.

"Hi, Honey," Kane said, his hand still on the doorknob. Perspiration beaded his brow and soaked the front of his plaid shirt. "One of the horses pulled a tendon and I'm in the barn with the vet. If you're hungry, everything is ready."

"How bad is it?" she asked.

Kane's brow lifted as if he hadn't expected her to ask. "Doc Hamil doesn't think the problem is serious."

She nodded, feeling at odds. "You better get back. I'll wait for you. Do you want a baked potato?"

His smile lit his dark brown face and lifted his mustache. "They're in the warming oven."

"Oh."

"I better go. I'll be back as soon as I can." He turned, then paused. "Thanks for being willing to wait. I enjoy my meals better with you."

Victoria stared at the closed door a long time. Didn't Kane have any walls, any defenses? He wasn't the least bit bothered by letting her see he was genuinely happy to see her. Then, she remembered their talk in the meadow. She wondered when his patience would run out and he'd get tired of her, and of cooking all the meals.

* * *

After two weeks of marriage, Kane continued to have meals ready when Victoria arrived home. Sometimes he treated her more like a guest than a wife. Other times, he let her know he expected her to be an equal partner in the marriage even if she wasn't sure about anything else.

"I am not getting on that animal."

"Tory, the only way to really see the ranch is on horseback," Kane explained.

Arms held stiffly by her side, Victoria stared at the sleek black horse being held by Kane. "I'm sorry, but horses and I don't get along very well. One threw me in summer camp when I was in the sixth grade. I made a promise then that if they'd keep away from me, I'd keep away from them."

"The counselor didn't put you back on?"

"He tried." The lift of her chin spoke volumes.

Another case of not trusting, Kane thought. Tory wasn't much on giving anyone, man or beast, another chance. Yet he had to teach her to try. She had to learn she could trust him with her emotions as well as with her body.

Kane glanced around and saw Pete heading for the barn. He was the oldest of Kane's hired hands and the hardest working. The retired bull-fighter wasn't happy unless he was busy.

"Pete, take Mirage back and unsaddle her, then come back and get Shadow Walker's saddle."

"Sure thing, boss." Pete's gloved hand closed over the reins. Passing Victoria, he tipped his battered straw hat. "Evenin', Mrs. Taggart."

"Hello, Pete," she said absently, her gaze on her husband instead of the wiry ranch hand.

Kane unsaddled his quarterhorse, then tossed the saddle on the top rung of the coral.

"You aren't angry, are you?"

He sent her a look over his shoulder. "I told you that you can say 'no' to me anytime." Catching the horse's mane, he swung onto its back. "Some things I'll accept. Your fear of horses isn't one of them. Come here."

Victoria took a step backward. Riding bareback with Kane would be more terrifying than riding by herself. Lately, when he smiled at her, she had the craziest urge to touch him. She looked toward the security of the house, a hundred yards away.

"I don't know if I mentioned it, but I've been riding since I was three years old. I'd catch you before you got ten feet."

Her chin went up again. "I'm not some animal."

"No, you're my wife. All I'm asking is that you come over here and close your eyes. Think of something nice and before you know it, you'll be up here with me. If you're still uneasy, I'll put you down." He held out his hand.

She shook her head, sending her ponytail swinging. "I just finished dinner."

"If cowboys waited for the meals to settle before they got on a horse, the West would still need settling," Kane told her.

"They were used to it. I'm not." She took a step backward, then another.

"Then you're going to give up, and let me be embarrassed in two weeks?" he asked mildly.

She stopped. "What are you talking about?"

"Every year I have a group of kids from the Fort Worth Youth Center over for an old-fashioned hayride and barbecue. I wanted you riding beside me."

She knew she was being set up. The trouble was, she didn't see how to get out of it. Yet. "I'll ride with the driver of the hay wagon."

"Counselors already have dibs on those seats. Of course you could ride in the back with the kids. I'll get you some ear plugs to protect your ears from their loud radios."

"Kane, don't think for a minute I don't know you're doing a number on me."

He grinned. "Guilty, but I'm also telling you the truth." The grin dissolved. "Last year Pete was sick and I drove the wagon. I wanted them to have a good time, so I didn't complain about the noise. The counselor said the kids say music sounds better if it's loud. It must have sounded fantastic."

Her resistance faded. So she wasn't the only one Kane gave to. He was genuinely kind. "If I fall off that horse and get killed, I'm going to come back and haunt you." Taking a deep breath, she walked to his horse and closed her eyes.

Warm hands closed around her waist. She concentrated on them. "You all right?"

Her eyes opened. She sat sideways on the horse. Kane's arm circled her waist and brushed the underside of her breasts. Careful not to look down, she nodded.

"Slide your leg over to the other side and lean back against me."

Swallowing, she slowly complied. Heat and conditioned muscles pressed against her back, and on either side of her legs. This was worse than she imagined. She tried to swallow again and couldn't. Her throat was too dry.

"We're only going a little ways. Since you don't have a saddle to keep you on the horse I'm going to keep one arm around your waist so you won't slide off. All you have to do is lean against me. I'd put you behind me, but I don't want you letting go and falling or shutting your eyes so tight you don't see a thing."

The horse took off at a slow walk. Victoria clutched the muscled arm circling her waist. She felt off-balance by the rocking motion as much as by Kane's closeness. "Kane?"

"I got you, honey. I'll have you riding in no time, but then again, this is more enjoyable." His warm breath caressed her ear. "Just relax, try to feel the motion of the horse and think of something pleasant."

All she could think of was Kane. She never imagined horseback riding as being sensual before, but her mind was conjuring up all sorts of things. None of them conducive to remaining impartial and upright. She was relieved when he stopped by the bank of a small stream.

Getting off, he pulled her into his arms and started walking toward a crop of trees. "Won't your horse run off?"

"Shadow Walker is too well mannered for that."

Victoria had a feeling that if anything or anyone was foolish enough to run away from Kane he'd come after them. "It may come as a shock to you, but I've been walking since I was nine months old."

"I like carrying you. Besides your fancy outfit would be ruined." He gave her oversized white blouse and black gabardine slacks a sweeping glance. "I thought we discussed your getting some other clothes."

Feeling more at ease, she smiled into his frowning face. "We did, in passing. The only things sturdier I have are a fantastic denim skirt and shirt trimmed in turquoise leather with a matching pair of custom-made boots. I wore them to a dance to celebrate the contributions of black men in settling the West."

"The 'forgotten cowboys'," Kane said. "One in every five cowboys was black."

"Exactly. I didn't know until that night that a black man named Estavanico helped discover Texas." She tried to look up in Kane's face. "I would think you would have been there. Cleo Hearn of Lancaster and a lot of other cowboys like Donald and Ronald Stephens from Oklahoma were there." She frowned. "Despite their last name, they were very nice. I met my first authentic cowgirl, Marilyn LaBlanc. I'm surprised you weren't there."

"I'm not much on social functions." Kane stopped beneath a willow tree on the sloping bank of a stream and sat down with her in his arms. "We'll go into town tomorrow and get you some jeans and proper boots."

She jerked upright in his lap. "My outfit will do for the youth outing."

"Not if you want to blend in. Besides, I told you I like riding every day, and I'd like you to go with me. I don't mind riding double, if you don't."

She looked into his stern face. "I'll pick up something after work tomorrow."

"Jeans, but I'd like to go with you to get the boots. Buy the wrong pair and your feet will pay the price forever."

She started to tell him she was capable of buying a pair of boots, then changed her mind. Kane had a stubborn streak sometimes, and she knew he wasn't above putting her in the truck and taking her despite her protests. The trouble was, his stubbornness was usually for her benefit.

How do you fight a gentle, protective man who has your best interest at heart? "All right. I think I'll walk back."

"Not in those play shoes." Gathering her closer, he rose in one lithe movement. "Once we're home you can walk around until you wear a trench in the yard."

"Anyone ever tell you how bossy you are?"

"Once or twice."

CHAPTER 11

The next day when Victoria came home from work, Kane was waiting for her. Black Stetson pushed back on his head, one booted foot crossed over the other at the ankle, he leaned against the porch post with folded arms. "You ready to go shopping?" he asked as soon as Victoria's sandaled foot touched the bottom wooden step.

"I suppose if I refused, your reply will be 'walking or over your shoulder'," she tossed, feeling unexpectedly jubilant at the thought of verbal sparing with him.

"Actually I was thinking of something else," he drawled.

"Such as?"

Unfolding his arms and body in one fluid movement, he walked to the edge of the porch. "This." Strong hands lifted her; gentle lips closed over hers. The kiss was slow and drugging. After a long moment his head lifted. "Do we go shopping for your boots or keep on kissing?"

Heavy-lidded eyes opened. Victoria realized her feet were on the step again, but their bodies still touched. She looked at Kane's lips, felt the erratic beat of his heart, knew hers wasn't any steadier. For the first time the knowledge didn't frighten her. From Kane she had known only tenderness, the same tenderness with which he now held her.

"What's the third choice?" she asked breathlessly.

He blinked, then threw back his dark head. Velvet laughter rumbled from his throat. "Tory, you finally got one over on me." Curving his arm around her waist he started for his truck, parked in front of her Jaguar.

"I told you I would." Smiling, she started to get into the truck, then stopped. "You opened the wrong door."

"No I didn't. If you're going to be the wife of a cowboy you might as well learn how to properly ride in a truck." He urged her inside on the driver's side. "Couples sit so close you can't tell where the man stops and his woman begins."

Victoria inched across the seat. "Kane, I'm not so sure we should carry things this far."

"I am. In fact I've been thinking about it all day." He slid in beside her. "You aren't afraid are you?"

"What do you think?" she answered evasively.

"I think you're the most beautiful woman in the world and I'm proud to call you my wife," Kane told her softly, his knuckles grazed across her jaw.

Her heart skipped a beat. "You're not so bad yourself," she said just as softly.

Kane started the engine and pulled out. "After we get your boots, we better have your eyes tested."

"My judgment is faulty at times, but my vision is twenty-twenty." Tentatively, she touched his hand, trying to give him the reassurance he had given her so many times. "In the ways that count you have no equal. No matter what happens, remember that."

"I'll always remember everything about you." He turned onto the Farm and Market Road. "I think you might look good in red boots."

Victoria willingly let Kane change the subject. "Only if you get a matching pair."

"You're getting too good at this."

"Ain't I though?"

"Mrs. Taggart, thank you again for letting the kids come out so soon after your marriage. We are all so thrilled for you and Kane. You two looked good riding side by side."

Victoria smiled at the elderly black woman. "Mrs. Sanders, please call me Victoria. I'll let you in on a little secret. Kane only recently started giving me riding lessons."

The gray-headed woman stopped dishing out potato salad. "No wonder Kane offered to let you ride on his horse with him."

Victoria blushed. "Kane likes to tease."

"He looks happier than I've ever seen him and we've been friends for five years," the other woman said.

"Mrs. Sanders, am I going to get any potato salad or not?" asked an ebony-hued teenager.

She glanced at the young man, an ear stud in his left ear and three inches of hair sticking up from the crown of his otherwise closely shaven head. "Keep on with that attitude and you might not."

The boy behind the impatient youth snickered. Mrs. Sanders shot him a look. "That goes for you too, Emmanuel."

Both boys cut their eyes at Victoria and tucked their heads. "However, since it was my fault for not paying attention, I apologize. Can't have the two star players of the baseball team hungry." She dumped an extra portion on both plates.

The young men straightened, their pride intact, and moved down the line to where several other volunteers handed out beef brisket, corn on the cob, and soft drinks.

"You handled them well," Victoria commented.

"I didn't always. You should see Kane with them. He's a natural father."

Victoria's hand paused in serving baked beans on the plate of the last person in line. "Yes . . . he's very caring."

"Forgive me for saying so, but you're not what we expected." Steadily working, Mrs. Sanders kept talking. "We all saw your picture in the paper with the announcement, and you looked a little tight in the shoes."

Victoria recalled having the picture taken for her thirtieth birthday. She had looked straight at the camera as if daring it to do its worst. It had. "I didn't want my picture made, but my grandmother insisted. I'm afraid it showed."

"I liked it."

Victoria glanced up to see Kane grinning at her. He did that a lot lately and more and more she found herself grinning back, as she was doing now. "You're just asking to wear these beans."

"On my plate is fine," he said, waiting until she complied, then he moved down the food line. Shortly, he returned holding a cardboard bottom of the soft drink case he had converted into a tray. Inside was a plate laden with food. "I've already staked us out a quiet spot."

Trying to ignore Mrs. Sanders's indulgent smile, Victoria followed Kane to a blanket under one of the many oak trees in the back yard. In the middle of the blanket was a card that read 'reserved.'

"Quite inventive." Victoria sat down and crossed her jean-clad legs over her new black eel-skinned boots.

"I thought so. Here, hold this and I'll go get us a couple of drinks."

Leaning against the tree, Victoria watched Kane cross the yard. The graceful power of his muscular body drew her eyes like a magnet. He had only gone a few feet when he was stopped by one of the youths, then another youngster joined them. A couple of times, he glanced back as he moved slowly toward the ice cooler. She waved her hand in understanding.

The teenagers, between thirteen and sixteen, vied for Kane's time and his attention. She couldn't blame them. She had sought solace in his arms and had never been disappointed. Kane gave without making you feel less for needing to ask.

She wasn't surprised when five of the twenty kids came back with him. He looked apologetic, then pained as another youngster dropped down on the blanket, music blaring from his boom box. Kane glanced at Victoria.

She shrugged her shoulders. "When in Rome."

"I brought my algebra grade up and I'm going to pass," boasted a pimply faced boy, his baseball cap on backward, his teeth bared in a wide grin.

Kane slapped him on his broad shoulders. "I told you. Some of us have to study harder than others."

"What did you ever have to do that was hard?" snarled a voice that plainly couldn't decide what pitch to maintain. "You have everything. A nice place. A rich, pretty wife."

Kane lifted a brow at the thin young man standing belligerently over him. "I worked on my father's farm two hours before school and until dark after I got home. I didn't expect people to give me anything. The world doesn't owe you anything, Ali, and thinking that it does is going to leave you bitter and angry."

"I've got a right . . ."

"Says who? You're barely sixteen. If you want to reach seventeen happy, change your attitude and try to figure out how the system works instead of working against it."

"That's selling out."

"That's surviving. Then you can help someone else have a better life."

Ali dug the toe of his well-worn sneaker into the lush grass. "I'll think about it," he said sullenly.

"You do that. In the meantime, stop standing over my wife and have a seat." Kane said. "And if you keep on trying to ruin the day for everyone, I might put Mrs. Taggart on your softball team as a pitcher."

The young man looked horrified. Victoria glared at Kane. "Did I ever tell you that the year I was the pitcher on the girls' softball team in high school we went to state?"

Kane's mouth dropped open.

"I know it's hard to close your mouth with your foot inside, but try," Victoria said sweetly.

The kids looked from Kane to Victoria, then they all burst into laughter.

Kane took the converted tray out of her hands and pulled her into his arms before she could protest. She could only accept and enjoy the brief kiss he gave her.

The boys whistled. The girls giggled.

He lifted his head. "I've got a feeling I'm going to pay for that remark for a long time." Sitting her upright, he picked up their food. "You know I was kidding, Tory. We're a team. We're going to beat all comers in every event."

"Event?"

"Three-legged race, sack race, water balloon toss." He eyed her cotton blouse. "Maybe we won't enter the balloon toss."

Victoria smiled. "Yes, we will. I am going to show you exactly how good I can throw."

Victoria and Kane lost every event.

In the three-legged race she fell on top of him within five feet of the finish line. They lay grinning from ear to ear at each other. Two hops and she was out of the sack race. Kane landed beside her. The softball game was a tie between the adults and the youths. Victoria pitched to Kane's loud praise and encouragement.

When it came time for the water balloon throw, the counselor couldn't find the balloons. From the shrugs and grins the boys were giving each other, Victoria deduced they had helped a little with their disappearance. One of the girls suggested a dance. The boom box blared out.

"Wanna dance?"

Leaning back on the blanket, Victoria glanced at Kane beside her. "I don't think my feet can move that fast."

"They don't have to." Pulling her up and into his arms, he held her close. "Listen to the music inside your head."

Her head pressed against his chest, she followed his lead. As warmth and need coursed through her, everything else ceased to exist. She felt cherished, needed, wanted.

The intrusive noise of whistles and applause caused her to lift her head. All the other couples had stopped dancing and moved back to watch Kane and Victoria. A few of the women counselors were dabbing their eyes, the men were giving Kane a thumb's up sign, the young girls looked dreamy, the boys surprised but pleased.

"It's nice to know love still exists," Mrs. Sanders said. "We've taken up enough of your time. You've only been married a month. Come on, people, and let's get the place cleaned up."

With a light squeeze and a brush of his lips, Kane went to help. Her mind in a turmoil, Victoria didn't move. She had forgotten about her boutiques and their business agreement. Frantically, she thought back and realized she had stopped thinking about the reason for their marriage after Kane kissed her earlier on the blanket. She had been a woman enjoying the day with a man she cared about.

"Tory, are you all right?"

She glanced up into Kane's ruggedly masculine face. If she didn't watch herself, when the time came, she wouldn't be able to walk away. "I'm just tired."

"Go on inside and rest. I'll explain to everyone."

"No, I'll be all right. You go on." She watched Kane help load up the van and knew she lied. She would never be all right if she didn't stay away from him.

Something was wrong. Kane knew it, but he wasn't sure what to do about it. He looked across the breakfast table at Victoria's bowed head. The only reason she sat there was because this morning she had been unable to think of an excuse fast enough. This was the first meal they had shared in a week. Where he was, Victoria wasn't.

It was usually dark when she arrived home. Mumbling that she had work to do, she closed herself in her room. He didn't know what had changed at the outing, but maybe tonight after the banquet they'd have a chance to talk.

"I'll pick you up around four."

Her head jerked up. "For what?"

"The banquet in Houston honoring black men who have made a significant difference in the community. A friend of mine is flying us down," he explained patiently. "I told you Monday."

Victoria put her fork beside the uneaten stack of pancakes. "I was out of the shop last Saturday. I can't be gone again."

"You can if you want to." Some of Kane's patience slipped. Maybe it was time to push again. "I made room reservations so you can rest and get dressed in Houston. After the banquet, we can stay over and fly back tomorrow."

"No." She stood. "I have to stay and work. You go and have a good trip."

"It's important to me that you go."

She stopped, but didn't turn. "I have things to do. Perhaps it's best if we don't become too involved in each other's lives. Remember, our marriage is only a business agreement."

Kane's large hands fisted on the table. "I thought we were . . . never mind. I'll see you tonight."

She glanced over her shoulder. "Since you'll be late coming back, I think I'll stay at my place."

Something hard flashed across Kane's face. "*This* is *your place* and you had better be *here* when I get home or I'm coming to get you."

"I'm tired of you bossing me. I can't wait until my time is up so I can get back to living my own life," she snapped, then ran to her car.

Tears rolled down her cheek and splattered on her blouse as she drove out of the yard. She didn't notice or care. She remembered the pain in Kane's face. She fought against going back and telling him she was sorry. For her own protection, she couldn't.

If things continued, she'd end up in Kane's bed. Once that happened she would be more vulnerable than she had ever been in her life. She couldn't put herself in that position again for anyone.

Victoria had the worst morning of her life. Realizing she wasn't going to be any good on the sales floor, she called in a part-time sales clerk and went to her office. However, she couldn't concentrate enough to work on the books, the time schedule, her summer sale promotion plans or any of the dozen things that needed her attention.

Each time the phone rang, she'd look at it and wonder if it was Kane. Then when her intercom didn't light up, disappointment would wash over her and she'd wonder how he was doing.

As the clock moved toward three, her restlessness grew. She wouldn't put it past Kane to make her go. Then she remembered the look on his face and knew he wouldn't come for her. Whatever feelings he might have had for her, she had effectively killed them. That had been her intention, but she hadn't counted on the pain for either of them.

It was after one in the morning when she pulled up in front of the ranch house. A single light burned in the kitchen. She didn't know if Kane had tried to make good his promise to come get her or not.

Ten minutes after three, she had left the shop and gone to an eight-screen theater. She hadn't been able to sit through more than three movies before the theater closed. Getting out of the car, she didn't know whether she was happy or disappointed not to see Kane's truck in the driveway.

Unlocking the front door, she reached for the light switch.

"So you finally decided to come home."

Fear splinted through her at the rough, unfamiliar voice. She fumbled for the switch. Light flared. Frantically, her gaze searched the room until she located Matt standing at the foot of the stairs. A part of her wanted to relax, but something about his eyes wouldn't let her. "Where's Kane?"

He didn't say anything, just continued to stare at her. "Answer me. Where's Kane? Has something happened to him?"

"Would you care?" he asked, his voice as hard as his face.

Fear congealed in the pit of her stomach. She ran toward the stairs. "I'll find him myself."

"He's not there." His words stopped her midway across the room.

"Where is he?"

"He went looking for you. For the life of me I can't understand why, after what you put him through tonight."

"What are you talking about?"

He snorted. "Don't try to act innocent. Kane knew he had a good chance of receiving the Man of the Year Award tonight. He asked you to go with him, didn't he?"

Victoria felt ill. "He asked, but . . . I didn't know he was up for an award."

"He won. His family was there, but not his beautiful bride. She was too busy with her stores to bother coming. Every man sitting on the platform had a woman with him except Kane. He refused to let Mama or Addie take your place. You can imagine some of the things people said."

Victoria closed her eyes, her heart going out to Kane. She had hurt him, trying to protect herself.

"What's your price?"

Her eyelids flicked open. "Price?"

Matt's smile left her chilled. "I'm going to save Kane from the hard lesson I learned about beautiful women and lying eyes. One Taggart strolling in hell is enough." He took a step closer. "A blind man can see Kane cares about you, but only a blind man would believe you cared about him in return. Name your price and walk away. I'll give you whatever you want if you'll go upstairs and pack your bags before he returns."

"If you weren't Kane's brother, I'd ask you to leave. I'll wait for Kane upstairs." She started past him.

"In your own solitary bed no doubt."

Surprise stopped her as effectively as if she had run into a glass wall. Words of denial formed in her mind until she saw the derision in Matt's eyes, heard it in his voice.

"I just discovered why Kane was so insistent that I not return with him. There's only one guest bedroom and you're sleeping in it. The others are full of unfinished antiques. He's too good to get kicked in the teeth like this."

"I wouldn't hurt him." Even as Victoria spoke the words, she knew that was exactly what she had done over and over.

"You don't think sleeping in the guest bedroom would hurt him? What kind of wife are you? You wouldn't even give him that little of yourself."

She flinched.

Unrelenting fingers grabbed her arm. "Name your price."

"Let her go, Matt." Kane ordered.

CHAPTER 12

Matt neither moved nor did he take his cutting gaze from Victoria's uplifted face. "I hope no one uses you the way you're using Kane."

Without thought Stephen came to Victoria's mind. Bile rose in her throat. My God! Had she treated Kane the same deplorable way Stephen had her? The realization that she had, struck her with the force of a physical blow. By trying to protect herself she had hurt Kane with the same selfish ruthlessness Stephen dealt her.

Matt's fingers slowly unclamped. Stepping back, he faced his brother. "I'll sleep in the bunk house."

Kane kept his gaze on Victoria until he heard the front door open and close.

"Please forgive me. I didn't know," Victoria cried, anguish in her voice.

"Like you said, we have to get used to each other not being around." He walked past her and up the stairs.

Not knowing what to say, Victoria went to her room. Restless, she paced the floor. She knew from experience the pain Kane must be suffering. Even when she no longer cared about Stephen, the idea that he thought she wasn't woman enough, intelligent enough, beautiful enough, hurt. A caring man like Kane didn't deserve to be hurt because she was a coward.

Trembling fingers opened the door connecting their bedrooms. What she saw made her heart constrict. Kane, his elbows bent, his bowed head resting wearily in the open palms of his hands, sat in an overstuffed chair in the far corner of the room. "Kane."

Abruptly his head lifted. For a moment he looked like a wild animal trapped in his lair, then his expression became guarded. "What are you doing in here?"

Knowing she was to blame for the bleakness in his once-tender voice, she took a tentative step toward him. "Trying to apologize *again.*"

"If you don't mind, I'm tired." Pushing to his feet, he pulled the dangling black bow tie from around his neck and flung it toward the bed. It missed. So did the black tuxedo jacket that followed.

For once he didn't appear concerned with neatness. Victoria was all too aware of the reason why. "Matt told me you won the Man of the Year Award. You must be very proud." She glanced around the room she had always been afraid to enter. She wasn't surprised by the antique mahogany furniture, but she was by the massive sleigh bed. Then she remembered the yearning she heard sometimes in his voice, saw in his face. Kane was a romantic. He still dreamed, and she had taken one of his dreams. "Where is your award?"

"In the car." His shirt landed in the vicinity of the other discarded clothes. Unbuckling his belt, he stared at her. "Do you mind?"

Victoria looked into his drawn face and felt his misery and need as if it came from her own body. Kane needed her just as she needed him. "Of course not. "Pushing his hands aside, she pulled the belt from the loops.

"What are you doing?" Kane yelled as he staggered back.

"Helping you," she said, hoping she sounded braver than her shaking knees indicated. "I know I haven't been very good at it before, but I had you confused with someone else. I don't any more."

"That's not what you're doing," Kane told her. "I heard what Matt told you and I don't need your pity."

"I'm not giving you any," Victoria answered softly.

Kane was not convinced. "Then what do you call your sudden need to come in here?"

"I hurt you and—"

"I thought so," Kane interrupted, his eyes blazing. "I can do without you offering your body on the sacrificial altar just because you're feeling guilty."

Incensed, Victoria gave him glare for glare. "How dare you say I'd go to bed with you out of guilt."

"It's the truth. Nothing else has prompted you to approach me first." Kane shouted back. "I can count on one hand the number of times you've willingly touched me. Now you think I'm fool enough to believe you can't wait to crawl in bed with me? Well, I'm not that hard up or that stupid."

Grabbing her arm, he started for the connecting bedroom door. "I'm doing us both a favor. In the morning you'd feel sorry you ever let me touch you and run like hell."

"Not if you did it right," she blurted out.

Kane went deathly still.

Knowing she finally had his attention, she looked at his hard face and rushed on. "I know I haven't had much experience in these matters, but it seems reasonable that *if* a man can make a woman scream in pleasure, she wouldn't be sorry afterwards or in a hurry to leave."

Kane's fingers tightened on her arm, but he made no other move one way or the other. Victoria decided to push him a little. "Or was it just a cowboy bragging?"

His eyes drilled into her. Victoria lowered her gaze to the middle of his wide naked chest. "I might have known. In all the risqué discussions I've heard at the beauty salon about a man's prowess in bed, I've never heard of a man making a woman scream." She sighed dramatically. "You probably can crimp a lot of toes though. Ethel, my beautician, says if her toes don't crimp, she feels cheated."

Victoria glanced up at Kane's scowling face. "Oh, well, it was an interesting thought."

Powerful hands clasped her arms and jerked her to him. Nose to nose, eye to eye, he snarled, actually snarled, at her. She had the feeling that Kane fought the urge to shake her. With her feet dangling in the air, he started for his bed.

"So you think I was bragging. So you think you might like to scream. Well, Victoria Elizabeth Chandler Taggart, you pushed this cowboy too hard this time." He tossed her on the bed.

Victoria bounced up, her arms flailing out to maintain her balance. Once equilibrium was achieved, she brushed her hair out of her eyes and wished she hadn't. Hands on hips, feet spread apart, Kane looked dangerous but didn't move from his threatening position. Then she remembered that this was Kane. He would hurt himself before he harmed her. He wanted her to run.

"If your intention is to make me scream by glaring at me, it won't work. As much as I enjoy looking at your magnificent body, I'd much rather have it next to mine."

"You're asking for it, Tory."

She tilted her head. "Am I going to get it?" she asked, her voice husky. "I want to be able to touch you without debating the wisdom of doing so. I've been running from you all week because I knew if I didn't, I'd run *to* you. I had stopped thinking of you as my business partner and started thinking of you as a man I cared about, a man I wanted to be intimate with." She took a deep breath.

"Despite everything I know about you and our agreement that I be there for you, I ran. I disregarded your feelings in an attempt to protect mine."

"Tory, don't—"

"Even now, you're trying to spare me. Not this time. I was wrong. It was utterly selfish of me to run out on you yesterday. I . . . I know that nothing I can say or do will erase the pain I caused, but I am sorry. The odd thing is, running only made me more miserable."

Hope and tears gleamed in her eyes. "I want to stop being afraid of my emotions. No other man can give me that freedom except you. I know I'm asking a lot after the way I behaved, but . . . but I thought since I was giving this time too, and I'm a little scared how this is going to turn out, it might count for something."

For a long time, Kane simply stared at her, then his hands moved to his side. "It counts for a lot."

"Oh, Kane." Victoria scrambled to her knees and into his arms. His lips took hers in a kiss filled with passion and long-suppressed hunger. She trembled, loving the feel of his warm muscled flesh beneath her seeking fingers. Their mouths clung as if both were starved and were finally feasting at a banquet.

"Please be sure. There isn't anything I wouldn't give to be buried so deep inside you that there would be no beginning and no end. To hear your cries of passion and know I pulled them from your lips." His hands trembled. "I'm not sure if I can stop once we start or if I could survive if you turned away from me."

Shaking fingers smoothed the frown from his brow. "I'm sure. The lack is mine, not yours." Her gaze fell. "I-I'm not very good at this."

Kane snorted. Hard fingers lifted her chin and pulled her closer. His hips moved. Victoria gasped as she felt the frank hardness of his desire. "If you were any better, I don't think I could stand it. Last chance to run for the door."

She kissed him, giving him everything, holding back nothing of the hunger she felt. She was tired of being afraid. Need shimmered through her. She leaned back and Kane followed her down into the waiting softness of the mattress. His body against hers felt glorious, but she wanted to know how it would feel if there was nothing between them.

Her breath caught when he started to unbutton her blouse. He released the front fasteners of her lacy blue bra. Air rushed over her lips in a ragged sigh. His callused hand cupped her aching breast. She wanted to moan with pleasure and scream with impatience at the same time. "Kane?"

"We waited so long, Tory. You feel good, too damn good," Kane growled, his mouth closing over her nipple. Then his hand swept up her skirt, over her legs, between her thighs. Instinctively, her knees clamped together. But as Kane's gentle finger stroked her inner softness, she arched against his hand in pleasure. A moan slipped past her lips.

"You were made to be loved by me," Kane half-groaned, half-growled. Quickly, he dispensed with her clothes, then tore open a foil package.

Finally she was beneath him, feeling the heat and hardness of his body. Their eyes met a second before he eased into her.

Kane wanted to keep his eyes open, to watch the emotions sweep across her face, but the pleasure was too exquisite, too intense. His lids fluttered. Her long sleek legs wrapped around him, drawing him deeper inside her satin heat.

When the scream came, neither knew whose it was.

Victoria woke slowly, savoring the delicious way she felt. Opening her eyes, she saw Kane, his elbow bent, his chin propped in his open palm, staring down at her. Sunlight flowed over his broad shoulders, bronzing his skin. He looked beautiful and glowing. She had put that look on his face. She was wildly pleased.

She smiled shyly. "Good morning."

Leaning over, he brushed his lips across hers. "Now it is."

"I-I planned to be up first and serve you breakfast in bed," she said, her voice quaky as his thumb stroked her rigid nipple through the sheet.

Kane's eyes shimmered. "Exactly what I had in mind." The sheet slid away. His mouth closed over the pouting point.

"K-Kane." Victoria's voice broke; she tried again. "I need to go to the kitchen . . . oh, goodness." His head moved across the flatness of her stomach, going steadily lower. Understanding dawned. "Kane, you—" Victoria sucked in her breath as Kane found what he sought.

Victoria's last coherent thought before pleasure overtook her was that besides making her scream, Kane was probably the best toe-crimper in the world.

Much later that morning, hunger drove Victoria and Kane to the kitchen. Kane had on his jeans; Victoria wore his white shirt. Kane had personally put it on her and rolled up several inches of dangling sleeves, saying she wouldn't stay dressed long enough to bother putting on anything else.

Arms folded, Victoria leaned against the counter and shamelessly studied Kane's hips as he bent to pull out a package of giant blueberry muffins from the refrigerator. To think, she had once been afraid of showing her emotions around him. She felt freer and happier than she had in her entire life. Closing the door, he turned to see her appreciative smile.

"You have a nice set of buns, cowboy."

Kane gave her a crooked grin. Setting the muffins aside, he pulled her into his arms and nuzzled her neck. "You think so, huh?"

"Hmm," Victoria almost purred as she arched her neck. "If you don't stop doing that, the bacon will burn."

"I might consider it, provided you stop moving against me as if you have an itch only I can scratch."

"One of us has to be sensible," Victoria said, then nipped his shoulder.

His hands cupped her hips and fitted her softness against his hardness, his lips searching for hers. "I don't think it's going to be me."

The back door opened. Through the half slit of her eyes Victoria saw Matt, his jaw slack, poised in the doorway. With a shriek, she tried to hide behind Kane, who had turned toward the door.

"Morning, Matt," Kane said, his voice strained. "Can you come back in a little while?"

Matt shook his dark head. "Just wanted to let you know, Pete is driving me to DFW to catch a flight home."

Kane nodded. "Have a safe trip. I'll call you later."

"Are you sure this is what you want?" Matt asked, his probing gaze searching his brother's face before going to the tousled head of black hair that had momentarily popped from behind Kane's back.

"Yes." Kane spoke without hesitation.

He nodded in resignation. "Then I'll see you at Addie's graduation ceremonies next weekend." The door closed.

"I don't think he likes me," Victoria said. "But then I haven't given him much reason to."

Kane stroked her face with his knuckles. "He'll come around. He had a bad experience with a woman and he doesn't want me to do the same."

A look of shame crossed her face. "I never intended to hurt you, but I did."

"You were afraid to trust. You've taken a big step and we'll take one day at a time."

"Is that what you want?"

Kane brushed her hair away from her face. "No. I'm a greedy man, I want it all. But like I told you once, I'd settle for a lot less."

Victoria breathed a little easier. She wanted it all too, but she learned long ago that wanting wasn't enough. In time, maybe they would learn what was enough. "I think I'm a little greedy too."

"I aim to satisfy all of your needs." A flick of his wrist cut the burner off, then he pulled out a chair. Victoria gasped softly to find herself straddling Kane's legs. "Scared?"

With her knees on either side of his waist, she was exposed and vulnerable. Her hands clamped on his shoulders felt the heat of his flesh even as she felt the tender way his hands held her waist. "Not me. Are you?"

"I like a sassy woman." He devoured her lips. When he lifted his head, both were breathing a little harder. "I was a fool to start something I'd have to wait to finish."

"One of us is crazy." She moved against the obvious proof of his ability to finish what he had started.

He laughed wickedly. "Me." Standing with her in his arms, he left the room. "Breakfast will have to wait."

"Why are we going back upstairs?"

"Birth control. I told you I'd always take care of you, and that means no unplanned pregnancy," Kane said. "I'd be the happiest man on earth to have a child with you, but I don't think you're ready for that big of a step in our relationship."

She blushed and buried her head between his neck and shoulder. After all the things she had done with him and to him, the subject of birth control shouldn't have embarrassed her. But it did. It also reminded her of how caring Kane was of her. She just wasn't sure if this time she agreed with him.

"If they don't stop ringing the doorbell, I'm going to strangle them," Kane growled, positioning one jean-clad leg between Victoria's bare ones.

"M-Maybe it's important," she said, her voice breathless and thick.

"Nothing is more important than this." Kane's tongue swept inside her mouth. Instantly her tongue sought his. Her arms tightened around his neck. Her body yielded. Desire rocked through him.

He pressed her deeper into the mattress. Restlessly, his hand swept over the silken skin of her stomach to the soft inner flesh of her thigh. Blunt-tipped fingers lifted the edge of her panties.

The chime of the doorbell was suddenly accompanied by what sounded like a fist pounding against the door. With a muttered expletive, Kane rolled from atop Victoria and snatched his shirt from the floor.

"I have to go to work anyway," Victoria said huskily. Sitting up, she fumbled with the clasp of her lacy red bra. "Mondays are always hectic at the store."

"Don't you move from that bed," Kane ordered. Shoving his arms into the shirt, he reached for the doorknob. "For their sake, I hope they have hospitalization."

Kane recalled few times that he had been so angry. He had finally managed to get Victoria to change her mind about going to work, and now some nut was making a nuisance of himself. During their lovemaking, she held nothing back and came to him with a passion and need that equaled his own. She cared about him, and soon she would learn to love him. She was his wife in every sense and she was going to remain his wife.

Stalking across the living room, he jerked the front door open. Seeing his business partner didn't take the sting out of Kane's words. "You better have a hell of a good reason for disturbing me."

William Conrad, who had never been the object of the full force of Kane's anger, stepped back. Mouth agape, his cigar teetered precariously between his teeth.

"Spit it out," Kane demanded. "You were anxious enough a moment ago."

"Kane, if you'd stop yelling at the poor man perhaps he could tell you what you want to know."

Kane glanced over his shoulder to see Victoria at the foot of the stairs, her hair softly mussed, her face flushed and beautiful. Her red knit dress clung to every glorious inch of her fantastic body and reminded him of the lacy undergarments he had almost removed before . . . He whirled back to their unwanted guest.

"I'm waiting, William."

Apparently, the reprieve had been enough time for William to regain his composure. "After the decision was made to go into men's skin care you said you wanted to make some changes in the marketing strategy and that you'd get back to me. The press conference is tomorrow to announce the start of Cinnamon II, and I wanted to know all the facts before then."

"Didn't I tell you last week that I needed to check out a few details and I'd get back to you before the press conference?"

"Yes, but—"

"Have I ever lied to you?"

"No, but—"

"Been late with a report?"

"No, but you've never been married before either," William said in a rush.

"I don't think we've been properly introduced." Victoria smiled sweetly as she stepped between the two men. "I'm Victoria Taggart and you must be William Conrad, Kane's partner."

William appeared dazed by the beautiful woman standing before him. It took him a couple of seconds to notice her extended hand. "Hello, Mrs. Taggart. You're lovelier than your picture."

Something that sounded suspiciously like a growl came from Kane. William snatched his hand back.

"Mr. Conrad, you must know that Kane is as dependable as the sunrise," she chided gently. "You can't have worked with him all these years and not learned how trustworthy and responsible he is. If he said he'd have the report to you, he'll have it to you."

The tension eased out of Kane. His wife was defending him again. It was almost worth William's interruption. Almost.

"I suppose," William admitted grudgingly. "My wife calls me a worrier. I like to know where I'm going."

"In other words, you like being in control, and you've found out you can't control Kane," Victoria guessed.

William's startled gaze flew up to Kane.

"I've known you were that way since our first meeting," Kane told him. "But in taking me on as a partner, you showed me you wouldn't put your personal feelings above the company's. You were also willing to work as hard or harder than I was in saving Cinnamon. You didn't sit around crying and feeling sorry for yourself. If you had, I would have walked away even if you had offered me twice the percentage at half the price. I don't have any patience for people who won't help themselves. You were then and you still are, a valuable asset to the company."

Once again, William appeared stunned. "You've never told me this before."

"I don't like explaining myself," Kane told him.

Victoria stared up into her husband's face and recalled all the times he had patiently explained things to her. She was married to a very special man. He almost made her believe in happily ever after.

William extended his hand, the lines of worry around his eyes gone. "Thanks, Kane. Sorry I disturbed you. It won't happen again."

The older man's hand disappeared into Kane's larger, stronger one. He decided to be as gracious as his partner. "I've already taken care of the changes I wanted, including reserving advertising space in newspapers and magazines for December, talked to a photographer about giving the layout a more outdoor feel, and started searching for another male model who doesn't look as if he hasn't started shaving yet."

"Why didn't . . ." William smiled and shook his graying head. "I almost forgot you don't like explaining yourself. In this case I can guess. Since you left, I've become more demanding. You wanted me to get the message that you won't be pushed."

Kane glanced down into Victoria's upturned face. "Only one person can do that."

"Kane likes for people to trust him," Victoria said.

Once again William's gaze went from Kane to Victoria. "It won't happen again." He went briskly down the steps.

As soon as his partner got inside his car, Kane closed the front door and picked Victoria up. "I thought I told you to stay put."

Victoria wrapped her arms around his neck and laughed. "You don't sound as if I can make you do anything."

Kane's lips found hers. The kiss was hot, quick and deep. He lifted his head and waited until her eyelids drifted upward. "You make me burn, Tory. You make me fight for control each time I take you in my arms."

Her trembling fingers touched the hard line of his jaw. "You make me feel the same way."

His black eyes blazed. He started for the stairs at a fast clip, carrying her as if she were as weightless as a shadow. The soft outline of her body against his chest proclaimed she was a flesh-and-blood woman. *His* woman. Nudging the bedroom door open with his shoulder, he sat her down and drew her dress over her head in one coordinated movement.

"Don't think I'm easy because I decided to let you have your way with me," she said, and pushed his shirt down his muscular arms.

"If you hadn't, I probably would have kidnapped you." He laid her in the bed, then stripped out of his jeans and undershorts.

With unabashed pride and longing Victoria stared at Kane's powerful, naked body. He was superb in every breathtaking detail. He had taught her so much, given her so much. She didn't know she could be this happy. "You would have made a magnificent knight."

Kane came down on the bed and gathered her into his arms. "Only if you were the prize."

"Words." Victoria licked the hard brown nub of his nipple and smiled at his groan. "I'd like to see some action."

His hands closed over her lace clad breasts, and when they lifted, the fragile scrap of material was gone. His head bent. "Your wish is my command."

The following days were filled with revelations for Victoria. No longer did she try to analyze her emotions. She reacted on impulse and continued to be rewarded with more happiness than she had experienced in her entire lifetime. To her added pleasure, she quickly discovered, she couldn't have been more wrong in telling Kane she didn't want whispers of sweet nothings. She unashamedly relished every sensual promise he made . . . and its fulfillment. One night after dinner, she told him as much. He smiled like a conquering knight, swept her into his arms and took her to bed. The next day, Bonnie and Clair Benson took credit for the glow in Victoria's face.

Bonnie she teased about no longer being afraid of getting an arrow in her back. Her grandmother she let think what she would. Victoria knew Kane deserved the real credit. At Addie's graduation, she and Kane were never more than a few feet apart. Relatives of Kane's she hadn't met gave Victoria as many hugs and congratulations as they did the graduate.

"I don't think I've ever seen Kane this happy."

Victoria turned to see Matt standing beside her, but his gaze was on Kane taking a picture of Addie in her cap and gown, with their parents. "He might not have been if you hadn't set me stra—"

"Forget it," Matt interrupted, his eyes finally coming back to her. "Just keep him happy."

Victoria frowned at the odd inflection of his voice. "Was that a threat or a command?"

"Both," he said, and walked over to drape an arm around Addie's shoulders.

"What was that all about?"

Startled, Victoria glanced around to see Bonnie. "He's afraid I might hurt Kane. I wouldn't do that."

"I hate to bring this up, but what are you going to do when your time together is up?"

The question was one Victoria had refused to let herself think about. "I don't know, but I'm not going to hurt Kane."

Uneasiness crept into Bonnie's expression. "If you leave, I don't see how you're going to be able to avoid it . . . hurting him and yourself."

CHAPTER 13

Thirteen days. Thirteen days were left of the three months she had agreed to spend with Kane. It seemed rather prophetic that she and Kane had eloped with thirteen days left on the deadline her grandmother had given her. She had known what to do then. She wished she knew what to do now.

At least she wasn't still hung up on her hatred of Stephen. The previous night in Dallas, at a performance by the Black Dance Theatre benefiting the Museum of African-American Life and Culture, she had looked up during intermission and seen her ex-husband. Seeing her, Stephen almost ran from the lobby of the Majestic Theatre.

Instead of rage, she felt sadness that she had wasted so much time hating. She had glanced up at Kane and wanted to be home and in bed with her husband. She whispered her own sensual promise in his ear. Hand and hand they quickly left the theatre.

A secret smile on her face, she leaned back in her chair and looked around her office. For once, it was free of the usual clutter of shipping boxes, lingerie, freestanding racks, mannequins, props, and an odd assortment of other things. Kane had "organized" things for her. She would have gotten around to it before the big summer sale, but he seemed to enjoy helping her.

Men and women customers certainly liked having him around. They weren't bashful about asking his opinion, and with a wicked gleam in his eyes, he had been quick to point out his preference. Sales had soared.

Customers had actually been disappointed that morning to learn he wasn't coming in.

Victoria couldn't blame them; she didn't want to think of a day without seeing Kane. Each minute she spent with him, she wanted a hundred more. She was actually looking forward to his college reunion the following weekend. Yet she wasn't so naive to think that the first bloom of passion would last forever. There had better be something to take its place. She smiled to herself. Passion wasn't so bad, for the time being.

An hour later, Victoria pulled up in front of the ranch house. Grabbing a bag of groceries in one hand and a picnic basket in the other, she went inside. She had two hours before Kane expected her home. She was going to surprise him with a picnic, and herself. Laughing at her own boldness, she set the bags on the counter.

The sound of an automobile pulling up outside had her rushing to the window. At the sight of a red truck, her shoulders sagged in relief. She went back outside.

A middle-aged man climbed out of the pickup and tipped his straw hat off his balding gray head. "Evening, Mrs. Taggart. I'm Nate Hinson."

"Have we met before?"

"Not in person." He smiled at her confusion. "Kane came into my antique shop about eight years ago and we hit it off right away. I've been out here too many times to count with deliveries. One time he showed me a beautiful, hand-carved cradle. Seems it had been handed down through his mother's family, and she insisted, as the oldest, he keep it. Kane showed me a picture of a pretty young woman about two years ago and told me she'd either be the mother of his child or he wouldn't have one."

"Kane showed you a picture and a cradle?"

"That he did," Mr. Hinson repeated. "The refinishing job on the cradle is one of the best I've ever seen. He put a lot of love into that job. Used to keep it in his workshop covered up and waiting. There's not a person around who isn't happy for him getting married. We sure would have liked to have been there to see it."

Kane had refinished a cradle for another woman. Pain ripped through her. Only years of training kept her upright and helped Victoria to mumble, "I-I'm sorry."

"Don't you go apologizing. We are all fond of that husband of yours. Everyone around knows what a good man he is and how much he loves kids." Mr. Hinson shook his head. "If you need help with a project with kids, just ask Kane."

She pressed her hand against her empty womb. "Yes."

"Nice seeing good things happen to a good man like Kane." Hinson glanced around the well-tended yard and the painted buildings beyond. "This place was going to seed until Kane bought it. That barn had a hole in it as big as my truck, and this house hadn't had a coat of paint on it in years. Good thing it was built to last. Never saw a man so good at turning throwaways into something worthwhile."

Victoria thought of herself: thrown away by Stephen and refurbished by Kane—but she was just a substitute.

"Here I am running on and you probably need to be getting on with supper. I saw this rocker at an estate sale yesterday and thought of Kane and the cradle." Unhooking the tailgate of the truck, he unloaded the high-backed mahogany rocker and set it down on the porch. "When I saw Kane in town a couple of weeks back I asked him if you were the one in the picture and he just grinned. Never seen a man so happy or proud."

Victoria's gaze clung to the rocker. Her throat clogged. Tears stung her eyes.

"It's my wedding gift to you and Kane. I better be going. The way those clouds are rolling in, it looks like we might have a bit of a storm." Closing the tailgate, he got inside the vehicle. "Good day, Mrs. Taggart."

The instant the door closed, Victoria tore down the steps and around the house to Kane's workshed. It took less than a minute for her to locate the small object, covered by the type of protective padding movers use. Her hand trembled as she lifted the cover.

A cradle. Not a speck of dust touched the gleaming mahogany surface.

Tears rolled down her cheeks. Kane might have wanted a substitute wife, but not a substitute mother for his children. He still loved another woman. Agony rolled over her in waves. Somehow, she managed to stand. She had one thought: to leave before Kane came back. It wasn't his fault she had played her part too well. She hadn't realized until that agonizing moment that she had confused passion with love. She loved Kane.

Her fingers clamped and unclamped on the smooth wooden surface of the cradle. Wearily, she turned, took a step, and came to an abrupt halt. Kane filled the doorway.

Pain and misery washed over her. And the one person in the world who she would have run to for consolation was the person who had caused her such pain.

"Honey, come inside and let's talk."

She watched him move closer and lift his hand toward her face. "Don't. Don't touch me."

Anguish ripped through Kane's gut. Having Victoria recoil from him now was worse than anything he had ever experienced. He had met Hinson a mile from the ranch. At the mention of the cradle and rocker, Kane had gunned his truck. It had taken less than five minutes to reach her, but he was too late. Victoria might want his body, but not his baby.

"Things can be as they were before. Forget about the cradle," Kane told her, aware of the pleading note in his voice and unable to do anything about it.

Victoria flinched. She looked at the man she loved. Big, brawny, and gentle, he still had the power to make her knees weak. If she thought there was a chance for him to forget about the other woman, she might stay. But two years and a cradle were too much to fight. She walked past Kane as if he didn't exist.

She knew he followed her inside the house and up the stairs. There was nothing she could do about that now. All her concentration was on getting her car keys and going someplace to nurse her pain in private. She was paying the price for caring, for being vulnerable.

"You're not leaving."

She opened her mouth, felt the sting in her throat and in her eyes. Her hands clamped on the keys. Closing her eyes, she said one word, "Please."

"No. You have thirteen days before the bargain is over and you're not going anyplace," Kane told her.

Her lids lifted. She saw the tortured look on his face, a look she was sure mirrored her own. No matter what, she was sure of one thing: Kane hadn't meant to hurt her. "I can't stay here."

He stepped toward her. "Tory."

"Don't." She bit her lip to keep from crying. "Just let it end."

"You owe me thirteen days, and unless you're ready to let your grandmother in on why we got married, you're not going anyplace," Kane warned, his voice as expressionless as his face.

"You wouldn't!"

"Try me."

Victoria took one look at his unyielding face and knew he spoke the truth. Kane didn't bluff. "Why do you want me to stay?"

"You haven't stopped running from life. Maybe in the time left you'll learn not to," Kane told her.

Any hope left within her died. Kane didn't want her to stay because he loved her. He was right about one thing—she was too cowardly to stay and see kindness instead of love. "Call her."

Shock rippled across his face. "You don't mean that?"

"I'm leaving."

"You hate me that much?" he said incredulously.

She wanted to shout that she loved him that much, but she couldn't. She was afraid that if she did, she'd fling herself into his arms. At least she'd leave with her pride intact.

Narrowed black eyes studied Victoria's determined face for a long moment. "There's a thunderstorm blowing in. Give me your car keys. I'll drive you."

Kane's voice sounded as bleak as he looked. Victoria dropped the keys in his outstretched hands. Both of them were at the end of their rope.

Inside the car, she watched the approaching storm and wished the thunder would drown out her thoughts. Kane wanted a woman he couldn't have. She wanted Kane. She bit her lip to keep from crying out or worse, turning to him and asking why he couldn't love her. Blinking back tears, she huddled against the door.

"Dammit, get off that door," Kane snapped as he stopped at a signal light. "I know you don't want me to touch you."

"If only that was true," Victoria whispered, but not softly enough.

"What did you say?" Kane demanded, ignoring a honking horn behind him.

"I want to go home," Victoria said, her voice raw.

"You want! Do you ever think of what someone else wants? Other people get hurt. Other people have dreams. Other people—" He broke off as other motorists made their displeasure known by blasting their car horns. The Jaguar sped through the light on yellow. "I thought you were a woman, not a selfish child who runs when she can't have her way. Maybe it's best you leave."

Victoria shuddered.

"In the morning, I'll have my lawyer draw up the papers for a legal separation. I know you don't want any problems getting a divorce when the year is up. I'll take full responsibility for the marriage failing." He pulled under the covered concrete canopy of her apartment.

She studied the taut lines of his face. "You aren't going to tell my grandmother?"

"What do you think?" he asked impatiently as he got out of the car and opened her door. As soon as she straightened, he held out her keys. When she didn't move, he grabbed her hand and slapped them into her open palm. Without another word, he walked into the driving rain.

Shoulders hunched, head bent, he continued down the street as if impervious to everything. Victoria knew he wasn't. He hurt. So did she. They had hurt each other. All she had to do was go up to her apartment and her life would be as it was before. All her things—her thoughts came to a shuddering halt.

Even after they started sleeping together, she hadn't taken one household item from her apartment to indicate she wanted to make a life with Kane. How was he supposed to know she wanted to stay with him?

She ran after him. He had given her everything she thought she wanted, but it didn't mean anything if she lost him. She realized that, just as she realized she loved him enough to swallow her pride and make a fool of herself if necessary. She had enough love for both of them. She gasped as the cold, driving ran hit, soaking her within seconds. She ran faster.

"Kane!"

He turned, his voice as thunderous as the skies. "Are you crazy?" He didn't wait for an answer, just picked her up and sprinted back under the protection of the overhang.

Victoria clutched his neck when he started to put her down. "Don't go. I don't care if you are in love with that woman you're keeping the cradle for. I'm not giving you a divorce."

"You think I—" Kane broke off abruptly as he noticed that several people who were entering the building had stopped and turned to watch them. He headed inside. Neither appeared concerned with the questioning looks and whispers as they crossed the lobby, rode in the elevator, went down the hallway.

Nor were they concerned that they were soaking wet and dripping water everywhere. As soon as Kane closed her apartment door, he stood her on her feet and barked. "Talk."

Misery welling up inside Victoria, she brushed away the wetness on her face, unsure if it was tears or rain. "The antique dealer told me you showed him a picture of the woman you planned to marry."

"You didn't think to ask me about it," Kane said. "You just assumed and ran."

She sniffed and brushed her hand across her face again. "I couldn't stand to hear about your wanting another woman. But it's better than losing you. You hadn't promised me anything."

"Hadn't I? I remember promising to love, honor and cherish. I remember promising in sickness and in health, until death do us part."

His voice still had a rough edge to it, but the words curled through Victoria like wisps of sunshine lighting all the dark places in her soul, in her heart. "But it was because of the business arrangement."

"Was it? Did you ever think it might not be? Did you ever think that what we had in bed and out of bed was something special?" Hands on his hips, he glared down at her. "I'm tired of you running to me, then away from me. Make up your mind now if you're going to stick with me in good times and in bad."

Tears, this time she was sure, started flowing. "You mean for the next thirteen days?"

"Damn the thirteen days," he shouted. "I'm talking about a lifetime. But you better be sure, because I'm not taking any more of this foolishness from you if you decide to stay. If there's a problem, we talk it out and we always sleep in the same bed. No sulking and no running away." He glanced around her apartment. "And you get rid of this place."

Anger worked its way past her misery. "You expect me to do all the giving. What about all the talk about us being a team? I may be in love with you, but you're not going to dictate to me."

Kane looked stunned. "You love me?"

"Of course I love you. What do you think I've been trying to tell you? What woman in her right mind wouldn't love someone as handsome and kind and tender as you?"

"Then you have to trust me, Tory. Trust me enough to know I wouldn't sleep with you, make you care about me, if I loved another woman. Listen to your heart. Take this one last step. For me. For you. I promise I won't let you down."

She heard the love in his voice, saw it in his beautiful black eyes, and launched herself into his arms. The one place she had always known solace and comfort. "I love you, Kane. I love you," she repeated through her tears.

He hugged her so hard her ribs hurt. She didn't care, she just held on. "Tory—" His voice broke with emotion. "You did it." He reached for his wallet. "I want to show you something."

Victoria leaned against Kane and waited. Not a shred of apprehension touched her. Love meant trusting and she trusted Kane. He held up a worn and creased black and white newspaper photograph. Her eyes widened. It was a picture of her taken four years earlier, when she had been interviewed about the success of Lavender and Lace. Her confused gaze flew up to his.

"I've thought about you off and on since the night of the storm at Bonnie's house. I agreed to help you because I wanted a second chance, to see what might have happened between us. It wasn't until you turned me down at the coliseum that I realized I loved you." His lips brushed against her damp forehead. "I cut your picture out of the newspaper on the pretense of giving it to Bonnie. Instead I tucked it in my wallet. Mr. Hinson saw it when I was paying for a washstand.

"What I told him was more wishful thinking than anything. I had held you once, on a night during a storm like this, and went down for the count. You touched me with your determination to be brave for Bonnie, your love for your grandparents, your innocence. You were beautiful and rich, yet down to earth and strangely insecure. When I picked you up to put you in Bonnie's bed, I didn't want to let you go." He shook his dark head.

"I felt ashamed for wanting you, and you were Bonnie's friend. I tried to forget you, but you'd pop into my head at the strangest times. After your divorce, Bonnie told me you were down on men, so I let it go. At her wedding, I saw you give more than one guy the cold shoulder so I didn't think I'd do any better. I dated, but it never seemed the right combination. After we kissed that day in the truck, I had to find out if you were the one woman for me."

"What is the right combination?" Victoria asked breathlessly.

Only after his mouth took hers in a deep, searing kiss did he answer her. "Love. Commitment. Trust. Fire."

Her trembling hand touched his lips. "Love. Commitment. Trust. Fire," she repeated solemnly. Tears pricked her eyes again. This time they were tears of joy. "It may sound selfish, but I'm glad another woman wasn't smart enough to make you love her."

"That couldn't happen. I'm yours for a lifetime. I was so scared I couldn't get you to care." His lips grazed against her palm. She shivered. "Your loving me was something I didn't dare let myself dream of."

"I love you with all my heart. Now that you have me, what are you going to do with me?" she asked as she looked up through a dark sweep of lashes.

He smiled devilishly. "First, we're getting you out of these wet clothes." Scooping her up in his powerful arms, he headed for the bedroom.

"What about you?" she asked as he put her down. "I don't have anything for you to put on."

"Neither one of us will be needing clothes for a long time." He began unbuttoning her dress. He paused on seeing the black lace merrywidow. His questioning gaze met hers.

"I had planned on taking you up the hill for a picnic, then making you an offer you couldn't refuse," she said, her hands busy undoing the buttons on his shirt.

With impatience, Kane finished first. The soggy dress plopped around her feet. She stood before him with the garter straps of the merrywidow taut over a black G-string bikini and the lace hem of black stockings. Kane sucked in his breath. "You're the most beautiful woman I've ever seen."

Her lips grazed his chest. "You make me feel beautiful."

"You make me feel beautiful too," he said without thought.

Victoria raised her head. Her eyes shone with love and wonder. "I'll never doubt you again. I love you, Kane Taggart."

"I love you, Victoria Taggart."

"Then give me something I want."

"Anything."

The zipper rasped on his jeans. "Give me your baby."

EPILOGUE

"**K**ane, come to bed."
"In a minute."

Since over the last two months Victoria had learned that Kane's "minute" could easily turn into an hour, she walked farther into the connecting bedroom.

"I still can't believe they're ours," Kane whispered in awe, his gaze switching back and forth between the two black-haired babies asleep in the spindle cribs.

Victoria smiled and leaned into Kane's hard body, felt his arm curve around her waist. "They're so sweet, the hospital staff probably can't either. I shudder to think what my grandparents and your parents put them through."

"I probably wasn't much better. I've never been so scared in all my life."

"Except when we repeated our vows at church," she reminded him. "You weren't much better at the private reception we had at my grandparents' house."

"That's because you waited until that morning to tell me you were pregnant. I didn't know whether to shout for joy or put you to bed and forbid you to move," he said, defending himself.

Victoria's smile broadened. Kane was still bossy. His fraternity brothers at his college reunion had teased her about being married to such an opinionated man. "If I didn't know how much you love me, I might be jealous of Chandler and Kane junior. The moment the sonogram confirmed twins, you and Mr. Hinson started searching for another cradle. Not that they ever get to be in them, except downstairs, because you think it's too drafty for them."

"A man's got to take care of his family." He pulled her closer.

"We couldn't ask for better." She turned in his arms. "Thank you for not giving up on me. Most of all, thank you for awakening me to love."

"You're my own Sleeping Beauty. I told you I wasn't afraid of a few thorns."

"So you did." Victoria smiled. "But unlike the fairy tale, the thorns around me didn't turn into beautiful flowers."

"No, like you, they turned into something much better, hidden treasures." His compelling black eyes blazed, his voice dropped to a velvet drawl. "How about we go to bed and thank each other?"

"All right. And this time I'll pretend I don't hear you scream," Victoria said, her eyes alight with amusement as she turned and ran for the bed. Grinning, Kane was right behind her.

BEGUILED

EBONI SNOE

With love, I'd like to dedicate this book to my husband Larry and all of my children, Na'imah, Ali, Dawn, and Larry, Jr.

CHAPTER 1

"*I just can't handle it, Raquel. It's over, that's all. I don't have anything else to say.*"

The finality of Clinton Bradshaw's words echoing in her head made her insides churn. After four years, all she'd gotten was a phone call to tell her they were through! Clinton hadn't even had the decency to tell her to her face. That phone call had been six weeks ago, and she hadn't seen or heard from him since.

Raquel Mason's trembling fingers twisted the top button of her neat, high-necked blouse. It was one of the many nervous habits she'd developed recently, although no one at the clinic where she was a social worker seemed to notice.

Raquel was an uncommonly beautiful woman whose velvety brown skin had a hint of red. Her thick, curling black hair, which she wore pulled severely back, framed a face with huge, sable eyes, a delicate nose, and full, sensual lips. Always conservatively dressed and perfectly groomed, Raquel appeared completely in control and coolly serene, no matter how heavy her caseload. But over the past few weeks, only Raquel herself knew how dangerously close that flawless facade had come to cracking.

She hadn't been paid in weeks, she was two months behind in her rent, and her other bills were mounting up. Everything in her life was going wrong, and Clinton's abrupt rejection had made matters even worse.

I have to cope, she told herself. *I can't let myself fall apart. I'll manage somehow . . .*

"Hey, ma'am, you gonna pay for that?" The cashier's voice broke into her thoughts, and Raquel realized she was holding up the line.

"Yes—of course. Sorry." Embarrassed, she placed the mango and the banana on the counter. The pearl button she'd been twisting popped off and fell beside them.

"Eh, pretty lady, what's wrong?" a young, deeply accented male voice asked from behind her. "Why you stand there breaking the buttons off your little blouse? You uptight 'cause you ain't got no man?"

Another young man began to laugh. Raquel ignored them both as she carefully counted out the money and put the fruit into her briefcase. With her back stiff and her head held high, she walked swiftly to the exit, her full, colorful skirt swirling around her slender legs. The *whoosh* of the automatic door wasn't loud enough to drown out the first kid's words.

"Next time you need somethin' to hold onto, baby, you just give Roberto a call, okay? I got plenty." More raucous laughter followed Raquel into the street, and she realized that she was trembling again.

I ought to be used to comments like that by now, she thought wearily, as the warm, humid evening air surrounded her like a damp blanket. She knew the young guys in the neighborhood didn't mean any harm. Raquel might even have seen Roberto's mother or sister at the clinic for counseling, and his mother would be the first to say she had tried to teach him better than that. Ordinarily, Raquel would have paid no attention to the boy's words, but tonight she was so tense that his sexual innuendos made her heart pound with irrational fear.

It was at moments like this, all too frequent lately, that Raquel realized what power her own mother's unreasonably strict religious upbringing still exerted on her. Even after all these years, she could hear Lucy Mason's shrill voice warning her against the dangers of the "sinful world," threatening her with the wrath of God if she ever strayed from the paths of righteousness and the fires of Hell if she sampled the forbidden pleasures of sex unsanctified by marriage.

Well, Mama, maybe you were right about that one, Raquel thought, as Clinton's image flashed before her mind's eye. Handsome in a conservative, buttoned-down sort of way, he was a rising CPA in a small but successful Miami firm. *I'm suffering, all right, but I'm twenty-six years old, and Clinton's the only man I've ever been with. I honestly thought we were going to be married. That's what he told me. He said we'd be married in a church . . .*

Much of Raquel's youth had been spent in church or participating in church activities, always with her mother. Lucy was grimly determined to balance the amount of time Raquel spent among the unrighteous with a steady diet of her own joyless, repressive brand of religion. The only fun Raquel had gotten out of it was once a year at a church-sponsored summer camp she was permitted to attend by herself. She had looked forward eagerly to that one precious week when she could mingle with girls her own age, free from her mother's eagle-eyed supervision. Always the overachiever, even at camp, Raquel had excelled at weaving beautiful, elaborate baskets which were then sold to raise much-needed money for the church. She had once brought one home as a gift for her mother, who had grudgingly allowed that it was almost—but not quite—perfect.

As far as Lucy Mason was concerned, nothing less than perfection would do in every aspect of life—perfection and careful planning. Day after day, year after year, even now, when she was bedridden in the nursing home, she said the same thing: "Take control of your own life, Raquel. Never leave anything to chance. Trust in the Lord. And most important of all, don't depend on no man. They'll let you down every time. Believe me, I should know!"

Raquel would then be forced to listen to the story of how her immigrant father, frustrated at being unable to learn English or find a job here in Miami, had finally returned to his home in the Dominican Republic, abandoning his wife and baby daughter. Lucy always finished by saying, "That man left us dirt poor, you and me, but we didn't stay dirt poor for long, no sir. I worked my fingers to the bone for you, Raquel, and don't you ever forget it. The Lord will punish an ungrateful child. You pay me back by making something of yourself, you hear?"

"Yes, Mama, I hear," Raquel always replied, and she had. She worked hard, she planned carefully, and she strove for perfection. Was her mother proud of her for putting herself through school and becoming a social worker? Did she love her for it? Did she love her at all? To this day, Raquel didn't know. "Love" was not a word that had ever been spoken between them.

As she walked along the cracked, uneven sidewalk in her practical, low-heeled pumps, avoiding the crevices that might cause her to trip, Raquel felt her racing heart gradually regain its normal rhythm. She absently returned the friendly greetings called out to her by the people sitting on the steps of their rundown houses, knowing that even though it was getting dark, she had nothing to fear in this low-income, mixed-race neighborhood. She was a familiar figure here—the clinic was only a few blocks away, and that was where she was headed now.

Conscientious to a fault, Raquel had recently made coming to work in the deserted building after hours a part of her daily routine even though her salary was so far in arrears. Without the distractions provided by her co-workers, she found its peace and quiet conducive to studying and evaluating the cases she'd dealt with during the day. By focusing all her attention on her clients' problems, she was able to forget her own for a while longer.

As Raquel approached the clinic, a streetlight flickered on in front of it, revealing a man who stood outside. He seemed to be doing something to the double doors. Was he trying to break in? Raquel slowed her pace, prepared to turn and run if that proved to be the case, but as she came nearer, she saw that he was putting a padlock through the door handles. The man wasn't breaking in—he was shutting *her* out!

"What's going on?" she called, striding up to the man and glaring at him.

"Por favor, señorita, no hablo ingles," he muttered, sounding apologetic.

Just like my father, Raquel thought bitterly. Although she knew he couldn't understand, she cried, "You're locking up the building where I've worked for two whole years, and you can't even tell me why?"

The man shrugged and repeated, *"No hablo ingles."*

Controlling herself with effort, Raquel took a deep breath. She knew she hadn't been fair. She'd needed to lash out at someone, and this man, who was probably just following his boss's instructions, had borne the brunt of her ill temper.

"Sorry," she murmured.

He shrugged again, then turned away and crossed the street. Raquel watched him climb into a battered pickup truck and rev the engine. As the truck pulled away from the curb, her dark eyes widened in disbelief. The back of it was filled to overflowing with furniture—the office furniture from the clinic.

Raquel turned to stare at the padlocked doors. This couldn't be happening on top of everything else. It just wasn't possible! She'd known for some time that her job was in jeopardy, but she had never dreamed that the administrators would simply close the clinic without a word to any of the staff.

What am I going to do? Raquel wondered, panic-stricken. *I'm unemployed, I can't pay my bills, or Mama's at the nursing home. I'll be evicted from my apartment. Before I find another job, I could be homeless!*

A Latin song blaring at top volume from a passing car jolted her out of her daze. Shaking her head to clear it, Raquel started to walk slowly, stiffly, toward the lot where she had parked her car earlier that day. She was still so overwhelmed that she didn't even hear the whistles and lewd suggestions from a group of young men hanging out in front of the coffee shop across the street.

When she reached her Toyota, Raquel popped the trunk open and tossed her briefcase inside. Closing the trunk again, she leaned against the car, her knees suddenly too weak to support her.

"Damn it! They could at least have warned me!" she moaned aloud, as the tears she had been fighting began running down her cheeks.

But in a way, Raquel knew she had been warned. She had just been too blind, too trusting—or perhaps too naive—to read the handwriting on the wall. Week after week, the administrators had promised to make good on the back pay they owed her and the other employees, but no checks had been forthcoming. Twice Raquel had approached the director of the clinic, inquiring about its financial stability, and each time he had smilingly brushed her off with a lot of double-talk. Why had she let him get away with it? She should have insisted on a reasonable explanation and demanded a straight answer. Now it was too late.

The only faintly bright spot in this whole disastrous mess was Raquel's knowledge that her mother would continue to be taken care of, at least for the time being. Four months ago, when Lucy's multiple sclerosis had advanced to the point that she needed professional care, Raquel had had no choice but to put her in a nursing facility. She had located one with an excellent reputation not far from the apartment she and her mother had shared, and since Raquel was still receiving a salary at the time, she had paid Lucy's board six months in advance.

Although Raquel felt no great love for her mother, the decision to entrust her to the care of strangers seared her with guilt. Clinton, however, had been wonderfully supportive. He'd seemed delighted that he and Raquel would at last be able to spend night after night making love, now that she didn't have to race straight home to tend to Lucy's needs. At first Clinton's ardor was all Raquel could desire. Thinking about it now, she realized that it was only when she revealed how much Lucy's nursing home was costing that he began to cool toward her. Was he afraid he would be responsible for Lucy's bills if he and Raquel married? Was that why he had broken off their relationship?

But at the moment, none of that really mattered. What did matter was that Clinton was gone, her job was gone, and Raquel was virtually penniless. She was also terrified.

The stumbling footsteps of a man who'd had more than enough to drink aroused a different kind of fear, making her realize how dangerous it was to be standing alone in the dimly lit parking lot. Raquel quickly got inside her car, locking the door behind her. Tears still clouded her vision, and she fumbled with the key before she was able to put it into the ignition. Her hands were shaking so much that she could hardly fasten her seatbelt.

I can't drive like this, she realized. *I might kill somebody—maybe me.*

Taking a tissue from her purse, Raquel carefully dried her eyes. Then, folding her arms on the steering wheel, she rested her head on them and took long, steadying breaths until she was sure she could function normally. Only then did she trust herself to drive out of the lot.

As she stopped for a red light at the corner, Raquel watched the usual Friday night crowds pouring into The Sunbreeze, a popular Caribbean nightclub. Snatches of laughter and a sensuous tune could be heard each time the green door opened. Raquel felt a sharp stab of envy at the sight of the carefree couples lured inside by the festive sounds and flashing lights. She sighed heavily. If only her life were as simple as theirs appeared to be . . .

The music was seductive, hypnotic. Raquel leaned back against the headrest, soaking up the sound as she waited for the light to change. Ever so slightly, her body swayed in rhythm to the beat. It would be sheer heaven to dance, to laugh, to have just a moment's release from the worries that burdened her so heavily.

A car behind hers honked when the light changed. Sitting up, Raquel inched the Toyota forward, but instead of crossing the intersection, she impulsively flipped on her turn signal and swerved into the parking lot of The Sunbreeze.

"If I'm going to be homeless in a few days, I might as well spend one night trying to drown my sorrows like everybody else," she declared with a defiant toss of her head.

She got out of the car and quickly made her way to the club before she could change her mind.

Once inside the green door, Raquel found a line of people who she assumed were waiting to pay the cover charge. As she opened her purse and searched for her wallet, a pang of guilt hit her. How could she spend part of what little money she had left on a frivolous night of drinking and dance? She'd never done anything like this in her life.

I must be out of my mind, she thought. *I'd better go home right now!*

Turning to leave, Raquel bumped into the man behind her. He was tall and dark-skinned, and he had a beautiful smile as he openly assessed her. When he spoke, his rich, deep voice revealed his Jamaican origins.

"Eh, lady, you lookin' good tonight. Would you like to spend some time wit' me? I got moanee, plentee of moanee."

With one glance, Raquel could tell this man was not accustomed to being turned down by women. The sparkle of many conquests lit up his dark gaze, so she was sure her refusal would not put a damper on his night.

"I don't think so," she said, tentatively returning his smile. "But there must be plenty of other ladies who would be glad to take you up on your offer."

He shrugged his broad shoulders. "You may be right, but plentee women are plucked. It is the few, like you, who are chosen."

Raquel blushed but made no reply, not wanting to encourage him. Seeing that her exit was blocked by the noisy crowds surging in, she was forced to move forward. When she reached the front of the line, to her surprise, there was no cashier. Instead, a husky woman approached and began patting her down, searching for "hardware." The shock of it immobilized Raquel. Did the woman actually think she might be carrying a gun?

"Could you step on through the door, please?" the woman asked politely. "There are quite a few people waiting to get inside."

Disconcerted, Raquel did as she was told, emerging from the partially lit search area into a dim world of throbbing music, drinking, and dancing she'd previously witnessed only on television.

Despite the restraints her mother had placed on her, as Raquel had grown older, she'd occasionally been allowed to date, and the boys had sometimes taken her to clubs. But those were nothing like The Sunbreeze. There was a flagrant sensuality exhibited by the dancers here that created a familiar tingle deep inside her. It reminded Raquel of hot summer evenings long ago when she would sneak next door to Paulette's and watch her perform her native dances. Paulette was Jamaican, and her daughters, Dottie and Pauline, were young teenagers like Raquel.

Naturally, Lucy Mason thought all dancing was sinful, particularly the kind of dancing Paulette enjoyed. That's why those stolen Friday evenings at Paulette's were so exciting. Their neighbor would treat herself by listening to all her favorite island tunes, accompanied by a bottle of rum and frequent closed-door visits to a little room in the basement. A pungent scent mixed with incense would always accompany Paulette when she returned. Then she would laugh and dance as if all her cares were gone.

One evening when Raquel's mother was attending church, Raquel had feigned illness in order to stay home, then run to Paulette's.

"This time, *you* dance," the woman said. "There be no young men aroun'. C'mon girl, it not be wrong to dance here in my basement. Your mama, she so afraid of anythin' resemblin' sex. How she think you got here, girl?"

Surprisingly, Raquel's first efforts weren't too bad. But it took several more secret Friday excursions, listening to Paulette's instructions to "bump, grind, and roll," before Raquel became really good. Once she had mastered the technique, she discovered that dancing at Paulette's released something wild, sensual, and free within her, something that had been rigidly suppressed all her young life. Raquel had not danced that way for many years.

Now she caught herself staring at a particularly handsome couple whose simulated sexual gyrations were hotter than any of the others. Embarrassed, she began twisting at one of the remaining buttons of her blouse and turned away, looking for a place to sit. All the tables were taken, but when a tall, slim man rose from his place at the bar, she rushed over and slid onto the stool.

"Do you have any piña coladas?" she asked the bartender nervously. He grinned. "Sure do."

"Are they made with real pineapple juice and real coconut?"

"Nope. All we got is mixes."

Raquel frowned. "I see. Well, in that case, I'll take a lime daiquiri."

"Frozen?" the bartender asked.

She nodded, and turned back to survey the crowd. Even though the evening was young, most of the dancers had already worked up a streaming sweat. Some of the men had opened their shirts to get what little air they could and to show off their muscular, glistening chests. One woman held melting ice cubes in both hands, rubbing them over her sweltering neck and then depositing them between her ample breasts.

"Here you go—one frozen daiquiri," the bartender said.

"How much?" Raquel yelled over the music.

"No problem. The gentleman down there has taken care of it." He indicated a man sitting at the end of the bar. "Pretty lady like you'll get plenty of free drinks."

Raquel glanced at her benefactor, smiling in gratitude, but made sure their gazes didn't meet for very long. Lowering her lashes, she sipped thirstily at her drink through a plastic straw. It was cold, sweet, and delicious. She hardly ever drank anything stronger than the herb teas she concocted to ease the pain of a tension headache, so the alcohol gave her an immediate, pleasurable buzz. The daiquiri was gone far too soon, and Raquel ordered another, paying for that one herself. She tried to drink the second one more slowly, reminding herself that she had a twenty-mile drive back to her apartment.

The stifling heat of the club combined with the rum she had just consumed was making her perspire, and Raquel opened the top two buttons of her blouse, fanning herself with a cocktail napkin. The tapes and CDs had now been replaced by a live band kicking up a fantastic beat. Colored lights flashed on and off, further contributing to the crowd's mood of abandonment. The dancers seemed to have let go of all their inhibitions, if they'd ever had any to begin with. As she had in the car, Raquel swayed slightly to the music's pulsing rhythm, her eyes half closed. Was it her imagination, or was that one of the tunes she'd danced to long ago in Paulette's basement?

"Eh, beautiful. Come and dance wit' a man like me," purred a voice close to her ear.

Opening her eyes, Raquel saw a slim, sinewy, dark-skinned man stretching out his hand.

Why not?

Almost without her own volition, she put her hand in his and let him lead her to the dance floor. They found a space barely big enough for the two of them, but there was plenty of room for the languid, undulating moves of Caribbean dance. Shedding her inhibitions as the others had, Raquel surrendered to the music as the singer crooned, *"All we have to do is live in love and harmony."*

A tendril or two escaped from the tight knot on the crown of her head, clinging to her damp face. Then the knot itself loosened as she moved, and a stream of thick black curls cascaded over her shoulders and back. Feeling the beat deep within her, Raquel raised her full skirt high on her thighs as she descended slowly, her legs spread apart, swiveling and pumping her hips in a provocative rhythm. Completely unaware of her partner, or of anything else except the music, she deliberately made her mind a blank. As long as she was dancing and more than a little drunk, it was easy to blot out the things she didn't want to remember.

Her partner, however, was not content to be ignored. Aroused by Raquel's seductive movements, his hands roamed eagerly over her body, clutching at her buttocks and caressing her full breasts. Under any other circumstances, Raquel would have been outraged, but tonight it didn't seem to matter. Nothing mattered anymore. Laughing almost hysterically, she responded to his amorous pawing.

Three men in business suits sat at a table nearby, watching Raquel's gyrations intently.

"I t'ink we've come to the right place," the one in the brown suit said to his companions.

"I think you're right," said the man in gray pinstripes. "She's not her twin, but pretty close to it."

"Yeah," the first man said, licking his lips. "Everyt'ing about her looks perfect, right down to her little round—"

"All right, Benjamin, that's enough. Watch your mouth," the third and most elegantly dressed man snapped.

"I'm sorry, mon. No need to get excited, since it's not your sistah anyway. Can I help it if this one does what she's doin' so well?"

"This looks like it's going to be easier than we expected. One club, and we find the right girl." The third man rose, a faint smile on his thin lips. "Fifty thousand should do it, but that's the limit. I'll be leaving now. Make sure you two don't let her get away."

Brown-suit grinned. "Don't worry about a t'ing, mon. We got it covered."

As the third man made his way to the exit, the throbbing island music eased into a slower song. Raquel lifted her dark curls from her perspiring neck and slipped out of her nameless partner's grasp. She waved goodbye to him and quickly lost herself in the crowd, searching for the ladies' room. Glancing briefly over her shoulder, she saw him gazing after her with a wistful expression on his lean, dark face.

Less than an hour later, Raquel pushed open the double doors and stepped outside. Humid though the night air was, a cool breeze pressed her sweat-soaked blouse against her breasts and back, making her shiver.

Eboni Snoe

Wearily she headed for her car, feeling completely drained. The frenzied euphoria of the past few hours was gone. Though many strangers had bought Raquel drinks, the liquor's effect had been dissipated by her strenuous dancing. Now that she was cold sober, the memory of all her troubles returned in force, and with it a deep depression. She had no lover, no money, no job, and soon she would have no home. Raquel had always prided herself on her ability to take charge of her life and to overcome a number of obstacles that would have daunted many others. Yet all her hard work, resourcefulness, and careful planning had led only to this dead end. Try as she might, Raquel could think of no way out.

Head bowed, she did not notice the black limousine parked around the corner near The Sunbreeze. But at the sound of brisk, determined footsteps following her, Raquel was instantly on the alert. It sounded as if there were two of them. This was a bad neighborhood after dark. Were they muggers? She quickened her pace. The footsteps quickened, too. What if they had knives, or even guns?

With a bravado born of desperation, Raquel stopped under a streetlight and spun around to face her pursuers. After all, she had nothing to lose but her life, and bleak as her future seemed at the moment, that wasn't worth much.

Eyes flashing, she shouted, "Go away! Leave me alone!"

"Calm down, lady," said the taller, slimmer of the two. He wore a brown business suit and an ingratiating smile. "We not going to attack you or do you any harm. We jus' want to make you a business proposition."

Raquel was so amazed by this unexpected statement that all she could do was stare at him.

The shorter man in gray pinstripes pulled a large brown envelope from inside his jacket and thrust it into her hand. "We want to solicit your services this evening. These papers will explain everything. You might be interested to know that there is also one thousand dollars cash in the envelope, the down payment on the deal, should you accept. You'll receive nine thousand more if you come with us to the appointed spot, and a final payment of forty thousand dollars will be forthcoming when you complete the assignment."

I must be dreaming, Raquel thought, stunned. *Either that, or I'm so upset by everything that's happened to me lately that I'm having some kind of wild hallucination! This can't be happening!* Still speechless, she stared from one man to the other.

"If you will be so good as to supply us with the name of your bank and your account number, the forty thousand will be deposited there," the man in the gray suit went on. "I hope that's satisfactory?"

Raquel finally found her voice. "Satisfactory? *Satisfactory?*" she echoed. "What is this, some kind of a practical joke?" Then her eyes narrowed.

"Oh, now I get it. You're undercover cops, right? If I accept your 'business proposition' and your money, you'll arrest me for prostitution. Well, thank you for your kind offer, gentlemen, but no thanks! I may be on the streets in a few days, but I'm not there yet. Now please let me pass!"

But the man in the brown suit, still smiling, grabbed hold of her arm before she could turn away. His grip, like his voice, was surprisingly gentle. "Pretty lady, you got it all wrong. We talkin' real business—no sex, no drugs, nothin' illicit. This a job, and you the only one can do it."

"I'm sorry if you feel the amount is insufficient," the other man said. "Unfortunately, we are not authorized to offer more. On the other hand, perhaps you don't need the money . . ." His voice trailed off as he watched Raquel closely.

"Not need the money!" She gave a short, strangled laugh that was more like a sob. "Oh, my God, if you only knew!"

In Raquel's present circumstances, fifty thousand dollars seemed like a vast fortune. With that much money, she could make a new start. She could pay all her bills and Lucy's with plenty left over. She wouldn't be evicted. She could take as much time as she needed to look for another job, a much better one than the one she'd just lost.

"What—" Raquel swallowed hard. "What would I have to do?" she whispered.

Gray-suit said, "As I told you before, the papers will explain everything. Please open the envelope."

Raquel's hands were trembling so much that she could hardly do so. When she did, the first thing she saw was a neatly banded sheaf of ten hundred-dollar bills.

"Why don' you put the moanee in your purse?" Brown-suit suggested, releasing her arm. "It be a shame to drop it on the ground, the way you shakin'."

Numbly, Raquel placed the packet of bills in her handbag. Then she took out the letter and began to read it by the light of the street lamp.

CHAPTER 2

"Would you care to hear some music?"

The chauffeur's disembodied voice drifted to Raquel's ears over the intercom in the sleek black limousine as it purred almost soundlessly along dark, tree-lined streets. She thought they were somewhat in the vicinity of Fort Lauderdale, but for all she knew, they might have been in the Kingdom of Oz. So many bizarre things had happened during the past few hours that at this point, nothing seemed impossible. Looking down at the scarlet, stiletto-heeled pumps on her feet, Raquel was reminded of Dorothy's ruby slippers. Would they protect her from evil influences?

"Music, madam?" the chauffeur repeated mare loudly, breaking into her thoughts.

"Yes, please," she replied.

"What kind? Rock, rhythm and blues, reggae, pop, or classical?"

"Do you have any jazz?"

"Yes, I do. If you care for anything to drink, the wet bar is in the compartment directly in front of you."

Moments later Raquel heard the plaintive wail of a jazz saxophone coming from the speakers. *Branford Marsalis?* she wondered vaguely, leaning back against the plush seat.

Raquel had no interest in the contents of the liquor cabinet. Instead, she turned her attention to the scene passing swiftly by the limousine's tinted windows. This was obviously an affluent neighborhood, where

mansions set back on lush, floodlit green lawns were barely visible behind high walls and wrought-iron gates. Presumably she would soon be
delivered to a similar mansion where she would embark on the assignment she had agreed to accept. Would she be equal to the task? What if
she blew it? The two men who had hired her insisted there would be no
danger, but could she believe them?

Thinking of the ten thousand dollars safely tucked away in her purse,
Raquel decided she could. The second payment had been delivered exactly as promised, and it was hers to keep. Even if the additional forty
thousand dollars was never deposited in her bank account, which she realized was a distinct possibility, she would still be better off than she had
been before Brown-suit and Gray-suit had approached her.

Raquel closed her eyes, picturing in her mind the beautiful, smiling
face in the photo that had been enclosed with the letter and the first
thousand. The young woman's caramel skin tone, bountiful black hair,
dark eyes, and generous lips bore an uncanny resemblance to her own,
but there was one major difference: Jackie Dawson had disappeared, and
for some reason as yet unknown to Raquel, she had been hired to make
one public appearance at a Caribbean soirée tonight, pretending to be
the missing girl.

Opening her eyes, Raquel picked up her handbag, took out her compact, and studied her reflection in the small mirror with something approaching awe. A turban in a wild floral print of red, green, and mustard
yellow crowned her head, concealing her unruly black curls, and huge
gold hoop earrings dangled from her ears. Her face was heavily made up
with vibrant purple eyeshadow and brilliant red lipstick. Raquel hardly
recognized herself beneath the elaborate mask. The only other time she
had worn so much makeup was on the rare occasions when her mother
had allowed her to attend a masquerade party in the church basement.
But Lucy would have tanned Raquel's hide and locked her in her room if
she had ever attempted to leave the house dressed as she was tonight.

Glancing down at the costume she was wearing, Raquel felt her cheeks
burning, glad that her mother couldn't see her now. Little was left to the
imagination. A skimpy bralike top in the same print as the turban revealed far more of her full breasts than it concealed. The flounced skirt,
above the knee in front and dipping to ankle-length behind, flared from
Raquel's hips well below her navel. Brown-suit, who was called Benjamin,
and Gray-suit, known only as Mr. Smith, had presented her with the outfit in their hotel suite less than two hours ago, telling her that it reflected
Jackie Dawson's flamboyant tastes.

Raquel was appalled. Even at the beach, she never wore anything so
bare, preferring a simple one-piece in a dark, sober shade. How could
she possibly appear in public half naked? She had been tempted to

refuse, but the thought of all that money and what it could mean to her and her mother was a powerful incentive. Casting modesty to the winds, Raquel had donned the borrowed finery, telling herself that it was merely a costume to be worn, part of the role she had been hired to play. Now, although she was still somewhat uncomfortable, she also felt a tiny thrill of excitement at the prospect of submerging her own personality in that of a woman who was obviously the complete opposite of herself. It was nothing but a masquerade, and after all, it was only for this one night.

Raquel dropped the compact into her purse, then picked up the brown envelope lying on the seat beside her and took out the papers. Back at the hotel suite, she had gone over them several times. Benjamin and Mr. Smith had coached Raquel endlessly about the woman she was to impersonate, but now, in the soft glow of the limousine's courtesy light, she carefully read yet again the information concerning Jackie Dawson to commit it to memory.

Actually, there wasn't all that much to remember. Jackie was twenty-six, Raquel's own age. Like Raquel, she was an only child. Unlike Raquel, however, Jackie was the ultimate party girl. She lived with her father, who was something of a tyrant and strongly disapproved of his daughter's frivolous ways. Her mother was dead. Jackie's personal preferences and political views were briefly mentioned, and the names of some of her friends were listed, along with the restaurants and clubs where her crowd hung out. Mr. Smith had assured Raquel that she had nothing to worry about. The information contained in the letter, meager though it was, would be sufficient to see her through the festive evening. But when she asked why it was so important that the other guests at the party think she was Jackie Dawson, his expression became suddenly grim.

"As we have already told you, Ms. Dawson is missing. You are impersonating her tonight in order to buy us more time to find her," he said. "That is all you need to know. You are being paid—and paid very well, I might add—for what is really a very simple job."

Benjamin's perpetual smile had held more than a hint of lust as he'd looked Raquel up and down. "I know 'bout pretty women. Pretty women like pretty t'ings. You jus' enjoy the party, and t'en tomorrow you take some of the moanee and buy yourself somet'ing nice, okay?"

Raquel had asked no further questions.

Now, as she put the papers back in the envelope, she glanced out the window again. They were driving along a road bordered by tall palm trees and a massive stone wall which blocked her view of whatever might lie behind it. Suddenly the car slowed its pace. Looking up ahead, Raquel saw the red taillights of many other vehicles that were waiting to make the turn into a gateway in the wall. Two huge wrought-iron gates stood open, and the gateposts were topped with crouching jaguars carved in stone. A uniformed attendant checked what appeared to be an invitation handed to him by the driver of each car before allowing it to enter. Feeling a surge of panic, Raquel realized she had reached her destination.

As the black limousine inched forward, following a gleaming silver Porsche that had just been permitted to pass through the gates into a floodlit courtyard, the chauffeur rolled down the window and presented a white card to the attendant. While the attendant scanned the invitation, Raquel read the words *Glimpse of Glory* inscribed on a bronze plaque behind him. Apparently that was the name of the estate where "Jackie Dawson" was to do her thing.

Raquel's nerves seemed to be vibrating throughout her entire body, and there was a weird ringing in her ears. She knew these symptoms heralded the onset of one of her tension headaches, and desperately wished for a cup of soothing herb tea. Since that was not a possibility, she steeled herself to resist them. The thought of the money in her purse calmed her somewhat, but she had been instructed by Mr. Smith to leave the purse in care of the chauffeur when she entered the mansion. Unsure whether this man whose face she had never seen could be trusted, Raquel furtively took out the banded stack of ten hundred-dollar bills. Breaking the band, she quickly tucked them into her top, placing five under each breast. Even if the chauffeur absconded with the rest, she would still be a thousand dollars richer.

When she looked out the window again, the limousine was making its way around a circular driveway to the entrance of the mansion which was built of stone the softest shade of pink, in the style of a Mediterranean villa. Through its tall, arched windows, Raquel could see brightly attired revelers, laughing, talking, and drinking.

It's like a fairy tale—or a movie, she thought, *one of those made-for-TV movies about the rich and famous that aren't anything like real life. I never knew people actually lived this way!*

The sliding glass panel that separated Raquel from the chauffeur opened soundlessly, and a dark hand presented her with an ivory envelope as the limousine glided to a stop in front of the broad staircase that led to the mansion's main entrance. Another uniformed attendant stepped forward, bowing and opening the car door. Clutching the envelope in her hand, Raquel got out. With a pounding heart, she ascended the stairs behind a couple whose scanty costumes were adorned with multicolored feathers. Compared to what they were wearing, her outfit was positively demure, and Raquel began to feel less embarrassed about the amount of skin she was showing.

When she reached the top of the stairs, she followed the feathered couple's lead, placing her envelope on an embossed silver tray proffered by yet another attendant. Then she passed through a vast, marble-paved entrance hall lit with crystal chandeliers into an even larger and more impressive chamber. It was crowded with guests, some of whom were fantastically costumed, while others were formally dressed. Drinks and hors d'oeuvres were immediately offered to Raquel by an obsequious waiter. Sipping a crystal flute of champagne, she assumed the persona of Jackie Dawson and casually looked around her.

It was obvious that her arrival had caused something of a stir. Various couples and groups of people whispered and threw surreptitious glances in her direction, but no one approached her. Was that because they knew Raquel was an impostor? Had the attendant to whom she had given her invitation realized that she was not who she claimed to be and alerted the others? Was someone even now preparing to throw her out bodily?

"Ms. Dawson?" The tentative voice addressed her from behind. Turning, Raquel saw a tall, slim young man in an immaculately tailored white linen suit.

"I presume you're Jackie Dawson—that's what everyone is saying." He smiled shyly. "You see, we've never met before, but I spoke to you on the phone about three weeks ago. You *do* remember, don't you? My name is Johnson—Derek Johnson. Jim, a mutual friend, encouraged me to call."

Raquel did the only thing she could under the circumstances. She furrowed her brow as if she were trying to remember. "Derek? I'm not sure . . ."

"The conversation was very short. Your father was furious because I called you, and he cut us off before I could tell you why I was phoning."

Thinking fast, Raquel said, "Oh, yes! Now I remember. I'm terribly sorry things didn't work out for us, Derek."

"Me, too." He seemed satisfied by her apology and hurriedly walked away.

Raquel thought that her conversation with Derek might have encouraged other of Jackie Dawson's acquaintances to approach her, but none of them did. Puzzled yet relieved, she finished her champagne, placed her empty glass on a passing waiter's tray, and took another.

As the evening progressed, champagne and colorful drinks that Raquel didn't dare sample flowed endlessly. Soon the lights dimmed, replaced by flashing red bulbs. Couples began to dance as the music changed from laid-back, standard pop tunes to reggae and rhythm and blues. Wandering through a pair of French doors onto an enormous flagstone terrace, Raquel saw that servants were placing flaming torches all around it and along the wide steps that led down into a beautiful tropical garden. Obviously preparations were being made for some kind of special event, but she had no idea what it could be.

"Eh, babee. Where you been?" asked a deep, insinuating voice behind her.

Startled, Raquel spun around and found herself face-to-face with a well-built man in a tuxedo. He was standing much too close, and the smirk on his face conveyed that he knew a lot more about Jackie Dawson than the other man who had approached her. Who was he and what did he want? she wondered apprehensively. Unsure of how to respond to his question, Raquel remained silent, regarding him with a cool, supercilious expression that belied the frantic pounding of her heart.

"I didn't hear from you for so long that for a while there, I thought you'd left the city. Why you leave me hanging like that, huh?" The man moved even closer, so close that she could feel his hot breath on her cheek as he whispered, "I thought we had a real good time the last time we were together. That glass dick was fire."

Fortunately, at that moment people began surging through the French doors onto the terrace, separating Raquel from her unsavory companion. Quickly losing him in the crowd, she could hardly believe what she'd just heard. *Glass dick?* Many times at the clinic she had heard her clients use that term for a crack pipe, but it was difficult to imagine how a woman whose life was so rigidly controlled by her father could be involved with crack cocaine. Her curiosity about Jackie Dawson increased, as did her apprehension. If the woman was deeply into the drug scene, Jackie might very well be dead by now. *Oh, God, just let me get out of this without anything going wrong,* Raquel prayed silently, and checked her watch, relieved to find that in only thirty more minutes the limousine was scheduled to pick her up and take her home.

By now the guests had arranged themselves around the terrace. Suddenly there was an explosion of color and sound as twelve male dancers burst onto the scene with a loud shout. Their faces were concealed by elaborate masks made of red and black feathers, and the torch-light flickered on gleaming bodies that were bare except for the briefest of feathered trunks. Accompanied by the throbbing music of wooden instruments played by a group of musicians in the garden below, the dancers leaped and whirled, letting out barbarous yells that sent chills down Raquel's spine. Still, she couldn't help being fascinated by the frenzied performance. Caught up in the display before her, Raquel didn't notice the man who had taken his place at the top of the stairs until a passionate drum combination attracted her attention.

The drummer was a magnificent specimen of manhood whose very posture exuded power. A tall drum sat between creamy brown thighs that tensed and bulged each time he rose to the balls of his feet in response to the drumbeat. Taut muscles rippled in his arms, and his hands moved so rapidly that they were nothing but a blur. Raquel couldn't tear her eyes away from him. She felt something stir deep within her that blotted out all conscious thought, a primitive, sensual response to the hypnotic rhythm.

The dancers had begun to entice some of the female guests to join them, and when one of them took Raquel's hand, she was powerless to resist. Dancing with even more abandon than she had at The Sunbreeze, she lost all track of time. When the dance finally ended, she was horrified to discover that more than half an hour had gone by. What if the chauffeur had gotten tired of waiting for her? If the limousine had come and gone, not only would Raquel have no way of getting home, but the precious nine thousand dollars would be lost as well.

She pushed her way through the crowd blocking the terrace doors and raced back into the mansion, retracing her steps to the entrance. As she ran outside, to her great relief, Raquel saw the black limousine sitting in the driveway. An attendant opened the door for her and she slipped inside, sinking down into the plush seat with a grateful sigh. One quick glance assured her that her purse was where she had left it; another glance inside proved that the money was all there.

As the limousine circled the driveway and passed between the jaguar-crowned gateposts, soft jazz began to play—the chauffeur had remembered her preference. Leaning back, Raquel closed her eyes and smiled, completely relaxed for the first time in weeks. It was over, all over, and so were her worries. Soon she would be home safe and sound and solvent. She might even use some of the money she had earned to take a long-delayed vacation. Only one problem remained: Raquel had promised her employers she would tell no one about tonight's adventure. That in itself didn't concern her, but sooner or later she would have to come up with a plausible explanation for her sudden wealth. The lottery, perhaps? Or a legacy from a rich relative? Raquel laughed out loud. It was all so incredible! Only a few hours ago she had been frantic because she had no money, and now she had to figure out what to do because she had too much!

Lost in her pleasant reverie, Raquel didn't notice that the limousine was slowing down, but when it came to a halt, she sat up and opened her eyes, a puzzled frown wrinkling her brow. They couldn't have reached her apartment already. Perhaps there was a problem with the car. She peered out the window, but saw nothing but pitch blackness since the moon had disappeared behind a bank of clouds. Not knowing how the intercom system worked, Raquel decided to attract the chauffeur's attention by tapping on the glass partition. She had just leaned forward to do so when there was a terrible crashing sound as the window through which she had just been looking was savagely smashed.

Raquel screamed and covered her face to shield it from flying glass. In a flash, someone reached through the broken window and unlocked the door. Almost before she knew what was happening, she was being dragged out of the car by strong hands. She couldn't see the man's face. Limp with terror, she didn't resist. If her attacker wanted money, he could have all of it as long as he let her go. Then, as the moon emerged from the clouds, Raquel saw the figure of another man standing beside the open door of a nondescript car in front of the limousine. It was one of the masked dancers from the party. Panic-stricken, she began to struggle with all her might, kicking and scratching at anything within reach as she tried to break free of her captor's grasp. Her nails raked away skin, blood, and a feathery mask, causing the man to curse and momentarily loosen his grip. Raquel lunged forward, and the other man yelled, "God damn it, hold her! Hold her, I said!"

"I'm tryin', but this one fierce bitch!" her assailant grunted, throwing both sinewy arms around her. "She clawin' me to death!"

She aimed a vicious kick at his shins with one sharp-heeled shoe. He let out a yelp of pain, and as his confederate ran to his aid, two other men jumped out of the car. Outnumbered and overpowered though she was, Raquel continued to struggle, kick, and scream while one of them yanked off her turban and slipped a pillowcase over her head.

"Lady," a silky, threatening voice warned from a few paces away, "we don't want to hurt you, but we may have no choice if you don't shut up."

"Hush, mon!" said one of the others. He sounded nervous. "You must not offend her, or you will be offending the *gubida* as well."

"Ah, but so far we have no proof that she is linked with the ancestors," came the casual reply.

The two men holding Raquel dragged her forward, and one of them shoved her into the waiting car's back seat so roughly that she fell on her hands and knees. As she scrambled upright, she heard the same voice that had just spoken address the man who was getting into the seat beside her. This time his voice was not sensual or silky at all.

"That's enough, Jay! There's no need to be so rough."

"I should've done more t'an t'at," the man called Jay muttered. "My face is bleedin'! Besides, I don't remembah anybody puttin' you in charge, Meester Nate Bowman. We were told not'ing about t'ese changes you talkin' about."

"I put myself in charge. Would you care to challenge my authority?"

The question was asked very softly, but there was such menace in it that Raquel shivered. The man called Jay made no reply.

"As for your face, don't worry—you'll live," Nate Bowman went on. "If the lady is too tough for you, I suggest you consider backing out while there's still time."

"She not too tough! *I'm* tough, or I would not be a membah of Shango!" Jay blustered.

One of the other men got into the back seat on the other side of

Raquel, effectively blocking any possibility of escape. The third man and Nate Bowman got in the front seat, and the car lurched forward as the driver stepped on the gas.

Crushed between two of her abductors, unable to see, barely able to breathe inside the bag that covered her head, Raquel had never been more terrified. Her thoughts spun wildly out of control. *Shango? Gubida?* What were they talking about? Where were these men taking her? What did they want with her? Suddenly she gasped. As far as the kidnappers knew, she was Jackie Dawson. If she told them she was not, they might let her go!

Before she could speak, the man called Jay gave an unpleasant chortle. "You right, Meester Nate. Another woman I would kill for what she done to me, but I will not hurt Mees Dawson. She is too valuable to all of us." He gave one of Raquel's breasts a painful squeeze. "But I cannot promise anyt'ing else. It's goin' to be a long trip to Dangriga."

Realizing how close she had come to signing her own death warrant, Raquel slumped over in a dead faint.

Raquel remained unconscious for several hours, coming to only when powerful, unseen hands shook her awake and led her out of the car. Stumbling over rough terrain, Raquel would have fallen many times if it had not been for the two men who gripped her arms on either side, their fingers digging into her soft flesh. As her captors led her down a treacherously steep slope, the foul stench of rotting fish and stale urine accosted her nostrils and she fainted again. One of the men must have carried her from that point on. When Raquel awakened the second time, she was dimly aware of being set on her feet and pushed through an open doorway. A moment later, she heard the door close behind her, and the sharp *click* as someone turned a key on the outside, locking her in. Still groggy, Raquel ripped the pillowcase from her aching head and took a deep breath of salt-tinged air as she looked around.

The tiny room in which she found herself had no window and was so dimly lit by the single flickering candle that even without the bag, she could hardly see. Taking a tentative step forward, Raquel promptly banged her knee against a sharp object. It turned out to be the corner of a bed that jutted out from one wall and took up most of the floor space. There was only one other piece of furniture, the small bureau on which the candle sat, and practically no room to walk except for about two feet at the bed's end and along either side. Leaning down to rub her throbbing knee, Raquel suddenly felt the floor heave beneath her, knocking her off balance. As she sprawled on the bed, she realized that she must be aboard a boat. And from the way the rocking motion continued, that boat was most likely heading out to sea.

Raquel plunged into total despair. On dry land, there was always the chance, however small, that she might attract the attention of some passerby or even make a desperate run for it. But on the ocean, there was no way to contact a potential rescuer and no possibility of escape. Burying her face in the bed's small, hard pillow, Raquel surrendered to a storm of hopeless tears until, exhausted, she fell into a troubled sleep.

CHAPTER 3

For the first few seconds after Raquel opened her swollen eyes, she didn't know where she was, but too soon the memory of all that had happened to her came flooding back. Sitting up on the bed, she squinted at her watch, trying to determine how long she had slept, but the crystal was cracked and the watch had stopped. The candle had almost burned itself out. Afraid that once it was gone she might not receive another one, Raquel quickly pinched out the flame.

The tiny room, however, was not completely dark. She realized that what little light there was came from a plastic hatch in the ceiling of the stuffy cabin. Desperate for fresh air, she stood on the bed and pushed against the hatch, but it wouldn't budge. Frustrated and more furious now than frightened, she shoved it with all her strength. Suddenly the hatch sprang open an inch or two, and a cool, salty breeze carrying the scent of the sea embraced her. Peering through the crack, she could catch a glimpse of moonlit sky. Over the sound of waves she heard two male voices. Standing directly below the hatch, Raquel listened intently to their words.

"He jus' don't understan'," one voice declared. "No one orders Jay, *Dada,* aroun'."

"No one, my brother?" asked the second. He sounded skeptical.

"No one! I simply obey the *buyei* because of my respect for him."

The second speaker said something else, but apparently the two had moved away, because Raquel couldn't hear what it was.

Sinking back down on the bed, she tried to gather her wits about her in an attempt to make some sense of her situation. These men who had kidnapped her were very strange. They spoke English combined with a language foreign to her, and they seemed to think that she—or rather, Jackie Dawson—was connected in some weird way with their ancestors. Raquel remembered one of the men warning the one called Nate Bowman not to anger the ancestors. He seemed to be afraid of them, and fortunately for her, that meant he probably feared Jackie, too.

It was also clear that the group's loyalties were divided. The man named Jay did not like the one he called Mr. Nate. From the snatches of conversation Raquel had heard, she gathered that the four men had never worked together before. So why had they conspired to kidnap Jackie Dawson? And why were they taking her to Dangriga, a place she had never heard of? Who owned this boat on which she was a prisoner?

Wondering if she would ever know the answers to her questions, Raquel lay down, but even exhausted as she was, it was a long time before she fell asleep. In that cloudy world between sleeping and waking, one of the words she had heard that night suddenly struck a familiar chord.

Shango or *Chango,* the god of power and passion. Paulette had once spoken of him—or was it one of the other gods of the Santeriá religion? They all sounded so much alike. Paulette had warned her never to speak of them to her mother and she never had . . .

Finally, Raquel dozed off again.

Jay's hands were sweating as he slowly turned the key that had conveniently been left in the lock of the woman's door. Nervously, he glanced over his shoulder, but the narrow passageway was empty. He had never thought it would come to his confronting Jackie Dawson face-to-face, but as things stood, he had no other choice. He had to get rid of her, somehow making it look like a suicide. Then Nate Bowman would never be the wiser.

His bulbous eyes gleamed in the darkness as he cautiously pushed the door open. Pausing for a moment, he took in the woman's voluptuous figure lying on the bed and licked his lips. Perhaps he would make one small detour from his intended plan . . .

The slight scraping sound of the door closing roused Raquel from her slumber. She could barely make out the shadowy figure before he was on top of her, pawing at her flounced skirt and parting her thighs with strong, eager hands. Although she was still half asleep, Raquel fought like a tigress, biting and clawing at him with talonlike nails.

"So you want to hurt me again, do you?" His hot, fetid breath scorched her cheek. "First I pay you back for what you did to my face. If you try to scream, believe me, I will make it very painful for you."

Raquel did not scream, but neither did she stop struggling. Before she gave in to this animal, she would gladly die. She raised one leg and kneed him accurately in the groin.

With a yelp of pain and outrage, Jay grabbed both her hands with one of his and pinned them above her head while with the other hand he ripped off her lacy underpants.

"Get off of me, you big ape!" Raquel screamed, writhing beneath him.

"I strongly suggest you do what Ms. Dawson says, Jay."

The silky voice from the broad-shouldered figure silhouetted in the doorway caught her assailant unawares and he momentarily froze.

"Screw you, Meester Nate!" he growled. "I do what I want to do, and what I want to do is t'is!"

Raquel heard a faint metallic click.

"Really. And now—do you still want to do it?" Nate Bowman spoke almost in a whisper and his face was shadowed so that she could not see his expression, but the menace in his voice was unmistakable.

He moved with the swift, lithe grace of a predatory animal. As Jay's heavy body rose abruptly from Raquel's, she saw moonlight reflecting from the switchblade Nate pressed to Jay's jugular vein.

"I'm warnin' you, Meester Nate. You will find yourself in big trouble if you mess wit' me," her attacker muttered.

"I'm willing to take that risk. At the moment, however, *you* are the one in big trouble." Nate Bowman grabbed Jay's beefy arm and hauled him to his feet. "Now, listen carefully, because I'm only going to say this once. While we are on this voyage, *no one* is to touch Ms. Dawson in any way, understand? I would appreciate it if you would relay this message to your brother, Al, as well."

"What you care if we have a little fun wit' her?" Jay asked truculently.

"If she is linked with the *gubida,* you will be grateful to me for stopping you. If she's not, I don't care what you do with her. But until we find out, Ms. Dawson is not to be touched, understand?"

Nate stepped aside and Jay edged out of the room, cursing under his breath.

When he had gone, Raquel wrapped the longest portion of her skirt around her and huddled near the head of the bed, trying to control the frantic racing of her heart. Had this man saved her from Jay only to use her for his own lustful purposes?

Although Nate Bowman was still shrouded in shadow, a ray of moonlight from the partially opened hatch touched Raquel's tumbled curls and smooth bronze skin. Looking at this beautiful, desirable woman, Nate knew that she had every reason to be wary of his motives. He could hardly blame her. In spite of what he had said to Jay, why should she trust him right after one of his henchman had attempted to rape her?

"Ms. Dawson . . ." he began, but Raquel cut him off.

"I suppose I should thank you for rescuing me, but gratitude isn't uppermost in my mind right now," she said acidly. "If you expect me to repay you with sexual favors, you are very much mistaken! Please leave me alone."

Responding to the challenge she offered him, Nate moved forward. He flashed the switchblade once more, then he murmured, "I don't take orders from anyone, lady. Just because I'm protecting you from the Shango doesn't mean you can do or say anything you like. I'm in charge here, and don't you forget it."

Raquel caught her breath. The lips of this man whose face she could not see were only inches away. Terrified though she was, she refused to grovel.

"Get out," she grated.

"That was my intention, and this time I'll take the key with me. But first . . ."

His mouth descended on hers. With a gentle sucking motion, Nate captured her lower lip, exploring it with the tip of his tongue. Before she could react, he strode out of the little room, closing the door behind him, and she heard the key turn in the lock.

Trembling violently, Raquel wiped her mouth with the back of her hand in a gesture of disgust directed as much at herself as at Nate Bowman. Try as she might, she could not deny the tiny spark of desire his kiss had ignited. What was wrong with her that she would respond to him this way? Knife or no knife, she should have lashed out at him as she had at Jay, but there was something masterful about him that had melted her resistance. He had proved his point. Nate Bowman was definitely in charge.

In an attempt to erase the memory of her disgraceful reaction to his kiss, Raquel decided to focus on the issue at hand. Nate Bowman had said he was taking the key of her cabin with him, and she was fairly certain that she had nothing to fear from him. But that might not be the only key. If Jay had another one and planned to attack again despite Nate's warning, she was determined to be ready for him. The first thing she had to do was provide some light.

Turning to the bureau next to the bed, Raquel opened drawer after drawer, fumbling in each one until she found what she sought—a book of matches. When she had lit the stubby candle, she rose to her knees and began looking around the cabin. She discovered the long strip of cloth that had formed her turban lying on the floor along with her ripped panties, but that was all. Raquel's abduction had happened so fast that she had left her purse in the limousine, which she now realized was providential. Though she regretted the loss of the nine thousand dollars, the purse also contained her driver's license, credit cards, and other information clearly establishing her true identity. If she had taken it with her, there was no doubt in her mind that the kidnappers would have opened it, and when they'd discovered she was not Jackie Dawson, Raquel was sure they would not have hesitated to kill her on the spot.

Thank God for small favors, she thought. At least she still had the thousand dollars she had tucked into her top. It might very well come in handy at some point. But at the moment, she had to do something about her half-naked state.

Since her underwear was beyond repair, she pulled the tail of her skirt between her legs and began tucking it into the waistband in order to transform it into a pair of ruffled, knee-length pants. Intent on what she was doing, she didn't hear the key turn in the lock. Suddenly the door swung open. Primed for Jay's second assault, Raquel opened her mouth to scream, but the scream died in her throat as Nate Bowman reentered the room.

"Did I startle you? Sorry—I didn't know you were dressing. I suppose I should have knocked," he said.

For the first time, Raquel was able to see the man's face, and she couldn't help staring as the flickering candlelight cast strange shadows on his ruggedly handsome features. Nate Bowman's skin was the color of cappuccino, his nose broad and well formed. Black hair, cut close, hugged his shapely head, and dark brown eyes fringed with long, thick lashes regarded her with cynical amusement. Full, smooth lips beneath a pencil-thin mustache quirked in a slight smile. It was the kind of mouth Paulette used to say could "turn a woman inside out."

Lowering her gaze, Raquel took in the man's slim yet muscular physique. A white shirt, open to the waist, revealed his glossy brown chest, and skin-tight jeans outlined powerful thighs and calves. As he lounged in the doorway, every inch of him exuded a confident masculinity that made her heart pound erratically.

Embarrassed and ashamed by her reaction, Raquel tore her eyes away. Yes, Nate Bowman was attractive, more attractive than any man she had ever seen, but he was also a criminal, and she was at his mercy. While they were on this voyage, he would protect her, thinking she was Jackie Dawson. But once they reached their mysterious destination, there was no telling what would happen. She shuddered as she remembered his words to Jay: *"If she is linked to the* gubida, *you will be grateful to me for stopping you. If she's not, I don't care what you do with her."*

Raquel had no idea what the *gubida* was, or how the woman she was impersonating might be "linked" to it. But since she was not Jackie Dawson, no such link was possible, and when Nate Bowman found that out, he would turn her over to day without a qualm—unless she could somehow manage to escape after the boat docked. That hope, faint though it was, bolstered Raquel's flagging courage and steeled her against her captor's insidious appeal.

"What do you want?" she snapped, scowling at him.

His reply surprised her. "I brought you something." Raquel had not noticed the small bag he held in one hand until he tossed it on the bed. "I planned to give you these when we reached Belize, but perhaps you might like something less—shall we say, *revealing*—than your present outfit to wear in the meantime."

Peering into the bag, she saw that it contained what looked like a shift of some sort, undergarments, and a pair of flat shoes. "Thank you," she said grudgingly. Then it hit her. "Did you say Belize? In Central America?"

Nate raised one dark brow. "Is there another Belize? Come now, Ms. Dawson. Has it been so long since you visited Dangriga, the home of your ancestors?"

She paused. "Yes. Yes, it has."

"It's a shame you must be taken to Belize by force." His apology actually sounded sincere. "But you should have more respect for your ancestors and their beliefs."

As Raquel gazed into his dark eyes, she thought she saw a flicker of compassion there. Seizing his hands in hers, she cried, "You talk about shame, but it's *you* who are forcing me, *you* who should be ashamed! Mr. Bowman, I beg of you, let me go! I promise I won't tell a soul about any of this!"

She must have imagined the hint of compassion, because his eyes now glittered as hard and black as obsidian. Looking down at her hands, he sneered as though they were dirty, unworthy of touching him.

A hot wave of humiliation washed over Raquel, and she quickly released him. "I should have known I couldn't expect the likes of you to do what's right!" she snarled.

Nate Bowman regarded her with undisguised contempt. "Right, Ms. Dawson? I doubt if you know the meaning of the word!"

With that, he turned on his heel and left the room. In a fit of impotent rage, Raquel took one of the shoes out of the bag and hurled it after him, but it bounced harmlessly off the closing door.

"You bastard!" she hissed through clenched teeth. "You no-good, arrogant bastard!"

CHAPTER 4

Whehen she had calmed down a little, Raquel noticed that the light coming through the hatch was much brighter now. Standing up on the bed again, she looked out and caught a glimpse of azure sky. Obviously it was early morning, and Raquel suddenly realized that she was ravenous. She had had nothing to eat since noon of the previous day except for the hors d'oeuvres at the party. Surely her captors didn't intend to starve her!

She got off the bed and marched over to the door, intending to yell at the top of her lungs, demanding that somebody bring her food. Raquel had just raised her fists to pound on the door when to her surprise it inched open and a young man stuck his head in. He was slighter in build than either Nate or Jay, his skin was chocolate brown, and he was holding a tray of fresh fruit, bread, and cheese.

"Good morning, *pataki*," he said softly. "My name Art. Meester Bowman say to bring you breakfas'. May I come in?"

His demeanor was so different from that of the other men Raquel had encountered that she felt no fear of him. Stepping aside, she allowed him to enter. As he placed the tray on the little bureau, he kept casting furtive glances at her over his shoulder. When he turned around, he actually bowed.

"Is there anyt'ing else I can do for you, *pataki?*" he asked, regarding her almost with reverence.

Raquel couldn't figure out why he seemed so much in awe of her, but it was such a welcome change that she smiled at him. "Well, now that you mention it, there is. I assume this boat must have a bathroom some-where. Would it be possible for you to escort me to it?"

Art hesitated. "Meester Nate didn' say nothin' about bathroom."

"I hardly think he will object. After all, I can't very well escape while we're at sea, now, can I?"

"I guess it will be okay," the young man finally replied. "Come with me, *pataki.*"

Wondering what the strange word meant, Raquel followed him into a narrow passageway to a small door. Art positioned himself outside while she used the facilities, then washed her hands and face thoroughly using a sliver of soap and some paper towels she found next to the tiny sink. There was no mirror, which was probably just as well, Raquel thought. She must look a mess. Running her fingers through her tangled hair, she stepped outside and followed Art back to her cabin.

Before he left, she said, "There's one more thing you could do for me, Art. Do you know if there's a needle and thread on board?"

"I do not know, but I will see."

Art bowed himself out and Raquel perched on the edge of the bed, de-vouring every scrap of her breakfast. When he returned, he handed her one needle and a spool of thread, then picked up the tray and left the cabin.

Raquel had once made many of her own clothes, and now she wasted no time converting her turban fabric into a sleeveless shirt. Although she was determined not to give Nate Bowman the satisfaction of seeing her in the clothing he had provided and had shoved the shift and shoes into a bureau drawer, she was unaccustomed to going without underwear. She took off the skimpy top she was wearing, careful to remove the thou-sand dollars she'd stashed there, and put on the bra and panties, which fortunately appeared to be new and spotlessly clean. Next she slipped out of the skirt. Examining the waistband carefully, Raquel distributed the ten hundred-dollar bills along the inside facing and sewed it securely to the body of the skirt before she put it back on. Then, after recreating her ruffled pants, she slipped into the makeshift shirt, securing it around the waist with the costume's original top. On impulse, she concealed the needle in a fold of the shirt's fabric. It wasn't much of a weapon, but it was the only one she had.

All dressed up and no place to go, she thought, surprised that under the present circumstances she still retained her sense of humor.

Just then Raquel heard a soft rapping on her door, and her tension re-turned. "Who's there?" she called out.

"It's Art, *pataki,*" came the young man's soft voice. "Meester Nate say you can come topside now if you want. The door not locked anymore."

Heart pounding at the prospect of release from her prison cell, Raquel leaped to her feet and quickly opened the door. Art smiled shyly at her. "T'is way, please." He led the way along the narrow hall and up the companionway at its end.

When Raquel stepped out onto the deck, her eyes were so dazzled by the brilliance of the sun that for a moment she could see nothing at all. Then her vision cleared, and as she looked eagerly around her she discovered she was on a sailboat. The motor she had heard the night before must have been used to propel the boat out of the harbor, but now pure white sails bellied out against an incredibly blue sky as the boat skimmed over the water. The craft was good-sized, maybe forty feet or so, with ample sleeping space for the four men aboard and their prisoner. Glancing into the main cabin, Raquel could see that its couch had obviously been used as a bed—Nate Bowman's, she assumed, since he was the boss.

Filling her lungs with clean salt air, she knew the sensation of freedom she felt was only an illusion, but still she reveled in it. Raquel had always loved boats, and knew quite a bit about them. One of her high school teachers, a sailing enthusiast with his own boat, had formed a sailing club. Amazingly enough, Raquel's mother had not objected to her joining, so she and several of her classmates had spent many happy hours learning all Mr. Rutherford could teach them about the art of handling a sailboat. Raquel, always an apt pupil, had often earned his praise for her skill at the sport.

Deliberately ignoring Nate, who was manning the wheel, she sat in the corner of the long padded seat, lifting her face to the wind and gazing out across the bluish green water. Raquel was a strong swimmer. If there had been any land in sight, however distant, she would have considered jumping overboard and taking her chances. But there was nothing but water as far as the eye could see, and Raquel knew that was why she was no longer locked in her cabin. The only possible escape would be death by drowning, and she refused to surrender to despair. She was a survivor, and survive she would.

Nate Bowman studied her as the wind whipped a tangle of black curls away from her beautiful features and pressed that ridiculous outfit she had concocted against her body, molding the fabric to the curves of her ripe breasts. He knew perfectly well why she had refused to wear the clothing he had given her. She was stubborn, proud, and strong, qualities he couldn't help admiring. Her fiery temper and rebellious spirit both infuriated and impressed him, and he had an inkling of how much it had cost her to beg him for her freedom the night before. Looking into her dark, pleading eyes, there was a moment when he had almost weakened. Instead of the shameless woman he knew she was, he saw one of the young women of Dangigra who had pleaded for mercy on that terrible day so long ago. It was a day Nate would never forget.

Ironically, it had begun as a day of celebration. A truce had been called between the two warring religious groups, the Garifuna and the Shango. The festivities commenced at noon and continued all day. He and his cousin Cecilia, both in their early teens, were having a wonderful time. Nate's mother had raised Cecilia from infancy, feeling it was her responsibility to give the baby a loving home when her sister died in childbirth. Cecilia's father had totally abandoned her shortly thereafter when he'd taken another wife.

The Shango had traveled the long distance from Punta Gorda to the outskirts of Dangriga with slabs of *gibnut* in tow. Armadillo and brocket deer were stewing in pots over huge open fires, along with a medley of seafood, cow-foot soup, beans and rice, and various vegetables and tropical fruits. Wine made from cashew fruit was offered to everyone, even youngsters Nate's age. His people believed that it strengthened the blood, and young men needed to be strong so they would sire many healthy children when they came to manhood.

Everyone was in a happy mood, and there was much dancing in addition to eating and drinking. Nate smiled, remembering how for the first time Cecilia had joined the dance of the young virgins. She was so lovely, so slender and lithe. Occasionally she would giggle when she caught the eye of an interested Garifunian male, but she was still too young to do anything but flirt. Nate himself had been very proud because he was allowed to join the band, playing a large drum his father had fashioned for him. Everyone had praised him, saying how much his drumming added to the ensemble of instruments.

Slowly Nate's smile faded. As the day wore on, people from both villages mingled freely, enjoying each other's hospitality. Like many of the Garifuna, some Shango men found Cecilia beautiful and desirable. Unlike the Garifuna, however, the Shango were unaware of Cecilia's extreme youth. That night, as the wine flowed freely and the dancing and celebrating reached fever pitch, several Shango men who desired Cecilia refused to be dissuaded by her objections. Some young women from Dangigra willingly went into the brush with the Shango, but there were others who were forced. Cecilia was among them.

When this outrage was discovered by the Garifuna, fierce fighting broke out between the two factions. Eventually the Garifuna were able to drive the Shango away, but not before some people were killed and many others injured.

The days that followed were sad ones for the entire village, and especially so for Nate's family. Cecilia's young, tender body had been so badly abused that his mother had sought out the priestess to help heal her. Despite the woman's assurances that Cecilia would survive, her condition worsened every day. After two weeks, the priestess declared that there was nothing further she could do. The girl had lost her will to live. Something inside her fragile spirit had been broken and she no longer wanted to remain on this side of life. Nate and his family sat helplessly by, watching Cecilia die.

Even though he was little more than a boy, Nate vowed that when he became a man, he would never force himself on a woman no matter how much he desired her, nor would he permit any other man to do so if he could possibly prevent it.

That was the last time the Garifuna and the Shango had come together in peace. Now a truce was being called because of a prophecy—and Jackie Dawson.

Nate's eyes flickered over the young woman sitting on the bench. Like Jay, he was sexually aroused by her, but he would keep his distance and make sure that Jay kept his. She was Nate's responsibility and he would not allow her to be harmed in any way.

Following Raquel's gaze, he saw that she was watching Art, who was looking at the fluttering mainsail, a concerned expression on his face.

"We're losing speed," Nate called to him. "I'm going to sail her straight into the wind, so prepare to jibe."

Art nodded, and Raquel watched him trim the jib sheet, then slacken the lines to allow the boom to swing.

"*Pakati,*" he said, bowing to her, "you must move now. The boom soon be swingin' in your direction and I would not want you hurt. It would be best I t'ink if you go below."

Touched by his concern for her safety, she smiled. "Very well."

Raquel rose and headed for the companionway. Art was the only man aboard whom she did not hate or fear, and she wondered how he had become involved in this criminal undertaking. Suddenly she stopped in her tracks. If she made friends with Art, he might help her escape when they reached Belize! She would gladly pay him the entire thousand dollars if he would.

Lost in thought, Raquel didn't notice the short, stocky, light-skinned man who sidled up to her.

"My brother Jay tells me the big man says we cannot force you, eh? Maybe I won't need force. Al got somethin' here the ladies like." He grabbed his manhood through his pants and grinned suggestively. "How 'bout you and me havin' some real fun?"

She was about to brush past him when Nate's shout of "Jibe-ho!" rang out. Raquel ducked just in time, but Al wasn't so lucky. The heavy boom struck him a cruel blow before continuing on its way, and the man crumpled like a rag doll at her feet, blood flowing from a deep gash on the side of his head.

Jay had come up from below deck in time to see the whole thing. Dropping to his knees, he called his brother's name, but Al did not answer. He looked up at Raquel, and the malevolence and fear on the ugly face she had scarred with her nails made her cringe.

"It's your fault, woman!" he accused. "You are *echu!*"

Nate suddenly appeared behind Jay. "This isn't the time to talk about whose fault it is. Let's pick him up and carry him into my cabin."

"Stay away!" Jay shouted. "You say this woman be a link to the *gubida,* but I say she *echu,* an evil spirit! Look what she done to my face, and now to my brother. I take care of him myself!"

Nate shrugged. "Do as you please. It's no concern of mine."

Bulky muscles straining, Jay began dragging Al's limp body to the stern of the boat, and Nate turned his cool gaze on Raquel.

"Al was our cook," he said. "From now on, you have kitchen duty. You *can* cook, can't you?"

Raquel stared at him in disbelief. "Cook? You're asking me if I can *cook* when one of your men has been badly hurt? You should turn this boat around right away and take him back to Miami where he can get proper medical care!"

"Lunch is to be served at noon, and supper no later than six," Nate continued, as if she hadn't spoken. "You'll find everything you need in the galley. If you don't know how to operate the stove, ask Art."

He returned to relieve Art at the wheel, leaving Raquel sputtering with rage. Even she, who detested both Al and Jay, felt compassion for Al's plight, but Nate Bowman felt nothing at all. The man must have ice water in his veins! Unfortunately, however, she was his prisoner. She had no choice but to follow his commands.

With Art's assistance, Raquel soon familiarized herself with the galley and prepared lunch. When it was time to eat, Jay eyed both the meal and her with suspicion and emphasized his distrust by spitting at her feet. He grabbed a can of baked beans from a shelf and returned to his brother without a word.

Jay's lust had frightened Raquel, but it was nothing compared to the enmity he expressed from that day on. For the rest of the voyage, she avoided him as much as possible, spending most of her time in her cabin. But whenever she came topside, Jay's vengeful eyes never seemed to leave her.

One day Raquel heard Nate tell Art they would arrive in Belize tomorrow. That night her heart pounded in wild anticipation. By now she was sure that she would be able to persuade Art to aid in her escape, and as she went to bed, she planned to offer him the money first thing in the morning.

She was awakened in the middle of the night by the boat's wild bobbing. Angry waves were crashing and pounding the hatch above her. Mingled with it was another noise, a high, constant screech like the cry of an animal in pain.

From the hallway outside her room, Raquel heard loud voices.

"Meester Nate need you to help bring the sails down or we will lose them," Art was shouting.

"Do it yourself," was Jay's angry reply. "I got to look after Al. Don' you see how he's actin'? He's out of his mind! What if he gets out of here and jumps overboard?"

"Al just one man. If we don' take care of the boat, we will all drown in t'is storm!"

"Go to hell! I'm not leavin' my brother. I don' know nothin' about sailin' a boat, no way. You and Meester Nate were supposed to take care of t'at!"

Of all the odds that confronted her, Raquel had never contemplated the possibility of going down with her abductors in the Caribbean Sea. Now, because of Jay, their chances of survival were almost none!

She leaped out of bed and pounded on the cabin door, which was still locked every night for her own protection. "Art! Can you hear me?" she shouted. "Let me out of here! *I know how to sail!*"

It was several agonizing minutes before she heard the key turn in the lock and Art opened the door. "Meester Nate say you will only be in the way," he told her apologetically. "But he know an extra pair of hands better than none, so he say come on."

Since Raquel slept in her clothes, there was no need to change. She raced after him down the hall and up the stairs. As soon as they reached the deck, the howling wind nearly knocked her off her feet, but she quickly caught hold of some rigging. Torrential rain mixed with seawater immediately drenched her as she turned to Nate for instructions.

"What do you want me to do?" she yelled.

"Can you steer?" he yelled back.

"Yes!"

Nate turned the wheel over to her. "Hold her as steady as you can." To Art, he said, "We have to bring those sails down fast!"

Raquel planted her feet wide apart to steady herself, holding onto the wheel with all her might. The cool metal burned the palms of her hands as she squeezed it tightly. Already the forty-foot craft was heeling dangerously as it battled the waters.

Nate and Art scurried to bring down the jib sheet, the wind whipping the material in their faces, fighting them every step of the way. Finally, they managed to tame it, tying it off just enough to secure it against the storm's vengeance.

Nate exuded sheer power as he fought the elements. Every muscle in his upper body was tense. His eyes burned with determination.

"Now the mainsail," he shouted above the storm, then turned to Raquel. "You're doing fine. Just keep holding her steady."

The wheel resisted her effort to control it, and she bent her knees, giving her more leverage against its opposition. Her eyes and face stung from the savage lashes of the seawater, yet she never slackened her grip.

Nate and Art tried to haul down the large sail, but something was caught. Several other attempts to free it resulted in one of the main lines disengaging.

"I've got to go up there!" Nate determined. "It's the only way we're going to get it down."

Art stepped between Nate and the mast.

"No—I better go," he shouted. "You bigger and heavier than me. I'll be able to cling closer to the mast. The wind will have a smaller target."

There was only a moment's indecision before Nate nodded his approval. As Art turned toward the mast, Nate suddenly grabbed his forearm, concern burning deep within his gaze. "Be careful."

Clutching the mast, Art shinnied his way to the top. Raquel could see his brown hands grabbing for the evasive hook as it swung wildly in the storm. He leaned out further, finally catching the rope in his hand, but at that moment a mountainous wave crashed against the craft, forcing Nate to grab a block attached to loose rigging, and casting Art into the raging waters.

Raquel screamed as she witnessed Art's slim body disappear overboard and with it her hope of escape. She nearly let go of the wheel to reach out for him, but she stopped herself just in time. It would have meant instant death for them all.

Nate hung onto the rigging for dear life. The white cresting waves went washing over him time and time again, while his black head resembled a bob on the end of a fishing line. Raquel watched in sheer horror, knowing there was no way she could help without causing all their deaths.

She had no idea how long she steered, but suddenly it was all over and the storm dissipated as quickly as it had appeared.

Once the waves became smoother, Nate collapsed onto the deck, weak from exhaustion. Upon seeing him, Raquel released the wheel, her arms and legs shaking uncontrollably from the ordeal, and knelt down beside him.

"Are you all right?" Her voice came raspily.

He nodded his head once; he could do no more. It was hard for him to believe the woman he had placed in such danger had actually saved their lives.

Consciousness was beginning to evade him, but he could hear her breathing deeply beside him and felt the wet mass of her tangled hair lying limply over his arm. He wanted to thank her, to touch her. Then all went dark.

Raquel lay upon the deck, exhausted, allowing the boat to drift in whatever direction the wind took them. She was too tired to care or even cry.

Looking at Nate's inanimate body, she realized that now he was the only one she could depend on. Art was dead. There was no way she could trust Jay, and she knew his brother Al was an invalid. Suddenly she found herself clutching at Nate's bare chest and she began to sob against it. He mustn't die. He mustn't!

Almost as if from a distance she heard her own hysterical laughter, and she tasted the saltiness of her tears mixed with seawater upon his muscular chest. As Nate lay unconscious beneath her, Raquel knew with every fiber of her being he was her only chance for survival.

CHAPTER 5

The shady porch of the inn was only several feet away, but Raquel was unsure if she would be able to make it. The storm had caused them to beach much farther south than Nate had planned, and considering the condition of the boat, they were lucky to reach Belize at all.

Nate turned to see how far she lagged behind. After reassuring himself of her closeness, he switched his heavy duffel bag to the other shoulder. Heavy lines appeared in his handsome brow. Now his initial plans would have to be altered. It could take another day or so before they reached their intended destination. He entered the inn deep in thought with Jay and Al following closely on his heels. Nate was uneasy about what this unexpected change would mean for the woman.

On top of all that had occurred, Raquel was badly shaken by Art's death. The fact that he was an accomplice to her kidnapping was of little importance. She had never before seen another human being die.

Nate, however, showed no outward signs of being affected by the drowning. He appeared totally preoccupied with his own thoughts. So despite the closeness they experienced while battling the storm, their relationship was barely cordial.

Raquel's thoughts drifted back to before they had reached Belize. They had exchanged a few unkind words after he'd criticized her sailing. His thickly lashed eyes had appeared worried, and his handsome features had displayed lines of strain around the mouth. He was impatient with their lack of progress and accused her of not concentrating. She couldn't believe his audacity. She was literally a prisoner helping to sail a boat to God knew where . . . and he had the nerve to be rude and ungrateful!

Angrily Raquel lashed out at him. "You don't care about anything but what you want. You don't care about anybody else, do you?" Her dark eyes were cutting and cold as she spoke. "I have feelings of sympathy for someone like Art. But I believe you choose to be the way you are just so you can justify anything wrong and ugly that you do."

For a second, the anger in his eyes made her think that he would slap her. Then his face became the image of controlled rage and he simply walked away.

After Art's death, Jay had been forced to perform more of the duties on board. Al was of little help. The blow to his head had deeply affected his ability to reason. His sentences were disconnected and his ability to concentrate was minimal. In other ways he exhibited the behavior of a man who'd gone completely mad. He ate ravenously, as if he didn't know how to stop, and his sexual penchants had become disgusting. Foul language poured out of his mouth at the most peculiar times, mixed with a tongue Raquel did not understand.

After a particularly vulgar outburst, Nate suggested Al should be locked in the cabin until they beached the craft, but Jay would have none of it.

"It is your fault, as well as the *echu,* that he is like t'is. Now you want to lock him away so you don't have to see what you have done. No way, Meester Nate."

Raquel felt that in some perverse manner Jay took pleasure in Al's demented behavior, especially when it was directed at her. She could not pass within arm's reach of Al without being mauled openly. A glazed look would enter his eye and a string of the foulest terms she'd ever heard would tumble from his slack lips. Jay laughed hysterically during these uncomfortable moments—daring Nate to stop his brother's actions, knowing a man whose mind was as disturbed as Al's appeared to be was not responsible for the things he did.

The tension between Nate and the two brothers seemed to worsen as the journey progressed. Raquel was concerned over how things would go now that they had reached land. Jay needed Nate in order to reach Belize. But now that they had arrived, she feared Jay would not hold back his negative feelings toward either one of them.

They had little trouble during the long trek up the coastline of white, sandy beaches but the sinking sand made the journey difficult. As Raquel passed by the last clapboard house in a row of six, the heat of the sun was nearly unbearable—even her tongue felt dry as she tried to swallow. Still her tired, anxious eyes scanned the place for a building that might house the local authorities. But from the look of the tiny, underdeveloped settlement, the inn was the only place of business other than a poorly stocked, smelly fruit stand. There wasn't even one telephone pole in sight. The settlement seemed to sit in the middle of nowhere, with a thick, imposing forest on its inland side.

Suddenly, Raquel found it hard to breathe. Here she was on foreign soil, totally ignorant about the country or their present location. Could a somewhat modern city be beyond the wall of trees and brush? Or was her nearest possible avenue of escape miles away?

Raquel had been holding on to the belief that once they reached land she would find a way to contact the authorities and get help. But seeing what awaited her drained all hope. It felt as if the last ounce of physical strength she possessed was replaced by anxiety and fear. It was hard for her to think straight, and she had to force herself to mount the stairs to the inn. She felt as if heavy weights had been tied to her feet, making the simple motion a strenuous task. As she looked around, it was evident the inn was not a popular spot for tourists. From the look of the settlement, she doubted they received any tourists at all.

Inside, the furnishings revealed that one would get nothing but the bare necessities at this inn. There would be no modern conveniences. Yet compared to the straggly clapboard houses with little shade from the hot, tropical sun, it was a virtual Shangri-la.

Raquel sank into a large chair that had obviously seen better times. Dog tired and mentally worn, she watched Nate negotiate with a short man behind the counter. The language was totally foreign to her.

Out of desperation she considered throwing herself on the innkeeper's mercy until his dark eyes focused upon her. With one sweeping gaze he took in the dirty, flamboyant costume she wore, and his conclusions were plain. Scorn filled his eyes before he looked away. Humiliated and helpless, Raquel knew he had no room for understanding and any attempt to garner his help would be futile. And she knew she had to be careful—she did not know how her kidnappers would react to an attempt to escape on her part.

"There is only one room left, and that one is mine," Nate informed her. "I've arranged for you to have part of the back porch area that's sometimes used for guests. You can bathe in my room if you like."

Since the storm, Nate had begun to treat Raquel with a little more respect; still, he did not speak to her unless it was necessary. She knew she should not have expected him to give her the one room that was available, but somehow she had hoped. Her sable eyes mirrored her disgust as she listened to his decision.

Behind them, the Creole innkeeper eyed Al as he walked over to a bowl of fruit and began to take bites out of each one. The innkeeper, waving his arms emphatically, called to Al to stop. Finally, he snatched the bowl away, then placed his flat palm under Al's nose, demanding payment for his deed.

A verbal spat ensued between Jay and the Creole. When Jay pressed the man about a place to sleep, he turned over the small registration tablet and gave it a final slap. With an extensive stream of words Raquel did not understand, he pointed toward the door, then determinedly showed Jay and Al his back. Raquel felt a tinge of relief knowing at least that night Jay and Al would be sleeping under another roof.

Slipping into the sudsy water of the old-fashioned tub, Raquel felt her feelings of fear and anxiety float away like the bubbles of her bath. She lay in the steaming, soapy waters at her leisure, wondering how she would be able to gain her freedom. The warm water soothed her aching muscles and eased her mind.

Her thoughts unwittingly drifted to Nate as she wondered where he was and what he was doing now. He puzzled her more than she cared to admit—he had kidnapped her, yet he had protected her from Al and Jay. But he wouldn't set her free and he wouldn't say why he'd kidnapped her. Raquel was sure he needed her for some mysterious purpose.

Nate had taken his time in the bath before he'd allowed Raquel in the room. When he'd opened the bedroom door, she'd noticed his dark hair glistened from being freshly washed and he smelled of soap and a mild spicy scent. His carmel colored skin was freshly shaven, leaving only his trimmed mustache.

"How much time do you need?" he asked, buttoning his shirt over his bare chest.

She averted her eyes, yet a hazy vision of his powerful brown chest remained with her. "I don't know. Do I have a time limit?" she asked sarcastically.

"No," he replied, then extracted several Belizean dollars from his billfold and placed them on the bed. "Take your time. You can buy a meal downstairs once you're through." He disappeared down the hall without a backward glance.

She didn't bother to thank him. If it wasn't for him she wouldn't be in the situation she was in. Raquel thought of the thousand dollars sewn inside the belt of her costume. She hoped at some point it would come in handy, perhaps as an adequate bribe to get someone to help her. Ironically, it was a need for money that had gotten her into this situation. Hopefully, money, and lots of luck, would get her out.

As she allowed her fingers to float upon the water, she realized her kidnappers apparently had no intention of killing her, at least not yet. Her presence—or rather, Jackie Dawson's presence—was needed for something special, and that something was keeping her alive.

Raquel did not really believe Nate would harm her. But she wasn't sure. There was something beneath his cool exterior, an ability for cruelty if the need arose. Whereas Jay was a different story altogether. She believed the two men's desire for Jackie Dawson's presence was connected, but the motive for it was not the same. There was little doubt in her mind that Jay would kill her with pleasure, if the proper moment arrived, but only after degrading her further.

An involuntary shudder ran through her at the thought, and she reinforced her decision to be wary of him.

Raquel put on the shift Nate had given her. Afterward she washed the costume she'd worn for the past two days. The truth was, the frilly material had been extremely hot and uncomfortable, and already she could tell the airy shift would be much more practical. After all, she shouldn't cause herself more discomfort just to annoy her taciturn abductor.

Instead of going to the small dining room as Nate suggested, Raquel settled herself in the functional space provided for her. It contained a cot, and a battered nightstand that served as a dresser. The mattress was soft enough, and the linen was clean. Raquel needed food, but right now her need for rest was greater, and she tumbled into a deep sleep moments after her head lay on the flat feather pillow.

A feeling of disorientation swept over Raquel when she opened her eyes and it remained dark. Finally, she realized she must have slept through the entire afternoon and it was night. The distant sound of a guitar came from the direction of the dining room, along with several unusual but delicious smells. Raquel's stomach grumbled in response to the aroma.

The outside wall of the meager dining room was constructed of netted wire, enabling a constant flow of cool air to come off the sea. There were few decorations other than plants which grew lushly in the tropical climate.

Raquel felt self-conscious as she walked into the room filled with men and one female whose purpose was plain. Her tattered shift hung unattractively on her slender frame, and the only thing that appeared remotely appealing was a lock of shiny black hair that hung from beneath a dirty scarf she wore.

Because of the young Indian woman's unkempt appearance, Raquel could not imagine anyone wanting to take her up on what she was offering. Yet only moments later, when several pairs of lustful eyes focused on her, she was glad for the woman's presence.

An older female, whom Raquel assumed to be the innkeeper's wife, ambled over to the table where she sat. There was no menu and the woman spoke no English—from this Raquel knew her choices for a meal would be nonexistent.

The woman stood over her smiling and gesturing expressively with her hands. At the end of her presentation, she pointed to the plate of a man sitting nearby. Still smiling and in a heavily accented voice she nodded affirmatively toward Raquel. Raquel had no choice but to agree. She would eat whatever the woman was offering.

Nate sat silently by himself in a corner. Two bottles of wine were the only things on his table. One was totally empty and the other was half full. With barely focused eyes, he stared at this woman celled Jackie Dawson. Out of the colorful frock and heavy makeup, she was still lovely. *More lovely than any woman has the right to be,* he thought bitterly. But he knew about women like her, and despite her beautiful face and desirable body, he wanted nothing to do with her. He would do his job and leave her alone.

Raquel looked uneasily around the room and felt a sense of relief when she saw Nate. She had the urge to get up and join him until she saw the bottles of wine on the table and the blank look in his eyes. Raquel returned his look with disgust. Not only was he a criminal; he was an alcoholic as well.

Jay and Al had come to the inn for dinner, and were conversing with two other men as they shared two bottles of wine and food. Raquel was amazed to hear the language they spoke was different from the one used while communicating with the innkeeper, and she wondered how many languages were spoken in Belize.

Deep-pitched, raunchy laughter erupted in the room as one of the men grabbed a slim cheek of the prostitute's bottom. The woman gave no sign of rejection or acceptance in response to his actions. Moments later, as the innkeeper's wife served Raquel her food, the two of them disappeared down the hall, noisily shutting a door behind them.

The dish Raquel saw before her resembled a gumbo, containing pieces of fish, shrimp, rice, and beans. Raquel ate gratefully. She finished her meal quickly, rinsing it down with a glass of cool limeade. To her dismay, as she emptied the glass, Al took a seat beside her. His breath stank of liquor and onions as he breathed heavily through mouth, which was slightly open.

Al's bleary eyes focused on her breasts. A shaft of light angling off of a small lantern nearby made them clearly visible through the flimsy material of her shift.

"Juicy hooters," he slurred, making obscene motions with his mouth and tongue, then looking expectantly into Raquel's face.

Jay laughed boisterously, followed by a low remark to the men at the table. Their deep guffaws joined his.

It wasn't enough that she had been kidnapped and shanghaied clear across the sea. She also had to stand being ridiculed and degraded by this group of degenerates!

"Get the hell away from my table!" she hissed, dark eyes flashing with rage.

Al's idiotic features suddenly sharpened into a mask of livid sadism.

Quick as a flash he had his large hand about her neck and his eyes were bulging with madness.

Raquel sputtered and gagged as she tried to remove Al's hand, but his grip was like steel. The weight of his large body caused the chair to tip over and they fell to the floor. Somewhere in the room she heard glass shatter as she kicked and squirmed to break loose from Al's deathly hold.

"Call him off, Jay, or I'll split his throat wide open," Nate's voice cut through a haze. "Now! Or he's a dead man!"

Raquel could see blood trickling down the side of Al's heavily veined throat. The tip of the jagged wine bottle, which Nate held, was already cutting deep into his skin.

"Stop, Al. Stop!" Jay called to his brother. "It is *Dada* who speaks to you."

Like a mad dog with a cherished bone, Al was reluctant to let go. Jay's insistent tug on his wide shoulders finally persuaded him, and Raquel rolled on her side, coughing and clutching her throat, while Jay led Al out of the building.

Raquel still held her throat as she tried to catch her breath. She could barely focus on Nate as he knelt down beside her, allowing the dazed young woman to lean on him as she stood.

"Are you all right?"

Raquel nodded blankly, even though she wasn't very sure. Stunned, she let him accompany her back to her place. Tears brimmed in her eyes, but she refused to cry. She'd cried more in the past two days than she had in her entire life. She would not cry again.

For a moment their eyes met, and Raquel thought there was something Nate wanted to say. Instead, he silently left her alone in the semi-darkness.

The thought of sleeping unprotected on the porch without a door with a lock petrified her. She could still see Al's insane eyes and feel his iron grip about her throat. There was no way she could stay there without protection. Desperate, Raquel ran after Nate.

"You cannot leave me out there alone!" Her voice was nearly hysterical as she stopped him outside his door. "What do you think they will do to me while you sleep?" Her frantic gaze searched his, and she noticed his eyes were slightly bloodshot.

"So what do you want? I'm not sleeping out there."

Stung by his apathy, Raquel retorted, "Then I'll just have to sleep in here with you."

A veiled look descended over his dark eyes. He did not answer her, and his steely gaze pinned her against the door.

Raquel was afraid his silence meant he would not accept her suggestion. She had noticed Nate kept to himself, never shared moments with anyone for the simple sake of company. It was obvious he treasured his privacy. Even his strange reaction to Art's death was a sign this man danced to a different drummer. She guessed that somewhere inside he carried a deep scar, but he had gone beyond the need to heal it. Perhaps that scar was his motivation. Somehow, she felt Jackie Dawson's presence in Belize was a key to his personal dilemma.

Desperate that he would reject her, Raquel resorted to the only weapon she possessed.

"I'm not that bad to look at, am I?" She spoke the suggestive words softly, looking deep into his eyes.

Never in her life had she propositioned a man, and the meaning behind the words she had just spoken caused her heart to pound. Through the years more than once her mother had accused her of being hot-blooded, and had made her pray for hours for what she called her sinful actions. And now here she was, offering herself to this man like a common prostitute. Was there a chance that her mother had been right?

Fortifying herself against her own traitorous thoughts, Raquel drew in a deep breath and her almond eyes narrowed. *I am nobody's prostitute, and I intend to survive all of this. Right now, this man is the only thing I can count on. Once we leave this hole-in-a-wall settlement it will be a whole new ball game.*

Her sense of survival was strong, and her own brazenness amazed her. A slightly trembling finger lifted to his neatly trimmed moustache. Systematically she began to run it through the coarse hair, then placed it upon his smooth lips.

Like lightning his hand caught her wrist, giving it a slightly painful squeeze.

"This is not a good time to tease me, lady." Nate's dark, thickly lashed gaze penetrated hers.

"Who's teasing?" was her raspy response. She was breathless from fear.

Something like a low growl emanated from his throat as he caught a handful of Raquel's curls in his fist. She winced with discomfort as he slowly drew her head toward his, then buried his face in her ebony tresses. Seconds later he lifted her off the floor and carried her inside, kicking the door shut with one foot.

"So you have decided to *give* it to me?" His hot breath heavy with alcohol grazed her as she lay pinned beneath him on the tiny bed.

"Yes." Her whisper was almost inaudible.

"Then you must show me how much you want to." A knowing glint entered his eyes while he straddled her.

Raquel's sable gaze widened. He must know she did not want to go to bed with him. But his need to control everything was surfacing in his words. She would ultimately seduce Nate, but he would remain dominant by telling her how.

The young woman wrestled with her outrage and her need to survive. It was only a matter of moments before survival triumphed. Without Nate's protection, she would be lost.

"All right."

With her consent, he rolled off her, and she climbed to her feet, standing a small distance away from the bed. Slowly she removed the shift.

Her body trembled ever so slightly, and the brown tips of her breasts hardened from an inner chill. She stood naked before him, allowing him to soak up the even, copper-brown softness of her skin. The tender valley between her breasts, their dark peaks, and the lush, curly triangle below were the only visible variations in color.

Raquel forced herself to look into his face and felt humiliated when she saw how impassive his expression was as he sat on the side of the bed. His hooded eyes made it impossible for her to read their message.

"Come here," Nate huskily commanded.

The young woman stepped forward, closing her eyes to brace herself against his rough exploration.

He watched her come toward the bed with her eyes clenched tightly closed, her face an anxious mask surrounded by masses of shiny black curls. She was breath-taking in her nudity, her womanly curves at full blossom. He observed the tip of her tongue darting nervously about, licking her full bottom lip in tense anticipation of his actions. Like this, she exhibited none of the fire he knew burned deep inside her.

An audible intake of breath escaped Raquel as he gently slid his hands around her hips and drew her body closer, placing his face against the swell of her lower abdomen.

The sting of tears burned behind her eyes, tears that she would not release.

"If I take you like this," his voice was silky and low, "it would still be taking you by force, and that I don't plan to do."

Raquel's eyes flew open, relief flooding their depths, and she looked down at the top of his head as it rested against her.

"But I intend to have you, now that you have offered yourself to me." He stared up into her face intently. "I've wanted you ever since that first night on the boat, but taking a woman by force is not what I'm about."

Her shapely eyebrows rose in astonishment. Here she stood, his captive, and he spoke to her of his principles!

"I did not say I am without faults. I am simply saying I am no rapist," he concluded. Then he released her.

"You are welcome to sleep here," he indicated the bed where he sat.

Raquel bent down to retrieve her clothing from the floor, but Nate's strong grasp stopped her.

"No. You must sleep just as you are."

At first, humiliation filled her richly lashed gaze, but it quickly turned into a stubborn glint.

"I will not," she hissed between clenched teeth. She had stooped as low as she intended to go by offering herself to him. She would not sleep beside him in the nude like a willing lover.

Once again she kneeled down to get her shift. This time he did not interfere.

Raquel walked around him, climbed into the bed, and slipped beneath the plain white sheet. She turned her back toward him, and her eyes rested on the fiber-board wall in front of her.

She was totally confused by this man. He was her abductor! He had forcefully brought her to an unknown land, and now that she had offered herself to him, albeit unwillingly, he refused her, saying he would only do it when she was willing. How could he expect that would ever be?

Nate climbed in the tiny bed beside Raquel. Gently he drew her body against his, and she could feel his heart beat, as well as his hardness against her. Raquel stiffened from the contact, but forced herself to remain deathly still, feeling small and helpless against his strong, masculine body. Protectively a muscular arm lay draped about her waist, and the top of her head fit perfectly in the space beneath his raised chin.

Minutes later she found her guarded state unnecessary as she heard his even breathing. Relieved to know he had fallen asleep, eventually she slept as well.

CHAPTER 6

"**P**unta Gorda is much closah," Jay snapped, his chin lifting to a challenging angle. "We should go there first, before travelin' to Dangriga."

Nate's voice remained icily calm despite the opposition Jay presented. "Our plans never included going to Punta Gorda. The main *dabuyaba*—temple—" he explained for Raquel's benefit, "is in Dangriga. That's where we planned to go in the beginning, and that's where I intend to end up."

"Have it your way, Meester Nate, but Mez Dawson is goin' to Punta Gorda wit' Al an' me." Jay tried to look beyond Nate into the bedroom.

Nate shook his head, a snarl of a smile crossing his lips. "That's not going to happen. Anyway, I doubt if she'd even arrive in Dangriga if I left her alone with the two of you."

"Ah, that's the key to this situation, Meester Nate," Jay said with a malicious smile. "There is only one of you, and two of us. How are you going to stop us?"

For the first time Al stepped from behind Jay, like a trained animal responding to its master's command. Nate's cool, steely gaze took in the two of them, and his half-nude body moved slowly from its relaxed position where it blocked the half-open bedroom door.

"Don't worry about me, Jay. I can be quite resourceful."

He purposely allowed the two men a better view of the dresser behind him, where the sun's early rays reflected off the Glock compact pistol that lay menacingly out in the open.

"Now, you may want to take a chance and try to overpower me, but I assure you, I'm a man who never addresses an unknown situation empty-handed."

Jay's glance darted to Nate's right arm that lay relaxed against his side. Then, for the first time, he became aware that his left arm remained hidden behind him.

Throughout the exchange Raquel lay very still, listening. But the sight of the deadly weapon lying several feet away from the bed caused her to start. She had anticipated a confrontation, but she'd had no idea it would happen so soon. Like Jay, Raquel wondered if Nate held another weapon in the hand that was also hidden from her sight, and she gasped.

Jay heard her quick intake of breath, and saw the slight movement of the sheet on the bed.

"That would not be Mez Dawson in your bed, would it, Meester Nate?" He tried to conceal his anger. "Not aftah you have warned us to stay away from the precious piece. You haven't broken your own rule?" His voice turned derisive.

"Whatever I do is none of your business. But rest assured, there was no force involved." Nate gave a meaningful smile. "You see, unlike you, I am man enough to arouse a woman."

It took all the control Jay could muster not to strike out. The side of his face twitched with unleashed anger, while his eyes burned into those of the man in front of him.

"T'is must be your lucky cycle, Meester Nate, because once again you have won. But we are in Belize now, and t'ings will be different. Al an' I have rented the only four-wheel drive vehicle available here, so travelin' won't be too easy for the two of you," he smirked, then continued. "We are goin' to Punta Gorda. A healin' must be performed on my brother by the *buyei*. But after t'at, at anytime, Meester Nate, be assured, you will look up one day and I will be right t'ere. And I promise you t'en the situation will go the way I want it to go."

Nate waited for them to walk away before he closed the door. Veiled eyes cast a glance in Raquel's direction before he strode over to the dresser and placed the Glock in his pocket. Raquel saw his right hand had been empty.

Nate turned a knowing, steady gaze in her direction.

"Well, I guess you heard all of that. We've got a long journey in front of us, Miss Dawson. I hope you realize it's not going to be easy, and I believe if Jay has anything to do with it, it's going to be rougher than anything you have ever experienced. Just don't make any waves and you'll do fine."

Raquel held the sheet up against her as she sat bolt upright in the crumpled bed.

"You're forgetting one thing, Mr. Bowman. If it wasn't for you and those two goons, I wouldn't be here in the first place!" she snapped. "So don't give me a pep talk like I'm a partner in crime, or something. I'm the victim here, and if you just happen to wear a similar hat at this moment . . . that's your problem."

"You know what? For someone who's in the position you're in, you sure talk a lot of stuff." He gathered the rest of his belongings together and began to pack them in the duffel bag. "But if I were you, I would be getting dressed. You see, it's still the rainy season, and the tourist trade will continue to be slow for a few more weeks. And let me inform you, there's not much law around here. Nobody cares about this little area. It's not a big money-maker as far as crops are concerned, and it sure as hell ain't no great tourist attraction. So if you want to remain here and become like the woman you saw in the dining room last night, I'm sure those men would be more than happy that you decided to give her some help."

He turned his bare back to her as he sat on the side of the bed and began to put on his shoes. Defined muscles rippled and spread out powerfully as he bent over to tie the laces.

Frowning, Raquel looked out the window at the elegant palms and profuse ferns basking in the dazzling sunshine. It hadn't rained during their long walk to the inn, nor did it look like it would rain anytime soon. What if he were lying just to scare her? With Jay and Al gone, she could refuse to go with him, and she definitely had enough money to buy her way back home.

The young woman brushed the thick black curls that hung in her face back in a defiant gesture. "I don't believe a word you're saying," she stated. "I'm not going with you. So what are you going to do, shoot me? If so, you better do it now."

She stood up in the path of the sun's revealing rays, challenging him with her eyes, her breasts rising and falling rapidly beneath the flimsy shift as she backed against the flatboard wall. She could hear him cuss beneath his breath.

"*Pataki* . . . don't push me." His response was threatening. "We crossed a sea to get here. And now that we are here, and things have developed as they have . . . I intend to do whatever I have to. And there's one thing you need to understand. I need you with me in order to accomplish that. So . . . no, I won't shoot you, but I can make your backside so sore that you may wish that I had."

"You'd *spank* me?" Raquel gasped incredulously.

"Right where the sun don't shine, baby." His features remained impassive, but his eyes gleamed wickedly. "As a matter of fact, I might find it quite enjoyable . . . so might you."

Raquel stood rooted to the spot.

"So, are you going to get dressed? Or am I going to have to give you a sample of what I'm talking about, while you're so conveniently attired?"

The thin shift did little to conceal Raquel's voluptuous body. Almost by instinct she could feel Nate's mind turning from business to pleasure. His dark gaze became smoky with desire as he stood staring at her for the first time during their entire exchange.

Nate's searing look made her pointedly aware of her nudity beneath the material and the very vulnerable position she was in. His long legs were spread apart as he watched her in a stance of readiness. Raquel knew, feeling fear mixed with excitement, whatever task he took on he would do it well, be it fighting, lovemaking—or tanning her hide. Just the thought of his ability to master her in whatever way sent an odd tingle through her body. Yet it appalled her to realize how much he fascinated her.

She weighed her chances of escaping Nate Bowman. He was far more powerful physically than she and knew Belize far better, too. She was fairly confident that he wouldn't rape or kill her, but Raquel had no such guarantee with the men downstairs. She reluctantly admitted to herself that Nate was her best and only hope.

Stoically the young woman dropped her gaze and crossed to the bathroom in silence, where she noisily slammed the door behind her.

Nate let her go, but he was quite aware of the variety of thoughts which plagued her. They were plainly written in her dark, sable eyes. He knew that she feared him, but she had come to him, seeking refuge from an even greater threat. Just thinking about making love to her aroused him. It had been torture lying next to her last night. And he was irritated that his body had betrayed him. She was so beautiful, and there was something about her that touched an instinctive part of him. It felt almost like a kind of integrity, something he had come to believe no longer existed.

"Integrity?" he chided himself. "How did I come up with that? Women like Jackie Dawson are a dime a dozen!" Whenever he took her, she would willingly give herself to him, just as he believed she had given herself to countless other men.

Raquel let out a startled shriek as several frantic turkeys and an armadillo were chased out of the abandoned clapboard building, heading right in her direction.

The meaty arms of the innkeeper's wife waved menacingly behind them before she turned and gave a broad smile to Nate, then gestured toward the rusty minibus inside the dilapidated structure.

It had been only moments earlier that the woman's now beaming features had been a mask of anger. It was when the young Indian prostitute attempted to interrupt her conversation with Nate. The disheveled female kept repeating the words "Nim Li Punti," after Nate had mentioned the unfamiliar phrase. Raquel thought she acted like a woman possessed, until the hefty female threatened her with the back of a raised hand. Finally, she shied away like a frightened animal. Until that moment Raquel had not realized how young the prostitute was, and she couldn't help wondering how she had ended up in such an awful predicament.

Nate circled the vehicle kicking its tires, and checking under the hood before he began to haggle with the innkeeper's wife. In the end their negotiations didn't take very long. Nate needed the minibus, and that was all there was to it. It was the only transportation in the settlement, and therefore could be had at whatever price she demanded.

Despite its run-down condition the van didn't need much coercing before it raucously cranked up and headed for a well-hidden road. Raquel didn't know what was worse—the road, if you could call it that, or the nonexistent shock-absorbers of the squat vehicle. Large plants brushed and pressed against the filthy windows as they drove down the narrow route, its uneven surface causing them to bounce about on the torn seats.

Raquel had refused to sit beside Nate as he drove, so she chose the longer seat behind him. She sat where she could have a clear view of the path, even though that was of little consequence; there was nothing to see outside of the thick foliage. Suddenly she realized the road was so narrow it would cause a major problem if another vehicle approached them traveling in the opposite direction. One of them would have to completely drive into the brush in order to allow the other to pass. In all her life the young woman had never seen anything like it. This was truly a wilderness, and her apprehension began to mount as she anticipated what could be in store.

Raquel would have chosen to sit on the back seat, if it had not been covered with old blankets and clothes that looked as if they had been there forever. Their musty smell floated toward them from the rear, causing her to cover her nose in disgust.

Raquel hated to admit to herself the other reason why she wanted to keep a safe distance from Nate. She found his nearness much too disturbing.

Looking at the back of his head and broad shoulders led her thoughts to earlier that morning, when the two of them still lay in bed. She had been strongly aware of the feel and smell of the man beside her. It had been warm and vibrant, almost comforting, unlike the cold nights and mornings when she'd gone to bed and awakened alone during her months of celibacy.

Raquel had offered herself to him the night before as a matter of survival. But it was hard to accept even the slightest possibility that she might actually want him, in light of all that had passed.

It took both hands to unlock the rusty device that controlled the sliding window. Sweat glistened on her limbs and face after she managed to open it. Abruptly a large branch forced its way inside the vehicle, leaving some of its leaves as the minibus continued on.

Nate glanced back over his shoulder. "I don't know if that's such a good idea."

"Why not?" she asked, plucking at the front of her shift to stimulate a flow of air.

"First of all, you never know what insects may want to hitch a ride. But mainly it's because some of those plants are poisonous. If they just touch your skin, you could be in a world of trouble."

"I'm already in a world of trouble," Rachel shot back. "But right now, I'm extremely hot as well."

"It won't be long before this road widens a bit. Until then you might want to remove some of those clothes you have on beneath that shift."

"No way! I'm fine just like I am."

In the bathroom that morning, Raquel had donned the bralike top of her calypso costume, and had turned the turban into a slip of sorts underneath the creamy fabric of the see-through shift.

"Suit yourself, then," he replied with a shrug.

Taking his own advice, Nate took off the shirt he was wearing, and unsnapped the waist of his jeans.

It was unmercifully hot inside the van even with the window open, and the clothes stuck to Rachel's back and under her thighs where her body made contact with the vinyl seat. Yet she preferred enduring the discomfort to following his advice.

Soon the road broadened as Nate promised, but this was accompanied by the inconvenience of enormous potholes. Raquel could see where the Belizean government had attempted to modernize the road. A thin strip of asphalt ran down its center, but after years of neglect, huge sinkholes dotted the sides, making it that much more dangerous. It was impossible to travel at a speed that would create a welcome breeze since the roads were so treacherous.

The clunk of tires moving in and out of potholes was soon accompanied by an occasional spatter of raindrops. In a matter of moments the rain became heavier until it developed into a torrential downpour. A deluge of water found its way through the window and into the vehicle. *So this is what the rainy season is like,* Raquel thought. Grudgingly her thoughts drifted back to Nate's warning, and just for a moment, she was glad Nate had persuaded her to come with him.

It didn't take long for the shabby roadway to run into a muddy trench. The potholes filled with water, causing the minibus to spin its wheels in an effort to drive through the mud. The rickety windshield wipers did little to clear the sheets of water streaming down the front window, and Nate peered uncertainly out at the road in front of him.

Suddenly, an unexpected drop into a massive pothole halted the vehicle with a jerk. The continuing whir of the minibus's tires buried the vehicle even further in the mire.

Raquel watched as Nate got out to evaluate the situation, fastening his skintight jeans before stepping out into the downpour. Repeatedly he wiped his thickly fringed eyes as he looked down at the embedded wheel, torrents of rain spilling over his muscular chest and back. He cursed savagely as he looked about him, deciding what would be the next move to make.

A gust of water blew inside the van as he climbed back into the driver's seat, and began to don his shirt over his drenched flesh. Impatiently Raquel waited for his assessment of the situation, but he didn't speak.

"What are we going to do now?" she prodded, after her nerves could take no more. Her question was met with silence as Nate slipped back out into the downpour and disappeared into the forest.

The thundering rain that assaulted the minibus increased in intensity as the minutes ticked away. Raquel could feel panic rising inside her with the steady tilting of the vehicle into the massive hole. Where was he? Had he left her here in the middle of a Belizean forest just so he could save his own tail after finding their predicament impossible? A man like Nate Bowman, a criminal, was capable of that and more.

Scraping sounds from the back of the bus caused Raquel's heart to lurch and the hairs on the back of her neck rose up. The thought of a savage animal awakening from slumber flashed in her mind, but it was quickly cast away by the sight of the prostitute from the inn rising out of the pile of foul-smelling blankets on the back seat.

Two pairs of frightened eyes stared at one another.

Suddenly the girl lunged for the door nearest the driver's seat, and the stench that surrounded her nearly caused Raquel to gag. She watched as she bounded out of the minibus into the rain, then stopped. The driving rain pushed the filthy scarf she wore onto the back of her neck.

Raquel was surprised to see straight, jet black hair hacked to shoulder length, and a hint of deep reddish brown skin beneath the film of dirt on her face which washed downward in the rain.

The young woman stood as still as a doe listening for danger, then her head swiveled to survey the landscape. Suddenly she stopped and stared far into the distance. Raquel darted to the opposite side of the bus to try and see what had captured the girl's attention. Through the wall of water it was hard to make out the large object far to the east of them, but it resembled an enormous hill or mountain, and a large portion of it was covered with trees.

Eyes filled with excitement and trepidation focused on Raquel once more, before she too disappeared into the thick foliage.

"Wait!" Raquel yelled. She rushed out into the rain after the only human connection she thought she had.

"What's the matter?" Nate's voice projected from behind her.

She whirled about to see him stepping out of the thicket.

"That girl was in the bus all the time," she explained excitedly, her face lighting up from the thought of it.

Nate's countenance reflected his confusion as he approached her.

"The young prostitute. She managed to hitch a ride with us and we didn't even know it. Don't you see? She escaped under their very noses," she yelled madly above the downpour. The young girl's victory was a cause for jubilation—there was hope in this ugly jungle.

Nate watched her with the rain plastering her inky curls against her face and shoulders, causing her clothes to cling enticingly to her breasts, hips, and thighs. The sparkle of life glistening in her eyes at that moment struck a cord of longing deep inside him, a long-forgotten yearning for that kind of belief in the good things of life. For here she stood, a captive in a strange land, not knowing what fate would befall her, but having the faith and courage to rejoice in the happiness of someone else.

Raquel's wet feathery lashes shielded dark, shining eyes as she looked at him. He knew she saw him as her enemy. What else would a kidnapper be? Yet he longed to possess her, to consume the light of faith that burned so brightly about her. Maybe it would help resurrect his own.

Yet, to Nate Bowman, possessing this woman did not simply mean possessing her body. She had already offered that to him out of a pure need to survive. No, he wanted more than that. He wanted the fire that he knew would consume her when she gave herself fully to a man, not the ember of fear.

"We're going to have to leave the bus here," he stated, climbing back inside to retrieve his duffel bag. Once outside again, he looked around him. "Which way did she go?"

"She entered the forest there," Raquel pointed. "It was like she recognized something. I think it was that mountain in the distance."

"Well, let's head that way. It's better than nothing."

"What do you mean, it's better than nothing?" Exasperation was apparent in her voice. "You mean to tell me you don't know where we are?"

"That's right *pataki,* at the moment your guess is as good as mine." A half smile crossed his rakish features. "I couldn't very well take the main roads, could I, even though there aren't that many here in Belize. This is a small country, everybody knows everybody, and we would be easy to find."

"In other words, to cover up your criminal activity, you brought us out here in the jungle and now we're lost!" she accused.

"Partially."

"What do you mean, partially?"

He entered the slumping vehicle again, leaving her standing in the rain while he rummaged through the articles in the back. Momentarily, he emerged with a couple of blankets and a rusted ax, then he picked up their conversation where he left off.

"If you want to make it easy for Jay to find us, that's your business. I just think it would be better if he and his brother had a somewhat difficult time doing it. Maybe we can make it to Dangriga before they do."

Raquel reared back and looked at him skeptically. "I don't understand this. All of you were together when you kidnapped me. Now all of a sudden you expect me to believe it's you and me against the world and all that jazz? Do I have this right?"

"You can believe what you want to believe." He entered the forest at the spot where Raquel had indicated.

"Well, I want you to know, you're no better than they are," she responded, annoyed by his offhanded remark.

"Maybe so, maybe not. Here, carry these blankets while I try to cut down some of these bushes." He tossed the smelly objects into her arms.

"I don't want to carry these!" she sputtered, imagining some of the filth had involuntarily flown into her mouth.

"That's up to you. I've got something inside here to use in case I need it tonight. You're the one who's going to need it, not me."

Reluctantly Raquel tried to fold the sodden covers so they would be easier to carry. The wet moss, leaves, and dirt beneath her feet had begun to soak the cheap shoes Nate had provided for her, making the trek that much more unbearable.

They walked for what felt like hours before the torrential rains stopped, giving way to a glistening green world sprinkled with vivid color. It was almost magical, the moment-to-moment transformation that occurred. Like a conductor motioning for an orchestra to commence, the sun's rays struck the flowering plants and trees causing them to come vibrantly to life, the cries and calls of numerous birds and animals only adding to its complexity.

Raquel was out of breath when they reached a partial clearing. As she began inhaling deeply, the rich smell of damp earth and plants was powerful. She plopped down on a rotted trunk covered with lichen and other symbiotic plants.

Nate stood not far away. He dug into his duffel bag, producing several soggy fry jacks, breakfast leftovers from the inn. Reluctantly Raquel accepted the limp corncake he offered her but threw it down in frustration after it crumbled when she attempted to bite it. She watched Nate impassively chew the crumbly mess.

"How can you eat that?" Her stomach growled in frustration as she observed him consume it.

"Simple." His dark gaze raked her insultingly. "There's nothing else to eat, and won't be until we come across something edible, or run into a McDonald's. Whichever comes first."

Nate's sense of humor was quickly becoming irritating to Raquel. She looked down and observed the yellowish hunks she'd thrown on the ground being quickly devoured by a swarm of ants. Hunger caused her to raise her eyes longingly toward the last morsel Nate was popping into his mouth. It surprised her to see the young prostitute quietly watching them several yards away.

"Hey," Raquel whispered. "That young woman is standing behind you."

He turned just as she called to them in a strange language, then motioned for them to follow her.

"She's a Mayan," he said, fastening the duffel bag and rising to his feet. "That could be lucky for us."

"A Mayan! I had no idea there would be Mayans so near the shoreline."

"We have traveled much further inland, *pataki*. It's quite widely known that the Kekchi Indians live near this area."

She paused, then asked softly "Why do you call me *pataki?*" The foreign word was difficult on her tongue. "Art referred to me with the same word." Her rich gaze clouded over with the memory of his being thrown into the sea.

"I remember, and that is one of the reasons I use it."

Raquel looked at him in surprise.

"It means 'legend,' " he informed her. "But I am sure my reasons for using it are quite different from Art's, because he has never seen you naked, as I have." His dark, smoldering eyes appraised her reaction to his words, then he continued. "But you are also believed to have a connection with the *gubida,* the spiritual ancestors of our people. That is why Art called you *pataki.* "

Raquel swallowed hard, then looked again for the girl. She was gone.

"Hey! Where in the heck did she go?"

The Mayan's quick disappearance was like magic.

Raquel knew they needed the girl, since Nate wasn't sure where they were.

"I don't know, but it would be to our benefit to find her."

They gathered up their belongings and hurried further into the rainforest. They were so intent on finding the girl, they almost stumbled over her as she knelt down caressing the purplish petals of a flower growing in the midst of several other plants. As they watched, she began to dig with nimble fingers until she unearthed a large tuberous root.

"It's a sweet potato!" Raquel excitedly announced, bending down to dig up the root of a similar flower.

The girl's blackened teeth dominated her smile as she showed her pleasure in presenting the food to Raquel and Nate. Nate swaggered over and took the vegetable from her hand. "Well, well. I think we've made a rare but valuable friend."

The Mayan's grin broadened and she returned to the task at hand. After digging up several of the orangish-yellow roots, the girl took them to a rock overhang.

Looking at the curious pair, she struck one hand repeatedly against the other.

Nate shrugged his broad shoulders, "What is it? What are you trying to say?"

Sensing his confusion, the girl turned her imploring eyes to Raquel.

"She's hitting her hands together," she said almost to herself. "Hitting . . . *striking* her hands together. She's striking her hands together! I bet she's asking for a match," Raquel adeptly guessed, then pulled a book of matches out of her bag.

The girl shook her head affirmatively, pleased that Raquel had understood. Next she began to gather a small group of dry twigs and leaves which she found nestled against the wall beneath a large, jutting stone. Once she felt she had enough, she made a fire, then dug a hole for baking the roots. It wasn't long before the sweet potatoes, encased in packed mud, were cooking in a smartly built natural oven.

Raquel was amazed as she watched the girl. Some of the history and stories she had heard about Mayans and their culture buzzed through her mind. Her thoughts of grandeur and power were such a contradiction to the young woman who stooped before her.

The filthy, tattered shift she wore barely covered her small breasts—the armholes of the garment were cut so large. She would have been a pitiful sight if it had not been for her eyes, which were extremely alert and knowing. She watched Raquel and Nate with the same intensity as Raquel watched her.

Nate, on the other hand, proved to be more restless than they. Constantly he rose and entered the forest, each time in a different direction. He always returned to the overhang within moments, his face a taut mask. On his third return the Mayan girl went into a string of words ending with "Nim Li Punti," patting her breasts, then pointing into the forest.

"So that's it. She hitchhiked a ride with us because we were headed in the direction of the Mayan ruin, Nim Li Punti."

After hearing Nate say it, the girl repeated the phrase.

"Did she come from there? And if so, how did she end up at the inn?" Raquel wondered aloud.

"I doubt it. Some archaeologists began digging out there about ten years ago. There were several reports, but I never heard about people actually living there. There is a Mayan village not far from it, but I would think someone as young as she would have learned either English or Spanish as a second language if she lived there. No," he eyed the young girl speculatively, "I think she's from one of the more isolated Kekchi settlements. Of all the Mayans, they are the ones who have attempted to remain less dependent on other cultures, keeping to themselves."

The young girl's almond-shaped eyes lit up as Nate mentioned "Kekchi," then quickly dimmed with some unknown understanding.

It didn't take long for the sweet potatoes to bake. Raquel felt as if she were cracking an egg as she burst open the hot-baked mud surrounding her meal. Piping-hot steam rose off the tender root. She had to remind herself to be careful as she plunged into the soft orange insides, burning her fingers in her hunger.

Once their meal was completed, the girl covered the still-smoldering fire with lumps of mud before the group continued on. Refreshed, Raquel followed the young girl and Nate, and the impact of how her life had changed over the last few days pressed upon her.

This was a far cry from working in the Miami clinic and her quiet nights alone reading, listening to music, or taking in an occasional television program. She wondered how her mother was faring. She knew she would be worried—hardly a day would go by without them talking, at least by phone. She hoped Lucy had concluded she'd taken that long-awaited vacation she'd mentioned for the hundredth time during their last visit.

Raquel knew her mother still felt guilty because of her breakup with Clinton. Sometimes, when she wasn't quite herself, she would babble about it. Many times Rachel had wished she hadn't broken down and told her why she thought they parted. Now, over six weeks later, walking through a Belizean jungle, with a Mayan prostitute and a handsome kidnapper, she knew the truth. Clinton simply hadn't loved her enough to chance it. That was all.

Rachel's bundle of blankets began to unravel, causing her to lag behind. Muttering to himself, Nate approached her, offering to take the awkward package, only to be stopped by the Mayan girl.

Astutely she began to look around. After measuring several vines, she chose one she felt was right for the task and motioned for Nate to cut it. In no time at all she had rolled the blankets into a neat bundle and strapped them to her back. She turned and smiled her not-so-attractive smile in Raquel's direction before continuing to lead them through the woods.

The sun was beginning to lower in the sky when they reached a roughly constructed highway that crossed a smaller road. As they were stepping out of the thicket the Mayan girl's frame abruptly stiffened, and she held her lean arm out to prevent them from passing in front of her.

Instinctively Nate and Raquel followed her actions as she knelt behind a lush plant.

"What's going on?" Raquel queried, her heart pounding.

"I don't know, but I guess we'll find out in a few minutes," was Nate's composed response.

It was less than that when three Mayan men, shirtless and dressed in calf-length pants and sandals, passed on the opposite side of the highway, then entered the forest. The girl stooped lower as their voices floated toward them. Raquel caught a hint of humiliation and remorse in her eyes as she glanced in their direction.

"This must be the Southern Highway," Nate whispered. "And if so, Nim Li Punti is not far away. Those men are from one of the Mayan villages, and from her reaction I would say it's the one she comes from. I can't imagine why she would hide after doing all the things she's done to get here."

The girl's sad eyes roamed over the stained, torn shift she wore, and Raquel understood exactly why the girl had reacted the way she did.

"Did you say there may be a couple of Mayan villages in the area?"

"Yes," Nate answered, curious at the intense sound in Raquel's voice.

"Are there any stores in them or nearby that would sell clothes or material?"

"Why?" He eyed her suspiciously.

"Can't you see the girl's embarrassed to return to her people looking like this? God, sometimes you men don't know anything, and are blind as bats on top of that!"

"You trying to tell me that this—*woman* is ashamed?" A hint of mockery lay beneath his words.

"And what if she is? Are you trying to say she shouldn't be? We don't know how this girl fell into that situation back there. And neither one of us is in a position to judge her. She just wants to go home."

"Are you speaking for yourself or the Mayan, *pataki?*" His voice was soft, knowing.

For a moment dark, fanlike lashes concealed her feelings, but when she looked into his face again, determination edged her soft features.

"What difference does it make? Would you be willing to forget about what you're doing and see me back safely to the States?"

Nate never answered but his steady gaze remained on her face.

Taking his silence as a negative, Raquel continued, "Well, then, why did you ask? Without this girl we might not have made it this far. At least we can go and find her something decent to wear."

The Mayan girl's discerning gaze locked on the two people who knelt beside her.

"Decency is not my forte." His voice was low and silky. "And how do I know this is not a ploy to help you escape?" he asked warily, his lips close to her ear.

Raquel forced a chuckle. It was a defense against the electricity his close contact roused in her. Suddenly she stood and switched her round hips back and forth in front of his face sassily.

"And just where would I go, Mr. Bowman? I guess I'll just take a stroll down that big old highway into the city, and catch me a plane back to Miami."

His strong fingers caught hold of the soft flesh of her upper thighs, eliciting a quick intake of breath from her.

"Don't taunt me, *pataki*. I am immoral enough to take what you offered me, right here in front of the girl." His unyielding gaze assured her this was no idle threat.

Raquel caught his large wrist within her hands, challenging him with narrowed eyes. "And what you would get would be about as fulfilling as that hole she dug in the ground a few hours ago!"

"Do you think so? There are many ways to light a fire. Some are easier to start than others if the wood or charcoal is primed just right." He let his fingers drag enticingly along her inner thigh before withdrawing his hands.

She shivered involuntarily. Their battle of wills was over, at least for the moment.

Slowly he stood beside her, taking out his map.

"Well, now, at least I know where we are," he looked around them. "Right over there is Big Falls, the only warm springs known here in Belize. You two can stay there and maybe bathe while I go to the village." He looked at Raquel pointedly. "Now, I'm telling you this for your own good. You need to find a place where you're out of sight, because you'll be trespassing on somebody else's property. Of course, you might come up with the bright idea that they might help you, which indeed they might. But keep in mind, the fellow you seek help from could be as bad or worse than Jay," he warned, leaving her to make her own decision.

At first the Mayan girl tried to follow him, but Raquel held her back, speaking slowly and signing that he would be back with clothes or material. The Mayan girl's eyes shone brightly, not quite understanding what Raquel was trying to say, but obeying her command anyway.

Moments later the two women headed in the direction Nate had indicated. It didn't take long before they arrived at the bubbling mineral waters. Just the thought of submerging her exhausted body in the vibrating liquid began to relax her, but the warning Nate had given surfaced in her mind. Part of her wanted to take the chance and see if the people who owned Big Falls would help her. But what if they *were* like Jay and his brother Al? Or what if Jay was actually there?

A streak of terror ran through her, an aftershock from her encounter with the two gruesome Belizeans. No. She was safe with Nate, as safe as she could be, under the circumstances.

She looked around cautiously, then pulled the Mayan girl into the safety of several bushes beside her. As Nate suggested, the women waited until the sun had been completely replaced by the bright half moon before they entered the soothing waters.

Activity in the Mayan village of San Pedro was grinding to a halt when Nate entered its midst. It was nothing like the dusty clapboard settlement in which they'd slept the previous night. No, compared to that, it seemed like a unique metropolis.

The houses, though a few were constructed from clapboard, were much more creative in design. Well-built thatched-roof structures constituted the most popular design. Most had strong stilts, with wooden stairways leading up to a platform which allowed one to gain entrance. Some had wooden verandas surrounding the one-story edifices; others were less endowed.

Not many people were on the narrow roads as evening began to turn to night, and Nate knew if he were to have any luck at all in locating a merchant who would be willing to sell to him at this late hour, he would need to hurry.

Nate saw a construction of thatched-roofed stalls as he entered what appeared to be a main road. A Mayan man busied himself inside one of the areas, putting away items he obviously had not been able to sell. Two Mayan women dressed in long wraparound colorful skirts and Latin-style blouses were leaving his store carrying baskets filled with goods. Shyly, they looked at Nate as he passed by.

The salesman stopped his removal of several items and eyed him with interest.

"Yoo need help?" The merchant's English was oddly accented.

"Yes, I do," Nate answered. "Do you have any women's clothing?"

"Yees." A spark of interest shone in the man's deeply creased eyes. "Ovar theere." He pointed out several folded squares of colorful material stacked neatly on a handmade bench, then crossed to the objects to display them for his unusual customer.

"They arr the skeerts our women wear. Eer arr the blooses." He held up several tops adorned with embroidered yokes. "The woman yoo arr buying theez for, she deed not want to come?"

"No." Nate turned hard eyes upon the little merchant.

"I oonderstand. Eet eez late. Maybe she deed not want to come out at sooch a late hour," he tried to appease the sullen man. "Arr yoo stay here at the lodge?"

"No."

"Oh." Curiosity continued to burn in his deep-set eyes. "Then where . . . ?"

"We're not staying in the village."

"No? But there eez not many place nearby to stay. Punta Gorda eez near, but eet eez too far to travel een one night by foot, and yoo do not have a carr." He looked around a second time to make sure.

A wary tone crept into the nosey merchant's voice. "There eez two other village. The Forbidden Village eez one of them. But they would not welcome your keend there. Sometime toureests do not understand thees." He tried to see if his words had sparked a response in the stand-offish man, but seeing none, he continued, "No doubt, they arr my brothers and sisters, but they arr the Kekchi, who have held to the ancient ways more than eeny of us. Theirs is a strong hate of change. Ponti knows how mooch," he pointed to a young Mayan crossing the road in their direction.

"Tell him, tell him, Ponti, he would not be welcomed een the Forbidden Village, would he?"

A strange mix of emotions crossed the young man's face as he looked at Nate.

"You're planning to go to *Balam?*"

The man's impeccable English caught Nate off guard. He eyed him suspiciously before answering.

"No, not necessarily."

The merchant seemed to perk up as he waited for Ponti to speak again, and Nate noticed how the younger man watched the merchant warily. Finally, the man Ponti decided to continue on his way.

Nate was on the verge of telling the curious merchant to mind his own business, for he quickly realized it might be to his benefit to listen to what the young Kekchi had to say. With purposeful strides he caught up with Ponti.

The young man stopped, still eyeing the disappointed merchant several yards away.

"Forgive me. Usually I'm not this rude, but the merchant loves to spread everybody's business across the village. Right now I have enough troubles already."

"So, is what he says true?" Nate questioned. "Is staying away from Balam a wise thing to do?"

"I can assure you it would be. I was born there," he paused.

There were lines of frustration marring his young features. Nate waited patiently for him to continue, and when he did it was as if he were finally relieving himself of a burden.

"I did not want to spend my entire life living the way my people have chosen to live. So I ran away, then worked and went to school in Belize City for a long time. Finally I acquired the papers I needed to go to the United States for college," he kicked at a stone near his foot. "But my school aid was soon cut, and I had to return to Belize. I had missed my family over the years, so I decided to come back to Balam. They would not even let me in," he commented with exasperation. "I was told to wait here for word when I would be allowed to reenter the village. That was over a week ago. No word has come, yet. So as you can tell, if they are hesitant to let me come to the village, strangers would not be welcome at all."

"Interesting." Hooded lids descended over Nate's dark gaze, "Thanks for the information." Nate and Ponti parted ways.

Bent on completing his task with as little conversation on his part as possible, Nate placed several Belizean dollars in the merchant's hands before he picked up two skirts and two blouses. "I think that should do it."

Then without another word he nodded his goodbye, and headed down the moonlit road.

Through trial and error the two women found a smaller offshoot of the heated springs, nestled in the middle of a clump of trees and bushes. Stealthily they removed their clothes and entered the luxurious waters.

Raquel lowered her eyelids as the heated currents surrounded her. The sensations were so satisfying she succumbed to their bewitching powers, completely becoming oblivious to her surroundings. Like the swaying watch of a hypnotist, the moon hobbed back and forth in the heavens to the rhythm of the currents that propelled her body. With time, the sounds of the Mayan girl splashing along beside her became one with her state of relaxation.

Raquel had no idea how much time had passed when two hands gently embraced her waist. Startled, she opened her eyes to find Nate inches away from her. A groggy look of surprise crossed her beautiful features as he easily moved her into a pocket of intensely bubbling water, in a private nook along the densely forested shore.

"What—what are you doing," she stammered, blinking away the drops of water that had attached themselves to her long, curly lashes. Strangely she realized there was no fear as he touched her, only a sense of unsolicited excitement.

"Hush *pataki* and continue to relax. I just thought you would find this portion of the water . . . what should I say . . . more stimulating."

The pocket of currents in which he had maneuvered her ran and bubbled more rapidly than the others. The vibrations of the silky, warm water massaging her body felt like knowing, insistent hands. She tried to fight the relaxing sensations the flow encouraged, but her tired body betrayed her as it gave in to the wet caresses, enticing her mind to relax and enjoy the pleasurable feelings.

Nate's muscular thigh rubbed against a smooth boulder submerged under the vibrating waters. It was just what he had been searching for as he forced Raquel's nude frame gently against it. He could tell she was giving in to the gripping motion of the water as she let herself relax upon the stone. Her elbows easily supported her on its moss-covered surface, and her legs hung limply down the rock's smooth edges.

A thick feathering of dark lashes lay upon her high cheekbones as she totally gave into the wonderful sensations. Nate watched as her well-formed chin tilted upward toward the splendid star filled sky, and her inky hair formed countless curly locks, the lower strands floating and bobbing within the animated currents.

Each forward movement of the water threatened to encase the top of her slender shoulders, yet a backwards motion, just as natural, temporarily revealed a wider glimpse of her rich velvety brown frame.

Raquel was aware of her nudeness, as well as his. She told herself there was nothing she could do under the circumstances. But a voice deep inside insisted she lied. She could leave Nate here in the water and seek the safety of the shore, reconfirming her stance of wanting to have nothing to do with him. Then whenever she did give in to him, if she did, it would be him forcing her hand.

Yet, she felt helpless as the mesmerizing sway of the bubbling waters held her captive. She was tired. Tired of fighting the inevitable. If he was to take her, let him do it now in her state of lethargy. Her eyes remained closed as she anticipated his move.

Silently she waited with masses of soft, stimulating bubbles forming around her. A forceful current had formed between her legs, massaging her inner thighs. Almost unconsciously she allowed the silky flow access to the most sensitive part of her. A natural expression of mild surprise and pleasure crossed her beautiful features.

Part of her wanted to move, to extract itself from the vulnerable, yet needy feelings that rose within her. But the sexual desires that were awakening inside her were so strong, she could not pull herself away.

The soft, but lapping current worked its way deeper within her, and she found herself welcoming it with a further spreading of her slender thighs. The pleasurable sensations began to build in intensity and Raquel wantonly gave in to her feelings, forgetting about the man who stood within the waters not far away, watching every change of expression that crossed her sensuous features.

They were expressions he wanted to arouse in her, and he longed to be where the pulsating water churned, evoking the looks of delight nearly bordering pain, that arose consistently as her body thrilled to nature's caress.

Raquel could not believe the height of excitement the gushing waters were propelling her toward. She lay there a prisoner of her own desires, her body soaking up each silky stroke.

Suddenly the current stopped. Raquel's shocked, lust filled gaze opened to find Nate standing between her legs. His eyes were full of the knowledge of her readiness, and the desire that encased his features told her, he too, was near the point of no return. She rose up further upon her elbows to see if his shaft would substantiate her belief, and she saw the shadow of it beneath the somewhat calm waters was immense.

Abruptly, an involuntary moan escaped her lips as she thought of it entering her.

Their smoldering gazes met, then held, and Raquel wanted to scream out her impatience, but her pride wouldn't allow it.

Nate was very much aware of the flicker of emotions passing over her moonlit features. His body trembled as he restrained the most natural thing in the world to do, while he watched Raquel's body arch in readiness. Yet, he knew it was her eyes that told the true story. She wanted him, yes. But her desire for him, even now, could not mask an even stronger resentment.

Somehow she knew the moment when he had changed his mind, and she reluctantly opened her eyes again. It was as if a light had been turned off behind his dark penetrating gaze, and the fire between them had turned cold.

Confusion flickered over Raquel's features as she watched him, standing like a statue with a half-moon upon his shoulder. A soft glow of light ran between the tiny waves of hair upon his head as the moon's light played up his chiseled cheekbones, creating interesting shadows upon his handsome features. He was so alluring as he stood there. So strong. So masculine. So virile.

She saw his lips move, and somehow her mind, through the fog of desire, was able to comprehend the simple words he said.

"I will wait, *pataki*, until you unconditionally want me. I don't want a small part of you. I've got to have it all."

Then he turned his massive back toward her, and headed toward the shore.

Suddenly the breeze that blew upon her face was cold, and she found her nakedness embarrassing. Never before had she felt so rejected and empty. Hesitantly she looked toward the shore, and saw the Mayan girl, wet, in her tattered shift, kneeling on her haunches watching Nate's advance. The expression on her face glowed with womanly approval as he shamelessly stepped out of the water and retrieved his pants. Then the girl's dark eyes looked uncertainly at Raquel, for it was clear to her, this man was most certainly a prize.

It took all the nerve Raquel had to rise up off that stone and walk towards the shore. She tried to walk confidently with her head held high, but she found it was of little consequence whatever manner she chose.

Nate never looked in her direction as she made her way towards camp, and for some reason she felt even more humiliated because of it. Quickly, she donned the shift and combed out her wet tresses with trembling fingers.

Without another word, Nate made himself a spot to bed down for the night. The two women followed suit, Raquel sharing one of the old blankets with the Mayan girl. He never mentioned his trip to the village, nor could Raquel find the courage to question him about it. She was so confused. A kidnapper who was caring enough to find clothes for the hapless Mayan girl, and desired her, yet wanted her mind to want him as well as her body.

As she lay there beneath the beautiful Belizean sky, she became angry with the strange man who lay only several feet away. Angry because she did not understand him. But also she was angry at herself for beginning to have a certain amount of grudging respect for him.

There were other feelings inside that were beginning to stir, but she dared not explore them. Somehow she knew if ever released, they would change her neatly packaged system of the rights and wrongs in human relationships. A system that had formed her foundation ever since she began studying psychology; its logic and borders safe, and not the least bit frightening.

Raquel balled up in a fetal position upon the thickly covered ground; the musty smell of the blanket wrapped tightly about her, not because she was cold, but because it provided a sense of security that she longed for.

Yes, no doubt she was afraid. She was afraid if she looked deep enough inside herself, she would find out how much she wanted Nate not only because he could protect her, but because his virility aroused her in a way that she had never known before.

Behind her tightly shut eyes, unwillingly, Raquel kept picturing his hard, muscular, nude body poised to enter her, and a searing spark began to throb between her legs.

She did not doubt he knew a lot about women and how to please them. He had purposefully led her to those waters where he knew she'd find pleasure, and she knew, he knew, she could have been his. But obviously, to Nate there were things more important in life. She had to admit it surprised her to know, just to have a woman sexually wasn't enough. He needed her completely in his corner, trusting him under the most untrustworthy circumstances.

Yes, Raquel was beginning to find out Nate lived by a strange code of ethics, possibly different from any she'd ever encountered before.

Like a fish out of water Raquel flipped abruptly onto her opposite side where her eyes rested upon his outstretched body, still and lifeless, well on his way to slumber. It was his prostrate figure that entered sleep with her, but it was a totally virile, unabandoned Nate, who possessed her dreams.

CHAPTER 7

The Mayan girl's black eyes shone brightly as she emerged from behind the cover of bushes, wearing the colorful wrap skirt and white embroidered blouse Nate had presented to her earlier that morning. With her face clean and her hair brushed through with the aid of a bristly, but strong plant, an unusual kind of beauty had been awakened in the girl. There was a kind of regalness about her. Raquel knew, this was the real person behind the filth and tattered rags. The dignified tilt of her shiny black head, and a knowing calm behind her dark eyes reflected that. Nevertheless Raquel couldn't help but marvel at how remarkable the transformation had been.

Nate too, was pleased by the girl's metamorphosis, a slight nod of his head indicated his approval which was answered by a quick, beguiling, black-toothed smile. A resourceful twinkle in her eye, accompanied it, showing her memory of Nate's physical assets was still fresh in her mind.

A tiny tightening in Raquel's chest at their exchange surprised her. Why would she be jealous if Nate found the Mayan girl attractive?

Quickly she averted her gaze, just in case her heightened feelings could be read upon her face. For some reason, just the thought of Nate turning to the Mayan girl to find pleasure, deeply disturbed her.

Judging the girl's existence at the inn, she had to be profoundly aware of the things that really pleased a man. Could it be she was afraid once Nate had the Mayan girl he would no longer find her desirable?

As if by intuition, the girl approached Raquel with the second set of clothing, offering to show her the proper way to wear the multicolored wraparound skirt. Her black eyes searched deeply into Raquel's sable ones. It was an offer of friendship and trust.

After checking a shirt that he'd laid across a bush to dry, Nate swaggered down toward the opposite end of the concealed springs.

He watched the silent exchange between the two women, and he wished he'd been able to see the message the woman called Jackie had relayed in her eyes. Had the Mayan instinctively picked up a message of jealousy or disdain before she offered her visual bond of friendship? He didn't know for sure. But one thing he did know, the few days he had spent with this woman, her ways and actions contradicted the things he thought he knew about her. There was an inner strength and resolve he had not expected from a woman of her caliber.

Nate knew he was a good judge of character, and a damn good judge of women. Why hadn't she crawled up beside him last night to quench her own desire? It had been so apparent in her face, even her body poised and ready to receive him.

Back in the States he thought it was obvious she had been with many men, showing little concern about when or where. A woman as loose as that had needs and desires of her own that would eventually have to be fulfilled.

At first he'd thought the anger and frustration resulting from being kidnapped was the reason she had not given in to her promiscuous sexual nature. So he'd responded accordingly, playing the little game that many women liked to play. And hell, he didn't blame any woman for not wanting the likes of Jay or Al. But to be brought to the brink of pleasure that she'd reached last night, and not reach out to fulfill it . . . there had to be other reasons. This woman was either totally different from what he had expected, or she was a damn good con artist. His instincts told him it was not the latter, and that bothered him.

Yet, he couldn't be concerned with that right now. They had to reach Dangriga. Once there, the whole thing would come to an end, and maybe by then he would have the answers he needed. Until that time came, he would protect her any way he could.

It took only moments for Raquel to don the simple Mayan outfit. The knotting of the tangerine, red and mustard-colored wraparound skirt, riding low on her curvaceous hip, had been accomplished easily enough. Afterwards the Mayan girl helped her comb out her tangled locks, which had dried into a voluminous head of wild, somewhat cottony, black curls.

Speaking in her own language, the girl gesticulated and exclaimed over the texture of Raquel's thick mane, then demonstrated how it would be a magnet for bugs and other bits of nature if it remained loose.

Resourcefully the young girl produced a flowered vine. Starting at the crown of Raquel's head, she ornately, but delicately, twisted the strong plant through the locks until she came to the base of her neck, where the remainder of Raquel's hair was gathered in a large ball surrounded by several vermilion blossoms. The heady aroma of the flowers was heavenly, and Raquel closed her eyes as she sampled the scent.

As she opened them, she could see the look of admiration and approval on the Mayan's face, but unlike her she did not seek a look of approval from Nate.

Beneath profuse lashes, she watched him stride slowly back in their direction, then stop directly in front of her giving her a thorough and possessive going over.

"It looks good. Now you should really blend in, should the need ever arise."

For a moment his words of approval seem to lighten the emotional turmoil Raquel was feeling, but that moment of respite was quickly doused when she understood he was only concerned about her not being discovered, therefore keeping himself out of jeopardy.

Contempt filled her dark gaze before she turned away from him.

"Well, I guess this means we are ready, ladies," he signalled for the young girl to proceed before them. "Lead the way."

They reached the outskirts of the Mayan girl's village in a short time. Raquel hadn't realized how close Nim Li Punti had actually been the night before, but as they circumvented the large Mayan ruin, she found herself gazing with astonishment at the sheer size of it.

There were numerous, intricately carved stelae towering eerily, their etched stone faces and figures telling a tale of long-gone Mayan triumph and tragedy. The smell was a strange mixture of stagnant air, weathered rock and plant life.

From what she could see, the majority of the ruin had not been reclaimed from the possessive forest whose vine-draped trees and shrouded bushes covered several buildings, creating large, uniquely shaped, foliage-molded mountains. Only a small section had been partially cleared. Raquel assumed this had been done by the archaeologist Nate mentioned the day before. It was around this section that they used the most care.

She understood Nate's cautious reaction, but not the one exhibited by the Mayan girl. There was a feel of fear and reverence about her as she skirted it. Her slightly slanted eyes were full of curiosity as she passed. She stole only covert glances whenever she dared to look at the ruins.

Raquel was surprised to see the gathering of thatch-roofed buildings hidden within the forest not far from Nim Li Punti. For some reason she had pictured the village sitting neatly on a plot of land totally cleared of foliage. This village, like Nim Li Punti, had an untamed feeling about it, as if it and nature were one.

The Mayan stopped several yards away from the unnaturally quiet gathering of thatched, single-room buildings. There was no speech or laughter to be heard, a strange feature for a well-kept village where people obviously lived.

Silently they advanced closer to the nearest cluster of edifices until an extremely large congregation of the occupants came into view.

A meeting of the entire village had been called. They had gathered upon the grass and moss, in what Raquel now recognized as the center of what appeared to be separate living communes.

A lone man was approaching the group. As he came closer Nate recognized him. It was Ponti, the man he had been introduced to the night before in the Kekchi village. His keen eyes narrowed as he surveyed the scene. Could the Mayan girl be from the Forbidden Village?

All eyes were turned in Ponti's direction as he crossed perpendicular to Nate, Raquel and the girl. Several of the men rose from their leadership seats upon the ground. They were followed by countless others, women as well as youngsters.

The women were dressed in the same manner as Raquel and the Mayan girl who stood silently beside her. The majority of the men were shirtless, wearing loose-fitting, white, calf-length cotton pants.

The entire scenario reminded Raquel of an old Western, the scene: A Mexican village, except the adobe buildings and dusty roads had been replaced by thatched buildings and an immense rain forest. The people bore a resemblance to Mexicans, albeit their straight black hair was of a finer texture.

Nate guessed Ponti had received the message he'd been waiting for: he'd gotten permission to see his family.

The three of them watched as he approached the crowd several yards away, and a burst of what the two observers assumed were shouts of welcome were heard. Suddenly, to Raquel and Nate's shock and amazement, Ponti was swallowed up in the swell of exuberant, trotting Mayans chanting and wailing, loudly. But their forward movement did not stop as they engulfed him, instead it increased in velocity pushing forward in their direction, only to halt when they enveloped the Mayan girl.

Inevitably, all four of them were caught up in the triumphant frenzy, but it was the Mayan girl who became surrounded by a small inner ring of elderly women, assessingly touching her face, skin and hair.

As the space between them widened, the young girl's eyes once again sought out Raquel's. The look within them alarmed something deep inside her. It was a look of resolve laced with fear.

In the midst of the excited Mayans, Raquel found herself beside the stranger who'd first attempted to approach the group. He looked out of place with his American-style haircut, jeans and T-shirt.

"Well Ponti we meet again," Nate's rich voice boomed above the throng's noise. "Strangely enough, it seems like we've been given quite a joyous welcome."

Raquel's eyebrows lifted with surprise to hear Nate address the man by name.

"Yes, in some ways this is a happy occasion, at least many of the villagers feel that way. I don't know about Mircea, the girl who returned with you. I think she probably feels quite differently."

"Mircea . . ." Raquel reflected upon her friend's name. "Why wouldn't she be happy to return to her own village?"

Ponti looked at the petite woman edged so closely against him because of the crushing crowd. He could see true concern for the girl's welfare written all over her attractive features. For a moment he hesitated, remembering the warnings of his parents and ancestors, "Never allow an outsider even a glimpse into our sacred rituals." But the beseeching look on this beautiful woman's face assured him, hers was not an exploiting concern, but a human one.

"She ran away to escape the fate that everyone here believes she was born to. A fate of blood and sacrifice."

Ponti realized he could not tolerate the look of shock and horror that spread across the woman's features as his words sank in. It was because of his feelings opposing these kinds of rites that he left his family long ago. Yet the rites were tradition—they would always support the elders, who never strayed from the laws of the tablets.

Rumors of these bloodletting sacrificial rites ran rampant amongst the nearby villagers. It was because of them that Balam had been given the name "Forbidden Village." Their Mayan brothers and sisters in nearby settlements had long ago let go of these ancient rituals.

"Sacrifice" the hushed word rolled numbly from Raquel's lips.

Nate remained quiet as he listened to the exchange, and his dark eyes surveyed the raucous crowd of Balamians. No doubt he felt for the Mayan girl's plight, but uppermost in his mind was what this could mean for himself, and Jackie Dawson.

As the Mayans' fervor heightened, they found themselves being carried along inside a huge crowd of Balamians as they proceeded back to the center of the village. The shrill note of handmade flutes shrieked loudly, and the older villagers began to stomp their naked feet upon the grassy plaza. Even the tiniest ones followed suit, their ignorance of purpose apparent in their darting eyes and fun-filled faces.

Raquel could see Mircea standing a slight distance in front of her on top of what must have been a stone slab, her eyes focused straight ahead of her, bizarrely glazed. Several feet away, a withered man with a leathery sack hanging heavily about his neck, commenced a ritualistic strut through the inner circle of women surrounding the tiny platform. He was minute in stature and weight, yet despite his deeply wrinkled face, his hair shone as darkly as a jaguar's black coat.

Once having danced his way to the altar, he removed the well-worn pouch from his neck, dug nimbly inside with knurled fingers, then finally extracted a curious shiny, black object.

As Raquel watched with intense curiosity, she saw Mircea accept a shallow pottery bowl filled with what appeared to be a string of narrow white rope. She held it with steady fingers just below her face, then she extended her tongue to its fullest length above it.

"What are they about to do?" Raquel asked as the aged man approached the girl. Nate responded by pulling her back against him, placing his strong hands protectively about her upper arms.

As quick as a wink the shaman took what looked like a spike of black glass, and forced it through the thickness of Mircea's tongue. There was no reaction of pain from her friend as he did so. To Raquel's abhorrence, this was followed by a threading of the white, bark cloth from the bowl through the open wound, and as the red of Mircea's blood crept down the thin stretch of paper, turning its paleness to crimson, the pitch of elation amongst the villagers was almost unbearable.

Stunned, Raquel turned her horror-stricken face into the safety of Nate's broad chest as her insides began to churn.

The excited group found joy in the Mayan girl's eyes glassing over from the pain. For it was the pain, the Balamians believed, that would allow her to communicate with the gods. This was her heritage. This was Mircea's legacy.

Time seemed to stand still for Raquel as she clutched Nate's shirt and tried to make sense of the willful suffering she'd just witnessed, but her clouded mind could not make sense of what she'd just seen. *Mircea, dear Mircea,* she thought.

After a sufficient amount of her blood had been shed, the young girl's limp body was hustled off to one of the living units by a tiny group of Mayans whom Raquel assumed to be her family. As she disappeared inside the wooden door of the building, the jubilant sounds ceased, only to be replaced by a deadly silence as a sea of dark eyes rested on the intruders.

Shocked beyond belief, Raquel feared they would be chosen next for this grotesque show of pain.

It was Ponti's voice that broke the unnatural stillness. His tone was strong, yet it held a note of definite respect as he directed his words toward three of the Mayan men. Two of them waited as the shortest of the group responded. His words were rapid, his stance, stoic, yet his eyes held a tenderness no one could ignore. There was no doubt this man was Ponti's father.

Slowly the young man crossed the space between them, and was received by a tight embrace with arms so deeply bronzed they reminded Raquel of copper. This open display of love and tenderness contrasted peculiarly with the ritual that had just passed moments before. Raquel's diminutive frame trembled as she continued to lean against Nate for support.

Verbal exchanges continued amongst the group, yet Nate's perceptive ears and eyes could tell when the conversation no longer centered on Ponti, but on himself and the woman he held tightly before him.

Strong head and hand gestures passed between the elders, and Raquel could tell something was afoot as the trio delivered cold calculating looks in their direction.

Barely moving her lips, she spoke so only Nate could hear.

"What do you think they plan to do with us?"

"It does not matter, *pataki*. I have plans of my own, and they do not include the Mayans."

Raquel gained strength from the conviction of his words, and even now in the height of her fear, she was painfully aware of his physical strength and virility. It was a heady feeling to know he would protect her no matter what, a potent aphrodisiac, for a moment she regretted not making love to him the night before. Looking at the intense faces surrounding them now, there was a chance neither one of them would ever make love again.

Raquel watched as Ponti leaned over and spoke into his father's ear. Contemplatively the older man nodded his head in agreement, his dark, perceptive eyes resting on their faces. Then he silenced Ponti with a final movement of his hand, and began to speak to his peers. At first they answered with silence, then reluctantly they agreed with his decision.

It was a stone-faced Ponti who approached the two outsiders.

"There's no easy way to tell you this," he solemnly informed them. "It's unfortunate that you were allowed to witness Mircea's initial bloodletting. If it wasn't for that, I'm pretty sure I could have convinced my father to talk the others into letting you go. So for right now, all I could do was buy you a little more time. You are to be the . . . guests of my extended family until the main ritual takes place tonight, during which you will be presented as part of the ceremony, the sacrifice," his dark eyes looked heavy with the burden of his words. "If I hadn't spoken up for you, it would have been over quickly, on the same small altar that Mircea's bloodletting took place."

One of the men loudly addressed Ponti, irritation apparent in his voice. In submission he nodded toward the Mayan and began to move in his direction. He spoke to Raquel and Nate over his shoulder. "It is the best that I can do," his eyes pleaded for understanding. "Now, you need to follow me."

On legs that felt like stilts Raquel walked behind Ponti. Nate's head towered above the crowd as they passed through it. By nature, the Mayans were a short people, and from the looks on many of their faces they found Nate's huge stature to be intimidating.

The two of them followed Ponti into a cluster of buildings not far from the one Mircea had entered. It was a single-room structure of medium size. A door on the opposite wall had been left ajar, allowing a view into a quadrangular-shaped patio. It was closed in by several other buildings, just like the one in which they stood.

Some of Ponti's extended family had entered behind them, their voices blending together as they offered their opinions, but it was the females who ended up with the last say, directing Ponti to take Nate into another building on the opposite side of the patio, while Raquel remained behind.

She proved to be quite a curiosity for the Balamians, especially for the children, but after a few sharp words from an elderly female, they ignored her.

She leaned back against the wooden walls of the room and watched the family as they went on with their daily chores and made special preparations for the night to come.

Wood was brought in and piled in the middle of the room. It was stacked beside the place where the cooking was always done. Three large blackened stones were the base of the fire; deep grooves had been dug in the ground to make them a permanent fixture. Other articles, like herbs, vegetables, cooking and cleaning utensils were hung about, and Raquel got the feeling this room served only as the kitchen and eating area.

She could see other Balamians traversing back and forth between the buildings. There was a unity displayed in their actions that bespoke of more than family—but rather gave a sense of an interdependent existence. Raquel admired this sense of camaraderie.

Raquel thought about the people and the neighborhood in which she worked back in the States. She knew if this kind of thinking could be nurtured and carried out back there, many of them would not feel so alone when they fought the daily battle of survival. She determined, when she returned, she would initiate an extended-family program as part of her counseling.

A burning sensation commenced behind her dark eyes as water welled up inside, causing them to glisten. The clinic was no longer open where she could implement such a program, and right now, her chances were very slim of returning home at all.

She tried to feel anger towards Nate for putting her in such a predicament, but now it all seemed like such a waste of energy. Whatever had driven him to be a part of the kidnapping ring that abducted her, had to have meaning in his life, for she knew now, he was not a criminal at heart, but a man of strong convictions.

The fire burned brightly, its smoke adding to the already soot-covered rafters above. Soon the smell of chili, sweet potatoes and tortillas wafted throughout, and Raquel's hunger mounted. Throughout the afternoon, groups of family members came in and partook of the delicious fare, but none was offered to Raquel.

Finally Ponti returned, his bronze features clouded with thoughts of the night to come. In a casual manner he walked near Raquel, secretly dropping a folded piece of beaten bark in her lap. With nervous fingers the girl clasped the paper, tucking it into the folds of the wraparound skirt. Her heart drummed inside her chest as she tried to imagine what had been written, and how she could read it without being discovered. For Raquel knew, even though it seemed no one watched her, the oldest female had taken it upon herself to keep a close eye on her.

After a few minutes of deciding what to do, she began to nod her head like a person fighting sleep. Several times she went through the jerky motions until she finally decided to stretch out on the dirt floor, eventually turning her back to the room as she deceitfully found a more comfortable position. It was there on her side, that she was able to read the note addressed to *Pataki*.

Make move at right time. Get close together.
Watch me. Don't be afraid.

Once again Raquel's heart thumped wildly. How could they ever escape from all of these Balamians? Already she could feel her adrenaline building, readying for fight or flight. If need be, it would be both, but she had no intention of dying here.

She thought of the fire that must have burned deep in Nate's eyes as he penned the scratchy note upon the rough paper. She could tell he was a man of deep passions and one day, she determined, she'd find out just how deep.

Lying on her side for as long as she could without slapping the troublesome fleas that nipped and bit at her ankles and arms, Raquel called upon the inner strength she knew she'd need in order to win. Like an invisible source, it had always been there whenever she needed it, and she knew the supply was infinite as long as she believed it was.

The young woman sat up, adjusting her skirt about her legs and feet, then patted the dust and dirt from her still neatly twisted hair. To the Balamians it looked like an accident when she broke one of the large, now withered, vermilion blossoms from the shriveled vine that encased it. But Ponti knew otherwise, when she sought his eyes with hers, then gazed longingly at the wrinkled petals. The flower would serve as her answer to Nate's message.

Gathering up left-over tidbits of tortilla, Ponti tossed the thick dough in Raquel's direction. Quickly the dogs pounced upon it slobbering, smacking and growling as they jostled for the offering. While retrieving several pieces that had fallen too close to the girl, he picked up the blossom and carried it out quickly in his hand.

The old saying, "funny how time flies when you're having fun" hammered in Raquel's mind as night descended quicker than she'd ever known it to do before. She surmised that whoever coined that line had never been faced with a time when they were scheduled to die. Now the young woman knew, time also flies when death is approaching your door.

An uncanny quiet descended within the complex. Most of the women and children had long gone, leaving several of the men to watch over her. A group of candles had been lit inside, casting powerful shadows upon the walls, making the atmosphere that much more macabre as she thought of the fate the Balamians had planned for them.

Raquel sat ghostly still as she tried not to think about how these people steeped in ancient tradition planned to carry out the sacrifice. After what had happened to Mircea, she knew her imagination probably could not conjure up the likes of what they would do to two outsiders if they had the chance. Her breath started to come in short snatches at the thought of it.

Yet Nate had promised her their plans would fail, and despite all that had passed between them, she trusted his word.

Unknown to Raquel, Nate could see her as she sat drumming up the mental courage and fortitude she'd need to face the Balamians. The room in which he sat was dark. No candle had been left for him, only the moon's light outside provided some illumination in the simple surroundings.

He could tell from her posture that she was afraid, but he could also tell she would do whatever it took to save herself, and that was all he could ask of her. It was his fault that she faced such a horrible end, and it was his responsibility to make sure she never had to endure it. But how could he have known things would get this far out of hand?

It was an understatement to say that Nate was glad the Balamians did not think it necessary he be searched. That was one aspect of their cultural thinking that would work to his and the woman's advantage. As the day wore on he had paid close attention to their ways, and had concluded the Balamians would feel guns and modern weapons were the tools of cowards. Well, if need be he would be marked a coward, but he had no intention of being sacrificed.

As a child he'd heard stories about relatives of the Kekchi Indians who lived isolated in a village amongst the ruins. They were bloody, gruesome tales of pain and visions. That's why he'd known when Mircea extended her tongue what she was offering to do. Had she been a man, the piercing would have taken place through the male organ.

The veins and muscles bulged in his tan arms as he made rock-hard fists when a group of Balamians appeared and motioned for the woman to follow them. The depth of the need to protect her sprung up from deep within. Although it shocked him, he did not question its origin, he only knew he would protect this woman with his life, if the need arose.

Moments later he too was commanded to follow several escorts. Nate complied willingly, anticipating the right moment when they could make their move.

Raquel had expected to exit the building to a waiting crowd of anxious Balamians. Instead a stark, empty village awaited her through which she was quickly directed. Soon she realized she was headed for the ruins of Nim Li Punti. The instinct to flee was rising fast, and she turned to see if Nate was anywhere near her as they led her toward the sacrificial ground. As soon as she turned around to look, a massively built Balamian prodded her forcefully in the back, insisting that she keep her eyes straight ahead.

As they progressed, shouts and shrieks pierced the night. This was accompanied by drums and the jingling and clanging of metal. A fire which the Balamians built in the center of what appeared to be a large plaza, blazed wildly, illuminating the lichen-painted walls of Nim Li Punti.

No one noticed Raquel and her escorts when they arrived. All eyes were riveted upon the mass of swirling, animated bodies not far from the flames. At first Raquel thought they were fighting amongst themselves. Half of the Balamians caught in the quick of action wore brightly colored headgear decorated with red feathers, while the opposers wore bright feathers of yellow. Swords rose and fell methodically between them, while others tussled on the ground, brandishing wicked-looking knives and daggers, as their kindred spirits on the sidelines chanted and keened.

For a second Raquel was disoriented. Her nerves were as tight as a bowstring. Did they also plan to kill their own kind to appease these gods that they favored? But then it became clear to her, she was witnessing a mock battle.

Picturesque stelae loomed around them. Some of them depicted warfare, lovemaking and bloodletting. Others sported strange hieroglyphics Raquel had no way of understanding. The largest one lay like a sleeping giant wearing a huge hat.

Not far away Raquel could see Mircea seated trancelike upon another altar. Hordes of vine-shrouded bushes and trees, sprinkled with bromeliads, orchids and other blossoms provided a magnificent backdrop for the eerie scene.

Mircea now wore a piece of colorful cloth that barely hid her tiny breasts. Her head was crowned with a headdress decorated in both the red and yellow feathers of the mock warriors.

Raquel was pushed in the direction of the platform on which Mircea sat, though she ended up only several feet away, her friend never acknowledged her presence. She was like a shell of herself, her tiny body motionless as it sat before the mass of clangorous Balamians.

Then the old shaman appeared out of the shadow of several tumbled rocks, gingerly carrying a sheathed dagger—the hilt of it, a masterfully carved jaguar. He lay the menacing object upon a special stand not far from Mircea. Like her, the shaman wore a headdress of mixed feathers. Several bowls of the ropelike beaten bark were also placed near the stand.

Raquel looked out into the excited faces of the Balamians, many of them waving spiked objects high above their heads as the momentum of the ritual heightened. Some of their wrists were entwined with strands of the beaten bark, waiting for the moment when they could give of their blood to the gods, their offering for the continuation of life as they knew it.

Raquel's dark, anxious gaze fell upon Nate as he was being brought up the opposite side of the sacrificial altar. His tough visage found her and rested there. A slight snarl raised one corner of his ample lips, assuring her they would not be sacrificed without a fight, even though two strongly built Balamians held both wrists behind his back.

Ponti's tormented features were taut as he watched the scene upon the platform. The sight of Mircea offering herself as a sacrifice tugged at his tender heartstrings. His eyes rested upon her tiny face, then her slender hands. They were so delicate and beautiful, something to be treasured not destroyed. Yet, like the other Balamians, he too held a bloodletting instrument, made from a stingray's spine, within his grip, and the telltale sign of the ceremonial paper was also wrapped about his wrists.

It was not a coincidence the elders allowed him to return the day before the Vision Serpent ritual. His father had warned him, "the only way we will believe that you, Ponti, have truly returned to your people, will be that you too give of yourself during the Vision Serpent rites, so the cycle of life can continue here in Balam."

Ponti was very much interested in life, for at this very moment his highest concern was for not a single life to be lost.

Demonstrating his power, the shaman raised his aged hands, and the crowd as well as the warriors brought their revelry to a climax, but the low steady beat of a drumlike instrument continued its motion. It was time for the ritual to begin, and with squat, animal-like movements the shaman commenced his portion of the ceremony.

It was obvious to Raquel that he was telling a story as he swirled, dipped and swayed, motioning to the various stelae; the light from the huge fire made his shadow a live thing amongst the carvings. He danced until he worked up a steady stream of sweat that careened down the deep groves in his withered face. It was amazing a man of his age was so limber, displaying the stamina of a man much younger than himself.

A recitation of rites followed his performance. They were long and tedious, read from a book that Raquel thought resembled an accordion. She could not tell how old the book was, but it was terribly worn, and fashioned from the beaten bark the Balamians used for so many things.

Although Raquel was aware of the powerful movements of the shaman, the fire and passion that burned in Nate's eyes as he looked at her brought an unexpected twist to the scene. Here she was, on the brink of death, and she could not draw her frightened gaze away from the message deep in his eyes.

He told her with his eyes how much he wanted her, to make her his and his alone. Even at this desperate hour, it was his deepest desire.

Raquel was overwhelmed, and his visual announcement to possess her was fervently met by one of complete surrender. She promised him with her gaze that she would be his if only they could survive.

Moments later, through apprehensive eyes, Raquel watched the sweating shaman approach her, an obsidian spike held calmly along his side. At first she was petrified, but as the elderly man drew closer, Raquel's instinct to fight back gushed forward.

She would not die this way. *No!* She shouted to herself. "No!" she shouted to the shaman. With a strength Raquel never knew she possessed, she freed herself from her two guards, and struck the shaman who was poised for the bloodletting.

Her defensive attack shocked everyone, and Nate took advantage of the moment. Through pure brawn, he tore away from the men beside him. He executed a deadly blow to one of their windpipes with a steely elbow, then struck the other in the groin with a forceful knee. Both men clutched their bodies in pain, falling to the ground. In a matter of seconds Nate was at Raquel's side, wielding the 9mm pistol, hidden in his pants.

The Balamians nearest to the altar recovered quickly from their initial shock and several men launched a menacing attack. Adhering to the promise that he'd made to Ponti, to kill no one unless he was forced to, Nate shot one Balamian in the thigh, the other in his shoulder, causing another attacker to rethink his move.

"Let's go! Now!" he shouted to Raquel, tugging at her arm, directing her to the vine-draped bushes behind them.

Without thinking, Raquel made a swift move for the ceremonial dagger that lay on the pulpit—at least Mircea would be safe. It would have been the last move she made had it not been for Ponti, who blocked the blow of a livid Balamian wielding an ax.

The sound of the sharp weapon crashing down on the cracked pulpit nearly split her ears it was so close.

"You little fool!" Nate shouted, then grabbed her arm before leaping into the dark foliage.

CHAPTER 8

J ay watched the *buyei* carefully light a long-stemmed, hand-carved pipe. Strands of blackish monkey hair hung uniformly from its bottom, shaking as the old high priest's unsteady fingers gripped the wooden object. His bulbous eyes stared, as the older man slowly inhaled the pungent herbs, then blew out a steady stream of greenish smoke.

Jay's gangly body swayed impatiently from side to side as he waited for the *buyei* to answer the question put before him. He did not care what the other Puntaborok villagers thought. He wanted to be done with this situation as quickly as possible, and that meant finding the girl and getting rid of her.

He rolled his yellow-stained eyes in the high priest's direction. It was obvious the priest was getting too old to run things. Even now, he didn't really know all the things that went on amongst the Shango, Jay thought with a smile. It was time for someone younger and stronger to take over.

"I think someone else should accompany you to bring the girl back. Al must wait here until a healing can be performed. Until then he cannot be trusted or controlled," the Shangoain dialect poured slowly from his lips.

"But, mighty *buyei,* he is my brother. We have always worked together. He would not go against my word, plus I will need his strength in case the girl resists."

Another green stream of smoke floated above the *buyei*'s head. Pupils that used to be dark, but had succumbed to the grey tint of time, focused on Jay as he squatted before him.

"Jay, *Dada,* I feel there are other reasons you want Al to accompany you to bring back this girl." After a controlled pause he continued. "She is not to be harmed."

The *buyei* picked up a root carved into the shape of a woman from the divination basket, and tossed it between them.

"The fork of change is near." His tough finger poked the dried, blackened object. "We cannot change what was meant to be, *Dada.* "

Jay lowered anger-filled eyes away from the knowing stare of the high priest. A familiar quiver surfaced in his stomach, reminding him that he knew the powers the *buyei* possessed, and it would not be wise to force his desires too strongly upon him. He glanced at his brother as he sat cross-legged beside him, playing with a large, unhappy centipede. Finally he nodded his head in compliance with the high priest's order.

"Take three of the other men with you. They will more than make up for the physical strength of your brother. The four of you will leave day after tomorrow."

Keeping his head bowed as he rose to his feet, Jay began to take leave of the high priest. It took several strong taps on Al's shoulder before he followed suit, mumbling to himself that Jay was interrupting his playtime.

There was no warm reception as the man and his brother entered their home, a stilt-topped building not far away. Acting more like a servant than a wife, Jay's spouse, Eva, lowered her head and shoulders as he came in, then muttered an offering of food. He gave the thin figure little attention as he crossed the room to a collection of containers, withdrew a crumpled envelope out of one of them, then stuffed the paper into his pants pocket.

"I am goin' out."

His wife's lowered eyes opened in surprise at this offering of congeniality. Their communication over the last three years had deteriorated to nothing, after it had become evident that she couldn't bear a child. Now she was a servant in her own home. It was only because of the *buyei* that they remained together.

As her dull eyes sought her husband's face, Eva realized he was not addressing her but his brother. Quickly she lowered her head again, and returned to the furthest corner of the one-room house, not wanting to draw too much attention to herself. She'd learned she was better off that way. Yet, she was very curious as to why Jay would leave Al behind; usually they did everything together. They were virtually inseparable. Maybe the *obeah* woman they had brought back from America had caused the change.

Eva's brown eyes shifted back and forth anxiously as she pondered the situation. Just the thought of any female having control over her husband pleased her. During their short marriage she had come to know just how much Jay disrespected women. To him they were simply objects to be used at his whim. With anticipation she concluded the power of the *obeah* woman must be very strong to bring about a change in the relationship between her husband and his brother.

Large leaves lashed against her face, and Raquel stumbled over vines and fallen branches as Nate pulled her behind him at an exhausting pace. The shouts of their pursuers grew closer as she began to tire, still her mind urged her body to continue.

"Where are we going?" Gasps of air laced her words.

"I don't know where. Are you thinking about going back or something?" he replied, as they continued to run.

The sounds of the jungle seemed to come alive as night descended over the thick foliage, "No. I'm not."

"If you think about it, maybe they wouldn't be so hot on our trail if you hadn't stopped to take that damn dagger!"

"I couldn't just leave thinking they were going to carve out Mircea's tongue with it. So I took it!"

"Not her tongue, sweetheart. It was going to be her heart. So you better hope they don't catch us 'cause it'll be ours instead," he chastised her. "Because of your heroism, you may have made it easier for them to get two for the price of one."

The thought of letting go of the large hand that clasped hers as he dragged her along, flickered through Raquel's mind. Here he was blaming her for their predicament, and if it hadn't been for him, they wouldn't be in Belize in the first place.

"Don't blame this mess on me!" She tried to dig her fingernails into his firm skin for revenge. "If it hadn't—"

"Save your breath for running," was Nate's curt reply.

Minutes later, starving for air, Raquel's breaths turned into gasps as her intakes became more and more labored. She wanted to beg Nate to stop, but she was so out of breath she couldn't speak.

Nate listened to the strained breathing of the woman behind him, and he knew they would have to stop if only for a brief respite. Hastily he pulled her down with him behind a large hyacinth bush as he listened intently for the group of Balamians not far behind.

He was grateful for the cover of darkness, but he also knew the sounds they made crashing through the rain forest kept the Balamians on their trail. Nate looked at the woman hunched over with her hands on her knees, desperately trying to catch her breath.

"Are you ready?"

She answered weakly, and they were off again.

Suddenly, Nate released a sound of intense pain although he continued to run. Raquel assumed he had scraped his leg, or slightly twisted an ankle, because the sound was accompanied by a slight break in his stride. It wasn't until he spasmodically released her hand, collapsed, then nearly rolled into a partial clearing, that she knew it was much more than that. His body began to shake as if he were experiencing a chill.

"What's wrong?" she fell to her knees beside him.

He attempted to sit up, "I think it's a s-snakebite." Nate tried to look at his leg, but was overtaken by another, progressively stronger quiver.

"Oh God, not now!" she heard herself say as she peered down at the limb he was holding.

A small circle resembling a bruise could be seen above his ankle, it was too dark to see the punctures.

Frantically the young woman tried to think of something she could do as she heard the Balamians closing in on them. Maybe she could lance it like in the movies, and suck out the poison before it got into his bloodstream, but that would take time, and time was something they didn't have. She examined the ominous-looking bite once again.

A tightness gripped Raquel's chest when she raised his pants leg and saw a dark line forming, progressing up towards his heart. She thought *Somehow I've got to stop the poison from traveling upward! At least try to slow it down.*

Swiftly she grabbed a stick that lay near them on the ground. With trembling, but strong fingers, she tore a length of material from the rim of the shift she wore. Putting the cloth around Nate's leg about two inches above the menacing dark line, she tightened it with the stick in an attempt to stop the flow of blood between his heart and the venom.

Then unexpectantly, a crumpled vermilion blossom fell out of the denim material onto the moss-covered floor of the forest. Raquel clasped its withered softness in her shaking hand, "Oh, Nate."

She thought of the longing that filled her in the Balamian village when she sent the meaningful flower to him, and how passionately, with their eyes they had taken that silent vow. Somehow it was wrong for such a tiny thing as a snakebite to bring him down. His strength and passion for life was much more than that. He did not deserve to die like this.

Raquel knew she had promised herself she would never cry again, but now she saw, rather than felt the large bits of moisture dropping onto the tawny colored material of his shirt, forming dark circles as they landed.

Instinctively her hands went to his head and she gently lifted it, placing it upon her lap. She stared at his blank features as she rubbed his forehead, his face, his hair.

With resignation, Raquel waited for the Balamians to overtake them. Somehow her will to live had become connected with the man's life whose head she held upon her lap. A man who had kidnapped her, yet had protected her every step of the way. If he was to die, this would be the only embrace she could give him.

Raquel gazed affectionately at his strong face. Strange how in her mind the now-continuous quivering did not jar the handsomeness of his features. She marveled at how his thick lashes had formed a dark half-moon upon his high cheeks. Softly, as in a daze, she traced the shape of his broad, tall nose down to his lips, that even at first sight she knew could have shaken the very foundation of her. Purposefully she placed a soft, lingering kiss upon them.

Out of the darkness, a figure appeared in the clearing. Raquel looked up with tired eyes expecting to see a Balamian with sword or dagger drawn, and a thick wrapping of beaten bark about his wrists. Instead a female approached.

Being overcome by exhaustion and mental strain and slightly relieved, Raquel calmly returned her remote, troubled stare to Nate's visage. Placing her face close to his, she began to hum a gentle melody as she continued her gentle administrations. If they were to die by the hands of this stranger, they would die together.

In silence, the odd figure exposed a large machete. Raquel did not flinch as she raised it high above her head, then brought it down with remarkable force for a person her size. A splintering sound ensued as the woman hacked off a long strip of a large thorny plant nearby. She brought it over and dropped it upon Nate's legs.

At that moment two Balamians burst into the clearing, then halted abruptly as they surveyed the scene in front of them. Their gaze darted between Raquel, who appeared to be unaware of her surroundings as she embraced the barely conscious Nate, and the bush doctor, who pinned them with an unwavering stare.

It was she who spoke first, rapidly and authoritatively, raising her arms, then grabbing and shaking a talisman that she wore about her neck. By that time, several more Balamians had gathered, and disbelief and fear plastered their faces as they gawked at the shamaness. Suddenly they began to back away when the commanding figure took a powerful step in their direction. One last menacing word from her caused them to run in fear.

Squatting beside the man and the woman, she stretched out one of Nate's arms, and began to measure the strip of cockspur against its length. Carefully she cut the severed plant's dimensions to match his, then with wrinkled fingers, she forced the plant into his mouth, clamping it shut.

Through a mental haze Raquel heard the woman's rough accented voice.

"You make yo'r man chew this. He must chew it good an' swallow the juice, but he must not swallow the plant. The juices will fight the poison that has entered 'is body," Strong, heavily lidded eyes focused on Raquel as the woman spoke.

Following the stranger's instructions, the young woman began to massage Nate's jaws as she spoke to him.

"You hear that, Nate? She says you've got to chew this. It's going to help you. Do you hear me? Please, just try," her hand mechanically opened and shut his mouth as part of the plant lay inside. Slowly he began to respond, unconsciously chewing on his own as she stuffed the remainder of the cockspur strip past his lips.

Satisfied with what she saw, the shamaness returned to the same plant. This time she used the machete to dig around and expose its root. She began to slice pieces off of the hard bottom.

"Remove the chewed plant from 'is mouth an' place it on the snakebite," she instructed over her shoulder.

With thumb and forefinger Raquel obeyed her command, patting the wet, sticky lump on the spot above Nate's ankle. He jerked as it made contact with his swollen skin.

"Now, one more time," the woman's raspy voice announced, as she stuffed the piece of cockspur root in his mouth. "Tis won't cure him, but will delay the effects of the venom until we can get him to my hut."

Moments later the two women were balancing Nate's heavy frame between them, his arms draped about their shoulders. Dark, badly crinkled fingers extracted the chewed root fiber from Nate's loose lips, then threw it on the ground. Satisfied, they began to make their way further into the rain forrest.

CHAPTER 9

A fter Jay turned up the controls, the old air conditioner blew smooth gusts of cool air directly upon him as he lay on top of the knitted bedspread. He watched the sides of his mud-caked shoes slap together, while he waited in the comfortable surroundings of the Punta Gorda hotel.

This was the life he was meant to live. Not locked away in a village of elevated huts where the most modern of conveniences was a wood-burning stove, and the women smelled like dying fish. No, that was not the life for him. He was born to have money and power and he meant to have both.

Jay walked over and drew back the floral printed drapery, peering at the bright lights of the disco not far down the street. He had a little more than an hour before he was to meet Ricky Flint and his friends, and he planned to make good use of the time.

He withdrew the crumpled joint from his pocket, then lit it with an engraved sterling silver lighter that Ricky had given him almost a year ago during their first meeting. Running his thumb over the smooth-textured surface, he anticipated the time when items like this would be a dime a dozen amongst his possessions.

Jay chuckled to himself as he thought about his future. He would be in charge, never to bow to any man again. Soon, he would have the power he knew he was meant to receive. Soon, he would have everything.

Jay blew out the small flame that was swiftly progressing up the rolled cigarette. As he held the end near his wide nostrils, he inhaled deeply, enjoying the thick pungent smoke that drifted away from it.

Confidently, he walked over to the hotel door making sure it was un-locked, then climbed back upon the now-rumpled spread. Several deep pulls on the marijuana cigarette caused a forgotten seed inside to sputter and pop, the man smiled to himself at the familiar sound as a heady feel-ing descended upon him.

Jay was feeling the heat on his fingers from the almost consumed ciga-rette, when he heard a light tapping on the door. He extinguished the tiny tip in a glass ash tray on the nightstand beside the bed.

"Yeah?"

"It's Lindy," a soft female voice called from outside.

"Come on in and lock the door."

A rather petite woman wearing a lilac-colored spandex minidress and heels entered the room. Shutting and locking the door behind her, she leaned enticingly against it.

"Hello. I understand you're looking for some company for about an hour," Her manner of speaking was intelligent and her carriage just a slight bit haughty.

Jay had seen her several times before when he was in town. She worked out of the same house as Candy, his regular. But for some reason he'd never requested to see her even though he'd had the hots for her, and now he knew why. He had always felt he didn't deserve her, and that she felt she was better than he, no matter what her occupation.

Lindy's heavily lined eyes sized up the man on the bed. A precisely manicured hand smoothed the sides of her French rolled hair away from her rich brown skin. She could smell the lingering scent of marijuana in the room, and knew that accounted for the glassy look in his eyes. She could also feel something else she couldn't quite put her hands on.

"Yeah, t'at's about right, but I want more than your freakin' company. So why don't you come on ovah here and get to work," Jay commanded, wanting her to know her position.

A light of understanding clicked behind her dark eyes, and she slowly sauntered over to the dresser and placed her purse on its top. Silently, she pulled the elastic material of the dress over her shoulders, wiggling temptingly. She eased it over her rounded breasts and hips, until it was a purple pile at her spike-heeled feet. Keeping her eyes on the man on the bed, she kicked it away from her, then stood with her legs spread apart and her hands on her black-gartered hips.

Despite the calm Jay was determined to display, he licked his lips in an-ticipation as he assessed her almost-nude frame, wearing only a garter, silk stockings and purple heels.

A look of triumph curled the corners of her pouty lips as she saw his reaction, and noted the growing bulge in the front of his pants. She'd seen his kind before. Straight from the forest, wanting to be big city. It was according to their frame of mind as to how they would react, so she'd have to be careful, for they could be unusually cruel, or as obedient as a trained seal.

The woman's change in expression coupled with the effect of the marijuana, conjured up another image in Jay's mind and he touched the pale scar on the side of his face. He could see the woman, Jackie, standing before him naked and ready to give of herself, letting go of the pretense that she did not want him. He remembered how his desire for her had nearly driven him mad. Her and her high-handed manners. He'd bet a hundred dollars she'd buck and scream like any other whore if he ever got inside her. He would still get his chance, he chuckled to himself.

"First, my money," Lindy held an outstretched hand in front of him, interrupting his drifting thoughts.

Harshly he slapped a fifty-dollar bill in her palm then rose to take off his clothes. No matter what women said, there was always a price for their stuff.

In the beginning he had believed otherwise, especially during the early months of marriage. Eva had been a virgin, and he remembered how proud he felt to have a woman that no other man had ever touched. Still the price for her virginity had been high.

She was young and inexperienced, and just the thought of that used to get a rise out of him. But he was patient, telling himself it would take time. Eventually he became her servant. She had him at her beck and call doing his work and hers. For certain she'd acted like she was the pot of gold at the end of the rainbow, and she had him believing it, because she was young and tender, and she knew he wanted a child.

The shaman had said if she was fertile a baby would be conceived within the first six months, but if she was slow to conceive, it would be at least a year. So he had waited. Settling for her lying there beneath him like a dead woman, giving little or no response only to find out she was no woman at all, and unable to bear him a child.

Jay's face relaxed into a satisfied smirk.

Well, after that, she got what was coming to her. If he was going to have to take care of a woman who couldn't satisfy him in any way, she'd work hard for that support. He wouldn't have a female that he was pumping into night after night remaining silent beneath him, openly denying his manhood. He had developed ways that would issue a response, be it pain or pleasure.

Before Lindy knew what he was about to do, Jay grabbed a hold of the mass of curls sitting on the top of her head, then bent her down over the full-size bed. Roughly, he kicked her ankles further apart with his still mud-caked shoes.

"If I'm going to have to pay you, bitch, you're going to work for your money," A snapping swat resounded off her rounded buttocks.

An appropriate whimper gushed from her lavishly painted lips,

"Whatever you say, baby." She braced herself with strong arms as she bent forward.

Taken over by a lust-filled stupor, at first Jay didn't hear the knocking on the door until it turned into forceful pounding. The loud noise caught him off guard causing him to spill forth prematurely and a disappointed moan oozed from his puffy lips.

"Are you in there, Jay?" a deep voice demanded.

"Yeah. Yeah. I'm here."

"Ricky's waiting for you at the disco."

"Ain't you a little early?" Limply Jay pulled back, giving the prostitute room enough to saunter to the bathroom.

A paused ensued. "Do you want me to tell Ricky, *you* want *him* to wait?" The question was richly laced with insinuations.

"Na-aw." Panic struck him. He swallowed deeply before he continued. "Tell him I'll be right over."

He dressed hastily, leaving Lindy in the hotel room as he closed the door behind him. It didn't take him long to walk to the disco down the street.

"What is wrong with you, mon?" a woman snapped after Jay rudely pushed her chair forward while making his way across the crowded club.

He heard her irritated voice but didn't bother to respond. His gaze remained focused on Ricky, sitting at the table with two other men. One he recognized; the other, a large hunk of a man, was unfamiliar.

Rising out of his char: Ricky extended an out-stretched hand. "Jay, good to see you again, man. You remember Rock, don't you?" he motioned to the familiar guy.

Jay nodded in agreement as Rock sat chewing enthusiastically on a stick of gum.

"And this is Mane-Mane."

He looked in the new guy's direction. His large, braided head remained lowered as he meticulously lined up several cigarettes on the plexiglass table.

Jay wondered which one of the Americans has threatened him with telling Ricky he wanted him to wait, as he gave them a none too friendly going-over. Both of their receptions were cold, and he decided he didn't care for either one of them. After all, they were nothing but Ricky Flint's flunkies, jumping whenever he said jump, and asking how high. Dudes like them would eagerly do his dirty work because they didn't have brains enough to do anything else.

During his first meeting with Rock, Jay found out how he believed the Belizean drug supply was an open playground for the States. So he had attached himself to Ricky Flint. He guessed Mane-Mane had done the same.

The sound of Jay's chair scraping the club's floor was drowned out by the loud reggae music. He looked across the table at Ricky's sparkling eyes, and wide, easy smile. His wavy, dark brown hair was pulled back to form a ponytail at the base of his neck.

He knew this man considered him as just a pawn in the game, and that's all he was when it came to Ricky's side of the board. But here in Punta Gorda, he could be the big man, the *oba*.

"Care for a drink?"

"Sure."

Ricky had barely raised his hand before a tall, chocolate brown waitress in a fuchsia cat suit appeared. Her wide smile was genuine as she glanced around the table.

"What d'ya having?"

Ricky motioned for Jay to place his order first.

Jay leaned back in the wooden chair, eyeing the woman's ample tush. "I'll have a Beliken & Crown."

"Make that four," Ricky added, patting the waitress's backside. "That's one thing I can say about you islanders, you have plenty of everything," He watched the woman's rounded bottom rumble as she walked away, then grinned. "Everything that counts, that is." He winked at Jay. "And of course that's why we're all here." A fluff of lint on his designer shirt drew his attention, and he aptly flicked it away. "Once you're able to tap into a supply like this one, the need keeps growing and growing. Some might think that's bad, but we know it's only bad for those who really don't count. For folks like us, Jay, it's a virtual gold mine."

Ricky waited for the waitress, who had hurried and filled the order, to pour his beer into a heavy mug. Lifting the glass with a manicured hand, crowned by a tiny gold pinkie ring, he boasted of things to come.

"This is to the future. After tonight there will be a helluva future to look forward to."

Jay clinked his mug with the man's across the table. By now he was full of anticipation, and the color of the man's eyes had become an omen. They were a deep green, the color of money.

CHAPTER 10

Large rivulets of sweat ran down Nate's face onto the woven pad beneath him. Raquel sat nearby, drinking a mixture of herbs forced upon her by the shamaness. The strain of the Balamian incident had taken its toll, but she would not give in to rest until she witnessed the strange woman use her knowledge of herbs and roots to help Nate. She watched silently as the shamaness performed her task. Finally she was satisfied when the woman promised he would not die after all.

She sipped the relaxing mixture that tasted of chamomile, cinnamon and another flavor she did not recognize, and watched the older woman revive the fire inside the small, dirt floor hut. It startled Raquel that she was not more panicked, that she felt so relaxed. She looked at the cup of tea in her hand and wondered if it was the herbs. She wondered if it was her trust in the shamaness. She wondered if she would feel this calm all the time if she simply knew Nate was nearby.

Skins and dried parts of various animals hung along the walls, mixed with different sized roots, carved figures and dried plants. The smell was a strange mixture of tangy sweetness and a gamy scent. Raquel was vaguely aware of how the hot liquid she drank helped to quell her desire to gag.

Eyes that appeared to be ancient would rest on her from time to time, while the elderly woman went about her tasks. She was distantly aware of the curious glances, but they did not move her either way. Nor did the figure's hunchbacked, skeleton-thin frame, crowned by a disarray of thick and thin dreadlocks, cause her the least bit of alarm. This person had brought them to a safe haven—one where the Balamians had not attempted to follow and were obviously afraid to trespass upon.

Outside, another pair of yellowish eyes watched the scene from the pitch blackness beyond the open flap of the hut's door. Raquel's hand paused in midair as she watched them come closer, until the slender, grayish body of a jaguarundi walked menacingly through the opening. A low growl rumbled in his throat as his almond-shaped gaze seemed to take in everything, paying special interest to the man who lay prostrate on the reed pallet. Slowly the shamaness turned toward the wildcat, and for a moment their eyes made contact. Now, the animal, like Raquel, seemed to freeze in midmotion, all except for his long swaying tail. Afterwards, as if receiving a message Raquel did not hear, the jaguarundi made a wide circle, only to retrace his steps and settle comfortably right outside the hut's door.

All this time she had witnessed the scene in the room through a kind of fog, and it was at this point the objects in the room began to swim about her. Moments passed, and before she knew it, the animal skins sans their hosts, began to come down off the walls and parley about the fire. Several ceremonial masks that hung in the corners provided peculiar sounds and chanting for the skins' bizarre dance.

Raquel never remembered at what point she lay down beside her very ill captor, placing her arm about his feverish torso. Nor did she know when reality turned into dreams, as she slept fitfully, surrounded by visions of warriors and jaguarundis.

It was early in the morning, and the young woman felt a deep urge to join her scream with the resounding noise of the howler monkeys perched in the rain forest trees. Their loud calls were free and uninhibited, making Raquel aware of her restricted existence.

She imagined it didn't matter if they were happy or melancholic, their voices would still ring out, and if they were lonely and feeling desperate as she felt, their loud cry would always be an outlet.

A day and a half had passed and Nate remained delirious, feverish. After the first night the shamaness decided he should be moved to a smaller hut beside her personal dwelling.

More than one of the forest animals had made their home in the vacant hut, and to her dismay, had to be chased out and shooed away. It was obvious the animals felt very comfortable with the old woman's company, and she with theirs; therefore, they didn't quite understand why this human creature did not find their company as appealing.

Raquel recalled staring down at the continuously bubbling broth, boiling in a large earthen container above the small fire. She didn't dare ask about the contents of the brew she'd been instructed to give Nate throughout the day. Its aroma reminded her of souring broccoli, the color being an appropriate vibrant green. Yet it was obvious to Raquel that the woman possessed a vast knowledge of the use of herbs and roots, unquestionably paling her limited wisdom, and for that she was grateful.

Raquel believed she could have stomached her outlandish surroundings much more easily if there had been any meaningful communication between her and her hostess, but there was none, not a mumbling word. Even carrying Nate to the other hut, and the shamaness's instructions to feed him, had been a series of head and arm movements, coupled with numerous glances from the woman's liquidy eyes.

It would have been different if she thought the woman could not speak, but she could, and that disturbed Raquel even more. It also made her wonder why the woman had intervened in the first place, when the Balamians were on the verge of killing them.

Had she not been standing in the midst of the rain forest, it would be easy to convince herself that being kidnapped, shanghaied and nearly sacrificed by a group of modern-day Mayans with ancient beliefs, was nothing but a bizarre dream. Now to be stuck with this person was almost more than her overloaded psyche could endure.

Suddenly, along with the mounting squeal of several howler monkeys, the young woman let go a releasing yell, but because her sound was foreign, it caused the familiar forest clamor to come to an abrupt halt.

Raquel didn't feel the least bit embarrassed when the old woman stepped to the door of her hut and looked at her with blatant curiosity. As a matter of fact she felt somewhat satisfied that her crude therapy had drawn a reaction from her distant caretaker.

Minutes later, with nothing to do, she went back inside the hut to tend to Nate. She sponged down his hot face and neck with a dampened rag, dipped in a bowl of water made available for that purpose. His uncomfortable features tended to seek out the cool cloth, turning in the direction from which it came as he felt it make contact with his hot body.

His sensuous lips had become cracked, puffy masses because of the fever. Ever so tenderly, Raquel placed the damp cloth against them, hoping to ease their soreness.

She wondered what events in life had made this man of strong convictions take a path of crime. Somewhere deep inside her she felt it was all such a waste. Considering his demeanor and leadership abilities, he could have been anything he aspired to, yet he had chosen a life that could eventually lead to prison.

Raquel lifted one of Nate's limp, warm hands into hers and began to study his strong fingers topped by amazingly well-kept, wide nails. She couldn't imagine his strength being contained behind iron bars, but more than that, it dawned on her, she couldn't imagine being the reason behind his incarceration.

Suddenly a strong urge to protect him surfaced inside her. The strength of it shocked Raquel as she looked down into his unconscious features. Small wrinkles creased his forehead as he turned uncomfortably. She reached out a gentle hand to smooth them away.

My God what was happening to her? Why should she care if he were imprisoned? It was crazy to worry about a man who had kidnapped her and placed her in such danger. Her whole life had been turned upside down because of him. If she made it back to the States, which was definitely uncertain at this time, she would have no home, and no job. And if she never made it back . . .

Suddenly she realized how unwise her near-reclusive lifestyle had been, and how her adult life of separating herself from others mirrored her loner childhood. The only two people who had been close to her were her mother and Clinton Bradshaw. There was no one else who would really miss her.

Nate began to make small, silent motions with his parched lips, and Raquel wondered if he mouthed the name of a lover he'd left behind. Against her will the thought of it bothered her, and she had to admit she longed to know more about him, his childhood, his loves and dislikes.

Confused, her troubled gaze stared out into the kaleidoscopic rain forest, trying to discover her own feelings.

And what if he *didn't* survive. What would she do then? She'd be forced to find her way out of the forest, alone. But how would she do that with no knowledge of this country? Maybe she would eventually run into someone who would help her, or maybe Jay and Al would find her before she could . . .

No. He will not die. I will make sure of that. I will personally make sure of it.

They had gone through so much together. Was that a sign they could possibly have a future despite their dire beginnings? Was there anything he could say or do that would make her accept him after all of this? Would he want to?

The onslaught of thoughts and emotions was nearly unbearable, so Raquel grabbed on to a more logical, clinical approach. Maybe the deep feelings she thought she was developing were simply a temporary reaction to the recent traumatic events. After all, for her, it was easier to sink into the comfort of loving feelings than confront the uncertain future she now faced. For there was one thing she did know—under extreme stress it was hard to calculate how a human being would react.

In the end it felt safest to look at their situation from a professional point of view. As a psychologist she had never come across a person as complex as this man, and naturally that would spark her interest to know more about him.

Raquel found a temporary comfort in her final conclusion, and she ignored the nagging gut feeling that told her it was not totally the truth.

The young woman reached for the wooden ladle lying on top of a large, pointed, clover-shaped leaf. She dipped it carefully into the broth. Patiently, she blew on its contents before administering it to the man before her. Droplets of green became caught in his mustache as she gently forced him to take in the liquid, afterwards wiping his mouth and chin as if he were an infant.

She readjusted the thin roll of cloth beneath his head and walked back outside. There she saw two porcupines eating contentedly in front of the shamaness's hut.

The image of a short-legged wildcat floated into her consciousness, and a nonverbal communication between him and her hostess ensued. She wondered if she'd dreamed it, but somehow the porcupines' presence insured her she had not. Plagued with loneliness, boredom and curiosity, Raquel walked past the undisturbed creatures and entered the doctor's home.

The even swishing of a jaguarundi's tail as he lay in a corner, proved to Raquel, that the encounter between the doctor and the animal had not been a dream. At first, she allowed the animal's piercing gaze to prevent her from entering, as did the somewhat cynical glance of the shamaness. Raquel's discomfort was obvious to her, yet she did not speak a word of welcome or motion for her to come inside.

A deluge of emotions ran through the young woman. Infantile feelings of wanting to shout at the crouching figure surfaced first. Would it be so awful to invite me in? This is ridiculous! Why did you bring us here anyway, if you really didn't want us here? Raquel could feel the muscles tightening in her face as her eyes narrowed in confrontation.

But it was the low growl of the wildcat that convinced her this would not be the route to take. The carnivorous sound made the hair stand up on the back of her neck and she thought, if this woman can communicate with the animals of the rain forest, what would she be able to do to me as well as Nate, who was virtually dependent upon her care?

So with a thrusting back of her shoulders, reliable logic won over emotion, and the young woman stepped further into the hut. Once again the overwhelming smell of animal remains mixed with various scents assaulted her, but this time she was determined to control her body's reaction.

A shallow woven basket filled with dried, crushed blossoms, caught Raquel's eye, so she sat cross-legged beside it, hoping their sweet fragrance dominated the space around them.

The jaguarundi released something akin to a purr, while a steady, smooth, grinding noise was being produced by the bush doctor as she ground a tiny pile of crushed green leaves into powder. She watched as the woman performed this task using a well-worn flat stone as the mortar, and another elongated rock served as a pestle.

As the young woman looked around, she began to wonder why this woman, who obviously lacked human companionship, had stored and prepared an untold number of liquids, powders and roots. Had the loneliness of the Belizean rain forest driven her to the brink of madness, as she felt she was being driven?

A nervous unbearable energy surged within Raquel as she realized, even though she had forced her presence upon her, her hostess had no intention of initiating communication between them. There was the possibility they could be there for countless days on end, and this woman would not have a need to act other than she was acting now. She was accustomed to not hearing the sound of a human voice, but Raquel was not, and to save her own sanity, she decided to do something about it.

"So . . . what are you preparing over there?"

A grayish yellow brow rose interrogatingly as the shamaness looked at the intent young woman, then returned silently to her work.

"Okay, so that's the way it's going to be," an unthwarted Raquel continued. "Well it really doesn't matter. You don't have to talk back. Just hearing the sound of my own voice feels like therapy enough. As a matter of fact it feels pretty good, and I'll just continue, if you don't mind?"

She spoke of her past job, her clients back in the States, and her practice of shaitsu and use of herbs. She spoke of her mother and her illness and her disappointment with Clinton Bradshaw. As time passed, it didn't matter that the old woman didn't participate in the conversation. Ironically, she thought of it as a visit to a psychologist like herself, but this time she was the patient, and the expressing of her thoughts and feelings began to have a cleansing effect.

She was careful not to speak of how she had come to Belize. Although, she really didn't know why. Not that she felt it would make a difference if this woman knew the man she was taking care of was part of a kidnapping ring. Living in the wild as the shamaness did, the laws and rules of society probably held little or no value in her eyes.

Time passed effortlessly, with the younger woman's continuous chatter. If her talking bothered the shamaness, she never expressed it, for in the midst of Raquel's talking, she had converted several small piles of herbs into medicinal powders, and stored them in dried, hollow guards.

Finally, feeling drained, Raquel decided to take her leave.

"Well, I guess that will be about all you can stand for one day. I can't promise this won't continue, at least until Nate is able to talk to me. How long do you think that will be?" she rambled on without expecting an answer. "Not that we've done that much talking in the past. But hopefully, soon he'll be well enough, and we can be on our way."

Raquel rose and dusted off the bottom of her wraparound skirt. She was surprised to glance down and see a papaya lying at her feet. It was rather strange. She didn't remember seeing the fruit when she initially took a seat on the ground.

"A papaya! Do you mind if I eat it?" Her wide, bright eyes searched out the elderly woman, but found only her back, cascaded with numerous dreadlocks. Then ancient eyes turned in her direction, examined her for a moment, and smoothly released her. Suddenly the thought appeared in her mind the shamaness had given her the succulent fruit. Astonished, she stared at the odd figure.

"Aw-aw . . . is this a gift for me?" she asked her reluctant hostess. But the shamaness simply turned away. Uniquely satisfied with the outcome of her visit Raquel left the hut to minister to Nate.

The following day mirrored the previous one with Raquel taking care of her recovering captor. Nate's fever had broken, but for some reason he slept continuously. It dawned on her, the brew she fed him probably contained a powerful, natural sedative.

Raquel gave a start as she saw the willowy figure of the bush doctor stooping near the fire—her entrances and exits were amazingly quiet, almost magical. She wondered about the woman's age, and how long she'd been living here, alone, in the middle of a Belizean rain forest.

She watched as the shamaness scraped what appeared to be a combination of finely chopped vegetables into the constantly boiling mixture, then she rose up and walked over to the young woman and man.

With nimble fingers she removed an old poultice that had been applied to Nate's leg the night before. She replaced it with several boiled leaves, still intact, that Raquel thought resembled wild burdock. Carefully she wrapped the pliable plants around the wound, then with her task completed, the bush doctor returned to her own hut.

Earlier that morning after finishing a breakfast of pineapple, banana and breadfruit, Raquel decided to visit with the distant shamaness, but to her dismay she found the hut empty. She was glad when the woman returned and she joined her in the space next door. This time she didn't take a seat on the dirt floor, but began a closer study of some of the objects, herbs and roots hanging profusely about. She was relieved to find the strong smell of the hut had little effect on her, and she marveled at how quickly the human body adjusted to its environment.

Her perusal was tentative at first, allowing the bush doctor to voice opposition if she chose, but as the moments passed and there was none, Raquel became more animated, calling out the name of herbs as she recognized them, though these were few and far in between. She imagined the number of herbs growing in Belize was astronomical, and that there must be many which even the most knowledgeable herbalists in the States had probably never heard of before.

For despite the emotional strain and circumstances under which she'd been forced to visit the country, its wild untapped beauty had not been lost upon her. It felt good to know the groping hands of civilization had not exploited, controlled or choked out the very essence of this country, as it had done to many others.

"And what in the world is this?" Raquel bent to touch a piece of bark that resembled the badly matted coat of a burnt red, shaggy dog.

"Don' touch that," the shamaness abruptly called out.

Raquel snatched her hand back as if she had been bitten.

"It ez gumbo-limbo. Your hand will burn an' blister if you touch it," the rough, accented voice of the bush doctor alerted her.

"Thanks for warning me," Raquel endeavored to keep a rousing satisfaction out of her voice.

"I see you have knowledge of the healin' plants," the raspy voice continued.

"Yes, I've worked with herbs. Still there are so many here I've never seen before. It's amazing. It must have taken you forever to gather all of them."

"Time for me ez of little importance, as it ez for you who live on the outside. Yet it was of the greates' importance for your man. Had he tended to the snakebite with the proper herbs when it first happened, the poison would not have had a chance to grab a strong hold on his body. But he did not and now he ez sufferin' 'cause of it," her liquidy eyes watched her. "But still, he ez young and strong, and it will not be long before you two mate again. I am aware of your anxiousness."

"Well, I—I," Raquel sputtered at the woman's directness. To say the least, it caught her off guard to go from having no communication at all with the woman to discussing such personal matters.

"Actually he is not—*my* man, so to speak."

Knowing dark eyes rose to the young woman's face. "Um-m," was her sole reply.

Now that the door of communication had been opened, Raquel refused to let it close again. "Do you think you could teach me about the herbs you have here and their uses?"

"Why?"

Startled again by her tactlessness, Raquel spoke the true answer. "Because I'd like to know more."

"There are many thin's that ordinary souls desire to delve in that are not the path for them to take."

"So are you saying I am ordinary or that you are extraordinary?" Raquel matched her insolence.

"Neither." The shamaness's thin frame lifted to its full height, but was still lacking because of her hunched back. "One must determine to be extraordinary if they choose to venture down the path."

"I didn't think that wanting to know more about herbs and their uses made me a wanderer down a particular path."

"It ez all a part of the whole. The healin' abilities of the plants cannot be separated from the spirit energy that created them. You must know the spirit in order to fully understand the healin'."

Once again, Raquel was impressed with the shamaness's wisdom, and her thoughts automatically centered on her own predicament.

"Tell me, what kind of people believe in the *gubida?*"

She tried to ask the question nonchalantly, attempting to draw attention away from her words by stepping up close to a mask of wood and fiber, examining it with great pretense.

"I do not mess in the affairs of others. That ez why I live as I do, so that my life can not be controlled by any group of people, or beliefs," the woman's voice was strong, resentful. With even steps she strode to the entrance of the hut, picked up a machete that lay nearby, then left without another word.

Raquel watched as the shamaness was swallowed up by the foliage of the rain forest. She reprimanded herself for being so impatient. Why couldn't she have waited awhile before she started asking questions about the customs and beliefs of the people in the woman's country? From her reaction there was no doubt she had hit a sore spot. It should have been obvious to her, there was a reason the shamaness had chosen to live alone. Now, at the moment when she had begun to open up and talk to her, she had pushed her too far. Raquel sincerely regretted her prying words, but she was only trying to seek help for herself.

"Get your lazy, stinkin' tail ovah t'ere and fix me some breakfas', but make sure you wash your hands before you do it," Jay roughly shoved his wife in the direction of the stove. "An' I don't want no more of those damn Johnny cakes. I want some fried feesh an' creole bread. Hurry up, too. I need to leave here by midday."

Eva shuffled toward the front door.

"Where you t'ink you goin'?" Jay demanded.

"I need to get some fresh feesh an' a few other thin's to cook wit'," she muttered.

"No, t'at's alright. I bought everything you need wit' me when I come in t'is mornin'." He looked at her suspiciously. "And the way you been lookin' at me, I don't trust you noway. You might try to put somet'in' in the food t'at'll make me sick," he stood menacingly close as he spoke. "So I'ma tell you right now, if anyting happens to me, today or next year, I'ma blame you. So rememba', if I don't die quick, you will go before me. You watch what I say," he clutched her pointed chin between his thumb and bent index finger, then pushed it back forcefully.

She caught her breath, inhaling the distinct smell of sweat, perfume and sex that still hung about him.

Minutes later, unchecked tears rolled down her dark face as she mixed bits of seafood and batter together to make the creole bread. Mucous ran from her wide nose, the result of her tears. Eva reached for a nearby cloth to wipe her face, then changed her mind. Using her open palm instead, she cleansed it, then immediately fashioned the chunky balls that would make the dough.

Jay gulped down the remainder of thick coffee and sat back after his meal, satisfied. He was glad Al had obviously drunk heavily the night before, for he had not budged from the pallet on which he slept. It would be easier this way, he and the men could leave without a scene.

He could hear Eva breathing as she sat on the edge of the bed with her back to him, and he wondered why she didn't eat the remainder of the creole bread as she usually did.

For a moment he slipped into the past when everything about Eva had once been smooth and round. Her cheeks, breasts, buttocks and calves, absolutely stimulating to see and touch. But all of that femininity had gone to waste because she wasn't able to bear him a child.

Ah! he thought. Why should he care if she ate at all? As long as she had the strength to cook his food, take care of his clothes and this house, it didn't matter if she ate.

A familiar feeling of resentment set in, and Eva's distorted unattractive features cast the older images aside. He deserved a better woman than Eva anyway. And when everything started rolling smoothly, he would have one.

The sun beamed high above when Jay joined the three other men inside the *buyei's* house. He was pleased with the selection of traveling partners the shaman had chosen.

"I plan to start the *dugu,* for Al in four days," the shaman's worn voice barely carried throughout the room. "The healing would be good if the woman could attend at its peak, her powers would be of great benefit. Either way, all of this must be settled before we go to Dangriga." His huge, tired eyes looked at each of the men as he continued. "The woman's presence with us will make the Shango that much more acceptable and powerful. When she is here, we will have time enough to convince her of our sincerity in wanting to reunite with the Garifuna, and she will understand why we have brought her to Punta Gorda." He sat quietly for a moment, then continued. "Already the scale is tilted in their direction, because the only *dabuyaba*—is housed on their land. Having her with us, will give us stature in their eyes." He drew a long breath. "Yes, scores must be settled, debts paid, but I am old now." His thin shoulders seemed to droop with the admission. "The Shango must not be left without a *buyei*. We are the ones who must present ourselves humbly. Still it can not hurt to have the link already united with us. It would be a powerful sign."

Jay and the others nodded their agreement.

"Now go, my sons," he raised bent arms in release, "and let the spirit of the mighty *orisha*, Shango, be with you."

Consumed by thoughts of the shamaness, Raquel returned to the hut where she and Nate slept, and to a basket she was attempting to weave. She had given the man a mindful glance before turning to the container of slender reeds soaking in a dish of water. His eyes were dosed, and there appeared to be no change in his condition.

The young woman scrutinized the irregularly shaped bottom that was to be the foundation of the basket. Slowly she began to shake her head. No one could ever have convinced her that those basket-weaving classes during summer camp would come in handy one day. Yet here she sat, seeking solace in the task.

Hesitantly Raquel inserted the damp reed into what she hoped was the proper opening to begin her work again. Her smooth brows knitted together as her fingers tussled with the wrapping motions. A thick, black plait she had twined at the crown of her head unraveled and landed on her bare shoulder as she worked, contrasting attractively with her copper skin, and the blood red color of the wrap she wore.

Earlier that day, it surprised her to find the roll of vibrant material beside her clothes when she emerged from bathing in a small nearby pool. Through experimentation and luck, she fashioned a combination African-like sarong from the folds. The soft linen felt good against her skin, and she wondered where the shamaness had bought it, for there was no evidence of a loom, and the material appeared to be quite new. She nearly laughed when she tried to picture the elderly woman sorting through piles of cloth choosing different patterns and colors for herself, when it was obvious from the nondescript robe she wore, and the way she had allowed her thick hair to naturally form into dreadlocks, such worldly things were not her concern.

Raquel looked down at the bright material, and she knew if she'd had her choice, red would not have been her preference. As a youth, her mother had always associated the color with sex, the devil and loose women. The latter term had included their next-door neighbor, Paulette, who loved red, and would allow Raquel to paint her nails in a variety of crimson shades, which sent her mother into a hissy fit every time. She recalled, there had been no love lost between the two women. Even on the day Paulette moved away from the neighborhood, the last words between them were ugly—her mother telling Paulette she was bound for hell. Paulette in turn dooming her mother to a life of pain and misery because of her "restrictin' nature."

Her mother's feelings about the color red had stuck with her, as had so many of her opinions and fears. You would not find anything red in Raquel's closet back in the States. It would be full of the proper clothing for a "professional" woman. Anything else would mean she was teetering too close to the edge, at least that's what she had always believed.

A pang of fear, anger, then regret, coursed through her. The chances of her having an apartment, let alone a closet of orderly clothes and shoes back in Miami was slim. They probably had been tossed out on the curb as she'd seen done before when a tenant was evicted for being delinquent.

A distraught, contempt-filled glance traveled in the direction of where her captor lay, and she was more than surprised when it was met by an unwavering stare, a fully cognizant gaze.

"Well, hello there." She placed the unfinished basket onto the dirt floor, then crossed the room to kneel beside Nate. Her depressing thoughts were quickly supplanted by relief to see him conscious for the first time since their arrival.

"Hello." The word was raspy, as his veiled eyes turned from the woman and looked around the hut.

"Where are we?"

It was difficult for him to speak, his voice was softer, strained, like a person finding out they could speak after a bout with laryngitis.

"You tell me," she offered him a sincere smile, then pivoted to dip a cup in a pail of cool water. "I've been here weaving baskets and studying herbs, while you decided to cop out and take a long, long nap."

Dark, inquisitive eyes searched her face. He was about to speak again, but she pressed the moist cup, with a hollow reed in its midst, in his direction. Automatically he attempted to rise to his elbows, but was overtaken by a dizzy spell. His chin slumped to his chest.

"Be careful," Raquel placed her slender arms about his shoulders, "You've been out of it for about two days. You have to be rather weak."

She didn't know why she wanted to comfort him, to make his awareness of his weakened condition more palatable, but somehow she felt it would not sit well with him to realize how bad off he had been.

Nate shook his head defiantly. He was unaccustomed to being pampered and catered to in this way, and he found his dependent state most annoying. With trembling lips he sought out the makeshift straw she offered him, quenching his dry throat, and stealing a moment to gather his strength. Feeling uncomfortable under her velvety compassionate gaze, he spoke roughly to her.

"And I guess I'm supposed to believe you hung around the entire time just to take care of me?" Cynicism edged the ungrateful question.

Nate knew he was being unfair, but it was shame that made him act this way. Contending with his weak physical condition was one thing, but to think this woman whom he had kidnapped and forced to come to Belize had stayed by his side, caring for him throughout the ordeal—that struck a sound blow.

Guilt and remorse churned inside him—they were feelings he had not experienced since childhood. It was all so foreign to him now, totally unsettling. It was as if a knife had cut into his armor and he felt weak and vulnerable as a result of it. Weakness was something he could not tolerate, and if this woman could bring out that side of him, he wanted nothing to do with her.

Raquel sat back on her haunches. "What if I say I did?"

"I'd say you were a fool, or worse."

Her eyes narrowed in anger. "Well I'll just be damned! And I'd say you were right!" She struggled to rise to her feet, but the cumbersome wrap prohibited a quick ascent.

Hastily Nate placed a solid but weak grip about her wrist.

"No, I'm sorry, *pataki*. Please, don't go," the words tumbled out before he could stop them.

Their eyes met for a moment before he closed his, then lay back inhaling deeply. His words were almost a whisper when he spoke. "I want to thank you." The message in his dark gaze as he looked at her again, was clear.

Raquel's shoulders slumped in resignation. She was tired of being on the defensive, tired of swimming against the current that had totally disrupted her life. Theirs was a most curious relationship. It would be almost comical if it weren't so intense.

She kept her eyes lowered as her mind filtered through her confusing thoughts, her small but able hands lay within each other in her lap. Maybe she could have left him with the shamaness and tried to find her way to civilization and freedom. But something wouldn't allow her to forget how he had never deserted her, and no matter how they had come together, she could not have left him at his weakest.

"*Pataki.*" His long fingers, thinner than before, reached up to caress the side of her face, "Why couldn't things have been different?"

His simple words melted away the small amount of restraint she had managed to hold onto, and her smooth, petite hand reached up to cradle his. Moistness appeared in both sets of eyes, but Raquel's spilt over, dampening his hand as it remained there.

"I don't know why, Nate. I don't know why."

She mouthed the statement over and over again, crying out her anguish at the unfairness of life in presenting her with a man she knew she could love, but who was ultimately her enemy. The young woman turned her tear-stained face and lips further into his receptive palm.

Gradually, Nate allowed his hand to slide around to the back of her neck where he gently drew her down toward him, until he cradled her in his arms, mouthing terms of assurance and support—tender things that his mother had said to him when he was a child.

He turned and placed a kiss in the cluster of cottony, black curls that had formed around her hairline, then drew her in closer to his body, until he could feel her damp cheeks and nose pressed against his neck. She felt so small and soft against him, and he worried that she'd lost weight since the day she'd sat so defiantly on board the sailboat, the wind pressing against her face. All of that seemed so long ago.

Raquel found it was hard to breathe with her face buried so close against him, but it was oh, so comforting. Here within her captor's embrace she felt safe, even cared for. Here she didn't want or need to analyze her feelings, her thoughts, only to give in to them, for never had she experienced such an intensity of emotions.

Somehow they both knew they were crossing over into uncharted waters as they lay within each other's arms. Neither of them was willing or ready to tell the other the truth about themselves, but both were unable to ignore feelings that had developed between them. At the moment those things did not matter; for right now this was enough.

CHAPTER 11

It was barely dawn when the cry of a young animal woke Raquel. Heavy-lidded eyes forced themselves open because of the nagging noise. Outside, the sun was painting breathtaking strokes of gold, orange and rose across the sky. Carefully she slipped out of Nate's sleeping embrace, and ventured into the cool morning air. As she stretched outside the hut, feeling more alive and happy than she could ever remember, the long whining sound began again, and Raquel realized it was coming from inside the shamaness's hut.

With her features clouded over with concern, Raquel quickly entered the space, fearing it was the old woman, in pain or worse, dying. To Raquel's surprise she discovered the shamaness was not alone. Another woman, kneeling against a tree stump that served as a table, was with her, and she in turn held on to the object which was the source of the noise. It was a baby.

No sooner had the crying stopped, than it started again, as the shamaness took a large gathering of fresh herbs and swept them just above the young child's body in cleansing motions.

If the two women were aware of Raquel's presence, they gave no indication of it. The mother's eyes remained riveted upon her squalling child as the shamaness executed several more thrusting motions with the plants, accompanied by words Raquel did not understand.

Had Raquel been thinking dearly, she would have left once she came across this obviously private affair, but the entire scene caught her off guard. It was like watching the enactment of a story Paulette once told her involving an illness and a powerful cleansing. More than once she spoke of almost unbelievable spells and cures she attributed to the *orishas* or gods of a religion called *Santeria*. Raquel had been warned never to repeat these stories to anyone, and she hadn't.

Now that the ritual was complete, two sets of eyes turned in Raquel's direction. The mother holding the now-cooing baby, examined her with avid curiosity, while the shamaness's stare was almost piercing.

"Oh. I'm—I'm sorry. I didn't mean to interrupt anything. I just heard the baby crying and I didn't know . . . I'll just go back—" she nervously turned to leave.

The shamaness's voice halted her. "No. Wait."

Startled, Raquel stopped dead in her tracks.

Hearing the woman's command for Raquel to stay, the grateful mother spoke rapidly, bowing her thanks for the shamaness's help. Agilely she bent down and picked up a small basket covered with a white cloth. She offered the package to the older woman as she revealed its contents, a selection of colorful bird feathers.

Never once offering a smile, the doctor stoically accepted the basket from the beaming mother; and yet her distant attitude did not seem to bother the woman. Instead, shyly but with apparent admiration and a touch of awe, she looked into her stony features as if she wouldn't dare expect more from such a powerful person. Then, her eyes bright with joy and relief, she briskly walked from the hut and joined two other women Raquel hadn't noticed sitting in the rain forest at the edge of the clearing. Chattering like eager birds, they pointed excited fingers in the direction of the hut.

"You are ready to learn more about the 'erbs?" the shamaness addressed her. It was more of a statement than a question.

"Yes. I am if you are ready to teach me."

"What wisdom would there be in discussin' it if I were not ready?" she retorted, as she bundled up the ritual herbs that she intended to discard.

The woman's change of heart toward teaching Raquel was unexpected. She didn't know if she should be grateful or apprehensive.

"None, I guess," she remained rooted to the spot near the hut's entrance.

"Do you expect me to teach you from there?" her dreadlocked head tilted to the side, as she placed bony fingers on hips totally hidden underneath her clothes.

"No of course not. It's just that I need time to get ready."

A perturbed, mostly grey eyebrow rose to show the bush doctor's impatience with her would-be student, forcing the young woman to explain.

"Nate . . . the man I came here with, became conscious for a while yesterday evening, and I'd like to check on him this morning before we get started."

Without addressing her further, the shamaness crossed the room and exited the hut. Raquel didn't know if she had offended her again, so she sought to appease her. "I mean, I will do it that way if its all right with you." She followed her, surprised she was headed for the second hut.

"You should have told me when he awakened," she rebuked her. "His broth mus' change now so that he can quickly regain his strength."

"Well everything happened so fast I didn't have time to think about it." Somehow the woman made her feel like a careless child.

The shamaness swept into the hut with her pendulous dreads reaching out about her, like antennas tuned to receive the vast messages of the universe. She was not pretty to behold. Actually she was a forceful sight, and this caused a wide-awake Nate to question his lucidity. He had no memory of the aid the woman had given them, and was more than a little relieved to see Raquel in her wake. Her presence assured him that he had not crossed over to the other side while he slept, that he still resided in the land of the living.

"You have been your own wors' enemy, man. Not takin' care of that snakebite when it first happened. The forces mus' be with you, a weaker person would have died. Of course, I did not tell your woman that." She jerked her head in Raquel's direction.

Raquel was forced to hide an amused smile behind her hand at the absurd, confused look that appeared on Nate's face. He looked in her direction as if asking for reassurance, all she could give him was a comical hunching of her small shoulders.

"A combination of beans and my special 'erbs should get you started." The shamaness raised his pants leg and checked the punctures, then shook her head with satisfaction. "That ez after you've drank plenty of the juices I will give to you."

Raquel just stood there looking rather dimwitted. She didn't know what to think of this talkative creature who had replaced the silent bush doctor of the last few days.

With uncharacteristic strength for her age, the shamaness removed the hot pot from the makeshift rack above the fire.

"Give it a few moments to cool, then throw the broth out into the forest, afterwards take it to the pond an' rinse it thoroughly, by then I will be ready to start the beans. Then you," looking directly at Raquel, "will be ready for your lessons."

A shroud of roped hair framed her angular face as she turned back to Nate, "Two days with my medicines an' you will be strong enough to travel, that ez if you don't use up too much of your strength on other things," she announced insinuatingly as she rose to depart, leaving Nate and Raquel stunned and amused by her last remark.

"After seeing her, I'm sure I have missed quite a bit over the last few days," he shook his head with disbelief, a half-baked smile on his face. "So you've got to fill me in whenever you get a chance, that is, between the chores you've been assigned and your other duties that have been heaped on you by your great and powerful master," he broke into uncontrollable laughter.

A picture of the dreaded, hump-backed shamaness pointing a bony finger and ordering the docile and obedient young woman around, replayed in his head. This was the same woman who had almost fought him every step of the way since he met her, even though he had to admit, she had reasons for wanting to go against him.

At first Raquel assumed it was the stress and strain, and powerful herbs he'd been forced to take, that had finally taken their toll on him. She had never seen this man truly smile before, let alone laugh, and somehow she didn't feel comfortable thinking that she was the prime target of his glee.

"What's so funny?" She attempted to keep a straight face, but it was all in vain, for his laughter was contagious. Before she knew it, she had joined in with the raucous noise, flopping down on the hut's dirt floor and laughing until tears ran down her cheeks.

Neither one of them really knew what was so funny. If they laughed at themselves for being in such an extraordinary situation, or at the outlandish statement the bush doctor made before she left.

Their unabandoned outbreak seemed to excite the animals in the rain forest as well, and their chatter and cooing swelled with the continuous laughter inside the hut.

Doubled over with hysterics, Nate stretched a frolicsome arm out and caught hold of Raquel's ankle. His touch sent tingles up her leg, and she playfully kicked at his hand so he would release her. They continued to laugh, both of them lost in a moment of complete camaraderie. It was marvelous to behold the twinkle of joy in the other's eyes, the sound of the other's laughter unknowingly becoming a treasured jewel.

Even in his semiweakened condition, Nate proved to be the stronger as he lay on his stomach supported by his elbows, holding tightly to both Raquel's feet. Still she resisted him, her knees pumping mechanically, while she attempted to pull down her wrap which was inching up because of her thrashing movements.

Suddenly two pairs of glistening, velvety dark eyes met and they stopped their childlike play, panting and catching their breath in the aftermath. In an instant an atmosphere of lighthearted laughter had turned into a communication of electrically charged passion, and a barrage of emotions surfaced in their eyes as they watched one another closely.

Nate's light grip on her ankles was doing strange things to her breathing, and Raquel could feel her heart begin to flutter.

"Pataki—"

Afraid of what he was about to say, as well as of her own response, Raquel cut him off. "I think the broth may have cooled a little by now," she looked for an inconsequential end to the awkward moment. Gently she extracted her legs from his hold, he, in turn, did not resist her.

Although the pot still steamed, she found two large cloths to shield her hands and aid her in the removal of the metal container. She had to do something. Anything. The feelings that had arisen inside her as she looked in his eyes were powerful, more powerful than her ability to refuse him, more powerful than her ability to refuse herself.

Silently, Nate watched her movements with veiled eyes as she carefully walked to the entrance with her load.

"Pataki," the name was thick with passion.

"Yes," she barely recognized her own voice. It trembled with a tingling fear, a heightened anticipation. Feathery lashes raised to view the man who sat behind her on the dirt floor. Cordlike tendons within his firm arms stretched to their limits as he balanced himself, his fists, large balls in the dust, his knees spread evenly apart.

"You must give in to me willingly . . . or not at all."

She nodded her head before walking through the opening.

Nate eased himself down onto his side. He could tell he was far from being his normal self, but from what he could remember, he felt much better than the day before.

Nate thought about the amount of time they'd lost, nearly four days. If his calculations were right, it would be about three days before they held the main ceremony in Dangriga. Initially he had planned to get there well ahead of the festivities, but it was far too late for that now. He would have to work within the time frame they had, hopefully nothing else would hamper their progress. Involuntarily his thoughts switched to Jay and Al.

It was obvious by now, Jay had a hidden agenda outside of wanting to have the woman present for the spiritual ceremony. Nate only wished he knew what it was. Yet there was one thing he did know. If he was right about Jay, it wouldn't be long before he would come looking for her, and he wouldn't come alone.

Nate's pulse quickened as his mind digressed to the feel of the woman's slender ankles within his grip. They were tiny and feminine, like her smooth feet beneath them. He wanted this woman in a way he had never wanted anyone else. If he could make her come to him willingly, he knew that he could truly possess her, and it was so very important to him that he did.

It had taken him years to feel as if he really controlled his life, his environment. That's why it angered him so that he could not have foreseen all the things that had taken place since they reached Belize.

For years his family ties had made it hard for him to be in control of his own life, and now that he possessed control, he would never relinquish that power to anyone.

Nate remembered an awful time when he had felt totally helpless. Life's tragedies had poured their fury upon him, leaving him stunned and confused. Death is never an easy pill to swallow. It is doubly hard when it takes people you love, like Cecilia . . . and his mother.

Ever since he was a little boy, she had always taught him to have faith in the powers, allow them to mold his life, they would not guide him wrong. In the end, both Cecilia and his mother had died, a result of his people's faith. Their deaths did not destroy his belief, but they forced him to understand he must always have control of his own life, that way, the choices and their consequences would be of his own making.

That is why his feelings for this woman vexed him so. They had surfaced unexpectedly, an overpowering need to love her, protect her.

Nate knew he was an excellent judge of character, but if he went by what he'd gleaned since she'd been forced into his life, he would consider her a good woman. A strong one. The kind that he seldom came across in the circles he chose to travel in, and when he did he shied away from them. With his lifestyle, he'd found they were a hindrance and managed to complicate things. No. He preferred women with whom he knew where he stood. And all that was important to them was compensation in one way or another. That way there were never any strings attached, for he had learned the hard way, if you could love, you could also be hurt.

He wasn't so sure about this woman. But in the beginning he thought he knew what kind of woman she was. That she lived life in the fast lane, and that meant she carried all the baggage that came with it. Men. Alcohol. Drugs. Maybe the telltale signs had been stripped away here in the wilderness, but they would probably surface overnight when she was back in her own environment, he cautioned himself. Yes. She was doing what she had to do to survive, like a chameleon, adapting to her environment. Still, he had to admit, she was doing a damn good job of it. But he convinced himself, staying by his side and taking care of him was all a part of her game, a masterful con. That way, when he came to, he'd be beholding to her.

Nate rubbed the new growth on his face as he gathered his thoughts. The reality was, she could not have found her way out of the rain forest without help. Even if she had tried, her chance of finding someone who would really help her was very slim. Strange things had been known to happen in Central America. Women being sold into slavery was simply one of them. No, she'd played it safe, and he'd played right into her manipulative hands. Sure he was weak for her, and any man near death could have a change of heart. He would just have to remember who she was.

Purposefully he pushed away the nagging uncertainties about the woman. But one thing would still hold true—he would still have her on his terms. Then when they reached Dangriga their unholy alliance would come to an end.

He gathered himself together to try and stand. He had to start exercising, regaining his strength so they could leave tomorrow.

Slowly he rose to his full height, clasping his hand over his eyes as a lightheadedness overtook him. His left leg, adorned with the remnants of the bite and a dark poisonous streak was weakest, but he forced it to hold its own. He hobbled around the interior of the hut, grasping hold of convenient supports along the way. A pile of vibrant floral material caught his eye—it was the wrap skirt he'd acquired for the woman in the Mayan village. Immediately strong stirrings erupted inside him.

"Dammit! I'll have her tonight. Then this *obedah* will be out of my system. That's what I need to do," he tried to convince himself. "After that I'll be just fine," but a small voice inside of him wasn't so sure.

Raquel's hamstrings felt tight from all the squatting, as she tried to concentrate on the flowering plant the shamaness now insisted that she focus upon. Hours had passed since they'd entered the forest and the old woman began pouring out her knowledge of plants and herbs, their hazards and their positive qualities. Raquel could not figure out how the woman expected she would remember even one fourth of the things she'd been told. Even if she'd had a photographic memory, it would have been impossible.

Yellow pollen covered the tips of the shamaness's forefinger and thumb as she plucked the daisylike, tiny, white blossom with yellow interior from its downy stem. It was pleasantly aromatic with yellowish-green leaves.

"This plant's name tells of its main purpose, feverfew. It can break a fever." Her liquidy, heavily hooded eyes locked with Raquel's. "It was one of the 'erbs I mixed into your tea the first night, it ez also good to help calm a person, help them focus."

Raquel shook her weary head in understanding.

Briskly the shamaness stood up and made her way further along into the rain forest. Stooping again, she called to the young woman. "Here ez a very powerful 'erb," a gravelly chuckle rose in her throat. Raquel stood above her gazing down at the profuse, dotted leaf plants.

Impatiently the shamaness motioned for her to come closer.

"Smell."

Obeying her instruction, Raquel bent over stiffly, and inhaled the scent of the small leaves. She nearly choked from the unpleasant odor.

"It ez St. Juan's wort," the elderly woman informed her, satisfied that she would not forget its potent aroma. "It flowers yellow in the summer, and both its flowers and leaves can be made to give a red oil. It ez good for many thin's from stomach pains to asthma. But it can also bring on wonderful feelin's, if taken in larger amounts."

Raquel continued to hold the back of her hand against her nose, then allowed it to travel up to her eyes, where she gratefully closed them.

"I'm really thankful for all the things you've been telling me, but I'm so tired. Do you think we could do the remainder of this tomorrow?"

"I do not think you can afford to be tired."

With furrowed brows Raquel looked at her, confused. "What do you mean?"

"You will need much knowledge to fool the Garifuna an' the Shango, or the *gubida* will not come through you."

Raquel stood stunned at the woman's words. Why would the *gubida* come through *her*? What was she in Belize for? What was going to happen to her? Questions raced through her mind, as her knees buckled and she almost sat down in the midst of the St. John's wort.

"What do you mean?"

"You are not Garifuna or Shango," the shamaness barked at her. "If you are to be in the ceremony, there is much you must know."

Raquel felt the hairs stand up on her arms as she took in the eerie vision of the shamaness who remained on her haunches beside her.

It was late afternoon, and the setting sun's dying rays emanated brightly behind her powerful countenance. Several thick dreads that grew from the top of her head, appeared to be alive with energy, as dazzling hues of gold, orange and red sparkled about them.

How could this woman have known why she was here in Belize? Did her powers go beyond her knowledge of herbs and roots, into realms that Raquel had been reluctant to even acknowledge? She had mentioned the *gubida* only once, and that conversation had ended in vain. Never had she spoken of the Garifuna and the Shango, yet the shamaness knew her very safety depended on her assumed connection with these groups.

"I—I never said I was," Raquel stammered, feeling it was useless to deny the truth.

"You know many believe you are," she squinted her ancient eyes perceptively, "if they did not, you would not be here, or . . . you would be dead."

The grave truth of her statement made Raquel acknowledge a fear that she'd lived with since the beginning of this nightmare. If it were ever found out that she was not Jackie Dawson, her life would not be worth a penny.

Immense anxiety began to rise inside her as she thought of Jay and Al, a more poignant shudder shook her as she thought of Nate.

"But how did you know about this?"

"I may live alone here in the forest, but there ez little I don't know. Villagers like the women you saw this morning come to me for 'elp when they feel there ez no one else they can turn to. It ez at those times I am told many thin's," she licked her leathery lips. "She told me of a woman, a descendant of the Garifuna an' the Shango, a connection with the *gubida*, ez expected to attend the settlement ceremony in Dangriga. It ez a very important time. It will mean the bringing together of the Garifuna an' the Shango. A rift tore the groups apart many years ago.

"The diviners of both sides say the signs show this woman can speak to the dead ancestors of both the Garifuna an' the Shango. There must be communication between the ancestors, before there can be communication between the livin'. This ez what they believe."

The shamaness plucked two tender leaves from a group of St. Juan's wort, carefully she placed one upon her thick tongue, the other she offered to Raquel. Stunned, the young woman accepted the piece of plant, then mimicked the woman's actions.

"These are secret rituals. It ez taboo for outsiders to know about them. Never are they involved. It would be dangerous for them to do so." Intently her old eyes watched as Raquel's frightened ones expanded as she listened. A strange smirk appeared amongst her wrinkles, as if she were drawing pleasure from the young woman's fear.

"Not because the Garifuna or the Shango would 'arm them, even though there may be some with powers who would place what ez called as *bilongos*, black magic spell, on the outsider. The real danger may come from the *orishas* for dabbling in their affairs. But if an outsider were to pretend to be one of the Garifuna or Shango, there would no doubt be those among the groups who would want to 'arm them."

Raquel swallowed visibly after the threat. The bitter taste of the herb was strong but seemed to have a rejuvenating effect upon the shattered woman.

Angry thoughts stormed through her mind as she thought about her unsavory position. She had not asked for any of this. There was nothing for her to gain. But here she sat in the middle of a Central American rain forest, staring into the face of a woman who spoke poignantly about her pending death. Defensively, Raquel struck back at her.

"So why are you telling me all this? You know I am not this person that they think I am, so why didn't you just tell them and get it over with?"

A spark of amusement appeared in the greying eyes.

"Because it would please me to play a part in foolin' those who did not want to acknowledge my power, simply because I am a woman."

Several brown nubs where teeth used to be appeared as she skinned her lips back in what was supposed to be a smile, then her gaze took on a distant look.

"Yes, they all knew I had the abilities an' the knowledge, but they refused to accept me as a shaman, because I was female," she continued.

"I grew up in a small settlement between Dangriga an' Punta Gorda. Most of the people who lived there were Shango, although there was a Mayan village not very far away, so there was much mingling between them. That is why I am a mixture of Shango an' Mayan," she proudly stated. "I was a curious child, an' had been allowed to attend a small school for all of the children in the area. Because of my seekin' nature, the teacher, an Englishwoman who had settled here with her husband, an archeologist, would send for special books for me to read. I became very knowledgeable about many thin's, but I also burned to know more about my people an' their beliefs, so I sought this knowledge any way I could. For years it did not matter, but as time went by and I matured, my Mayan father felt the time had come for me to wed one of the villagers. He felt I was becomin' too independent in my thinkin', and I was. I did not want to marry the villager he had chosen or any other man," she defiantly declared.

"The wisdom I had gained through the years surpassed any of the males in the village, even the *buyei*, an' I told them so. I told them none of the men were worthy of me, an' that I should be *buyei* of the village. Had I been of Garifunian descent this may not have been a problem, even though my arrogance must have roused them deeply. But being of Mayan and Shango ancestry, it was unthinkable. It ez important to the Shango that the *buyei* be male because they are named for the powerful and violent *orisha*, Shango, who ez the perfect symbol of the male sex.

"After that they tried to force my hand, but I ran away an' retreated far into the rain forest, to the place where I live now.

"Through the years my wisdom an' therefor' my power has grown. With time, there were incidents that spawned rumors of my abilities, frightening stories," her eyes gleamed wickedly. "Since then no one has dared to cross me, only those seekin' my help venture near to my home."

"So that is why the Balamians were afraid to attack you?"

"That ez why," she nodded gravely, then an impulsive glimmer entered her gaze. "But through you I can seek my revenge. The ultimate shame would be for an outsider to take part in their secret rituals, and by powers acquired through me, deceive them."

"So that's it," Raquel rose on to her knees. "You want to use me." Her anger and frustration mounted as she glared at her. "Just two weeks ago, if I hadn't agreed to being used by someone else, I wouldn't even be in the mess I'm in now. Once is enough. Thank you. After all of this, if I survive, maybe I will have learned my lesson."

"Ump . . . maybe. But there ez no other way for you to get through this without being discovered. I want to use you, but you need me in order to survive." The shamaness rose to her feet. "You are a very open spirit. What I want to do would be impossible if you were not," she eyed her appreciatively. "Word ez, a group of Shango men are headed this way, lookin' for a man and a woman. The woman ez the link to the *gubida*," the shamaness announced. "It will take them another day or so before they reach this area. You would do well to use this time wisely," she warned, then continued. "Let me pour the needed knowledge into your mind an' spirit. I swear it will not 'arm you. In the end, it will only aid you in the spiritual evolution that all human beings must go through."

Raquel looked at the strange woman who stood before her. She had called her an open spirit. The words struck a deep cord within her. Even as a child she had sought refuge in quiet moments alone. In her desire to escape her restricted environment her ability to open herself to her imagination had become acute.

Raquel couldn't help but think of how throughout her life, she had been plagued by the consequences of her mother's past. The lines and perimeters had been drawn early. Without a male in their house, and because of her mother's fervent religious beliefs, she had grown up under stringent rules. There had been rules and times for everything, and the system of rules could never be broken without dire consequences. Every good and evil deed one committed was being recorded, but her mother eagerly informed her, it would take many good acts to lessen the effect of just one sinister deed, and to her mother the simplest of mistakes was considered signs of wickedness.

Lucille Mason could see wickedness everywhere. She saw wickedness in the outside world and insisted Raquel remain within the walls of their home where it was safe. She changed her name from Mercenez, a constant reminder of Raquel's father's wickedness. Raquel would never forget how Lucy saw wickedness in a fatherly hug Raquel received from a fellow church member and loudly banished Mr. Harrison from their household.

In order to understand her mother's obsessiveness, Raquel decided to become a counselor and so that one day she would be able to help other people understand themselves.

She watched as her mother became more withdrawn and judgmental through the years, obviously fearing her daughter's march toward adulthood, and her inevitable leaving. Constantly, she cast taboos and roadblocks into her young fertile mind about many things, but especially when it came to the opposite sex, not knowing the long-term effects they would eventually have.

She knew it was bizarre to think, but somehow, at first, she felt her mother was almost relieved to hear she had developed multiple sclerosis. It was something else to permanently bind her daughter to her side.

"You won't be able to leave me now," she had pleaded, eyes brimming with tears, but not a trace of sorrow in their depths. "It was because of my love and concern for you that I remained here, instead of following your father to the Dominican, where I could have been happy." Then she pointedly asked, "You won't leave me, will you, Raquel?"

Of course, every time her answer was no.

Now she believed it was her strong unyielding stance, demanding her mother be allowed to live with her and Clinton when they got married, that had put a strain on the relationship. Yet, there was another disturbing reason. She realized that her mother's spoon-feeding her negativity towards men throughout the years had been very fruitful.

It had taken years before Clinton had been able to coax her into making love, but then, the few times they had, it had been extremely unfulfilling for her, and undoubtedly for him. During their last words on the telephone, he had called her "cold and ungiving." It had hurt badly, but deep inside, Raquel felt his painful words were not true.

She knew there were times when consuming waves of emotions would rake through her. Like at the sight of a couple in a heated, mounting embrace in a movie, or while reading a romance novel, and now, at the touch or even a glance from Nate.

A sudden panic enveloped her. What if Clinton were right? What if her mother's teachings had helped to mold her into a woman who was simply unable to really give of herself? That she was able to feel at a distance, but when the moment of truth arrived she would completely shut down. A woman like that could never satisfy and hold Nate. He would only desire someone whose passion was as fiery as his own.

Now, once again, she faced being a pawn to someone else's past. But this was different, she thought, as she stared into the foreign, weathered face that watched her closely. The bush doctor's revenge on her past could be Raquel's ticket to life.

"What must I do in order to receive this knowledge?"

"I must make your mind an' spirit willin' to accept it. As you know, we don't have much time, but through your open spirit and the use of 'erbs, mainly the blue passion flower, I can mold them to what we both need."

The young woman's face was a concentrated mask when she gave her answer. "Then let's do it quickly, before I change my mind."

Dusk was fast approaching when Nate looked out the hut's entrance for the umpteenth time. He couldn't understand what the woman and the shamaness could be doing in the forest for so long. It worried him a bit, but he felt if anyone knew these parts the shamaness did. So he would just have to wait patiently until their return.

The bean soup she'd prepared for him had become ready much earlier during the day, and he'd eaten most of the tasty concoction. Some of the seasonings were familiar, bringing up memories of when his family resided in Dangriga. But other tastes were odd—still it all comprised a unique blend.

As the day wore on, and he felt his strength returning, he became anxious for something to do. As he looked around, one of several pieces of wood he discovered during a walk around the clearing caught his eye. Picking it up, he turned it over in his hands, exploring the grainy surface. It was a beautiful chunk of dead cypress, and Nate thought it was large enough for him to carve a simple drumlike box, but he would need some kind of tool to do it. Because he had explored the hut thoroughly, he knew there was nothing here that could serve his purpose, so he decided to look in the shamaness's shanty.

It was Nate's first conscious visit inside the hut, and the variety and number of objects he saw amazed him. Slowly, his dark eyes began a perusal of the room. He was inside the cluttered space only a few moments, when his curious examination was cut short by the menacing growl of a lounging jaguarundi. Caught off guard by the animal's presence, he grabbed a nearby rusted knife. He quickly backed out with his carving tool in hand.

It took some time before the dull knife was sharp enough for carving. Being a perfectionist at heart, he attempted to remove all the rust on its surface against a flat stone. He had carved a lot as a boy, and he knew the edge had to be just so before the blade would render its best work. Finally he was ready to begin, and after removing the bark, he placed all his creative concentration on the light-colored wood. Time passed effortlessly as he worked, and before long the instrument was almost complete.

With proficient eyes, Nate checked to make sure the sides and the bottom of the hollow box fitted together smoothly before he began to place a carved top into place. He had cut different designs into the flat piece of wood, most of them long and slender, some with bulbous ends, others

with prongs that stretched outward like fingers. The wood that remained, when struck, would yield a range of deep melodious plucking
sounds, characteristic of a highly tuned bongo.

Satisfied the box was snug, he snapped the instrument's lid into place,
then ran practiced fingers across its surface and sides. Using a rod he
fashioned specifically for this purpose, he struck several of the prongs,
and they yielded a lavish range of sounds. Yes, he thought, in such a short
period of time he'd done well.

Settling with his back against the wall and the bongo box in his lap, he
struck the prongs again, making himself familiar with each sound. It was-
n't long before he began to beat out the rhythm of a familiar tune, while
he waited for the women to return.

CHAPTER 12

Raquel stared at the beautiful flower sheltered underneath the thick cover of a healthy fern. Large yellowish petals, with a vibrant center of bluish-violet spikes, were crowned by pistils and stamens of equally complementary hues. Yet, what amazed her most, was the orangy fruit that had grown in the midst of its picturesque center.

"This ez what you shall eat," and the shamaness bent down and extracted the fruit from its home. "It ez very sweet an' delicious, an' will shield the bitter taste of the St. Juan's wort that you must also ingest." The elderly woman surveyed the area around them. "It ez good this passion flower has grown so close to the pond, for the water will aid me in what I must do."

Raquel looked out onto the tranquil water where the moon reflected luminously against its surface. Calmly she sat down beside its shore, and held the fruit that had been broken open by the bush doctor's withered hands. Determinedly she took a healthy bite from its center.

There was no doubt in her mind what she was about to embark on would be considered an evil deed by many. Anything that acknowledged powers outside the church's belief in which she had grown up, would be considered a product of the devil, of Satan. But for her, that inner battle had been rectified long ago when she became interested in the Eastern way of healing. She realized there was so much she did not know or understand.

Her explorations had led her to shiatsu, a form of massage using acupressure. Now, as an adult, she believed anything that brought relief and joy could only come from the highest source, no matter what name a person chose to call it. She finally had begun to free her mind from the shackles of fear put inside her by her mother's misgivings. Yet Raquel knew that a part of her mind, the part that controlled her body, still remained in chains.

The shamaness was right. The blue passion flower's fruit was delicious, and she gratefully munched on its yellow pulp, avoiding the many seeds. Every once in a while she would place a leaf from St. Juan's wort into her mouth, until she had consumed more than she could remember of the tiny pieces.

As she neared the end of the second half of the fruit, she involuntarily began to focus on the moon's reflection in the pond. Like a giant luminous ball, it quivered ever so slightly in the water. It turned into a beckoning hand and seemed to draw her towards it.

Somewhere in the back of her mind she heard a plucking noise, and the reflection began to dance back and forth to its beat. Her transfixed eyes remained glued to the enticing surrealistic orb, as it bobbed to the rhythm of the pond's ripples.

Raquel thought she heard the shamaness chanting softly beside her, but she wasn't sure, nor did she care, as the most wonderful feeling began to embrace her. Willingly she gave in to the power of the moon's reflection and the vibratory hum of human sounds being whispered in her ear. Over and over again they would swell and fall in unison, until she anticipated the crescendos and valleys of the rhythmic noise. The young woman could not remember when she and the intonations became one, and time passed without notice. Her only recollection was of a wonderfully talented light, who could dance, sing and practically fly.

Some time later, Raquel's dark, flashing eyes began to focus on the weary ones before her. The shamaness looked exhausted, while she felt mildly energized but normal. There was no tingling in her fingers, she did not see a glow emanate from her body. Did the "magic", the power transference, work? Was her soul open enough to accept what the shamaness had to offer? Would she be able to fool everyone, including Nate?

"Are we done?" she asked nervously. "I mean, did it work?"

"Yes," the shamaness answered wearily. "The transfer ez complete." The old woman sighed as she recounted how there had been resistance in Raquel's mind before the channeling of her own mind's power and wisdom could be completed. With a satisfied smile, the shamaness watched her.

A deep sigh escaped the shamaness's pleated lips. "You won't see or feel a change, girl. The knowledge will only arise at the appointed time.

That ez, when the *orishas* are called durin' the spiritual ceremony. Your life will remain the same," the elderly woman assured her. "The small leather pouch that I have placed on a cord around your neck, 'olds several very powerful female objects. A necklace of white and blue beads, seashells and stones found by the seashore. When the time ez right, you must place the beaded necklace about your neck, an' clasp the shells and stones tightly within your palms. You must think of the sea, an' the ocean, an' imitate its movements with your body, the rest will take place naturally," she balanced the tightly packed, small leather sack in the palm of her hand. "As for tonight, on an' off, you will continue to feel the euphoric, sometimes hypnotic effect of the 'erbs, but even that will be gone by mornin'."

Sensuously, Rachel began to rub her tiny hands across her head, but found her hair was no longer braided. Thick locks hung spiritedly about her shoulders, the moisture in the air adding to their volume, puffing them up into a black voluminous cloud.

"My hair—why is it loose?"

The shamaness managed a weak smile.

"Many do not understand the power of a person's hair. When allowed to grow freely an' in its natural state, it ez like a virtual tribute to the female energy in creation. Fertile understandin' an' yieldin' energy. It ez a tribute in its own right and should be worn proudly."

Raquel watched as the woman rose slowly to her feet. "Now, it ez time for us to go. I am finish."

As they approached the clearing in which the two huts stood, a soul-stirring rhythm of bongo beats could be heard. As if with the approaching steps of a powerful animal, they pranced in the dark, complementing the natural night sounds. The closer they came, the more compelling the music became to Raquel. By the time they reached the clearing, Raquel felt as if the beating had somehow entered inside of her. Sensually, with eyes closed, she moved her head from side to side, mimicking the sound with her continuous motions.

Despite her fatigue, the shamaness's eyes shone with anticipation. Secretly, she had known of the lustful effect the transference and wearing off of the herbs would have on the young woman, but she had chosen not to tell her. Her eager body would have no choice but to reflect the dose of spiritual power her mind had gained.

"It ez the life of the music you are feelin'," the grated voice whispered. "Some believe music ez a connection between the all powerful an' the mortal. So enjoy, young one. Bathe in the sensations that will arise in you, the emotions that will master you, for tonight will be a great night of blue passion."

With those parting words the shamaness entered her hut, leaving

Raquel standing alone, just outside the place where Nate played the erotic sounds.

Slowly, but with excitement, the young woman approached the entrance, then stood with eyes aflame as she watched him play beside the fire.

Inside, searing tongues of orange and yellow appeared to leap to the beat, casting hypnotic shadows on the walls of the small hut. The entire scene was an aphrodisiac, fanning the flames of Raquel's potent desires.

Unaware of Raquel's presence, Nate's muscular shoulders were intensely hunched forward as he played the coercing cadence. A pumping bulge appeared and disappeared in his upper arm as he gripped the stick that ignited the carnal sound.

Thick lashes cast shadows upon his cheeks as he closed his eyes, oblivious to everything else. Suddenly, the soft pink tip of his tongue flicked onto the upper corner of his lip, as he leaned forward toward his instrument, feeling the beat he'd made.

Raquel's breaths began to come in deep rushes as his virility seemed to reach out and touch her. She grabbed hold of the sides of the entrance as a rousing tingle coursed through her, causing her to become weak in the knees and lightheaded. There was no doubt she could blame the surge of lustful feelings that were spilling over within her on the shamaness's herbs, but she could not deny the seed for them had been there all along. The herbs simply allowed them to break free.

It was at that moment Nate felt her presence. Purposeful dark eyes turned to embrace her, then became hooded at the unexpected carnal picture she made.

Raquel's head had dropped with the unexpected rush of desire. Now, as it subsided, she threw back her head, causing the jet, cottony billow surrounding her narrow face to quiver ever so slightly. It was then that their eyes locked, hers full of passion, his with a dawning curiosity.

Nate never stopped beating the box as his eager eyes traveled up from her trim ankles to the wide expanse of firm calf and thigh visible through the opening in her wrap. As a matter of fact, he began to beat the instrument even more intensely, beckoning her to join in with the rhythm, as he rotated his shoulders enticingly. He remembered how she had danced in the club before, and the thought of it caused his loins to tighten.

Nate had no idea what had occurred in the rain forest, but there was no doubt in his mind that the sensual creature standing before him would be his before the night was through. Somewhere, she had cast aside her reluctance to give herself willingly, and that suited his purposes all the more.

Abruptly, as if commanding her to begin, he struck a rapid succession of notes, then rose slowly to his feet. Taking catlike steps he began to cross the room in her direction. Each move, accompanied by the same five primitive sounds. By the time he had traveled halfway across the room, Raquel's body was replying to his unspoken challenge.

She began to anticipate each succession of beats, her frame swaying to its rhythm. Raquel would thrust her full breasts forward, leaning temptingly toward him long enough to entice him, only to withdraw as he stepped toward her. Her backward step rivaling his forward one.

It was only for a short period of time that Nate allowed the dance of prey and predator, for he couldn't help but be mesmerized as he watched her backing closer and closer to the flame, their shadowed forms reflecting the erotic scene on a gigantic scale.

Subconsciously, Raquel still played out her unwillingness to surrender to him through their mock chase. But because her dark gaze remained riveted upon his, she knew when he began to tire and wanted more. So like a sensual animal, she implored him to continue, promising him more if he would give it. It was the only way she could cope with the seething physical need that always existed, but had been made unbearable by the herbs. Her body yearned to be touched by him, but deep inside she was still afraid to surrender. So she siphoned off pleasure from the passion in his eyes, seeking its nourishment.

"Don't stop, Nate," she purred. "I will dance for you, if you don't. I will do anything for you, Nate, if you don't stop." Teasing, heavily lashed eyes taunted him from beside the fire.

A deadly glint entered his dark eyes, and he caught a portion of his generous bottom lip within his teeth. He held it there.

"Oh-h. Do you promise?" was his husky response, and she nodded affirmatively, her pouting lips parting ever so slightly. "Um-m," the sound vibrated deep in his throat. "Well, I'm going to play for you, baby. Don't you worry about that." He picked up the pace of the sensual tune.

With lingering fingers, Raquel traced the rim of the wrap across the tops of her copper mounds, until they rested on the knotted material that held it all together, certain his gaze would follow her every move.

Unyielding, his eyes froze on her lithe hands as she prolonged the teasing motion, then laughed somewhat wickedly, before snatching it apart and thrusting the length of material to the other side of the hut.

Nate felt and heard his breath catch in his throat as she flaunted her nudity before him, the fire giving her reddish-brown skin a golden overtone. He knew he had seen her nude before, but this time, there was pure passion exhibited by every part of her. He allowed her a few more moments as the swaying, gyrating temptress, but he had come to his limit in visual fulfillment, and was ready for something much more tangible.

Displaying the agility of a panther, he lunged forward and grabbed her by her slender waist, drawing her into his bare chest, the leather pouch the only barrier between them as he held her possessively.

"I am through playing, *pataki*," he stared down into her smoky eyes. "Playing is for children and I am nobody's child."

The shock of his quick embrace helped to clear the lust-filled fog she had been under. A flicker of fear flashed in her velvety eyes, and her mouth parted slightly as if to murmur a sudden protest.

His perceptive gaze detected the ember of apprehension, and a deep growl emanated from inside his throat, "Ah-h, it is far too late for that, little one. There is no way I am going to let you change your mind."

A strong hand reached up to cup her chin, swiftly followed by his soft but firm lips upon hers. The height of desire Raquel had evoked in Nate was apparent through his searing kiss. With dauntless fervor his tongue sought out the moistness within, as his eager hands traveled down the length of her back to cup her exposed bottom. At first her mechanical response went unnoticed by him, until he sought to mold her more deeply into his hard frame, only to find what had been a lithe beckoning body, had now turned stiff and unyielding.

Abruptly he grabbed her shoulders, then shoved her far away from him in order to see the entire length of her. By now he was totally angered by her less-than-ardent response.

"Woman, I'll be damned if you will deny me tonight," he swore. "Who do you think you are, playing with me like this?" he demanded, shaking her. "Or is this part of the cat and mouse game you play in Miami with all the men you go to bed with? Do you like to hear them beg for it?"

Once again he cupped her chin, but this time his hold was rough, demanding. "I will not beg."

Raquel stood speechless as she watched his fury mount. She was confused by her own actions. She knew she wanted him, her body cried out for his touch, but her mind remained a captive of years of primness and order on which she prided herself. All her grand education helped her to analyze herself, but it couldn't free her. She felt so ashamed. How could she blatantly flaunt herself before him, then turn as cold as ice when he began to collect what she had offered.

"I'm not playing a game, Nate," she finally managed to say as his thumb and third finger pressed hard into her jaw bone.

There was pure anger in his eyes, but further inside their depths, there was a tinge of hurt. It was the latter that made Raquel continue.

"How can I make you understand when I don't quite understand myself," she pleaded. "I want you Nate . . . but I am just afraid. Afraid of you . . . of all of this . . . but also afraid of things from long ago that you had nothing to do with." Her slender hand came up to enfold the taut one that remained on her face. She shook her head passionately. "If we do this, what will it mean when this is all over? There are so many things you do not know about me, and I know so little about you." Her troubled eyes searched his for answers.

Nate did not know what kind of response he had expected from this woman, but he was sure it was not the sincere outpouring he had just heard. Overwhelmed by emotion he gently drew her head into his chest.

"Dammit, what kind of woman are you, *pataki?*" he swore at her softly, stroking her ebony cloud of hair. "I didn't come here equipped with a crystal ball so I can't say what is going to happen. But I promise one thing, as long as you are with me no harm will come to you. You have touched me in a way I've never been touched before."

Relief flooded her as she heard his reassuring words. Tenderly she looked up into his face. "And you have touched a place in me, Mr. Nate."

She rose on to her tiptoes and placed a lingering kiss upon his lips. "Two people couldn't go through this much together without consequences."

Nate's dark eyes clouded with emotion, then he sighed, deeply.

"*Pataki,* sometimes it's strange how life brings people together. And I know, it can't get much stranger than how we got here," he looked down at her intently. "But you've got to begin to trust me, and I've got to begin to trust you. In the end our very lives could depend on it."

Raquel studied her captor's sincere features, and strong feelings began to stir inside.

"I may end up feeling like a fool, but for now, I know I must try."

Nate's gaze drifted from her ebony eyes to her promising lips as they formed the reassuring words. A sheen of moisture caused their fullness to shine, beckoning him once again to touch them with his.

This time as his head descended toward her, he could feel her hands reach up to aid its progress, and his loins stirred with the promise of her touch.

A chilling weakness encased Raquel as his mouth covered hers. The utter softness of it began to unravel her and she whimpered.

Nate's deepest desire was to feel her give in to his touch, and from the moment their lips met, he knew she was all there for him.

With lingering motions he explored the inner sweetness of her mouth, feeling as if he could drown in its softness. Longingly he rubbed his temple against hers, then sought out her willing mouth again.

Feeling her flame of passion ignite, Raquel wanted Nate to know the depth of her desire, so she withdrew her mouth from his, tracing tiny, suckling kissing about his lips, as she murmured, "I want you, Nate. I want you." He enfolded her even more tightly inside his embrace. His caress was so intense she feared she might break from the strength of his arms.

In his fervor, he raised her inches off the hut's dirt floor, then kissed and plied the tender spot at the base of her throat as she wrapped her arms tightly about his sweltering shoulders.

Then like a man possessed, he snarled, "Now you shall have me, baby." He swept her up in his arms and carried her to his pallet.

With dark eyes smoldering, Raquel lay back with anticipation as she watched him unbutton and remove the cut-off jeans he had conveniently fashioned. She had no idea if the herbs had taken effect again, but she did know the hunger that churned within her was real and needed to be fed. Then as she watched the denim material slide to his muscular thighs, there was no doubt in her mind, Nate had the ability to fulfill her craving.

His eyes burned when he crouched above her, pinning her forearms to the natural material. Deliberately, he dragged his gaze from her face to her heaving breasts, causing their budded tips to constrict. He gave each darkened peak an encouraging lick to further their response; then cooed like a bird in the rain forest as they tightened even more.

"*Pataki,* you are so beautiful." He rose again to give her a lingering kiss, only to withdraw before her lips were quenched.

Briefly his gaze returned to her swollen crests, only to travel further down her frame. Finally it rested on the profuse knoll of black curls, lying between the valley of her thighs. His eyes squinted intensely, as the involuntary pink tip of his tongue traced the shape of his own lip. He looked up into her eyes drunk with desire as he ground his teeth together, "Woman, I have waited for a long time. Now," he murmured, "you are mine."

Nate rubbed his face back and forth upon her curly mound, as if inhaling the female scent. Raquel's reaction mirrored his, as her head writhed from side to side anticipating whatever might be in store. There had never been this kind of intimacy between her and Clinton Bradshaw.

Nate enclosed the width of her waist within his hands before burrowing further into her center. His wetness sought out hers, and they mingled a honey sweetness, causing Raquel to cry out in sheer delight. He assaulted her over and over, until her hips began to rise and fall in a demanding motion.

"I can't take this," she moaned, "I feel as if I'm going to explode." And she grabbed his head, drawing it closer to her own.

Seething with his own desire, Nate released her, then readied himself in order to make them one. "Oh no, *pataki.* It is not nearly time for that. You must wait for me."

His possession was smooth. Hungrily Raquel arched her back as she received him, her moment was so close at hand, but Nate lay very still inside her, waiting for her passion to draw back from its crest. He wanted them to mount the peak of pleasure steadily, together. Raquel reluctantly followed his lead, too far gone to do anything else, hoping in the end to satisfy the exquisite ache he had initiated.

When he felt the time was right, he began to thrust inside her, causing ripples of pleasure to shoot through him. This taste of bliss naturally incited his motions, and his pace began to accelerate as he sought the sensations over and over again.

Never before had Raquel been pleasured so intensely, and she greedily wallowed in each stroke. He could feel her tighten selfishly about him, and he reached down further seeking to touch the very core of her.

Raquel and Nate clung to one another passionately as they rose, he whispering provoking words in her ears, assuring her of the pleasure she was giving him. His sensual words fueled their fire, and she met his thrusts, her voice turning raspy as she answered his erotic questions; the knowledge of her gratification fueling his own.

Suddenly the passion became unbearable and she cried out in her frenzy.

It was Nate's cue to join her as they clung to the peak of pleasure, then tumbled into a world of satisfaction.

CHAPTER 13

The tricolored heron extended its neck ever so slightly. It resembled a stuffed bird, it stood so still. Its ruby-colored eyes remained fixed on the moving water below, watching and waiting for the right moment to surprise its morning meal.

Raquel sat quietly as the blue, maroon, and buff-colored bird stalked its prey, then with lightning movements, immersed its dark plumed head under water, afterwards emerging with the catch.

She'd come to the pond early that morning, memories and scents of the night before clinging close about her. She had intended to float in the forest's calm waters, but found it teeming with animal life. They, of course, were operating to nature's time clock.

At first, her disruption of the natural gathering caused some of the animals and birds to scatter, leaving behind a stubborn agouti on the opposite bank. His rabbit-sized body remained poised for flight as he assessed the unwelcome visitor.

Finally, he decided to continue his rapid lapping of the pond's water, concluding she was much too far away to do him any harm. After the agouti's bold stand, some of the other animals and birds began to return, but they were ready to retreat if she made even the slightest threatening move.

Raquel hugged her knees close to her newly awakened body. Parts of her still throbbed from the lovemaking the night before, and she knew it wouldn't take much to ignite the barely dormant stirrings within her.

Sooty lashes swept down on to high cheekbones, as she marveled at the ability human beings possessed to give such pleasure to one another. Still basking in the glow of her first true experience of being fulfilled, she wondered how her mother could ever have misled her to believe this natural thing between male and female could be wrong. It was all so powerful. And maybe that is where the problem rested. This kind of power used abusively could be devastating, but with love, it was the most wonderful thing on earth.

Raquel placed her flushed face against her updrawn knees. Love. How could she use the word in referring to a man who had participated in abducting her by force? Yet, amazingly, she had no doubt about the way she felt.

In deep thought, she dug her toes into the moss upon which she sat, and she knew her feelings for the man, Nate, had not just begun the night before, but days before.

Here was a man who didn't even know her real name, or who she truly was, and she claimed to be in love with him. Had she been back in Miami, counseling a young woman who spoke of being in love with a man in less then a month's time, a man who had committed a criminal act against her, she would have cautioned her to examine her feelings further. Might they be a strong case of infatuation? Or maybe even some kind of obsessive fantasy? She would kindly inform the misguided girl, that it takes true love a long time to grow and develop. She would say, "Most certainly it wouldn't be directed toward a man of this nature."

Raquel searched her logical mind for an answer to her own confused feelings. Maybe all of the things they had experienced together since coming aboard that sailboat, had sped up the natural ties and bonding that usually takes months and even years to develop. On the other hand, there is no way anyone would consider their "courtship" as natural.

The sound of nearly demented laughter echoed about her as she laughed at herself and the emotional predicament she found herself in, and the young woman covered her tangled hair with a settling fold of her arms.

Nate's search for Raquel had brought him within several feet of the water before he saw her. The strange laughter she expelled nearly sent chills up his spine, and his dark features clouded over with concern. It caused him considerable pain to see her in such mental agony.

At the moment there was nothing he could tell her that would ease her distress. He knew the words he might have chosen could even add to her heavy load. So he chose to remain silent, announcing his presence from the brush to warn her of his coming.

"So here you are," his tone was deceptively cheerful. "I wondered where you had gone so early this morning," he stooped and placed a playful kiss on the back of her neck.

Just the sound of his rich voice caused butterflies to appear in her stomach, as his cool lips upon her back began creating a tremor. She dared not turn and look in his face, for she knew how she felt about him had to show in her eyes. So she attempted to match the nonchalant intonation of his greeting.

"Morning, Nate."

"Hey, this is a great idea," he said with a wide smile. She watched him stride purposefully toward the pond's edge. "I think I'll go for a swim."

Lithely he removed his cut-off jeans. Raquel couldn't help but stare with unabashed adoration at his athletic body. It was well defined, starting with his wide shoulders, his narrowing waistline, and firm buttocks. His legs and thighs were muscular like a runner's. Of all the animals she had seen at the pond that morning, Nate was undoubtedly the most beautiful.

Flashing her a pearly smile, he dove into the blue-green pond. Large spurts of water splashed her face from his body's weight, feeling cold in the early morning air. Nate emerged yards away, shaking water from his drenched face and head.

"What are you waiting for, *pataki?*" he called to her. "The water feels good, come on in."

She watched him float luxuriously on his back, as the soft rays of well-awakened dawn beamed down upon him. Raquel reminded herself that getting into the water was her sole reason for coming to the pond that morning, so she quickly unfastened her wrap, then tiptoed to the water's edge. She was on the brink of jumping into the chilly water before she remembered the leather pouch that hung about her neck. Protectively she removed it, hanging it on the sloping branch of a tree. She walked into the pond's refreshing embrace, closing her eyes as it rose higher about her body, until it reached her throat. Finally she struck out with a powerful kick, then turned on to her back, so the sun's rays could rest upon her face.

Nate watched her float alone, although he was very aware they could not waste much time this morning. Today was the day they would have to push ahead, Leaving this semi-private haven, to face the fate he had chosen for them. Had he known what he knew and felt now, he dared say he would not have involved her in this tangled web.

With powerful strokes Nate swam to a fringe of the pond where tall, slender reeds grew in abundance, and he broke off several handfuls of the plant. Straight away, he lit out to join Raquel.

Paddling on his back beside her, he told her to follow him in closer to the shore. Finally, they stopped, once her feet could firmly rest upon the ground beneath the water. Exposing her wet breasts to the morning air caused the tips to contract—the sensation deliciously reminded her of the night before.

"Here, let me show you."

Balling up the plants in his hand, he rubbed them vigorously between his palms until a soapy film began to form. Afterwards he circled behind Raquel, and began to gently rub the natural suds against her back. She moaned at his gentle, cleansing administrations. His hands felt strong as he lathered her back. To her pleasure, he did not miss the opportunity to explore the fullness of her buttocks, teasing her all the while.

"Oh, sorry about that," his lips touched her ear as he taunted her, "for a minute I forgot what I was supposed to be doing."

Raquel couldn't help but giggle at his mannish ways as he turned her to face him. "Oh boy, now look what you have done," he remarked, then smiled wickedly, but continued his mischievous bathing.

The reeds began to fall apart and lose their usefulness, but that did not stop the fond explorations of Nate's hands. Finally they could not resist the other, and they found a secluded spot to continue their lovemaking. The night before blurred in Raquel's memory—she was lost in the moment with Nate. Raquel wanted to remain in his arms, feeling his touch and his kiss, but there was a growing tenseness about him. She knew it was time for them to head back to the hut.

"I guess we need to be going back," she announced. "From what I understand we've got quite a way to go before we reach Dangriga."

The veiled look that appeared in Nate's eyes was not lost on the young woman, and she wondered what thoughts he hid behind it. Now that she had the shamaness's power within her, she hoped she no longer had to fear being exposed as a fraud during the ceremony. She was torn inside, because out of desperation part of her believed all the shamaness had told her, but another part of her still doubted if it were possible.

The shamaness had been the only person to tell her about the ritual. Nate had not, because he believed she was Jackie Dawson. How would he feel about her once he found out the truth? For him to have gone to the lengths he had to bring Jackie Dawson back to Belize, and to protect her to such extremes—how would he feel about Raquel Mason from Miami?

Raquel couldn't help but feel threatened by such tenacity. She knew from personal experience he was not an easy man to comprehend. Now her fear was twofold. Could she live up to what was expected of her once they reached Dangriga? And it frightened her to think of losing this man because of who she was not.

Neither spoke as they dressed, and they walked back to the clearing in silence.

"Nate!" an excited voice called as they stepped out into the open.

Both Nate and Raquel were surprised to see a somewhat bedraggled

Ponti, safely standing several feet away from the shamaness and her mascot, the jaguarundi.

In his hands he carried a bundle of familiar objects, Raquel's belongings which she had left behind in Balam, and Nate's handgun, which he lost while fleeing from the Balamians.

If it hadn't been for Ponti, more than likely they would have been killed. In Raquel's exuberance, she gave the Mayan a friendly hug, causing him to flush with embarrassment. The damp material of her wrap still clung enticingly to her body.

Raquel noticed the flustered look on his face and stood back modestly, smoothing out some of the folds in the damp cloth. Still she couldn't contain her curiosity.

"How is Mircea?"

Ponti gave a boyish grin. "Fine . . . now that you have stolen the ceremonial blade. The elders are in an uproar. Most of them say there can be no more sacrifices until it is found. You see it has been in our village for thousands of years. Some believe it was used during the ancient bloodletting rituals," he rolled his eyes into his head playfully. "I don't know if it is that old, but there's no doubt it would be hard to trace its true origins back to the very beginning. So you see—" he stopped in midsentence realizing he did not know her name. "I'm sorry. I don't know your name," he confessed, abruptly.

"Ra—um-um." Raquel acted as if she needed to clear her throat as her real name nearly slipped off her tongue. "It is Jackie. Jackie Dawson," she weakly replied.

"So you see, Jackie, you have become a legend in our village. There are elders who are wondering if it is not a sign that the sacrifices and bloodletting should come to a halt. Maybe this will be the beginning of change for my people."

Raquel nodded with anxious appreciation.

Nervously, she felt for the leather pouch that usually hung about her neck. In a panic, she realized she had left it at the pond. Her wide eyes flew up to the shamaness's wrinkled face.

Turning hurriedly to Nate, she explained, "I forgot something back at the water. It won't take me but a few minutes, but I've got to run back and get it." Before he could answer she had dashed back into the forest.

Swiftly her feet crashed through the foliage. She was excited because of Ponti's presence, and to hear that Mircea's life might be permanently spared as a result of her efforts. She wondered if she could ever make such a difference back home.

She saw the pond in the distance. Oddly, there wasn't an animal or a bird in sight. Mildly curious, Raquel wondered if her rapid approach had frightened them all away.

Raquel could see the pouch hanging from the swinging branch as she approached it hurriedly. It took two hands to untangle the cord from the fingerlike limb. Specks of loose bark clung to it, and a few remnants flew into her eyes as she replaced the sack around her neck. Instinctively, her hands flew up to rub them.

Suddenly, a pair of rough hands covered her mouth and grabbed her about the waist. She kicked and squirmed wildly, although it had little effect on her abductor. He made no sound as he carried her rapidly away through the forest.

Raquel's eyes teared painfully as she tried to see who was responsible for the act, but the flecks in her eyes prevented her from opening them. In horror, she wiped at her face over and over again, feeling totally helpless.

Finally she was placed on the ground, and through blurry vision she whirled to face her assailant. But it simply made it easy for an accomplice to forcefully place a gag in her mouth, then tie another rag over her badly watering eyes. Frantically, she clawed to keep the wrap about her body, as her abductors dragged her through the rain forest.

They finally burst through on to what felt like a dirt road to Raquel. Somewhere near she could hear the laboring engine of a badly maintained vehicle. Suddenly, the motor revved up and the car's noise advanced towards them at a dangerous pace. Two strong arms reached down and pulled her into the car. Then just as swiftly as the car had pulled up beside them, it sped away down the bumpy road.

Nate offered Ponti the only seat there was in their small hut, as he told him of his snakebite, and the care and housing the shamaness had provided for them in their time of need. He was surprised to find out none of this was news to him.

"The villagers who chased after you came back and told of how 'the powerful one' would not allow you to be harmed. After that, rumors abounded. They were saying the woman who would be a shaman was housing the man and the woman responsible for the loss of the ceremonial blade. Although everyone believed this, no one from the village would dare to venture here to find out for themselves if it was really true."

"That is, besides you," Nate acknowledged.

Ponti nodded his head proudly. "I have always gone against the grain, but because I am smart, when I want to, I am able to hide the things I do that would upset my people most. When I left and went off to school, I did not care what they would think. Eventually I felt they would accept me again. And now that I have proven myself by trying to stop those who would steal the precious ceremonial blade," he said with a wink. "Now, I am very trusted in Balam. So much so, they charged me with getting rid of the belongings of the perpetrators. They do not want your negative energies in the village. So here I am getting rid of them." He placed Raquel's bundle on the floor and handed the handgun to Nate along with a roll of money.

Then a serious look blanketed Ponti's youthful features.

"I do not want to lead you to think that I do not love and respect my people. I just know that things must change," he sought Nate's understanding, "There are many things that the Balamians know that could be of exceptional good for the rest of the world, but I know as long as we continue to do bloodlettings and sacrifices, we will be looked at as nothing but senseless barbarians."

They shared a moment of companionable silence.

"I can't tell you how much I understand being connected to a group of people with ways that are not always understood by others," Nate said smoothly. "Things that as a young man I found hard to accept. And now as an adult, I fear, what I shall call . . . modern-day sacrifices. Either way, Ponti, the way of the Balamians or this more evolved way is wrong," he gazed off into the distance.

"Here in Belize, we are such a diverse people. Our heritages nearly span the globe. The tree is here, but it has been fed from as far away as Africa to China. In many ways, it is one of the most primitive places that lies in the midst of the civilized world. I think it will be quite some time before all our beliefs become tame . . . if ever."

"Yes, at times, we are far from tame," Ponti shook his head in agreement. "And that is the main reason I chose to bring these things to you this morning. I have news for you." He bent forward conspiratorially. "Late last night, the merchant that you met in the Kekchi village, was forced by a group of men to come and talk to us in Balam. They knew that an outsider would not be tolerated in the village. So they found the merchant, and they counted on his Mayan blood to allow them access. But before they came to Balam he says they had asked many questions, and evidently the merchant's answers led them to come to our village. He was very frightened, and more than a little pleased when he saw that I was one of the persons the head men chose to speak with them. From what I can understand, these men were very interested in your and your Jackie's whereabouts."

Nate's body became still as stone. His eyes took on a deadly glint, yet his voice was deceptively calm. "Were they Shango?"

"Yes." Ponti noticed a frightening change in his friend's persona. Slowly he eased back from leaning so close to him.

"They heard about the missing blade and the possibility that you may be staying with "the powerful one.""

"Were they still at Balam when you left this morning?"

"I cannot say. I had to come here in secret."

The thoughts in Nate's mind turned like a well-oiled wheel. He cursed under his breath for underestimating the speed in which Jay would come back to find the woman. It was evident they had not come by car, or they would have arrived in the area earlier. Nate did not think Jay would allow the shamaness's presence to keep him from coming for her, especially if he had back-up. Now he was sure the man's plans for the woman involved far more than he had confessed.

Suddenly Nate was keenly aware that Jackie had not returned from the pond. Without warning, he grabbed the firearm, checked it, strode forcefully toward the entrance of the hut, then broke into a solid run once he got outside. A startled Ponti was close behind.

Powerfully he shoved aside the large foliage that would block his way as he bolted for the water, his ears straining to hear the slightest indication that the woman was in trouble.

Yards away he crouched upon the ground, then began to crawl on all fours with the gun still held within his hand. He prayed Jay had not found her, but if he had, and there were more of them than he could handle, he would have a better chance by sneaking up on them; but most importantly, he did not want to unnecessarily jeopardize her life. Nate knew how badly Jay hated the woman, and that he would kill her without a second thought.

With cautious movements, he extended the length of his body outward, until he was on his belly, then made his way closer to the water by using his elbows. His muscular chest was still bare, and he knew that what he was doing was extremely dangerous—he had already had one encounter with a poisonous snake, now squirming along the rain forest's floor, his chances of being bitten a second time were very high. Abruptly he stopped, lying there for seconds at a time, listening. Then slowly he rose, peering at the water. His greatest fear took hold when he spotted the edge of the pond, and found she was not there. Instantly he rose above the foliage, forcing a school of startled reddish egrets to stop their morning hunt, and head for safety in the sky, in a red, blue-gray flurry.

Tense, he looked for signs of a struggle, but there were none. Yet he knew in his heart she had been taken, and taken by force.

He gripped and released the handle of the Glock pistol as a cold chill crept up inside him. Only once before in his life had he felt such uneasiness, but the memory of it lingered as if it were yesterday. Like a flash his mind went back to a time when he was a boy.

* * *

For Nate's mother, his father had been everything. Even after he was born, and Cecilia came to live with them, he remained the center of her life. Nothing had been too good for him in her eyes, she loved him so deeply. The fact he in turn loved her, couldn't have made her happier.

After Cecilia died, she began to change. The thought of a loved one dying frightened her terribly. The powers that be had failed her by not protecting the girl and in taking one so young. Since his mother was a person of deep beliefs, the impact of that event had a most profound effect. Even then as a child, Nate felt he could handle his cousin's death better than his mother, and he tried to comfort her the best he could. So did everyone else.

At that time, he was nearly twelve and had finally surpassed his mother in height. He had never noticed how small and delicate she was until then, and she became even more frail as time passed. Then slowly another problem surfaced. She became peculiarly paranoid about the dangers she said stalked her family.

The rift between the Garifuna and the Shango had caused a spiritual weakening of their villages. No longer was there a *dabuyaba*, religious temple, for the Garifuna to hold their important ceremonies. Now the only temple was located in the village of the Shango, and his mother viewed that as an extremely evil sign.

Nate's father tried to reassure her that things would be all right, but she clung to him even more. She always needed to hear that he would never leave her, even in death. And he would never love anyone else the way he loved her.

Then one day a young Shangoain woman appeared in Dangriga. All eyes were upon her as she walked through the small village. People appeared in the broken doorways of the clapboard houses, puzzling over what could have made this woman come to the Garifunian village, ignoring the awful split that had occurred nearly a half year before.

Nate remembered watching the woman progress up the dusty pathway between several of the buildings. He had been sitting outside his home finishing a drum his father had helped him fashion. The woman walked as if she were in a processional, carefully placing each foot in front of the other, until finally she reached the door of their house. His father was not home at the time, and it was his mother he called to speak to this unorthodox visitor.

Already fearful, she approached the door warily. Her apprehension grew when she realized the woman was Shangoain, her eyes widening with suppressed fear. Cautiously she spoke to her, then immediately asked what was her purpose for coming to the village, especially to their home.

Without an invitation the Shangoain stepped past his mother inside their front door. She never said a word as she started to unwrap the many folds of cloth that surrounded her thin frame. From the beginning, Nate had noticed how strange her dress had been, she was wrapped so completely. It was peculiar because it was a sweltering day, and he wondered how far she'd walked in the heavy, dark material.

His mother tried to discourage the woman's bizarre unveiling, but she ignored her as she continued to undress, keeping her steadfast gaze fastened to his mother's increasingly frightened features.

It had to have been obvious to the Shangoain that his mother was not well, for even at such a young age her fragile hands shook uncontrollably at her sides. She had to clasp them together in order to cease the embarrassing trait.

Eventually his mother saw her demands for the woman to stop her disrobing would continue to go unheeded, so she motioned for Nate to leave the doorway. Reluctantly he did so, yet he remained conveniently close to the house only a few feet away.

Moments passed, and suddenly he heard the swooning sound of a female voice. This was followed by the slamming of one of the doors inside. Shortly thereafter, the Shangoain woman appeared outside again, fully clothed. She turned a superior eye in Nate's direction.

"Boy, I want you to deliver a message for me."

Hesitantly he had nodded his head, all the time wondering why she had not passed the message on to his mother. It would have been far more appropriate for it to be delivered by another adult, because whatever her reason was for coming to Dangriga, it had to be of the utmost importance, and therefore a matter to be handled by the elders of the village.

His gaze fixed upon the woman's dark features which had the distinctive trait of the Shangoains, eyes that were extremely large. The shape of her face was round, and in its center was a nose so flat it was buttonlike, yet her lips were extremely thin. Large twists of hair rippled back from her face, gathering together in the crown of her head.

"Tell your father, he no longer has only one child. Soon there will be another. Tell him the mother is Vita, the Shangoain. He can find me in the town of Barooch, if he wants me." Stoically she turned and walked away.

It took Nate a few moments to recover from the woman's stunning words, but when their meaning set in, he quickly entered the house looking for his mother.

An eerie feeling crept up his back as he stepped inside. The uncomfortable feeling confused him, for this was the house that he had grown up in, and had never known another. He called to his mother from the doorway, but she did not answer. Concerned, he crossed to his parents' bedroom door, pressed his lips to the crack of it and called her name several times again. Still, she did not respond.

By now he was extremely afraid, he tried to open the door and found the knob turned easily. He called to her once more in vain. It was then that the most soul-shaking chill descended upon him as he walked into his parents' room.

At first he surveyed the entire area and did not see her, but as he turned to go back out of the door, he saw her small, slouched frame in the corner behind it. A thick flow of blood oozing from the deep cuts she had made in her wrists.

From the amount of blood she had shed, he knew he did not have time to run for help. So the boy did everything he could to stop the blood from flowing, but even while trying to save the last breaths of life in his mother's body, he knew that she was dead, perhaps had even died before he'd found her.

It was there on the floor that his father found them together. A disbelieving look of utter horror and shock took over his father's handsome features as he stared, but still, Nate had no merciful words to offer him.

"I don't know why you're standing there surprised." Nate's voice was inappropriately calm. "It is all your fault, you and that Shangoain woman, Vita, who says to tell you she is carrying your baby."

It was the first time in his life he had ever seen his father cry. It was an outpouring of deep, racking sobs that continued even while Nate was gone to bring back one of the village elders.

His father's depression went on for weeks, leaving him to fend for the both of them. Ironically, it was the act of a desperate man, one who didn't care about the future, that ended up changing their entire lives.

Ponti finally caught up with Nate, the latter's guerilla-like techniques had caused him to fall far behind. The lethal look on his companion's handsome features said everything, so the man waited to hear what plan of action he had decided to take.

"I'm going back to the hut for our belongings, and then I'm going after them. They haven't been gone long, so they couldn't have gotten far." He checked the handgun again to see if it was in good working order. "Hopefully she will try to slow down their progress, then I—"

"I don't know," Ponti cautiously interrupted. "By now they could have gone quite a ways if their vehicle was parked near Southern Highway."

"What vehicle?" he asked roughly.

"The men . . . persuaded the merchant to let them use his jeep. He was in it, sitting outside his stall last night when they came up to him. They checked it over, found it was in good condition and had a tank full of gas. So they kept it."

Hearing this, Nate wasted no time in heading back for the clearing. This changed everything. Now he would have to find a car, and fast.

"Does the guy who runs the store at Big Falls still have a couple of four-wheel-drives that he rents out?"

"The last I heard, he does."

"Then I'll have to go there first before heading for Punta Gorda."

Nate knew there was no chance the owner wouldn't recognize him. Through the years he'd come through his place too many times. But now he had no other choice.

Hastily he threw on a shirt and a long pair of jeans as Ponti watched. The only belongings he had were his duffel bag and the things that belonged to Raquel, so he threw them all together. He was set to go when the shamaness entered the hut, like a watchdog, the jaguarundi was not far from her side.

There were signs of strain and fatigue edging her aged face, and for a moment Nate imagined her features had been altered in a kind of bizarre way. The change made her facial likeness more akin to the feline that was her constant companion.

Her voice was raspy when she spoke. "You are leavin'."

"Yes." His steely gaze rested on her. "Some men have taken the woman. These are men that will do her harm if I don't stop them, so I must go and find her."

"Oh-h yes," she shook her dreadlocked head in agreement. "But before you leave, I want to reassure you, that no one can stop the change. No one. She will remain safe," her commanding gaze locked with his.

Nate made a slight tilting of his head, a gesture of thanks and recognition of her power. With this, the shamaness stepped aside and allowed them to pass.

Already Nate was several steps ahead of Ponti, determined not to lose even a minute's time. The youth was like a puppy, yapping at his heels.

"Maybe I should go with you. I could be of help."

Nate stopped momentarily at the edge of the rain forest. "I won't say I couldn't use it."

Ponti's brows knitted together as he thought it over. "First I will go back to Balam and tell my family I have some unfinished business I must settle before I completely return to the village. I'll tell them it will take me a few days to do it." His youthful eyes shone with excitement. "After that, I will meet you at Big Falls."

"All right. It is up to you, but I want you to understand two things Ponti," his visage hardened as he turned to face the young man. "One. This is not a game and someone will probably get hurt. And two, if you are not there when I climb into that four-wheel-drive, I will leave without you." Without waiting for his response, Nate disappeared into the foliage.

Nate's thoughts were like a tornado, churning round and round, at its center was Jackie. Loving, passionate pictures of her that morning and the night before flashed through his mind, and he hoped he would find her before it was too late. Just the thought of it caused beads of perspiration to break out on his forehead and above his lips.

He tried not to think of the horrible things Jay and Al would have done to her had he not been there, but there was no way to avoid it. Before he knew it he had called out in the wilderness, "I will kill them if they hurt her."

Exotic bird noises enveloped him as he progressed; the mocking sound of macaws and parrots were the most disturbing as they seemed to warn him in their humanlike voices, "rrah-rah, rrun, run, run . . ."

CHAPTER 14

It was hard for Raquel to breathe folded up on the hard floor of the jeep. The humidity outside made the small stream of air where Raquel lay stifling and thick with the musky smell of her new abductors. Two pairs of legs stretched out over her, concealing her from prying eyes and limiting her already restrained movements.

The young woman's hands remained tied behind her back making her arms ache despite the extra pad that had been placed on the jeep's floor for her supposed comfort.

Her eyes itched and burned something awful beneath the tight bandanna, and she could feel they were swollen. Maybe it was the kind of bark that had fallen into them, or the combination of that, along with the tightness of the scarf that had complicated their condition; but through a rising panic, she was sure, even if the bandanna were to be removed, her eyes had become so badly infected it would be impossible for her to see.

She strained to catch even the slightest indication of a human voice, but was only assaulted with the loud roar of the vehicle's engine. She couldn't imagine her captors sitting quietly for the period of time they'd been traveling. No, that wouldn't make sense at all. So she surmised, because of the open vehicle, the men's voices were being snatched away and carried outward by the wind, even making it difficult for them to hear one another.

Raquel's logical side urged her to be alert and listen, so she could be prepared for what they had in store for her, but another voice inside the horrified young woman warned her to remain in ignorance as long as she could. Deep inside she knew who was behind the kidnapping, and she knew the horrible things he was capable of doing.

Prolonged sounds of whimpering began to gurgle up in her throat as she shivered and wallowed in deep self-pity and fear. She buried her dirt-streaked face in the pad beneath her.

The nonchalant hand of one of her kidnappers reached down and shook her shoulder. She refused to respond.

"Heh, *obeah* woman, what is this?" His heavily accented voice sounded as if it were coming out of a vacuum. "You no can breathe with your face in there like t'at," and he turned her head to the side to insure she could. "We be there soon enough, and we can let you loose, okay?" he chuckled and patted her suggestively on the buttocks.

Raquel winced from his touch, and it was followed by an endearing pang. She allowed her mind to take her back to hours before when she had not shrunk from the hands that touched and caressed her. Mentally she cuddled up to the thoughts of security that Nate's memory provided.

Moments later Raquel's comforting thoughts were interrupted as the jeep pulled off the road into the brush. Who would ever find her if they went off the path? Once again panic set in as her thoughts raced to try and anticipate what would happen next.

The squeaking noise of rusted hinges scraped her dark environment, then she felt a rush of fresh air upon her face and shoulders.

"Right here is as good a place as any," the voice said, and the swishing sound of feet parting grass followed.

Raquel lay as still as death, as if her immobility would help protect her.

"Well, I might as well join you," a second voice called, the same one that spoke of their impending arrival. She could hear the man grunt and groan as he removed his stiffened legs from about her, and joined the other outside the jeep.

Next, the distinct sound of a projected stream of liquid followed by another could be heard, all of this accompanied by one man's sigh of relief. Now Raquel knew they had not arrived at all, but that one of her captors had decided to make a pit stop, and a second had conveniently joined him.

"You t'ink we need to go off t'is highway before we get to t'at road t'at will take us straight in?" a third voice near her inquired.

The muffled response of a fourth person followed.

"Yeah, we've made good time haven't we *Dada?*" a now somewhat familiar satisfied voice called from outside the jeep. "It wasn't too hard findin' and catchin' her," his voice grew closer as he stepped back into the jeep and repositioned his legs. "And why didn't you tell me what a

good-looking package the *gubida* had chosen to speak through." A fumbling hand reached down to find an easily accessed breast, squeezed it
forcefully, then rolled the unwilling tip between its fingers. "Maybe aftah
the ceremony is over, the *buyei* won't mind if we poke around a bit. I bet
she has some other abilities we can appreciate besides speakin' with the
ancestors." The man next to him laughed, while a third reentered the
jeep, slamming the door behind him.

Their laughter was short-lived, as a frightfully familiar gruff voice
barked, "Keep your willie to yourself, David. Plans have already been
made for her."

The only sound that followed his brusque words was the gunning of
the jeep's engine, and that loud noise was blocked out in Raquel's mind
by the beating of her own heart. There was no doubt who that last voice
belonged to. The knowledge of it caused her to lay frozen, stiff with fear
in the bottom of the jeep. One of her greatest fears was happening. Jay
had found her, and was taking her away, and only God knew what was in
store for her next.

Nate waited impatiently while the store owner took care of two groups
of eager tourists, one a family of five and the other, two women.

Although the father was ready to pay for the objects picked up by his
brood, the two youngest children kept changing their minds as they
came across new, more exciting souvenirs near the cash register. He
looked grateful when the mother, who was straining with the hand of an
unhappy two-year-old, put her foot down and told them to make up their
minds or go without. Nate chuckled gently to himself before returning to
the matter at hand.

Before coming inside he checked to see if there were any vehicles left
to rent. To his relief, there were two parked out back.

Nate's anxious gaze drifted over to a taxi driver with his foot conveniently planted beneath the mandatory green license plate of his car.
Even in this position he managed to rotate his slender hips to the blaring
reggae music blasting from the car's crackling radio. Every once in a
while, the driver would flash a wide smile in the direction of the two
women whom he obviously had driven to Big Falls. One of them acknowledged him, while the other cast interested looks in Nate's direction. Nate raked over the woman once with an apathetic glance—who
could compare to Jackie?

Out of his peripheral vision, he saw the tall, shapely blonde bend over
and laughingly whisper words into her companion's ear. The other in
turn looked to size him up, then reciprocated her friend's whisper.
Seconds later the blonde walked over in his direction.

"Excuse me," she breathed, batting generously lashed blue eyes, then purposefully squeezing her tightly shorted hips between Nate and a nearby wall to look at the contents in a glass case behind him.

Wordlessly he shifted his position, leaning his hard frame a foot or so down from where he previously stood.

The blonde leaned over at an angle with rounded breasts thrust in his direction. The fashionable aqua-colored summer top revealed a substantial amount of cleavage, but her angle exposed even more to his conveniently positioned gaze. With slanted eyes he watched her with mild inquisitiveness.

A sheet of white-blonde hair draped over the side of her face as she stooped, covering her ploy. She daintily swept it to the side with a brightly polished hand, displaying two expensive diamond studs in one ear.

"May I help you?" the store owner called in his next customers, then for the first time he noticed the man leaning against the distant counter. "Nate Bowman," he exclaimed, "How are you?"

Nate gave a quick nod of his head as an answer.

"I'll be with you in just a minute. I've got to take care of these two ladies. They were here first." He then turned his attention to the redhead who was walking over to his counter, followed by the blonde sauntering enticingly behind her.

"Yes," she replied, her American accent ringing in the air. "We'd like to rent one of your cars."

"Well I've got to tell you you're just in time. We've only got one more that's working. It's the black four-wheel Suzuki Samurai in the rear. Why don't you follow me outside, and I'll show it to you."

Nate's eyes narrowed with the man's pronouncement. "Do you mind if I come with you?" His voice was low, calm.

Before the store owner could answer, the smiling blonde extended her invitation. "Of course not, honey," she gave him a meaningful glance.

The four of them rounded the back of the building arriving at two mud-caked vehicles.

"I really hate that that other car isn't working. I don't like driving those things," the attractive blonde complained. She pushed her bottom lip out seductively, while eyeing Nate.

"I'm sorry," the store owner apologized, "but it's all I got."

"I tell you what," Nate quickly assessed the situation. "Since you two pretty ladies don't want to be bothered with it, I'll be willing to take it."

The redhead looked at him shrewdly, "I guess you would. There's nothing else here to drive. So you wouldn't be doing us any kind of favor if you took if off our hands, so to speak."

"Oh, but I would," he smiled slowly, showing even white teeth, a dangerous glint entering his darkly lashed eyes. "I'd be willing to talk the cabbie into taking you back where you'd be sure to get a nice air-conditioned automatic, and that way, you two lovely ladies could ride in comfort."

"Doesn't sound too bad to me," the eager blonde chimed in, but the redhead wasn't totally convinced.

"Ah come on, sugar," the blonde gave her companion a familiar hug, flashing her blue eyes in a way that was persuasive, then shimmying closer into the embrace. "Who knows, maybe we can convince this handsome fellow to come visit us while we're in Belize City," she turned insinuatingly to Nate. "We can pretty much guarantee you'd have more than your normal amount of fun," she smiled seductively.

Dark eyes gleamed knowingly. "Well I can believe that," he continued to smile. "Why don't you tell me where you're going to be staying, and I'll have to look you up when I get there."

The redhead's eyes lit up with anticipation. "Sounds pretty good to me. We'll be staying at the Chateau Caribbean. Donna and I will look forward to seeing you," she blew a kiss to Nate.

Nate reciprocated with a snarl of a smile. "Well . . . ladies, let me go and speak with the cabbie."

"Sure," the blonde acquiesced. "I saw a couple of things I'd like to get before we leave anyway. Coming with me, sugar?" she asked her girlfriend.

The two of them smiled and followed the store owner back inside.

"How do you come off askin' me to take them to Big Creek, now? Me and the redhead had some urgent plans, and she never even mentioned drivin' there," the irritated cab driver retorted.

"Well take your plans to Big Creek." Nate's voice was deceptively calm. He'd used up all his diplomatic abilities on the women inside, and he had no intention of furthering his skills in that area when it came to the cabbie. "I will pay you, for your trouble," a visible muscle in the square of his jaw began to pulsate.

He was grateful the Balamians weren't even interested in receiving the negative energy off of his money, and he peeled off two bills from the roll returned to him by Ponti, pressing them forcefully into the driver's palm.

Grudgingly the man took it, and watched Nate walk away with purposeful strides. On the way he passed the two women with a similar amount of impatience. Once inside the store, he placed what he knew was more than a week's rental money on the counter.

"Keep the change, Pete. I won't be bringing the vehicle back here. I'll make sure someone delivers it to you out of Dangriga in no more than a week."

Nate didn't wait for the store owner's response, he simply headed for the Samurai.

With a powerful tug, he pulled back the stick to reverse, and stomped down on the gas. Quickly, Ponti swung himself into the vehicle just before Nate made a screeching one-hundred-and-eighty-degree turn. With the gas pedal to the floorboard, the Samurai almost leapt forward as they bounded past the front of the building, leaving the blonde, the redhead and the cabbie in a hail of mud.

CHAPTER 15

Weak from fear and stress, Raquel placed her hands against her caked and swollen eyes as she kneelt. The stiffness in her arms made her discomfort that much more agonizing, but the feeling of utter helplessness because of her loss of sight preyed on her mind.

She tried to open her matted lashes, but it was to no avail. The tight bandanna had aided the infection. She had to accept that she was sightless and at the mercy of Jay and the Shango. The realization was stunning, and Raquel fell forward on her elbows with the heavy weight of it. Afraid, she listened to the voices around her.

"By the *orishas*, what happened to her eyes?" an ancient male voice asked.

Jay looked at the unkempt figure that crouched in front of them. Her black hair was full of remnants from the rain forest, her wrap, crumpled and spotted with dirt and oil.

"It is not our fault," he said smugly, speaking English so Jackie was sure to understand them. He wanted her to know how little he cared about her welfare. "Her eyes were already becomin' infected when we foun' her. We had to keep them covered so she wouldn' see where we were bringin' her, *buyei.*"

"What is t'at?" the shaman asked abruptly. "Evenshally she would know anyway. T'is woman lives in the United States. At no time while bringin' her here was she a physical threat to you." He got up and crossed over to Raquel. "And look at her wrists, they are already raw the bonds so tight around t'em. *Dada,*" he turned an accusatory eye in Jay's direction, "t'is is the woman who will speak to our ancestors. She should not have been tied up like a animal for slaughter an' kept in the bottom of t'at car until you arrived here," his filmy eyes flashed. "It was not necessary and you know it. T'is is a shame before the *orishas!*" his lank arm trembled with anger.

Almost in a fog, Raquel listened to the defending words of the older man. Seeking any comfort she could, she reached out blindly in the direction of his voice, feeling the dust of the dirt floor beneath her hand until she came across the rough skin of the shaman's bare foot, she touched it imploringly.

"I have warned you, *Dada,* the *orishas* are not to be shamed in any way. T'is should not have happened."

"I was told to bring her here, an' I did," Jay could barely contain the anger in his voice. "Now I am to blame for her condition?" he spat back.

"Are you not *Dada,* named for the brother of the mighty *orisha, Shango?* It is to his brother t'at the real responsibility for the continuance of his good name is given. When I gave you t'is name, when you were only a young man, it was because of your love of *Shango* and your desire to protect what was *Shango,*" the high priest proclaimed. "Aftah the split with the Garifuna, your father let you come under my wing, an' for a long time I thought t'at you would be the next *buyei* for our village. But as you got older *Dada, I* could see in you a weakness for worldly t'ings t'at should never be present in a *buyei.* It is for t'at reason, and t'at reason alone t'at you have only been given the initiations of the seventh rank. I could not as *buyei* initiate you further. But because of my love for you, I have kept you close by my side. Do not make me t'ink now, *Dada,* that you were not even deservin' of it, because of your lack of understandin' and compassion."

The shaman pinned Jay with his fiery gaze.

Just for a second Jay felt the urge to challenge him, but it was a fleeting need. Quickly he dropped his subservient gaze to the hut's floor.

"Now you will be responsible for cleanin' her up, an' make amends to the *orishas.* Take her to your wife, Eva. Tell her what I have said. Afterwards, she is to stay in the house where Grace lived until we go to Dangriga. It is empty now, her burial was yesterday."

Surprised, Jay looked from Raquel to the shaman.

"What about the *dugu* for my brother. Is it not to be tonight?"

"There will be no *dugu,*" the elderly man replied. "At least not here. More time was needed to prepare. It will be joined with the ceremony in Dangriga."

With shaky hands the elderly *buyei* reached down to aid Raquel in getting to her feet. "Here let me help you," both of them unsteady, he, from age, and she, from the trauma of the entire ordeal.

"Come here, *Dada,*" he motioned for Jay to approach them, "take her to your home an' have Eva look aftah her."

With determined control Jay took Raquel's arm, offered to him by the *buyei*.

"No! Don't touch me!" she screamed out, stumbling to the ground as she blindly tried to put space between them.

Jay clenched and unclenched his fists as he glared down at her.

"You see! She do not want any help. I do not feel anyt'in' for her," he touched the thickly scabbed scar Raquel was responsible for placing on his face. "From the very beginnin' of t'is she has been a negative source, so let her suffah. Just like Al is sufferin' now."

Wearily the shaman looked at the young man he had nurtured since he was a child, the dimness of sad acceptance blanketing his features, "You are wrong, *Dada*. She does not want *your* help. Now go an' get Eva. Bring her here an' let her take the woman to Grace's."

Angrily Jay stalked out to return minutes later with an ill-at-ease Eva. She tried to keep her face averted from the shaman's perceptive gaze. In an uncharacteristic fit of anger she'd threatened to go to the *buyei* about the treatment she was receiving from Jay and his brother. Jay warned if she did, he'd make sure Al had a new focus for his attention, her youngest sister.

Eva's calloused hand tugged lightly on Raquel's elbow, encouraging that she come with her. As the young woman obeyed and turned her badly infected features toward her, Eva looked uncertainly at the *buyei*.

"Take her down the street, child. Clean her up an' make sure she is well taken care of."

The woman nodded, obediently.

"An' Eva," the *buyei* called just as they were to pass through the door. "Aftah the ceremony in Dangriga we must talk, all of us." He turned an assessing gaze in Jay's direction.

Raquel allowed the thin woman to lead her silently down the path. She could hear several voices at a distance as they progressed, there was a hint of uneasiness in the low tones, and no one came up to them.

She guessed by now everyone had heard about her, and some of them like Jay, gave her no sympathy. But still, she could also feel their fear of an *obeah* woman, and what she might do should they cross her.

If Nate's initial feelings about Jackie Dawson shed any light on the situation, there was quite a bit of animosity toward her for abandoning her homeland and the responsibility she had in bridging the gap between the Shango and the Garifuna. Raquel surmised, maybe if Jackie Dawson had returned to Belize willingly, things would have been different.

The sun blazed hot on her face, causing the already-sensitive skin around her eyes to sting and burn. Even the protective touch of her own hands appeared to aggravate the condition. Unsure of herself, Raquel held on tightly to the arm of the woman beside her.

Finally the sound of broken clay erupted, startling the sightless young woman as they entered a house. Blindly, she had kicked an object just inside the doorway, causing the unexpected clatter.

Eva looked into Raquel's distorted face and could not help but feel sympathy for her. Word of how the young woman had arrived in the bottom of the jeep had spread quickly through the village. Eva assumed Jay was taking revenge against her for the magic she had worked on him and Al during their trip from the States.

Many of the villagers were afraid of the consequences such treatment of a *obeah* woman would have on the town. Others felt she was deserving of what had happened to her—she knew her responsibilities, but still had to be forced to do them.

As she looked at Raquel, Eva could not take sides. All she saw was a person in pain. She understood how it felt to have your face and body marred, to be used and to feel like a prisoner, having no control over your own life. Jay's wife decided to make her stay as comfortable as she could. It was something to take her mind off of her own troubles, and a reason to stay away from her home and Al.

"Don't worry," Eva spoke softly as if she were speaking to a child. "It is nothin' put a piece of the clay vessel from Grace's burial. It is a Shangoain tradition, but of course you should know t'at."

Raquel nodded her head.

"Now you sit here while I set up the tin tub for you to bathe. Grace did not have a bathtub, but she's got runnin' watah. I will heat some on the stove as well, 'cause here it is easy to use up the hot watah, even if you run it for jus' a short period of time. Not much electricity here in Puntaborok."

Eva talked to Raquel continuously as she prepared for her bathing. It was if she had not talked to anyone like this in a very long time, and the young woman found her steady voice comforting. She couldn't help but think how horrible her life must be, being married to a man like Jay.

She remembered the revengeful, sadistic way he began to look at her after she scratched his face and Al had been hurt, and she knew he was a man capable of deep cruelties. Raquel was very aware, with the condition she was in now, there was no way she could defend herself should Jay decide to take action against her.

"Eva? Your name is Eva, isn't it?"

"Yes."

"Is there anything here that I could use to put in my eyes?"

"Maybe, Grace used to grow all kinds of herbs in the back of her place. There may be somet'in' t'ere."

Raquel's spirits brightened a little when she heard this.

"Yes, there may be," she thought out loud and she began to search her mind for the names of herbs that would best serve her purposes. "Do you know anything about herbs, Eva?"

"No ma'am, I don't"

"Well maybe someone else in the village does."

"The *buyei* does, but his eyes are bad now an' it is hard for him to get around. He has not dealt in the herbs for many years." Eva looked over at Raquel's anxious face. "The only other person in the village who knows 'bout the herbs has already gone to Dangriga. A group of people who are helpin' to prepare for the ceremony, left a few days ago. I wouldn' trust anyone else here, ma'am, when it comes to somethin' like t'at."

Raquel's shoulders drooped with disappointment. If only she could see, she could choose the proper medicine herself. Her thoughts focused on the shamaness and the extensive lessons given to her in the rain forest. There were several herbs she had shown her with antibiotic qualities. How could she identify what she needed if she were blind?

It was at that moment Raquel made up her mind.

"Eva would you take me back to the garden? Maybe I can still choose the right herbs."

"I will if you like," was Eva's leery response.

"I will need something to place over my eyes while we are outside. The sun is awfully tough on them right now," she admitted.

After Eva provided a clean cloth that she gingerly tied on Raquel's face, they made their way to the garden.

"T'ere aren't very many of t'em, ma'am," Eva warned her as she looked around.

"Well maybe that is good, this way it won't take long." Remembering the shamaness stressing recognizing a plant by sight and smell, Raquel hoped she learned her lessons well. "Now if you would break off small shoots of the different herbs and bring them to me. Maybe I can discern through smelling them which one I need."

All of her life she'd been told when one of your senses is lacking the others become stronger to compensate for the inadequacy, and as she accepted the herbs from Eva's hands she prayed the saying was true.

Minutes later, several plants had passed beneath her nose with no luck, and frustration began to set in. Perspiration streamed down her face from the heat, and the salty solution burned as it touched her eyes beneath the cloth.

"T'ere are only two more," Eva said as she watched her.

"Okay, bring them here."

Hesitantly, she inhaled the first of the last two plants. An intensely thick scent wafted into her nostrils. It was sharp and leafy, and she could feel her heart quicken as she inhaled it. She thought she recognized the scent but she wasn't sure. Again she inhaled the small plant with shaking hands, this time, taking a deeper, surer breath.

"Eva, I believe this is an herb called Golden Seal," she announced excitedly. "If it isn't, it is something in the same family, and it must have the same qualities. Pick some more of these and we'll take them inside and boil them. I will need the liquid to bathe my eyes in. From the rest I'll make a poultice."

From the distance, the sound of several drums and a wind instrument reached them. The music was accompanied by a lone voice chanting a spirited tune. It was a vigorous sound, surrounded by the occasional howl of a nocturnal animal stirring for the first time as night began to descend.

Eva looked off in the direction of the sounds.

"They are beginnin' to prepare for the journey to Dangriga. Tonight there will be much singin' an' dancin' an' drinkin' of cashew fruit wine. In Dangriga they started weeks ago preparin' for Garifuna Settlement Day. It is a yearly holiday usually attended by tourists, but because of the uniting ritual, which you will be in, an' the *dugu* for my husband's brothah, many special things must be provided. The ritual and the *dugu* will take place first, an' it will be held in private. You see, our people must be in a receptive mood when they arrive in Dangriga, an' the celebratin' tonight should bring about the feelin's needed."

Raquel noticed a change in Eva's voice as she spoke of Al, and she wondered what kind of encounters she had had with him since his return from the States. From her own experience, she knew they could not be pleasant ones.

Eva poured several containers of hot water into the tin tub she had partially filled from the tap. The remaining water would be used to boil the Golden Seal. A generous handful of the dark green leaves was used to make the medicine, and she allowed them to steam and bubble just as Raquel instructed, until the water turned dark green. Eventually the plants were removed, and for a brief period the extract was allowed to cool.

Afterwards, she located a small swathe of white linen cloth. A part of it was torn off and dipped into the soothing liquid. With it Raquel carefully cleaned her own eyes, allowing some of the pungent brew to seep inside. Once the cleansing was done, Eva placed two poultices made from the remainder of the cloth, and filled with golden seal and chamomile, on Raquel's swollen eyes. The young woman sat back gratefully and hoped it would work.

Minutes later, Raquel sank gingerly into the lukewarm water with Eva's steady arm around her. Because the tub was small, it was necessary for her to keep her knees close to her body as she lowered herself into the soapy water. At last, for the first time since her second abduction, Raquel was able to breathe a sigh of relief, and pray that Nate would soon come to find her.

It wasn't easy to hide the Samurai in the densely treed forest, so they parked it quite a distance from the road that led into the village. Although Ponti was the younger man, his knees and back ached from remaining in the same position for such an extended period of time, and for the umpteenth time, he shifted his weight. He marveled at the control of the man beside him as he remained as still as death, watching the activities of several nearby musicians.

They had waited until almost dark before they ventured this close. He knew the man Nate's patience was wearing thin, and he contemplated how long it would be before he would take action.

"I wonder which house she's in," Ponti asked, feeling the need to talk. Nate had said very little since they left Big Falls. The feel around him was volatile, and Ponti thought it best not to breach the silence, until now.

"There's no telling. So we've got to wait for some kind of sign. Other than that, anything we do might put her in jeopardy, and I'm not taking a chance on that. Whatever move I make will be treated as the final one, because I'm going to do whatever I have to do to get her out of Jay's hands."

Ponti's stomach growled loudly as if it was responding to Nate's brusque words. The smell of roasting armadillo, and beans prepared with sweet potatoes was strong. He regretted not eating earlier. Their chances of eating anytime soon appeared very slim.

Several men and women had begun to gather in the area of the musicians and the food. One small boy, who looked to be no more than three, broke away from his mother to sway to the beat of the double-headed dundun drum, smiling all the while as a few people in the crowd egged him on. Systematically, other young males would break out into an energetic dance, with powerful movements and widespread steps.

"They're preparing to go to Dangriga," Nate informed a curious Ponti. "They believe everyone's spirits and energy must be at their highest to get through the ceremony that will go on for a few days. Right now, it would be good to be able to count on that belief but that just ain't the way it is. There are a couple of guys involved in this that I know you can't trust, and one of them has it out for her."

Several feet in front of them, a young man held up a goatskin fashioned into the shape of a hornlike pouch. Turning it up, he drank eagerly from its contents. Some of the liquid flowed from the corners of his mouth as he squirted the potent brew into the cavern, afterwards wiping his mouth with the corner of his free hand. With rhythmic weaving motions he made his way over in front of a young female. She in turn, kept her eyes focused on the ground as he danced animatedly before her. The small crowd roared with laughter when she made mockery of his movements once he turned his back and danced away.

At that moment a crashing noise erupted inside one of the clapboard houses. None of the villagers, neither Nate nor Ponti, could hear the sound, as the drums beat loudly, and the spirit of the evening's festivities were being launched to new heights.

"I never go wit' you no more," Al whined as he threw the large pottery bowl against the wall. His features showed his distress as he closed his eyes and roughly pulled the skin of his face downward. "You left me here fo' days. And now you want to go again wit'out me."

The childlike statement from the large man appeared out of place, and Jay sought a way to comfort his distraught brother. It was hard for him to see him like this, and his anger against Jackie Dawson was fueled.

"Aftah we go to Dangriga, Al, I will take you everywhere wit' me. It will be like it was befor'. You and me. Inseparable."

Al's thick lips turned down into a pronounced pout. "After Da-Da-Dangriga?" he repeated questioningly. "You told me tonight, Jay. Tonight I would go wit' you. You say there would be a parry for me. Now you say another time. I no believe you, Jay. I no believe you."

He paced around the room in a circle, repeating the statement over and over again. Jay wished what he had promised Al was true, but the *buyei* had changed his mind and there was nothing he could do about it. Because of the condition Al was in, there was no way he could afford to take him with him tonight when he met with Ricky Flint and his men for the transaction.

His eyes were concerned as he looked at his brother. It was at times like this when he was lucid and thinking logical thoughts, he was sure he might be getting better. But it was the other times, when he was totally someone else, that worried him. Jay wondered if the healing ceremony would be of any use.

"Look, Al. I can't take you wit' me, mon. I just can't. But aftah tomorrow, I will stay here an' travel wit' you to Dangriga, an' I promise you t'ings will be fine from t'en on."

Startled, childlike, accusing eyes focused on Jay.

"I know why you won't take me. You are goin' to your secret place." A bizarre pride gleamed on Al's face as he spoke. "See I know, I know, about it. You did not want me to know, but I know, 'cuz I follow you there, the first night you left me."

"What are you talkin' about?" Jay's bulbous eyes narrowed with concern.

"You know. You know where, Jay."

Al sat down in a kitchen chair, and started flapping his knees together, vigorously. A dim-witted grin crossed his face as he licked his lips with his wet tongue.

Jay stared at his brother. He wondered if what he said was true. In the beginning, he had planned to bring him in on everything once they got back to Punta Gorda, but the accident happened, changing all of his plans.

"No, I don't Al, tell me. Where is my secret place?"

Al replaced his leg movements with an aggravated rocking as he eyed his brother, then he abruptly stopped. His mood changed from excited to sulking almost in a split second's time, "I don't know, Jay. I don't know."

He laid his head within his arms which he folded over a badly nicked wooden table. He began to whine again like a baby.

Jay walked over and placed a comforting hand on his brother's shoulder. "It's gonna be all right, Al. T'ings will be jus' fine," he assured him. "Do you remembah that girl on the boat, Al? Do you? Well, she is here in Punta Gorda an' I have plans for you an' her."

Al peeped out at his brother from beneath his large forearm. Back and forth he wiped the mucus from his runny nose against it.

"You did like her didn't you?"

He shook his head, numbly.

"Well tonight when I come back, we're gonna pay her a visit."

"W-w-where she now?" Al blubbered.

"Eva is gettin' her ready for you, down in Miss Grace's old place. She's cleanin' her up to make her smell good all just for you, man. Now I want you to do one t'ing for me, and t'at's stay here until I come back to get you. Then we'll go and get t'at girl for you. All right?"

Grunting in between snorts of laughter Al answered him affirmatively.

It wasn't until Jay walked briskly out into the open path that Nate spotted him. The numerous trees hanging umbrella-like around his house, made it impossible to see the comings and goings there without being in the direct path of the moonlight.

A man on a mission, Nate watched as Jay paid no attention to the group of festival-goers. Hurriedly he strode pass them, then continued to walk towards the end of the village. As he passed one of the dwellings he was stopped by an elderly man. Nate assumed, by his dress, that he was the *buyei*. He could tell by Jay's stance that he was impatient and wanted their talk to end quickly. After another few minutes' delay, the two men parted company. The high priest headed for the celebrations and Jay continued on his chosen path. Nate and Ponti followed Jay under the cover of the surrounding rain forest.

CHAPTER 16

E va helped Raquel pull the plain shift over her head. It was necessary since her arms remained sore and hard to lift. Afterwards she busied herself carrying buckets of water out back as she emptied the tin tub. In the short amount of time they were together, the two women had developed a strange sort of camaraderie. The helping hand Raquel extended to Eva had served as a salve for her own dampened spirits. In turn, her comforting deeds and words could not have been offered to Raquel at a more needy time.

Once again the young woman touched her infected eyes. The itching and burning had ceased, and some of her sight had been restored. She was able to see through hazy slits, the results of the medicinal herbs.

As she combed through her wet hair, she thought of the shamaness, and felt gratitude toward the elderly woman who'd chosen an eccentric life of solitude, instead of a subservient one.

Suddenly, the clatter of an empty bucket being tossed to the floor startled her, and she turned in the direction from which it had been thrown.

Eva was standing just in the doorway, her eyes bulging with fear.

"What's the matter, Eva?" Raquel asked. Instantly her nerves became tight and on edge.

Before the woman could answer, Al pushed her inside, an unnatural look in his eyes as he salivated and grinned madly. Shocked, Raquel jumped to her feet, knocking over the wooden chair she was sitting on as she looked from Eva's horrified features to Al's deranged ones.

All was blurry because of her limited vision, but she could tell Eva was petrified with terror. Then she saw why. In Al's left hand an old-fashioned shaving blade, rusted with time, loomed threateningly at his side.

"What do you want?" Raquel murmured, as her mind wrestled with the scenario before her.

Al continued to grin stupidly. "I want you," he motioned with the blade. "Jay told me you were here wait'in for me an' later were we gone come get you togethah. But I—I didn't want to wait."

"Okay, I understand," she replied in an effort to reason with him. "But why do you need the razor?"

"So you won't run away. It wouldn't be nice fo' you to run away."

"I won't run, Al," Raquel lied as she tried to calculate how quickly she could get to the door without Al catching her. If only she could see clearly!

Taking a chance, Raquel made her move, heading for the door. Unluckily her foot caught on some object causing her to fall, but still she managed to grope for the knob. Just as she was opening it, Al's large frame slammed into her, knocking the breath from her body, and shutting the door once more. Raquel screamed over and over again hoping someone outside would hear her, but her cry for help was drowned out by the loud music of the preparatory celebration.

"You lied," he harshly whispered in her ear as he picked her up off the floor, and carried her with one arm around her waist. "I don't like people who lie. Jay lied. He told me he would take me wit' him tonight an' t'ere would be a party for me, but it was not true," his voice was wounded and childlike. "T'at's why I lied to him 'bout his secret place. I said I did not know where it was, but I do. It's the *dabuyaba* an' I'm gonna take you t'ere wit' me," he said decisively. "I'll show you what I do to liars. I don't break my promises."

Aimlessly Raquel kicked, squirmed and screamed as Al carried her out of the back door into the darkness. "Oh God, Eva-a-a, help me. For God's sake help me, Eva."

Inside, Eva remained petrified, tears flowing unchecked down her cheeks.

Minutes later Jay stepped up to the doorway of the last house in the village. At first, he acted as if he were about to knock and go inside, then suddenly he turned and backed into the shadows. Nervously, he looked to see if anyone saw him. Feeling comfortable that no one had, he ran across the path's end into the rain forest.

"Where do you think he's in such a hurry to get to?" Ponti enquired.

Nate didn't bother to answer. Wherever Jay was off to he didn't believe it had anything to do with the woman. Back at the celebration he'd overheard a conversation between two of the village women, talking about the *obeah* woman that had been taken to one of the villager's homes.

Stealthily, he made his way to the house Jay had stopped in front of, pausing at the door to hear if there was any noise coming from the inside, but there was none. He motioned for Ponti to hurry to his side.

"I don't know whose house this is, but it's as good a place as any to start looking for her. Now Ponti, all I want you to do is to stay back, because if I'm hurt we're going to need somebody to drive us out of here, and that somebody's going to have to be you."

Ponti nodded. "But what if you should get killed?" Fear of the unknown behind the wooden door weighed heavily on the younger man.

"That's a possibility, but not a probability," Nate calmly replied.

Vaguely satisfied, Ponti backed into the shadows.

Adjusting his stance, Nate gripped the Glock in his right hand as he tried the door knob with his left. His heart beat heavily at the thought of being discovered but he was counting on the majority of the people being at the ceremony as the probability that weighed in his favor.

The knob turned easily in his hand, and he cracked the door, then waited for some kind of response from within, but only silence greeted him. Cautiously, he pushed it open with his right elbow, and the light from within the small house spilled out onto the path. As the opening widened, he could see there had been a struggle.

Nate was surprised when he saw the woman sitting passively on the back stoop with the door wide open. Her badly scarred back was exposed. Nate knew she had to have heard the door open, but she never turned to see who was entering the place.

Stepping inside, he inspected the room. Lying next to a tin tub he saw the bright red wrap Raquel had worn earlier that day.

Gently, he stooped down beside the woman whose salty tears had left white tracks on her dark skin.

"Where is she?" he asked then repeated the question. "Where is the *obeah* woman?"

Blankly, Eva looked into Nate's worried features, then with lips barely moving. "Al's taken her to the old temple. He say, he gone do to her, what he did to me."

As quick as a flash Nate was at the front entrance. "Ponti," he called. Instantly, the Mayan appeared out of the shadows.

"Go and get the Samurai, and meet me at the end of that road that forked off from the main one, coming in to the village. Do it! Now!"

Nate crashed through the foliage as he headed for the abandoned *dabuyaba*. He remembered its location well, for at one time, while he was still a boy, it was the only temple used by both the Shango and the Garifuna.

Branches and vines whipped at his face as he ran, the sight of the woman's scarred back spurring him on. He had to get there before the same gruesome thing happened to Raquel.

Al dragged Raquel into the thick darkness of the neglected building. The only illumination came from a small stream of moonlight that infiltrated through a crack in one of the dirt clogged windows. Holding on to her wrist tightly, he closed the door behind them, then he pulled her resisting body further inside. They passed between several rows of dusty benches before they reached the front of a large room.

Because of the darkness, Raquel's limited vision was practically useless, and an unfathomable panic began to rise inside of her.

"Let me go, Al," she pleaded. "You don't want to do this. It's bad! What you're thinking is bad, I tell you. And you're not a bad man, Al," she tried to reassure him through his demented mind.

Al was quiet as he looked around the dilapidated room. "We should go in t'ere." He dragged her behind him as he kicked open the door of a smaller room jutting off to the side of the large one. Bright moonlight streamed in as the door gave in to the weight of his thrust, and he slammed it behind them.

Satisfied, he let go of Raquel's wrist, and she peered helplessly into the semidarkness around her, frantically searching for an avenue of escape.

Strangely, this room was much cleaner than the first. Several large objects were lined up neatly against the wall. Remnants of broken benches had been piled in one of the corners, but the majority of the space was wide open.

"Yeah I like t'is room. It's much bettah than the first," Al rambled madly. "I can see bettah in here, and I want you to see what I do to you," he wiped the back of his hand across his nose.

He backed up to one of the containers against the wall, and placed the shaving razor on it. Then keeping a watchful eye on Raquel, with jerky motions, he began to strip off his shirt and remove his pants. Finally he stood stark naked before her, grinning dementedly all the while. His thick, muscular body in contrast to the bizarre smile on his face.

A sickening bile began to rise in Raquel's throat as she watched him; the thought of what he planned to do to her was utterly revolting.

"You gotta take off your clothes too," he stated, his tone absent of threat or anger. "I want to make pretty pictures for you." His eyes gleamed.

"I can't, Al. You've got to help me," she coaxed, her mind working quickly. Raquel began to back towards the stack of wooden remnants. "It will be better if you help to undress me," she said in a quivering voice.

Al started across the room just as Raquel's back touched the wooden slats of the wall. Suddenly she turned and groped for one of the smaller pieces which lay near the edge. She grabbed it, sending a splinter deep into her hand. The pain was intense but Raquel did not care as she blindly swung the plank with all her might in Al's direction.

The wood landed with a sickening thud as it caught him across the face, breaking the skin with its force, its uneven edges cutting into the tender meat. Even so, the blow barely rocked him, and a cry like that of a mad, wounded animal rose from deep in his throat.

The unnatural noise horrified Raquel, and with a counter-swing she wielded the board again, this time catching him in his throat, causing him to grab it and double over with pain.

Seeing her chance, Raquel tried to skirt his massive body, but with one arm he reached out and caught her by the waist, as the other hand remained protectively about his own neck. She screamed again as he grabbed her, and in blind terror, she swung the slat wildly over her head, striking Al repeatedly. The powerful and mad Al shook her as if she were a rag doll, then released her as a piece of the splintering board pierced one of his eyes.

Like a cornered animal she dropped to the floor, scrambling to get behind him and to the door. With every ounce of strength she had she rose and lunged for the knob.

By now, Al's face was bleeding profusely. Seeing Raquel through a stream of blood, he caught her leg, forcing her to tumble sideways into the containers against the opposite wall. Raquel gasped as the board fell from her hand into the darkness of the room. With a triumphant laugh, Al climbed on top of her, placing his large hands about her throat. With eyes blazing wildly, he pressed her head back into a white dust that surrounded them, as he reached for the razor he'd placed on top of the containers.

She started to scream as his hand found the weapon and he raised it high above their heads. She closed her eyes to block out the horror of what was about to occur.

Suddenly, two loud bangs rang inside the room causing Raquel's eyes to fly open. For a second, Al's demented features seemed to freeze before he tumbled over to the side of her, dead from two bullets to the heart.

Raquel began to cry and shiver uncontrollably as Nate took her in his arms.

"It's all right *pataki*. It's all right. I am here now," he spoke to her comfortingly. "No harm will come to you, now, baby. No harm at all."

She clung to him, burying her face in his chest. "I thought I was dead, and I'd never see you again," she managed through racking sobs.

"No baby, it's all over, just like a bad dream."

Gently he picked her up in his arms and carried her out of the temple. Moments later a set of headlights beamed in the distance, then pulled up beside them.

A silent Ponti looked on as Nate placed the young woman's limp body into the back seat of the car, then climbed up beside her, continuing to cradle her close in his arms. He rubbed her face and tangled hair, kissing her repeatedly, as he murmured reassurances.

As they drove down the moonlit back road, sprays of white powder floated inside the vehicle. Blotches of it were on Raquel's face, and a fine dusting was in her hair and on her shift.

"What the hell is this?" Nate muttered as he looked at it. Then he stuck a finger into a thick batch clinging to the side of Raquel's face and placed it in his mouth.

Smacking his lips experimentally, he exclaimed, "I'll be damned. It's cocaine."

CHAPTER 17

"Shut off the lights!" Jay ordered, his voice hushed, excited.

Mane-Mane cut resentful eyes in Jay's direction. "What the hell for? Look man, you're getting on my freakin' nerves with all this bull—"

Reaching over Mane-Mane's muscular arm, Jay extinguished the lights as a nude couple full of cashew fruit wine stumbled drunkenly toward them. Their inebriated state was evidence of the orgiastic climax of the waning Shangoain celebration not very far away.

High-pitched squeals of pleasurable glee erupted from the female as the male's hands intentionally groped over her full frame. With anticipation, the couple fell to the ground continuing their sexual escapade. Quickly the woman's laughter was replaced with guttural moans of pleasure as they concluded the unabandoned foreplay exhibited only moments before.

Mane-Mane leaned over antagonistically towards Jay. "Don't you all have beds out here in the jungle to do that kind of thing? Or are you just so savage you all prefer making out on the ground like animals?"

"I wouldn't expect you to understan'," Jay retorted as he slid further into the car seat. Ricky's men acted as though they knew everything, that they were in control. But this was Jay's country, Jay's people. Soon he would control everything and these men would not talk to him with disrespect. He could almost taste all the power he would have if everything went according to plan. "It's the kind of t'ing only real men an' women know about," Jay continued to Mane-Mane. "Not punks who hide their true nature behin' big muscles, tryin' to make up for the tiny bulge in the front of their pants."

Mane-Mane's eyes lit up with anger, "You backwoods mother—"

"All right. All right. Cool it. Do you want them to hear us?" The other man, Rock, placed a calming hand on his partner's shoulder. "What the hell are they doing out here this time of morning anyway?" he asked Jay, irritated.

"T'ere was a celebration in the village. T'ey should be makin' t'eir way back towards the main street soon. Usually no one comes t'is far out. It must have been a very spirited ritual wit' lots of wine."

"Okay, we'll just wait them out."

Jay's prediction proved to be correct. Minutes later, the satiated pair made their way arm and arm back towards the distant music.

Still not wanting to take a chance, the trio started the car but kept the lights off; the moon provided enough illumination for them to navigate their way toward the abandoned *dabuyaba*.

"Mane-Mane, you and Jay go inside and take these sacks with you. Since this is our first haul we didn't stash that many bricks here, we're just starting to test the waters so to speak. If everything goes smooth tonight, the next haul will be much bigger," he looked encouragingly in Jay's direction. "Now, only three of the containers actually have cane in them, the others are just dummies with debris and other crap inside."

"Yeah . . . yeah, I know. Remembah I was wit' you when the first drop was made," Jay was anxious to show he knew what was going on. Already he was outside the car with two of the large cotton sacks and a small spotlight in his hand.

Rock fastened a barely tolerable stare on his lean, suddenly impatient companion. "Just chill, man. I know that. I'm just doin' my job," he paused to let his point sink in. He needed to remind the newest member, whenever Ricky wasn't around, he was the man calling the shots. "While you two go inside, I'll stay out here, and make sure we don't have any unexpected guests. Mane-Mane, once you all check the place out, and find everything is okay, come back and let me know before you gather up the bricks."

Mane-Mane's braided head nodded with understanding. Then he grabbed the remaining sacks and flashlight, and joined Jay as he walked toward the building.

Carefully they opened the large wooden door, switching on their lights only after it had been closed behind them. Breathing heavily, Jay peered into the semidarkness. He shone his minute spotlight around the dust-filled room making sure everything appeared to be the same.

Mane-Mane's eyes followed the path of Jay's light, from time to time blending his own luminous bubble with his partners'.

A hoarse laugh gurgled up from his throat.

"Shit man, I'm disappointed. Ain't no leftover shrunken heads or human skulls laying around. Ain't that the kind of stuff y'all use to hoodoo each other with?"

"Screw you, man," Jay threw back at him while he advanced toward the side door aided by the flashlight.

Suddenly, the light focused on a large, muddy footprint planted firmly upon the door. Jay stiffened at the sight of it, then turned to Mane-Mane, placing a silencing finger across his thin lips.

Now, as alert as a bird dog, Mane-Mane pushed him aside. Cautiously he touched one of the thickest edges of the print's outline, and found it was still damp under the dry outer crust. A fatal look replaced the playful visage the huge bodyguard had worn moments before. He let the sacks fall silently to the dirt floor, and stealthily retrieved a .38 from the front of his pants. He motioned for Jay to continue shining his light in the direction of the door.

With amazing swiftness and one smooth action, Mane-Mane forced the door open, entered the room, and stood poised to confront anyone on the opposite side. He was counting on the element of surprise, coupled with the pitch darkness behind him and the glare of Jay's small spotlight to throw any would-be-opposers off guard. His heart beat loudly in his ears as his deep-set eyes darted swiftly about the wrecked room.

"What the hell is this?" The words tumbled from his thick lips as his eyes landed on Al's nude, bloodied body against the tumbled containers, under a white coating of pure cocaine powder.

Pushing Mane-Mane aside, Jay forced his way in front of him. A painful pressure tightened inside his chest as he looked at his brother's lifeless body. Al's head lay cocked at an unnatural angle where the impact of the bullet had snapped his thick neck.

"Who's the dead freak lying in the middle of the stash, man?" Mane-Mane asked, not really expecting an answer. Before he could turn and look at his counterpart, Jay launched a mad attack on his back, a throaty scream of anguish echoing throughout the room.

"Don' call him a freak!" A thin but powerful arm locked about Mane-Mane's muscular throat, while Jay squeezed with all his might.

Gagging, the bodyguard tried to pry loose the viselike grip choking his neck. With fingers resembling talons, he desperately reached behind him, locking them into the side of Jay's thin throat. Squeezing his thick digits deep into his throat, Mane-Mane bent forward, and flipped him over onto his back. He followed Jay's fallen frame onto the ground, edging a forceful knee into his sternum, pressing his weight against his chest.

"What's the matter with you, man? Huh?" he managed between choking gasps, guardingly holding his throat.

Jay squeezed his eyes together, tightly, as he focused on the lingering pain beneath his jawbone. Tears edged their way from the corners of his eyes, and he fought against the pain and the mental picture of his brother's inert body.

"What's going on in here?" Rock spoke from behind them. His eyes were wide with foreboding and a few snorts of cocaine. A .38 similar to his partner's was visible in his hand.

"What the hell?" Rock reached down to pick up one of the hot spotlights, "All right, Mane-Mane, let him up," and he turned the light's glare on Al's stiff frame. "Damn, he sure is messed up. I wonder who he is," he shined the revealing white light upon Al's blank features, highlighting the thin covering of narcotics that blanketed the body and the area around it. "And look at all the cane that's on him. You got any idea who this is, man?" he turned to Jay, the situation and the drugs making his heart pump faster.

"He's my brothah," Jay stated as he weakly rose to his feet.

"Your brother." Rock's tone turned the innocent words into a crime. "What was he doing here?"

"I don't know," Jay held his shaking head in his hands. "As far as I know he nevah even came to t'is place. Nobody evah does."

"Well that's what you get for thinking village boy," Mane-Mane looked closely into Al's open eyes. "Rock ma-an, I warned Ricky against getting involved with folks like this boy. Now look-a-here. Part of the dope's messed up and we got a corpse on our hands. But see he don't want to listen to—"

"Shut up, man," Rock ordered. "He don't listen to you cuz you don't know when to be quiet. We need to find out how many bricks we still have left. We'll talk about everything else later."

Roughly Mane-Mane bent forward to move Al's inflexible body out of the way. Jay knocked his hand off of his brother's shoulder.

"I'll take care of my own brothah."

Rock and Mane-Mane rummaged for, then counted the remaining bricks of cocaine while Jay tried to cradle his dead brother's body in his arms, the natural effect of rigor mortis making his affectionate gestures nearly impossible.

"Nine, ten . . . Okay. That means we only lost two of them," the larger bodyguard concluded after placing the last pair of white rectangles in the sack.

"What do you mean, *only* two! Wait till Ricky hears about this. Those two bricks alone would be worth millions on the street," Rock's eyes flashed at his partner.

"Well hell, I didn't do it! Ain't no need to get pissed with me."

"Naw, you're right. But somebody's gonna have to pay for this."

Both sets of eyes focused on Jay and his brother.

"And I know jus' who," Jay said, almost to himself. "T'ey will pay for my brothah's death an' t'ey will not die quickly. I'm gonna make sure t'ey suffah," he spoke reassuringly to the corpse.

Rock and Mane-Mane looked at each other.

"That ain't the only thing around here that's gonna have to be paid for," Mane-Mane retorted. "Your damn brother getting killed is the least most important thing that needs to be considered."

A chill of fear ran down Mane-Mane's spine as Jay cast eyes shining with a bizarre light in his direction.

"I will put a curse on you . . . your mother, and every generation that comes after you, if you say anything else against him. I could be a *buyei*. Do not cross me. Do you understand?"

Mane-Mane knew about fighting with his hands and weapons, but being threatened with curses was unchartered territory, and almost frightened him more than a gun being pointed in his face. He threw up both his hands in a show of surrender.

"All right, man. All right. Yeah. Whoever monked up our stash . . . and did this to your brother, is gonna have to pay. They'll have to pay with their lives." He adeptly changed the subject. "I'll guarantee Ricky that."

"Yeah, you're right. We'll have to guarantee him something when we tell him about this," Rock sniffed and squeezed his nostrils out of habit. "But right now, we need to bury the stiff . . . I mean your brother, before this place is crawling with the law."

"No," Jay grabbed at Al's chest possessively. "He must be buried the Shangoain way. Not put in the ground like some worthless dog."

"Naw man, that's not what I'm sayin'," Rock explained, his patience growing thin, but like Mane-Mane he too was leery of curses. "Right now, it wouldn't do us, or your brother any good, if we get tracked down and put away before we can take care of the suckers who did all this. You see what I'm sayin'?"

Jay's bulbous eyes stared at him suspiciously.

"Since they offed your brother, I don't think they'll be running to the authorities right away. So we got a chance of finding them and paying them back. But if you take your brother back to your village like this, ma-an, ain't no way somebody dealing with the law ain't gonna hear about it. Now you want to get the suckers who did this don't cha?"

Jay nodded affirmatively.

"Then just do what I say, all right?"

Rock watched as Jay and Mane-Mane carried Al into the main part of the temple to be temporarily placed under the platform. His drug habit compelled him to dab his finger into a small pile of cocaine, then inhale it up his nostrils. The uncut narcotic caused his nose to bleed immediately. He patted it with a corner of one of the cotton sacks.

Eventually the three men returned to the vehicle, placing the remaining bricks of cocaine in the trunk of the car.

"Now, how do we find out if the people you think are responsible for all of this, are actually behind it?" Rock asked, gently rubbing his nose.

"It'll jus' take one stop," an unearthly calm laced Jay's words. "You all will have to stay in the car back off in the woods. If we drove up into the village, it would cause too big of a stir," he warned. "I'll tell you where to drop me off."

Jay entered the dark house silently. Once again, he waited to switch on the spotlight only after he'd closed the door behind him. His heart lurched as the light beamed directly onto Eva's emaciated, barely covered frame, hunched in a corner on top of a cot. Her eyes were wide open, but they did not blink from the glaring light. Any other time Jay would have spoken to her harshly, but her uncanny appearance made him think twice. Instead he cased the room with the unnatural light. Only after he was sure Jackie Dawson was not in the house did he address his wife.

"Where is the woman?"

Eva continued to stare directly ahead.

"D'ya hear what I said? Where is she? Did Al come here an' get her?" Jay demanded loudly, shining the light interrogatingly in her face, but to no avail. For a moment her features reflected fear as he mentioned his brother's name, but then that was replaced with the same blank stare.

Maybe he was tired from the entire ordeal, or even more unlikely he felt sorry for the pitiful picture his wife made, but for whatever reason, he didn't press her further. He switched off the light and closed the wooden door behind him. He didn't need Eva to tell him what had happened. The woman's absence told him everything he needed to know.

It was obvious Al had known about his secret place and had taken Jackie there. He had tried to have his way with her, she had fought him like the *echu* he knew her to be. Then Nate Bowman had come, probably during their struggle, killed Al and took her away.

Jay rounded the tiny house, only to stop on the side facing the rain forest. He needed a few moments alone before he joined the two men that waited for him. The intensity of the emotions rumbling inside him made it hard to think straight. It seemed like in a matter of minutes everything important in his life had been destroyed.

Al was dead, and his relationship with Ricky and the *buyei* would both be on shaky grounds after tonight. Even if he killed Nate and the woman, which he had to do to avenge his brother's death, it would not guarantee things in his life would be any better. Ricky could still decide he was too risky to deal with, and that would mean a loss of his future as he had dreamed of it; away from this village, living in Miami, having the best life had to offer. If that were taken away from him, as things would stand then, he would no longer have the high priest to support him. He would be ostracized, claimed dead to the Shangoains for killing the link to the *gubida*. The *buyei* would never forgive him.

Jay pulled hard on the reefer he'd automatically lit as his mind rambled through his current state of affairs. The one thing he was sure of, he had to make the people suffer who were responsible for his brother's death.

The man stared at the sky as he took several drags, then finished the hand-rolled cigarette, throwing the butt on the ground as he made up his mind.

He'd do everything he could to make Ricky give him another chance, that was the future he wanted, and that's what he still intended to have. After everything was over with, he would go back to the *dabuyaba* and give Al the best Shangoain burial that he could, but the truth about Al's death would have to remain a secret. He would convince the *buyei* Al had run off, and with his mind as scrambled as it was that would be easy for anyone to believe.

If Nate Bowman had killed him, which Jay believed he had, he figured Nate would not run and tell the authorities too quickly. So once he and the woman were dead, no one else would ever know what had happened. Most important, no matter how Nate end Jackie ended up dying, he'd have to convince Ricky and the others the Shango must never know he was involved in any kind of way. It would be the only way they'd be able to continue trafficking drugs in the area.

Automatically his mind went to Eva. She was the only person who knew enough of the truth to destroy the entire plan.

Jay's hand went to the switchblade he always carried with him. Already mentally drained, by now, he was almost acting entirely on instinct. He rounded the corner again and reentered the house, but this time when he turned on the spotlight, Eva was not there. His eyes went to the back door that was still ajar. She had managed to leave without him hearing her.

At first a feeling of unadulterated fear engulfed him, but that was replaced with a sense of relief when he thought of the threat he had made against her life if anything should ever happen to him. A satisfied smirk rested on his dark features. He knew his wife. The years had cowed her spirit. She would think long and hard before saying anything that could cause problems for him, and the state she appeared to be in, he didn't know if she was capable of thinking at all. Probably by the time she made her mind up to move against him, he would have found a more efficient way of taking care of her.

Jay let the calming thoughts wash over him, the effect of the marijuana aiding his endeavor. Feeling a sense of security, he shut off the spotlight and headed back to join Rock and Mane-Mane in the car.

CHAPTER 18

"How much farther is Dangriga?"

Looking into the rear-view mirror, Ponti's voice reflected his weariness of body and spirit. The events of the previous day hung in his mind like a nagging movie. He didn't actually see what had happened in the temple, but he'd heard the unmistakable gunshots, and from the state the woman, Jackie Dawson, was in, there was no doubt in his mind Nate had killed the man responsible for it.

Over the last twenty-four hours he'd come to admire the man's steely strength, but he had to admit that admiration was tinged with fear. He believed there was very little Nate was afraid of, and a man without fear could be a dangerous man.

Ponti watched as Nate gently removed the wild strands of wind-blown hair from the woman's face as she slept comfortably against his shoulder, his ability to show such tenderness starkly contrasted with the toughness he also possessed.

Thickly fringed eyes gazed out the window as he studied the very familiar territory. Because of Nate's knowledge they had been able to keep to the back roads.

"I'd say we've got ten miles to go, seven if we were able to cut through the forest," he responded to Ponti's question.

His deep voice caused movement underneath Raquel's closed eyelids, followed by the slight opening of her matted eyes. She could feel his arm draped snugly around her shoulder as thoughts of the morning's events drifted into her consciousness. She continued to remain very still, not wanting him to know she had awakened.

Raquel was afraid of what her reaction would be when she looked at him knowing he had killed a man, even if it were to protect her. Somehow her attempt to do the same thing in the heat of her struggle with Al did not lessen the weight of Nate's actions. She felt as if the arm about her shoulder was that of a complete stranger.

Truthfully, what did she really know about this man, Nate? That he had kidnapped her and forced her to come to Belize to be subjected to the horrors she had come to know? Yet in the midst of it all, had done all he could to protect her? That with the skill of a master sculptor he knew how to touch and caress her, bringing her to heights of passion she had only dreamed about? That he had killed a man, shooting him at point-blank range without a second thought?

The look in Al's eyes when Nate shot him forced its way into her mind, and a shudder ran through her, causing Nate to look down and find she was awake. Their eyes met briefly allowing him to catch the glimmer of fear in hers before she quickly looked away. Nate's dark gaze looked emotionlessly ahead as she lifted her face from his shoulder, turning it in the direction of the opposite window.

"Here," he offered her a small container of bottled water and several crumpled napkins he'd found on the back seat of the car. "You can try and clean your eyes with this."

Raquel accepted his offering wordlessly.

The tepid water felt refreshing against her skin as she cleansed her face. She was relieved to find her eyes were almost back to normal, even though that discomfort had been replaced by another. Jarring pains shot up and down the length of her neck from even the slightest movement of her head, an achy reminder of her most recent brush with death.

Natural reflexes caused her to flinch from a particularly sharp pain, and Raquel's slender hand raised to cradle her bruised throat. Tears stung the back of her closed lids as she fought against the physical and mental discomfort.

Raquel felt a warm, caressing feeling on her thigh. She opened her eyes to see Nate's large comforting hand reaching out to console her.

Suddenly the sight of this comforting gesture infuriated her. Like a volcano that had been waiting to erupt, her raspy voice struck out, full of insurmountable fear and pain. "Don't you touch me. If it wasn't for you none of this would have happened to me." Dark, injured eyes overflowed with tears. "I can't stand any more of this. I can't stand you."

Nate almost felt his heart stop at hearing the harsh words against him, nor could he stomach seeing her so distraught. Desperate, he enfolded her in his arms despite her loud protest, holding her tightly against him, willing the pain and hurt to go away.

Finally Raquel began to sob. It was a deep outpouring of the misery she felt as she gave in to the comforting embrace.

The fear Nate had seen in her perplexed eyes was more than he could bear. To accept that the woman you love, feared you and perceived you as a cruel and a heartless criminal, was hard to do. Yes, he had finally admitted to himself that he loved her. Seeing Al attempt to take her permanently away from him made his feelings clear: he desired her, he admired her and he loved her.

Yet Nate had mixed emotions about Raquel's reawakened fear of him. He knew in many ways they were still strangers. The moments of love they had shared were far less than the continuing nightmare she found herself in. He had no one to blame for that but himself.

As the moments passed, Raquel regained her self control, and she withdrew herself from his arms. Nate wanted to continue to hold her but he could tell from the stiffening of her body that she would not welcome him.

Raquel could feel his ebony gaze upon her willing her to look into his eyes. Curly, hesitant eyelashes fluttered during a moment of indecision before unveiling a tear bright, dusky stare. The unnerving chill of love, the warmest of emotions, trying to survive under these circumstances was felt by them both.

Although Nate's lips never uttered a word of apology, it was written clearly in the depths of his eyes. Raquel recognized the look but couldn't accept it.

Once again she was the first to break eye contact. He had saved her life and she knew she still loved him, but she couldn't reach out to him any further, not after what happened with Al.

As she returned to looking out the window, bright splotches of color could be seen in the distance. The rain forest was very dense and traveling had been slow. She could tell that the road they had chosen was not well used, because in actuality it was little more than a path. The humidity had begun to build inside the vehicle as the morning progressed, and even though it was quite early and the massive cohune palms and guanacaste trees blocked out the majority of the sun's rays, its strong influence was beginning to be felt. All the jeep windows were now rolled down, it had become too sticky and hot inside.

"Hey, Nate. There are a bunch of women and children to the far right of us. They look like they're gathering something," Ponti exclaimed with curiosity.

"Yes, you're right. They're digging up cassava roots. There will be a lot of *ariba* bread made and eaten over the next few days, so they are making sure they'll have enough throughout the ceremonies."

"It is like the Mayan tortilla?"

"Somewhat."

Nate noticed Raquel's eyes brighten as she watched two Garifunian women accompanied by a little girl heading back for the village. On top of their heads they balanced baskets piled high with roots from the shrublike plant. He felt relieved to see even the slightest positive change in her. So he continued to talk, avoiding the heavy silence of moments before.

"It is a flat, dry bread, that is the very essence of the Garifunian culture, a legacy of our Carib Indian ancestry," Nate continued. "I say *our* because my father is Garifunian, but my mother was Creole. I basically know about the culture because of that, but the Garifunian are very secretive about a lot of their customs. There are things they never share with outsiders, not even their spouses."

A surprised look crossed Raquel's features as she listened to Nate talk about his family. For awhile now, she had longed to know more about him. It was a revelation to hear his parents were of mixed heritages, even though they were both Belizean. She envied what little knowledge he had of his father's people, since she had grown up completely ignorant of her own.

"As a matter of fact Garifuna means 'Cassava-eating people' taking their name from the Carib word *Karifuna,* of the Cassava clan."

Ponti nodded his head appreciatively, always anxious to learn whatever he could. Since he had grown up in Balam, he didn't know much about the other ethnic groups that populated Belize. The elders did not find it wise to share knowledge about other cultures. They felt the Balamian way was superior, and knowledge of others only helped to confuse their own villagers.

By now all of the women and children had become aware of the jeep. They stopped in the middle of their tasks, watching the vehicle's sluggish progress no more than a hundred yards away.

The dresses the women wore reminded Raquel of floral printed dusters favored by some of the elderly females who frequented the clinic, but these women also wore bright head wraps and scarfs.

While the women continued to watch their progress at a distance, two of the young boys began to run in the direction of the four-wheel drive. With agile grace their bare feet paddled against the forest floor. As they got closer they picked up pebbles and began to chuck them at the jeep. But their impromptu fun was cut short when they were abruptly stopped by a particularly vocal and nimble female.

As the vehicle passed the harvesters, and the distance between it and the women and children increased, Raquel could see all of them hoisting their loaded baskets on to their heads, and in a staggered line heading for Drangriga. Their easy movements with such an arduous task made her wonder what kind of people would greet them there.

For some reason it was hard for her to connect Nate with the women and children she saw toiling in the rain forest. From the very beginning, he had stood out from her other abductors. His naturally quiet, reserved ways—until provoked—seemed to separate him from Al and Jay. He was a man whose presence exuded power, unlike Art, with his youthful penchant to take instructions instead of give them.

Raquel choked back the urge to demand from Nate an answer for all that had happened to her. Why he had kidnapped her, then had chosen to protect her? Why was it so important to him that she participate in the Garifunian ceremony, that he would risk his own life to protect her?

Yet she knew she was afraid of what she might find out, and it made her feel that much more vulnerable. She was afraid the answer Nate might give would confirm the worst of her fears. That he was not a man with morals and principles who had simply been caught up in a mad scheme beyond his control. That he was in his own way like Jay, all of his deeds a shield for his own selfish needs.

Raquel felt a powerful urge to look in to the strong features of the man whose face at times revealed boundless compassion. She sighed heavily. She hoped she was right about Nate Bowman. She wanted to be reassured that even if her logic had failed her, her inner guide, her sense of good and evil and right and wrong, had not led her astray. It was all so confusing. So much had passed between her and Nate in such a short period of time, she was having difficulty knowing what to believe.

Instead she looked down at her hands that were covered with dirt and her own blood. She was surprised to see a large splinter lodged in the fleshy mound of her palm beneath her thumb. As she picked at the splinter, she realized her mind had been so overwhelmed with the battery of recent events, and the engaging images before her, she had managed to block out the pain of the tender injury. Somehow seeing the violated flesh made her feel its pain, causing once again an overall feeling of defilement and uncertainty.

It had only been yesterday when she'd felt so sure about her feelings for Nate, and her abilities to carry out whatever was necessary during the ceremonies in Dangriga, but now she wasn't sure of anything.

Unable to remove the splinter, she reached instead for the small leather pouch that hung about her neck. Her soiled fingers clung to its smoothness as she searched for the power within herself to stay on the sane side of her emotions. At that moment it would have been so easy to cross the line, to let the current of the mental gap between sanity and insanity sway to the latter.

Oh God . . . Spirit . . . Will . . . whatever I should call you. I need you to be with me now. Just let me be able to hold on. Her mental cry to the powers that be vibrated from within her, creating a strong shuddering, as she moved her lips to the words of the silent prayer, her richly lashed eyes closed tight in her seeking.

The intenseness that surrounded Raquel during this prayer-filled moment was felt by both Nate and Ponti. The younger man watched with true concern through the rear-view mirror, while Nate's dark gaze burned with a well-known torture.

The one woman whom he'd loved the most, his mother, had lived her last years of life balancing on the edge of sanity. Events not nearly as violent as the recent ones this woman beside him had suffered, had placed her on that precipice. He did not know if he could accept finally finding another kind of love, just as powerful, then losing her to a similar fate. Only this time there would be no one to blame but himself.

"It all will be over soon, *pataki.*" He sought to say the only words that he thought would comfort her.

A heavy silence prevailed inside the tiny vehicle as they progressed closer to the village. Raquel watched as the landscape changed from a dense rain forest to rising hills. Finally they took an ill-kept road called Hummingbird Highway that quickly changed names prior to approaching a shabby bus stand with a sign pointing toward Dangriga.

Time passed slowly as they entered the town's vicinity, a dilapidated fruit-laden truck creeping along contentedly in front of them helped to prolong the journey. As the minutes passed, Raquel realized the city of Dangriga was not another isolated village like Balam or Eva's small settlement near Punta Gorda. Modern society had definitely made its mark here. From what she could see it was a neat, bustling town with restaurants, gift shops, a bar and a disco. Just like any city it had its more prosperous neighborhoods where the stilted houses were well kept, then, no further than a few blocks down, the housing climate changed, sometimes slightly, at others, drastically so. Just the sight and feel of the city gave her some reassurance that regular life still existed outside the bloodletting Balamians and vengeful Shangoains.

It was energizing to see a river flowing straight through Dangriga, populated with a variety of boats and people fishing. There seemed to be a festive attitude as they smiled, chatted and reeled in fish of all sizes and hues.

"Turn here," Nate instructed solemnly, pointing to the right. "It will take us down to the sea."

Ponti waited patiently as the traffic moved slowly through the streets.

Raquel could feel her spirits lifting as she watched the city's serene activities, but nothing was more healing than the inner calm inspired by the sight of the turquoise, clear Caribbean Sea. The spectable of its expansive waters lying before them assured her, there was definitely a master plan. One in which she and others like her had, in comparison, small but important roles to carry out. Raquel believed one either conjures up the faith to see oneself through or succumbs to the negative forces.

They turned down a road that ran along the meager beach. Like the river, it too had its share of people, but some of their activities were a little more puzzling to the young woman.

An older man placed a small colorful flag in the sand, carefully he began to smooth the surface of the tiny mound of sand around it. Raquel noticed the flag was one of several in varying colors, jutting out along the shore. The squeal of several frolicking adolescents drew her attention. There were several Creole boys chasing two girls of similar ages along the beach, the snapping pinchers of two large crabs helped to make the romp more exciting. The young females shrieked delightedly, as their dark, slightly waving hair, stretched out in the cool breeze. But their play was cut short by an older woman who beckoned the boys over in her direction. She and three other women were kneeling down beside what Raquel assumed was a large hole in the ground. Curious, she continued to watch, as the reluctant young males turned from their pursuit of the fairer sex and raced over toward the waiting older females.

One of the women was dropping what appeared to be several hot rocks, which she handled gingerly with a piece of heavy cloth, into the opening. Soon after the boys arrived with their catch, those crabs along with others were expertly bound in large banana leaves and what looked like sea weed, then placed in the gaping hole. Once the wrapped crabs were situated, the cavity was filled in with sand, and a small flag was placed above it to mark the spot.

With calculated timing, the two young females reappeared near the newly constructed oven, provoking the young males to go back to their previous chase.

The wheels of the Samurai crunched onto the pebbled lot of the Pelican Beach Resort. It was a good-looking hotel with a dock facing the sea. Several brown lounge chairs made with wooden slats had been conveniently placed facing the water, enabling guests to take advantage of the sun and the beautiful view.

It didn't take them long to check into the hotel where they secured two rooms. One for Ponti, the other for Nate and herself.

Rebellion wanted to raise its obstinate head when Nate directed her to their room and closed the door decidedly behind them. Had it not occurred to him that she might have wanted a room to herself? Even after all that had passed between them, did he still consider her his prisoner? She sighed, in actuality she still was. Not only because he had abducted her in Miami, but because in this short period of time he had managed to imprison her heart.

Never during her entire relationship with Clinton Bradshaw had she experienced such intense feelings ranging from fear to utter desire. It rattled Raquel to realize despite her cautious nature, what she did not know about Nate was less important to her than her growing feelings for him. She feared their intensity more than his cloaked past. Yes, she feared him, but she loved him more, and hoped her intuition was right: that he would never use that dark side against her.

The young woman inhaled deeply, her strong shoulders slumping with the weight of the past few weeks. There was so much to think about and do, now that they'd arrived in Dangriga.

A confused bird crashed into one of the windows of the hotel room, and Raquel's frightened eyes flew to the panes, expecting to see a vengeful Jay. She stood paralyzed until she heard Nate's voice.

"It is nothing to be frightened of *pataki*, only a bird," he crossed the room to place his arms about her. Nate felt her jump at his touch, then she began to shake uncontrollably.

He placed his bristly cheek against the cloud of black hair on top of her head, wrapping her even tighter in his strong embrace to still her trembling, and his fear of never being able to return to the blissful moments they had shared.

"You are my woman now, *pataki* and that means a hell of a lot to me. All I can ask is that you trust me to do the right thing by you. To take care of you. Can you do that?"

Raquel managed a few jerky affirmative nods of her head. But she was uncertain if she really meant it.

"Now, let's start with that splinter."

Nate had gotten everything he needed to remove the sliver from Raquel's hand when he checked into the hotel, and she and Ponti waited outside. The removal was painful, but necessary, and she couldn't help but be touched by the tenderness and concern Nate displayed as he carried out the tedious procedure.

"Now that wasn't so bad, was it?" he asked, dark, brown eyes looking deeply into hers as he held her hand, then placed a soft kiss in its palm.

"No" she managed, but was unable to respond further.

"Now let's run some hot bath-water. I believe I saw some bath crystals in here," he searched through the little set of bottles assembled in a decorative basket for the hotel guests.

"Here we go," he raised the small container with blue crystals for Raquel's inspection, then turned toward the bathtub. The rushing water thundered into the fiberglass tub, its contents turning blue as Nate generously added the bath crystals.

She watched his accommodating actions with interest and a warm feeling of appreciation.

"Do you need me to help you undress . . . I know right now, your hand may make it a little difficult for you." He said with a deep whisper.

"No . . . I can manage. Thanks."

Raquel knew from the smoldering look in Nate's eyes that his thoughts weren't only occupied with her comfort.

"All right. I've got to go and take care of a few things. If all goes well, this will be over with sooner than you think," he held her gaze meaningfully. "I'll just be gone for a little while. Maybe you'd like to take a nap after your bath or order something to eat. If so, just put everything on the room. You will find your belongings inside the duffel, over there on the floor.

"All right."

"And *pataki*." She turned her head toward him, her hair softly falling around her shoulders. "As soon as possible, we will need to let the Garifunian priestess know that we have arrived. It's a matter of respect."

He gave her a comforting smile as he tried to mask his growing concern. Nate knew that by following this protocol he would ensure the good tidings of the nearby villagers and priestess. Every moment counted now, and he wanted to do everything he could to protect her.

Raquel could tell he was anxious. His gaze continuously strayed to the window and out onto the street below.

"Nate, I've got to know what's going to happen to me." The statement loomed like an invisible wall between them.

"If everything goes right, *pataki*, you will be safe and on your way back to the States by tonight." Taking a deep, slow breath he looked down at the floor, then engulfed her with dark troubled eyes. "I never expected any of this would happen, but I will explain everything to you then."

"What do you mean?" Confusion and hope filled her weary eyes.

"Just trust me," his thickly lashed gaze implored her. "But I've got to go, *now*."

At first she hesitated. She wanted to force him into telling her everything right then. But from the look in his eyes she knew that would be impossible to do. As they stared at one another Raquel remembered how, up to that moment, he had never lied to her. She knew she would have to believe that he was not lying now. Feeling totally exhausted she nodded her agreement.

"Good." Nate breathed a sigh of relief before reaching out to squeeze her hand, and closing the door behind him.

Raquel soaked in the tub until she almost fell asleep in its comforting waters. Stepping out, she wrapped the large, plain bath towel around her, then decided to wash her hair in the sink. It reminded her of the way her mother used to do it when she was younger.

She patted her hair as dry as she could before combing it out. She was surprised to discover the costume she'd worn to the party was also in the sack. The thousand dollars that had gotten her into all of this was still stealthily folded and sewn away.

Raquel parted her hair down the middle and formed two French braids along the sides of her head, ending in two ropelike plaits dangling against her shoulderblades. She realized, as she inspected her features in the mirror, the style made her look much younger. She also noticed puffy sacks beneath her eyes, either remnants of the infection or visible signs of her weariness. Either way, the braids, coupled with the swollen areas, had her looking far from her best. But right now Raquel didn't care, she would try to impress the priestess and the others when she felt more up to it.

Raquel crossed the hotel room, patting the nape of her neck and her edges with a hand towel, her eyes straying to the window the bird had struck.

Several people paraded up and down the busy thoroughfare, going about their daily activities, oblivious to the tumultuous events that had taken over her life. She wished for the peace of mind they displayed with their contented wanderings.

She noticed a woman wearing a colorful skirt and watched her cross the street. Across the street, just inside the doorway of a small shop was a man placing a phone call. As she looked closer, she could see it was Nate. She wondered what nature of business had forced him to find a phone on the street instead of using the one in the hotel room.

Raquel watched as he hung up and made two other calls. His body and hand movements were intense as he spoke, making sure his back was to the street. Finally she saw him calm himself, then nervously turn to the street as if he were afraid he had been overheard. After forcefully hanging up the phone, Nate strode out onto the sidewalk, then stood looking over at the hotel.

Quickly Raquel stepped back from the sheer paneled window. Concealing herself against the wall, she hoped her rapid movement had not caught his astute gaze. It was an act that showed the lack of trust between them. His secretive calls outside the hotel, and her need for him not to know that she was aware of them.

Taking another covert glance, she watched as he made his way down the street, disappearing around the corner. Unnerved, she climbed between the warm covers of the bed, placing a dry towel on the linen-covered pillow to absorb the moisture from her hair.

It was about a half hour ago when he had asked her to trust him. Now, the uncertainty she felt as a result of his clandestine actions was that much stronger.

Raquel reached over to the nightstand and retrieved the leather pouch given to her by the shamaness. She placed the symbolic object about her neck. Normally she was not a superstitious person, but for some reason the small sack was the only thing that seemed to bring her comfort.

It was easy for her weary eyes to close as her mind brought up snatches of various thoughts between consciousness and sleep. Deep feelings of being trapped surfaced, telling her her choices were few. She could use the telephone to call the authorities, but she would be taking quite a chance. In a small city like this they were probably connected with the Garifunians. But even if they weren't, they probably wouldn't be willing to rub them the wrong way by dabbling in their religious affairs. As she drifted closer to sleep she came to the conclusion that trying to contact the States was out of the question. By the time help arrived all kinds of things could have happened. No, her best bet was to stick with Nate. She was afraid that if she might try to do something alone, Jay could be waiting for her. He would be ready, willing and able to snuff out her life in a moment's notice.

Feeling a kind of sickening fear wash over her, she submitted to the thought that Nate was her only hope. One that her heart irrationally placed complete trust in, but her mind failed to follow.

CHAPTER 19

"Get that out of my face!" the usual smooth tones of Ricky Flint's heavy voice exploded, interrupting his telephone conversation. The woman's thin but long eyelashes, swept down hastily, and her pretty features turned angry as she held her throbbing hand. A petite, silver, embossed tray lay face down on the sky blue carpet—its white contents almost invisible in its plushness.

Suddenly her anger dissolved into hurt, and the nostrils on her long nose slightly pumped in and out as her eyes glazed over with tears. One by one, crimson droplets spattered the carpet along with crushed pieces of glass; remains of the delicate crystal tube shattered by Ricky's blow.

Turning his back to the scene, the man pulled haughtily at the leather belt on his expensive pants.

"Just get over here," he yelled into the receiver. "Right now! You got that?" He slammed the custom-designed phone back into its cradle. Ricky turned his irritation back in the woman's direction.

"Why are you still standing there bleeding all over the fuckin' carpet?"

Not accustomed to this kind of treatment from her lover, the Creole woman struck back the only way she knew how.

"You *backra!*" Her dark eyes burned with harmful intent behind the racial categorization. "You can't talk to me like that."

Her timing was bad, and Ricky Flint delivered another blow. This time a backhand that sent her sprawling across the spacious sunroom floor. Classically designed billows of chiffon spread out delicately about her legs, and her heavy, dyed-auburn hair diffused in massive curls lay above it. Stunned, she sobbed uncontrollably upon the expanse of blue carpet.

"This is not the time to cross me baby. Somebody's messin' up my business and I have no patience for that." He walked over and kneeled down beside her and began to artfully arrange the curls away from her already darkening cheek.

"Call Carl in here to clean up this mess, and here," he placed a few hundred-dollar bills beneath her nail-art-bedecked hands. "Go to one of those all-day spas and get pampered for daddy. By tomorrow you'll feel as good as new."

He rose to his feet and left the room, leaving her to weep alone.

About two hours later Jay's gaze strayed to the window, looking down at countless living walls of sculptured hedges, strategically grown to form an intricate maze. The collective pattern resembled two shattered sphere halves with a stone pathway down its center. Resplendent orchid blossoms pushed their tongued heads through the green blocks in intervals, giving the illusion of small fluctuating rainbows in their midst. Jay's eyes gleamed brightly as he took in the opulence from this high vantage point. From what he could tell, Ricky had carved himself out a wonderland that took up acres of his native soil.

Envy boiled up inside as he thought of the pitiful plot of land his entire settlement occupied. It wasn't fair that an outsider should possess such wealth, and he, a Belizean, should be so poor.

A resounding crack drew Jay's attention back to the room in which he stood, and a beautiful porcelain head of an almond-eyed female rolled, then wobbled toward his feet.

"Your freakin' brother is the reason I've lost over a million dollars of cane . . . and you got the nerve to stand in here while I'm talkin' and look out the window!"

Ricky's aggravated tones hung in the air just like his hand, holding a completed karate chop above the broken statue's birdlike body.

Jay eyed the expensive head of the siren lying in the thick bed of carpet, thinking only of how much of a waste it was to destroy the collectible piece. An Englishman he'd worked for as a child had owned quite a collection of invaluable things. As a result of working around such splendor and returning to his own impoverished surroundings, Jay promised himself, one day, he would have what the Englishman had, and more. Ricky's childlike outburst did nothing but increase his feelings of being more entitled to the good things in life than his extravagant boss. He would appreciate them more.

Slowly Jay's haunted, obsessed eyes traveled from the broken porcelain to Ricky's reddened face.

"Leave my brothah out of t'is." His hands formed strained fists at his side. "Already his soul is in danger of not makin' the trip to the othah side because I had to come here first before buryin' him properly. I will not let you or anyone else provoke him further, and have his troubled spirit remain on t'is side, nevah findin' peace."

"I don't give a good god . . ." Ricky's insult ended abruptly as Jay's thin lips began to move silently as in a chant, a piercing light emanating from his consumed stare.

During his years in Belize, Ricky had heard of many bizarre things that had happened to both natives and strangers alike who had crossed or wronged an emotional Shangoain. These things were spoken of fearfully and in whispered tones, as if just the mention of them in the wrong way would bring about an undesirable end.

There had also been Benjamin, a virile Creole whom he'd hired to help his gardener. The young man had angered his Shangoain cook by fooling around with her young granddaughter. Ricky had seen with his own eyes how he ended up incapable of pleasing any other woman as a result of their bizarre magic.

The drug boss looked into Jay's glazed eyes and rephrased his reprimand.

"All right. All right. Let's leave the dead alone. But I want compensation for the drugs that I'm missin', and if I can't have it in money, I want it in blood."

"I want their blood too," Jay stated flatly. "I want the pleasure of seein' them die by my hand, especially the woman. But I will have to kill Meester Nate first befor' that happens."

"I can understand how you feel," he continued to placate the emotional Shangoain as he felt around for the right words to say.

Ricky was glad Jay wanted to kill the people responsible for messing up his haul, even though that was not his motivation. In the end it would make it that much easier for him. This way he'd be able to gain total control of Jay. Committing a crime like murder was one of the best hole cards he could have on one of his men. As a matter of fact, on occasions, he had "requested" that some of his men do a job in order to bind them more securely to him.

He looked at the dark, slender man who stood before him, his body tense and rigid. Ricky could tell it wouldn't take much to make Jay snap, and that wouldn't be good for any of them. He had to play him like a well-tuned piano. Hitting the right keys would create such beautiful music, but the wrong ones would be disastrous. Ricky didn't want Jay's enthusiasm to mess things up. Murder had to be approached with a calm hand.

"Look, right now I want you to know you are not alone. You've got family. Rock, Mane-Mane and myself. We're all part of a large close-knit group. So I tell you what," congeniality permeating his gaze. "If you can take care of the guy, somebody else'll take care of the woman. Okay?"

"They will be at the Garifuna Settlement Day ceremonies, day after to-morrow. I will do it then," Jay announced, ignoring the question posed by his drug boss.

Uneasily Ricky looked at Jay, then at the two men who stood a small distance away from him. Rock continued to chew his gum as he watched his boss's face, waiting for even the slightest instruction. Mane-Mane rolled his index finger beside his temple, giving his unsolicited opinion of Jay's mental state.

"All right we'll do it day after tomorrow," he cunningly agreed, know-ing Jay didn't care if he did or not. Under the circumstances Ricky knew he had to deal with him in a more subtle manner.

"Now that we've got business out of the way, why don't you and Mane-Mane step into the front sitting room and have Carl fix you some drinks. Rock, I've got a few things to go over with you, so you'll need to stick around for a few more minutes."

The two men watched as Jay and Mane-Mane filed through the double white doors, the latter closing the brass openers behind him.

"What d'ya think?" Ricky asked as he slumped down into the thick, ma-roon leather chair, placing his jeweled hands flat upon his desk.

"I think he's an uzi waiting to go off," Rock replied.

"Yeah, you're right," he began to drum his fingers. "But if we can point him in the right direction, he can do us a great service. The woman's got to be killed before she can complete that ceremony."

"There are going to be a lot of tourists and things hangin' around for that ceremony. If any thing goes wrong, make sure it can be pinned on the man, Jay," Ricky continued. "He thinks he's not dispensable, but he is. There's another guy in that village just as greedy as he is, and would be more than willing to take his place as our contact. I really don't care about this guy Jay calls Nate. As far as I'm concerned he did us a favor by wastin' his crazy brother." Ricky smacked his hands together abruptly. "Messed up over a million dollars in pure cane just tryin' to get some snatch. It is his brother and that woman who need to pay for fuckin' up my cocaine. But he's gone, and now we got two reasons to waste the woman."

CHAPTER 20

Raquel was grateful to step inside the plain, but clean house. It allowed her some respite from the prying, inquisitive eyes of the Garifunians, who stopped their tasks to watch them advance down the road. Many had called out friendly greetings as they saw Nate, but none of the amicable words or looks had been thrown her way. But unlike the Shangoains who seemed hostile and afraid, the Garifunians appeared to be more curious, observing her as one would study a queer specimen under a microscope.

Once they reached the door of the small house, there was something in Nate's mannerism that made her hesitate. Somehow she felt he was uncertain about her accompanying him inside. But before he could explain, a wisp of a boy with a smile appearing too big for his face, opened it, giving Nate a warm welcome by embracing his waist. In turn, the man began to rub his closely shaven head.

"Brandon, what happened to your head, man? Marjorie must have gotten ahold of you this time," he teased. "You know I told you to watch out for those females. They like to get a fellow where it hurts whenever they can," he continued his fond needling.

The boy's eyes burned with amusement, yet despite his display of open affection, he never spoke a word.

"By the way, where is Marjorie?"

Raquel watched as the smile remained on Nate's handsome features, but a solemn look appeared in the depths of his eyes.

Silently, the young boy pointed in the direction of a lone door, his brown eyes clouding over with concern. "She's in there," he responded in whispered tones, then looked beyond the front door, "Where's Art?"

Nate kneeled down in front of the boy whom Art's mother had taken in, bringing his face parallel with his. "He couldn't come with us, Brandon," he spoke the foreboding words, his voice raspy. "But let's talk about that later, because right now I've got something for you."

With the ease of any six-year-old, Brandon brightened as Nate pulled a cheerfully packaged box from the shopping bag he was carrying and presented it to the boy. Small, eager fingers ripped off the colored paper, removed the lid of the box, and dug into the cloud of thin, white tissue. He stopped abruptly at the sight of his gift, a loud, "Gosh!" verbalizing his feelings.

"It's *The Rendezvous,*" he exclaimed as he carefully reached down and retrieved a magnificently crafted sailboat. "Is it just like yours Mr. Nate?" bright eyes looking up at him admiringly.

"Just about."

"Wow, I've got to go show Chris," he ran for the door with his prize stretched out before him. Suddenly he made an abrupt turn. "Oops, first I gotta ask Big Mama." He headed excitedly for the room but Nate caught him by the waist.

"That's all right, you go ahead. I'll tell her."

"Thanks." The word had barely been spoken before he disappeared through the door.

Nate watched him for a moment, then he turned to Raquel.

"I think it might be best if you stayed in here," his features solemn as he addressed her.

The words were put in the form of a suggestion, but Raquel knew they were a subtle command, as he motioned for her to take a seat in a hardback chair at the table. She could feel all his attention had become focused on the room Brandon had pointed to only moments before.

Raquel watched as the door gave in to the even pressure from Nate's large hand. From her seat she could see inside the tiny room. It was barely large enough for the ornate, full-sized bed and dresser. There was a petite shaded lamp casting a soft glow throughout, and it was the only source of light, because the window shade had been drawn to completely block out the sun.

Nate approached the bed, somberly, even though it appeared to be empty from Raquel's vantage point. As he turned his profile in her direction, she could tell from his troubled features, someone of grave importance in his life was lying there. For moments on end, he stood in silence looking down at the still blankets. Finally, a slight arm rose up and reached toward him, and Raquel heard what she thought was a breathy version of his name.

Compassionately, Nate took the hand that reached for him, knelt down beside the bed, and placed it against his cheek.

"How is my favorite girl," He gazed down fondly at the weak figure in the bed, concern making the deep hollow beneath his high cheekbones appear even more apparent.

"Mind what you say, Nate Bowman. It's been a long time since I was a girl . . . and your favorite? That will be the day when you call any woman your favorite."

Raquel could barely hear the soft words, but hear them she did, and it weakened her crumbling belief that she was someone special in his life.

"You never could take a compliment," he countered.

"No, I never could stand for B. S. and I still can't."

A look of resignation descended over Nate's dark features. "Marjorie . . ."

"You don't have to tell me. I know. Art is dead. It came to me in a dream the night he left."

Nate nodded.

She closed her eyes as she thought of him. "About two days after I had that dream I began to feel ill, and I tell you I get weaker with each day. But I know what's going on. The will of Art's spirit has attached itself to me." A weak smile crossed her wrinkled face. "He don't mean me any harm, he loves me, and he was a man of faith. That's why he wanted to help bring Jackie back to Dangriga. He wanted me and the *orishas* to be pleased with him. And that's the reason I think he's holding on to me. He wants to be present with me at the ceremony tomorrow," she stopped to catch her breath.

"I'm glad the ceremony is only a day away, then he will be free, and so will I," she finished.

Unintentionally, Nate glanced up in Raquel's direction, causing Marjorie to do the same. Even this slight physical exertion resulted in her flopping back listlessly against the white sheets.

"Jackie . . . is that you, Jackie?"

Raquel's eyes opened wide at the mention of the name. Once again Nate looked at her, a veiled appearance fell upon his features.

Marjorie called out to her again.

"Ye-es," Raquel answered, hesitantly. "It's me."

A weak smile appeared on the woman's tired face.

She was the one who had shown Nate so much compassion at the time of his mother's death. Through the years he had done all he could to make her life as comfortable as possible. The presence of the modern furniture and fixtures reflected that, but even the generous contributions he made could not completely ward off the effects of the hard life Marjorie chose to live in Dangriga. She was stubborn about maintaining "the

Garifunian way," and he respected that. Still, in his heart, he had vowed to do whatever he could to help her.

He thought about how hard he had taken Art's death, even though at the time he could not show it. He had drunk entirely too much that night when they first arrived in Belize, as he dwelled on how he would have to tell Marjorie her only son was dead.

"I knew she would come," she said almost to herself. "The *gubida* would never desert us. Tell her to come closer," she implored as her eyes opened slightly, then fluttered shut again.

Nate motioned for Raquel to join him at Marjorie's bedside. Her body shook with each step as she crossed the small space, the moment of her undoing becoming imminent. As she stood above the fragile figure, the tired eyes flickered open for a look at her, and showed a spark of confusion. Then, the woman exhaled loudly and fell back into a deep, almost coma-like sleep. A trembling breath of relief eased out of Raquel.

"I don't think she would have recognized you anyway," Nate commented. "You were a little girl when you left Belize."

Startled dark eyes looked up in his direction. Was there a hint of collusion in his voice?

When Nate returned to the hotel no more than an hour ago he appeared tense and preoccupied. Appearing somewhat relieved to see her dressed, they wasted no time in heading for the Garifunian settlement. He had said very little during the short time it took to get there.

Quickly she looked down at the figure who lay before them.

"I think we should leave and let her rest," Nate said as he took her arm. "The priestess is also expecting us."

There was little if any indication that this small settlement on the outskirts of Dangriga had ever been touched by modern society. Some of the doors to the simple clapboard houses were open for ventilation, allowing anyone who felt like it to watch whatever was happening inside. After taking several quick assessments of the interior of homes displayed in such a manner, Raquel concluded that Marjorie's house was probably one of the best furnished, if not the best, in the entire settlement. Somehow she knew Nate was the cause of her good fortune, and she wondered what compelled this strange man to do the things he did.

"Well, well . . . look what de win' done blew in," a husky female voice called from the open structure they just passed. "If it isn't my mon, Nate, lookin' as good as evah."

An ebony-skinned female leaned against the inside frame of the weathered door, a set of perfect white teeth shining from her round face. Like the women in the cassava field she wore a dusterlike dress with floral print, but on her shapely frame, it was transformed into a provocative frock. The tiny buttons which traveled the length of its middle strained at their holes where her full breasts pressed against the light material, and groaned against the pressure her ample hips placed upon them. A wild arrangement of full hair framed her animated face, like a softly persuasive afro it reached out around her, touching her shoulders, giving way ever so slightly to the wind as she began to cross the space between them.

Raquel watched as Nate's eyes lit up with a familiar gleam that was quickly doused as a somewhat cynical, sideways smile forced its way onto his features. The woman passed by Raquel, completely ignoring her. A natural scent mixed with a tangy floral smell drifted around her.

"Why did it take you so long to come back and see about your Belinda, eh?" She donned a pouty expression as she placed her hands upon her hips, her body almost touching his.

"How are you, Belinda?" He spoke, his richly lashed eyes intent on her face.

Slowly her full lips spread into a winsome smile. "I am good now that you are here." She placed her palm upon his chest, rubbing it ever so enticingly.

"You probably don't remember Jackie, do you?" He turned in Raquel's direction. "You were both so young when she went to the States."

Her round eyes narrowed in speculation as they roamed over the silent young woman, stopping at her large, flashing eyes, "No, I don't."

There was no way for Raquel to deny the strong wave of jealousy that had washed over her as she watched the woman's exchange with Nate. It took all the control she could muster to keep from removing her clinging fingers from the material of his shirt.

"Strange that your sistah would be so jealous of you, Nate," Belinda's sultry voice took on a harsh edge. "But of course you have always been able to bring out the best and the worst in us females."

Nate's sister! But surely she was mistaken. Raquel opened her mouth to protest Belinda's words, but no sound emerged. Unsure of herself and shaken, she waited for Nate to straighten her out. Surely, she did not think Jackie Dawson was Nate's sister!

Just as Raquel expected, Nate addressed Belinda, but his words were far from what she expected.

"Maybe she wouldn't feel that way, if you weren't such a tantalizing creature," he continued to gaze in the woman's direction, the half smile fixed upon his lips.

With his words, Raquel felt as if she would faint—the switch from jealously to sheer shock was so strong Through an emotional fog, she looked at the man she felt she had come to know and love, and she realized she really didn't know him at all.

There was a falseness to the smile he gave Belinda, though the woman seemed not to notice as she laid her voluptuous body against his in an invitational embrace. Obligingly Nate placed his arms around her as she leaned her head on his chest. He turned to look at Raquel above

Belinda's mass of hair, the muscle in his strong jaw working convulsively. His dark eyes seem to burn into her.

"I will check back with you later," he assured the woman, but he continued to stare at Raquel while holding her in his arms. A flicker of remorse flashed in his gaze. "The priestess is waiting for us. Are you ready . . . Jackie?"

The name dropped on her like a heavy stone, and she realized Nate had never addressed her as Jackie before. She remembered how in the beginning he had called her Miss Dawson, in a distant way. But he never used the more familiar Jackie, because Jackie Dawson *was* his sister.

Before Belinda could remove her face from his chest, Nate reached out and clutched Raquel's arm. With his touch a feeling of total weakness seeped into her. All of a sudden she felt so tired. If only she had never accepted that envelope.

There was no logic behind what had happened to her over the last week. All of the time she had pretended to be Jackie Dawson, Nate had always known the truth. All the while she'd feared for her life and continued with the charade because of it, she had never been in any danger when it came to him. He had known all along she was an imposter.

From the flurry of emotions that flashed across her beautiful features, Nate could tell what Raquel was thinking. Belinda's timing couldn't have been worse. Any trust she had in him had been crushed, and right now, there was nothing he could do about it. But there was one thing she had to realize, this was not the time to reveal her true identity. She was in way too deep for that.

"Jackie," he shook her arm abruptly, causing the closest thing he'd ever seen to hate rise in her eyes.

"What is wit' her? She looks as if she was in a daze or sumt'in?" Belinda snapped.

"I'm surprised at you, Belinda, you of all people should understand. She's been sending herself through strong preparations in order to make a true connection with the *gubida* tomorrow, and it has not been easy for her after living such a pampered life in the States. But of course there's no need for me to remind you of this," he stroked her after speaking rather harshly in the beginning. "You have worked with the priestess, and have noticed the drain her spiritual travels can cause, something as plain as that would not get past a woman like you."

Belinda eyed Raquel with skepticism. "Yes, t'at is true. But t'ere is a weakness about your sistah that leads me to t'ink she will not be able to stand up under the power of the spirits tomorrow evenin'."

Belinda held her head up haughtily. She looked down on Raquel for allowing the city life to spoil her, but at the same time, she felt envious because of it.

"She is stronger than she appears, I can assure you of that," Nate said with a nod. Secretly hoping that the time would never come to prove Belinda right or wrong.

"Well, I hope so fo' the people's sake and fo' hers. The entire village and remainder of the Shango will arrive early tomorrow mornin'. They will all be countin' on her. If she is able to call up the spirits of our ancestors but cannot carry them, horrible thin's could happen, ya know?"

"There is no need for you to worry, Belinda."

Nate slipped a protective arm about Raquel's shoulder as he urged her forward. She flinched at his touch, a repulsive feeling rising inside. She wanted to scream at him and remove it. Yet she dared not react as they started down the dirt road, many of the villagers' eyes upon them.

There was a bizarre feeling of dejàvu as she realized she was back where she started. She was all alone, and she could not depend on Nate.

Her nervous fingers sought out the leather pouch that hung about her neck, a tool of deception. Strange how this entire ordeal had started out with deceit. But to find out she, the deceiver, had also been deceived by a man she thought she had come to love, was the most bitter pill to swallow.

CHAPTER 21

"Nate, there is no need for you to remain here and be burdened with our spiritual talk." The delicate voice wafted toward them from the opposite side of the room. The tone was imploring but Raquel knew it was still a command.

The woman who sat before them was nothing like Raquel expected. After witnessing the Mayan shaman at work, and being trained by the shamaness in the rain forest, she had expected the priestess's countenance to be more, for lack of a better word, mystical.

The woman's soft, but even gaze, continued to rest on Nate as he rose from the chair and obediently passed through the door.

On leaving Belinda, they had time for only a few words before they were confronted by the priestess. She had taken it upon herself to meet them on the street while the majority of the village looked on. As she approached—she was a generous figure in African garb with a wide sun hat upon her head—Nate issued a warning to Raquel, "Whatever you do, don't let anyone know who you really are!" It was those words that echoed in her mind as he left her alone with the Garifunian priestess.

With hands much like those of a baby, she produced a pack of cigarettes and a lighter. Hospitably, she offered the pack to Raquel, who promptly refused.

"It is a shame you did not return to us of your own accord, Jackie. I know the *gubida* would be happier if you had." The priestess's smooth English oddly comforted Raquel, but not enough to dispel all of her questions and confusion.

There was a pregnant pause as she waited for Raquel to offer an excuse or apology for her action. She continued when none was given.

"Your brother has gone to great lengths to bring you here. We are grateful to him, and so should you be. It is the youth like you, who have weakened our society by disrespecting their roots, discarding the beliefs of their ancestors, and trying to become something they are not. That is why our people grow poorer with each year. It is a dreadful cycle. The youth see no promise for tomorrow, therefore they leave. And in their leaving, they take with them any promises they could have fulfilled in the future. There are only a few who look back and try to give of themselves once they are gone. Your brother has been one of them. Now, it is because of the prophecy, that has been spoken of for many years, that you are here. You are that foretold female descendant of the Garifuna and the Shango. Born out of a union performed during the night of the split. You were the only child conceived that night, and as a result have been endowed by the *gubida* to speak for them." Her ample figure rolled to the side, choosing a bunch of grapes to appease her eager appetite. With hands accustomed to traveling rapidly toward her cushiony lips, she popped a string of the deep purple fruits into her mouth. Suddenly, she paused with an aggressive gleam in her eye which she pointed in Raquel's direction.

"I have felt the energy of those who are filled with the power of the *gubida* before, and somehow yours is different," she squinted her already small eyes even more. "Powerful but different. By now, I know if the *gubida* are truly with you, they have instructed you on what to do to prepare for tomorrow. Tell me what they have said."

The priestess's obvious test for Raquel, caught the young woman off guard. Instantly fear shot up inside her. She dropped her eyes to the floor to hide the emotion from the woman's probing gaze. For moments that felt like an eternity her crowded mind searched for what would be the right answer, as the silence hung heavily between them. Involuntarily her hand sought out the pouch around her neck.

Foggy images began to appear behind her tightly closed eyelids, they grew in clarity as she gave in to them. As these pictures appeared to her mental eye, she relayed them to the Garifunian priestess in a surprisingly calm voice. She told of her eventual experience with the shamaness of the rain forest, of the water, the moon, her consumption of the blue passion flower and the St. Juan's wort. She spoke of gathering together the objects which she now wore about her neck inside the soft leathery pouch, gifts of the sea, and the earth, amidst the sparkle of bright beads. She told it as it unfolded in her mind, but she didn't realize until her tale was complete, and she was looking at the beaming features of the Garifunian priestess, there was one thing missing. As the occurrences of that night replayed in her mind, she was alone.

"Ah-h the most powerful preparations from *Yemoja,* goddess of the ocean." She smacked her lips appreciatively as she finished the last of the grapes. "It must have created a great yearning inside you," her sparkling eyes commented knowingly. "Did you find a suitable male to appease the fire and consummate the ritual?"

"Yes." The single-word response gave no indication of the shock Raquel felt at the woman's perceptive words. For a moment she reflected on the first night she and Nate made love. She had no idea the Garifunian priestess would consider the act a consummation of one of their rituals.

"Good. Now that I am certain you have been touched by our ancestors, and the ways of an initiate have been given to you, we can talk about the present." She adjusted her large frame on the well-worn, cushioned arm chair. "A place has been made ready for you, along with an attendant. There you will have the privacy you need for your vigil tonight. Once she tells me you are ready, a proper receiver of your female energy will be sent to you."

All of a sudden, she repeatedly smacked the backside of one hand against the palm of the other, and a hefty young woman entered the room carrying a large bundle under her arm. She kept her eyes riveted on the woman who had summoned her.

The priestess spoke to her in a dialect Raquel did not understand as the young woman, dressed in white, nodded her head reassuringly.

"Well now, everything is ready. She will show you where you must go." Her dark gaze turned solemn, "And may the *orishas* be with you."

"I am proud, because I am the chosen one tonight," the sinewy young man boasted as he walked away from the fire. Several grunts and verbal acknowledgments of approval followed. The circle of males, young and old, agreed with him. They all considered being chosen as the receiver, an honor. Drawing their attention away from the fortunate villager, once again, a dried, decorated gourd, half full of cassava wine began to circulate.

With an air of insolence, the young man walked away from the group, a small burlap sack flapping against his hard hip. He had secured the hood beneath his belt after receiving it from the priestess. He wanted it to be handy whenever the time came for him to use it.

The feel of the cassava wine still burned in his chest, and he wished he could have stayed longer with his friends to help them finish the gourd. But he knew the time was drawing close, and just the thought of what was to come excited him. Through the trees he could see the lights from the houses, dotting the main area of the settlement, and even though he could not see it from where he walked, he knew, soon, he would be engulfed in the warmth of one of those lights, and in the arms of the one chosen by the *gubida.*

"Hey, what's your hurry?" a husky voice called out from the dark, causing the young man to turn abruptly.

"Who's askin'?" he replied, his rich, brown eyes searching the semidarkness.

Nate saw the telltale burlap sack hanging at the young man's waist, and his dark eyes narrowed perceptively. Night had arrived and there was no sign of the help he had expected. After the phone calls he had made earlier, he had been leery, but still hoped they would come back in time. Now he knew it would be sometime in the morning before they arrived. Nate had vowed to himself, and to the woman he had come to know as Jackie, that he would protect her, and protect he would.

He was glad he'd kept his word to Belinda, and had gone to see her no more than an hour ago. She had offered him a steaming plate of brocket deer and red beans and rice, prepared with coconut milk and spices. Belinda had always been a good cook, and he knew she would be insulted if he refused the offer. It was from her he knew a receptor would be chosen tonight.

"So, it is you who has been chosen tonight?" Nate added a bit of a slur to his speech, hoping the young man would not notice it wasn't there before.

Defined youthful features peered at Nate's face in the darkness. It was hard for him to see under the cover of trees and the influence of the wine. In the end, he concluded he did not recognize him, and he wondered how this stranger knew about such things. Secrecy in matters like this, when it came to outsiders, was second nature for Garifunians.

"What would you know about that?" his voice dripped with skepticism.

"Everything man. How old are you, nineteen?"

"Twenty."

"Oh yes, that explains it," Nate chuckled, turning up a near-empty bottle of cashew wine. "You were probably still a breast baby when I was taking care of business the way you'll be doing tonight." He made a show of draining the bottle. "I thought you looked pretty wet behind the ears. Are you sure you can handle it? Or are you going to need a little help?"

Nate made sure he remained in the shadow of the trees so it would be difficult for the young man to see his face, but he could clearly see the now-aggravated features of the fellow who stood before him.

"What you talkin' 'bout old man? I don't need no help from you or anybody else. My abilities around this village are well known. Maybe it's been such a long time for you, that you can't even imagine what I'm talkin' 'bout."

Tossing the now-empty bottle to the side and swaying a bit on his feet for emphasis, Nate made a show of attempting to open a second corked bottle with his teeth, loosening it just enough so it would come out easily with the slightest bit of pressure.

"I know more than you think I know, and ain't nothin' I can't take care of that you can," he baited.

"Yeah mon, I'm sure . . . just like that bottle cork."

Arrogantly the young man snatched the bottle from Nate's willing hands.

"Eh-h, wait a minute," he protested loudly. While inside he thought things were progressing even better than he planned.

With ease the young man removed the cork, and took a long swig from the bottle. Afterwards he wiped his mouth with the back of his hand.

"See there? I told you," he grinned as he held the bottle stretched out far from his side, then took another long, dramatic swill.

Yes, you sure did, Nate thought. But so did Belinda.

He was glad Belinda's penchant for young men and good wine had put her in such a good, relaxed mood. She told him all about this particular young man and where he could be found. Now he just hoped there was enough hop in that bottle to put him out for the night.

Raquel's eyes focused on the exposed beams of the ceiling and the wooden planks that lay in between them. Over and over she counted them with the aid of the moonlight. She would try anything if it would keep her mind from straying to the burning ache searing inside her.

It had begun after she drank the tea. The feeling started in the pit of her stomach, fluttering like excited butterflies. Slowly it turned into a stimulating quiver, then finally an aching desire, blazing a demanding trail to the core of her womanhood.

She remembered feeling relieved when the young female attendant left her. The nagging desire had begun to take effect, overpowering her thoughts of escape. Embarrassed, she did not want the woman to know of her sensual predicament.

For a while she thought the girl would never leave. Her well-trained actions made it unnecessary for Raquel to initiate any of the preparatory rites. Instead she just followed the young woman's lead, taking whatever was offered to her, meditating at the times when she stopped in thoughtful prayer; then in the end, allowing her to place a soft, azure blue, caftan over her frame. It was then, as the cottony material slid over her nakedness, she first became aware of an awakening feeling within her chest accompanied by a somewhat heady sensation. As time passed these feelings increased, in a strange way establishing a feeling of empowerment. It was if she was at the height of awareness. An awareness of her femaleness and its creative powers.

Raquel didn't understand why she was feeling this way—was she actually the chosen one? She didn't understand why the ceremony's preparations seemed natural to her, normal, as if she were indeed fulfilling a legacy. As if she, Raquel Mason, not Jackie Dawson, was anointed.

Raquel's thoughts returned to the shamaness who shared her power with her. Perhaps the shamaness was right, perhaps Raquel did have an open soul, perhaps everything the shamaness had said and done was real. Perhaps, Raquel thought as she ran her hands gently along her thighs, everything will be all right.

A pleasurable wave ran through her. Raquel moaned with the sensation, feeling as if all her senses had been intensified. Eager fingers began to trace the shape of her own firm thigh beneath the smooth material, and her nostrils flared with the scent of the oils massaged on to her skin. A bittersweet, somewhat familiar taste still lingered in her mouth, a remnant of the aromatic tea she drank with her meal.

Unwillingly, images of the first night she made love to Nate surfaced in her mind, causing a staggered intake of breath. In a remote way the erotic pictures helped to quench the mounting fire within her, but in a deeper sense they only fanned the flames.

Hastily Raquel sat up on the bed, placing her bare feet on the furry skin that lay beside it. She forced herself to think of Miami, and her mother, and assured herself all of this would be over soon. In the end it would seem like a distant dream, or a more accurate description would be nightmare.

Like a restless cat, Raquel began to pace the floor, the feel of the smooth material moving against her skin arousing her even further.

Thoughts of the shamaness of the rain forrest flitted through her mind once again and she wondered why she had not been present in the images she relayed earlier to the Garifunian priestess. Something inside told her this was significant, but at the moment she didn't have the will to peruse the possibility, the aching in her loins seemed to overpower all other trains of thought.

What sounded like footsteps and cracking branches outside the house made Raquel stop in the middle of the door. Dark, intense almond-shaped eyes focused on the door to the one room building, and her bosom heaved heavily as she waited for it to open. Exaggerated moments went by, followed by nothing but silence. It wasn't until that moment that Raquel realized she had been intently waiting for something. But what?

A mixture of a laugh and a sob escaped her lips, for she finally realized what she was listening for. The priestess's words "Did you find a suitable male to receive your female energies?" . . . "Once you are ready, a proper receiver will be sent to you," echoed in her head. There was no doubt she was waiting for that "receiver." A suitable male. Any male!

Abruptly Raquel sat down on the bed, she drew her knees up to her chest and clasped them tightly together. What kind of ceremony is this, she wondered, as she laid her tormented face on her lap, causing her knees to be engulfed in a dark, cloud of hair. Her mind strayed to Nate. If he truly cared for her, how could he bring her here knowing she would have to be intimate with another man—any man? And why did she still desire a man to be with her now?

A warm burst of air and dim light swept into the room as the wooden door swung open, and a hooded male stepped inside. Raquel stared up with wide, startled, damp eyes. Just the sight of him frightened and excited her, as he remained in the shadows near the door. She sat paralyzed as she gazed upon his massive, muscular frame, which in the semidarkness resembled a male statue. For a moment she thought there was something familiar about him. She cautioned her mind not to play tricks on her. Nate was the only man in this settlement that she knew, and the priestess would not send him, because she thought he was her brother.

Quickly she dashed away several tears that were making their way down her velvety cheeks. She tried to calm herself so he would not see how nervous she was, then she realized he could not see her, the hood was solid, making it impossible.

Just this tiny realization of his helplessness sparked boldness in Raquel. She knew her eager body had been well-primed with herbs for this male who stood before her, and the logical side of her nature was being silenced by an earthy desire.

Slowly she rose from the bed as several hedonistic tremors ran through her, like a spider with a victim in her web, Raquel became the predator, and she eyed her catch with anticipation.

The young woman took deep, trembling breaths as she crossed the room and stood before the man. This time, she allowed her gaze to linger on his taut frame as she assessed him, starting with his broad, tan shoulders, traveling downward. She could tell he was not nervous, his chest rose evenly, causing the sharply defined musculature encasing his abdomen to rise as well.

Raquel's dark lustful gaze stopped at the simple wrap he wore around his hips, a slight smile turned up the corners of her full lips as she thought of how easily it could be removed. This caused her sable eyes to become smoky with passion as she imagined what lay underneath it.

Possessively she reached out and touched one hardened pectoral, then ran her hand across his chest to the other. The feel of his rock-hard body caused her to moan again, and she closed her eyes as an exquisite sensation throbbed between her legs.

Almost with a will of its own her hand trailed down to the side of the wrap covering his maleness. With one swift motion she removed it, causing his shaft to spring forward. To Raquel's lustful eyes it appeared massive, and she longed to take it inside her.

Somewhere in the far recesses of her mind a small voice called out in protest to what she was about to do. But then another part of her, a strong inner-knowing, calmed her fears.

From that point on, not once did she question her thoughts or actions. She was being guided by a force, natural in its nature, but unnatural in intensity. It was as if she had become totally possessed by the spirit of desire, pushing her forward to assuage its needs.

Anxious, she led him to the bed and helped him lie down on the sheet. Her eyes never left his body as they burned with a dazed passion, soaking up his maleness which was in a state of semireadiness. She nearly tore the blue gown as she removed it from her body with such haste, and left it in an abandoned heap upon the floor.

With animal-like agility she straddled the man's strong body, as thoughts of impaling herself upon him engulfed her. Writhing because of the fire between her thighs, Raquel lowered herself upon his frame, needing to feel the closeness, but at the same time aware that he was not yet poised for entry. The feel of the rough hood against her skin, interrupted her sexual revelry, so with trembling fingers she grasped it, then hastily withdrew it from his head. Dazed with lust she did not focus on his features, at the moment they were not important. Nothing was important outside of the aphrodisiac's persuasive power, and ultimately quenching her own sexual need.

With hooded eyes Nate watched Raquel's passion-filled features as she threw back her head then arched her back. A mixture of emotions fought inside of him. The desire to fill her aching body almost overpowered him, but a nagging resentment echoed in his head as he realized she didn't care who fulfilled her need.

He had heard of how potent the possession could be. This, coupled with the proper herbs would be overwhelming. But to see the woman he loved eagerly mount a man she did not know only angered him.

"You want it so badly, do you?" his silky voice was laced with anger.

Raquel's dazed eyes tried to focus on the face of the man beneath her. His voice was familiar, but it sounded like a murmur against the waves of passion pounding in her head and through her body. Yet, somewhere deep inside she knew him.

Suddenly he grabbed her beneath her armpits, then easily turned and pinned her beneath him.

"The female spirit may be riding you, *pataki*, but I want you to know, that it's me, Nate, that you are giving yourself to. Do you hear me? You are mine, dammit, and no one else's!" He shouted as he clasped her chin in his hand.

He knew it was his fault she was in this predicament, but just the thought of her wantonly giving herself to a stranger had driven him to anger.

Nate's harsh words helped to clear Raquel's fuzzy head. Like a person functioning out of a mental tunnel, a vague realization of what was taking place began to unfold. Suddenly her almond-shaped eyes became lucid and full of loathing. Why hadn't he made her aware of who he was before now? He just let her go on humiliating herself in front of him! And now he was speaking to her like she was some common whore. It was his fault all of this—the kidnapping, the jungle, the ceremony—and she hated him for it.

"Who in the hell do you think you are, huh?" she insulted him. "I don't trust you one bit Meester Nate," she gave the best imitation of Jay's accent she could muster. "You drag me down here to this God-forsaken place and I end up going through hell and more because of you. Now you say I belong to you? I don't belong to you or anyone else." She raised her hand in an attempt to strike him.

Quickly he caught her hand, then forced both her arms above her head where he clasped her wrists together while his other hand descended over her mouth.

"What are you trying to do? Let your friend out there know we are having a disagreement." His eyes raked her features sarcastically. "Oh no, *pataki*, you must be quiet. This is not the time to let anyone know the truth about me or you. What would they say if they thought I had gone through all of this to be with my sister?" He placed warm lips against the hollow of her throat as he spoke, emitting a derisive snarl as she struggled against him.

"You keep moving like that, and it won't be long before you are raking my back in pleasure," he provoked her with a crooked smile. "I just wanted to make sure you knew who it was you were giving yourself to." He stared into angry eyes that were beginning to glaze over with passion. "We are not enemies, *pataki*, we just had a bad beginning. You'll see. And one day I will make it up to you."

Totally aroused now, his searing lips descended on hers as she lay pinned helplessly beneath him. At first she attempted to turn her head to avoid his assault, but he was relentless in his quest, in the end capturing them completely and forcing their surrender.

He kissed her long and hard, angry at himself and at how things had turned out. Never could he have imagined on that fateful day, when he first saw her, that things would get so out of hand.

The taste of her lips fueled his desire, and once again he sought out the hollow of her throat. It was as if he could not get enough of her. Drunkenly he blazed a trail of kisses from that tender spot to her taut caramel breasts below. He took each brown nipple between his lips, nibbling and sucking until they were hard and erect. Despite herself Raquel responded eagerly, thrusting the mounds in the direction of his hot lips, needing and wanting more of what he had to offer. As swiftly as her clearheadedness had descended it vanished, washed away by the passion he fueled and something else she did not quite understand, nor did she care.

The fire between her thighs flared, rising to a pitch that was unbearable. Like a wild woman, she bucked her hips against his torso seeking appeasement in any way she could. With strong hands Nate sought to restrain her, as he continued his downward descent. Firmly he covered her breasts with his large brown hands, molding the mounds into pliable flesh as she moaned her desire.

He entered his tongue into the heart of her blaze, and found it literally sweltering to the touch. Eagerly he sought to cool her while satisfying his own hunger.

The sounds of pleasure that rose from her were guttural and thick, she was beyond knowing who he was or even caring, but he knew it was he who was abating her flame, and for the moment that was enough.

From the time Nate entered her, he knew it would be like no other lovemaking he had ever known. She was an active volcano drawing him inward, clasping hold with an intensity that took his breath away. Even though he was astride, there wasn't much he could do but ride the wave of passion that spurred her on. He wrapped her tightly in his arms, murmuring words of endearment. It was all he could do to endure the journey, but when her time came he was ready to render his last most powerful strokes, sending them both over the precipice to the cliffs below.

Hoarsely he moaned into her ears, "I love you, *pataki,*" as they plummeted into the valley of pleasure.

CHAPTER 22

The gathering of Garifunians parted naturally as the Shangoain *buyei*, accompanied by the remaining villagers entered the settlement. Eva's eyes darted nervously from side to side as she progressed with the group. Like the others, she held her back rod-straight and her chin high as they moved along. She was glad one of the village women had given her a new shift to wear for it gave her the extra boost of confidence she needed. Still, she was glad to be walking deep in the midst of the crowd. It gave her a sense of protection.

A quiver of fear ran through her as she thought of what she had done, and what Jay would probably do once he found out. Then Eva calmed her own fear by thinking of what the *buyei* had promised. He assured her no one was put on earth to suffer, and if she left Jay she would be protected by the *orishas* and by the Shango.

Like the other Shangoains, Eva knew some of the Garifunians considered their coming to Dangriga an act of submission and admission of wrongdoing on their part. Yet they, the Shangoains, considered it more an act of faith. The prophecy said the special ceremony must take place in the *dabuyaba*, and Dangriga housed the only active temple of their faith in Belize. Obviously, those who could see the future had known this would be the only way to bring the two factions together, and outside forces had worked against the *dabuyaba* in the Shangoain village eventually closing it down.

Eva strained her neck to see the black and white feathers of the *buyei's* headdress as he led the group several yards ahead of her. Despite all its elaborate splendor, it was still hard for her to see anything but the tips of the piece, and the reason for this made her sad. Time had humbled the *buyei's* proud, erect posture. Now his shoulders displayed a pronounced droop, causing a need for him to crane his neck and head like a bird whenever he spoke to someone taller than himself. She pictured his almost feeble progression as he led them, and she knew it too pointed up their weakness in the Garifunians' eyes.

The gathering of Garifunians began to move in a parallel fashion along with the Shangoains, following them into the interior of the village. Several tourists who'd come early for the Settlement Day festivities focused their attention on the advancing crowd. They gathered together naturally in a curious bunch, in a place that allowed them clear view of the entire scene. Questioning glances and words passed between them as they checked their watches. It was only 11 A.M. and the ceremony wasn't due to start until that afternoon. An elderly man informed the others he'd been told they would have to leave and return at the proper time when the Settlement Day ceremony began. Several others chimed in they had also been told the same thing, and looks of excitement and apprehension settled on their faces as they wondered what was in store.

The tourists watched as the growing congregation made a large, thatched roof on stilts their final destination. The crowd began to speak in hushed tones, as they waited, and a feeling of anticipation surfaced. Suddenly all movement and sound halted as the Garifunian priestess stepped forward to meet and welcome the Shangoain *buyei.*

She looked quite different from the day before. Gone was her sun hat and scarcely matching African garb. Today's circumstances called for a more elaborate mode of dress. A well-twisted and coiled white wrap, sprinkled with gold threads, topped her generous features, and this of course, was accompanied by a matching outfit. Like a queen in all her glory, the Garifunians' religious leader calmly surveyed the group before her. If she had even the slightest feeling the Shangoains had finally succumbed to her people she did not show it as she tilted her voluminously enshrouded head, then extended a meaty arm inviting the *buyei* to join her under the cool thatched roof. It was amazing to see how elegantly the large woman maneuvered herself in the long fitted skirt and top; the sleeves so stiff it resembled a shield.

Looks of pride were exchanged among the Garifunians as they watched their opulent priestess accompany the waning Shangoain *buyei* back to their seats. A cool drink was offered to both leaders, and they sat in a companionable silence as they consumed it.

Without instruction, the Shangoains and Garifunians split up and joined their fellow villagers, who had already mapped out separate areas where cooking and other activities were taking place. Both groups knew after today's ritual, they would have to accept the other as their brother or sister in faith, yet, inside, they still housed a need to show that in some ways their own people were superior.

So with no open challenge spoken between them, they set out to out-cook, and out-perform what they considered the rival group. They knew their people were alike in many ways, but there were small things that drew a fine line of distinction, and their cooking was one of them.

In the Garifunians' camp, smoke rose from shallow troughs dug out and filled with wood to form an open fire, and large pots hung by their handles on branches stretched out well above the flames. Inside the kettles, a broth had just begun to form between the pieces of gibnut and armadillo. The meat would be allowed to stew until it was juicy and tender to the touch. Other dishes, seafood and vegetable alike, were prepared with coconut milk and spices indigenous to the area.

The Garifunian cooks carefully sampled all the condiments to insure their freshness and potency before adding them to the main fare. This was an important meal, and the women couldn't chance overlooking even the smallest detail.

On the other hand, the Shangoains' culinary talents had been largely influenced by the Spanish conquerors. In their camp, several females poked sticks into slabs of beef which popped and sizzled atop large piles of coal, as the meat cooked in the open. There were big iron pots nestled down in the red and white carbon, and inside, chunks of meat cooked slowly in a variety of tangy sauces. Looks and words of satisfaction or disapproval were passed between the concerned cooks as they tasted the spicy mixtures.

Not far away, huge tortillas were being stretched and made ready for the time when they would be filled with beef, eggs, or beans, either singularly or combined. One carefully rolled tortilla could provide a small meal for at least ten people after it was sliced and dished out. From the painstaking activity in the village, it was obvious both groups were intent on preparing their culinary best, which would be consumed by all.

While the women were busy with the food, the men continued to make last-minute repairs to the costumes that would be worn during the Garifunian Settlement Day ceremony. Over the years wear and tear had gotten the best of some of them, so with pride, they added new feathers or paint where they were needed.

Still groggy from the night before, the young man who had been chosen as Raquel's receiver, smoothed out the colorful feathers of the cape he would wear during the historical reenactment. Because of the power he received from the medium the night before, he would wear the most prestigious costume in the ceremony. He would be Chatoyer, the legendary leader of the Garifuna, who led their last historic battle against the British nearly two hundred years ago. Chatoyer's people had fought courageously, but still the confrontation ended with the surviving

Garifunians being captured and deported to the island of Ruatan near Honduras. The ceremony is held each year so they would not forget their ancestors' bravery.

Suspiciously, he combed the crowd of men for the one he met on his way to the medium's house the previous night. His mind was foggy about what had actually taken place, and even now his head seemed to pound and swell as he tried to concentrate. All he remembered was waking up in one of the hammocks hanging amongst the trees throughout the village for convenience' sake. He had no actual memory of last night.

Bursts of laughter erupted from the group of men beside him as the ever-present bottle of cashew fruit wine made its rounds. Just the thought of drinking it caused his stomach to churn, and a slow feeling of nausea to rise.

A strong hand clasped the young man's shoulder, and he looked up into a half-smiling face above him. The glare of the sun behind the stranger blurred his facial features as he began to speak words of praise.

"Congratulations, I hear you're going to be Chatoyer during the ceremony."

"Yes, I am," the younger man grimaced as he answered. In the back of his mind he thought there was something familiar about the man's voice, but he couldn't place where he'd heard it before.

"You should be very proud," Nate said, his voice like silk. "I happened to be turning in as you were leaving the medium's place last night. You deserve the honor of being Chatoyer after receiving such power."

"Uh . . . you saw, I mean . . . thank you." He donned a self-assured look as he acknowledged the compliment.

"You are welcome," Nate replied, his steely gaze boring into the young man's confused features before he rose and walked away.

A perplexed look surfaced on his face before he put his doubts to rest, accepting the man's word. He could be proud because he had performed his duty as the medium's receiver, and today during the ceremony he would be given even greater honor.

Nate frowned as he rested his foot in the low fork of a tree, and scanned the active crowd. It was almost noon, and soon the *gubida* ceremony would begin. He had never intended for it to get this far, and he scolded himself for not being able to get the woman back to the States before now. He knew it was now too late for that. Obviously she'd been able to convince the priestess of her authenticity, but Nate knew talking was one thing, performing the mystical tasks involved in the ceremony would be another.

His dark eyes searched the outskirts of the settlement. He knew it was still early, and he hoped Ponti and the men would manage to come in time. He was deeply concerned about her performance in the ritual—a ritual he had never witnessed before. He only hoped it would all be over soon. Then he would be in a stronger position to protect the woman from anything Jay and his people might have planned. For there was no doubt in his mind, they would make their presence known in the settlement, and when they did, their main objective would be to silence him and the woman.

A group of men in the Garifunian camp began a lively beat on a set of drums. This was soon answered by a similar cadence from the Shangoains'. It didn't take long before bands had formed on both sides, each one striving to out-play the other. Clusters of energetic children began to shuffle their feet and shake their hips and shoulders in a fashion they'd seen displayed many times by the adults. Nate watched as Belinda joined a group of them, showing them how a well-seasoned woman could spice up the moves. Her antics brought forth whoops and hollers from both the Garifunian men and the women.

Encouraged by their sounds of approval, Belinda danced toward the young man who would soon wear the costume of Chatoyer in the settlement day ceremony. A lopsided grin surfaced on his young features as he watched her, then with slightly glazed eyes he rose, and accepted to become her partner.

Feeling the music, his neck moved back and forth like a rooster as he danced toward her. Both sets of eyes were focused on the others, and they smiled the smile of lovers who knew the other could most certainly satisfy their needs. Once again this spawned a reaction from the crowd, but this time there were innuendos, sexual in nature.

As time passed, sporadic dancing and music broke out in both camps as the cashew wine flowed, and the people's spirits rose in anticipation of the events to come.

CHAPTER 23

Still drowsy, Raquel fought against the tangle of sheets binding the lower half of her body. At first she tried to block out the unwelcome sunlight that had awakened her, but eventually, her heavily lashed eyelids fluttered open to the demanding light. It took a few moments for her to orient herself, but when she did, her heart began to race within her as she thought of what the day would hold—coupled with flashes of the previous night.

Now, in the bright light of day, the night's events seemed almost impossible to believe, and she looked around the house to see if she could have imagined it. But the blue heap of material on the floor told the entire tale. It had not been a dream. What she had done . . . and how she had acted . . . it had all been real.

A slim, nervous hand reached up and pushed a mass of bushy hair away from her face. Afterwards she sat up, squinting in the direction of the window where the sun was forcing its way inside.

The sight of a large thatched roof on stilts caught her eye. Immediately she recognized the robust priestess, and she guessed the man who sat beside her was the Shangoain *buyei*. Without warning, an icy chill ran down her spine as she thought of the role she would soon play, and the danger she might meet should she fail.

Once again thoughts of running away entered her mind. Panic-stricken eyes searched the growing crowd outside, and her heart lurched as she saw a group of tourists standing idly by. To the north of them she could see several parked cars. If only she could get to them! Maybe she could get them to help her!

Without further thought Raquel threw on the light blue caftan and headed for the door. Maybe she could secretly hide out in one of their vehicles, and wait for the time when they would leave.

Excited by the thought of escape, she cracked the door to peer outside. After going over the area quickly, she thought there was a chance she could circumvent the center of the settlement, and approach the cars from behind. Shoving the door aside, she made her initial step to run for the cover of the nearby woods.

"Mornin'," a respectful, strong voice greeted her. "So you finally woke up, did you? I thought you would sleep the whole morning through. I was just about to check on you again. I been in there twice, trying to see if you wanted breakfas' or something."

Badly startled by the assistant's presence, Raquel answered a short, "No," then immediately closed the door.

Her nerves on edge, she tilted her head back against the wood, and with a trembling hand she squeezed the leather pouch hanging about her neck. Frustration filled her moist eyes as she looked down at the ill-shaped object. In so doing, she caught sight of a large, dark bruise on her forearm. The unsightly spot made her think of Al, then drove a horrible fact home. If she failed during the ceremony, the Garifunians and Shangoains might do her harm, but there was no doubt if Jay caught up with her while she was trying to escape, he would kill her.

Perspiration broke out on her forehead. Raquel decided she would be better off taking her chances performing the ritual. She would do as the shamaness of the rain forest advised her. She had said she was an open spirit. So she would will herself to open to the voices of her intuition, and simply allow that part of her to flow. Raquel knew for her, that was easier said than done. But if all else failed, she determined, she would put on a performance that would win her an academy award, if need be.

Raquel was very skeptical about her abilities to yield to such spiritual beliefs. All of her life she had purposefully kept that kind of thinking at bay. As the years passed, she had convinced herself those quiet moments of childish imagination were only possible because she had been so young. To her, intuition meant uncertainty, and she had no room for that. Controlling logic had been her foundation, and now her very life depended on being able to let go of that.

An insistent knocking erupted behind the door, followed by the assistant's voice.

"I know you said you didn't want anything, but I got a basin of hot water for you to wash up in, and some fruit for you to eat. Madame Sofea would never forgive me if I didn't take care of you right. D'ya hear?"

Raquel eased up on the pressure she was applying against the door. "Come in," she invited her, half-heartedly.

Obedient, the young assistant picked up a large bowl filled with steaming water and stepped inside. Her stride was purposeful as she crossed the room and sat the container on a handmade wooden table. Beside it she placed two washcloths. Raquel watched as she went out again, returning with a package beneath her arm. There was also a bowl of oranges, grapefruits and tomatoes.

"Once you have eaten and washed yourself, here is the dress you will wear for the ceremony." She laid the brown paper packet on the bed. "I will not disturb you again until everythin' has been made ready, and the people have gathered for the ritual." The young woman started to cross the room to the door, she stopped and looked back, "Should you need me, I will be waiting outside."

Raquel sat down at the table. Despite what she told the assistant, she was hungry, and she began to peel one of the aromatic oranges as her eyes traveled to the brown package on the bed. Now, there was no turning back. She would go through with the ritual.

Automatically, Raquel began to rely on her ability to carve out a logical understanding of how she could perform what would be expected of her. Through her years of study, she had come to know of a part of the mind, which, when given the right atmosphere, even under the most bizarre situations, would react impulsively, answering the need, even when it was totally opposed to the person's personality or abilities.

Images of the night before surfaced, and she was ashamed to think how unabashedly she'd responded, letting go of all restraints without hesitation. She had been ready to do whatever was necessary to appease the potent desire burning in her veins. It just so happened Nate had been the one to come to her. She was appalled to admit that, at that time, she would have given herself to anyone.

There was a part of her that was thankful it had been Nate. But now, knowing how he had lied to her, using her even after she thought things had changed from the time he'd forcefully brought her to Belize, she could find only a bittersweet comfort in it.

In some ways, it hurt even more to have given herself to him. It further cheapened her love, seeing how he had completely used and deceived her.

Raquel sat eating the orange in silence, and listening to the tangled sound of music outside the window. She thought of the men who approached her outside the Caribbean club that fateful night, and she wondered what connection they had with Nate, if any.

A sickening feeling churned in her stomach as she thought of how ruthless he must be to have deliberately put her in such a dangerous situation, just to satisfy his own means. She was stupid to trust him, and even nurse him back to health in his hour of need. How he must have secretly laughed at her kindness, and used what he considered to be her weakness to his advantage. Now that he was back on his home turf, he could afford to tell her the truth, because she had nearly served her purpose. Whatever that may be! Wouldn't it be most ironic if he and Jay were actually working together, putting on this outrageous farce for reasons they only knew.

Raquel's anger rose with a disappointed kind of fear as her mind conjured up all sorts of reasons for the last ten days of her life. She knew she could use the anger to give her the strength she would need to survive what was in store for her.

After finishing another piece of fruit, Raquel attempted to wash her body with a sliver of soap she found on a cabinet. Deep in thought, she dried off with the second cloth, then slipped back into the caftan.

Curiosity drew her to the brown package on the bed, with trembling fingers she unwrapped it. The objects inside were simple, a string of sparkling blue and white beads, a floor-length shift in a similar shade of blue, and a large-tooth comb missing several of its prongs. A cynical smile touched Raquel's full lips, such a simple outfit for a medium who was expected to perform such miraculous works.

With the comb she managed to style her hair. She thought it should reflect the simplicity of the dress and beads, so she decided to redo her braids. The two plaits began at her forehead, outlined the edge of her hair, and met in the back where she braided them together, making the final braid into a ball.

For some reason she felt an unnatural calm as she sat on the bed with her head against the wall, waiting for the time she would be summoned. Raquel closed her eyes, shutting out the world, and tried to focus on the center of peace she had come to know on rare occasions during her sporadic meditations. As she concentrated, she knew, no matter what methods she used to conduct the ritual, the answers would all have to come from inside her. She just hoped they were the right ones.

CHAPTER 24

"Hey, what is this?" the middle-aged, red-haired man protested. "I didn't come all the way down here in this god-forsaken mudhole to miss any of the action. I'm ready to par-r-tay. And I heard you've never been to a party till you've partied down here at one of y'all's festivals. And now you're telling me I'm not allowed," he raised his voice at the teenage Garifunians who had linked arms to block his way.

A group of tourists interested in the outburst lingered conveniently behind. Unlike the others who had contented themselves with shopping in the only gift shop, they wanted to see if there was even the slightest chance they would be allowed to see the forbidden ritual.

"This is not for outsiders," one of the louder, bolder teenagers replied, then clasped the wrists of his human chain counterparts even tighter, causing the others to do the same.

"Oh it's not? We'll see about that."

The large man attempted to shove his way through the teenagers' block, but he was abruptly stopped by two adult males approaching from the rear.

They didn't speak a word as they grabbed him beneath his armpits, and forcefully dragged him back to the middle of the settlement while he shouted obscenities and the other tourists shuffled off to do some shopping.

The red-haired man continued to grumble as he sat in the spot where he had been discarded by the two Shangoains, but he made no attempt to follow them as they entered the rain forest.

As the minutes passed Raquel knew it wouldn't be long before the assistant informed her the villagers were ready. Once again a light sheen of perspiration broke out on her forehead, and a little voice inside admonished her, calling her a fool for even attempting this. Maybe she was a fool. Maybe she had even become as confused as some of the patients she'd counseled over the years. But there was one thing she was sure of, that she was willing to do whatever it would take to bring this ordeal to an end.

Yet Raquel knew there was something else that compelled her, even though she would deny it if she could. It was a persistent, inner nagging, telling her there was more. Something on an almost imperceptible level coercing her to carry out this task, guiding her with forces she did not understand.

The young woman ran both of her hands over her eyes, and tried to rid her mind of that train of thought. It was futile at this point to try and reason why her life had led her here. It would only drain her, and she would need all the powers of concentration she could muster for the ritual.

A knock sounded at the door, and as Raquel rose to answer it Nate came into view far outside her window. He was carrying Marjorie, her small body appearing frail in his arms. Brandon's smaller steps looked hurried beside Nate's long strides as they crossed the mud-caked road to enter the rain forest. There was a scowl upon his handsome features when he turned and gave the settlement one hard, searching look before disappearing into the thicket.

Impatient from no answer, the assistant cracked the door and spoke into the tiny space.

"It is time for the ceremony to begin."

Raquel took a deep breath and steadied herself, "I'm ready," then she walked over to the door and stepped outside.

The assistant acknowledged her with a slight smile, but without further adieu she turned and walked toward the rain forest.

The green darkness of the tree-canopy-covered forest was a stark contrast to the tropical sunshine beaming down on the rest of the settlement. The transition was almost mystical, for this was a totally different world, ruled by nature and its forces. The assistant's movements through the brush seemed to reflect Raquel's thoughts. She was no longer the pragmatic creature from the settlement, but one who showed even with the slightest touch, that she honored nature and its gifts. Almost with reverence she pushed aside the branches and vines appearing in their way as they progressed deeper into the forest, her feet moving soundlessly upon the ground.

It didn't take long for them to reach the circle of villagers, gathered around a partial clearing. Immediately, countless pairs of dark eyes engulfed Raquel as they entered the center area covered by moss and other growth favoring a close relationship with the earth.

The Garifunian priestess and the Shangoain *buyei* sat on the opposite side of the clearing. In their hands were small gourds, covered with netting, connected by cowrie shells. Both nodded as she entered the circle, shaking the minute instruments in a welcoming salute.

It was then Raquel noticed the other musicians. They were seated on the ground with their legs crossed, holding the same instrument, varying in size.

Obviously the welcoming rattle was their cue, so with controlled hand and arm movements, they began a low, rhythmic, slating sound. Over and over they played the same pattern until their bodies naturally joined in, their upper torsos and heads following the repetitive beat. With perfect timing, the light, hollow pulse of a bongo drum fused with it, giving the cadence a lulling, resonate sound. Some of the younger Garifunians and Shangoains began to imitate the body movement of the musicians until the entire gathering seemed to sway in unison, beguiled by the trance inducing music.

A moment of confusion nearly disrupted the beginning of the ritual, when both the priestess and *buyei* attempted to speak at the same time. An awkward silence followed as they both gestured, indicating the other should be allowed to go first. Finally, the *buyei* accepted the priestess's act of courtesy, and spoke briefly to the crowd.

"We have waited a long time for t'is, and out of respect for the *gubida* we should not delay it any longer," his trembling, but strong voice floated outward. "T'is ceremony will renew the bond between the Garifunian an' Shangoain people, makin' it stronger than evah. An' through this unity our faith will also be strengthened by us giving the proper honor an' praise to the gods an' goddesses of our ancestors."

The *buyei* finished his introduction by picking up a small cup of water that had been sitting between him and the priestess. He turned and offered it to her. Following his lead, she accepted the object from his knurled hands and began to sprinkle several drops of the water on the ground. Afterwards she shook her rattle, and spoke in a loud voice.

"We praise Olodumare and all honored ancestors who live at the feet of Olodumare in the world thus to follow. We praise our personal ancestors and salute the priests of our houses. We also salute Yemoja-Olokun and Shango and the many gods of our people."

Verbal agreement resounded throughout the crowd at the priestess's words. Finally, when the crowd became silent, the music began again, but this time it was louder, and all eyes turned to Raquel.

Her anxious features searched the faces of the villagers surrounding her, then reluctantly her gaze stopped on Nate's concerned face and Marjorie's thin countenance, leaning against his chest.

She could feel the crowd's expectation as they stared at her, it was almost a suffocating feeling. She tried to relax enough to think of the advice the shamaness of the rain forest had given her, but her mind drew a blank. The music seemed to become more insistent, the sound of it feeling as if it were literally trying to enter her head.

Suddenly Raquel felt overwhelmed. She became lightheaded as if she might faint, and she dropped to her knees. Weakly, she leaned forward and placed her face against the cool moss blanketing the forest floor. It was hard for her to breathe, and despite herself, she tried to call out to Nate for help, but no sound came from her lips. Finally, her fading gaze connected with his, just as it looked as if he had decided to come to her. Then everything around her went dark.

There was a part of her that was aware of everything, but somehow time had been suspended. She could see her body crouched in the forest, the people around her, and Nate on a perpetual verge of reaching out to her.

The part of Raquel that was conscious, turned its attention toward the rain forest, then merely by focusing her thoughts on its interior, she began to travel at an amazing speed. All the colors of the forest blended together as she whooshed by, and before she knew it, she was standing outside a cave. Two bright eyes glowed from within it, then upon seeing her they began to move in her direction. It was an animal. A jaguarundi. When he emerged from the cave he came and laid his body down at her feet, as docile as a kitten.

As Raquel knelt to rub his soft fur, his piercing eyes seemed to draw her gaze within them, and an image of the shamaness of the rain forest appeared in their yellowish depths.

She was lying alone in her hut upon a pallet. The rise and fall of her thin chest was almost indiscernible beneath the numerous layers of cloth, and her once-powerful dreadlocks lay limply about her. The vision clutched at Raquel's heart, and her feelings went out to her mentor that she should be alone in her hour of death.

Then suddenly, as if she could feel Raquel's emotions, a slight smile appeared on the shamaness's withered face. Slowly she began to speak, and somehow Raquel could hear her coarse voice purring in the wind.

"Do not feel sad for me. Soon I will be totally reunited with the source of all power. And that ez the key to all knowledge, girl. All that lives has a spark of that power within, as you do. Clasp hold of the pouch an' give praise to the ocean an' her life-giving forces. Ask for her compassion, an' she will help bridge the two worlds that you seek. My timely passing will open the way for you." Her last words were only a blur, then her dried lips were still and Raquel knew the shamaness of the rain forest was dead. Oddly, at that moment, she did not feel grief. If she trusted her mentor, she would have to believe all that she had said. Maybe now she would find the acceptance she could not find here on earth.

Abruptly her mind focused on the pouch. She needed it to call on the ocean's power, yet it still hung around her neck as she crouched in the forest. A profound yearning to hold it overcame her, and with that urgent desire, in a split second, her spirit and body were reunited. During that second, she was totally aware of being in the clearing, the people, the music. But as soon as she called on the force of the ocean to show her compassion, her consciousness totally deserted her.

CHAPTER 25

She could barely make out the face above her, but as the moments passed, and her fluttering lashes halted their erratic movement, she realized it was Nate's face. Her confused mind began to fill with all sorts of questions. But Raquel knew they would have to wait, because breathing deeply was all she was capable of doing. She felt exhausted, even her head felt heavy as she attempted to turn it on Nate's lap. Finally she realized her portion of the ritual was over.

Two villagers had taken her place as the center of attention, and they were in the throes of what she could only call some kind of trance. The man and the woman resembled marionettes being controlled by invisible strings, their body movements jerky and unpredictable.

The music had also changed from the repetitive cadence she remembered, to a more animated, invigorating, sound. This was matched by the movements of the chosen villagers.

The entire crowd had become energized, and by the satisfied looks on the priestess and *buyei's* faces, she knew she had been successful.

"What happened?" she asked weakly. She found her throat was parched as she attempted to speak.

One smooth eyebrow raised, perplexed, "You tell me," Nate's dark eyes glistened as he looked down into her face. "You looked like you knew exactly what you were doing a little while ago."

She closed her eyes, not understanding what he meant, and too tired to reply. When she opened them again, she saw the assistant kneeling down beside her, offering her a drink. Hastily she took the container, gulping down its contents without a second thought.

A thin hand reached out to take the empty cup from her, and Raquel's eyes opened wide with disbelief when she saw it was Marjorie. She was deathly thin, but within the depths of her eyes was the sparkle of life.

"I want to thank you for releasing my boy," her voice was barely more than a whisper as she spoke. "Now it is time for me to rejoin the livin'. Brandon needs me, and I know now, Art has safely crossed over to the other side."

Raquel could only nod her head lamely.

As Marjorie walked away, two village women approached them and gently removed Raquel from Nate's care. She was moved to a seat of honor near the priestess and the *buyei*. There she was given time to recuperate, and with amazement, she watched the remainder of the ritual.

Raquel could tell, despite his helping her, Nate was grateful when the women took her from him. It was obvious he was on edge, and even the compelling activity inside the clearing could not hold his attention. His watchful, steely gaze continuously searched the surrounding rain forest. His concern was somewhere out there, not within the circle of satisfied Garifunians and Shangoains.

The young woman watched as the villagers, whom the priestess said were being ridden by some unseen forces, unexpectantly dropped with exhaustion. Quickly several caring participants came to their aid, and moved them to places where they too could rest. The music continued to play for a while longer. It was as if the musicians had to come down from the peak where their music had taken them. Shortly afterwards, the sound of the bongos and the rattles came to a halt.

A meaty, dimpled hand was shown to the crowd as the priestess sought to gain their attention.

"I know there is only one question that both the Garifunian and our spiritual brothers, the Shangoain, would like to ask the ancestors. And that is, "Are you pleased with what we have done here today? Has the spiritual rift between our people been mended by these works?"

Words of encouragement and affirmation intermittently rose from the crowd, and Raquel could tell this question-and-answer period was also a part of the ceremony.

The question had been asked, and now a divination would decide if the answer was a positive one. If it was, blessings would be bestowed on both of the villages, or if the contrary were true, afflictions would rage among the people for not pleasing the *gubida*.

The Shangoain *buyei* produced the divination tools from a sack he carried at his side. They were four hollow coconut shells, and Raquel could tell they had received much use through the years. What used to be their hairy outer part had been worn down, until now the fibers resembled a sprouting beard.

Ceremoniously the *buyei* wet each one of the shells. Once done, he cast all four on the forest floor. The villagers watched the process in a hushed silence. Three times he threw them, and three times they landed face up. Raquel had no idea what the results of the casting meant, until the last throw was met by exuberant shouts from the pleased crowd.

This time the priestess did not try to calm the congregation, so above the excited raucous shouts she announced, "We have surely been blessed today! Now let the Settlement Day festivities begin."

Jay grabbed the first painted mask and shirt he found. Working fast, he removed his top and quickly replaced it with the costume. His anxious fingers found the small buttons on the old rayon top difficult to work with, and he cussed at the shirt under his breath.

"Look through there, and see if t'ere's anythin' t'at will fit both of you," he instructed Rock and Mane-Mane.

Rock resented the authoritative attitude Jay had taken since arriving in the village. He would have made it known, but he realized nabbing some of the costumes that were to be worn during the ceremony wasn't a bad idea. This way their faces would be covered, no one would be able to identify them, and they'd surely blend in with the crowd.

He signaled his okay for Mane-Mane to search through the small stacks of shirts and masks as he kept watch. He could see one of their backups perusing the gift shop, while the other joined in with the large crowd of tourists waiting for the festivities to begin.

"You ain't found nothin' yet?" he barked, as he rubbed his index finger back and forth beneath his nose. "Hell no! These damn things are too little for either one of us. That goes to show you what I've been saying all along. These suckers, just like Jay, ain't nothing but—" he stopped and looked in the man's direction, to see if his remark would hit home.

But Jay's anxious eyes were focused on the spot where the villagers would reenter the settlement. He'd waited a long time to settle the score with Nate and the woman, and revenge was uppermost in his mind.

Unable to get a rise out of him, Mane-Mane continued.

"Maybe we should go back to our original plan and just wait for Jay to round up the woman. Once the guy sees she's missing, he's sure to follow, and we can take care of both of 'em at the same time."

Jay's eyes seemed to light up as he heard Mane-Mane mention Raquel. "Yes, leave the woman to me. I'll take care of her."

"What d'ya mean you'll take care of her?" Rock jumped in. "You're suppose to bring her to me, and I'll decide how it's handled from there." Hell, Rock wanted Jay to do the killing, but not out in the open where everyone could see. As obsessed as he had become, there's no telling what he might say and do that would ultimately connect him with their organization. He told Ricky this guy was going to be hard to handle. But all he could say was, "Just point him in the right direction, and let him do the dirty work."

Jay simply stared at Rock. It was a long hollow look, as if he could see right through him.

Rock hated to admit it, but ever since they found Jay's dead brother he'd begun to feel uneasy around the guy. There was something spooky about him, just like this stare he was throwing down on him now.

Jay insulted him in a voice as piercing as his stare. "I don't take no orders from nobody like you." Then he walked away, disappearing into the nearby brush.

The crowd at the clearing jumped to its feet no sooner than the priestess's words were spoken, and the musicians began to play again. This time the bongos and rattles were joined by other drums and an old guitar. The Garifunians and Shangoains joined their voices in song as they made their way back to the settlement. At first their revelry sounded like a low hum to the tourists, but it rose in pitch as they got nearer to the settlements border.

Raquel was well entangled in the joyous crowd. Despite her fatigue, she could almost feel the energy from their happiness. She knew, not even in a thousand years would she be able to explain what had happened back there, but explain it or not, something miraculous did occur, and she had played a major role. But her moment of triumph was cut short when Nate showed up beside her.

"We-ell, that was quite a show you put on back there, *pataki*, I didn't know you had it in you. Are you sure you haven't done this kind of thing before?"

There was a slight smile on his face, but his eyes were bright like an animal's whose senses were tuned for danger. Possessively, he placed his large hand around her forearm and held it tightly.

"If it isn't my dear . . . brother," she spat at him. "I'm glad my performance was greater than even you had expected. But that shouldn't surprise you. Being great performers and deceivers tends to run in the family," she retorted angrily, trying to remove her arm from his grasp with no avail.

"You can let go of my arm now," she hissed between her teeth. "Haven't I served my purpose? Or has that calculating brain of yours come up with some other way you can use me?"

"Yes, in a way you've served your purpose, and very well I should say," his voice was harsh. "And now I want to make sure you get to keep doing just that." His already-firm grip tightened at the anger and distrust in her voice.

Dark, almond eyes looked up at him with accusation, "Don't start that again." Wincing, she looked at his large hand on her arm. "And you are hurting me!"

Nate's voice softened, and so did his grip as he looked down at her. "I'm sorry, *pataki,* but we didn't make it this far for me to lose you now. I know after all this you may find it difficult to believe, but I only want to protect you. You see—"

"Liar! You're nothing but a liar!" she screamed cutting him off, then managing to yank herself free. But no one could hear her, or paid her any attention as the excited crowd burst out into the settlement.

The strong forward thrust caught Raquel up in the throng. They were joined by the tourists who were moving in closer to get a better look at the Yankunu dancers jauntily advancing toward them. Their costumes depicted the dress of the villagers' ancestors, some much more elaborate than others.

Large hand-painted masks covered their faces as they waved sticks and other objects, representing the weapons they used to fight the British during that fateful battle.

Raquel caught a glimpse of Nate's contorted features as she was carried outside of his reach. For the first time since she'd known him, she saw fear and apprehension in his eyes, and she knew without a doubt, those feeling were not for himself but for her.

The appearance of the dancers further enlivened the group, and almost everyone had joined in the celebration. Food and wine were being passed about freely, as the villagers celebrated Garifuna Settlement Day, and the favorable results of the ritual.

Staggered, boisterous phrases of praise resounded all around as the young man dressed as Chatoyer entered the scene. His bright feathers seem to vibrate in the sunshine as he twirled and turned showing his prowess, energized by the crowd's approval. Several eager villagers hoisted Raquel up and maneuvered her nearer to the symbol of their legendary leader, putting her down in the front of the crowd, so he would surely see her.

Just as the excited crowd expected, the young man's eyes gleamed within the ferocious mask when he saw the woman he thought he had coupled with the night before, and he began to prance saucily before her, surrounded by the other Yankunu dancers, drawing an even more jubilant response.

Raquel stood tensely before him with the villagers shouting words of encouragement at her back, not sure what they were encouraging her to do.

One of the dancers reached out and grabbed her by her wrist, and began to pull her into their circle as she was being pushed from behind. Energized, he began to cavort with her by his side. She could tell he expected her to duplicate his movements, but the picture of Nate's face only moments ago still loomed in her mind.

Suddenly a string of shots rang out from an automatic weapon. The eruption seem to come from the area where the tourists had parked their cars.

Raquel's heart lurched with fear at the sound of the loud blasts. It was Jay! He'd finally caught up with them. Suddenly all she could see was Nate lying in a pool of blood and Jay standing above him, a satisfied smile on his face after killing the man who'd fatally shot his brother.

"No—o!" The mad scream rose from the depths of her as she tried to break loose from the dancer who still held her arm. She had to find out . . . to go to him!

The sound of the gunshots caused panic to break out amongst the crowd, and people were shoving and pushing one another to find cover. In the pandemonium, the dancer who held her hand began to drag her in the opposite direction of where she wanted to go. Once again she tried to extract her hand from his, but he held it even tighter. It was then, she realized, she was being forcefully led by the masked man.

Jay began to lead her away from where he knew Rock and Mane-Mane were waiting. He would not allow them to tell him what he should do with the woman. He already knew what had to be done. She had to be made to suffer, just like Al suffered. And he would be the only one to do it.

"What are you doing?" Raquel screamed as her plight began to sink in. "You better let go of me!"

Furiously she fought against the iron-tight grip, trying to break free. The man was headed for the cover of the rain forest, and she knew she would be in even graver danger once they entered it.

Obsessed, Jay paid little attention to her pleas as he dragged her deeper into the forest. Sweat poured down his face beneath the mask because of the heat and the effort it took to control the woman. His breaths became ragged with exertion, and his heart pumped faster as he focused on the fear in her voice.

Finally reaching a point far enough within the brush, he stopped and removed the papier mâché cover.

A slow, unnatural smile spread across his thin lips. "So we meet again, *echu?*" A terrifying mixture of hate and lust burned in his eyes as he addressed her.

The shock of seeing Jay's face beneath the mask was nearly too much, and it took all the strength Raquel had to remain steady on her feet.

"You shouldn' be surprised to see me. Don' tell me you thought I wouldn' come aftah you." The sound of his large switchblade releasing sliced into his words.

"Yes. I knew from the very first you were bad luck," he spat on the ground beside her feet. "Yeah, I know of all 'e talk of you an' the *gubida*. But 'e stories are fairy tales, told to people who are afraid to take control of t'eir own lives." He meaningfully tested the point of the blade against his index finger, drawing a quick spurt of blood. Once again he looked up at Raquel. "You were bad for me an' my brothah, Al. But you were no good even before t'at. I tried to get rid of you, but somehow it didn' work. I would have taken care of you from the very beginnin' if it hadn' been for Meester Nate. He was *always* t'ere to protect you . . . but he isn't here now."

Jay's horrible eyes burned into hers as he grabbed her by the throat and drew her to him. "No, he isn' here now." Each word caused bursts of his coarse breath to blow into her face, and Raquel closed her eyes against him.

Grinning, he meticulously moved the blade from her throat downward with the needle-sharp tip of the knife. Putting pressure against the thin material of her shift. It pierced the papery fabric easily, drawing a pencil thin line of blood on her skin as he went. Savoring the moment, and his feeling of power over her, Jay stopped at the tender spot between her breasts.

"Yeah, the man who talked all t'at fancy talk 'bout protectin' you because of the ancestors, ain't nowhere aroun'," he snorted. "But now I know he jus' wanted to keep Al and me from you, cuz he wanted you himself," he applied more pressure against the knife. "I wonder where he is now, *echu*. I wouldn' be surprised if he isn' layin' not very far from here wit' his brains shot out by Rock or Mane-Mane."

"Guess again, Jay."

Raquel's eyes flew open to see Nate standing several feet behind the man, his gun drawn.

A flicker of surprise clouded Jay's bulbous eyes at the sound of Nate's silky voice, and he tightened his hold about Raquel's neck.

"If you have a gun Meester Nate, an' you decide to shoot me at such close range, the bullet will go right through me into t'e woman. Or by t'e time it enters my body, I will have plunged t'is knife deep into her chest. Either way she will be dead."

"That's true, Jay. You both will be dead. But I will be alive. And I'm the one who bent over and put my gun against your no-good, crazy brother's heart. Put him out of his misery just like a rabid dog. I killed him Jay. And once you're dead there'll be no one to avenge him," he paused to let his words sink in. "But if he were my brother, Jay, I'd want to kill the person who killed him."

Raquel could feel the knife quiver against her chest and she knew Nate's words had reached their mark. Jay's grip on her neck tightened and she winced in pain.

"You shut up 'bout my brothah, you no-good sonuvabitch! I will—"

"You will what?" Nate's voice was deadly smooth as he spoke. "Kill me, Jay? How you gonna do that as long as you're holding the woman? If you let her go, I promise you, I'll put down the gun and you can have me. I'm the one who actually killed your brother, not her. I'm the one you really want."

There was a moment of indecision before Jay spoke again.

"Well, you come 'round here where I can see you and t'en we'll talk."

"I'll come, but I don't want to talk. See there's a chance I can get near enough to you, and shoot you before you can stab the woman. And I'm willing to take that chance. So to keep it fair, I'm going to stop here and count to three. On the count of three, I will drop the gun, but while I'm counting, you better be pushing her away, and have released her when I'm done."

"One . . ." Nate's dark eyes narrowed as he watched Jay's veins in the hand around Raquel's neck protrude. "Two . . ."

Her breath was cut short as Jay began to push her over to his side. She could feel his fingers constricting around her neck, and she knew he was trying to choke her. Her hands flew up to her throat in an effort to pry his maniacal fingers from around it.

"Three."

Suddenly he pushed her on the ground, and she heard the thud of Nate's gun when it hit the moss-covered floor. Like an animal, Nate sprung toward Jay, grabbing the arm which held the ominous switchblade. Both men struggled, pitting their strength against one another, as they rolled through the brush.

Focusing his strength, Nate forced Jay onto his back, and applied his weight against the arm holding the knife. Jay's teeth ground together as he tried to hold onto the weapon, but finally Nate prevailed, and the switchblade was knocked into the thickness of a nearby bush.

Pushed beyond the point of anger, Jay let loose an enraged yell and kneed Nate in the groin, causing him to double over in pain. Jay knew he had to take advantage of the moment, and he lunged toward the Glock Nate had thrown on the ground. Panting and feeling the hard, cold metal in his shaking hands, he aimed the gun in Nate's direction.

"Now, not only am I going to kill you, Meester Nate, but I also get to kill the no-good bitch. No-ow," he groaned, "it will end as it should end by my killin' the two of you."

A broad, demented smile beamed on Jay's face as he pulled the trigger, only for the bullet to go off into the ground a couple of feet in front of him. Like a wooden soldier being pushed face down, Jay's thin body pitched forward. The butt of the switchblade sticking out of his back as Eva stood above him. Motionless she stood watching as his body convulsed with his last painful breaths. Then almost as if realizing what she had done, she abruptly looked up at Nate and Raquel, then turned and ran into the rain forest.

CHAPTER 26

A large, wet area was forming on the back of Mane-Mane's T-shirt, compliments of the sun. His muscles rippled underneath the soggy material as he adjusted his body, trying get more comfortable.

"Shit," he hollered loudly. "The hood of this damn car is burnin' my face," he complained as the top of his frame lay across the blue vehicle. His eyes rolled to the side as far as they could in an effort to see what kind of reaction his remark had drawn. To his dismay, it drew none. Sniffing, Rock lay beside him cussing beneath his breath. Both men were handcuffed. Their two accomplices were draped across the vehicle on the other side of the hood, bound in the same fashion.

Raquel tried to listen at a distance along with several villagers and tourists, to—as she guessed—law-enforcement officers haggling about what had taken place. It was hard to hear because of comments from curious onlookers.

A short man in uniform pointed an accusing finger toward Nate and the five men standing near him. She knew Nate had to have heard the remarks, but saw that he continued to explain events calmly to the group around him.

Raquel could barely concentrate as her mind and senses continued to reel from the scene in the forest. Once they had reentered the village, things happened so fast she could barely keep up with them.

She remembered Ponti rushing to their side, and upon seeing the blood from the shallow cut on her chest, asking if she were okay. Weakly she had nodded, and with his support walked with him and Nate across the main thoroughfare of the village. Abruptly Nate stopped, instructed Ponti to take her to a shady spot, and handed him the pistol Jay had attempted to use only minutes before.

"I think the danger is over," Nate cautioned, "but if not, don't be afraid to use it."

Still shaky, but pleased to have Ponti by her side, Raquel watched as Nate walked toward the parked cars where several men were being held at gunpoint by apparent tourists. Moments later, Belizean law-enforcement officers arrived on the scene, and after a few words with Nate and the other men, placed handcuffs on the prisoners, who were now lying across the cars.

A short official, obviously the one in charge, showed growing signs of irritation as he spoke to several other officers. Distrustful glances were cast toward Nate and the men around him as they continued their conversation.

Suddenly, the officer shoved his way through the ring of men surrounding Nate, and confronted him. The back of his hand smacked against his palm repeatedly as he spoke. All of his gestures were wild and irritated during the exchange.

Raquel looked on as Nate stood quietly, his tall frame looking almost relaxed as he leaned into one hip. Beads of perspiration gleamed on all of the men's faces as the sun beat down on the scene.

Several minutes passed and Raquel was slightly amused that the official had not run out of steam, but it was apparent Nate had heard enough. Interrupting the man's speech, he turned to one of the men behind him, and immediately produced several folded papers and a small, leather billfold.

The official was plainly offended by Nate's actions and placed his hefty hands on his hips as he watched him warily.

"What the heck is going on over there, Ponti?" Raquel asked totally baffled.

"It's a long story," he hedged. "Maybe I should let Mr. Nate tell you about it."

Surprised, and a little irritated, Raquel looked at Ponti's cloaked features, then back at Nate and the men around him.

After a minute's perusal of the paperwork the official abruptly flung them back into Nate's outstretched palm.

"I should know about things like this before they take place," he protested over the murmur of the crowd.

Further confused, Raquel watched as Nate spoke to the man, then showed him the contents of the leather billfold. The official shook his head as if he'd been defeated, asked—Raquel perceived—more questions, then threw his hands up in submission and rejoined his men.

Barking instructions, he watched as his officers placed the handcuffed men in the back seats of two of the four-wheel drive vehicles, then secured them further by handcuffing them to the interior of the car. Satisfied they had performed their duties in an adequate manner, he made a slight nod in Nate's direction, got into another vehicle and drove away, followed by the cars filled with two new sets of prisoners.

For a moment their eyes met, and Raquel was more aware than ever that she knew nothing about this man with whom she'd spent the most dangerous, yet fulfilling week of her entire life.

Nate's attention was drawn back to his men and they exchanged a few more words. Afterwards they dispersed in several directions, while Nate advanced toward the priestess and the *buyei*, who were seated beneath the large thatched roof.

Once again Raquel could tell that several questions were asked and Nate supplied the answers. On this occasion, taking his time to explain what had occurred, thus showing them more respect than he had shown the law-enforcement officer. Sporadically, the priestess and *buyei* nodded their heads in understanding as he spoke, until finally each one laid their hands upon him, giving him their approval.

Raquel wondered if he'd told them the truth about who she was, and if so, why were they still pleased with him? And the officers—they'd nearly treated him as if he were their equal. It was all so confusing, if he knew he had their trust, why had they hidden like criminals the entire time they were in Belize? And why had he actually participated in kidnapping her, if he was such friends, so to speak, with the law?

By now totally perplexed, she watched as the two heads of the Garifunian and Shangoain communities bid him a fond farewell as he began to cross the dusty road progressing in her direction.

There were so many questions she wanted to ask and things she needed to say, but once he reached her, she was speechless.

Nate understood the myriad of emotions playing across her still-beautiful, but somewhat-drawn features. She had lost weight, and the bruise on her face was at its peak. He wanted to take her in his arms and tell her everything would be okay, but coming from him, he knew those words would sound empty and meaningless.

"*Pataki*, we're ready to go home now." His expression was veiled as he looked into her face.

For some reason the phrase she had waited to hear for so long angered her. And the word which he had come to call her grated on her nerves. So after all this, he would simply tell her we're ready to go home! He didn't think he owed her any kind of explanation as to what had actually taken place! So . . . she should be grateful to be alive and that was it!

"Just wait a minute!" her incredulous eyes cut into him. "So that's it, huh? This is crazy! You think you can just walk over here and offer to take me home like we just went to the movies or something?"

"No," his eyes continued to search hers. "I understand—"

"We're ready to leave any time you are, Mr. Bowman," one of the men interrupted him.

"All right," he answered him, but his eyes stayed fastened on Raquel's. "Look, I've got a lot to tell you, and this isn't the place to do it. It'll be better once we're on the plane."

Their dark eyes locked in a silent battle.

Wanting and feeling like she deserved more, Raquel thought of protesting further, but another one of the men approached Nate, insisting he had some pressing things to discuss with him, then he began to physically pull him aside. After a few choice words in his ear, the understanding countenance he'd shown her only moments before disappeared, and he became engulfed in the conversation at hand.

Wordlessly he cut the man off with a movement of his hand, "We need to talk about this on the plane." The man nodded his head in agreement.

With distressed features, Nate turned and addressed Ponti.

"I've got to go now, but you know what to do."

"Yes, I've got it all written down right here." He patted a leather binder Raquel had not noticed before.

"Good, because from now on you're going to be one of my main people working between the States and Belize. Let's consider this as your first assignment." He patted him on the shoulder.

Happily Ponti nodded his compliance, then turned a more solemn face toward Raquel. "Here." He passed her the bundle filled with the costume from that fateful night, and a few other belongings. "These are yours."

She held the objects in front of her, staring at them. They brought back so many memories, she could feel unwanted tears gathering behind her eyes, stinging them. To hide her emotion, she quickly hugged him around the neck, "Thank you, Ponti," she murmured, as she tried to gain control of herself. "If you ever see Mircea again you tell her I will never forget her."

"I will see her. And I will tell her," he promised.

"Well, we've got to go now." Once again Nate took control, as he helped Raquel into the back seat of the four wheel drive. One of his men, already behind the wheel, revved up the engine once Nate seated himself.

Almost with disbelief Raquel settled back and began to wave to the many curious, but accepting villagers who remained behind. The *buyei* and the priestess both acknowledged her as they passed, and it wasn't long before she could hear a bongo beat, inviting them to forget the sorrows of the day, and join in the celebration. Only a matter of minutes had passed and they had left the village behind.

"The plane is not far from here," the man driving the vehicle informed Nate. "John brought it down in a nearby bean field."

Nate showed little reaction to the man's words. She could tell his thoughts were already far away.

"A private plane?" Raquel questioned.

"Yes," Nate replied, but would provide no further information.

"Well may I ask whose plane I'll be flying in, or is that too much to ask," she exploded.

Not liking the tone of her voice, the driver attracted her gaze in the rear-view mirror, disdainfully answering, "Mr. Bowman's, of course."

"Yours?" Raquel demanded of Nate.

"No. My father's."

It was a white and blue Beechcraft that seated six people. The pilot and two of the other men were already aboard. The cars they had used were turned over to two of the men from the village, who drove away before the plane took off.

All the men addressed Nate as Mr. Bowman, except for the one who said they had important matters to discuss. He took the seat across from Nate's, and began to immediately shovel papers in his direction. A fourth man, in his twenties, took the seat opposite Raquel. He had a no-nonsense look about him, and Raquel felt he would not be open to her questions or idle conversation.

As the small craft lifted off the ground the young woman's adrenaline soared with it. Taking one last look out the window, she spotted a large jaguarundi, standing at the edge of the rain forest, watching the plane's ascent. Goodbye, she called out to him silently, acknowledging the living symbol of her mentor's spirit.

There was a mixture of uncertainty and elation as they climbed and she realized it was finally going to happen. She was finally going home!

The flight was a relatively short one, but during the entire time not once did Nate attempt to speak to her. It was true the man who sat beside her constantly fed him information, but Raquel still felt that was no excuse for ignoring her. As the flight progressed, she felt more and more alienated from the man with whom she'd shared the last week.

Unfastening her seat belt, Raquel sat on the edge of the cushioned seat and placed a demanding hand on Nate's forearm.

"You've got to tell me what's going on here? What happened back there in the village, and who are these men?"

She tried to speak at a level that only Nate could hear, but no sooner had she said the demanding words than both of the men pinned her with an impatient stare. The one who seemed to have the closest tie with Nate handed him another envelope, emphasizing that he felt the business at hand was more important than Raquel's questions.

"*Pataki,* my sister, Jackie, has died." He paused a moment at Raquel's gasp. "And unfortunately, her death has set off a whole chain of events. I cannot tell you anymore right now. I promise we will talk once we reach Miami." His dark eyes were sad and sought understanding, but she could tell he was anxious to get back to his conversation with his aide.

It all felt very strange, for in a matter of minutes things had changed, drastically. In the primitive world of Belize they had depended almost solely on each other, but now as they flew back into the present, into their world, she felt as if they were becoming strangers once again.

The young man beside her leaned forward, "Is there anything I can get for you, Mr. Bowman?" his demeanor reflecting his willingness to serve.

Raquel never heard the response. She just watched as he returned to a restful position and looked out the window. His subservient attitude toward Nate only fed her uncertainty. The feeling was magnified by the respect all of these men showed him, men who obviously felt they owed him their allegiance. Who was Nate Bowman?

All of a sudden she felt out of place, and she glanced nervously about the plane with its immaculate interior, TV, VCR, and telephone.

Now, there were only two things she knew about the man, Nate Bowman. His family was far from poor, and from what she'd witnessed in Dangriga, they also had plenty of clout in Belize. Yet she knew there were all sorts of ways to make money and gain clout in a Central American country, and not all of them good.

Raquel looked at the young man who sat across from her, and almost by telepathy he turned his head returning her gaze. Quickly, she dropped her thick, lashes, but he continued to look, a long measuring stare. Self-consciously, she placed her hand over the bloodstain smearing the front of the slashed shift. Suddenly she realized what she must look like to this fastidious young man.

Embarrassed, and wanting to explain, she looked directly into his face, but she could see he had drawn his own conclusions. They were dearly written in his eyes. They were of two different worlds. She was not a woman who belonged in the world of private planes and the best life could offer . . . not this woman discovered in a dance club and given ten thousand dollars to play a game.

This time it was Raquel who turned and looked out the window, perturbed by Nate's silent and pompous judgment, and fearful he was not the only one who shared those feelings.

When they landed a small crowd of people met them at the Opa-Locka airport, all of them wanting to talk to "Mr. Bowman." At first

Raquel stood idly by, watching the interactions and waiting for Nate to look for her. But as the moments passed, and the men in their business suits, and a particularly well-kept female vied for his attention, she knew her chances of speaking to him would be slim to none.

A sick feeling of disillusionment began to rise inside her as the minutes rolled by, and she questioned her logic for remaining there. Why was it so important that she speak to him anyway? No matter what, he still played a part in the kidnapping, bringing her close to death more times than she cared to remember.

Still she stood and watched, her mind fighting with her emotions, remembering how it felt to be in his arms, the things he had promised, the moments they shared, if only . . .

The woman reached up and laid an affectionate palm against Nate's square jaw, her china-doll hair swinging back from her meticulously made-up features as she looked up at him, welcoming him back. This woman's actions forced Raquel to face reality. There was no reason for her to wait. She didn't belong here. Not because she didn't deserve the things they had, but because she knew nothing about them, and they knew, and cared nothing about her.

It wasn't hard for Raquel to locate the women's bathroom. Once inside, she washed her face and changed her clothes. Resourcefully, she donned the shift she was given when she first arrived on the sailboat, completing her outfit with the skirt from the costume.

With steady fingers she ripped open the bralike top of the festive outfit, and to her relief found the one-thousand dollars still inside. With unshed tears in her eyes, Raquel looked in the mirror, took a deep breath and patted the thick French braids that circled her head, "Well this is it, girlfriend, I guess it's time to go home."

CHAPTER 27

"Are you coming tonight, Sam?" Raquel called out as she headed for the door.

"I'm thinking about it." He frowned, then rubbed his hand through his hair. "You know how I hate politicking and all the brown-nosing that goes with it."

"Well look at it this way," Raquel advised, "It's a chance to get a free meal, and drink some good wine for a change."

She smiled at the man who had proven to be her right hand during the last five weeks.

She had been back only three days when she was contacted and told the clinic would be reopened, financed by a well-established foundation. They were also looking for a director to head it up.

Her aspirations had never included being director, and after Belize . . . she only wanted to practice her profession with a little more open-mindedness, and live her life as carefree as she could. So for her, taking on the director's position was out of the question, but she had someone in mind who would be perfect for the job. That person was Sam.

They had worked together before, and she knew he had plenty of expertise in business and social services, actually many more years than she had served as a professional psychologist.

So she called him up. Luckily his number was the same and he was between jobs, but she still had to convince him to take the position. With a couple of lunches and emotional support to persuade him, he finally accepted. Raquel knew Sam really loved his work, and just needed to get ahold of his midlife crisis long enough to join the world of productive human beings again.

"All right, you've said the magic words." Sam laid his grey head on top of the cubicle wall. "Where do I go and what time?"

"The announcement's on the bulletin board," she spoke as she headed for the door. "It's been there for a little over a week."

Even though Sam was the director, it was Raquel who had organized everything before the clinic opened. It had taken a couple of weeks, and both their efforts for the place to begin to run somewhat smoothly. It was at that point, she had warned him.

"Look, I wouldn't be doing this if we weren't friends, and if I had done any less than begged you to take this job. But now that the place is pretty much on the right track, this is it, the ball's in your court. You take on your responsibilities and I take care of mine."

Privately she was thankful for the onslaught of work, it kept her mind occupied, and her body tired.

Raquel felt truly blessed when it came to how things had worked out once she'd returned to the States.

Her fears of having been evicted were foremost in her mind as she rode along in the taxi. She expected to see remnants of her belongings littering the curb. But to her relief, nothing like that had occurred.

The landlord was the one who had been thrown out by the owners of the apartment building. She found a letter beneath her door, telling how he had "misappropriated and embezzled funds." It had stated they had no way of knowing who had actually been paying their rent and who had not. So under the new management, all tenants were considered current, and the upcoming rent would be due at its usual time.

Raquel couldn't have asked for a better arrangement. She had been given the break she needed, and with the ten thousand dollars she'd earned from her charade; she had enough money to catch up her important debts.

Yet it was the phone call from the Devon Foundation that truly seemed like a miracle; they wanted to reopen the clinic where she had worked. In contacting the previous director, they discovered he had already committed himself to other employment. But they informed Raquel he had spoken very highly of her, and of her dedication to the facility. With such a strong commendation, they wanted her involved in the reopening, if not as director, then as the resident psychologist performing the same duties she'd performed in the past. Strange, it was almost as if things were exactly the same. As if Belize was only a dream.

Raquel reached up in front of her and pulled down the sunvisor that sported a mirror on its backside. Immediately her dark eyes focused on the almost invisible line that traveled down from the pulse point at the base of her throat, then disappeared into the folds of her blouse. This faint scar, along with the objects she'd stored in a shoe box in her closet, were the only proof she had ever been to the Central American country. There were many things, however, she could not see that were also proof of her ordeal.

She had come to accept and believe the power of the human mind and spirit was far greater than she'd ever imagined, and she was determined to use her new-found knowledge in her work as a psychologist. In many ways she had been strengthened by the ordeal, gaining confidence in herself and her ability to perform and survive under the most demanding circumstances. Raquel was no longer afraid to trust her own instincts, to stray from the beaten path and go with the flow. Those were the positive things she had brought back with her.

But there were also the dreams that had haunted her since her return. Jumbled menageries filled with all sorts of things. Some of them frightening, some bizarre, most of them included Nate Bowman. She'd promised herself if they persisted, she would seek some kind of counseling. As a professional she knew it was the right thing to do. Yet she was hesitant to follow her own advice.

Raquel rolled down her windows as she got on the highway. The forceful movement of the muggy air helped to free her thoughts of Belize. Tomorrow she would take her mother the book she bought her.

She was relieved to find out she had worried very little about her, and had assumed she had taken that long-talked-about vacation. Everything was like before. Almost.

The young woman checked the address she'd written down on her pad. The even numbers were on the right hand side, so the Devon House would be located on the left side of the palm-lined street.

Raquel saw the lines of parked cars before she reached the address, so she decided it would be fruitless to try and find a convenient parking space; therefore she parked several houses away.

The neighborhood possessed a distinct character. The architecture of the old stucco buildings was unique, each house having its own special qualities, though they were no bigger than average in size. Most of the homes had been transformed into commercial properties, giving the businesses a personal touch.

Raquel's heels clicked on the flagstone walkway as she passed the ornately hung sign, and mounted the two steps to the entrance. The main door consisted of an oval-shaped glass trimmed in wood. Through it, she could see the people eating and drinking inside. She determined she would mingle with the crowd no more than thirty minutes. That should be sufficient time to pay her respects to her employers, and then she would slip away and go home. Sam was the one who was obligated to spend a more "meaningful" amount of time at the affair. He was the director.

"And your name is?" An elderly gentleman in a dated suit extended his hand in Raquel's direction.

"Raquel Mason," she switched the glass of wine to her left hand. "I'm the resident psychologist at the newly reopened southwest clinic."

"Oh, yes, I know all about it. My name's Robert Kellner. I'm on the Devon Foundation board. For some time we had been considering backing an organization like yours, and when we were told the clinic had recently closed, we thought it was a prime opportunity to pursue our goals." He smiled at her. "Let me show you around the Devon House. I've been involved with the foundation for many years. And I think we've done some pretty good things."

Raquel followed Mr. Kellner about as he showed her several rooms in the house, furnished with antiques and memorabilia from the foundation's various projects. Hors d'oeuvres and wine were available in two of the rooms, and Mr. Kellner took it upon himself to introduce her to the different groups of people they encountered on their tour.

Finally, they reached the last room which served as the foundation's museum. It housed their most-prized possessions. Raquel could tell Mr. Kellner got pleasure out of telling her the stories behind the objects that were displayed, and she listened contentedly, enjoying his company and the knowledge he shared with her.

"Hey Bob," a plump, middle-aged woman called from the door, "there's somebody who just came in who's looking for you."

Mr. Kellner apologized for having to leave so abruptly, then he disappeared after the woman who'd summoned him.

Raquel drained the wine glass and looked around for a tray to discard it.

"There's one over there," a silky voice spoke from the doorway.

Raquel nearly dropped the glass when she heard the familiar voice. She turned around quickly to see Nate Bowman standing behind her. He was dressed in a well-tailored, black, double-breasted suit. His hair and mustache were groomed to perfection. The sheer shock of seeing him was overwhelming enough, but the businesslike persona he carried compounded her reaction.

Still she held on to her composure as she crossed the room to the table he'd indicated, her heart pounding beyond belief as she spoke.

"Well, I see you're not wearing your kidnapping clothes today." Even to her own ears the statement sounded lame and somehow inappropriate.

"No, I'm not. That's because abduction isn't my usual occupation," his dark eyes were steady as he watched her. "Would you like to know what is?"

Her hands trembled as she turned to face him, "Should I?"

"I hope s—"

"Mr. Bowman," the deep voice cut into his words, "there's a guy downstairs who wants to speak with you."

Raquel recognized the young man who had been seated opposite her on the plane ride back from Dangriga.

"Not now," his tone was impatient. "I've had enough interruptions. This is important." He turned and looked at the young man, "This woman is important."

"Yes, Mr. Bowman," his eyebrows lifted in surprise. "I understand."

Nate took a step inside the room, then turned and locked the door.

"There's so much I've got to tell you, *pataki,* but I need to know that you are truly open to me, and willing to hear what I have to say."

He had crossed the room and was standing in front of her, a hint of cologne wafting around him. Involuntarily Raquel took a step back. Over the past five weeks she had tried to occupy her waking thoughts with anything and everything but this man and what he had awakened in her. She felt ashamed of her feelings for him—that she would fall in love with a person who had kidnapped and used her the way he had. There could be no doubt she had missed him. But somehow not seeing or hearing from him had made it easier. She could pretend it had never happened. It was all a dream.

Raquel looked into his face, and she didn't know if she wanted to slap or kiss him. Several locks of wild hair framed her features, expressing their independence from the ball she'd gathered at the crown of her head, as well as from a separate cascade of rich, black hair beneath it.

Her emotions were like an electrical current, each one touching off another until they flowed together in a powerful stream. Everything had been his fault, and now here he was again abruptly reentering her life, but this time he was offering an explanation for wreaking the havoc he had caused. Was she willing to listen? Could she? She had tried so hard to bury his memory. It had been the safest and most sane thing to do.

Nate reached out to touch her face.

"No . . . please don't," Raquel turned away from him, then her dark eyes flashed back at him. "What makes you think you have the right to touch me? We are no longer in the wilds of Belize, and I'm no longer your prisoner."

"All right," his eyes clouded with pain, "I won't touch you. But I want you to sit in this chair, and give me a chance to tell you the truth. That is all I'm asking. After that you can make up your own mind."

He went and perched on a nearby windowsill and waited for Raquel's answer.

Nervously she tugged at the top of her navy blue suit. She wished she could stop the blood that was racing through her veins as she looked at him, heard his voice. As he sat with the sunshine outlining his dark frame, she knew she had lied, for part of her was still his prisoner. She knew he still held her heart and always would.

Slowly Raquel descended into the chair he pulled up for her. She focused her eyes on her hands as she held them in her lap. "All right. I'm ready."

Relief flooded his rugged features as he watched her. Suddenly his neck settled down on his chest, like a man who had carried a heavy burden for a long time and now would be able to relieve it. "Where do I begin?" he said almost to himself as he turned and looked out the window. "I guess I should start at the beginning.

"You may not remember, but I was there the night Benjamin and Thomas offered you the money to impersonate my sister. We all sat together and watched you as you danced in the club, and I knew you were perfect for what I had planned. There was a strong resemblance between you and Jackie, your size, your complexion, and she wore her hair similarly to yours." His eyes focused on her face as if he were seeing her for the first time, then he continued.

"It was strange because, even then, I found you very attractive. But I watched as you danced so enticing and intimate with the guy on the floor that night. You made my blood boil, and I thought I knew what kind of woman you were. I have known so many, *pataki*. They have been the kind of women I have allowed in my life. The kind who always look for new thrills and do not have any problems getting paid for them, if they can."

Raquel looked down at her hands as she thought of the dire circumstances she had faced that night and how desperate she was. Now, when she looked back, she knew she had acted rashly.

"I watched them make you the offer through the window of a limousine parked out front, and when you accepted the envelope, I knew I had judged you correctly. It was after that when everything went haywire." He walked over to a nearby bookcase, and ran his fingers along the leatherbound backs. "You see my sister Jackie was very ill at the time." His eyes had a faraway look when he turned to her.

"From the time she came to live with my father and me, she'd been a very independent, high-spirited young girl. It was after my mother died and we were moving to the States. You see Jackie is my half-sister. Her mother was Shangoain. You know the story, the one conceived on the night of the rift."

Raquel nodded that she remembered.

"Well, when my mother found out about Jackie, her mother was still pregnant with her. It was because of my father's infidelity that my mother committed suicide. Afterwards my father nearly lost his mind. He didn't care about anything, me . . . the property . . . anything. He just wanted to let everything go. Not that we had much at the time, but we did have some land that had been owned by my mother's family. But as my mother became less and less competent mentally, my father had her sign owner-ship of the property over to him for safe-keeping." He laughed dryly to himself. "That almost ended up being a mistake with the frame of mind he was in after her death." He paused as if to gather his thoughts.

"You see my mother was Creole, and the land was located near Belize City where a lot of development was going on. Eventually some develop-ers felt our land was the best location for their project, and they offered us a small sum of money for it. My father was willing to let it go at that price, but I had heard stories about how a family could become rich off of the outsiders who were coming in, wanting Belizean land. I was a young teenager then, but I convinced my father to talk to one of the lawyers in Belize City before he signed the papers. The lawyer put together a real good deal, and invested part of the profits in some more land further in-land. We still own that land today. It's covered with orange and grapefruit orchards, where the majority of my family's profits come from. We pro-vide the citrus that grocery chain stores make their orange and grapefruit juices from, here in the States." He sat back down on the windowsill. "A very lucrative enterprise.

"A couple of years passed with good profits, we moved to the United States, and Jackie moved with us. Jackie's mother was ostracized by the Shango because her child was part Garifuna. Years passed before it was prophesied Jackie would repair the rift between the Shango and the Garifuna, and the year and the date when this would take place. Wanting the best for her child, Jackie's mother, who is now dead from cancer, gave her to my father. It was common knowledge amongst the Garifuna that she was my half-sister. Some, like Marjorie and Belinda knew her. But no one among the Shango knew.

"From the very beginning it was hard for my father to control Jackie, and as the money poured in, and Jackie became a teenager, it was almost impossible. I did the best I could while I was around, but at the same time I was trying to live my own life. I guess, because of the money, things came rather easy for us. And through the years I must admit I've done some things I'm not too proud of. It seems I've always been attracted to danger. Finally I learned how to channel that energy in a positive way. I began to spend a lot of time out of the country, in Belize in particular, and I started working with the National Drug Advisory Council. It's Belize's DEA. My father was having some problems with poachers trying to grow their drugs in our fields. Being a part of the NDAC gave me con-trol over the situation, I thought.

"Unable to control Jackie, my father hired a man to keep his eye on her because she started hanging out with all sorts of unacceptable people. But before he realized it, she had gotten the bodyguard under her thumb with her charms, and he ended up taking her to these places to meet these friends of hers. One thing progressed to another, and before you knew it the cans of beer were joined by marijuana and so on and so forth, until she started using cocaine, eventually freebasing.

"Everything happened so fast, by the time I caught wind of it she was a heavy user. Because of our family's wealth and our Belizean contact, she was getting the majority of her stuff from the homeland. Three nights before we found you, Jackie had smoked some coke laced with cyanide. The guy who my father had hired to watch her said she suffered a bad seizure as a result of it and that sent her into a coma. I knew it was no mistake she'd gotten a bad package." He pressed his hands deep into his pants pockets. "Someone wanted her out of the way, and I had to know why." Deep in thought, Nate turned and stared out the window, almost as if he had forgotten Raquel was there.

"At first I didn't tell my father. He's old and sick, and had never really recovered from losing my mother. I had to try and see if Jackie would pull through before letting him know what was going on.

"You know, in a way I felt personally responsible." His dark eyes searched hers. "Here I was a big NDAC agent, and couldn't even protect my own sister from the drugs they may have been growing on my own land. So I came up with the bright idea to have someone pretend to be Jackie at a big function. One that just about everybody we knew would know about. We'd make it invitation only, and that way we'd have a list of just about everybody there. So if any of the folks who attended the function had anything to do with Jackie receiving the bad package, I felt some kind of way they'd show their hand," Nate nodded his head in retrospect. "And they did. But it wasn't anything like I expected.

"Right before the party, I found out a group of Garifunians and Shangoains had banded together to take Jackie back to Belize. Evidently she'd been contacted several times by the priestess and the *buyei,* telling her about her spiritual obligations, and what it would mean to them if she would come voluntarily. But Jackie, being in the condition she was in, found the whole thing rather funny. I found some letters in a box she had under her bed. She had written on top of it with some red lipstick, marking it 'voodoo.'

"Well as you know, the spiritual heads of the Garifuna and the Shango didn't think it was a funny matter at all. They were dead serious about it, and so they decided if she wouldn't come on her own, they'd make her come. Once she'd performed her duties as the link to the *gubida,* they'd allow her to return to the States. But she was going to meet her obligations one way or another.

"Art was one of the men chosen by the Garifunians. Once he got on the mainland, he contacted me, telling me about the plan. *Pataki,* I felt responsible for bringing you into a situation that was about to get out of control, so I did the only thing I could think to do. I detained—with ample funds—the other Garifunian who was to be part of the kidnapping ring, and I took his place. Art simply thought I wanted to watch out for my sister. So it was he and I who met up with Jay and Al at the appointed time and place. It was easy for me to hook it up, by saying we were independent dancers and musicians hired for the party. We showed up with the rest of them, in costume, part of the entertainment for the evening."

Raquel reflected on the first time she'd seen Nate, his muscles rippling in his arms as he played the drum for the feathered dancers. She remembered there had been an animal magnetism about him that had strongly touched her.

Nate watched her eyes cloud over with memories and he wanted so much to make her understand, all along he had just wanted to protect her, even before he realized he had come to love her.

"I never intended that you would spend one night in Belize, *pataki.*" His thickly lashed eyes pleaded that she understand. "I had made arrangements for my men to meet us in Dangriga when the sailboat arrived, but after the storm, we landed much further south than I expected, and it became a totally different ball game.

"Jay was part of a grapevine between here and Belize. We intentionally put out that Jackie would be at the party that night, and that's why we hired you. Jay wanted to insure the job was done right the second time, so he made himself a part of the kidnapping gang.

"I knew things were going to be dangerous when Jay threw you in the car. I had to establish myself as the head of the group. I finagled using my boat and all to try and have as much control of the situation as I could.

"At first I just thought he was a bad apple, then I suspected more. I decided to take you through the ceremony because I knew there was a connection to Jackie's overdose and the reunification. It wasn't until you ended up in that abandoned temple where the cocaine was stored that I was sure about Jay. It was Jay who made sure my sister got ahold of the bad cocaine. In their ring, he was the only one who knew the Garifuna and the Shango wanted her to come back and perform the ritual bridging the rift between them. But Jay knew if she were allowed to do that, his little party would be over. If he got rid of Jackie before she ever came back to Belize, he could continue using the old temple as a storehouse for the cocaine until it was shipped to the States. The rift between the Garifuna and Shango would continue, and his life as part of the Belizean drug world would grow and prosper, and his pockets along with it.

"So you see *pataki,* I could not let you know that I knew who you were. I knew as long as you thought hiding your real identity was the only thing you had that was keeping you alive, you would play your role as Jackie Dawson to the hilt."

Raquel shook her head at the complex story Nate had laid out before her.

"So how did you find me? You didn't even know my real name."

"I had Benjamin inquire at the building where you'd left your car. He asked if they had towed a car fitting the description of yours. Of course they said yes, and they told us where it had been taken. They also said a pretty, young woman had been in earlier that day asking the same thing. You made quite an impression, *pataki*. We figured it was you, and we went from there."

"But that still doesn't explain what you're doing here."

"My father is on the board of the Devon Foundation. After I had you checked out, very thoroughly, I realized you used to work at the clinic that had closed down. I encouraged my father to suggest that the Devon Foundation take it on, and reopen it," he smiled at her cunningly. "I figured you would be attending this little get-together as part of your working duties."

"So after five weeks you finally got around to making time in your busy schedule for the charity case, huh?" Still, she could not help but distrust him. Unconsciously she sought a way to tell him so.

"Oh no, *pataki*." He walked over to the chair and bent down in front of her. "I had never planned to let you out of my sight once we got off that plane. But before we even left Belize, I was told Jackie had died, and my father was taking it very badly. My mind was in a whirlwind as all these papers were being put before me, getting things in line in case my father also passed away. If only you had waited for me, *pataki*. Once I was back in Miami, there was Jackie's funeral and so many other things that demanded my attention. It was impossible for me to break away. But there wasn't a day you weren't in my thoughts."

He covered her trembling hands with his.

"*Pataki*, I could never forget the woman I'd come to know in the rain forest of my homeland. The strength and the courage she showed, and her willingness to love me, no matter what. Did you think I could ever let you go after what we shared?" His voice almost sounded angry.

"Deep in that forest I promised myself, no one would ever have you but me. You were mine, and we would live to share our lives together. It was that hope, and that promise that kept me alive."

Raquel could feel her heart pound through her chest. "How can I believe all of this is true? How could I ever forget?" Her dark eyes searched his frantically. "*How* do you start over from something like this?"

"How?" he looked straight into her face streaked with tears. "Like this," and he wiped the tears away. "Hello, my name is Nate Bowman." His voice was low, silky, "What's yours?"

"Raquel," she answered uncertainly. "Raquel Mason."

"It is so wonderful to meet you, Raquel," His voice caressed her name. "Don't ask me how, but for some reason I just know, you're the woman I've been searching for all my life."

"I am?"

"Yes, you are."

Two pairs of dark eyes searched each other.

"Well, I want to warn you, the bad memories of what happened may be with me for a long time."

"And I'll be there for you, *pataki*, if you need me. Reminding you of how we discovered our love for one another, and if it hadn't been for those bad times, we may not ever have found each other." He touched her face tenderly.

"I'm afraid to try!" Her moist, dark eyes shone brightly, above her full quivering lips.

"Don't be," he reassured her. "Just call on the strength I know you have deep inside."

Their eyes held until their lips naturally gravitated together. Raquel and Nate kissed tenderly for a long time. Then, with his lips lightly touching hers she heard him say, "Now, *pataki*, now you are truly home."